Christopher Robin Cook is a Yachtmaster and an intrepid yachtsman and has sailed in both the northern and southern hemispheres; he has been a student of sea lore and an avid collector of facts and anecdotes of the same over many years. He and his wife and two children are presently residing in Australia.

See appended glossary of nautical terms

YACHT *WORIPPA*

Christopher Robin Cook

Gladken

Gladken Publications

Published in Australia by Gladken Publications 2012

ISBN-10: 0-9578595-2-X
ISBN-13: 978-0-9578595-2-4

g

Gladken Publications
Australia

For those in Peril on the Sea

CREW

Bill Corsham: Cellarman and cook.

Nicolo Frascati: Foredeck man.

Christian Lincoln: Crew.

Helmut Meissen: Crew.

Lionel Potter: Crew.

Gary Prestwick: Navigator.

Brian Ramsey: Owner and skipper.

Sharon: Gary's girlfriend.

Warren: Crew.

New Year

VICTORIA

MELBOURNE

Geelong

Port Phillip Bay

Western Port Bay

Gabo. Is.

Cape Otway

Wilsons Prom.

Cape Wickham

KENT GRP

KING IS.

BASS STRAIT

Grassy

FURNEAUX GRP

Three Hummock Is.

Hunter Is.

FLEURIEU GRP

Cape Grim

Bluff Hill Point

Sandy Cape

TASMANIA

(Hell's Gates)
Cape Sorell

Macquarie Hbr

Point Hibbs

Low Rocky Point

HOBART

Tasman Pen.

Port Davey

Nth & Sth Bruny

South West Cape

Tasman Head

MAATSUYKER GRP

South East Cape

SOUTHERN OCEAN
Roaring Forties

0   50   100   150
Kilometres

Chapter 1

Glimpsed and caught in periphery vision, and faintly surprised and vaguely disturbed and slightly taken aback – and those feelings fed to Lincoln's brain in a split second of time. Another *coupe d'oeil* recorded that she was a 'she', and looked as startled as Lincoln felt. The apparition presented took him another half a second to comprehend, assimilate, and then digest: a bright red headband affair above her forehead matched her bright red mouth – and in that order because it was the headband that had caught his eye first. The elaborate home, self-styled, silver-grey, failed coiffeur only registered after. Lincoln looked at her directly, and at her smudged, heavily lipsticked lips that stood stark and proud against her etched and wrinkled face and nondescript nose; and up at the large floppy bow above her forehead again, which, rather than a plain ribbon, partially but unsuccessfully hid a receding, thinning hairline and a sparsely curled crown. She a startled biddy, a grandmother, probably a great, great grandmother – and she was staring back and apparently frozen – an owl behind glass. Their eyes met momentarily again during her panicky exit, and her turning emphasised just how badly her back was hunched, and that the narrow elasticated waistband of her skirt ended directly beneath her breasts – she hadn't a perceptible waist! Just that one final furtive glance from her and then she was gone. There had been a frowning grimace on her face – there had been more than that, she had left Lincoln with an after-image – written there had also been disapproval, distaste, apprehension and . . . and fleeting fear? The thought eventually penetrated his mental fog and surfaced – not a happy lady, and that last departing expression didn't sit too well! Seemingly seconds later a hand and arm appeared and the glass panel slid back violently, rattling against its stops.

"Right, Mister, and what's your problem?" demanded the newcomer. "Have you been drinking?" An aggressive thrust of his ridged neck made the bristling unfriendly face follow the direction of the voice – straight ahead, uncompromising – and take no prisoners!

Lincoln twisted round, checking – yes, he was talking to him.

This hotel was what Australians, when polite, which in

Lincoln's experience was practically never, would label 'budget'. The foyer was reasonably clean and tidy, and yet not quite. Ahead were double doors and a sign above them read 'Dining Room', and not 'Restaurant', and that in itself told a story! Homemade steel 'hand' and 'kick' plates were attached to the doors and there were scuffed and scarred wear areas in the thick, lumpy, cream, dust-impregnated paint around them. The countersunk holes in the plates were, even from where he stood, too large and the attachment screws in them too small, and that the screws lent this way and that instead of fitting snugly was what actually had attracted Lincoln's eyes to them in the first place.

Squatting in the corner and far to the right of the doors and in a rusting tray there a dusty potted plant, and so placed that one of its extended, sparsely-leafed branches would intimidate patrons turning to climb. Towards Lincoln and in front of the plant and against the wall opposite was a flight of black-banistered, tiled steps – the pale green tiles were the same as those on the floor of the foyer. In front of him and opposite from them and below the screwed sign 'Reception', and placed centrally in the faded, finger-stained, flowered wallpaper was the now open glass-fronted hatchway. 'Slightly tired' sprang into Lincoln's mind: the sort of hotel that would typically, instead of sticking properly, nail down the peeling edge-trim of a dressing table's veneer surface!

Reflex dipped Lincoln's head and he automatically sucked in, gathering for the reply. A second downward glance bottled an erupting temper and acid retort. This man's hostility from his point of view (and the grand dame's) was, on second thoughts, understandable: it didn't improve your image by not combing your hair, washing, shaving, nor changing your clothes for five straight days. And thinking about it, weaving and swaying down the full length of Du Fresne Avenue wouldn't have gone down too well either, and that and encrusted and white with salt would not impress because people wouldn't have known that it was salt! Lincoln was also aware that his eyes probably did look bad, so little sleep had made them gritty, and they irritated like the devil: the salt around them got rubbed in after involuntarily satisfying their irresistible itching demand. And the subsequent painful stinging then watering made a person finally lose their temper and dance on the spot; and it didn't help knowing that it would take about two minutes to forget till – and then another silly repeat performance! Added to that, and even now, his grey matter still hadn't got the message and it was still trying to compensate for a yacht's motion in heavy weather – hence the lurching about. Potter had once described it accurately, that it was similar to stepping on or off a moving pathway at an airport – when a person mistimed it – when the thing was going too fast. When they stepped on and the speed shot their leg forward and they nearly fell over backwards – and ejected them off at running speed at the other end! Yes, on further reflection, little wonder that his future host (hopefully) wasn't too keen!

"No," Lincoln replied apologetically, "I haven't been drinking. Umm. I have a reservation?"

"What . . .?" he wearing his obvious disbelief on his sleeve, "At the 'Albany'?"

"Yes," Lincoln said, "I'm afraid so. A friend booked me in – should be under the name of Lincoln? Umm, Christian Lincoln?"

He looked at Lincoln doubtfully and then looked down, obviously scanning his register. "Right, right, right . . . Right!"

The last lengthened 'right' emphasised his comprehension – or miscomprehension, as it were.

Suddenly there was sunlight, and happiness dawned. "Ah, you're Mister Lincoln of Melbourne, I remember her, your friend . . ." He snapped his fingers. "You're the 'yachtie', right?" Lincoln's 'right' went over his head. There was suddenly concern on his face. "Are you all right, Mr Lincoln?"

Lincoln nodded.

He went on then, undaunted, unthinking, and putting all previous behind him in a single breath. "Wasn't too bad this year, was it – apart from the start – it looked bad off Sydney Heads, and the worst weather at the start in living memory, they said. Well, since the race began anyway, I watched it on the 'box' – exciting stuff."

"Wrong race," Lincoln said.

The hotelkeeper's head drew back from the hatchway, a puzzled frown on his inquiring face. It cleared as he bent forward again, further forward than before. "You been on the 'West Coaster'?"

Lincoln nodded confirmation. "Yes."

This time he stepped backwards away from the counter, and Lincoln did likewise and at the same time straightened.

Lincoln's concentration drifted. Who the hell built these bloody hatches all over the world anyway – he felt his temper slipping and was suddenly furious again. Instruments of torture: they ought to make the idiot who built them stand in front of one of his own creations for a few hours – and see how his back felt – and that apart from the indignity of having to crouch in front of one of the damn things.

Reality jolted back.

He wasn't bashful nor the retiring sort, this hotelier. "Christ, this is the first time I've ever seen one of you raving lunatics in the flesh – you're bloody mad!"

Unimpeachable, shy, reserved and retiring to his patrons – my word. Actually, to be fair, the man had a point, and Lincoln knew what he meant – two points if he had any depth. The hotel was too nondescript and, as Lincoln had found out, too far away from the quay – especially if a person had to carry any weight – so he probably wouldn't have that many 'yachties' staying, period. Happily the tariff reflected the quality, and presumably, the geography; still, if he followed yachting, as he implied, then Lincoln knew that that wasn't actually what he had meant at all . . .

The Melbourne to Hobart Race had, through tragedy, been under unofficial scrutiny in recent years, and many considered the west coast of Tasmania too dangerous, period – for any shipping, period. Certainly no place for a yacht race, especially as it included mostly amateurs. Not a view restricted to the faint-hearted either; some very prominent yachtsmen, as Lincoln appreciated, held the same opinion.

There was no question of a conflict of interest, those people above that – and professionals in every sense. Both the Melbourne and Sydney races started, for all intents and purposes, on Boxing Day: the Melbourne was generally a local affair, that is to say, few yachts from outside of Victoria usually participated. In truth, wrongly or rightly, and depending on one's point of view, internationally it was a non-event. Despite Sydney's renown as the most dangerous and gruelling yacht race in the world, for Lincoln's money, the Melbourne was, potentially, the worse of the two.

The reason became self-explanatory after a glance at any

half-decent school atlas: Tasmania lies, or rather clings to the underside of the earth, approximately between latitudes forty and forty-four degrees south, and smack-bang in the way of the world's worst prevailing winds and seas. Called the 'Westerlies' by some, but more popularly known as the 'Roaring Forties', and with a reputation awesome in maritime circles and not without justification: the ocean rolling right around the bottom of the planet, and often and regularly gathering furious momentum: its passage only partially obstructed by the tip of South America, and then over halfway around the globe again before the next interruption and landfall – and guess where!

Included in the 'West Coaster' package is a continuous lee shore, and if a vessel got into trouble there was simply nowhere to run nor anywhere to hide! Conversely, if the Sydney yachts were going to run into trouble it would usually be off the south-eastern tip of Australia, below Gabo Island, where the East Australian Coast Current meets and battles with the constricted outrunning, or outpouring, of the Southern Ocean Current. There, as they cleared the protection of land, the full force of the same 'Westerlies' hits and further stirs an unsure and tumbling sea.

The difference being then that one race was exposed to nature's wrath all the way while the other, apart from a dash across the Bass Strait, was sheltered by the 'Island' Continent and the 'Apple' Isle.

"You awake, the name's Urwin Edgehill – proprietor. Call me Urwin. Drifted around much did you last night?" Urwin grinned, unabashed.

Lincoln smiled faintly, their Urwin did know his onions then, and Lincoln understated dryly, "Yes, it can be a little, um, problematic . . ."

They had creamed up Hobart's main sea-artery, and then, true to the Derwent River's reputation, had died in the hole. They'd followed previous hard won experience and stayed on the left, to 'port', as they had closed the town proper, and they had all known that the usual replay was about to begin as the fresh breeze had failed on approach. Rarely was there a puff off the docks, through some quirk in nature, local geography, whatever, always there the night was still . . . excepting that dog's frenzied barking clearly heard echoing off the buildings in the city! At least on their side the occasional ripple or a cat's paw had broken the surface; over and away to 'starboard', true to formula, the water was an undisturbed mirror.

In the harsh glow of yellow-orange neon they had ghosted back and forth, tack and tack about, desperately trying to catch the tiniest, elusive whisper of wind in the mainsail and in the acreage of their gossamer-thin, lightweight headsail. Hour after hour they had drifted and only vaguely powering on an occasional erratic zephyr; and their cursing and swearing barely audible lest they further offended the wind gods: Adad, Aeolus, Auster and Notos. Despite endeavours, inevitably, they had ended up closing the same buoy – chance, wild coincidence – neither losing nor gaining an inch!

They had tried everything else to no avail, so, presumably, all their prayers had been answered by whoever's god had taken pity on them. Four hours after the first sighting of their too familiar, hated, enemy buoy, and right inshore where safety dictated they shouldn't have been, a back-eddy of the river slowly edged a boat full of very, very tired boys across the finishing line.

Potter's voice so loud in the drained communal silence, "You've got to admire the persistence of that fucking dog, haven't you!" That now famous and later often remembered line of Mister Potter's had been uttered in the vacuum just before the significance of a car's flashing headlights – when the official finishing signal had really registered.

His comment, of course, had broken the spell of the moment. The indignity and the injustice on top of such a trip: of sitting there helpless with huge white sails hanging slack and useless, and their immunity to all their combined efforts had damaged their self-esteem, had hurt their egos. It had affected and subdued – they were all terribly proud of their skills – and defeat didn't sit easily.

Surprise absolute; they had expected anything but cheering. Mainsail flaked on the boom and hidden by its protective canvas cover, and all headsails bagged and stowed, and warps attached and ready to throw. Most of them had been sitting on deck or perching anywhere convenient, and quietly contemplating and still in another world – and still numb. Not before individual voices could be distinguished, and then it dawned – the reception was for them!

Above the hubbub the skipper's wife could be heard, "What

the hell have you been doing out there? We've been waiting hours and I'm bloody freezing. Just wait till I get you home – you're going to get it!"

The crowd and themselves had laughed delightedly, and some enviously. They had always been in love, Brian and his wife, and there was little doubt what 'it' meant! Poor, lucky Brian, he could handle a yacht and crew in any weather, and handle business with enviable acumen, but after twenty years of marriage, or more, he still couldn't handle nor control Judy. A great sadness swept over them all as they watched for his reaction. One hand waved helplessly and then silently he began to weep: tears streaming down each cheek. They had quickly closed ranks, unrealised camaraderie coming to the fore; and his crew respectfully and sympathetically making room as Potter, after nodding to Helmet to take Brian's place, eased him from behind the wheel and had led him back to the privacy and shadows and the obscurity of the pushpit.

Urwin touched Lincoln's arm and Lincoln blinked and refocused, and came back to the present. "I'm sorry, Mr Lincoln, but you're much too early, it's only a quarter-to-seven – I'm afraid your room won't be ready for a while yet – they don't have to vacate until ten." He leant his head to one side, his eyes like polished beads – bouncy and perky like a sparrow. "They've started breakfasts, why don't you go and have breakfast? You must be hungry – at least that'll fill the time?" He pointed. "Leave your bags over there, put them under the stairs – nobody'll touch them there, it's not like Melbourne, you know – you can trust people around here." Urwin qualified that, "I went there a couple of years ago, to Melbourne I mean, and I didn't like it. The people . . . too many people – bloody unfriendly place – I hated it."

Lincoln sighed inwardly with disappointment – he felt so desperately tired. He really needed to be alone . . . Still, there was no point in getting upset at this juncture – if he had to wait then he had to wait. Anyway, Urwin was right, and Lincoln knew from experience that food would take away the bad persistent taste at the back of his throat and ease the 'sickly' feeling. It would also pull him back for a limited period and, as far as he could remember, they hadn't really eaten since yesterday tea.

Lincoln nodded assent. "Right, and thanks."

7

Urwin indicated the dining room doors. "If you'd like to step through they'll look after you." He called loudly, "Mum? Mum? Would you take Mister Lincoln through to the dining room, please? Put him in the corner – by the bar. It's all right, Mum," he reassured, "he's the yachtie."

"Chris, call me Chris," Lincoln said. "My name's Chris."

Urwin's Mum moments later partially opened one of the dining room doors; hers was the face that he had first seen in the hatchway.

"Gave you a fright, did I," Lincoln asked quietly, "earlier?"

A knowing look and a dry twinkle belying pretended petulance and grumpy disposition – and she over her fright and tougher than she looked. "Not exactly dressed for the 'ball', are you?"

Lincoln grinned. "No," he said.

Appearances could be deceptive, Urwin's mum had recovered remarkably quickly from the ordeal of meeting him – she led Lincoln through. Despite her fragility and pronounced stoop, Urwin's mother led him to his table with an agility and briskness that belied presumptions of her age and physical ability. She indicated a chair. "Sit here, at this table. Help yourself to cereal. I'll bring you your tea."

"Thank you."

Halfway through 'cereal' Urwin appeared behind the metal shutters of the bar. There was a stage, fronted by a small wooden-sprung dance floor, at the other end of the 'dining room'. Yes, typically 'budget': obviously the 'dining room' had to double-up for evening entertainment!

Urwin placed a large beer on the table and in front of Lincoln. "English breakfast," he enquired, "egg and bacon suit you?"

These people and their unpretentious natural kindness; Lincoln blinked away wetness – damned salt.

*   *   *

Helmut decreased their engine revolutions while discreetly observing Brian; there had been no need for verbal communication, they were in tune to each other and each other's needs. They would not dock until they were satisfied that Brian had gained his composure and was ready to face the world. Helmut eased their speed again and they knew he would, if necessary, mistime his approach and go round again, and do it at minimum speed. They would finally find an excuse to stand off if more time was required.

Hobart had done them proud, Elizabeth Street Pier had been thoughtfully laid out and mooring buoys spaced evenly and parallel to the pier, and the distance off more than adequate, and there enough space for the largest yacht. So many yachts converged there at Christmas and ingenuity crammed them into, as efficiently as possible, every available space. All the yachts there, Lincoln could see, were moored in 'continental' fashion: with vessels bow-on and at right angles to the dock. Judging from the number of masts showing, or rather, glinting in the reflection from the dock lights above the intervening buildings, Constitution Dock was already full.

Lincoln went forward to prepare the bow lines, Helmut had signalled with his thumb – Brian was now fit.

Potter materialised and took the starboard line from Lincoln, for all his bulk he could move quietly and quickly when he wanted.

"You awake, Pom?" he asked.

Lincoln grunted.

"Feather in your cap having the 'West Coaster' under your belt – you did all right."

Praise indeed, Potter was a man of few compliments, Lincoln had found, and never short on criticism and bitingly hurtful with his sarcasm. Many people couldn't stomach him – Lincoln had seen him operate under pressure in a nasty seaway – he had time for him!

"I think you're sweet too, Lionel," Lincoln answered, actually feeling embarrassed by his complement. "Is Brian okay?"

Potter seemingly hadn't noticed. "Responsibility of command – relief and all that. He'll be fine now, matie."

They heard the 'clunk' of the gearbox going into reverse and they threw their lines; they knew Gary would have slipped the stern rope through the horizontal rail welded around the mooring buoy off their stern. They had absolute faith in him, and tension would already be on, and it would be a comfort to Helmet too, any misjudgement on his part, like hitting the dock, would be neutralised.

Helmut, chagrined, had once, to their delight, crumpled the 'pointed end'; whenever, as Potter put it, 'he got up himself', one

9

of them would go forward and carefully inspect the bow. Helmut hated it, still, Potter was right – it did have the effect of 'normalising' him. Helmut at times could be infuriatingly opinionated and unbearably arrogant!

Lincoln only caught the one aside as they were both rudely pushed out of the way. "Nice of you both to acknowledge us!"

Potter and Lincoln looked at each other sheepishly for a second, and then they both grinned – it would be a brave man who got in Judy's way!

"Hello, are you awake, Mr Lincoln?"

"Chris," Lincoln mumbled as he swam up reluctantly to consciousness. All the previously empty tables were now filled – couples and families were smiling and grinning in his direction – and a little wave from here and there.

"Your room's ready for you now," Urwin said gently. "There're clean sheets on the bed – Room Number Five. The girls are up there, they'll show you where." Urwin hesitated. "Um, you'd better watch them – it's New Year's Eve and they've had a sherry." He laughed. "You'll have to hold onto your trousers!" Urwin turned serious then, thinking. "Umm . . . Um . . . They're good workers, and it's only fair that I turn a blind eye." He indicated with an arm. "As you can see, we're getting very busy and we're a bit stretched." He asked, "Can you see to yourself?" He grinned. "You should be capable of running the gauntlet – you being a sailor, an all." Then he thought better of it. "No, perhaps it'd be better . . ."

Lincoln hurriedly intervened, he didn't know what the hotelier was talking about, but nothing was going to stop him from getting into that bed. "That's all right," Lincoln said, "there's no need – I'm more than capable."

Urwin nodded. "Right. Thanks."

Back Lincoln went through to the entrance hall, come-foyer. With one elongated, waterproof, logo-sponsored holdal leading and another trailing he climbed the first flight, initially pushing aside and brushing past the olive-green, light-khaki spotted, diseased, dusty, waving leafed-tentacle of the lonely pot plant, and round then to the brown chocolate-carpeted landing and adjoining corridor.

There was a young lass just ahead, and leggy, and in a short, blue, nylon overall – vacuuming. The industrial motor that drove the thing was deafening – she switched it off when she saw him.   She was blond and wore no make-up . . . and pretty – and there an enquiring frown on her face.

"Um, Room Number Five?"

She just looked at him for a moment, and then she smiled. "Oh. Ah . . . You're the sailor?"

Lincoln half-grinned his confirmation. "That's right."

"Just finished." She indicated the room in front of them. "This one."

Another blue overall backed out pulling an oblong wicker of heaped bundled sheets, bedding and towels – she turned – and the same features, but younger. This 'Miss' didn't even blink. "Do you want me to stay and wash your back? You look a bit done in . . .?"

That sweet innocent smile – eyes and eyebrows another story!

"Sarah! For God's sakes," squawked the elder sister, or cousin. "She's man-mad!" she explained to Lincoln breathlessly. "Nobody can do a thing with her!"

"Go on." She shooed her sister off with a flap of her hand (Lincoln had decided that they were sisters) and then lifted some towels from the wheeled trolley. "In here," she said.

Lincoln followed and indicated, "On the bed'll be fine."

A snigger burst out from her and another from outside. "My God," she gasped, "you don't mess about, do you – I'd heard about you sailor-boys!"

"The towels," Lincoln said, now resigned.

"Oh." She smiled, and then said soberly, "We'll leave you to it then, don't take any notice of her – I mean, us. Not offended, are you? She's . . . we're not really like that – just a bit of fun. Um, Uncle Urwin'll give us the sack in the end – if he gets too many complaints."

Complaints? Lincoln had to ask himself – what exactly had they been up to, prior to meeting him? "No, course not," Lincoln answered instead. "Glad of the humour."

"Good, besides . . ." She paused before squealing, "I can wash your back better than she can – anytime!"

The door slammed and there was whispering and giggling in the corridor outside, and peals of laughter. Just kids and there no malice in them – it didn't do an old man's ego any harm though!

Chapter 2

The 'bit' of the drill screamed again as the power came on, and its tip bit into masonry. Lincoln slowly came awake and the dream faded and the drill resolved itself into a telephone's insistent ringing – Lincoln fumbled for it.

"Mister Lincoln, good evening. It's Urwin here. I'm sorry to wake you, but I've assumed that you'll be wanting to be up and out – after all, it's New Year's Eve in Hobart Town?"

"Thank you, um . . . Urwin," Lincoln mumbled, trying to stifle a yawn. "That's all right – what time is it exactly?"

"It's just gone half-past-six." Urwin half-asked, half-pleaded, "You were going out?"

Lincoln searched his mind. "I'm supposed to be at the 'Blue Lagoon' at seven-thirty."

"Right," said Urwin cheerfully. "By the way – what's the name of your yacht?"

Lincoln shook his head. "*Worippa*," he said.

Urwin sighed. "Did you have the press on board last night, and a camera crew?"

"Yes . . ." Lincoln said slowly. "The 'finishing' officials insisted that we wait for the press photographers; they got quite upset when some of our crew started to drift away." He thought back over the events of the night before. "We also upset a camera crew – we made them take their turn. They were an unfeeling lot and just a bit too mercenary and just a bit too pushy. We were all pretty tired and a bit flat."

Urwin's rejoinder was reconciliatory, "Don't be too harsh on them, Mister Lincoln, I don't suppose they ever get any recognition and would probably have been covering and filming the event all day and most of the evening, and, by the looks, most of the night as well – I expect they were all pretty tired too."

All this was going over Lincoln's head completely, and, anyway, it had been him who had been there and the conversation was just beginning to faintly irritate. None of it made sense anyway. "Why are you enquiring exactly?" he asked shortly.

"You were on the six o'clock news!" He could feel Urwin grinning down the phone. "I inadvertently hit the nail on the head, didn't I," and he added triumphantly, "I had it to rights, didn't I, you really did get stuck on the river, didn't you – sorry about that." Urwin, to his credit, and to Lincoln's relief, reframed from belabouring the point any further. "Actually," he confided, "it was the girls who recognised you, and they were right too, *Worippa* was the name of the yacht."

"Were we?" Lincoln hesitantly queried, and for the life of him he couldn't think of any plausible reason for their being on the news, or for their being remotely news-worthy . . . Those guys last night, not a word from one of them or even a hint had been dropped, and Lincoln, still perplexed and not quite fully comprehending, again concentrated on what Urwin was saying.

"Actually, that press and camera and news crew did you proud, they showed you struggling to finish and then explained how so many boats win or lose, and it depending on the conditions, the state and whim of the river, and so on, if you see what I mean – they featured your boat – they were quite sympathetic. They did a sort of mini documentary, they even explained why you were all hanging over the side and you all tipping the boat so as to keep the shape in the sails through gravity – you know, so as not to waste any whisper of wind. It was all quite interesting – that was all new to me – it was all good stuff. I can see why you were so tired this morning, messing about like that all night." Lincoln just had to smile, and shake his head in the end, the man was irrepressible. Urwin then changed the subject, and without an apparent pause for breath, "Oh," he said, "you'd better get a move on or you really are going to be late – time really is ticking. I've got to go, I've got a customer. And, well done."

Lincoln gently replaced the telephone, and laid back and tucked his hands behind his head and contemplated the ceiling. The silence was crowding in and it wasn't unpleasant: the absence of the constant crackle and chatter from the radio; of people moving about, talking; the muted shouted instructions and muffled movements on the deck; the straining, screeching, creaking and groaning from the hull and the rig; and the motion and discomfort of a racing yacht on its beam ends crashing and banging through a heavy sea he especially wasn't missing. Lincoln revelled quietly in the peace and the solitude, and luxuriated in the clean sheets and the room to spread and extend his legs unhindered.

Lincoln absentmindedly rubbed his chin, another shower

and another wet shave would, he mused, finally see him clean. Though half-expected, the smell of his own body when he'd stripped off thermal underwear had been a bit of a shock that morning. That smell had gone beyond the normal harsh, ripe, body odour of perspiration caused by hard physical exercise, rather, it had been a strong, deeply rancid, stale, dull, sweet, elusive musk. The intimate parts of his body, especially his testicles, they and the surrounding flesh had been clammy, sticky and slightly slimy.

What had really surprised Lincoln after he had bared his feet to the air was the absence of 'athletes' from his athlete's feet. It would seem that feet trapped in seaboots and letting them stew in their own juices, as it were, for a minimum of at least five days was positively beneficial! He had been cursed with that infliction all his life and over the years, and none of them effective, had tried every powder, cream and potion ever devised by man. Later, and after due consideration, he had attributed the 'miracle' to nature's antibodies being allowed time to work their own quiet cure. The implication, Lincoln thought, would go down like a 'lead balloon' in drug and pharmaceutical manufacturing circles!

Lincoln's body when he saw it in the full-length mirror hadn't looked like his: it was thinner, gaunt . . . almost emaciated. They had had a bad ride, he knew that, but even so, the bruising seemed excessive. Most contusions were a deep bluish-black in the centre turning to a deep yellow at the edges – and there was a proliferation of various sizes, although rather than on the extremes they were, for some reason, mostly concentrated on and around his ribs! And one leg, the right, looked particularly colourful: like a black and white horizontally striped pole! Certainly he couldn't remember that many collisions with immovable objects.

*   *   *

Soiled plastic-wrapped underwear and socks disappeared into the first public litterbin – they were too bad.

Two things Lincoln particularly found noticeable after being at sea: one was exhaust pollution and the other was an inability to judge general traffic speed – the velocity of vehicles always seemed to him to be inexorably excessive. He had already mistimed the crossing of two junctions since setting out – and nearly fatally on the second.

A taxi pulled into the curb just ahead and the rear door opened and Judy peered back at him – and that was a surprise because they were staying, Lincoln knew, in a one of better international hotels – so their route must have coincidently coincided with his. "You'd better get in before you kill your bloody self." She was clearly irritated. "What on earth do you think you're doing?" And without waiting for an answer she added, "You're late, get in."

Lincoln bent and looked to Brian for help, but he was pointedly staring out of his side-window, and Lincoln could see, and caused by the taxi's interior light, almost a grimace on his face in the reflection on that selfsame window opposite.

Lincoln explained mildly, "I thought the walk might get rid of the stiffness."

Brian finally turned and asked, and forestalling any further comments from Judy. "I take it that you've seen the news?"

Lincoln nodded and smiled. "Yes . . . Well, no, but my innkeeper told me all about it."

Judy turned and looked at him and gently shook her head, pursed her lips, and raised her eyebrows, presumably at his use of the word 'innkeeper', but didn't comment.

Lincoln saw the disgruntlement on Ramsey's face, and quickly added, "It didn't sound too bad . . ."

"Well, I wasn't too impressed," Ramsey aggressively stated. "We'll be known as just another 'nearly' boat now! I don't know what we were supposed to do, we tried everything – always the bloody bridesmaid, us. We could have won, you know . . ." Ramsey caught sight of the fleeting look of scepticism on Lincoln's face and begrudgingly qualified his statement, "Well, we could have – we were in the running. We would have been placed, anyway, wouldn't we?" Lincoln gently nodded his agreement – they had been in with a chance, certainly. "It almost," Brian added with not a little asperity, "seems to come down to blind, bloody stupid luck, doesn't it!"

Ramsey, Lincoln realised, was simply airing his frustration and letting off steam for what might have been, and Ramsey knew very well just how notoriously fickle the Derwent was – and better boats than theirs had been defeated as they had, some very famous boats, and better skippers too – and it wouldn't have taken a TV news program to tell him that!

So, for no other reason other than to lighten the mood,

Lincoln mildly and mischievously interjected, "Yes, it was a bit tiresome, I know, and all part of the rich tapestry of life, but never mind; however, you do know what they say, Brian . . ." Ramsey was petulantly looking in askance. "They say, 'lucky in cards, unlucky in love'!"

Ramsey was taken aback for a moment, but only for a moment. "I don't give a flying fuck," he spluttered, "about love or . . ."

Judy twisted round to Lincoln as she raised a cautioning finger to her spouse, and despite her barely contained humour – just that one penetrating look at Lincoln! Lincoln also just glimpsed, as she turned back, and in contradiction, at a coy, coquettish, tiny smile that minutely appeared on her lips. Her finger wagged and her voice was very quiet, "Careful, Ramsey," she warned.

Some quality in the very quietness and tone of that admonishment stopped Ramsey in mid-tirade. ". . . Um, yes, well . . . Umm, sorry . . ."

And then Lincoln saw a private and intimate look pass across Ramsey's face: some message had obviously passed between them, a message that Lincoln shouldn't have been privy to: a lover's look and message that had softened Ramsey's features and told one, and apart from their obvious recent activities in the marriage bed, just how deep his love, fondness and affection was.

He was silent for that moment, Ramsey, and then his eyes crinkled as he grinned at his wife. "Yes, well, all right . . ."

Lincoln simply raised his eyebrows and imperceptibly nodded, and they travelled the rest of the way to their destination in comparative equanimity.

Judy stopped them on the steps of the restaurant. She pulled at Brian's collar and brushed and then plucked, with exaggerated care, an imaginary thread from his shoulder. Lincoln stood there patiently as she tucked his shirt into his trousers and then eased it out over his hips. That she'd pushed his shirt down the front of his trousers, obviously, wasn't relevant to her though it did make Lincoln blink.

And her final comment gave him such confidence, "You look like shit, but you'll have to do." She stepped back. "Right, you two heroes – in we go."

Lincoln nodded and muttered his thanks and then looked at

Brian, who raised his eyebrows in tolerant resignation before motioning Lincoln to follow Judy in.

A cheer went up as they entered the bar, and Lincoln quietly stepped to one side as Brian raised his arm with palm out, both saying 'hello' and acknowledging and thanking them – and the two of them, Brian and Judy, they just stood there looking and smiling, and basking in the warmth of their reception.

Potter fronted up.

Judy focussed on him. "Were you late, Lionel?" she politely and, Lincoln thought, somewhat pointedly asked. "You don't seem to have a drink?"

It had always amazed Lincoln how she expected people to obey rules that she herself ignored, and especially when they were at least three-quarters of an hour late themselves, and that excluding his tardiness! Or was it him, had he missed the point, was she being subtly sarcastic? Lincoln grinned to himself, if she was then any subtlety would be completely wasted on Lionel – and it was.

"No, there just wasn't any point, Judy, in starting without you," said Potter, exuding a greasy, fawning affability.

Potter always made Lincoln cringe, the way he blatantly complemented and flattered Judy – and, Lincoln had to admit, in his own way he wasn't without a certain amount of charm – and despite herself, Judy fell for it every time!

She glanced past Lionel and her face suddenly changed. "Who's that with Gary?" she asked in a dangerously quiet voice – the edge on it would have cut through ice. "Wearing the handkerchief!"

Lincoln could see what she meant, there was plenty of exposed flesh and Lincoln gave an involuntary grunt as he studied the girl hanging on Gary's arm. "I wonder if she's got an elder sister?" he asked.

Brian followed-up on his comment, and he forgetting the risks in the heat of the moment. "I'd prefer to meet the younger sister, myself . . ."

Judy's head snapped round and Lincoln winced, and Brian lowered his eyes under her withering stare.

She turned to Lincoln and said with a quiet deadly condemnation, "You're married!"

Potter had been listening to their conversation – with his

head raised and his eyes piously looking to the ceiling.

Judy wasn't wearing it and she admonished him in turn, "For God's sake, drop it, Lionel – drop it. You weren't innocent when you were born!"

Potter contrived to look hurt – unsuccessfully.

She started forward like a battleship about to engage the enemy. They knew what it was about too: Gary's wife had died of cancer: of a strain peculiar to women. It had been a long, painful and agonising death, and, as with many of these things, it had left the living devastated. The trauma had left Gary a broken man, unable to cope and unable to pick up the pieces. The only reason he was there today was because of Judy: she had nursed, consoled, jollied, cajoled, persuaded, hectored and bullied him back into life.

Potter casually stepped in front of Judy and barred her way. "Hold hard, Judy, not too hasty." There was something in Potter's voice that made Judy pause. "Come on, think; anything that brings a semblance of a smile to Gary's face can't be all bad, now can it?"

She looked at Potter for a moment. She whispered, and her voice barely audible against the background din, "But he's so vulnerable, Lionel."

She turned in askance to Brian.

Impulsively Brian kissed her. "Let him make a fool of himself, Judy, if he wants. He's a big boy, it doesn't matter – and it won't do him any harm either – at least he's starting to live a little. It doesn't really matter if the company he's keeping is a little . . . um, inappropriate, does it – and even then, we don't know that?" The look on Judy's face said that she did know exactly that. Brian reached out and touched her arm. "Let him go, Judy, he'll be fine."

After a poignant pause, and talking to nobody in particular she quietly asked, "Can I have a drink, do you think?"

They collectively sighed.

Intuition had caused people to stay clear, and somehow they had known that it had not been the time to interrupt. Judy's request for a drink had broken that invisible barrier and they surged around them like a comforting blanket, talking and gesturing to them and to each other in turn.

Lincoln spotted him across the room and made his way across, and Lincoln stood there in front of him until he was sure that he had his full attention. "Christ, is that you, Bill, your mum dressed you, did she?" The comment Lincoln meant was that at another time and in another place he would have walked straight past him. In truth it was one of the few times that Lincoln had ever seen him tidy, and Lincoln reckoned he'd only just caught him – and that he was already deteriorating around the edges. The top button of his striped shirt was undone behind a sideways-edging tie; his hair still showed some semblance of behaviour but was on the edge of breaking loose. Soon, Lincoln knew, his shirt sleeves would be rolled up and, much to everybody's amusement, his shirt tail as he crossed the room on some errand would be seen to be hanging out, and only then would he be comfortable. How he had ever managed in the 'forces' Lincoln couldn't guess, though on thinking about it his unconscious resistance to anything smacking of dress code or formality was probably a reaction due to all those years in uniform.

"William Corsham done up like a dog's dinner." Lincoln sniped, unable to resist and turning the knife a little.

He was actually blushing under the scrutiny – he was genuinely a nice guy – and one of nature's gentlemen and to pursue the advantage further would be cruel.

To Lincoln's knowledge, William Corsham had never been seasick. To say that Bill was the cook aboard *Worippa* would be selling him short: he was a boon, an asset, and weight-for-weight, the most valuable man on board – and much more. And even if he were just the cook, a hot meal provided at the right time and in any conditions could make, literally, the difference between life and death – men make fewer mistakes on a full stomach!

Lincoln stood there looking at him . . . no, there was more to him than that. He was that bit older than the rest of them and he had abandoned the rigors of 'top side', and was now satisfied with the role of cook and chief bottle-washer below decks. Items required were found and passed up without fuss; all equipment, switches, valves and sundries he could literally find and if necessary operate in the dark. Doubling as 'cellar' man and manhandling up, dragging down, re-flaking sails and re-bagging *Worippa's* huge spinnakers. He was often up to his eyes in wet canvass, and more often than not forgetting, or not having the time to don his 'oilies'. He organised his twilight world, his world of damp fug like the ex-chief petty officer he was. To Lincoln personally he was adviser, friend, and mother hen.

He asked warily, "Have I done something wrong?"

"No." The question puzzled. "As far as I'm concerned, Bill, you couldn't do anything wrong."

"You were bloody staring, that was all." He shivered. "It was like you were looking straight through me." He brightened visibly. "We didn't do too badly, did we – did you see the news?"

Lincoln grinned. "We did do well. I didn't see, but I heard all about it – they were quite commiserative, I understand . . ."

Lincoln ignored Bill's slightly bewildered look and looked in question to the woman at Bill Corsham's side instead.

Bill caught up after blinking several times. ". . . Oh, sorry, Chris." He turned to her. "I'd like you to meet my wife, Jean. Jean, meet Chris."

She had her arm through his, and she was smiling faintly, and it was there for anyone to see in her face – she obviously adored her husband. "Ah, I've heard all about you, Chris, you're the 'Pom'." She sighed. "They're so rude."

"All bad, I suppose. No, it's not rude . . . Well . . ." Lincoln paused for a moment. "Well, yes, it was . . . Originally it was derogatory, but now it's just a habit. And sometimes, I like to think, even a term of endearment, though I'm probably only kidding myself." He added lamely, "Most of them don't even know what it means anyway."

She couldn't resist and asked, "What does it mean, actually?"

Bill leant forward.

"Oh, it stands for 'Prisoner of Her Majesty'."

They both leaned back and silent for a moment, and presumably reflecting on the reasons why, historically, such a macabre word had found its way into their modern, everyday Australian language!

Bill spoke finally, "Are you all right, you look like shit." He mildly added, "You hurt yourself badly a couple of times, didn't you?"

His observation surprised Lincoln and Lincoln said slowly, "Do you know, I don't really remember – but I feel fine."

Bill looked up at Lincoln speculatively. "No, you wouldn't,

you turned out to be a real tough bastard, and not a pleasant surprise for some of them. You drove that boat petty hard." He nodded across the room. "I don't think Warren's too fond of you either."

Although he couldn't possibly hear, Warren turned his head away as Lincoln also looked across.

The smack on the back nearly sent Lincoln sprawling. Nicolo Frascati, foredeck man extraordinaire stood before them: out of breath, flushed, grinning, and criminally handsome.

"Have you seen Gary's 'piece'?" he gasped, his eyes glittering.

"Piece!" Bill echoed, and then corrected him. "You mean 'young lady'."

"Yeah, that too."

They all smiled, to them he was Nick, and the baby of the crew – this Don Juan in him was always a bit of a surprise, still . . .

Lincoln winced and then raised his eyebrows and frowned in mock annoyance while Nick was trying to peer over the heads of the crowd – and he was using Lincoln's shoulder as a support.

"She's too young for him," he commented as he peered, he was on tiptoe and his head was swaying from side to side as he tried to peer between the various intervening people.

Helmut had come across, and he pushed Nick's hand off. "It is more like she's too old for you, you mean – she vould vant a real man."

"What, like you, I suppose?" Nick turned as he spoke.

Here we go, Lincoln thought.

"Ja, just like me." Helmut made a grab for his arm and Nick dodged out of harm's way, and Lincoln knew his concern, Helmut was unbelievably strong and if he squeezed your biceps – it apparently hurt.

Whenever Nick felt bored, which was often, he would bate Helmut, and Helmut to his credit never really hurt Nick, though Nick pushed his luck at times.

"So . . . that is vhy your face is red, you have been vanking over Mister Prestwick's new girlfriend – you dirty little foredeck boy."

Helmut's stage whisper carried far outside their circle and Lincoln glanced quickly and discreetly at Mistress Corsham before checking on whom else they had offended – her countenance gave nothing away, except for the bottoms of her ears, and they had turned a quiet shade of red!

Fortunately they were called into dinner before either of them, Nick and Helmut, could get into it any further.

*   *   *

The late evening air was pleasantly cool there on the steps of the Blue Lagoon restaurant – and the restaurant had done them proud – the food and the service had been superb. The background noise suddenly increased, which coincided with the opening of the restaurant entrance door behind Lincoln.

Both of them stood under the caress of the florescence thrown by the restaurant's brightly-lit sign, observing the night.

Lincoln didn't turn when Gary spoke. "I saw you slip out." He swallowed. "I just wondered?"

Lincoln pre-empted him, "Yes, I know – I look like shit."

Gary stepped around and peered directly at Lincoln, and there was puzzlement on his face. "No." He shook his head and then hesitantly continued on, "Look, please don't take offence, and it isn't meant as it sounds. I know you're a 'loner' – you don't need people – you have an indifference . . ." He paused again for a moment and then burst out, "You don't mind about Sharon, do you?"

"No." Lincoln said slowly, and now it was his turn to be puzzled. "How's that relevant, Gary?"

"Because, because . . ." They stood. "That stare, Pom. If you give her that, if you give her the cold shoulder . . . Well, you'll frighten her off."

Lincoln was shocked at his suggestion, and the implication. "Gary," he said reasonably, "you don't need my approval – nor anybody else's for that matter. If you like her." Lincoln shrugged. "Then go for it."

Gary reached out and held Lincoln's arm and Lincoln glanced down, and then Gary let go. "Sorry. You really don't understand, do you, if you accept her then the rest will accept her too."

Lincoln sighed, he was vastly overrating any influence he had, or for that matter was likely to have – and anyway, what did it matter. "Gary! I don't know her from a bar of soap, do I, but if you like her then that's good enough for me, and," Lincoln assured him, "it'll be good enough for everybody else as well."

They stood quietly. "Actually," Gary admitted, "I don't know her that well myself, I only met her this afternoon." There was a smile in his voice, "And I've had an erection ever since."

They started to laugh and as they did so the restaurant door opened again and quiet footsteps approached.

"Private party, is it?" she asked.

The question wasn't, hadn't been rudely put and it really meant: 'Is it all right for me to interrupt and join you?'

It was Gary who answered, "Yes . . . No . . . Sorry, Sharon, I didn't mean to abandon you, are you all right?"

There was placidity and certainly no malice in her countenance as she sighed, but there was something. "Yes, I managed to give Warren the slip and came to find you."

She was looking at Lincoln while talking to Gary. He was being weighed up like a piece of horseflesh, and he felt like a racehorse, or what he imagined a racehorse felt like, and he didn't like it. What she was doing was known in racing circles as 'weighing the potential'. This was no innocent virgin and bold eyes told a story, and this was trouble with a capital 'T'! Furthermore, and now Lincoln suddenly knew exactly what Gary had meant, more of her breasts were uncovered than covered and she obviously wasn't wearing a thing underneath, and her nipples were sticking out proudly and unashamedly in the colder, sea-chilled night air. And Lincoln could sympathise with Gary's physical discomfort, to resist ogling down her front took real willpower – and she knew and was fully aware of the effect she was having too, and it didn't worry her!

"You haven't officially been introduced. Sharon, meet Chris."

"Hi, Sharon," Lincoln said.

Sharon didn't drop or avert her assessing gaze, and she simply acknowledged the introduction by raising her arm and wriggling, palm forward, the pinkies on her languid hand.

Out of the restaurant rowdily spilled the rest of *Worippa's* crew and associated company, which curtailed further conversation.

Their walk down to the quay was an eye-opener, and in almost every doorway they passed were kids, and most of them either drunk or well on the way. Some, by their looks, were already unconscious – and it was not even twelve o'clock yet!

They side-stepped more than one violent shouting match and had to push their way through a street fight in progress. Lincoln thoroughly disapproved of Potter's answer to the problem – violence begets violence – and yet the shock of it did stop them . . . Potter, who was ahead of them, caught each with an elbow as he passed between.

They had to squeeze their way down Morrison Street, and the crowd unbroken from shop frontage, across the road and pedestrian walk, to the quayside. Their feet ground as they threaded their way along Franklin Wharf, without interruption, on broken glass, and only when they stepped off Elizabeth Street Pier and onto *Worippa* did the crunching stop.

A general call of welcome went up as they climbed on board; in the bedlam they hadn't noticed that the neighbouring yachts were nearly sinking under the weight of people. Lincoln laughed as he heard, above the hubbub, some wag call out, "It's the famous TV celebrity!" And another, "It's that television heart-throb!" And another, "Can we have your autograph?" The crowd laughed and Ramsey good-humouredly and tolerantly waved a hand in dismissal, and turned, embarrassed and crimson-faced, and obviously pleased, to accept a beer that had been passed up from below.

All of Hobart, it seemed, was there counting in the New Year, and they were all, the yachties, guests and the locals, in harmony by the seventh, and in complete unison on the final stroke of twelve. Emotions were still running high as the first opening bars of 'Auld Lang Syne' tentatively began, and it was gradually picked up as the crowd organised itself. Hands were joined after initial fumblings and the snaking, uninterrupted, up-and-down movement of crossed arms ran unbroken along the sea front, along the quays, along the wharves, and on the yachts – and squabbles and old arguments forgotten. The first firework, a rocket, and the timing was perfect, soared into the pregnant hush after the final note of that ancient song had died, lighting up the sky and the upturned faces, and the surrounding water.

      *   *   *

They sat there in the aftermath of the celebrations, in the cockpit, and contemplating their feet that were resting on the cockpit seat opposite. Lincoln turned his head, following – and he nodded at the passing launch. "There seems to be a lot of

Water Police about, Brian?"

Brian grunted. "A few kids, because of the press of people, got pushed off the quay a couple of years back, and the poor little wretches drowned before they could get to them – they don't want a repeat performance."

He indicated splashing and squealing across the way.

"Ah," Lincoln acknowledged and sat up as the horror of his, Ramsey's, few words drew a picture in his mind's eye, of the anguish of the parents, and brothers and sisters . . . and then Lincoln closed his mind to it, not wanting to face such thoughts on this, their anniversary night. Lincoln stood up instead. "Right, Brian, I'm off then."

"And us, I'll wake Madam." Judy was huddled in the corner and sound asleep. "Do you know, I'm still winding down – and even now, I still can't settle – I'm so tired I can't sleep." He closed his eyes for a moment, and then opened them and quietly admonished, "Don't forget Jamie, at twelve and here on the quay." He raised his eyebrows. "Yes?"

Lincoln nodded and half-laughed. "It would have been wild at his place tonight – the meeting of the clan." Lincoln paused, and then enquired, "Are we the last – is everyone accounted for?"

Brian puckered his lips and nodded slowly.

"Gary?" Lincoln asked.

Brian whispered, and wary of Judy even though asleep, and pointed to the hatch. "Below, with his new ladylove."

"Potter?"

This time he replied in a normal voice, which sounded overly loud, "Below – pissed."

Not until Lincoln had stepped around the mast was it that the figure, stationary on the foredeck, registered: it . . . he, or she, was resting on their hands and knees and just forward of the hatch. Whoever it was, his or her, their concentration was such that he or she didn't react to the quiet drumming of his footsteps. Recognition came as Lincoln lifted gently and led him unresistingly across to the standing rigging. "Come on, Warren," he urged, "don't be sick there."

Warren pulled his arm abruptly away as Lincoln tried to wedge him between two of the tapering, heavy, vertical, plastic-covered, wire mast shrouds.

"I'm all right," he muttered, leaning on the rigging while

looking down into the silvery-gold swirl of water below.

Lincoln left him there finally, and with alcohol and good company tempering and softening any previously conceived and perhaps too-hasty prejudices.

Chapter 3

Jamie obligingly stopped the minibus at a convenient spot on Rosney Esplanade so that they could stand and look at the panorama before them; they were on the other side of the river, on the east side and almost exactly opposite the city. Whether it was the cloud cover, imagination, or fact, there was an overall feeling, Lincoln felt, of sombreness, and of bleakness, and of . . . of indifference prevailing. The impression wasn't strong, but rather, just an echo from that beyond, and that 'beyond' was seeing Hobart crouched beneath Mount Wellington, and the mountain full in splendour and yet partially shrouded – and some of it was wreathed in faint tendrils of light mist. Just the same, that prominence soared above and belittled, and somehow threatened the huddled metropolis below.

From where they were and from their perspective, and it was only the token gesture of defiance from the central business district that averted total domination and marginally salvaged Hobart's complete subservience. Lincoln gazed: the various sized, grouped, tall, thin oblongs looked, from where they stood, like a child's play bricks stacked to different heights on a woven carpet plain, or, and at the other end of the spectrum, like isolated, bunched columns of gambling chips on a dark-green, baize table. In that clustered group, Lincoln knew, would be banks, hotels, head offices – tall, elegant, glass-faced 'insurance' columns and multinationals – a defiant little group of high-rise buildings and slim tower blocks reaching up.

The river before, the city's life's blood, was naturally deep enough to take ocean shipping, and miles wide in places, and surrounded and enclosed by rolling hills and high country. It was in total the junior reminiscent of a grand Norwegian fjord, and, for Lincoln, as before, this vista had that same slightly forbidding and intimidating atmosphere as well.

The bridge had been a surprise and stood whitely stark against the sober blue of the river and the, comparatively, dull green backdrop of the countryside. It was well to the right and north and upriver of the commercial centre, and at least as ambitious in its way as the Westgate Bridge in Melbourne, and it easily outranked Sydney, but was less in stature, than say, San Francisco. The road across, Lincoln noted, was supported on spaced concrete pillars whose feet were encased and rested in oblong, concrete, pontooned shoes. The pillar heights following a gentle, elegant, convex curve and the span a link to these eastern suburbs and beyond.

It was Lincoln who broke a rare silence of their party. "That's quite a bridge, Jamie – and very impressive. I can't say why, but I just hadn't expected to see a bridge of that magnitude here . . . to be here."

"Yes, and it nearly wasn't," Jamie replied dryly. "A ship ran into it in the fog about ten years after it was built . . ." He pointed. "It took out two pillars and a section of road."

They absorbed this snippet.

"People were drowned in their fallen cars, and some of the ship's crew were also killed in the collision, as well – and the ship actually sank!"

They all looked at the bridge with new eyes, and each, Lincoln presumed, presumably imagining that day.

Jamie didn't dwell on it, and asked, "Does it remind you of Scotland, Chris?" He turned with one hand held out, gesturing. "All this?"

Lincoln's eyes travelled the same arc as Jamie's hand and he nodded. "Very much, Jamie, have you never been there, Scotland, I mean?"

"No . . . I've just heard people commenting on the similarity, that's all, though I should dearly like to see for myself." There was a wistfulness in his voice. "It's probably why my great grandfather settled here – it reminded him of home."

"You're fourth generation, Jamie, you've surprised me." Lincoln was surprised too. "You've a faint brogue, did you know that?"

Jamie smiled. "You wait till you hear my grandfather, he's Tasmanian and has never been to Scotland, and his accent hasn't changed at all – he's unbelievably broad."

Nick snickered in the background and Jamie rounded on him, and correctly interpreting that it was he who was the butt of an implied, unspoken jibe. "You just can't leave it alone, can you?" Jamie asked.

Of late, Lincoln had noticed, Nick had had the edge, and Nick being Nick, he just couldn't help or reframe from probing any exposed nerves. "Don't be so touchy, Jamie." Nick replied and paused, and then he just couldn't resist. "Just because you piss out of your elbow."

It was as well for him that Judy had not been around, or Potter, thought Lincoln, but then, he wouldn't have dared that stupid, infantile, hurtful remark had they been.

A tactless, insensitive arrow and out of order and humiliating – and, as Nick well knew, or should have known, taboo in such mixed company, or in any company for that matter! They were all, in fact, more embarrassed for Nick than for Jamie – that someone could be so ... so insensitively callow. Jamie stepped forward threateningly, and the uncharacteristic depth of his anger measured by his action. Quite capable was Jamie, as Lincoln knew from past experience, of verbally and physically defending himself; it was the unspoken, understood, incestuous implication and innuendo of inbreeding that had aroused him. Australian humour, to Lincoln's chagrin at times, respected very little and Tasmanians, and New Zealanders, with their small populations, geographical remoteness and isolation were particularly considered fair game. It was an unfortunate flaw in the Australian character, and probably a defence mechanism – their casual, derogatory vindictiveness to their next-door neighbours and other Pacific neighbours, their indigenous peoples and their emigrant minorities. But that by no means excused Nick though, and Lincoln shook his head in disapproval – if anyone, Nick should have known better because he was of Italian descent and had probably experienced similar. If not himself, then certainly, and Lincoln was fairly sure, as comparatively new immigrants his parents and grandparents would have! They would have had to endure the same taunts, insults, innuendo and prejudice, and Nick's unthinking, base, idiot remark had been, as those past bigots, simply cheap points at another's expense for an audience.

Even Nicolo Frascati was not brash enough to push much harder and it was dawning even on him that theirs was a disapproving and quietly disgusted silence. What really underlined their condemnation was that they did not verbally rebuke nor chastise him, but that they had all looked in any other direction rather than at him. People like Nick, Lincoln knew, could stand any amount of haranguing, and, to a degree, even enjoy it, but indifference was something else. He had stepped over that line, and to make matters worse, Jamie was their host and had invited them into his family's home – and furthermore, Jamie was apparently the youngest in his family – he had four sisters! Lincoln shuddered, it didn't bare thinking about.

Helmut caught Nick by the arm, his, Nick's, vigilance, had been distracted; he wriggled and squirmed and tried to pull and break away. "So," Helmut grated. "You are being rude again, you are not funny, and nobody here thinks you are funny." Helmut nodded slowly. "It is a lesson you must have." Helmut shook Nick very gently. "You must say after your good friend Helmut . . . I am a fucker of kangaroos and I vill never be rude to my friends again." He shook Nick. "Say it!"

Nick struggled, half-laughing and half-crying – and even then not quite believing that Helmut was serious and, Lincoln could see it in his face, not believing that it was he himself who was being so humiliated.   He loudly protested, "Get off, Helmut, you're bloody well hurting. Get off."

He choked with pain as Helmut casually shook him harder. "Say after me – I am a fucker of kangaroos. Not nice, ja – to feel a little yourself belittled – say it!"

Nick winced and then slowly and painfully gasped out, "I am the fucker of . . ." He took a shuddering breath and then added quickly, a clenched grin twisting in pain, "A big fat German pig!"

They sighed – Lincoln sighed. Helmut shook his head and then let Nick go – he pushed him away. "I do not vant to talk to you again; you are a child – a thoughtless little boy.   You do not realise how you hurt people and humiliate – Jamie, the Pom, and me – me, the clumsy German."

Nick rubbed his arm and watched Helmut climb back into Jamie's van, and he then slowly turned and looked directly at a fascinated Sharon, he ignored Warren and then gazed at Gary, and at Lincoln.   Finally he pivoted around and stared at the departing backs of Bill Corsham and his wife.

That day, in Lincoln's eyes, Nicolo Frascati turned, faced, and took a major step towards manhood. "I'm sorry, Jamie," he apologised, "that remark was out of order – wrong time, wrong place . . . And wrong. I'm sorry."

He had meant it too, and Lincoln could hear it in his voice, the sincerity was there, and it had cost him a lot. Jamie went bright red for the second time, but this time with embarrassment of a different kind!

Nick looked directly at Lincoln and Lincoln nodded, and Nick then walked over to the van.

Helmut greeted him and patted the seat next to him. "You sit here next to me, Nick, ja."

Lincoln espied that Jamie's family home, which was situated off of Rokeby Road and a three-storey, ochre, sandstone house. The full width of the second storey was fronted with a traditional, white painted, iron-lace balcony. It was not luxurious, but rather, a practical house, and a little neglected and used around the edges and yet this not masking the fine workmanship and the quality of a bygone age. Lincoln noted that it had been built on a plot that was some way back from the foreshore and was quietly sitting in a screen of trees, and only a small park separating it from the River Derwent.

None of them were really surprised by an excited yapping and growling black-and-white border collie, and its sporadic greetings as it followed and then raced the van – it ignored tyre-thrown stones from a weedy, gravel drive. The dog reluctantly wound down like an old engine after Jamie's affectionate abuse and patted hello.

It was later in the kitchen where the enquiry ensued and it was Jamie's mother who had been most affected.

"What exactly happened, Jamie, she wouldn't hurt a person – he must have provoked her? And even then . . ." Jamie's mother was really quite upset and distressed, and close to tears.

Jamie began to stutter, began to choke, and there were the beginnings of a . . . titter, and that titter was gathering momentum!

"Jamie!" His mother's shocked voice stopped him. She looked from him to Lincoln, and her concern deepened. "What's the matter with him?" she asked.

Lincoln could only shake his head.

"Mother?" Jamie gasped, and regained her attention. "You should have seen him staggering around in the garden – with Trudy swinging in an arc and hanging onto his trousers' leg for dear life." The grim line on Jamie's mother's face softened slightly and Jamie quietened. "God. Mum." He shook his head. "It was so funny." He directed his next sentence to Lincoln and the humour in his voice died slightly, "That's the first time I've ever really seen bloody Warren move since leaving

Melbourne!"

Jamie's mother intervened, "Jamie . . . You'll be ashamed of yourself, your grandfather has said there's bite marks – Trudy's bite marks. You won't be laughing if he – what's his name . . . Warren, if Warren takes it further. We'll certainly have to buy him new trousers."

Her obvious concern and his respect for her feelings stopped short another outburst of laughter and Jamie turned and looked directly at Lincoln, and all his humour was suddenly gone. "I don't know that Trudy's far wrong, do you, her instinct's true. There's something really sleazy about him and he gives me the creeps." Jamie gave a shiver. "He actually makes the hair on my neck rise – he bloody well scares me." Jamie pulled a face. "And I, for one, won't be sad to see the back of him – I'll not grieve when he flies home."

Florence Montrose studied her son for a moment, her face still very white, and her disapproval gradually gave way to reserved neutrality – she gave her son a perfunctory nod before quietly leaving the room.

Jamie's eyes had only left Lincoln's face when he'd quickly glanced at his mother. "You've felt it, haven't you?"

*   *   *

Lincoln surveyed the Montrose's main living room, which ran the full width of the second storey and half the length. With the exception of hung paintings, three of the walls were bare and these were in contrast to the forth wall, which had shelves against and down its entire length, and some of the inch and a half hardwood planks incorporated in construction were warping downwards under their heavy load of books and tomes. Scattered rugs rested on a varnished, polished, Baltic pine floor and their bright colours broke up what could have been a rich-honeyed plainness. It had been Brian Ramsey who in a past conversation had mentioned to Lincoln the history of the now-fashionable popularity of Baltic pine floors in Australia – and Tasmania. Baltic pine had been used as ballast in the holds of the early supply and settler ships, which in turn had been used as flooring generally. This particular pine, Brian had told him, and, as Lincoln could see for himself, was very different to the modern farmed and processed pine – the old, tough, knotted texture, after a floor of the same had been sanded and treated, was rich-lustre beautiful. Brian had also informed him that only recently had a lot of Australians come to realise the true value, aesthetically, of what they'd been walking on and had had covered for years. This particular floor, Lincoln appreciated, had an air of age, and love, and . . . wax – Lincoln could just discern the faint, underlying, pleasant redolence of wax floor polish. The pictures, the floor and scattered carpets, and the books on their shelves, and what furniture there was . . . it all cancelled out to make a very comfortable room.

Lincoln and every man were aware of her presence and each of them couldn't help but occasionally glance in her direction: she sat in one of the comfortable, scattered armchairs and she was Jamie's eldest sister, Mary. Behind her and standing in attention and with his hand resting on her shoulder was her husband, one Andrew Pennine. He was a lucky man and, Lincoln was pleased to determine, looked as if he had enough sense to know it. It wasn't as if she was beautiful, though her inner beauty shone through; Lincoln contemplated, and it wasn't sexuality, nor, becoming though it was, her traditional highland dress. Leonardo's *Mona Lisa* was the most famous though a somewhat unversed example, and Lincoln felt, nevertheless, that she had that indefinable quality of a fine woman in her prime, at peace within herself and in love and secure in her children's and her husband's love – and on top of that was . . . Lincoln couldn't put it into words: she was secretly laughing at the world – and probably at them!

Grandfather Montrose broke Lincoln's reverie and it was only then that Lincoln realised that Mary's eyes and his had been locked across the room, and hers, though bold, held no message, and she, Mary Pennine, had just not found it necessary to look away.

"You're the English man?" It was a statement rather than a question, though not offensive and nor did he require, Lincoln instinctively knew, an answer. "Mary, whom you've been looking at is the eldest of Jamie's sisters – all bonny lasses. You'd be married yourself, I understand?"

Lincoln grinned at his so-obviously transparent enquiry – Jamie had quietly given him the 'inside story' earlier. Lincoln nodded solemnly. "Yes, I'm married."

Jamie's grandfather saw through Lincoln straight away and chastised him accordingly. "It's all right for you to laugh, laddie, marrying off four granddaughters is a serious business and up till now I've no been successful – except for yon Mary, of course."

Without thinking Lincoln asked, "Where's their father?"

Grandfather Montrose's face dropped.

Lincoln quickly apologised, "Sorry, I didn't mean to pry."

No preamble and straight out with it, "Ay, laddie, the wee man stepped off the pier one night – whiskey, blind drunk and that was that. We never recovered his body. We never found the body. And nare a body to bury – and I can't even go to the cemetery to have a wee word with him." Grandfather Montrose sighed resignedly. "The wee girls nor his widow cannot even put flowers on his grave." He was pensive then. "We do not talk about it in this house, ay, tis best forgotten – best not to go stirring up the memories." Which, Lincoln observed, was exactly what he was doing! "Ay, a waste, a dreadful criminal waste." And after a moment, which Lincoln was relieved to see, the gloomy look on his face cleared and he sat up straight. "Why I've confided in you, I don't know – you'll honour the confidence?"

"Yes, Mister Montrose," Lincoln replied, "I'll honour the confidence. I'm only sad that such bereavement had to take place."

Grandfather Montrose brightened up then, and actually rubbed his hands, and obviously happy in the pursuance of what had become an entertaining and, apparently, a somewhat provocative hobby. "Ay, well, we've managed. There are more people to come, I understand; now which of these fine young men are . . . Not the one with the dog bites – who's eligible?"

Lincoln grinned again; he just couldn't help it. "Well, there's only Brian and his wife to come, I'm afraid, and they're at a 'skippers-and-wives' bash – these are going to have to do, these are all there are. There's Lionel, of course," Lincoln was thinking as he spoke and said slowly, "but nobody's really too sure exactly what his marital status is. He's gone too, to the same bash, I mean, because he felt it discriminatory not to ask crew – and nothing to do with free drinks at the Sheraton, of course!" Lincoln asked, curiosity getting the better of him, though at the same time not really seriously believing that this conversation was taking place. "There are plenty of local young men available; surely they can't all be unsuitable?"

"Well apparently they are not good ... 'Bash'!" he suddenly echoed, and he raised his eyebrows with a certain mocking, taken-aback and pretended, derogatory contempt.

They both sat silently watching as another of his granddaughter's, bearing a tray, entered the room. She, like her elder sister, Lincoln observed, also wore tartan. The representation of a folded cloak was neatly draped over her shoulder; and the worked tasselled edges of each end hung equally at her back and front and both ended just below her waist. A heavily embossed broach, Lincoln noted, was pinned above and on the downward slope of her ample up-thrust breast and held the representation of the cloak in place, and it secured it to her white blouse. Her pleated tartan skirt swirled easily. To the garters, presumably, and just below her knees, and particularly catching his eye, were attached tartan chevrons. They, Lincoln conjectured, the presumed garters, held up white socks – which were covering a fine pair of shapely legs.

General conversation picked-up and Grandfather Montrose whispered an aside as she approached. "Margaret, the second youngest – twenty-five and rapidly heading for the shelf."

Grandfather Montrose leaned forward as Margaret bent and kissed her grandfather on the cheek. "You can strike this one off the list, lassie," he informed her, "he's already spoken for – save you a bit o'time."

Margaret quickly glanced at Lincoln and then away, her eyes flashing and her face crimson. "Bloody hell, Grandfather, what do you think I am – a bloody cow on the hoof."

She held the tray forward and to one side, putting Lincoln between the tray and her grandfather. "Would you like a vol-au-vent?" she asked demurely and then looked directly at her grandfather, her affection showing through her contrived haughtiness. "Grandfather doesn't want one."

The old man laughed outright. "It'll be a strong man who tames her, laddie, ay, and then only if she wants to be."

Margaret turned away before she could receive further damage, but ended the conversation with a passing shot over her shoulder. "He probably won't want ... if he carries on like he is, then he won't be getting his tea either!"

"Are you retired, Mister Montrose?" Lincoln politely asked, after they'd finished admiring Margaret's departing back.

"Ay lad, we have a small engineering shop. Service and

repairs to a lot of the ships that call – and local vessels, of course. I'm at work at seven every day," he said with some pride, and with a sublimeness which had to be seen to be believed, he added, "though 'tis Jamie's business now, only I just haven't got around to telling him yet! You'll be as well to call me James; it'll stop the confusion with Jamie."

A babble of conversation drifted round them, James Montrose was one of those few men who were quite comfortable and at ease with silent companionship. They contentedly watched the small groups talking.

Helmut was also silently occupied, his eyes had never left Margaret since her entrance, and their glances were meeting too often across the room for coincidence.

Helmut caught Lincoln watching him and crossed directly. "Chris?"

"Not here, Helmut," Lincoln interrupted and turned to James Montrose. "Could we use – would it be possible to use your balcony, Mister Montrose, please?"

Grandfather Montrose didn't turn a hair. "James," he corrected. Not daft, Lincoln observed, was James Montrose. "Ay, lad." He pointed. "The door's there, and it's not locked."

Helmut and Lincoln stepped out.

"It's better to talk out here, Helmut, it's private," and Lincoln added dryly, "and we won't have to shout." Lincoln's aside had obviously gone over his, Helmut's, head; Helmut didn't have time for it anyway!

"Chris, that is Jamie's sister, Margaret?"

Lincoln started to laugh.

"Vot is funny?" he demanded, and the anguish in his eyes showed.

"Sorry, Helmut. Okay, Margaret, what about her?"

"How can I talk to her? My English, I am German. Vot vould I say to that girl? Vould she marry a German immigrant? Vould her mother and grandfather stop her, do you think? And Nick standing there too – the handsome prick."

Lincoln took a step backwards, the outburst so intense – and passionate. As an irrelevant aside Lincoln faintly corrected him. "You mean 'prince'." And then asked, "You haven't even talked to her yet, have you?"

"No." Helmut rubbed his face, and his hand then cupped his chin and he stroked the bristle.

Lincoln gave up trying to work out if he'd said no to 'prince', or no, he hadn't talked to her yet. Either way it didn't really matter, he'd only left her two choices, and if he looked at her with those 'cow eyes' much more she'd either be sick over this balcony or she'd rush him straight into bed!

"Leave it with me, Helmut." It was unthinkingly uttered, and Lincoln smiled, Christ, look at him, any one would think that the marriage was already arranged for Saturday – and if it wasn't, it would be only one person's fault!

Lincoln stood, contemplating – bemused and bewildered. Helmut knew, without a shadow of doubt, that he had met his ladylove and soul-mate, and the next move was the wedding – and strangely enough, Lincoln knew it too! Lincoln hardly registered Helmut's departure, and not seeing either nor admiring the glorious view across the Derwent.

"Are you all right, Chris?" Jamie's mother stood in the doorway.

"Sorry, Mrs Montrose, I did ask James. He said it was all right to be out here."

"No, no, you personally . . ." She asked curiously, "Did Dad ask you to call him James?"

"Yes, is that all right?"

"Yes, of course," she answered slowly. "It's just . . . I can't remember when I last heard somebody call him James." She took a breath. "You must be a rare man, Christian Lincoln, if you're on first names with my father-in-law all ready."

After a moment Lincoln followed her in and sat.

"Everything all right, laddie?" James Montrose enquired.

"Hmm," Lincoln answered and then bent forward to better hear Margaret's enquiry. "You were talking to Helmut?" she demanded rather than asked.

Lincoln pretended to scan the room. "Who?"

"Helmut," she snapped. She stood defiant, refusing to look away, and wearing her heart on her sleeve. "Was he talking to you about me?"

"Margaret!" interrupted a shocked James Montrose. "Chris is a guest in this house and I'll no have you . . ."

He got no further and Margaret didn't even turn to look at him. "Grandfather, please. Just for once . . ."

Lincoln sighed, this was serious stuff and time to cut to the quick. "Margaret." Lincoln touched his lips with his fingers.

"He's a good friend of mine, and he hasn't got our sense of humour." Lincoln qualified that, "Well, he has, but not our type of sense of humour – you have to know him ... He's a marshmallow under that tough facade. He's the marrying kind; don't take him on unless you mean it." Lincoln looked directly into her eyes. "Please don't hurt him."

A stunned James Montrose and Lincoln watched her as she moved away.

It was he who broke their wondering silence. "Christ, the wee girl's been struck silly." He pleaded, "He's a bloody German."

Lincoln grinned behind his hand – it had been very noticeably that James Montrose, tough as he no doubt was, was neither game enough nor daft enough to confront, try to discipline or impose his will on the implacable spirit of his wayward granddaughter. He complained instead.

"I'm not too sure that I want a bloody German in the family."

"He's a precision engineer," Lincoln placidly said, "originally apprenticed to a world famous ship-builder in Hamburg."

There was a silence. "Glessen's?" Grandfather Montrose asked.

"Glessen's," Lincoln replied.

James Montrose looked across at Helmut thoughtfully.

They were silent then and Margaret's sudden bombshell apparently forgotten – as yet another of his granddaughters made her entrance. He pointed. "A grandfather shouldn't have favourites, but look at Sophia, the youngest, of course, and the apple of ..." He sighed and admitted, "I've spoiled her," and then to himself, "but then, she spoils her grandfather too, or twists him round her little finger more like."

Lincoln wouldn't have minded but he was looking him in the eye when he said it. "It's hard with granddaughters, laddie."

"I can see how you're struggling." Lincoln laughed and nodded to his favourite. "All have red hair, do they?"

"Ay, like their father."

"And you all wear traditional dress?" Lincoln asked, looking from her down to Grandfather Montroes's kilt.

"Ay, only on New Year's Eve and New Year's Day, laddie. My father was a whaling man, Hobart serviced the whaling fleet, he honoured his forefathers and for him the clans were part of everyday life and not a wee few facts in a dusty history book. He wore the tartan for them. New Year's for him was a time of memories, nostalgia and not a few tears." He blinked and added, "I hope the girls don't wear it just to pander to and humour an old man." And to Lincoln he said, "Do not throw away your heritage, laddie – it's important."

He ruminated for a few moments. "We've always been sailing people and the women folk 'medical' – the girls are medical." James Montrose paused. "Am I boring you, laddie, one of the wee problems with ongoing senility is that you tend to wander."

Lincoln smiled, James Montrose had all his marbles and they both knew it.

Sophia leaned with an elbow on one of the book shelves; and resting on one leg while drawing circles on the boarded floor with a soft, black, leather-slippered toe. Lincoln grinned inwardly, both with their heads down and she listening with apparent deep concentration to Nick's words – and his lips close to her ear.

Lincoln noticed James Montrose watching them too, so rather than open another can of worms he ignored their apparent intimacy and indicated Sophia only. "She's medical, is she, as well?"

James Montrose groaned. "Yon lad, he's Italian, isn't he? Ay, her and Margaret, they both do the nursing." He nodded across to Mary. "Mary was the surgical sister at the hospital; Andrew had to threaten to actually operate on her before she'd even look at him. Elizabeth's the doctor, a GP – always the bright one. Ay, and too bright for her own good, I've given up with her, she's thirty-four and actually on the shelf gathering dust. You'll maybe meet her later, she's up at the hospital at the moment – one of her wee patient's has been took ill."

"Leave him alone, Grandfather," a voice interrupted them, and she said to Lincoln, "You're Chris?"

"Sophia." Lincoln stood to shake hands.

"Only Papa calls me Sophia – you're to help yourselves to tea . . . Oh, and while I remember, your skipper has just phoned, they'll be a little late, they said." She pointed to a doorway at the back of the room. "Will you show him, Grandfather?"

Actually, it wasn't tea, and Lincoln just looked, it was high tea and in the fullest sense of the word. The table groaned under the weight of fare: smoked ham, cold roast turkey, cold roast beef, a leg of pork, warm roasted and boiled potatoes, warmed vegetables, salad, fresh cut loaves, butter, pâtés, dips, spreads and sauces. A large serving trolley carried deserts and 'finishers': gateaux, homemade fruit pie, fruit flan, fruit salad, fresh fruit and cheese-board. The girls had thought it out and Lincoln congratulated: a carving knife placed beside each plate of cold meat, and they themselves were to cut from whatever and help themselves from wherever. Plates and dishes were of the paper variety – and thus they wouldn't need to be served nor would there be any washing-up after.

It was an ignoble end to a beautiful day: to be impaled on the corner of a medical bag while stepping back into the living room!

Chapter 4

A white mist swirled and the world was a tenuous thing and the black-edged shadows hesitated: bordering on spreading, but still undecided. Lincoln from somewhere had felt his knees jar as they hit the floor and he had automatically changed hands as he had fallen, so that his right arm and hand were under and across and covering and thus protecting and holding where the bag had caught. The floorboards impressed themselves into and felt cold and dry and pleasant under his left forearm, and the cool boards contrasted the trapped heat and sweat that was between the skin on the uppermost side of his forearm and that of his forehead that rested on it. Lincoln was allowing his weight to rest on his right elbow and was using it to make space and create leverage for his pressing hand. No, he wasn't going to pass out – the pain wasn't going to allow that. Shallow breaths and concentration on the epicentre – the pain came in waves whose peaks were searing. Irrationally and for some unknown reason an association and comparison of two key words fluttered, and they were 'excruciating' and 'toothache' – though the slicing pain was far greater and deeper than the excruciating agony of any toothache in the night. Edging his right knee forwards and sideways and shifting more weight onto that joint eased the poignancy very slightly.

A voice gradually separated itself and surfaced from the confusion – the confusion and babble of voices. To Lincoln it was intrusive and loud and demanding, and the words made little sense; Lincoln listened, rather, to its tone finally, and there was concern and a soothing gentleness underlying the persistence. And it worked . . . the distraction worked and worked amazingly well. Lincoln noted that fact somewhere and stuck it into the back of his brain – to be remembered and considered later. The result of that deliberately distracting voice was impressive and it had impacted as a surprise, and it was elementally so obvious and yet so spectacularly effective. Once realised, then Lincoln's concentration was total and the diversion of the voice all-important because its cadence was splitting the pain and mixing and distracting away, and achieving, finally, a good percentage of switched attention. And it was just as well because never had Lincoln experienced, or been subjected to, or felt, or endured such explosive pain of such scalding intensity.

Cool fingers caressed and the voice gradually turned from gentleness to 'meant' insistence. "Are you concentrating – concentrate – listen." Fingers pulled at Lincoln's ear. "Listen to me – listen!"

Really sharp pain from his right ear lobe was beginning to annoy and the words were involuntary and spoken without conscious thought, and unfortunately without restraint. "For Christ's sake, don't do that – piss off!"

Lincoln regretted it as soon as he'd said it – why upset the voice!

Fortunately, the voice came again, though a touch dryer and a touch harder, and a touch more determined. "Very good. Now tell me your name? Concentrate and listen – answer me. What is your name? Come on, we're not going to sleep, tell me your name?"

Nagging bitch! . . . And annoyance flared with renewed intensity and in accordance the focus of sharp, piecing, writhing agony shifted and dulled and thankfully moved to one side. And strangely, if he looked only down the tunnel, then he could think round it.

"Chris," Lincoln finally replied.

The voice responded and Lincoln glowed in its pleasure and caress. "Good, just a little longer. My name is Elizabeth, Elizabeth. Now tell me my name?"

Damn, he just couldn't quite bring into or hold the focus long enough – oh, he understood her; it was answering that was the problem. He had experienced similar before, it was the same when drunk: the brain then was also a treacherous and slippery thing and the same drifting away and shifting before current thoughts and subjects were fully formed – and the same feeling of detachment and of no real sense of presence, nor importance, nor of reality.

The voice interrupted again and with more insistence, "Say, Elizabeth – come on, concentrate."

Lincoln involuntarily answered, "Elizabeth."

"Good – think, listen. My mother, Mrs Montrose, Jamie's mother – you remember Jamie's mother?"

Lincoln moved his head.

"Moving your head means 'yes', does it, Chris? Move your head again if it means 'yes' . . ." Lincoln did as she asked.

"Good. Now I'm going to lift your left hand and put a cloth under it – I won't hurt you, is that okay?"

Lincoln assented again and drowsed.   The voice moved away though her droning presence was easily distinguishable amongst other mumbled conversation.

Cool fingers rubbed and caressed his neck, Lincoln hadn't heard nor sensed an approach – and then the hand rested. "Are you all right," the voice murmured – her voice. "Not long now."

"Umm . . ." Lincoln murmured in return, "that's nice, don't stop."

There was a tut and the voice quizzically asked, "Grandfather's, Jamie's Grandfather, you remember Jamie's Grandfather?"

Lincoln gave another of his equivalents of a nod.

"Grandfather's room is next door, it's just a few steps, could you manage that?" The voice suggested and half-instructed at the same time, "You can walk in a half-crouch, if you want – we'll help you stand. You'll be more comfortable on his bed; you can lie on your side . . . We'll carry you otherwise, we'll carry you if you can't – if you find that you are unable to walk, that is."

Lincoln hated the thought, not about having to move, he'd dismissed that, but that his moving would spoil everything and the voice would go away, or change! No, Lincoln wanted that comforting voice to stay – and his reptilian brain analysed – there was unfulfillment . . . a sadness, a yearning, a wistfulness and something else that he could not quite grasp, something which was deeply hidden and camouflaged behind that voice, and it was he, Lincoln, who suddenly wanted to comfort and to hold and to protect . . . and to touch and to caress and too . . . too . . .

Lucidity was slowly coming back and those virtually subconscious thoughts washed away as the synapses connected – and she was right – he couldn't stay here, lying outside their doorway.   Lincoln took a deep breath and nodded, and he moved his head sideways and swallowed the dribble and then focused down the tunnel. "Elizabeth?"

"Yes," she immediately answered.

"Just lead me and I'll do it myself – it's going to hurt when I move, isn't it?"

"A bit, maybe, only you can tell." She advised hesitantly,

"Find, feel for it – you must search for the most comfortable way of moving." She obviously wasn't happy and it sounded as if she was having second thoughts. "Look, we could easily lift you, you know – it really wouldn't be any trouble to lift you. To be honest, I'd rather we carried you than have you trying to stand."

Lincoln was silent, no, it wasn't as cut and dried as that – for a start they wouldn't have a stretcher handy . . . and to be carried like a sagging bag of coal would hurt a damn sight more than him making his own way.

Lincoln made up his mind. "I'll walk," he said.

Well, at least she didn't argue, Ms Montrose, thought Lincoln, but the tightness in her reproving advice boded ill.

"All right, but don't do anything if there's pain, and if there is then we'll find another way – after all," she added wryly, "there's no shortage of manpower around here, is there!"

"Hmm," Lincoln muttered in agreement and a picture of the grinning hairy apes that Brian Ramsey had the cheek to call a crew flashed across and into his mind's eye. The depth of affection that Lincoln felt for them all surprised him . . . That train of thought was interrupted by Doctor Montrose, who was suddenly all business.

"Right, I'll hold your left arm – whatever seems easiest. When you're ready then," she ordered, and then contradictorily added, "take your time."

Hands grasped and helped as Lincoln straightened and got his left knee up, and that knee and his foot and calf were shaking uncontrollably under a trapped left forearm; thankfully, the weight of his upper body resting and balancing just about locked it into position. A right hand he kept protectively over the damaged area. It was a strange sensation – to be watching himself from somewhere – to be immune in the back of his brain . . . and calm and floating above. Lincoln could hear and feel himself taking more deep shuddering breaths and he waited until the cloth wiping his forehead withdrew. In a half-stood crouch Lincoln followed Doctor Montrose's guiding, supporting, directing and pulling hand.

*   *   *

A voice asked, "Where's the blood coming from, Elizabeth?" The voice then irrelevantly commented, or at least it seemed irrelevant to Lincoln. "Margaret and I, we step out for two minutes for a breath of fresh air and this happens, talk about a busman's holiday." He, whoever, cheerfully complained, "Nobody mentioned blood!"

Andrew Pennine, Lincoln thought.

Another voice answered him – and feminine – Elizabeth Montrose. "It's superficial, Andrew, it's coming from his left hand, his index finger – the nails. The middle fingernail should be removed – what's left of it. The bloody fool had band-aids around them, God, they must hurt." She paused. "They're not worrying me, the blood, or his nails, I mean, it's what's under his shirt, that's what's worrying me. I hardly touched him with my bag . . . At least, I didn't think I did . . . I'm doubting myself now . . ."

Andrew Pennine's enunciation changed slightly, "No, all you would have done, at worst, was wind him . . . No, there's more going on here, Elizabeth, he's now been, from what you've told me, unconscious for too long. No, either we wake him somehow or it's straight to hospital – at least we can wire and monitor him there."

"If we can get somebody in and get some X-rays done, Andrew, then I suspect they'll tell a story." Elizabeth Montrose sounded to Lincoln as if she were absently half-speaking to herself rather than to Andrew Pennine. "So . . . this is Jamie's hero." There was a momentary pause before she resumed her conversation. "He was slammed two or three times against the mast according to Jamie, freeing tangled halyards in a blow, and he lost his fingernail – nails then. Jamie said it was either free them or retire – or worse. They were trying to get a foresail down and a storm jib up – and he crashed heavily, really heavily, when they were lowering him back down." Her tone changed – and exasperation was creeping in. "You know what they're like, Andrew, they close ranks – it doesn't seem to occur to them that this one may have seriously injured himself. Knowing Jamie, a 'wee blow' was probably a howling force-twelve gale with waves the size of express trains and travelling at twice their speed!"

Little did she know, Lincoln thought.

And then exasperation changed to temper. "I'd put money on it, Andrew, it's self-induced, self-inflicted, and now he's sound a bloody sleep." Lincoln could almost hear her foot stamping. "He's damn well let go and ruined my New Year's

Day." She paused, and then continued on more slowly. "They've all said that, they all say that he hasn't slept since Boxing Day, apart from five or possibly six hours at the very most after they got in – they don't seem to know. Him and Brian, that's the skipper apparently, were the last to bed last night – no morning, I mean, this morning." Elizabeth Montrose calculated, "Just catnaps then, and not many of those as far as we know. Two beers he's had and drunk here, and . . . plus Mother gave him a card of Paracetamols," The rustling of the packet sounded very loud. "And going by how many are left, he's been taking one every half-hour – every half-hour, Andrew, God, his kidneys'll be under a hell of a strain." Lincoln was then, once again, roundly condemned. "He bloody well shouldn't be awake, he should be bloody dead, and he deserves to be – the irresponsible bloody idiot."

James Montrose was right about his granddaughter, Elizabeth Montrose, she was the bright one. Away in Lincoln's secret place and deep under the active brain he listened – their voices echoing in from a different plane. This is where he went off-watch, and the top active brain asleep, here Lincoln monitored the boat: it was a faint thread of consciousness ready to rouse and trigger alarms to the above should any alien or unusual sound or motion differ from the norm. Lincoln was aware and could debate with this inner self only when in the last stages of exhaustion.

"He'd have to virtually be a corpse before they'd X-ray him today, wouldn't he, Andrew . . . Damn it – I'll cut the clothes off him."

Andrew wasn't the brave one – my word, thought Lincoln, the medical fraternity was a bit of a worry – he could have been dying!

'Doubting' Andrew voiced his reservations, "He'll be bloody furious if we cut his jeans, Elizabeth, it won't matter that we'd have saved his bloody life. The rows we've had in casualty: bloody patients losing blood by the buckets-full and still insisting that we take their bloody jeans off intact – some of them even have the blasted effrontery to moan about their own blood on them . . ." Andrew Pennine half-coughed and sighed at the same time. "Still, not to panic, he's got a steady heartbeat and his respiration's fine."

"Right, Andrew, enough's enough." Lincoln grinned to

himself, at the determined sound of her voice as she mentally rolled up her sleeves. "Don't you worry yourself about his jeans, I'll sort them out. Now . . . we'll cause him only a minimum amount of pain if we're careful. I'll . . ." There was a snip, "Cut his belt – and I'll cut straight down the leg seams and then I'll cut his shirt away." Grim satisfaction was the only way to describe her self-justifying, self-satisfied, obviously unrepentant, final sentence. "He'll be a lot more comfortable anyway."

They had the sense to leave Lincoln on his side; Doctor Montrose and Master Surgeon Pennine were extraordinarily gentle and discomfort caused was minor. There was a sharp intake of breath from one of them, and he'd misjudged Andrew Pennine, his professionalism began to show – and his voice took on a different timbre.

"I need to see his reactions, I want him awake, Elizabeth, and I want him awake now – his torso's going to be worse."

She pushed the hair away from Lincoln's eyes, and he gave an involuntary grunt – the torchlight blinded.

"You should know better than to talk in front of the patient, Doctor," Lincoln murmured, "unconscious or awake."

Andrew Pennine's voice forestalled her answer, "How long have you been awake?"

"A few seconds," Lincoln answered.

"Then how . . . never mind, how do you feel?"

Lincoln considered, apart from the usual the specific pain had dulled to a raw tender throbbing. "Better," he acknowledged.

"Could you sit up, do you think? I'd just like to check for damage now that we've got this far."

Illogically, Lincoln felt like a child in front of them – a naughty child – awkward, self-conscious and embarrassed. In truth, Lincoln desperately wanted to be just left alone; oh, they meant well, he knew, but the urge to pull the blankets over and curl up was all but overwhelming . . . Just to close out the world and rest in his secret place – and lick the wounds.

Andrew Pennine must have glimpsed something of Lincoln's intentions. "Not yet," he said, "do this for me first and then you can."

Lincoln looked from him to a puzzled Elizabeth Montrose and then nodded, resigned to his fate.

"It'll perhaps be better if you stood; it'll be easier to get your shirt off . . . Well, what's left of it. I'm assuming, of course, that you can stand." There was a momentary pause. "Can you?" He added quickly, "Don't worry, we won't hurt you – we've done this thousands of times."

Lincoln shook his head as Andrew Pennine reached forward to help. "No, I'll do it."

In one smooth movement Lincoln rolled off the bed and onto his hands and knees – he took a few breaths and then stood.

Andrew Pennine shook his head.   "It never ceases to amaze me – the way the human body adapts.   It's been hurting for some time that, that side, hasn't it?   Sorry," he quickly apologised, "stupid question." He pointed and said gently, "If you can manage to drop that protecting arm for a minute, then we'll get your, um, shirt off."

Elizabeth Montrose stepped behind and gently slid Lincoln's shirt off his shoulders and eased it down his arms.

Andrew Pennine sighed. "You've been in the wars, Mister Lincoln." He just looked for a moment before commenting again.   "I'm not sure that you wouldn't be better off at the hospital."

Thank Christ my underpants are clean, Lincoln thought irrelevantly: they weren't of the latest style, but they couldn't have looked too bad!

"Sorry," Lincoln queried, "what did you say?"

"Just try to concentrate for just a little longer, please." Andrew Pennine looked down, pointed and nodded. "I assume you can move the toes of your right foot – all the feeling is there, is it?"

Lincoln came back again and nodded in turn. "Looks worse."

"Would you turn round, I'll just check your back."

The door opened as Lincoln turned and Judy and Lincoln looked at each other, and their eyes locked for what seemed to be an age. Lincoln was childishly pleased to see her – to see a friendly face – and he smiled just before she broke eye-contact. Her eyes dropped and roamed before coming back to Lincoln's face.   There something wrong – she bit her lip and then her face crumpled – tears streamed. Lincoln just hadn't the strength nor the will to go to her: he was fighting to stay upright as it was and he hadn't excess energy, nor initiative, even to call out. She silently and mutely shook her head before gently re-closing the door.

Lincoln turned and looked in askance to Elizabeth Montrose – and then promptly forgot what he was about to ask!

There was no comment from Elizabeth Montrose, she simply stepped forward and hooked her arm under his – beyond being proud, was Lincoln, and he gratefully leant on her shoulder.

"Breathe deeply." The cool stethoscope traced a pattern. "Tell me if any of this hurts?"

Lincoln grinned to himself – he'd tell him all right!

"Okay – would you turn again? Elizabeth?" Andrew Pennine held out the stethoscope. "Sorry."

She merely shook her head.

"Only a couple more minutes, Chris. Lift your right arm?" he instructed. "Okay. Trust me. Lift your left arm, please? Okay – don't force it."

Lincoln jolted as his fingers probed into his left collarbone, nevertheless, he was exceptionally quick, and thorough, he'd give him that. Lincoln gritted his teeth – waiting for – anticipating and dreading his touch on his ribs. That dread never fully materialised, and he thanked God, and Andrew Pennine explored with a feather light touch and only using minimal pressure.

"Okay, finished, you can lie down." He looked to Doctor Montrose and raised his eyebrows. "Elizabeth?"

Her reply didn't register as she eased him down onto the bed. Lincoln swung his feet up and round in one smooth movement, and then shuffled and wriggled himself into a comfortable position. The urge to turn on his side and pull up his legs had gone and Lincoln looked at the ceiling instead, eyes unfocused.

Andrew Pennine was scribbling notes, and his pen scratched: they all used 'fountain' pens! It was an irrational thought and yet in Lincoln's present drifting mood it seemed relevant: surely it hadn't gone unnoticed – other people must have noticed too, that doctors seem to take such . . . They get so much pleasure out of the ritual . . . and of decisively screwing the top back on!

"Right," said Andrew Pennine, "without X-rays . . .

Definitely a broken collarbone and three ribs cracked; one almost certainly broken, though at present the ends are obviously together.   Looking at the depth of bruising, and despite your assurances, your right leg could have a fracture – at least a hairline fracture anyway." Andrew Pennine considered. "You've been walking on it, which bodes well. We need to X-ray it to be sure, but be warned, any signs of pain and you disregard those warnings, then you'll damage it further and then it'll be pins! Understand?" Lincoln nodded. "The human body is designed so as to protect vital organs, fortunately for you, Mister Lincoln."   He looked from him, Lincoln, to Elizabeth Montrose and then back.   "Though then again and only going by the abuse and the evidence, I would imagine your kidneys ache like the very devil as well."

He suddenly shot out another question, "You've no blood in your urine, have you?"

Lincoln shook his head.

"None in your faeces? Not coughing up blood?"

"No."

"Do you remember hitting your head or damaging your neck?"

"No."

"Blackouts? Headaches? Vomiting?   Do you have any allergies? Do you react to any drug – penicillin, for example?"

Lincoln mouthed another 'no' and started once more to drift, something made Lincoln glance at him, and as he did so Andrew Pennine grimaced and lowered his face close to Lincoln's.   "Though not a pretty sight you aren't about to immediately expire – we'll sort it all out tomorrow."

The words echoed round.

"Sleep is what his body needs more than anything, Elizabeth – and time."   Although he was speaking directly to Elizabeth Montrose his words were indirectly aimed at Lincoln. "If he'll just give it half a reasonable chance then the damage'll repair itself – he's not the sort though, his type'd rather die." There was a rustling and a sound of tearing. "Still – we won't give him an immediate choice, will we." Silence reigned. "Both shots – one in each arm – one's a painkiller, the other's a sedative. I guarantee he won't catnap, he'll sleep though he'll wake if he feels any acute discomfort."

He dismissed Lincoln then, the job was done and Lincoln

was completely out of his thoughts – it's how you remain sane, Lincoln supposed, when you were in his line of work.

"By the way," he asked Elizabeth Montrose, "what did he mean when he referred to you as the 'dusty one'?"

There was an edge to her voice when she replied, "I don't know, Andrew, though I suspect my Grandfather might."

Words and their meaning faded and oblivion invaded the last bastion.

*   *   *

Not at this stage of the game, surely, with vision starting to blur and his mind beginning to go, and lungs bursting – and the creeping red mist enveloping . . . And Mother's face barely distinguishable – and so very sad. Nor would she answer – she wouldn't answer – and Lincoln called and called again, and again . . . and she just kept shaking her head. She had once been his true love, and the only one, and the only one with whom he'd place his trust implicitly: the one Lincoln loved the most . . . and Lincoln wept. Her face gradually faded and another slowly evolved out of the swirling fog. Oh God, now Father – but blind – and with sockets only . . . He'd have had to have been in the water for some time: he was so puffed . . . so putrefied. Then the image was wavering, and impaired, and the detail becoming indistinct. His saturated vision was hopeless without face protection – trying to see through water-filled eyes. Lincoln stood amongst swaying bottom-weed and ignored the various distractions: the fronds touching, the kelp caressing . . . and the siren whispering. Lincoln cursed, and scrabbled around in a panic – he had no wax! To foetal position and hands over ears instead – not to listen . . . not to listen.

His spear, Father's spear tip, hovered around in a jabbing, threatening circle – he feigned once and missed – and feigned again. It was in slow motion, but even so, Lincoln wasn't quick enough and the tip of the spear glanced off of his fending arm and went under before finally twisting away . . . and the agony . . . and the fire from a white-hot poker and spreading. There was no air left for screaming – only little spurts – only fine streams of bubbles to dribble out with the blood. Arms above head and frantically pulling down then, with every ounce of waning strength – and a final kick before having to breathe in . . . or to give-in finally, and inhale, and die. Lincoln blinked, and above was the dimpled, transparent, meniscus surface-skin of a benign sea. Lincoln broke through into the sunshine finally and lungs were filled with sweet oxygen, and he punched the sky with one fist above; loud and full of rigor and a full-throated yell of triumph – victory – to be alive!

The overhead light was blinding and it hurt – and disorientation was complete. Reality and realisation began to creep and Lincoln stared at the wall and at a curtained window across from the bed – James Montrose's bedroom. There was a supporting arm across, the hand of which firmly held onto his right shoulder, and there was another hand grasping his left; Lincoln turned around to see who it was and as he did so she shifted her head so that those emerald eyes were more imagined rather than seen. Furthermore, she'd placed her body in such a way so that Lincoln couldn't turn further, and the outline of her face, in periphery, was, disappointedly, only a blur in side-vision.

"You've been dreaming," she said softly. "A nightmare." Lincoln looked around again as she explained. "You're in my Grandfather's room, Jamie's Grandfather's – remember?"

Lincoln could hear quiet conversation, whispering and faces were peering.

Elizabeth Montrose gently released Lincoln and quickly stepped across and quieter words were exchanged from behind a partially pulled-to door. Lincoln just observed, and still in a faint daze: her left hand rested on the inner door handle and only her arm, side and back were visible as she leant around – and her dressing gown was of pale green towelling . . . and her hair a cascade of red.

She turned finally and just stood there, and not fully aware – standing silently, obviously considering.

"How often do you have that nightmare," she asked eventually, "that sort of nightmare?" She was suddenly brusque then and her quietly asked question apparently forgotten. "I'll find some more underwear while you're showering." She pointed. "There's an *en suite* through that door – the bed's awash and so are you. I'll change the sheets while you're in there."

She was right and Lincoln absently wiped away the sweat and then pushed the quilt back, but got no further – she'd sat herself in the way. She looked at him and he looked at her and they silently crossed swords.

"You haven't answered my question," she stated, and added archly, "and you're not going to, are you?"

"It's none of your business," Lincoln replied matter-of-factly. "Why should I allow you to cut my hair – who are you anyway!" Lincoln made to push the bedclothes back further. "Now, if you don't mind . . ."

She considered. "Macho thing, is it? Show no weakness in front of the opposite sex – it might damage your image?" The provocativeness in her voice was next replaced by concern – curiosity was still in there somewhere too though. "You haven't denied that you have had that dream before." She raised her eyebrows. "Often?"

Lincoln said tiredly, "Similar – at odd times – now and again."

And now it was his turn, and after raising his eyebrows, Lincoln belligerently enquired, "So?"

"Doctors are like solicitors and priests," she said solicitously. "I'm not here to take away your strength – any confidences I'll honour without question." Elizabeth Montrose looked serious – was deadly serious. "It maybe that you have a problem, please don't take offence only . . . I couldn't but help to have listened – I think you need professional help."

Lincoln's gentle laughter turned her complexion to a deep red – that deep red emphasised the white spots that had appeared on each of her cheeks. Real temper sparkled in her eyes and on the edge of slipping its leash, if Lincoln was any judge. Why, Lincoln couldn't say, it was the best-kept, buried secret of the century: sorry for her perhaps, and maybe touched by her sincerity, her earnest concern . . . something!

"In confidence, you said?" Lincoln asked.

She nodded, so intent – her curiosity was obviously killing her.

"It fits the facts too well, surely," Lincoln jeered lightly, "a little too pat even for a country doctor, I would have thought: huge, classic, Freudian problem: love mother, hate father, and all that?"

That she was furious with him was an understatement!

Lincoln just couldn't help but grin. Had she the insight though – did she have the maturity to realise the cost!

"I can't . . ." Lincoln said reluctantly – it was he who looked away. "I can't swim!" Lincoln stated finally.

53

Chapter 5

The air was crystal clear and too many deep breaths of the stuff and one would be drunk on pure oxygen. Lincoln, after he'd got out didn't turn as the engine revolutions of the taxi increased, nor did he when its tyres crunched on the gravel as it pulled away – and that was because he was too absorbed in the spectacular backcloth that was laid out behind the Derwent Sailing Squadron Clubhouse. Curiosity drove him around that building and onto their grass foreshore and to an uninterrupted view of a curving bay which the river had scooped out from the land. For all intents and purposes, Lincoln could very well have been looking at a very large lake, or a small inland sea rather than a river, considering the Derwent's width and the width of the bay from that point. The Derwent Sailing Squadron Clubhouse, and where he stood, was almost directly south and only separated from the city by Battery and Secheron Points. The clubhouse was actually situated and tucked in-between Secheron Point and the 'casino'-capped Wrest Point; and the bay, as measured on the chart, was, in fact, some one and a quarter kilometres in length, and half a kilometre in breadth. Of immediate interest were the many vessels moored within the bay's confines: tenders, rowing boats, speed boats, motor boats, motor cruisers, cabin cruisers, cruising yachts, racing yachts, cats – and even the odd trimaran. Yes, every colour, Lincoln noted, every shape and every design – a good many of Hobart's amateur water population must have been moored there.

Small ripples breaking the river's surface caught and reflected minute flashes from a sun that was well on the way to the meridian in the north and a prearranged zenith. This was one of those magical little respites which occur every now and again in everyday-life and make life worthwhile. And so Lincoln stood, oblivious to that other world, and just breathing in deeply and taking it all in and drinking up and savouring the atmosphere and surveying the vista – and the big sky, and the far horizons.

Lincoln turned eventually to retraced his steps, and then bulked before hurrying on, and bewildered and embarrassed by the seemingly hundreds of pairs of eyes that were staring out from behind the complete wall of picture-windows that were the seaward front of the clubhouse, as it were!

Stealthily, Lincoln opened and peered around one of the second sets of doors that guarded the club's main-street entrance. Judy smiled and gave a little wave; she was seated across the room next to Brian and amongst all the participating skippers and their wives. Also, at this end of the long rectangular hall was a stage, and on it had been placed a raised, white, table-clothed plinth, and behind which were seated 'tied' and 'blazered' officials, guests, guests wives and guest speakers, and other dignitaries. Down and filling the other end of the hall and furthest from Lincoln were the yacht crews, family, friends, audience and general riffraff. The speaker looked around questioningly as a muffled cheer went up – *Worippa's* crew was in a merciless mood and there was, Lincoln knew, going to be no quarter.

Lincoln had miscalculated badly and he hadn't banked on this; Judy caught his eye again and her smile had now gone and in its place was a frown. Lincoln knew her, she'd be working out time-frames – she pursed her lips and half-stood – and he could see her, literally, and like someone else Lincoln had met recently, mentally rolling up her sleeves! Lincoln hurriedly edged around the door and tried unobtrusively to join the crowd towards the back – it would have been better had the floor opened – the drumming of feet and banging of hands and implements on any surface stopped the 'prize giving' dead. Thankfully, the thin obscurity of the crowd ended it, still, anything was better than facing Judy . . . And even then, Lincoln wasn't necessarily safe – he wouldn't put it past her; she'd have the nerve to walk across, oblivious to any audience, and go for him there and then – and in front of everybody! It hadn't taken her long to work out: that Lincoln couldn't be at the hospital and here at the same time!

Lincoln decided, despite the risk, to stay on this side of the room; along this side they were only one deep against the wall and the crush, in his condition, would be too much amongst the main audience at the back. Needless to say, he noted, *Worippa's* crew had settled themselves in front of the bar and against and along its leading edge, and one of three forming the standard, mirror-backed oblong – the whole structure of the bar protruded out a fair way into the room. Lincoln looked down and silently congratulated himself – he'd remembered to wear his 'designer' top, and nobody, but nobody, could doubt which boat they all belonged to. Most yachts had individual sponsors, which is very nearly essential as the cost of running a competitive racing yacht, Lincoln knew, these days was bordering on prohibitive, even for medium, well-off individuals – it had become, unfortunately, sometimes a necessary evil. Other boats had beer, sail, yacht chandlers, paint, engineering and similar sponsors, and these providing crews with enviable, appropriately patterned, or featured, fashion tops. Brian's only comment was that he had to get his finance from somewhere and paranoiacally adamant that they wore theirs – and he just indifferently shrugged off all complaints. Still, their moans, and Lincoln sympathised, were understandable: cheap and poorly designed tee-shirts advertising 'rice puddings' and 'semolina' were not the most inspiring. Actually, the only people who really loved their tee-shirts were the other crews!

When Lincoln was sure that their attention was elsewhere . . . and only then did Lincoln furtively look in their direction; most of them had sat themselves on bar stools, with their sides against and their elbows on the bar's polished top. Jean sat next to Bill; Sharon stood leaning and facing the front and against and between Gary's legs; his arms, Lincoln noticed, were around her waist. Margaret was in front of Helmut and leaning against him, and that, somehow, didn't surprise him – that Sophia was in front and leaning against Nicolo Frascati did! Mrs Montrose stood next to a seated Lionel, which was typical of Lionel – him allowing a woman to stand while he sat; and Jamie, Jamie had a young, clean, nice-looking girl in tow. Warren stood in the corner and between the bar and the wall and alone, as usual. Lincoln had to grin, and like peas in a pod in their tea-shirts; what good sports they all were, and even Mrs Montrose from somewhere had acquired and was also wearing a *Worippa* tee-shirt!

Clapping gradually became automatic for Lincoln after the initial 'Line Honour' presentations, so many different divisions and classes existed these days, and so many prizes for so many yachts racing under so many different handicapping rules. Rating yachts so that they all have an equal chance of winning, and that despite differences in age, design, size, crewmembers and the rest is virtually impossible. As new computer-enhanced systems develop, and as far as Lincoln could keep abreast of, so these categories, ironically, had increased rather than decreased

– and there must be, Lincoln thought, a moral somewhere in there – and hence the confusion and Lincoln's wandering interest. Only when their class winner was called out, which immediately brought a ragged cheer, did proceedings regain Lincoln's full attention.

Finally they clapped that skipper after he'd made the usual winner's speech – and he having thanked the race organisers, safety vessel, race sponsors, his navigator and crew and everybody else involved for their generosity, time, help and support. To be truthful, Lincoln had thought, despite him being their class winner, his speech et cetera to have been as equally boring as most of the previous had he not have had to belatedly jump sideways – to avoid the unattached, falling, heavy, black trophy base which, despite his sudden alacrity, resoundingly thudded down between his feet! They all watched, transfixed, as it slowly journeyed across and off the edge of the stage before trundling its way, hypnotically, in a curved arc, and as if attracted by some divine force, precisely to Ramsey's feet. Ramsey no more looked at it before bending to pick it up. He lifted it to eye level to theatrically inspect, and then pretended to spit on it, before giving it a vigorous polish with his sleeve – and before stepping forward to the edge of the stage in order to hand it back to the winning skipper. That skipper refitted the base to the cup, and then to everybody's surprise, placed the heavy, newly assembled trophy on the stage floor beside him. He stood and next bent again to say something to Ramsey, and held out his hand, which, after a slight hesitation, Ramsey firmly shook. "Brian Ramsey, ladies and gentlemen, of the yacht *Worippa*," said the commentator, who had quickly understood, "and an inspiration to any would-be contestant and a shining example of perseverance, tenaciousness, the indomitable spirit, and the art of not giving up!" The applause was resounding, and whether that skipper knew Ramsey, Lincoln didn't know, or whether he had seen the wistful, pensive sadness and 'if only' bared on Ramsey's face, in his eyes and in his body language, as Lincoln had clearly observed, he didn't know either. Or whether it was simply that he had perhaps seen that same news report and had acted on impulse, Lincoln couldn't guess, but just the same, it was handsomely done! The whole episode climaxed wonderfully after Ramsey had returned to his seat; by Judy pulling his head down into her bosom, commiserating and no doubt, and judging by her up and down head and lip movements next to his ear, and going by the sublime expression on his face, obviously telling him how wonderful and what a tiger he was despite everything!

The applause, which had been loud, increased yet again as the winning skipper made his way back to his seat – and everybody cheered, clapped and stamped – and Lincoln realised that not only were the audience cheering him as the winning skipper, but also, and probably more so, for his generosity of spirit too.

Lincoln was slow to realise, but on turning belatedly became conscious that the clapping could also have been extended by another, because, and like any other male with half an eye and half an ear, he couldn't help but notice Sharon blissfully and energetically jumping up and down, with one arm, or arms raised, and at the same time cheering enthusiastically. None of them would have been human had they not been mesmerised by her unrestrained, full-nippled breasts bobbing and jiggling ebulliently beneath thin cotton. Gary obviously couldn't see from behind and perhaps wasn't aware – either way, on his face there was . . . pride of possession, pride in the admiration of others, ownership, belonging, and there was also, Lincoln could discern, something in the way he touched her back that indicated, to him anyway, perhaps the beginnings of something deeper. One thing though, Lincoln concluded, and whatever prejudgements he had made, and now felt, Gary was no longer unhappy, and not lonely – and one couldn't truly envy him, and Lincoln didn't doubt that those who knew him would all feel the same – and after the darkness, and despite everything, that Gary Prestwick needed and deserved all the light he could get!

Judy had quiet words in the car park, from which Lincoln came away somewhat scathed. Potter had inadvertently taken the edge off his chastisement – by sniggering and making faces and wagging an admonishing finger, and all this just out of sight and beyond Judy's predatory, eagle vision – and his antics, silly and childish though they were, had somehow saved the lustre of the morning. Jamie's people were very tactful and Jamie was, in fact, more concerned about his 'doctoring' sister: her tempers were notorious, which, from the little that Lincoln had gleaned, didn't surprise him. They were bad enough in comparison, apparently, according to Jamie, to make Judy's ticking-off look like a child's tantrum!

They ate a buffet lunch after the photographers, international, national, and the local press had finished with them all. Their mood slowly changed to one of quiet preparation – they were mentally gearing up for that afternoon's 'finale': the 'King of the Derwent' glory run.

*　　　　　　*　　　　　　*

They climbed into the taxi, and after Brian had given directions he addressed them. "They all want to come, all except Bill's Jean, she's taking Mrs Montrose with her, she reckons they'll have a few cocktails on board the flag ship and then look for a couple of likely sailors. Jamie's girl, by the way, has said she would like to come along too."

Their skipper, the new brave Brian Ramsey (because Judy was out of sight) took the initiative, though even if, albeit, somewhat defensively. "Well, they put up a good argument, though I could have argued if I'd wanted that it's going to be 'light airs' and therefore none of them can come because we need minimum weight."

Actually, the part about 'light airs' was, in fact, true, Lincoln knew, though they were all pretty sure that the midday forecast had no bearing on the matter at hand.

Potter, after a derogatory snort, countered Ramsey's argument, "I know we like to think it, but those 'sheilas', they're far from daft, matie, for a start they'll ask, Judy would anyway, as to why we aren't dropping a few of the regulars off. Especially you, Pom," Potter never could resist the odd little dig, "apart from being useless with those few minor injuries of yours, you aren't too popular with her at the moment anyway, are you!"

Lincoln had just smiled, because as Lincoln had surmised, Potter had always had this knack of giving the knife a friendly little twist – and not to react, he'd found, was the only real defence.

Ramsey dithered on, "I know we'll be still well under crew allowance, but it just makes me nervous that we'll be breaking some rule or other with all those extra people."

"You really mean all those women on board. No," Potter considered, "it's no different to racing in any other regatta,

Brian, you carry whoever's available from day to day – a lot of regular crew would have flown home already anyway, there'll be crew changes and locals aboard on every boat."

Lincoln decided to be nasty too and finish it. "Judy says she's coming," Lincoln said innocently.

Potter immediately picked up on and saw through Lincoln's comment. "You're a 'shit', Pom," he said, before turning back to Brian. "It'll be fifteen miles around the pins, Brian, and the sun's shining – stick 'em all on the weather rail, matie, they won't be a problem, and furthermore, their weight'll keep the boat upright. Come on, Brian," he said, apparently without guile, "it'll be the thrill of a lifetime for 'em."

Potter's remark, Lincoln discerned, would have been innocent and logical had they all three been unaware of the zero to ten-knot wind forecast – the three of them knew perfectly well that with the amount of people anticipated on the one side, *Worippa'd* virtually turn turtle! Potter's little sideswipe still rankled so Lincoln took that out, with pasted sarcasm, on 'weak-knee'd' Ramsey as well. "It's your plain duty, Brian; you might even convert one of them – maybe one who'll end up to be the world's best yachtswoman."

Lincoln waited, watching discreetly: some fell on 'stony ground', and Potter, he, Lincoln knew, was doing the same. It came as they were just beginning to wonder.

"Why don't you two fuck off!"

Lincoln didn't dare let Potter catch his eye and peace reigned only because they were pulling up next to the pier – the taxi driver, Lincoln had noticed, had been staunchly silent throughout the whole journey, which Lincoln thought in his own little way was also quietly humorous!

      *   *   *

"Right, the Navy's here."

"I can see one rowing boat, where's the other one?" quipped Potter.

Brian ignored Potter's smart remark concerning the Australian Navy's resources. "The gunboat will be at one end of the line, and that buoy there," he pointed, "next to the launch, will be the other. I daren't play around amongst this lot." He then addressed Lincoln, "Further up river, you judge when – take some bearings, Chris, would you, and then time our run-in to the start. That way we'll be on starboard and have the right of way – it'll be a damn sight easier than trying to manoeuvre." He motioned with a slow chopping hand. "We'll plough straight down the centre – straight through the lot of 'em. I'll aim for the centre of the line too, most of them won't bother to time their run-ins and with luck they'll hang back a bit – because their views'll be obscured. None of 'em'll want to pay the price of having to go round the ends again – and with luck we'll find a bit of clear air too."

Providing the wind stayed constant, Lincoln assessed, then Brain's strategy was sound, and to be honest, probably the only way under these conditions – and that also taking into account the novices that they had on board. Even at this moment in time, and despite the fact that they were out early, the congestion was formidable and they were, even now, going to have a job on sailing a pre-run. Thousands of spectators were already lining the quays, wharves and shoreline – and the press of spectator boats was already a hazard – and every vessel that could float was seemingly out here. Even the local ferry, Lincoln noted, had been commandeered, for town officials and local sponsors by the look; and several smaller oil and seismic explorers and working ships were also already standing off, close to the fleet, inshore. Even the Sydney and the Melbourne race escort vessels had been given over to sponsors and club officials, to crew, family and friends. The local fishing fleet Lincoln also observed, was also strongly represented, and present in force. These, and other big craft would cause problems, their wakes throwing up a considerable chop – and another reason to stay inside the fleet and keep clear – it took considerable power to punch through such turbulence, and considering the light winds . . . Estimates later, Lincoln had heard, numbered the spectator flotilla alone at around one hundred and fifty, such a relatively undisciplined mishmash caused and created major headaches: a race of this magnitude was almost impossible to police. In truth, Lincoln judged, unless by some miracle, collisions were going to be inevitable: the combined Sydney and Melbourne competitors on their own formed an armada in excess of sixty yachts.

"Are you happy with the time . . ." Brian hunched himself over the wheel.

They all ignored Ramsey's rhetoric because they were, Lincoln could see, and as Ramsey had obviously and subsequently realised, intimidated and awed. The silence lasted for the time taken for the majestic giant 'maxi', and one of three there at Hobart, to plough halfway down their length. The backs of the monster's crew, and in identical green and yellow uniform, sat in a line and there were, if Lincoln were any judge, at least twenty to twenty-five of them there on the far weather rail. All would have their feet, Lincoln knew, hanging out over the side, and that boat'd be quite a sight when viewed from port. They all turned and gave them a little wave, and those aboard *Worippa* cursed because the sails attached to their one hundred and ten foot mainmast were blanketing their wind – and the yacht's overall eighty-three foot length seemed to take forever to clear!

Potter knew the 'monster's' master and with his usual consideration for delicate ears and the 'fair' sex aboard both vessels addressed their skipper. "Will you get that great heap of shit out of the way, matie," he yelled in a foghorn voice, Potter waved his hand. "Go on, fuck off."

Wide grins were only part of their departing reply, Lincoln laughed to himself, and they must have practised because they then all held their middle fingers up to attention in timed unison!

"Chris, you stay behind me then." Ramsey checked round, making sure Judy could hear – it didn't pay, and they'd all leant that hard lesson too, not to keep a weather-eye on Judy. "Count us down; the final gun will be on the dot of two o'clock. Would you also help the girls, if necessary, get across on the tacks." He glanced again at Judy and then, presumably, after seeing her expression, remembered Lincoln's physical state. "No. No, no don't help the girls across, Judy and Lionel'll do that, you just give me the benefit of your advice."

He looked at Judy again and half-apologising, "After all that, our leaving early, we still didn't get around to entering the marks into the computer." To the rest of them and to Lincoln, he said, "We're clocking a constant fifteen knots of wind from the south-east, that won't be a beat, will it, Chris, rather, it'll be a close-reach across at an angle." He indicated with a hand. "Down river. About a hundred degrees magnetic plus maybe a bit for tide and leeway." He reasoned, "The big boys'll show us the first mark, they'll round it long before us – it'll be round it to port and then along and back across under spinnaker."

There was no need for a comment from Lincoln – he had it to rights.

Brian turned to the girls next; they looked snug, vulnerable and appealing in borrowed, out-sized thermal jackets – all two, three, four sizes too large. Lincoln was pleased to see that one of the boys had had the forethought – that out here tee-shirts were not enough, the water cooled the air to three or four degrees below that of the land, and again, even on the open water out here, the 'chill factor' of the wind could soon drop body temperature to dangerous levels.

His advice to the girls, again, Lincoln observed, was sound, "When we change direction, as we turn through the wind, the wind in the sails will slowly lessen. The sails'll hang empty for a moment on the centre line of the boat." Brian was mimicking how the shape of the sails would change with an upheld, cupping hand. "Then they'll fill again, but from the other side, the opposite side. The boom," Brian touched it with a finger. "This heavy aluminium spar under the 'mainsail' will swing across like a scythe, if you or your head are in the way it'll not notice you." He paused, presumably, Lincoln guessed, to let the significance of what he had said sink in. "So, when I yell 'ready-about', be ready to scramble across. And next, and when I yell 'lee-ho', then cross quickly, keeping your heads down." He added and was quite serious when he said it, "We don't need any cases of 'boom-rash' today, thank you."

They shy-reached for the first turning point, and heading towards, as Brian had predicted, the high, empty green hills across and down the river. They'd thrashed their way through a maze of competitors without incident and were now trailing behind about a third of the fleet, the majority of those ahead, for one reason or another, were simply physically faster. The race leaders, Lincoln saw, had already popped their huge, spectacular, multicoloured spinnakers and were now running back upriver and parallel to the river's edge – and to the second turning buoy and under the eyes of the massed spectators that lined the beaches, foreshores and vantage points of the suburbs opposite the city.

They found water at, and rounded the mark and executed their fastest spinnaker hoist ever.

Brian was impressed. "We'll have to have the girls along on every trip, Chris, that was just brilliant."

Lincoln nodded his agreement, and then pointed. "Look at them."

Without exception Nick, Jamie, Gary, Warren, Helmut, and even Bill, were grinning at the girls, and at them.

Lionel had been also watching from his vantage point. "Pitiful," he muttered.

Needless to say and Lincoln had half-guessed, it couldn't last, and it didn't, and 'it' happened as they rounded for the second upwind leg, and it due to Helmut making 'cow-eyes' at Margaret again.

"Holy fuck," roared Brian, "look at it – my best 'light-weight' fucked – Helmut, you fucking great lump of lard."

They all looked studiously about, and especially not at Judy – her silent 'hysterics' were catching – and anywhere but at Brian – and anywhere but at a crestfallen Helmut. The poor wretch, and Lincoln sympathised, had cranked the headsail onto and through the top spreader!

"Leave it, leave it, there's no point. We'll carry it," Brian screeched, "it's fucked anyway. Shut-up, Judy."

Reaching across the narrower two to three kilometre stretch of the river, off of the suburbs and in front of a packed audience – they stuffed up a second spinnaker hoist as well. This one being as bad as the other was good, and in the end they had to lower it and physically unwind the 'wine-glass' in the spinnaker's centre – though, to Lincoln's relief, it blossomed beautifully on the second re-hoist.

Potter, with his usual tact, commiserated with Brian after they had passed through the finish line off Sullivan's Cove. "Ah well, matie, at least we didn't have to send you forward to cut the thing away with a knife."

Brian glowered at him, his reply was terse, "Just go away, Lionel, please."

*   *   *

Judy, from the hatch, nudged Brian with a full, bubbling, plastic champagne glass. "I saved this for a rainy day," she said and started to pass other glasses around. "I'll take the headsail in tomorrow," she offered, "with a bit of luck they'll have it ready for the evening."

Helmut interrupted her, "I vill take it in, Mrs Ramsey."

Brian Ramsey's character came to the fore; he passed his glass to Helmut. "Drink your champagne, Helmut, there's no panic, and don't concern yourself too much, worse things have happened at sea."

Judy passed the next glass to Lincoln. "Here," she said, with slight acidity, "though you don't deserve it."

Lincoln looked at her directly, welcoming the 'olive branch' – for some reason she blushed very slightly and a little smile accompanied her silent nod.

A cheer went up suddenly from the yacht moored next to them; one of their female crew had stripped down to bra and panties; and taking a firm hold on a warp she dived gracefully off the stern and into the cold water. They shuddered as she swam confidently out to the mooring buoy and secured the trailing rope. Their yacht, in the late afternoon sea-breeze, must have been putting considerable pressure on the next boat down: they'd obviously missed or mistimed attaching their stern line when coming in. Two crew eventually lifted the game young girl back on board – mission accomplished, and she posed tantalisingly for only a second – her wet, transparent underwear left absolutely nothing to the imagination!

Judy interrupted their intense concentration, "Put your eyes back in boys." Then she pointed. "The next episode's over here."

The wind had somehow got a grip on the poor man's yacht and had trapped it at amidships against the next, but one, mooring buoy up. Windage on the exposed full length was, Lincoln saw, in turn exerting enough force and pressure to drive the buoy sideways and down: its, the buoy's, barnacled underside was now noisily gouging fibreglass gelcoat. Despite a crewmember who'd bravely jumped onto and was pushing and at the same time balancing on the buoy's welded, and now acutely angled, encircling mooring ring, and despite boat hook and fenders . . . The skipper finally had no choice but to motor. They gritted their teeth as the buoy rasped, scraped and ground its way down half the boat's length.

Only just heard was Brian Ramsey's awed whisper, "Christ almighty, look at that – and I was worrying about a ripped sail!"

Chapter 6

The light tapping on the door occurred again and Lincoln groaned as he moved – stiffness had crept in. Lincoln wrapped the sheet around in 'toga' style – anything was better than trying to struggle into underwear – and in all probability it would only be Urwin with an enquiry of some kind anyway.

And that sheet Lincoln nearly dropped, not that her calling wasn't surprise enough – it was the way she'd attired herself... Wow! Lincoln didn't move... Doctor Elizabeth Montrose stood there in the doorway, dressed to kill – and an absolute 'stunner'.

"Come into my bed," Lincoln stuttered and still taken aback. "I mean, come into my bedroom, I mean ... um, come in."

Lincoln backed into the room and was followed by an 'Aphrodite' – carrot hair piled up – and her hair and her make-up emphasising her white skin and startling clear emerald-green eyes. Doctor Montrose wore a short, sheer, black-sheathed dress under a cheeky, chic, high-backed, bolero jacket; and her legs in black silk and on her shapely feet were elegant high-heeled, leather, court shoes of the same colour. Her plain elegance was only broken by a single strand of glimmering white pearls and glimpsed earrings – and each earring on closer inspection was a single pearl-drop set in gold. The heavy, scarred and scuffed, brown leather medical bag that she held, or rather, that hung from her hand, jarred in disharmony.

Lincoln eventually asked, and not knowing what else to say, "Um, is something wrong?"

"No ..." She blinked and looked up and then looked at Lincoln directly, before looking away again. "I just called to check, that's all – I'm also here to pick you up."

Lincoln raised an eyebrow and grinned. "Really. That's nice."

Was there just an echo of defensiveness in her voice? "To check on you medically, I mean, and as I was passing anyway, I was volunteered to give you a lift to the dance."

Damn, there was a very slight flush spreading across her face – Lincoln obviously shouldn't have done that: he'd construed a *double-entendre* from an innocent sentence that had not been intended nor meant – and the last thing Lincoln wanted to do was to embarrass her or make her feel uncomfortable ... It was unworthy, and besides, many girls didn't like or appreciate that sort of innuendo – and truth be known, Lincoln didn't appreciate it himself! It had been quite few years since he had been so tongue-tied nor experienced more than a spectator's indifference. Lincoln sounded like and felt like an inept old man trying to flirt – he felt as if he was treading on glass – 'pick you up' indeed.

Elizabeth Montrose coughed lightly and broke into Lincoln thoughts. "Ah," Lincoln said dejectedly, "right." Why was he so disappointed that someone had volunteered her and that she hadn't really dropped by on her own accord! "Um, thanks, is it late – are we late?"

Something snapped inside of Lincoln then, during her next sentence, and he suddenly felt belligerent – and he gave up trying not to stare, and gave up acting as well ... Yet conversely, nor could Lincoln pay much attention or make any real sense of what she was actually saying to him – it was the brogue, the burr, the localism, and the cadence of her words that once again held Lincoln.

"It's seven o'clock," she had just observed when he refocused, "give or take a few minutes. Why don't you lay ... Why don't you sit back down on the bed, you don't look very comfortable?"

No, I'm bloody not, Lincoln thought, starting to get even more annoyed, and clutching at the toga – the damn thing had taken on a life of its own and was busily trying to expose various intimate parts of his anatomy. Lincoln gave that up too shortly and just sat on the bed as suggested – as directed.

Doctor Montrose, and on her own initiative, stepped across and quietly closed the hotel room door – the door to the outside world, as it were. "Sorry," she said as she turned back to face the room again, "I didn't mean to wake you."

"That's all right." Lincoln smiled. "You can wake me any time." Whoops, he hadn't given up acting apparently, or was it acting, the words had just slipped out – and yet again, and Lincoln felt strangely abashed, this wasn't like him, to be so ... so brash!

"I'll put the kettle on," was her only reply, "you must be dry?"

Lincoln watched her from the edge of the bed and at her

occupying herself with a domestic chore added to the unreality!

She glanced around. "Don't stare," she requested, "you're making me feel self-conscious enough as it is."

"Sorry," Lincoln replied, actually, Lincoln wasn't sorry at all.

"You're not aware, are you?" She'd turned and was now leaning against the small dressing table on which the white plastic kettle, tray, and other tea-making and coffee sachets and related paraphernalia resided. "You really aren't aware . . ."

"Aware of what?" Lincoln asked, nonplussed.

She sighed. "If I were your wife I wouldn't let you out – your stare.   Both my sisters simply melt when you look at them. Mary felt it, even my mother – they all do."

Now it was Lincoln's turn to feel self-conscious, really self-conscious, Lincoln could feel the blush spreading – and this the Doctor!

Her eyes flicked up demurely.   "You should have the decency not to stare into peoples' souls."

Lincoln took the proffered cup finally, and scratched, and looked at her. "Right," Lincoln replied. What else could one say!

The trend of conversation changed direction abruptly then, and it took Lincoln a moment to understand her question.

"How did you get on at the hospital?"   She had stepped across and now stood directly in front – looking down in askance – questioning.

Lincoln glanced away and then back furtively and then away again.

She was obviously puzzled and then said slowly, "You haven't been.   You haven't bloody well been.   You haven't bloody well been, have you?" Lincoln's face and expression must have given the game away. "Why? Why didn't you go?" she demanded. "Answer me . . ." She pushed Lincoln's face back round with a finger. "Don't look away."

And her standing there, hands on hips waiting for, expecting, and demanding an answer: her face red-tinged, breathing heavily, nostrils slightly flared and chest heaving. Jamie was right, Lincoln thought, this one really did have a temper!

Doctor Montrose turned and took a very deep breath – she must have spotted his, Lincoln's sailing jacket then, and thermal on the floor – and incredulous was the only word – and Lincoln cringed.

"You've been . . . you went sailing, you were out there this afternoon – out bloody sailing." She stared. "You're mad – you simply don't know the risks." Her eyes were suddenly distant – and her apparent mood change unnerving. "Andrew won't believe it, he'll be disappointed, he'd have thought you'd . . . He'd have credited you with more sense."

Lincoln sat there silently, looking at his feet – he had no defence to offer, and there was no point in trying to explain his irrational hatred of hospitals – and that the very smell of them nauseated and brought him out in a sweat.

Her temper had expired and the sun began to shine again and she said quietly. "No, that's not true, that's not the truth, he knew, Andrew knew. If you hadn't gone to the hospital when you were already suffering that amount of pain . . . He knew you wouldn't go and he as good as said so, didn't he." She calmly picked up and took a sip from her cup and their eyes met across the cup's rim and Lincoln felt like a little boy – that same little boy again. "Finish your tea," she instructed, "while it's hot."

Lincoln had only half-finished his cup when she became all business again and took and placed his cup on the side. She came and stood in front of him. "Right, bend forward." She pushed down on the back of Lincoln's neck, and then to add insult to injury, pushed it down a little further, further than necessary, and Lincoln bit down on a half-muttered curse. "Bend further forward and breath deeper."

The stethoscope, and true to comic strips, was cold.

"Further forward, deeper, big breaths – and now back this way – come on, I'm not going to eat you, you know."

She was standing directly in front and Lincoln was still sitting – and his forehead was now resting on her abdomen – and the heady fragrance of her perfume. If only she would, Lincoln thought!

Doctor Montrose moved around and next pushed a set of fingers into the side of Lincoln's back, Lincoln grunted – where, Lincoln wondered, was the gentle ministering angel who'd previously treated him.

"Does that hurt?" she asked.

Lincoln's right kidney shot into his mouth and Lincoln tried to keep his voice normal, "Yes," he replied, "but only when you push your fingers in."

Lincoln was pretty sure the extra dig of pressure was unnecessary, and either that or she'd turned heavy-handed during the night!

"Sorry," she blandly commented and ordered, "lie on your back."

Lincoln caught the slipping sheet and straightened it out; Doctor Montrose pulled it back down to waist level. She proved beyond a shadow of a doubt that collarbone and ribs were still very sore. Doctor Montrose was not mindful of modesty either; she pulled the sheet up – and her manoeuvrings with Lincoln's leg brought tears.

"Do you hurt anywhere else?"

"Those you've just broken are enough, thank you," Lincoln sarcastically replied. "Will it help if I apologise?" Her face fell and Lincoln was immediately sorry for the smart remark and amended hastily. "No, just stiff, is all."

"I can see that," she replied dryly, nodding downwards. "I'd heard all about you sailors too!"

Lincoln quickly glanced down as well, so she'd noticed his aroused predicament, and not that she couldn't help to – and Lincoln resented her commenting, it was tactless and as a doctor she shouldn't have been that surprised – and she should have known better . . . And apart from that, Lincoln had been desperately trying to think of something else, anything to stop the rising traitor – any diversion. All to no avail, even the sharp shock of acute pain and her somewhat painful manipulations hadn't deterred it – the bulge had grown! Betrayed by hormones, thought Lincoln, and hidden desires, or rather, plain naked desire . . . and her cool hands! A few weeks of celibacy? There was no excuse and no point in denying or trying to hide his obvious feelings – and a bit late anyway.

So, in the end, Lincoln just sighed and mussed up the sheets over the offender. "Sorry." Lincoln said.

"No, don't be sorry, I'm flattered," she murmured gently and bit her lip. "I'm the doctor; I'd better sort it out."

Disbelief! There was no other word!

Doctor Montrose moved across to the room's only chair and turned and slipped off her jacket. Her dress was haltered, Lincoln saw, and just a thin black strap from above her breasts and around her exposed neck. Her supple back, for Lincoln, shrieked desire – and Lincoln wanted to kiss it – eat it! The dress dropped to the floor, Doctor Montrose was something else again, she crossed to the bed wearing only a wide, black lace suspender belt, sheer black stockings and a flimsy piece of silk that was supposed to represent knickers – they weren't decent. Lincoln couldn't help but glimpse too, as she slipped out of them and pulled the sheet up and over, at a bright triangle of profuse, tangled, red pubic hair.

*   *   *

"Would you like a drink, Elizabeth?" Lincoln quietly asked and nodded to the whiskey bottle. "There's a choice, I can offer you scotch, scotch and water, or, water and scotch?"

"No," and a half-smile of acknowledgement accompanied her reply, "I'd better not. I'm supposed to be delivering you to the Wrest Point Casino Hotel. We're supposed to be there for eight o'clock – Brian invited the family to the 'prize-giving' dance. Another cup of tea would be nice though."

The boiling kettle roused Lincoln from his reverie.

She called, "You're not self-conscious, are you?"

Lincoln turned and looked at her. "No," he replied. "I don't ever think about it, nudity, I mean, only other peoples." And added with a smile and a salacious leer. "Especially yours."

The doctor took the offered cup and Lincoln climbed and sat with his back against the headboard as well. She lifted an arm above and massaged the back of her neck, and apparently unaware of Lincoln's glance, her eyes on the ceiling; her arm had pulled her breast upwards – and it was incredibly erotic – and Lincoln had the irresistible urge to reach across and undercup, and gently pinch and fondle, and slide a finger gently over and caress.

"You don't shave, Doctor Montrose?" A still non-thinking, non-censoring, stupid, inept brain had allowed those tactless idiot words to slip past even before he had been aware of framing the question.

Instead of quickly lowering her arm or quickly covering up, Doctor Montrose simply glanced casually down at her armpit – the question hadn't caused offence apparently. "No . . ." she said slowly, as if considering, "you don't approve?"

"Oh I approve." Lincoln murmured and then leant down

and twisted round and lightly kissed her there.

"Don't." She pulled her arm down abruptly and curled away, and in doing so splashed her tea.

Lincoln reached around her and gently took her cup. "Sorry," he apologised.

She shuddered and then squeezed her legs together on her hand. "God, I can't stand that, I can't stand being touched there, under the arms." She squeezed her legs together again and shuddered. "God, I'll wet myself."

And then, to Lincoln's intense relief, she re-settled herself, and caused a moment of indescribable well-being, trust, possession, elation: when she casually placed a limp elbow of that same arm on Lincoln's shoulder. That limp elbow represented so much more than just a languid extremity, to Lincoln it represented her trust in him, and that she possessed part of Lincoln; her caring and that they were . . . were in love – lovers . . . something? Her elbow spoke of things and feelings that defied literary translation.

"A bit of a risk, Doctor," Lincoln said eventually, "considering sex and its modern-day problems and its consequences: we haven't set the best of examples, have we?" Lincoln looked at her from under his eyebrows. "We didn't use a condom!"

It was obviously becoming a habit – who was this simplistic, idiot half-wit who kept uttering these idiotic words? Lincoln shut his eyes and shook his head and despaired. Lincoln, he thought, you're a complete and tactless, utter bloody fool!

She turned, her eyes travelling up and along her forearm and then directly at Lincoln. Her answer, her next few sentences shook to the very core – so casually profound. Those words didn't sink in immediately – the implications behind them though were to echo around in Lincoln's head for years to come.

"Do you have one?" she asked.

"No," Lincoln admitted with some embarrassment, wishing that he hadn't started the conversation and wishing that the ground would swallow him up.

"Well, it doesn't matter anyway," she stated matter-of-factly, "I know I haven't had any extra-marital affairs." She looked at Lincoln knowingly and then looked away. "Nor any other affairs for that matter, and anyway, I took a blood sample from you yesterday and one of the labs analysed it yesterday and the results arrived back this afternoon – there's nothing wrong with you, the only problem you've got is a slightly high cholesterol level." And with that she twisted and swung her legs around and sat up on the opposite edge of the bed. "Come on," she said, over her shoulder, "we're late, it's eight-thirty all ready."

*   *   *

The spokes-person representing 'the sponsor' of the Melbourne to Hobart Race was just winding down. "We hope you have enjoyed your stay amongst us here as much as we have enjoyed having you. No doubt you are aware that the Sydney-Hobart and the Melbourne-Hobart keep our town on the international map and is therefore of paramount importance to our place in the world, our international reputation and, of course, our prosperity." The spokes-person looked up from his notes and smiled. "I don't know how many of you have been drinking milk, but going by the sales figures of our beverages, there can't be many of you – fortunately for us, you milk drinkers are apparently a rare breed." He stood there, at the podium and waited patiently for the catcalls, cheers and ragged clapping to subside. "From my point of view," he eventually continued on, "that is, from my company's point of view, it has been our best year ever – we have broken all our previous sales records." He yet again waited for the cheers, whistles and applause to die down. "The town does, of course, also benefit accordingly – if indirectly, in turn." He waited patiently again – his timing of the pause was immaculate, and then finally, "The Wrest Point Casino Management have asked me, on their behalf, to invite you to feel free and to use any of the hotel's facilities: you all have honorary membership for tonight so you can, if so inclined, try your luck should you care to. Please bear with the hotel staff while they clear away the debris and the buffet tables . . . The 'disco' will commence at ten o'clock. A happy New Year and a prosperous one to you all. Thank you."

From past experience, Lincoln knew, as with many of these social occasions, they either fell by the wayside or they were a resounding success – and this one had started to rock after an hour. Lincoln noted that it had been Jean Corsham who had started the trend, and after inquiring about Lincoln's health, had insisted that they dance. Over the next two hours Lincoln had danced with all the girls, and Judy was his final partner; and she'd have to be the last, and fortunately for Lincoln, it was a slow number which was just as well because his right leg was just beginning to buckle.

"Did Doctor Pennine give you the 'bollocking' you deserve, I saw him wagging his finger at you earlier?" Judy enquired after they'd established their arm positions, stance, dancing style and roles.

"No," Lincoln replied mildly. Lincoln looked down at her and raised his eyebrows slightly and then added in a sublime, slightly disdainful, lofty tone, "He was concerned, that's all; he's all right – a good egg."

"Christ, you Poms." She raised her eyebrows in turn, apparently in incredulous disbelief. "'Egg'!" she echoed.

"What?" Lincoln asked.

"Never mind, are you all right? You're beginning to look a bit tatty around the edges."

"Yes, I have to admit," Lincoln confessed, "I've just about had enough, it's been nice, but I'm just about ready for bed."

"I'm sure you are," her riposte was the riposte of a master swordsman . . . woman – and straight to the heart. "the question is, Mister Lincoln, who's? I hope the hell you know what you're doing?"

Lincoln looked down at her in astonishment . . . and then dismay.

"It's fairly obvious," Judy continued on, "you've danced with everybody else, including sisters, and mum: but you've studiously ignored Doctor Montrose. You've both been discreetly making eyes at each other – the pair of you have been sending silent messages all night." Judy looked into Lincoln's face, she must have seen horror there, and then she looked away and sighed. "Don't worry, I doubt anyone else would have . . . has noticed." She turned her head and looked at Lincoln directly again. "That was 'bullshit', wasn't it, about her not being able to wake you, I mean, wasn't it?" Judy being Judy, she wouldn't, of course, let the subject drop without some comment. She gazed up at him for an expectant moment longer and then said, "It must be annoying for you." She blinked slowly. "With every man and his dog fighting to dance with her."

What she had said, and apart from her last sentence, was, of course, a flat statement of fact and not debatable, and she knew beyond a shadow of doubt and denials would insult her intelligence. Judy waited, and her worth showed, she'd not judged . . . at least, Lincoln hoped she hadn't – and anyway, he had nothing . . . there was nothing he could say.

Judy sighed finally, hopefully realising and apparently accepting that she wasn't going to get an answer. "You're a silly boy, Chris. Brian and I are around if you need us." She kissed Lincoln's cheek. "I can't condemn her, but you I can." She breathed out heavily through pursed lips and, thankfully, decided to let it go and changed the subject. She nodded across the dance floor. "I'd better go and sort out Warren, look at him; he's really 'tiddly'. He's just about dragged every poor girl onto the dance floor tonight, Gary'll end up thumping him, he won't leave Sharon alone – look at him."

They served coffee in a quiet area, back through and past the 'gaming' machines. Lincoln sat in one of the thoughtfully placed armchairs.

"Will you take me home?" Elizabeth was leaning over and was resting one elbow on the upholstered back of the chair.

Lincoln twisted round – bits of him creaked. "Now?" Lincoln enquired.

She nodded. "You're shot anyway."

"I'll get your wrap." Lincoln said.

She waved an end of it next to her face. "I've got it."

Neither of them thought about her coming up to Lincoln's room, she just did; and a natural presumption on both their parts.

She leant her back against the door finally, as Lincoln fumbled for the key. "I'd like that drink now," she murmured and her eyes met Lincoln's, "especially as I won't be driving again tonight!"

*   *   *

"Yes, I realise that, but why do you really?"

Lincoln rolled over on his side and propped himself on an elbow, a hand supporting chin and cheek. "I don't know, it's hard to describe, even to yourself – that's if you even bother trying – you see pictures in your minds-eye rather."

"Try, please, it interests me."

Lincoln hesitated, searching for the words. "Well, there's a freedom out there, and . . . and every now and again there's a moment of beauty: a sunrise, a sunset, a cloud formation, moonlight. You . . . you feel an insignificance: a humility, an unimportance, a humbling – there's a sort of peace." Lincoln took a breath. "It's clean; it's somehow like coming home. It's all that, those things and more . . ." Lincoln felt embarrassed, opening one's heart to someone and displaying such innermost thoughts was something Lincoln didn't do – so he gently edged around the subject. "Incidentally," he said, "it's why the armed forces have 'training' ships. They know, or they used to know, that you can't hide out there: your true character shows quickly: it exposes your best and worst innermost traits for the entire world to see. It'd take years, if ever, to know someone as well as you know a sailing companion. It's something akin," Lincoln was struggling to find the right words again – struggling to at least give the gist – to convey an echo of what he meant. "It's something akin," Lincoln repeated, "to having a brother or sister, though not quite: you accept their faults and love them just the same – if they're worthy."

Elizabeth was quiet for a moment. Her next question Lincoln found a little odd – and just a little out of text . . . and loaded. Or was that conscience?

"You don't sleep on board with the other single men, do you, and I presume that you'd pre-booked your – this hotel room, why's that?" She glanced up quickly and raised her eyebrows fractionally. "You know what I mean."

Lincoln shrugged. "No, conversely, you can all 'fall out', or some of you anyway, and end up to be the bitterest of enemy's – there's been murder committed on a boat more than once. I didn't know how we'd all get on, and besides, four or five days is enough for me – I like to be alone."

They were silent; Lincoln reached across in that silence and pushed her hanging fringe away from her eyes, and caught her studying him.

"Can I see your wee boat? she eventually asked, "I'd like to."

Lincoln smiled inwardly – he'd noticed before – the odd word and the Scottish inflections surfaced now and again.

She looked at her watch. "It's seven; I don't have surgery till ten. There won't be many people about at this time – this town is like a village – I'll have to be careful."

Lincoln laughed at the thought.   "If you go out in the 'rig' that you wore last night," he said, "then everybody'll know you've been a really naughty girl."

"I've got 'runners' in the car?" Doctor Montrose retorted indignantly."

"Okay." Lincoln smiled. "I've got a pair of clean jeans and a spare tee-shirt, if you want – you'll have to anyway, you certainly can't drive about town in that thing you call a dress."

She pulled a face and stuck out her tongue. "We can have breakfast at my place afterwards – that's if you want?"

"Is that wise?" Lincoln asked.

"Probably not," was her terse reply.

*   *   *

There were quite a few people about despite the early hour; they just stood and looked at *Worippa* from the quay.

Elizabeth gazed down the length and then up at the mast. "It's far bigger than I imagined – close up, I mean."

Lincoln nodded down the river and raised a quizzical eyebrow "It quickly gets smaller out there." Lincoln shivered inside and after a moment he returned his full attention back to Doctor Montrose. "Come on aboard," Lincoln said brightly, "I'll show you round."

Lincoln stepped out and stood on the bowline as on a tightrope, over the water, with one steadying hand on the pulpit. Lincoln's full weight on that warp brought the heavy yacht gently towards them, till the stern ropes tautened and restrained further forward movement – till the bow was not quite touching the wharf. Elizabeth clambered over and it felt good when she held onto Lincoln's shoulder for support. Lincoln followed her slowly along the deck until they were just abeam of the mast, and once there she stepped across and stood directly in front and with her straight arms together in front of her she finally leant against it, and then peered up. She shuddered and said wonderingly, "You were actually up there? You're all . . . you were all so bloody casual, I'd no idea."

"Don't be fooled, Elizabeth, it's safe enough," Lincoln said casually, but nevertheless, Lincoln couldn't help but feel the hero, "we were in a seaway, that was all."

She gave Lincoln a 'knowing' look and then stepped around, she stopped again when she was about halfway down the length of and parallel to the boom, she'd been trailing her hand along it for support – she pointed here and there at the deck.

"Winches," Lincoln said.

"There's so many of them." She gazed upwards and around and then turned three hundred and sixty degrees, she seemed to be almost in a trance. "So many bits of string," she said.

Lincoln smiled; it usually did seem that way to a newcomer. "It's not that complicated, Elizabeth, nowhere near as complicated as the human body, for instance. Sorry," and Lincoln added quickly, "that was a naive and an insultingly simplistic comparison." Lincoln hurried on before she could comment, "You only have to follow one piece of string and see where it leads and what it does," Lincoln shrugged. "As with a lot of these things it's only people who try to complicate, it is, in truth, very simple."

Lincoln steadied her as she climbed around to behind the wheel, and as she placed her hands on its rim, as if on cue, Helmut's head appeared, framed in the companionway hatch that was directly in front of them. He nodded pleasantly to Elizabeth before addressing Lincoln.

"So, it is you, Mister Mate. You are just in time for breakfast, you vill come below?"

"Thanks, Helmut." Lincoln nodded sagely and what he hoped was casually. "We'll be there." They moved slowly around and across. "Climb, descend facing me, Elizabeth, just as you would a domestic ladder."

Lincoln waited for her to get clear – people objected when you stood on their fingers when descending ladders!

Elizabeth's furious voice erupted, echoing up from below, "You too, Sophia, Jesus Christ, what is this, a bloody love boat?"

Lincoln's mouth dropped, blasphemy from the good Doctor – and all too easy to guess why!

Lincoln quickly followed her down and stepped through to the entrance of the main saloon. The subjects of Elizabeth Montrose's ire sat in a line against the hull and along the padded settee behind the ship's fiddled table. Sharon was furthest away – and she and Margaret wedged Sophia between. They looked, from where Lincoln stood, as if they wore only *Worippa* tee-shirts (exactly like Elizabeth's!) and apparently nothing else!

Helmut calmly emptied another egg onto a plate; he

stopped and looked from the Doctor to Lincoln. "I promise you, Chris," he said, and he was talking to Lincoln but was actually looking the Doctor in the eye, "ve have done the honourable thing, Nicolo and I." Helmut indicated Nick with a thumb. "I have to hurt him only just a little," he said with a certain satisfaction, "only enough to make him behave, you understand." Helmut overrode Nick's attempted interruption. "The girls, they have slept in the bereft bunks, ve in our usual bunks."

Lincoln half-smiled – the use and meaning of the word 'bereft' was new – but his meaning was quite clear ... conscience clear – clearer than his!

Gary and Nick sat opposite the girls: on the padded, buttoned top of the engine cover – its length doubled-up as a centre bench. Nick was silent for once and Helmut's little sideswipe forgotten – he and Gary stared from Helmut, to Elizabeth, and then to Lincoln in turn – in unison – for all the world like two owls roosting on a branch.

It was Helmut who broke the silence finally, "Do not look at me, Chris, like that, it is true." After a moment's silence he added heavily, "I cannot speak for Gary though, the boat this morning vas swaying, the mast back and forth so." He held up the skillet vertically, tipping it back and forth and using the handle's in-built hanging eye, or hole, as a pivot – a graphic example of the mast's movement.

Lincoln put a hand over his mouth and looked away, desperately trying to bottle it – the heat from Gary and Sharon's red faces burnt.

Lincoln had long resigned himself: Helmut's Teutonic sense of humour could at times, to say the least, be a little offbeat. Coupled with that, he also had the bad habit of mentioning the unmentionables in mixed company: things that were somewhat indelicate, or, by their standards, to be frank, in bad taste. Only this time he had really put his foot in it – this latest attempt of his at drollery had obviously been much too close to the truth for comfort!

"Where's Warren?" Lincoln asked, desperately trying to keep a straight face and change the subject at the same time. "You haven't shut him out, have you? You haven't excluded him – that wouldn't be fair – he's crew too."

Lincoln pushed away the mental picture that the sentence

he'd just uttered conjured up: of the whole lot of them ensconced all together, in the altogether, and in one bed!

"No, that is not the case." Lincoln blinked and tuned back into what Helmut was saying. "I pour him out on the forward bunk and I check him last night and this morning – he is alvays on his side – I vished him not to choke even though he has been silly vith his drink."

"Thanks, Helmut." Lincoln nodded – what more could one say!

"You vish breakfast, ja," he was obviously, happily oblivious, seemingly, poor lad, to the gaff he had just made. "I have done plenty."

He didn't get to answer; Doctor Montrose hadn't finished yet. "How the hell are you two going to explain your absences to Mother?" she demanded of her sisters and placed her hands on her hips and lent aggressively forward as she spoke.

Good old Maggie was not going to be intimidated and a nasty glint appeared in her eyes. "Well," she said sweetly, "we're going to use the same excuse that you're going to use when explaining your new trousers!"

'Touché', Lincoln thought.

They all looked: jeans about three sizes too big, with folded turn-ups that were excessively heavy from too many rolls of rolled-up material. Those turn-ups were hanging and swaying very slightly and looking for all the world like two stalled pendulum weights affixed to two denim pendulum rods!

Chapter 7

"Look, the first thing we've got to understand . . . do . . . Umm, allow to sink in, is that . . ." Ramsey was holding out his hands, palms upwards, in mock supplication. "We're now on holiday." He grinned, took a breath and raised his eyebrows. "We're to unwind – there are no more races. We've all been under a fair bit of pressure, let's relax and start enjoying ourselves. There are not many chores and we've plenty of time." Ramsey turned his attention to Lincoln. "Chris, if you would help Lionel fit the roller reefing – it clips on just behind the forestay – Lionel knows. We'll top up with water and diesel this afternoon. Jamie has kindly volunteered to take us into town, we'll get all the stores and any shopping, Judy'll go with us, she's not flying home until after we sail. If any of you want any treats, favourites, alcohol, wine, more beer, put it on the list – it's now or never. From a cooking point of view – is there anything else?" Ramsey looked from one to the other and at each of them in turn. "You're all happy? You've got everything you need to cook your favourite meal with?" Ramsey turned slowly on one heel, encompassing them all again "Good . . . Helmut, sorry?"

"Ja. Nick and I." He made a grab for Nick and as he did so Nick casually shifted his shoulder an inch back, and just enough to only allow Helmut's frustrated outstretched fingertips to just brush. Helmut settled back and continued on with his conversation after giving them a complacent dry look. "First ve vill help Bill, he goes to lunch with his beautiful vife. Ve to help him to re-flake all of the sails properly ve now do not use, ve make sure they are dry and then pack them avay. Ve vill sort out and have ready the storm sails: jib and trysail." Helmut looked to them. "Then, if it is necessary ve help Lionel and Chris vith the roller sail. Sharon and Varren vill . . . they are going to vash and clean, ve vill also help them – ve must have a boat clean, ja?"

Nick interrupted, "Yes," he said, "and while we're doing that we'll stick a couple of broom handles up our arses and we'll give the decks a quick scrub while we're at it."

Ramsey closed his eyes for a moment and then ignored Nick's dripping sarcasm. "Clean boat," he corrected Helmut. "Good. Right then. Oh, and Gary's offered to give me a lift with the stores – we're off." Ramsey indicated with his hand, "After you, Gary."

Lionel and Lincoln climbed, following the shoppers topside.

"Have you used roller reefing before, Pom?" he asked.

"Not really, Lionel."

"They're simple; Brian designed and made this one: it works pretty much like a domestic roller blind in any house, except it's hung vertically, of course. It's not bad considering." He explained, "Brian used an old foil and a redundant Number One heavy, needless to say it's a bit stretched here and there."

They strolled forward to the bow. "The main drum is shackled to that eye aft the forestay," Lionel pointed as he spoke, "the whole thing: foil, top drum and the rest are hoisted aloft on the two jib halyards – to spread the load. That way we leave the original foil and forestay 'intactus', if we really get in the shit then we drop everything and slide up the storm jib, get it?"

Indeed Lincoln did.

They, Potter and Lincoln, finally winched the whole lot above after they'd threaded the old headsail's bolt rope into the foil and had shackled its head. They wound the sail on, the main drum being turned by the 'furling' line.

Potter directed, "Take the line to a spinnaker winch, through that snatch block, the one next to the cockpit, matie." Lincoln followed Lionel's instructions as he was talking. "That way we don't have to go forward, Pom, we stay all comfy in the cockpit and forget about getting a square arse and freezing our balls off on the weather rail." Lionel placed his hands on his hips as Lincoln finally took a couple of turns around the aforementioned winch; Potter surveyed his current kingdom with obvious satisfaction. "Pissed and paralytic all the way home – dry, snug and warm. Sheer luxury, ay, Pom, no beating into the wind, aerodynamically this rig is hopeless, the wind gets too far forward of the beam then on goes . . ." He pointed and bobbed a hooked finger downwards. "We fire up the old 'iron horse'. Below five knots, on it goes – we'll be home in no time!"

Little did Potter know what the Gods had in store for them!

       *   *   *

"You didn't really get a 'quiet little drink', did you?" persisted

Potter knowingly.

Lincoln ignored the wealth of meaning in Potter's raised eyebrows and took his comment, deliberately, at face value only. He was on the surface referring to the huge drinking bout: a marathon session the boys entered into each year at one of the local hotel's – which usually involved girls in 'wet' tee-shirts and other unsavoury antics.

"Next year," Lincoln said shortly.

How much he knew or had guessed Lincoln didn't dare ask.

Potter was not to be put off. "You'd be a brave man, or a fool, if you sail into this port again next year, matie."

Fortunately and thankfully, and did Lincoln but know it, this would be one of the few times that Potter would refer to his entanglement.

Lincoln quietly fumed, the 'Doctor' had been right; Potter aside, Hobart was a small village and Hotelier Urwin Edgehill had caught up with Lincoln that morning. He'd tactfully and discretely and apologetically warned Lincoln off, apparently James Montrose had a reputation and was known for his bad and violent tempers where his granddaughters were concerned – and a married man had never, to his, Urwin's knowledge, been associated or involved with one of his girls! Talk about what webs we weave!

*　　　　　　　*　　　　　　　*

"Chris?" Brian beckoned from the quay. "You too, Lionel, come on, we're going for a drink."

This was definitely out of character, especially as Lincoln knew that Brian didn't drink in the dinner hour as a general rule, and especially not when they were in the middle of preparing *Worippa!* More trouble then – or was it conscience! They walked, Brian and Potter and Lincoln, to the pub on the corner. They waited to be served; surprisingly and considering the hour they were amongst a goodly number of patrons. They were served eventually, and from there they collected their drinks and edged their way around and made their way to the back of the saloon.

Ramsey waited until they'd settled and after they'd all sipped and tasted. He spoke to Lincoln directly, "The thing is, Chris," he said hesitantly, "Gary has asked if Sharon can sail home with us."

Lincoln had expected anything but certainly not that: a girl on a boat for a prolonged period, one way or another, usually caused strife; and there generally was, in his experience and past experiences, enough natural competitiveness on board without adding to it. Furthermore, it was only a certain type of girl who could 'mix it' with men, and Sharon was certainly not, in his, Lincoln's opinion, that type.

Lincoln shook his head emphatically. "Won't work – she's trouble."

Brian voiced his doubts. "I'm not so sure you're right, you know, originally yes, a bit promiscuous maybe . . . No, that's not the right word, a bit . . ." he waggled his hand, "a tad flighty perhaps, but underneath the protective shell I think you'll find she's all right. Had, have you . . . did you notice that neither Judy nor the Montrose girls put her down? If the surface picture was true then we'd not have a problem," and he added wryly, "Judy would have already sliced her out with a scalpel and thrown her away." He mused for a bit. "There's more to her, it came out yesterday: she's a postgraduate, you know, she attends both Melbourne University and the Royal Melbourne Institute of Technology." Ramsey stared straight at Lincoln. "Yes, surprised you, hasn't it, Pom, surprised us all, studying 'pure mathematics' would you believe – 'pure mathematics'."

The intensity of Ramsey's stare faded. "Despite his situation and everything, Gary's not daft – it just isn't, it just can't be coincidence that he loves fiddling with figures as well, can it?"

Potter was incredulous and not a little awed. "I knew there was something about her."

Brian beat Lincoln to it, "Fuck off, Lionel." He turned back to Lincoln. "Look, Chris, if we only manage five knots all the way home, which I can't believe, but even if we did, it's our worst scenario – agreed?"

Lincoln reluctantly nodded.

"Then it'll only be four days, tops, right. If Lionel would keep a watch with Warren, that'll be four watches with me floating."

Lincoln quickly interrupted, "Hold on, hold on. How come Warren's name has suddenly appeared? Where did he come from? I thought he was flying home?"

"He's changed his mind," Ramsey blandly admitted, "he's asked if he could sail back with us, he hadn't booked: he had intended to fly out on the first available empty seat."

Lincoln looked at Lionel; Brian's statement had truly surprised him, more so, for some reason than the Sharon scenario. Potter answered the look after an aside to Brian. "Thanks very much, that'll really 'make' my trip back – partnering Warren. Don't look at me like that, Pom, I object to it, it's new to me too." He was hesitant just for a moment. "Come on, Pom, let's at least consider, let's at least take a moment to think about it." Lionel absently placed his fingers on the rim of his glass and rotated it on the stained beer mat beneath. "Providing that there's not a major falling out." He held up a finger as Lincoln tried to interrupt. "Hold on, as I say, presuming that we all somehow manage to get along then . . . then it'll probably make all the difference between a pleasant voyage on the one hand, or a hard slog on the other. If the numbers are right then we'll, in theory, only need . . . we'll only require two on watch, that'll mean two hours on and six hours off. If a watch needs a hand that still leaves another two watches snoring, and that's excluding Brian. It'll make all the difference to the trip home," Potter continued on reasonably, "adequate sleep and leisure and energy to be able to take it all in – and as Brian said earlier, we're all still pretty tired, you know."

To say that Lincoln was exasperated, irritated, upset and bloody annoyed would be an understatement. Lincoln objected to Lionel's reasoning with dripping sarcasm, "It all sounds very logical, Lionel, but, the girl's never been on a boat, she doesn't know what she's getting into, and any sailing trip for her would be an adventure. To take her for her first outing up the east coast of Tasmania is doing her a disfavour. Christ, she doesn't even know if she's going to be seasick, it's no trip for a lady – it's not only stupid," Lincoln said flatly, "it's irresponsible to even think about taking her."

Both Ramsey and Potter were silent, and then they looked at each other before he, Ramsey, dropped the final bombshell, "Ah." Ramsey placed his fingers on his lower lip and pulled down. "Um." He grimaced and then bared his teeth and bit them together. "Actually, Chris, we hadn't, um, intended to go back via the 'east coast'!"

It Lincoln's turn to look, from one of them to the other, face grim, all humour gone. "You weren't thinking of going back via the 'west coast', were you," Lincoln ground out, "you'd be mad enough to go back that way on your own let alone take a novice with you!" Lincoln added harshly and thinking on the run, "I don't believe it!" He stated it coldly then, as the full picture blossomed, "Neither do I believe in taking unnecessary risks, especially with other people's lives – especially mine."

Both were silent, Brian broke it and he said quietly, "That's a bit strong. Look, both Nick and Helmut want to get home; Bill has to be at work for the ninth, this way he's virtually guaranteed a day's rest. The west coast's the shortest route, all right, I know it's thin," and he added finally and lamely, "but it just wasn't in me to refuse him – Gary, I mean."

Now they were getting to it, or part of it.

Lincoln carried on relentlessly, "You know damn well there won't be an escort ship with us on the way home – no help, no relay! At least up the east coast there'll be plenty of other vessels about: other ships, other yachts and a choice of places to run." Lincoln asked innocently, "By the way, that reminds me, will we be travelling in company?"

Their answer – silence again.

"You never enlightened me, did you, Brian, that's what I find as objectionable as any of it – you hadn't intended to, had you. Where I come from that's called 'lying by omission'." Lincoln stated it flatly, without tact, without niceties: in black and white – he was furious.

Brian retaliated with alacrity – stung by the words, "They're harsh words, Chris, unjustified and unfair and I take strong exception to them: you can be a rude, offensive fucker when you want to be, can't you?" Ramsey's eyes didn't waver. "What are you saying then," he asked finally, "that you aren't coming, is that it?"

"That's right, Brian, you've got it in one, I'll be catching the first available plane out." Lincoln nodded to them, pushed his chair back and stood, there was nothing else left to say. Brian stood also; he walked round the table as Lincoln stepped out from behind his chair – he barred the way through to the street. "You would, wouldn't you; you'd 'walk', just like that. You're a hard man, Chris; hard right through – no compromises with you, are there, no give, no softness, and no compassion." He stood his ground. "I'll not let it end, not with a stupid argument. You're in the wrong; half in the wrong anyway – sit down . . ."

He nodded his head. "Please. We'll either sort it out or we'll all be flying home. Please . . . I'm asking you – sit down." They finally sat; Brian looked at Lincoln for a minute. "All right, I agree you might not have realised which way we intended to go back, but despite your accusations I'd not consciously kept it a secret from you. I could argue that we'd have more trouble trying to get from the top of 'Tasi' sailing against prevailing wind and current, westwards to Melbourne – but I won't. I could also argue that there are plenty of places underneath where we can run if in trouble. There's Port Davey further up, then Macquarie Harbour. Oh I don't deny it's rugged country but there are a surprising amount of places to shelter – you only have to look at the chart."

Lincoln cut in on him then, "Do you think for one moment that I haven't, Brian," Lincoln demanded, "most of them are marked 'unexamined', aren't they. We'll not even have Jamie on the return trip," Lincoln added bitterly, "so what little local knowledge he has won't be available to us."

Ramsey suddenly slumped. "Yes all right," he said quietly and there was hurt resignation in his voice, "Okay, you're right, I'll check and see who else is going back at the same time, the same way as us."

"I haven't said . . ." There was no point in completing the sentence because Ramsey wasn't listening, wherever Brian Ramsey was, it wasn't with them: he was obviously far away and viewing another world in his mind's eye. There was an expression on his face that gave Lincoln pause to interrupt his obvious meditations. "Did you know," he said eventually, "that Jamie's great grandfather, he was a whaler. Jamie, when he was a child, can still recall him talking and describing the albatrosses – it was he who was actually the one who told Jamie that they were supposed to be drowned sailors that had been washed overboard, that they followed ships because they were looking for the one that they had been washed off from . . . Do you remember him telling us that, Lionel?" Lionel didn't comment, he merely grunted. "Yes," Ramsey almost absentmindedly commented, and obviously to himself as much as to company, "the wandering albatross." He looked at them, seemed to shake himself and then said brightly, "Men have always been fascinated by the albatross, I'd heard or read about what Jamie's great grandfather had said elsewhere, of course, but still . . ." He gave Lincoln a start when he suddenly and quickly leant forward in his chair, Lincoln had been lulled by the softness and entranced with his . . . his foilibility. "You've seen them, Chris," he said earnestly, "those birds: their gracefulness, their beauty, and the way they cruise. Officially a wing span of some thirteen feet, that's conservative you know, they're only some of the few they've managed to get around to measuring. We've seen . . . Royal Albatross, maybe." He shook his head in what Lincoln could only say was wonderment. "They're way in excess of that, some of them – bloody huge. You saw them for the first time on this trip – the way they examine you as they sweep past the boat; and the humming sound of the air as it flows over their wings." Ramsey pointed. "I watched you," he accused, "your heart wept didn't it, you were crying inside: the yearning in the chest hurts, doesn't it. Your soul is with the albatross, you flew with it – I saw your face, I know. You'll be with us next year, with Bill, Lionel, with Gary and me. They'll never discontinue the Melbourne to Hobart race," he stated with absolute conviction, "despite the periodic rumblings, the race isn't what it's about – it's about God's country." Brian's dreamy, far-away look had faded with his last couple of sentences and he was now fully back in the present. "The trouble is Gary's told Sharon; he's told Sharon all about it." Ramsey pursed his lips. "Gary's a romantic, you see: the albatrosses, the prolific bird life, the whales, the wilderness and the rest, they're all . . . Well, their postal addresses are all on the West Coast, if you see what I mean!"

Lincoln sighed. "Gary's a romantic," Lincoln remarked dryly, "not alone, is he. Are all the chores finished?" Lincoln asked and stood up.

Brian nodded. "Helmut's still got the light-weight Genoa to collect – a few bits and pieces otherwise. Yes, they're just about be finished by now."

"What time are you intending to slip tomorrow?"

Brian gazed up at Lincoln. "I'd like to be away by about ten – half-past at the latest."

"Make sure Gary buys her her own seasick 'patches'," Lincoln said without inflection, "they're too expensive to give away – I'll see you both in the morning."

*   *   *

"I'm telling you, that Pom's got his hands into more knickers than you've got pairs of drawers in your top draw!"

Lincoln coughed and deliberately reframed from lowering his head immediately, and not really wanting to see to whom Mister Edgehill was talking to in the office beyond the glass hatchway.

Urwin at least had the decency to be embarrassed. "Sorry ... err ... a couple of messages for you." He said quickly and picked up a pad. "Oh yes, Judy called." He coughed again. "She said to tell 'the sailor', her words," he said apologetically, "she'd like to get it off – get off earlier. She'll meet you on the pier at nine, not ten; her husband's getting fidgety and anxious!"

Lincoln nodded his understanding, straining to keep a straight face.

"The same woman who booked your room phoned," he continued on, "she'll be ready-and-waiting, she said, so call when you get in – she'll be out tonight."

"Right." Lincoln said.

"And," he pointed, "there's another young lady waiting for you in the wings." He nodded to the stairs and his head bobbed up and down. "Um, she seems to be a bit upset."

Lincoln turned and looked through the vertical steel banisters; Sharon sat on the bottom steps.

Lincoln thanked Urwin and then stepped across, Sharon stood up when she saw him, Urwin had been right: her eyes were red-rimmed – she'd been crying.

"What's the matter?" Lincoln asked, concerned. "What's wrong? What's happened?"

"Nothing," Sharon kept her eyes downcast and would not look at Lincoln directly, "I wanted to see you, that's all, about the trip." She hurried on before Lincoln could comment, "I just wanted you to know that if you weren't keen I'd make up a plausible excuse and pull out. Gary said it'd all hinge on you." She made eye contact then. "I'd rather not go if there were objections: we'll probably never meet again – there'll be no repercussions. Gary won't be any the wiser, so no hard feelings."

She'd got him, bloody hell, Lincoln could argue against a demand, belligerence, selfishness, aggression, but against this type of approach he felt defenceless – crashed and burning.

Brian had been right though, there was more to her: either

she was a bloody good psychologist, or genuine – Lincoln gambled on the latter.

"I hope you know . . ." Lincoln reluctantly forced out the words. "I hope you realise what exactly you're trying to get into. There are risks, serious risks; we'll be sailing up the west coast of Tasmania, one of the worst pieces of water in the world: it may not be a picnic even though it's summer – freak storms, the Southerly Buster, huge waves – you can quite easily lose your life out there, people have, let alone somebody as inexperienced as you." Lincoln bulldozed on as she tried to interrupt and added on a couple of finishers for good measure, "There's no privacy on a yacht, you know, and I mean no privacy! You could be seasick, it'd be pretty miserable for you if you are – you can forget the romance . . ." and Lincoln added nastily, "and you can forget sightseeing at the bloody penguins too, despite what Gary says . . . you know what I mean."

That she was indignant and furious an understatement, and interrupt she did. "Give me credit . . ."

Lincoln held up his hand and cut her off abruptly – the battle was lost. "Don't bother," Lincoln snapped irritably, "it was settled this afternoon – you're going."

Toe-to-toe one minute, her arms thrown around him the next – like the bloody weather . . . Lincoln wouldn't say it wasn't pleasant, but, to tell truth, the kiss was just a bit too long, just a mite too enthusiastic!

Lincoln didn't see, hear, nor sense the smack coming till the palm caught – just below the eye, high on the cheek. And he glimpsed only a pair of very clear, emerald-green eyes in a distorted, flushed face.

Smashing glass registered somewhere but not foremost, and that was because Lincoln was laying on something and the pain that it was causing in his back put paid to any other diversions. Furthermore, the discomfort increased twofold every time he tried to push Sharon off, thankfully, she rolled off on her own accord eventually – and in her own sweet time, that is, or so it seemed. Lincoln took a breath and breathed out loudly and then lifted a shoulder and reached under and pulled the tray out from beneath, it clattered when it landed; Lincoln sat up finally and propped on his hands behind and pushed with his feet, he ignored the lumpy debris and shuffled backwards on his bottom and only stopped when his back was resting against the wall. Lincoln had to grin despite everything; Sharon lay in and amongst the remains of the pot plant, the pot splintered beyond recognition or repair: spilled earth layered the floor and branches and leaves partially covered them. The rusty 'catch' tray buckled and bent was across from them, where it had landed, and two of its edges were now flat from their combined weights.

Sharon's awed whisper interrupted the abrupt silence, "Was that . . .?"

Lincoln nodded and closed his eyes. "Yes."

"Oh . . ." She thought about it for a second . . . "Oh!"

Lincoln turned and looked at her directly and then raised his eyebrows. "Um, I would appreciate . . ."

Sharon was quick – Lincoln would give her that. Her sarcasm didn't help, and for some reason she'd turned huffy – really huffy. "So sorry if I've caused you a problem and got in the way; you don't have to worry about me, I'm the last person you have to worry about. I'll . . . I'll be the soul of discretion." Then she added sweetly, "I won't tell anybody about the Doctor giving . . . sloshing you one in the eye – your indiscretions are safe with me."

Why was it that she didn't sound reassuring, why was it that she was already beginning to really worry Lincoln – Christ knows what made them tick!

Into shadow and Lincoln squinted up at Urwin Edgehill and after a moment nodded to his smashed front doors, and the glass from the panes of each that littered the floor. Lincoln enquired, "She did that?"

"I don't think Doctor Montrose was very happy." And Lincoln noticed in passing that there was an echo of smugness rather than annoyance in Urwin's demeanour.

"You'd better call somebody in." Lincoln peered round. "Sorry about the mess, Urwin." Lincoln sighed. "You'd better put it on the 'bill'." Lincoln sighed again. "I'll be shipping out in the morning, you'll be glad to know – that's if I live that long."

Foolhardy rather than brave maybe, pushing his luck just a little all the same, nevertheless Urwin measured up. "I'd be more worried about your eye," for some reason the ill-concealed smirk on his face wasn't offensive, "and don't worry about the damage, sad to see you go, the inconvenience has been a cheap price to pay for the entertain . . . Um. It's going to be a beauty," he pointed, his finger a little too close for comfort, "it's swelling already." He muffled an uncharacteristic titter. "If I were you I'd be more concerned about showing . . ." He swallowed. "If I were you I'd be more concerned about getting a doctor to have a look at that!"

Chapter 8

"A door, a door you say, matie, you walked into a door?"

"Look Potter," Lincoln said tiredly, "sod-off, will you – enough's enough. Judy'd not bloody-well leave it alone, then Nick, now you." Lincoln pointed. "And you're about all I need – you're about as useful as a chocolate fire-guard, aren't you. Exactly how much mileage do you all think you're going to get out of it anyway?"

"There's plenty more in it yet, Pom," came back Potter, "plenty more, we've got to make sure we don't get bored."

Brian tentatively and a little sheepishly half-apologised for his wife's insistent, over-zealous interrogation of that morning. "Tut, that's women for you, they love the gory details – don't we all." He quickly then moved on to another subject – the business at hand. "I'll give Radio Melbourne a 'bell' in a minute; I'll give them our sailing schedule, ETA and everything else." But not for long – and he, Ramsey, just couldn't resist not adding his two-pennyworth either. "Now, do you want me to ask them to put a doctor on, Chris?" he asked. "He'll talk to you directly from the hospital, probably advise steak." Lincoln shook his head resignedly – they weren't going to give it up, not for a while anyway. Lincoln waited for Ramsey to spit it out – he was desperately trying to contain his spluttering and finish the sentence. "Not going to be enough, is it, the way you're going, I'll tell 'em to send a bullock, I'll tell 'em not to worry about the horns, we'll pull 'em off here. Ha, ha, ha!"

The joy the man got from his hopelessly inadequate jokes, and sometimes they all cracked into fits simply because he literally giggled himself silly on his own daft, farcical humour – and offence Lincoln simply couldn't take. And although the planning and thought of sailing for home had made him, Ramsey, understandably anxious, nevertheless, one couldn't help but notice the change in him. His earlier comment, that the pressure was off and that cruising wasn't same as racing showed in spades! The comparative lack of responsibility had relaxed him and although it obviously just didn't compare to that other heady mix of race hyper and associated acute butterflies, just the same, it did not quell the suppressed nervous excitement that he clearly and transparently felt. It was the same excitement that they all felt or experienced, to a greater or lesser degree, at the beginning of any sea voyage.

Added to that adrenalin, Lincoln knew, was that *Worippa's* motley crew had had enough of the drinking and late nights and felt a relief at the prospect of being out of it and at sea and going home, just as he, Lincoln did . . . didn't he?   Ramsey, his last stutterings just audible, and that just before Lincoln could voice the two appropriate expletives, had the sense to smartly disappear below!

It hadn't been an easy morning and if Lincoln had not known better he'd have believed Judy to be pleased – she'd virtually ran the last few steps down the pier. That is to say that she'd got quite excited examining the latest damage and was really and genuinely quite surly when Lincoln had not been forthcoming with details. Her women's intuition, which at the best of times was frightening, had unerringly told her that it had been caused by something other than an accident – her 'you can tell me', be damned. Her's and others' questions, innuendoes and sly and humorous comments and enquiries, Lincoln had endured it all stoically, even Sharon's sweet smile. To tell the truth Lincoln's mind then had still been elsewhere, so most, to their, and especially hers, Judy's annoyance, had gone over or around Lincoln's head.   Jamie and his sisters, with their usual native politeness, had pointedly ignored the subject: no doubt they'd guessed exactly, if not the reason, from where Lincoln had acquired his decorative disfigurement.   Lincoln hadn't really helped himself either because he simply just couldn't be bothered nor had he the inclination to think up a half-reasonable covering story, not that it would have been believed, so what the hell.

What to do about Elizabeth Montrose, that was the thing: she dominated Lincoln's thoughts.   Would it maybe and in the long run be better for both of them to use their parting 'fiasco' and end it! The trouble was Lincoln had committed himself to something when he had allowed her to climb into his bed – and not so simple; she'd been and was fretting, hurting and pensive inside, and nursing some deep need that Lincoln had instinctively felt and knew, and had known intuitively. Her mercenary approach had been out of character; perhaps and hopefully the shortage of time had forced her to be so forward. Elizabeth Montrose, Lincoln knew beyond a shadow of doubt, was not the 'one-night stand' type and not one who'd dabble in a night's philandering: the ferocity of that smack, and more relevant, the hurt in those green eyes had exposed too deep the depth of feeling. What she definitely hadn't required was somebody kicking her and wounding her further. From her point of view it'd been Lincoln who had been 'one-night standing' all over Hobart!

There was no weight on the momentarily resting hand and Potter climbed round, and not turning to face forward stood behind Lincoln's shoulder, next to the wheel, and looking astern. "Can't you drive this thing straight, Pom, our wake looks like a dog's hind leg!"

Lincoln half-grinned and gave a nod, nor did Lincoln need to turn, Lincoln knew the remnants of the track that *Worippa* had cut through the water would be like a ruled line. Lincoln allowed his head to hang. "Sorry, Lionel," Lincoln said, affecting a deferential, chagrined humbleness, "I'll try harder, I promise."

Lionel grunted, he didn't turn but he stayed where he was and kept his back to their embryo small world. "Chris?"

Something really was wrong, thought Lincoln, he only ever called him 'Chris' when in real earnest – or in deep trouble!

"Introversion's no good, not at your age, matie, that way can mean problems, especially for someone like you: thinking too much and brooding leads to depression, and depression's catching – it's an illness." Lionel must have caught the look of 'spare-me' on Lincoln's face and he abandoned the fatherly tone. "I mean it, matie, I'm serious, better men than you have got themselves into a state over a woman – best you stop now. I don't know what went on and I don't want to know what went on, what I do know is that you've got to put it away. The people on this boat are relying on you, they, or we, rather, look to you for a lead. If you're unhappy, they're . . . we're all going to be unhappy." The timbre of forcefulness in Lionel's voice gentled and changed to gruff advisory, "It pays to be cheerful, Chris, it's important, this country'll shrink you to insignificance. It's intimidating enough where we're going even if morale is high. You owe them, us . . . me. Your first loyalty is to the boat."

Lincoln felt a sudden anguish . . . and a nameless yearning, and a hollow feeling of despair. Lincoln said it quietly. "I like her, Lionel."

"And she likes you, I know that, matie," and then there was a very faint, ironical, tentative sparkle of humour in the cadence of Potter's consolatory words, "Nobody slams a door that hard into someone's eye if they're indifferent." Unfortunately, Lionel's further advice and his attempt to lighten up and bolster Lincoln's outlook was just a little too pat, a little too glib, and a little too shallow for Lincoln's taste. His subsequent efforts smacked too much of clichés, and, in Lincoln's present mood, neither applicable nor relevant – though Lincoln didn't doubt that he meant well. "Take solace from those who have gone before, Chris," he instructed, "your 'comrades in arms': those sailormen down the ages, going back through to the mists of time, they all had to leave loved ones in foreign ports. You won't believe me now but you'll like the next one too, they can't have left you alone much, whatever 'it' is – you've got 'it'!" Lionel continued blindly on, and was sublimely oblivious and obviously completely unaware of the implied presumption concerning Lincoln's assumed promiscuousness. "Life's like a glass, Chris, depending on how you look at it: is it half-empty or is it half-full – be thankful for the memories." Lionel changed tack then and his voice suddenly became business-like, "Meanwhile, just take a look at this country." His arm swept encompassingly around. "You haven't got time to be maudlin – no brown studies. You're about to embark on a sea voyage going where the scenery and associated 'goodies' are second to none in the world – they're unique. And furthermore, we're going to have time to look." He smiled with benign pleasure and nodded, and then they were both oddly silent for a moment, and any indignation Lincoln had felt was now somehow inconsequential. It was Lionel who broke that odd moment of introspection and Lincoln could almost see him shrugging off the sombre mood that he had added and inadvertently introduced. "I'll put the 'main' up," he said with false and forced joviality, "We'll get wind further down the river, we might as well be ready for it, and in the meantime we might as well use the 'lift' – it'll give us at least another half-knot for free."

Potter wrong, even though he meant well, thought Lincoln . . . or he might be right! One wouldn't, if one had any sense, be completely fooled by Lionel's bluff exterior. Lincoln certainly wouldn't put it past Lionel to have the sensitivity to read between the lines and take it upon himself to give him a little 'talking to'. Would that it be so simple, yet Lionel's advice and his wishing, and to an extent Lincoln's also, wouldn't make it so, Elizabeth Montrose was very special and not a toy to be put down . . . she wouldn't let him put her down anyhow. Vivid haunting pictures of her kept appearing unbidden in his mind's eye: her image, a look, an expression, a pose, her face, her breasts, an intimacy. She'd roused Lincoln's curiosity, touched a deep nerve, and to his surprise, those images and affined feelings only got worse as time passed, and not better – and tormenting!

*   *   *

A whisper of wind gently rattled and tugged at the mainsail and set it quivering in anticipation of the voyage.

Brian reappeared, a stereo speaker in each hand. "We must have all been pretty busy," he said as he stepped clear of the companionway steps, "nobody's had time to set up the 'stereo'. Do you like music?" he asked as he stepped around and behind Lincoln, he didn't wait for an answer. "We've got all sorts, I made Judy bring a bag full of cassettes as hand luggage, she got a bit 'shitty' about it – still, 'all's fair', yes."

He straightened up after he'd clipped the second speaker to the middle rail in the starboard corner, which was directly opposite to the one he'd already carefully attached and positioned in the other corner, on the port pushpit rail. "Don't go away, you can tell me if they're both working. I'll knock the engine off – got enough, have we?"

He was asking about the wind, of course. "Yes, filling-in all the time."

Brian turned and faced Lincoln after he'd climbed back around. "I'll send some bodies up." He pointed a finger downwards and grimaced wryly. "They're round Sharon like bees round a honey pot – you'd think they'd at least be curious, wouldn't you, about what's going on up here . . . Yes, all right, take that 'I told you so' look off your face, I don't need reminding." There was a lopsided, half-smile of tolerance on his face as he said it, Lincoln noted. "You'll see, we'll be all right once we start watches and are sailing."

"Your misinterpretation, Brian, all I'm doing," Lincoln partially turned and indicated with a hand, "is taking in the scenery. The high country, the peaks, Brian," asked Lincoln, "are they always hidden – shrouded by cloud?"

"Sorry," Brian apologised as he scanned around, obviously with new eyes. "No, not all the time, though Mount Wellington has been on nearly every trip I've made." He turned slowly around again then and took time to look in every direction. "It does have a quiet magnificence, doesn't it," and apparently irrelevantly and absentmindedly, and almost without pause for breath, he added, "It doesn't pay to let your imagination run – the land time forgot!" Brian, did he but know it, was echoing Potter's earlier observations and Lincoln's thoughts, he could almost see Ramsey mentally shake himself as he indicated gently with his thumb. "As soon as the sun breaks through, which it'll do shortly if I'm any judge, then it'll change its character completely: it'll have a softer beauty then." He nodded and then turned; he paused with one leg over the hatchway coaming. "I'll knock the engine off, give me a second and then turn the key, would you."

*   *   *

"Chris."

"Bill. All settled in?"

"Here's your jacket, I've put your stuff away behind the lower port bunk – usual place, and I've asked Brian to put us on the same watch – you don't mind, do you?"

"No, Bill, delighted." And Lincoln genuinely was. "Who makes up the other watches? No, I can guess, there's a natural order."

"The two hour watches start at twelve noon," Bill informed Lincoln, "with Nick and Helmut; Lionel and Warren are next at fourteen hundred. We'll be relieving Gary and Sharon – we'll be watch 'four'."

Lincoln reached down and turned the key and the engine spluttered and then died and *Worippa* joined her natural environment, free again; the intense silence after the noise of the engine hurt.

Bill's voice assaulted that silence, "Tell me when I've let enough headsail out, would you?"

He eased out the furling line then sheeted in the headsail, and doing it alternately – playing till they were happy.

"That's fine, Bill," Lincoln advised eventually, "six knots, she's pulling like a train. There's no point in putting her on her ear, we'll shakedown first – that'll give everybody a chance to get used to the motion again." Lincoln blew out through inflated cheeks, "And me most of all."

"Never have got over it one hundred percent, have you?"

"No," Lincoln admitted, "and you can count yourself as lucky – having that cast-iron stomach."

"I do, don't worry."

"These seasick 'patches' they recently brought out have saved the day – they actually work. I was in real trouble when they took those seasick tablets off the market; they were the only ones that worked – for me anyway."

Bill was curious, "I never really did catch up with that; what exactly did go on?"

"The kids were apparently taking them with alcohol to get 'high', the chemists were only allowing one customer the one box after they'd first realised what was going on. Those kids, and adults presumably, soon got around that: the cheeky beggars bought one packet from every chemist in town initially. They were only available on prescription after that – then, thank God, they finally came out with these lifesavers." Lincoln pulled his ear forward and exposed a half-inch, circular, waterproof plaster, and then absentmindedly touched and rubbed it with a finger. "It's impregnated and dribbles the appropriate dosage of drug in through the pores of the skin – it lasts for about three days – by the time it runs out you're supposed to be used to the motion – that's if you're lucky."

Time passed and both of them busy in their private worlds; Lincoln's inquiry broke their companionable silence. "You've been down here before, Bill, haven't you?"

Bill understood the meaning behind Lincoln's question and the accompanying raised eyebrows and indicative look to seaward. He nodded confirmation. "Yes, this'll be my third time. Our biggest problem will be clearing South West Cape; we'll be comfortably reaching like this till Cape Queen Elizabeth – off the bottom of North Bruny Island." He accented his next sentence with an out-held, upright hand: a hand that represented *Worippa's* angle to the wind. "It'll be tighter and tighter onto the wind after that, and finally on the nose after we clear Tasman Head; there won't be a let-up then till we turn at Whale by South East Cape." Bill, and Lincoln picked up on the fact with quiet humour, with a sort of morbid relish that all sailors seem to quickly acquire (seasoned or not), went on to embellish on detail. "The year before last we ended up dropping the roller reefing and had to put up the Number Three – that was the only way, it was just impossible to bash through it with this rig, too inefficient. If we get a south-westerly 'buster' it'll be hard on the wind and we'll be doing the same again, so pray for a southerly – we'll just scrape around with that. You look slightly anxious, does it worry you?"

Lincoln had to smile to himself, if it didn't before, it would now, after his confidence-inspiring description! Another thought flashed through Lincoln's mind: both Brian and Lionel had forgotten to underline those few little facts during their tête-à-tête!

Lincoln said slowly, "Mm, it does worry me, Bill, though not that particularly – that what you're been telling me about. I've got the jitters, that's all. I feel jumpy." Lincoln started to explain, and as much as to express the hollow feeling that lay in the pit of his stomach to himself, as to him, Bill. "Being an Australian, you probably wouldn't understand . . . I stood on Ninety Mile Beach – that's where it first hit home with a vengeance – that's where I first felt the feeling that I'm feeling now. On either side of me when I stood on that beach there was nothing. What I mean is," Lincoln said, labouring for the words, "for hundreds of miles either way there wasn't a soul in sight. There were no people, no sign of human habitation – there was absolutely nothing on the high-water mark to even suggest that there was human habitation or that humanity had ever existed. There wasn't a bottle, a piece of plastic, a shred of rope – not a thing!" Lincoln took a deep breath and then gestured with a hand. "Here is worse, I find it unnerving." He rubbed and pinched his lips ruefully, and admitted to cover his embarrassment, "I must be a city boy at heart." Bill glanced at Lincoln and then looked forward again; and his silence, for some reason, compelled Lincoln to explain further. "Both Lionel and Brian commented on this ruggedness and its effects," Lincoln pointed, "but what they were talking about isn't what I'm feeling." Lincoln breathed heavily through his nose. "In England the press of people is such that you can never really get away from them – it doesn't, or didn't seem to matter where you were, or went. As a kid, for instance, you couldn't find a place to take a girl for whatever: somebody would appear from behind a hedge, a man walking his dog'd pass by, there'd be someone about – always. It's no people – I mean 'no' people." Lincoln really emphasised the words 'no' and 'people', trying to get his meaning across. "It surprises me, but in truth, I find the absence of people disconcerting, uncomfortable, and . . . vaguely threatening."

Bill had turned to face Lincoln during his last few sentences. "Don't worry about it," he said easily, "Australians feel the same way – it's a big, empty continent, Australia. There are only seventeen million people and the size and remoteness of the country defies the imagination – your body-senses . . . Err . . . you know what I mean – your instincts – they know though. Four million there are in Sydney, and another four million in Melbourne." Bill nodded his head. "A million or so in each of the other cities and other odds and ends spread about. It scares the shit out of all of us, all but the hardiest of types." He quickly went on, "Have you noticed that Australians have comparatively big families: three, four kids, even more sometimes. That's part of the same symptom – we're still pioneering." He gestured, as Lincoln had done earlier, but there was more strength and meaning in his gesturing encompassing arm and hand. "They'll be lucky if they exceed more than four hundred and fifty thousand here in Tasmania, and those are mostly concentrated in pockets – don't kid yourself, out here it is one bloody big, empty and lonely place!"

*   *   *

"Those swells are getting more pronounced, Bill."

Bill indicated the approaching open water. "If you look carefully you can just make out the 'Iron Pot', that white, square tower out on the low wedge of rock – see it? That's the light that we were looking for when we were coming in – remember?" He looked in askance.

"Yes, that's something I'll never forget," Lincoln said with feeling, "it was like a candle in the window welcoming us home."

Bill nodded acknowledgement and the understanding that passed between them went far deeper than any words: that feeling of relief, the draining of tension, and happiness and excitement . . . and exaltation when approaching and entering a safe haven after a hard and rough voyage could not be expressed, only experienced – it was, to use Potter's words, 'comrade-in-arms' stuff. Bill, after a moment, continued on with his quiet commentary, "That light was convict-built; they used to boil down whale blubber there in the early days, hence the name." He redirected Lincoln's gaze and indicated with his right hand. "A gap in the cliffs will slowly open on this side, to starboard – where the land ends is Piersons Point. And if you look carefully you can just make out a white structure amongst the eucalypti." He pointed again for emphasis. "It's got a mesh . . . it has a wire fence round it, it's a bit far off yet . . . It's virtually on the summit, see it – you can just make out the light and walkway on the top?"

Lincoln could too, and acknowledged the fact.

"That light," Bill explained, "also mark's the entrance to the D'entrecasteaux Channel. That's a scenic lookout point up there, there's a car park and whatnot, it's called the Tinderbox. The tower actually stands on the grassed-over roof of a dug out: a reinforced concrete, gun emplacement. You'll see for yourself when we get closer, it was built during the Second World War – to cover the river against invasion." There was a ruminative and an echo of things-that-were-not-to-be in Bill's next sentence, "That's probably where we should be going, in there is protected water – you can follow it right through and finally come out at Whale Head. That way is too time-consuming for Brian, though he's right in a way, you must see it in daylight to appreciate it – it's spectacular country. In there are probably some of the most scenic, unspoiled cruising grounds left in the world." Bill sighed and the regret in that sigh was palatable, as was, as Lincoln realised, the disgruntlement in his next few words. "Though the longest route, in theory, it'd not necessarily take the most time!"

Bill pointed yet again – though quieter; Lincoln silently acknowledged that his local knowledge was also formidable. "A line between 'Piersons' and the 'Pot' is about three miles, once over it then we're in Storm Bay. You know, now that you mention it, I've got a lot of affection for the old Iron Pot," Bill shaded his eyes with a hand and peered intently. "Hm, it's too far away to make out that much detail; it's not a manned lighthouse any more, they knocked all the maintenance buildings, power and lighthouse keepers' houses down, their foundations are still visible though." He turned and spoke to Lincoln directly, "Not too friendly to mariners this bit: Storm Bay by name and Storm Bay by . . ." He gestured. "There's a fair few wrecks hereabouts, an awful lot foundered in the early days; they still foundered even after the 'lights' were introduced, though not as many as previous, of course. You still get the odd one even now, this can be a real nasty and treacherous piece of water when the wind's wrong, this can."

Chattering company curtailed any further discussion between them, and presumably *Worippa's* more pronounced motion and Brian's admonishments had driven everybody up from below.

Brian's head appeared above the hatch after they had exited the companionway and had crowded the cockpit. "The Iron Pot should be on our beam." He too placed a hand above his eyes to shade the sun. "Good," he commented as he spotted it. He looked at his watch next. "It's near enough to twelve o'clock." He turned and addressed Helmut, "Helmut, you and Nick are taking the first watch, aren't you – would you take the helm, please."

*   *   *

There was one ingrained unwritten law and a rule that they never neglected when onboard *Worippa*: whatever current conditions prevailed, they always ate well. Like many Australian boats, climate and storage ensured that *Worippa* had a huge fridge and freezer built into her. On an ocean-going boat of her size bottled gas was neither desirable nor practicable, and fuel availability and safety dictated the use of methylated spirit. A built-in tank also fed a large cooker and oven.

If Lincoln were forced to name one of the most important pieces of information that he had gleaned from sailing in hot climes, from *Worippa* especially, and there was absolutely no reason why the same should not apply equally to cold climates, apart from mentality, then near the top of the list would be the value of an in-built freezer. Pre-made, homemade, individual frozen meals, Lincoln acknowledged, were the prerequisite for ocean racing, and these being sealed in aluminium foil trays, or containers, and were a winner. Experience had obviously taught Brian Ramsey that a planned and balanced diet of ingredients particularly liked by an individual was the answer and partial cure to a lack of appetite, and therefore energy, that accompanies foul weather, impossible conditions, and seasickness et cetera. Happily, there was also a side-bonus, as Lincoln could attest: it also solved the onerous problem of washing-up! Like so many good ideas it was so laughably simple: each individual delivered their frozen choices, ready-labelled for contents, day, and for which meal of the day; they were then separated into appropriate piles, and finally, just prior to sailing, conveniently packed into chronological layers – easy! He was so right too, Brian, thought Lincoln; although slightly nauseous you tended to pick at a meal of your own choice, especially if bland, and once started then you often managed to get a portion down somehow. Energy foods that are easily digested were the most successful, never mind the Sunday dinners and other rich cuisine, anything with potatoes, pasta or rice. Still, a week of this sort of plain fare is enough and after a trip such as Hobart most of them were fairly seasoned: thus if the weather clement they turned to and often cooked, and ate 'gourmet' meals with impunity, on board when after-race cruising. One of them, as Lincoln had witnessed, would get fed-up or bored, and then they'd all dwell on the evening meal. Dinner would be planned in the cockpit or on deck, and they'd each have their say and add to the meal's recipe or to the menu generally.

Again, he'd been clever, had Brian, and Lincoln admired him for it: the incentive: that whoever was excused a watch if cooking . . . and also excused from clearing away and also from whatever washing-up there was! The rule was based on sound common sense: deliberately tackling from the onset and judiciously trying to persuade crew that domestic science was a useful and worthwhile hobby. That rule, his rule, intentionally encouraged everybody to cook and, in fact, changed an onerous chore into a pleasurable pastime, with everybody sharing and not leaving it all, as on most yachts, to the hard-core few.

Over a period of time this crew, Lincoln had come to see, in their own ways had all become proficient and each had one or two recipes that they'd perfected. What was unusual about this crew, however, which Lincoln sincerely applauded, was a common factor that applied to them all: they all, without exception (including him) specialised in cooking 'curry'! Contrary to popular belief, their concoctions had never caused any of them digestive problems: curry was the answer to a maiden's, or a hungry sailor's prayer anyway: the ideal alternative and all in a single pot! Anything could be thrown in and nothing was wasted: leftovers: vegetables, apple, potatoes, eggs, pasta, oven chips, baked beans, any sort of meat – they'd even put 'rhubarb crumble' in once. Lincoln grinned to himself: all had eventually claimed superior skill and had changed: from initially sharing recipes to being very secretive. Curry was their *piece de resistance* and all without exception had come to love them with a passion.

Lincoln shook his head mentally – Bill Corsham had gradually given up protesting, in his world deep rumblings, flatulence, volcanic explosions and associated vapours were the accepted norm, and erupting and wafting gases from various bunks part of everyday seagoing life!

Awkwardness, Lincoln knew, over this now ingrown habit made most of the crew feel uncomfortable: most were natural gentlemen and it offended their sense of decorum to execute such bodily functions in Sharon's presence. It was Potter strangely, who became especially inhibited and restrained when women were aboard. Lionel was not actually a crude man, Lincoln admitted, but rather, still a child in this one area: of never having outgrown a child's delight in 'willies and bums'. One of his pleasures and entertainments was to watch peoples', or rather, victims' faces, and sniggering from below blankets; and with only his glittering eyes visible when the silent creeping gas, let loose by a lifting leg, offended an already polluted atmosphere. Lionel already, to Lincoln's knowledge, had had two serious mishaps caused by over-enthusiasm: twice this year he'd had to strip his bunk, wash and disinfect it, and blankets too!

Sharon was obviously not aware of how deeply honoured she was by this commendable conservatism, though how long his, Lionel's, and the rests' perception of priority would last was, Lincoln thought, another matter. A point of sensibility, or redemption, had long been passed amongst them, and revenges paramount, it had become every crewmember's ambition: a matter of honour, even duty, to pay Potter back – with interest!

Chapter 9

"Just a little 'touchy', aren't we?"

"Gary, you I don't need at the moment," Lincoln said tiredly, "just slide out and let me in."

Gary slid on his bottom and slowly pulled himself along and out from behind the chart table, Lincoln eased him gently to one side after he'd stood and slid along into his place. A pencil, which was folded into the closed log and trapped, marked the current page; Lincoln inserted a thumb and gently flopped the log book open.

"When, Gary," Lincoln looked up from the log, "at what time did you start? When did you write in our first log entry?" Lincoln ran a finger down the page. "I take it that this is our first barometer reading, is it: one thousand and thirty-nine millibars?" Lincoln glanced at him again and raised his eyebrows. "It was you, wasn't it; it looks like your writing?"

Gary, with his shoulder leaning against the leading sole-to-deckhead upright, which, apart from supporting the deck overhead, had been utilised and was also now an integral forward part of the chart table and an instrument-bearing, chin-height partition, answered slowly, considering Lincoln and obviously puzzled. "Yes, it was me, as you well know; the time's there and the barometer reading is as it says: thirteen-thirty."

Lincoln reached forward while Gary looked on and gently tapped with a finger, the tap dropped the barometer needle half a point and then, while ignoring the large ship's clock which was directly in front of Lincoln, asked him. "What's the time now, Gary, please?"

"Fifteen forty-five."

He interrupted, and not comfortable with the silence finally, and looking from Lincoln to the entry in the log, to the ship's instruments and back. "It's only dropped half a millibar, that's not significant, it'll vary a bit ..." He hesitated before changing his confident flat statement to a tentative trailing inquiry. "Won't it?"

Lincoln ignored his question. "We should be noting the temperature as well! Why don't we?"

Gary bristled, "You know we don't, we used to try and then we gave it away because it wasn't really practical. We could never find a real use for the information anyway – you can't easily relate it to anything." He gave up trying to answer Lincoln's implied criticism finally and, his exasperation obvious, asked, "What have you got the shits about anyway – in a bad mood, are you?"

"What." Lincoln absentmindedly replied.

He was silent again for a moment, looking at Lincoln and understandable curious despite Lincoln's imagined criticisms, and then, when Lincoln didn't continue on further, eventually enquired. "Are you that worried . . . Why?"

It was not easy to answer that question; the trouble was, thought Lincoln, that it was nothing specific, and yet . . . something! An increase just noticeable: a barely perceptible shift in the wind: a touch colder perhaps? Up top he had observed and if you looked closely, high cirrus was subtly being overtaken by cirrostratus; and an odd, globular, isolated puffball of cloud was floating across here and there. Messengers? Were they forerunners? Also, he had observed, it was just a touch hazy and there was, it seemed to him, a vague halo around the sun – the signs were, he had to admit, subtle and difficult to discern. There was chaotic cloud only just visible above an obscured and misty horizon – were the tops of those faint sun-touched anvils peaking? There had been, and there still was, an almost invisible yellow tinge all around; the sea and the swells were like glass. Lincoln sat staring into space – he had seen something like this before – not exactly the same, but echoes of! Lincoln pictured what he'd been observing minutes earlier again in his mind's eye: it had seemed to be darker there, in the south, where the sky met the sea on the edge of the world . . . or was it no different from average? Damn, sometimes it was so difficult to tell . . . Lincoln bit his bottom lip, it was all too easy, at sea, to let your imagination run away with you and get into a hollow-stomached animal panic. Sailors, and Lincoln mentally acknowledged himself as one of their number, were notoriously superstitious – tiredness, loneliness – their . . . your tininess and the immensely huge, indifferent sea. Was what he was seeing an unheralded forewarning for those who had eyes, an echo of things to come, or a flight of fancy and imagination running riot – like bogeymen in the dark? Bugger!

Lincoln turned to Gary who had just been swaying there

patiently and tactfully waiting and saying nothing. "I'm not very happy, Gary." Lincoln shrugged his shoulders. "It's just a feeling, that's all." Lincoln looked at him directly and held out an indicating thumb. "Is there much static on the radio?"

Gary clicked his tongue on what sounded like a tooth crevice, and his reply – even that was like the previous – inconclusive. "A bit, maybe."

*   *   *

They all ate in the cockpit when the weather permitted, and some, especially Lincoln, even when it didn't – the lack of fresh air, despite ventilation, and the smell of food, especially on their first day – queasiness would send Lincoln back up top. Those who were fortunate, Lincoln had long ago noted, and didn't particularly suffer from seasickness also preferred topside if given a choice.

Not a thing was said when their first offering was served, Lincoln smiled in dry humour; a light meal had been expected because there'd not been time enough to prepare anything elaborate. Even so and despite the fact that they couldn't possibly be hungry after the breakfast they'd had and the incidental cups of tea, cold drinks and biscuits between, yet there a was certain sullenness, an air of disappointment, a hunching of shoulders, a vague element of displeasure.

Lincoln looked down: a meal made up from shop-bought meat pie, boiled potatoes, peas and gravy seemed like a near miracle to him when you considered exactly how much time Bill had had to prepare and the distractions he'd had. Besides socialising, everybody had been busy putting and packing personal things away and generally getting themselves settled.

It was generally the same at the start of any voyage, people were tense and excited and the chatter and laughter loud. Sharon's presence, he knew, and the associated focus, curiosity and flirting had added to that, and it'd probably be late evening before that nervous excitement finally tailed off. That nervous energy would take its toll and finally tiredness and the oncoming of darkness and the night would cause the establishment of a ship-going routine – tomorrow would be time enough, he felt, for the allocation of mundane chores and the preparing and cooking of meals. Bill had had to work around that initial enthusiasm: the queries, the questions and the general hubbub. As well as the preparation of this meal he had also spent most of the morning showing and putting stuff away, and that without complaint, and that apart from getting the boat organised and shipshape generally!

Another thought followed closely on the heels of that one: they all knew the score and, of course, had anyone of them a mind to then any one of them could have given Bill a hand, and yet, to a man, none of them had! Lincoln felt an unrepentant embarrassment creeping: what a thoughtless, selfish crowd they all were: and what made it worse, even if Lincoln, Lincoln personally, had had the knowledge of hindsight at that time, he still wouldn't have – he just simply couldn't, that excepting queasiness, have been bothered nor cared a less!

Lincoln witnessed the world-renowned red bottle doing the rounds; and each plate being flavoured and enhanced, or drowned, with lashings of tomato sauce. That red catsup dressing appeased the atmosphere somewhat, and the meal, it seemed, after all, might be just acceptable!

Despite their beautiful surrounds, the accompanying noise of the sea and the relatively balmy sea breeze blowing over them, it was Potter whom quietly broke the ensuing silence, inquiring too quietly and too casually of Sharon. For Lincoln, and others it seemed, alarm bells began to ring – she'd not been eating her food – her meal was growing cold resting there on her knees.

Helmut clamped a hand around Potter's wrist before Sharon's plate reached his lap. "You have forgotten, Lionel." Helmut was looking Potter directly in the eye and nodding his head at the same time. "On this boat there is a democracy – ve share; nor do ve not take food from the mouths of babes."

Potter grinned painfully. "Sharon doesn't want hers," he wasn't quite pleading with Sharon, but it was close, "do you, Sharon?"

Helmut enquired, "This is true, Sharon, you are not hungry?" Helmut leant forward, turned and ducked his head in order to look directly into her face. "Vot vill Gary say," he asked, "is not good, you must eat – do you really do not vont it?"

Sharon gently pushed Helmut away and just sat there regarding them, she looked ill and overlaying that paleness was puzzlement, and also something akin to consternation, and . . . and distaste! Sharon gently shook her head and the frowning, questioning creases in her forehead deepened – Lincoln concluded that it was bewilderment that they were mostly seeing: bewilderment that had been caused by the abrupt change of mood and the swift departure of *bonhomie*. She had witnessed and had been thoroughly shocked by the commencement, or rather, the re-establishment of a code of unwritten laws that allowed and made it possible for a group of confined, competitive, testosterone-laden men to live together in comparative peace. From an outsider's point of view, Lincoln could easily perceive, from her point of view, it must have looked like a pack of wild dogs snarling over the entrails from the underbelly of a ripped and bloody carcass. Her confusion, concern, disdain and disgust showed, and that was because she didn't understand. To be fair, what she had seen and was witnessing, Lincoln knew, was, in fact, very complex and most of the subtleties had been established prior to today – all she was seeing, or had seen, was the obvious surface re-establishment of previous, loose conformances . . . Lincoln sighed mentally, in simple terms it involved and all came under the heading of pecking order!

Helmut feigned with her plate. "I throw over the side then?" he threatened.

Sharon only nodded.

Helmut was satisfied. "If you do not object then, Sharon, if you really do not vant to eat it and if you really have no objections, then ve vill share it out, okay?"

Sharon again mutely nodded her consent.

Helmut addressed Lionel directly, "Equally, that is fair, Lionel, I vill see first that there is no more below."

Some hopes, Lincoln thought.

He reappeared a few moments later shaking his head. "The cupboard is bare." Helmut turned to Lincoln. "Chris, you vill cut and share to every vun equal portions, please?"

All eyes watched carefully as Lincoln sat Sharon's plate on his lap and deftly divided her abandoned meal into equal parts: each received a square-inch of pie, a small portion of potato and a teaspoon of peas; each then retired to eat having been satisfied that fair play had been seen to be done – and, of course, the sauce bottle did its inevitable rounds yet again.

Bill Corsham's head appeared in the hatchway, he'd obviously been listening in – he tried to lighten the atmosphere.

"No bite-marks needing bandaging, are there? No blood in the cockpit!" He grinned. "Who wants semolina then?" He peered enquiringly round. "Come on, it's on the stove, don't be shy." He counted. "Okay, six portions. Sharon?" he asked to make sure. She shook her head. "No, right, six portions up here then, with, wait for it, strawberry jam!"

Pretended groans followed Bill's departing head.

Whether due to *Worippa's* motion or the incident she'd just witnessed, Lincoln couldn't tell, but Sharon's pallor had gone from a milk-white to a paler shade of green! Lincoln looked at her more closely, if she was sick now what would she be like and how would she cope once they'd cleared the lee!

Lincoln leant across. "Sharon, show me your ear?"

She just looked at Lincoln – uncomprehending.

Lincoln pulled back her hair, she made no effort to evade or stop him, nor were there any objections. Putty, Lincoln thought, she was well past the first stage – at the stage where they stop thinking – bloody Gary. "Try to hold on to your seasickness, Sharon; I'll get you something that maybe will help."

Lincoln stopped by the chart table and waited for Gary to finish pencilling. "Why haven't you given Sharon something for her seasickness, Gary?" Gary just looked at Lincoln. "Christ, I'd have given you more credit." Lincoln harshly criticised, "I'd have thought it obvious, it isn't as if we haven't already discussed all this, is it: it'll mean the difference between her enjoying the trip on the one hand and it being hell on earth on the other." Lincoln paused for breath and Gary didn't take that opportunity to defend himself, he still just looked. Lincoln enquired, puzzled, "Didn't Brian mention it, I'm sure I heard Brian say something about it to you earlier?"

"Actually," Gary slowly and reluctantly admitted, the words coming out like pulled teeth, "Brian did," then he added the clincher, "but I forgot."

That was when Lincoln exploded. "Jesus. Come on, Gary, she's your girlfriend, and she's a novice, you've got to think – think for her. You know that as well as I do, it would have been be a hundred-to-one fluke if she'd of not suffered from seasickness, there's not many who don't suffer from it first time out, you know that, and especially where we're going – this lop'll be nothing! Anyway," Lincoln looked at him knowingly, and concluded cynically, "I guess it's not relevant now, is it – because suffer from seasickness, she does."

Even now, Lincoln didn't think that Gary had realised the enormity of his irresponsibility . . . and theirs, and his, by association: it wasn't beyond the wildest realms of possibility that this girl could be laid up in her bunk for the rest of the voyage and be very, very ill, to boot – perhaps critically ill. It would be unusual, he admitted, but it wasn't unheard of. Lincoln knew he was going over old ground but the reality was quite different from conjectures and decisions that had been made whilst sitting comfortably in the back of a pub!

Gary didn't allow Lincoln to dwell on his welling and serious misgivings, and nor did Lincoln get to voice the suggestion that now was the time to turn around and return Sharon to shore. It was the blatant belligerence written there on Gary's face that overwhelmed those thoughts. "You know the rules," Lincoln said through his clenched teeth, trying to rein a slipping temper, "she's your guest and therefore she's your responsibility. It's probably too bloody late now, as you know full well, pills and whatnot aren't usually that effective after the event," and Lincoln added, seeing Sharon's face in his mind's eye, "the poor little bitch."

On the defensive, Gary, and he was quick to pick up on an incidental – though reluctantly, Lincoln had to admit, he did have a point. "Mind your tongue, Chris, she's not a bitch. I wouldn't talk about your wife in that way, so don't talk that way about my girlfriend, all right."

Lincoln took a few deep breaths and shook his head. Lincoln hated the kind of tactic that Gary was using; it was what he called 'diversionary flack'. In essence an adversary diverted a person's attention away from the main point by picking upon an incidental fact that was, in truth, whether right or wrong, irrelevant to the main argument. Furthermore, Lincoln knew, if a person did allow themselves to get embroiled and diverted up that side-street and if that adversary was good at it, then before that body knew where they were they'd suddenly find themselves on the defensive!

"Sorry," Lincoln said with dry irony, but nevertheless meant it, and Gary knew full well that his irony was for him and that Lincoln had not meant to be personal about Sharon. "I apologise, all right – I spoke out of turn."

Lincoln gave it away then; further argument wasn't going to get them anywhere. He held out his hand. "Here, give me one of your patches." Lincoln looked him in the eye. "Better late than never!"

Then suddenly that initiative was back into Lincoln's court again, and an unwelcome and unwanted initiative. Gary was just sitting there looking: mute, miserable and pathetic.

"God. You haven't got any!" Lincoln said, and turned and then walked away in disgust.

Lincoln handed Sharon a paper towel. "Here, wipe the skin of your neck behind your ear, it doesn't matter which one. Do it carefully."

She did as instructed and harshly scrubbed the skin behind her right ear. "Good, hold your hair back," Lincoln instructed and peeled and stuck a pad tight in, and smoothed it down with a thumb.

From his pocket Lincoln took a small, oblong, aluminium foil card and popped three pills out. "You'd better take these as well, Sharon." Without comment and like an automaton, she held out her hand and Lincoln dropped them into her cupped palm. "They're going to make you drowsy – seasick pills tend to. I've given you too heavy a dosage so they'll probably send you to sleep – if you can sleep, it'll help."

Sharon just sat there with her hand still out. Lincoln reached out grasped the lapel of her jacket and shook gently, "Are you still with us, Sharon," he asked, "are you listening?" Sharon mutely nodded, but she didn't lift her head. Lincoln lifted the bottle of lemonade that always rested by the side of the hatch, undid the top and held it out to her. "Take them," Lincoln said.

Bottles of drinks were always available and put in set strategic places on deck aboard *Worippa*. Lessons learned: there a danger of dehydration: not so much in these latitudes, though he had been surprised by just how much body fluid could be lost, even down here!

"Listen, it's important." Lincoln paused for a second, just to make sure that she was listening. "Despite what you think and what a lot of folk assume – the only other way of getting over seasickness, the only other way that I know of anyway, apart from enduring, that is, is to go below and climb into a bunk." Sharon lifted her head to look at him, Lincoln regarded her:

those words had got her attention, if nothing else – so at least she wasn't completely out of it! Lincoln explained, "You'll have to fidget around until you find a position for your head where you can hang onto the nausea. There may only be one head position that works, often it's a position where your head twists and rests in the crook of you arm: your elbow. You know," Lincoln demonstrated, "your arm above your head, your body twisted and half on its side – so that your body's sort of locked – all right?"

The poor girl, Lincoln thought, really did not look too well – poor thing. He pulled on her collar again. "Sharon, if you decide to go below and get into a bunk, you must be quick or you'll be sick before you can get there. You're talking to an expert here, Sharon – I suffer from seasickness myself." And to assure her and allay any disbelief that she may have concerning what he had been telling her, added, "A lot of people that I know of actually get undressed in the cockpit and often it's a race between being sick and getting horizontal. There's a lot of us in the same boat," and Lincoln had to grin to himself as he said it – the pun wasn't intended, "and suffer cruelly from what you're suffering – you'll be all right, don't worry, once you've got your sealegs." He sighed, and hoped to God for all their sakes that she would indeed eventually find her sealegs. "I'm afraid that's all the advice I can offer you. All I can suggest is that once you're down you try to daydream: it won't happen straight away, but with luck you'll find your daydreams will get longer – the thoughts of being sick less regular. Try to cope with it, give the pills and the patch a chance to work." Lincoln turned as someone shuffled in the hatchway. "She's all yours, Gary."

As Lincoln gently took the lemonade bottle from her unresisting grasp Sharon admitted miserably. "It's the smell down there, every time I turn my head to go down . . . it makes me feel worse."

It hadn't taken them long to get over their bashfulness then – and Lincoln knew exactly what she meant – all of half a day!

     *   *   *

"I'll hurt you a good deal more, Brian, if you don't listen."

"You're fucking mad, Pom. Let me go. Let go, that fucking-well hurts."

Lincoln pushed the side of Brian's head down harder

against the top of the chart table and pushed his arm up his back just a little further at the same time. "Are you going to listen to me now or am I going to have to stick your head under this desktop and slam the bloody thing down on it."

"Just fuck off," Brian spluttered, "and let me go, you're a fucking lunatic."

"Right." Lincoln said, and he wrenched him back and lifted the lid and then, and despite his struggles, forced his head in. Still without letting go of his arm Lincoln carefully edged sideways from round behind him till he could turn in the isle and face the stern. Once there and with his right hand and arm now over Brian's left shoulder and still levering up, Lincoln rested his hip against the end of the table – and then leant gently on the hinged, wooden desktop.

Brian muttered a curse as the pressure from the lid increased, it wasn't very loud because he was using all his breath and strength in a bid to lever himself free. Actually, he was light-years too late: Lincoln was in an unassailable position: with his hip where it was and pulling gently on his arm and at the same time leaning his weight on the desktop, Lincoln had found a sort of balance and he wasn't uncomfortable – he could wait! After another couple more efforts to break free Ramsey finally gave up and relaxed for a moment. His voice when he spoke again was muffled and Lincoln had to bend to hear.

"Jesus, you've got a fucking bolt loose."

Ramsey was a 'tryer', Lincoln'd give him that – his yells for Lionel in the desk's interior, in-between ineffective efforts to break loose, even though muffled, were enough to raise the dead.

Lincoln finally managed to get a few words in edgeways after some more particularly energetic strivings – after he'd stopped once again to catch his breath. Lincoln leant and spoke into the gap between the chart table lid and its base. "Don't take the piss when I'm talking to you, Brian, I don't like it. Life and death is what I'm talking about – and I get really serious when mine's involved, as I told you before, the least you can do is have the politeness to listen."

Potter clattered down the companionway steps. "What the fuck are you doing, Pom, let 'im go. Christ, you're breaking his bloody neck."

It wasn't fair, poor old Potter had not been expecting it; Lincoln had grabbed Brian again before Potter's knees hit. The punch caught Potter with his stomach muscles slack and had left him blowing like an old carthorse . . . and partially acting the part too – Lincoln knew.

The opportunity was too good, so Lincoln pulled Potter's face into his crutch for good measure.

"Vot is going on, Chris, vot are you doing? You cannot . . ."

Where he had appeared from, Lincoln didn't know. "No closer, Helmut," Lincoln threatened, "don't make me hurt you as well."

He was cool, was Helmut, he deliberated for a moment, then, "I do not believe that you could. I cannot let you hurt people, this you cannot do."

He took a step towards Lincoln.

"Have you ever had a premonition, Helmut?"

Helmut stopped, obviously puzzled, he considered. Lincoln hoped nobody'd ask him a question in the future in a situation where time was of the essence – and when he was just about to save his, Lincoln's life! "Ja," he replied eventually, "I knew ven my Mother died, I felt it. I vas here, she in Deutschland. That is vat you mean?"

"I come from the east coast of England, Helmut," Lincoln answered, "generations of seamen; my people were old when they watched Captain Cook leave Whitby." Lincoln eased his weigh off and lifted the lid and prudently let Brian go, and stepped back away from Potter.

Split between throwing a punch, furious yet curious, Ramsey – yet his sense of humour was winning. Despite himself, Lincoln could see it coming to the fore, and he was also responding to Lincoln's gentle touch on his arm and grin. "Premonitions," Lincoln quietly said, and Lincoln had them – they were listening despite themselves. "My people used a 'lode' stone to steer by, and steered using a board: an oar outside the hull on the starboard side, yes? They crossed the North Sea from Norway in open wooden boats. They saw Iceland, Greenland, and they landed in Newfoundland." Lincoln paused momentarily, as much to collect his thoughts and for effect as anything else. "I can feel it in my water; we're in for the storm of storms." He looked at each one of them in turn. "Can't you

116

feel it – can't you sense it?"

Despite all the shouting, threats and physical of previous, there had been an underlying element of . . . not exactly humour, but rather an underlying tacit, unspoken agreement that nobody would get hurt nor truly upset by the rough-and-tumble. It had been, rather, a sort of trial of strength and bugger-about, although an outsider probably wouldn't have been aware of it – certainly Helmut probably wouldn't have been, thought Lincoln, although you never knew with Helmut? Lincoln shivered as the strongest premonition of doom that he'd ever felt overlaid all other thoughts. "Forget everything; if we don't secure this boat . . ." and almost to himself Lincoln added, "I'm not so sure that we're still going to be here after tomorrow anyway, despite whatever we do!"

Nicolo Frascati's head materialised in the hatchway above Helmut, eyes like saucers, though filled more with excitement rather than fear. "The 'Seven-Year' storm?"

"No, Nick, nothing so mundane. This is going to be the 'Seventeen-Year' storm and, quite frankly, I'm getting . . . I'm getting so scared that I'm very near pooing myself." Lincoln tried to grin. "And the quicker you all are too, getting scared, I mean, then the happier I'll be."

Brian eased the chart table lid down with one hand; he rubbed his neck ruefully with the other. "You prick, Chris, that fucking-well hurt." He pointed a finger. "I'll not forget – fucking stupid thing to do to a person; and belting Lionel one, he doesn't deserve that, he's older." Ramsey stared: already knowing – giving himself time to think. "Are you really serious, or pissing about?" Ramsey answered his own question. "No, you're not pissing about. Are you really that nervous?"

Lincoln nodded.

Brian mulled that over. "Fucking hell. There's nothing to support what you're saying: there was nothing mentioned in the forecast at eighteen-fifteen: no storm warnings from Melbourne or wherever – none." He squinted down, leant across and then tapped. "The barometer hasn't dropped that much, has it . . ." Ramsey scratched at the stubble that covered his chin. He turned to Potter. "What do you think, Lionel?"

"Not so much of the 'older', that's what I think." Lionel grunted as Lincoln helped him to straighten up. "For Christ sake's, do whatever he says." He indicated to Lincoln with a thumb with one hand while tenderly rubbing his tummy, the consummate thespian, with the other." I don't think I can take another punch like that." Lionel took a deep breath and then expelled air noisily out from full cheeks. "Anyway, they won't necessarily be aware, will they, the Met, especially if it's local or a one off!" Lionel took another deep breath and turned directly to Lincoln. "He's right, Pom, you really are a right prick."

"Vot is it that ve do?" Helmut nodded to Lincoln. "I believe, Mister Mate." He looked down and lightly caressed his forearm. "The hairs stand on end, on my neck also."

Ramsey was sarcastic, "Well there's evidence."

It was Nicolo Frascati's turn next. "Yeah," he drawled excitedly, and then hit Helmut hard on the top of that same 'hair-standing' arm. "And not only that, I haven't got time to hang around, I've got things to do next week, let alone today." He hit Helmut again and outlined a female shape with his hands and then raised his eyebrows. "Haven't we, Helmut?"

Helmut rubbed. "Do not be rude about the girls," he admonished and wagged a warning finger. He smiled wistfully then. "But yes, Nick is right, ve have things to do – definitely."

Helmut's haymaker whistled – Frascati, fortunately, was no longer there. Helmut looked round questioningly – from face to face. "Tell me again, vot is it ve have to do?"

Lincoln shook his head, he was something else, was Helmut!

"Go back on watch with Nick, Helmut," Brian instructed, "we'll get back to you, we've got a bit of time yet." Brian turned his attention from Helmut to Lincoln. "I don't know why I believe you, Chris, but I do." He shut his eyes and shook his head. "God knows." That statement was not without an attached, half-hearted proviso. "Mind you, I'll quickly come after you if you're wrong, I just prefer not to chance it just in case you're right, that's all . . . And anyway, you're too sure." Ramsey ignored Potter's knowing smirk and suddenly his demeanour was without humour. "Okay, it's your ball-game then, seriously, what do you suggest, and you, Lionel – what's to do?"

      *   *   *

"Gary, get Sharon out of that bunk and strip her. Dress her in thermal underwear and then a layer of fleece, all right. Jamie's 'oceans' are forward, she'll have to wear them, I don't suppose Jamie'll mind, considering." Lincoln continued on before he could interrupt. "Connect a safetyline to her harness, loop it over her shoulders and around her neck and clip it back on, then put her in a bottom bunk." Lincoln pointed. "Over the keel, Gary, the motion'll be less pronounced there – and double-lash the lee cloth."

"Yeah, but she'll melt . . ."

Lincoln took a threatening step forward. "Gary!" Lincoln looked at him. "All right, leave the zips down, but not completely undone – she'll be wanting all the warmth she can get, especially later when the evening draws in." Lincoln added with a half-smile, "You can zip them right up again later, when it turns."

"Okay, okay." Gary held up his arms. "Fuck, I'm doing it; keep your Pommy hair on."

Lincoln turned to Ramsey. "What's the worst you've been in with this boat, Brian? How does she handle? How, where, what's her . . . when is she most comfortable?"

They got no further, Lionel really tried to look angry – he was looking past them. "Who the fuck are you looking at, Corsham? You won't be laughing, walking round with that ladle sticking out of your arse – it won't be the handle end going up first either."

Bill stood in the galley; he'd certainly been privy to all that had gone on. His hands rested on either side of the sink: he leant on them, arms stiff, head down. Lionel's threat set him off, he didn't or couldn't lift his head for laughing – all he could do was shake it. "Christ," he addressing Lincoln, "I wouldn't want to be around when you really get upset, Pom, you're absolute fucking-hell on wheels."

He dropped the façade then and was suddenly serious. "Sandwiches, soup and tea in the flasks? Have we got time for a hot meal? How long we got before it hits, do you think?"

Brian and Lionel were silent; Lincoln had their full attention yet again.

"Probably three hours, or less, Bill, maybe six, with an outside chance of nine . . . No, strike that, not that long." Lincoln hesitated; to overestimate would be stupid, if not criminal. "In your case, Bill, to cook a meal: depending on how quickly the seas build, probably no more than an hour and a half, two at the most, that's all."

"I'll start now – straight away." Bill stepped away from the sink. "I'll do sandwiches and soup first, and then prepare the meal after – that's if there's time."   He nodded to them. "We'll be right."

"Where's Warren, Bill?" Lincoln asked, suddenly aware that he hadn't caught sight of him for some time. "He might as well help."

Bill's half-laugh was tinged with both concern and contempt. "He'll be shitting himself in the heads by now. You lot really did frighten him, he thought the fighting was deadly serious." He sighed. "Just give him a little more time to collect himself – leave him be – I'll go and get him when I need him, all right?"

Lincoln thought about that, and Bill was right, if he was in a state he'd probably be more of a hindrance than a help. "Okay, I'll leave him to you then, thanks."

Brian's mind had clearly been elsewhere – he voiced what had obviously been dominating his thoughts without prompting. "I think our best bet would be to run before it – tow warps if necessary, if the waves get too big." He held up a hand to stop any interruptions. "The chances are that we won't get pooped, I'd chance that, *Worippa's* stern is very light." Brian spoke directly to Lincoln.   "To be honest, Chris, as far as I know, *Worippa* has never fired a shot in anger, at least, not while I've owned her . . . The worst we've experienced is a seven – we've been lucky, right, Lionel?"

Lionel didn't answer straight away and it was with obvious and serious reluctance when he did.   "The mast's too tall."

Lincoln blinked – this was new!

"It's no good looking like that, Pom; it's not uncommon to add a few extra feet in this part of the world."

Lincoln blinked again – a few feet?

"We spend nine-tenths of the time bobbing around looking for wind down here, or barely ghosting more often than not, so don't go getting on your high-horse."

Lincoln just looked at him: sooner or later they were going to pay their dues for altering the marine architect's specs, unfortunately, for him, Lincoln, it looked as if it was going to be sooner. No, he was being a little unfair, some naval architects did err too far on the side of safety . . . Thing was though, Potter would never have admitted that little gem unless it was relevant, and then Lincoln wondered exactly how long his two feet actually was!

Lionel bulldozed on, ignoring the look that was obviously written there on Lincoln's face, and ignoring the bland, pretended, worried innocence that was on Ramsey's: as if the little 'gem' concerning the mast would go away if ignored, and not wanting to discuss it. He was right, of course, Lincoln admitted to himself, Potter was right; any discussions on that subject were now redundant! "She won't be comfortable," he continued, "nor happy lying a-hull – under bare poles. In my view we'd be better off to keep canvass on her – she'll pendulum like a pig even then, should we decide to heave-to." He sighed. "No good, is it?" Potter had been watching Lincoln closely. "D'you know, I've never seen you like this, Chris." He pointed. "You'd better stop biting your lip; you'll be drawing blood in a minute. You'd better tell us the worst, by the look on your face there's obviously more to come?"

Lincoln started to mentally assemble an overview – and Lionel, unfortunately, misinterpreted Lincoln's silence.

"Go on, fucking stare, Pom, we're not children, you know, matie – we all knew and have always known the risks, and have willingly accepted them before we sailed."

Some of us hadn't, Lincoln said in his mind, some of us hadn't known all the risks though, had they – and some on board were innocents – Potter knew that despite his empty, reflexive admonishment. Lincoln didn't look round at Ramsey; it probably hadn't sunk in yet – let's hope, Lincoln hazarded, that it would never have to.

They rode and adjusted to *Worippa's* motion without conscious thought and without taking any notice of the familiar creaks and groans, and the muted sound of the sea and wind. Lincoln reached out in that silence and touched Potter's elbow. "It'll come from the south, Lionel, maybe a little west by south. I don't think we've got a choice, if you think about it, whatever – whichever way you look at it we're on a lee shore. We're going to have to try and sail through it, any other way and the wind and leeway'll eventually push us up on the beach. Forget about the extra few feet on the mast, only just pray to God the rig's strong enough and will take it, irrespective, that's all!"

Potter was curious, Lincoln didn't doubt for a minute that

he now believed him, Lincoln had accomplished that much, at least. "How are you so sure it'll be coming in from the south?" He shook his head. "Or wherever?" he asked.

That question was too complex to answer, and furthermore, Lincoln didn't know that he could even if he tried. "Well, that's easy, Lionel. Every time my back faces south, my rectum puckers and the cheeks of my backside clamp and pinch up so tightly that it makes them ache."

Potter grinned.

Ramsey smiled, despite himself. "That's it then, we're really in for it. If I didn't believe you before I believe you now. Silly us. Why didn't you say so in the first place, that your arsehole's been playing up, it would have saved you, and us, all that fucking about." He looked down and pulled the edges of his jacket together before looking at them directly. "We better get started then, hadn't we – up and at 'em."

Chapter 10

"What you doing, Pom?"

"Putting on a tape. I wouldn't mind to hear something in the background, other than," Lincoln jerked his head and raised his eyes to the deckhead, further elaboration wasn't necessary, Potter knew that Lincoln meant outside, "and I find music soothing."

Potter complained, "Not now, surely? Can't it wait? Come on, from what you say we're going to need to have this Council of War as soon as."

"Yes, I understand, Lionel, just give me a minute."

The general chatter slowly died and the silence gently crept as the melodic strains imposed and made themselves heard.

Ramsey's head appeared around from behind the locker bulkhead. "We ought to keep the stereo on topside, you know, things aren't so bad with a whole orchestra for company; we can use the dimmer down here if it disturbs people's sleep too much." His remark caused Lincoln to inwardly smile. "What is that, Chris, there's something about . . . I know that piece from somewhere . . ." His eyes narrowed and then his face lit. "That's one of my recordings."

"That's right, and I put it on just for you, Brian – everybody hates it and didn't want me to put it on, but I know you like it, so, and at great personal risk, I put it on anyway!"

"No, come on, don't fuck about, Chris, you know what I mean – what is it, what'd it say on the box?"

"*Mendelssohn*," Lincoln said.

"Yes . . . And?"

"*Symphony Number Three in A Minor*."

"Yes, I remember now, now that you've told me – that's also known as the '*Scottish*'." Ramsey's face turned pensive. "And recorded and tacked on the end of that symphony as a filler, if I remember rightly, is an overture called '*Calm Sea and Prosperous Voyage'*. Bloody ironical when . . ."

Ramsey's pensiveness changed and a resigned dryness, not quite outright distaste, took its place as he turned to address Potter directly. "You're an uncouth pig, Lionel."

Lincoln had turned also. "He's right; you're a bloody uncouth Philistine, Lionel."

"You fat bastard," iterated Ramsey, wrinkling his nose.

"Fart-arse," Lincoln added.

Potter had loudly emitted wind in the first silence, between movements one and two – and their concerted attack and admonishings had left him completely unperturbed.

"Trombone's a bit flat." He looked at them. "Come on; snap out of it – for fuck's sake, we'll all be weeping in our beer next."

*   *   *

"If it were me, I'd get the roller reefing off her straight away, while we've the chance and motor while we're doing it. Gain as much sea-room as we can and sneak every inch of offing while we can.   It'd be prudent to top-off the batteries anyway." Lincoln paused as another thought struck. "The storm jib, Brian, does it have cringles up its luff, has it – is it a belt-and-braces job?"

"Christ, I'm starting to get scared now." Brian searched Lincoln's face. "Yes, it can be secured to the foil independent of the bolt-rope, that's if the foil fails and the bolt-rope pulls out, I assume that's what you mean?" He looked at Lincoln. "Um, we'll just have to make up some short rope lengths to attach it, that's all.   Don't look at me like that, Pom – we've used the storm jib before obviously, but we've never been in the sort of blow where we've found them necessary – to be honest, I've always felt that they were a bit over the top . . . I'll do it now – all right, satisfied!"

Lincoln ignored his sarcasm and didn't bother to point out what was patently on his mind: that short lines for reefing should have already and permanently been rove through and ready, and that they'd probably already be heading for trouble when they pulled the storm jib from its bag, period, and that in such a given situation there wouldn't be time for such niceties. What Lincoln didn't mention was that there was a school that believed in keeping it simple with storm jibs, and they didn't use the foil at all, just the rope reefs, or ties, that were knotted around it – the jib slid up outside and independent of the foil – so, in fact, to do both was in a way double-insurance. The thing was that it wasn't entirely his fault either – preparation at sea was everything – and Lincoln should have checked himself!

Lincoln, ignoring Brian's grimace at his silent implied criticism, quietly continued on, "You've got a trysail, I know, the track for it is on the mast and I heard Helmut mention it. We'd best fit that as well – while we've the time, yes?"

Potter spoke next, "The main's got four reefing points in it, you know, Pom. We've only ever had to reef down to that fourth reef – what, Brian, three, four times, maybe?" Ramsey nodded. "As far as I can remember, we've never fired the trysail in anger, right, Brian?" Ramsey nodded again. "We always thought . . . Well, we've always felt that the trysail was, well, was a bit of overkill." Lionel's voice had run down like an old clock towards the end of his sentence and he added lamely, "There's not much canvass left when that last reef goes in, I can tell you that, matie."

Lionel clearly already knew and that his last sentence had been fatuitous and for Lincoln to say so wouldn't help – now was the time for tact. "It'll be a lot cheaper if the 'try' gets blown away, Lionel – we're going to need that main later." Lincoln redirected their discussion. "Anyway, it's the storm jib that's more important, as long as the storm jib holds then we'll be able to keep way on." Lincoln turned to Ramsey in order to change the subject again, and to discretely let Lionel off the hook. "It's just as well she's a 'masthead', Brian, at least the pole's supported all round: no breaks in the triangle of strength."

"Well, I'm glad you're pleased about something," Brian observed ironically, and he opened his mouth to comment further but was interrupted by Potter barging in.

"We're a bit old-fashioned on here, matie," stated Potter, with a self-satisfied, superior air, "we've never felt quite comfortable with a 'three-quarter' – we've never liked that unsupported bit at the top. I don't want to tempt fate, but you'd have noticed – it's always the 'bendies' that seem to break under the strain?"

It never ceased to amaze Lincoln, and not so much Potter in this instance, but generally: to what lengths people would go to, to save an imagined vestige of pride, or to keep on top. To resurrect and refer back, or to cover a point, as Potter was doing – it simply emphasised that point – a point that was past and forgotten anyway, if only he did but realise it. Brian caught Lincoln's eye with raised eyebrows and a knowing look, and then they both looked away.

Potter was oblivious, "And talking about fate, what you said earlier, Pom, about 'your' people: you can quickly get into their minds, can't you, you don't have to be out here very long before you understand why they were so superstitious. Were you really serious about them yesterday, I wouldn't have had much time for that mystical shit, but today I'm not so sure."

Worippa heeled and they held on – *Worippa* was already beginning to travel a bumpy road – and occasional, pronounced dips and lurches were beginning to be noticeable.

All over the place was Lionel – that would be stress. Lincoln said gently, "You'd be making a serious mistake, Lionel, if you didn't listen to your inner voice. Don't you believe in ancestral knowledge – inherited instincts of the species – all that? On second thought's, if you haven't, I hope you don't experience them. You'd have to be on your last 'knockings' to do so; most people will only acknowledge them then. Why do we have a bowel movement when we're faced with a violent end: our last hope is that the smell: that the stink'll put the predator off. There're lots of examples of primeval impulses at work around, Lionel, if you do but look."

Brian's retort was a comfort to Lincoln, he'd started to think: to get into the right frame of mind. "Let me tell you, Pom, and you're getting as bad, Lionel, like I said before, if your intention is to put the fear of Christ up me then you've succeeded handsomely." Ramsey turned to practicalities then, "She will sail under main alone, by the way, but only just. We'd better get moving then." Brian puffed out his cheeks and expelled a long breath. "The trysail, it's brand new, and we've only tried it the once – the day after it came from the sail-maker's." He held up a refraining finger. "No, Chris, it's all set – remember, Lionel?" He turned back to Lincoln. "Lionel and I set it up the day after it was delivered – we tried it – remember, Lionel?"

"Yep," confirmed Lionel. "We're good to go."

"Okay, said Ramsey, "what else do we have to do after we've bent that on?"

Lincoln didn't doubt Brian – if he said that he'd set up the trysail, then that's what he had done . . . What was really starting to hit Lincoln was his neglect, and thinking about it, that he, well they, had never had, and Brian had confirmed that, practised and familiarised themselves, himself, with putting up *Worippa's* storm sails – and sorting out their particular peculiarities. One of the first safety procedures that should be regularly practised on any yacht – let alone one roaming the worst seas in the world, was setting storm sails – elementary

126

stuff!

Ramsey should have, and Lincoln also included Lionel in that, he was experienced enough . . . But then so was Gary, and Bill – and, come to that, the rest of the crew too! No, Lincoln castigated himself, he should have checked and never mind about casting about and apportioning blame – bottom line, it was him, Lincoln, who had been criminally neglectful.

Brian and Lionel were both looking at Lincoln expectantly. Put it away, Lincoln thought, all that can be thought about later. He took a breath. "Okay, as you say, let's waste no more time. Brian, what about if I take Helmut with me and fit the Number Three? Actually," Lincoln admitted, "I might have been a bit hasty – we don't need the storm jib quite yet – just so long as it's ready and to hand." Then Lincoln added a proviso, "So we'll have time to attach those earrings." It was a barely disguised order, and best, thought Lincoln, to hurry on before further sarcastic rejoinders were made. "What we really need to do is keep the power on while we can, and punch through it, and, as you say, gain sea-room." Lincoln was working out assignations as he was talking, "Nevertheless, I think it would be wise to get the trysail on her – again, as you say, we're a little unfamiliar with that – bend that on while conditions are still reasonable."

Brian nodded and touched a finger to his chin and gestured for Lincoln to continue on.

Lincoln looked at them. "Well, perhaps if you would take Nick with you, Lionel, and bend on the trysail – you're familiar with it. Then, if we put Gary on the helm then that'll leave you to sort out the engine, Brian, which you know better than anyone." Lincoln paused, and then added a suffix to that, "That's if our sailing speed drops below our engine speed, if you see what I mean – which I actually doubt now. But what you really need to do is radio in our 'lat-long' and situation – yes? We'd be in a much better position with those radioed in and under our belts: I know I'll be a bloody sight happier anyway."

"Right." Brian confirmed with a nod of his head. "Okay." He turned to Potter and diplomatically asked, "Have you got anything to add, Lionel?

"No," answered Potter placidly, also without acrimony, "it all sounds fair enough to me. The 'try' sheets run through the leading blocks that we attached to the toe rail, right, and then round the spinnaker turning blocks and then back to the spinnaker winches, right? "

Ramsey confirmed, "Yes." He added a qualifier, "Attach those tackles I had made up to either side of the boom, will you, Lionel – position it horizontally with the topping lift, then make sure that the mainsail sheet and boom downhaul are nice and tight. If I remember rightly, the tackles are . . ."

Lionel interrupted, "I know where they are, matie."

Ramsey hesitated, and then said it anyway, "I know I don't have to say this, Lionel, and I don't mean to be insulting, but please just double and triple-check everything – all we'll need is that thing to come loose and be scything about – the weight of that boom, it'd maim somebody for life if it were ever to come loose in a seaway."

When Lincoln was sure that Lionel had nothing more to add – he actually didn't have to, his look said everything!

Ramsey looked at Lincoln – Lincoln looked at Ramsey. "Don't you drop the boom and lash it to the deck then?" Lincoln harshly and in a criticising tone asked.

"No," answered Ramsey firmly, "we've tried that in the past, on a previous boat – fucking useless. Gets in the way all the time – everybody tripping over and having to climb over the bloody thing – too bloody dangerous. Furthermore, that last time we did it, the sea washing over it put so much pressure on the stanchion it was trapped against – it just about ripped that stanchion out of the deck."

There, Lincoln thought, was a yacht owner's answer. He made to retort, and then stopped . . . Actually, it sounded safe enough to him, provided that the tackles that Ramsey had said that he had had made up were heavy enough – and the mainsail track-trolley was controlled and restrained by a winch at each end of the mainsail track too.

Lincoln then asked the obvious, "Um, the topping lift . . .?"

"Wire," said Ramsey conversationally, "strong enough to lift a train."

"Um, those tackles . . .?"

"Each from this end of the boom directly to a U-bolt next to the toe rail opposite."

"Um . . .?"

"Spare me," said Ramsey. "They're four-part tackles and strong enough."

"It might be," Lincoln said, knowing it sounded like he was questioning Ramsey's competence, "prudent to run all the reefing lines to the main, ready – before we put it to bed – just in case. Ready for when we do go to use it again – if you see what I mean?"

Ramsey merely nodded.

Lincoln breathed deeply and relaxed. "Just one last thing then, Brian – one other option. When you do check our position, we may still have enough time to run back into Hobart – I realise that we're on the edge of our range and you might well, if there's no other way, have to run the engine at full bore – thing is, is it still a choice?"

Ramsey didn't hesitate. "No, we've come too far now, Chris, and the very thought of getting caught going in – Storm Bay, for instance." He shuddered. "I'd prefer to put my faith in *Worippa* and take my chances out at sea – it'll be safer."

"Okay," Lincoln assented, and he agreed with him, "Skipper's decision."

Potter's hand stopped Lincoln from standing. "Very nice all this – all this common-sense you're spouting, Pom. Just one minor point, matie," Lionel pointed and wagged for emphasis, underlining each word, "you stop your antics. Horseplay's all very well, Brian and I know there's no malice in it, the trouble is, nine-times out of ten it'll end up backfiring." Lionel pushed Lincoln down again as he started to rise. "And another thing, don't involve poor Helmut, he's on a totally different wave-length as far as humour is concerned – he has trouble handling it. Also, it's all very well you telling us, but you're just as bad, and if what you say is true and I don't doubt that it is, then you've got to stop yourself risking further injury. Brian might not have thought of it, but I have – one good belt in the ribs and it'll be 'goodbye' to you for the rest of the trip. We're going to be short-handed enough as it is, so don't you go damaging yourself further: I suspect we're going to need you – need everybody." Potter crossed his arms in front of his chest, swaying. "What we don't need is a member of crew laid up in a bunk, or even worse, having to be lifted off." He nodded. "Your Achilles Heel – don't forget about it." Lionel plainly hadn't finished with Lincoln yet, and he held out a threatening finger while exploring his gums with his tongue; next, with exaggerated deliberation he sucked on and then wiped them, his gums and his teeth, with the edge of his hand. He grimaced. "And don't stick your 'dick' into my face again either, matie, it wouldn't have been so bad if you washed it now and again." He raspberried spittle onto his fingers and massaged his lips at the same time. "Taste was awful!"

*   *   *

"What do you think, Lionel?"

"The bloody mast'd have to pull out before that canvas'd give way, it's so stiff you can't bend it, matie – it's like a piece of bloody board."

A pair of hands finished pulling hard on the boom lashings and then dropped to the underside of the boom; Nick's face appeared momentarily before he ducked under and joined them. "It's turned colder, really cold." He shivered and stumbled slightly; and the engine's exhaust gurgled as *Worippa* lifted and leaned in the swell. "Started hasn't it – the sea look's evil."

Potter calmed and comforted, "Don't let your imagination run away with you, Nick, it always seems worse when the light's going – indifferent and impartial, is all. And, as you say, it's starting to get cold too and that won't help: it's cold because the wind's coming directly off the icepack, nothing to stop it: there's nothing between Antarctica and us. You have to dress for it, Nick, or it'll leach the stuffing out of you – keep yourself well rugged-up and you'll be right, matie." Potter turned to Lincoln. "I'll have a word with Brian, Pom, let him know we've finished." Lincoln nodded assent. "It might be wise," Potter added thoughtfully, after glancing around and staring into the twilight, "to head in a bit: Sidmouth, Eddystone, Pedra Bronca and Flying Scud Rocks are all out there somewhere: we won't see them in this murk, not till we hit – they're all unlit." Potter held out and waved an all-encompassing hand. "Bloody place seems to be strewn with rocks just waiting for the unwary, it would be a bit ironical if we bumped into one of those instead, wouldn't it!" Talk about first boosting up their morale, mused Lincoln, only to drop them straight down again! "Right," he abruptly said, "enough," and turned till Lincoln was in his sights again. "Come on, Pom, you'd better come below with me, you're dripping blood all over the deck, Brian won't like that."

Lincoln hesitated as he lifted a leg to climb over the companionway coaming, and bent his head down instead and sniffed at the aroma wafting up. "Hark at that smell, Lionel, a 'William Corsham' curry special for dinner tonight – that'll put extra powder in your musket."

Potter, never one to be slow on the uptake, parried without apparent thought. "Let's just try to keep it dry, matie, that's the trick, nothing more disappointing than a misfire – come on." He gave Lincoln a gentle push and turned and spoke to Gary as he did so. "We'll send someone up ASAP, Gary, as soon as we're sorted."

*   *   *

"No, not according to our position on the GPS." Brian puffed up his chest and blew noisily through his lips.

Surprisingly, they didn't have to talk overly loud to be heard above the rumble of *Worippa's* engine, and that it was just a little too powerful, in Lincoln's experience, for a yacht of *Worippa's* size happily negated the necessity of having to run it at high revs, and that factor and that it was well maintained and well insulated ensured minimum engine noise.

Brian still hadn't got over his latest navigational acquisition. GPS stood grandly for 'Global Positioning System', and they'd not really got a proper look yet because he was still guarding it with a vigour that they found most unbecoming. They were only and grudgingly allowed to play with the 'Sat Nav' now that it was, in his eyes, old hat! That the Sat Nav was situated below the GPS had saved them a couple of times from being caught: another furtive pastime of theirs was to fiddle with his new toy when he wasn't around.

"We're through them," Ramsey stated, "Cape Bruny Light should be back off our beam. The light marking the entrance to Recherche Bay and Actaeon Island Light will be just forward of it. You can't miss Bruny, it's a powerful, elevated monster – throws out mega-candles, and it should be with us for miles – and it'll be the major navigational aid for us."

Lionel yawned, and a deliberate casual act, which in a stroke effectively deflated Ramsey's schoolmaster-to-pupil pomposity, as it was meant to do. "What did Melbourne Radio have to say, matie?"

Ramsey's look of disgruntlement disappeared almost immediately and was replaced once again with keen enthusiasm, though of a different, admiring sort this time. "They're good, those blokes, they put me through to the 'Met' after recording all our details – they certainly didn't laugh. The 'weather' people advised me – us, I mean – what they said basically was to run with the feeling in our ... well, Pom's 'water'. They said that they've already plotted a 'low' and they know that a front's coming in; as he said, their weakness is always time: they sometimes have difficulty in judging exactly and specifically how fast a low is moving at any given time, and hence they can't tell you to the minute at what time it'll arrive in your area – they do give you a window though. Anyway, they reckon its centre will follow a fairly standard route and track to the northeast – they reckon it'll pass to the east of Tasmania. They also said, coincidentally, that there's a high in the Australian Bight that probably wouldn't be too influential, but on the other hand, it won't help. It doesn't sound it the way I've put it, but like I said, they were, in fact, very helpful. They asked for air pressure, wind speed, direction, sea-state – the works. He pushed an A4, pre-printed, blank weather map form of Bass Strait across – he'd filled in the lows and highs and relevant information as dictated by the Met people. "Ten-out-of-ten, Pom." He indicated with a finger. "The synopsis shows the left-hand side of a low, rotating clockwise; and as you can see, eventually it'll be directly over us." He looked across to Lincoln. "That's your southerly, Chris." Ramsey traced with a finger. "The right-hand edge of a high, rotating the opposite way, its centre ... here." He tapped his finger on it for emphasis. "In the Bight. In my opinion it looks as if it will add to it, despite what they say." Ramsey squeezed and pulled at his nose with his left-hand forefinger and thumb. "The barometer's dropped to one-zero-three-one millibars, and it's still dropping!"

*   *   *

Those that could be were present: silence ensued and Brian's pupils glinted as his encompassing passing glance briefly focused on Lincoln before moving on. "Which two are officially on watch now?" he queried, and didn't wait for an answer. "Thing is, we've been a bit lax with watches up till now, but from here on in I suggest that we re-establish our watches; only from now on we'll have four people on each watch." He didn't wait for a consensus. "Right, and I'll double-up for Sharon as and when necessary. We'll keep just the two on watch now though, then once we've finished sorting the boat and ourselves out, then, as I say, we'll have four on each watch, but only two up top – the others in the watch are to be dressed and ready to go topside if called." Brian clarified, "The less people we have up top, the less people are likely to be washed overboard – in truth, you really only need just the two, and if it really starts to build, then it'll actually, though you might not think so, be safer below."

Brian continued on and what he had said obviously wasn't up for discussion. "As soon as anyone has completed their chores, then they're to get their heads down – if you can't sleep then just rest – everyone, by the looks of things, are going to need as much rest as they can get, time allowing." Brian looked down and then up again. "That's excluding any other emergency, of course." His eyes circled around again. "You're all to carry your knives, just in case; there's one attached permanently to the life raft forward of the mast," he stated meaningfully. "The other life raft is aft – you all know where – and I don't have to remind you to attach the 'painter' before you throw it over, do I?" Nobody answered. "Nor see to the 'Emergency Position Indicating Radio Beacon'!"

It took Lincoln a second to comprehend his last sentence and what it meant – Lincoln raised an eyebrow, Nick's face was completely blank. Brian's exasperation showed and he pointed a finger at Nick. "You mustn't . . . whatever you do, don't forget that – it's our one certain ace in the hole." Ramsey wagged his previously pointing finger vertically in the air so as to include – and addressed everybody who had quietly gathered, rather than just Nick. "It's not like the old days, that signal'll be automatically picked up – they'll find us within a couple of hours." Ramsey looked directly at Nick again. "EPIRB – remember? The orange-red thing with an aerial hanging upside-down," he nodded, "over there, on the wall?"

Puzzlement cleared and enlightenment dawned on Nick's, and other faces too, truth be known – and everybody was happy again!

Actually, and despite his emphasis, Brian had understated – and Lincoln was sure that few non-professionals had sat down and had truly absorbed the reality – the immeasurable value – and the significance of that electronic, hand-sized, bulbous, float-shaped, plastic-encapsulated miracle. Lincoln assessed in his mind: EPIRB's were, as far as recovery was concerned anyway, the most revolutionary piece of safety equipment ever devised by man. It was originally conceived, he knew, and designed to trace 'downed' aircraft (in hostile terrain – land or water), and until recently had had its limitations when operating in a marine environment: it had had a defined range width and therefore could be only utilised when a vessel sank, foundered, or was in trouble near a flight path – but preferably under a regular commercial aviation route. The distress signal, prior then, had been bounded – and furthermore, had been only capable of being picked-up by another over-flying relation – in other words, a ship or boat in remote seas could not be heard and was on its own if away from a frequented air corridor. Thankfully, and Lincoln was eternally thankful, the program had been upgraded and an umbrella of satellites now existed – the last only recently launched – and the system now covered ninety percent of the world's oceans!

As Brian had pointed out, they'd be pinpointed and picked-up within two or three hours – the ultimate in rescue. There was another wonderful and further bonus after that as well – a sort of quiet, dull, inward warmth momentarily glowed in Lincoln – the initial price of an EPIRB was well within every yacht owner's budget, and the service free thereafter: it had and would save millions; and mammoth expensive man-hours; and associated dangers to the rescuers; and resources not spent looking. They all, thought Lincoln – everybody won!

Something in the tone of Ramsey's voice re-attracted Lincoln's wondering attention – there was a firmness in Ramsey's voice that hadn't been there before, and also quiet determination. "Well, we might as well get it over with, as you all know, or should know," he indicated with a finger, "the grab bag lives in the locker below the EPIRB, and everything that we could possible want in an emergency, everything that I could think of anyway, is in it. The wire cutters are in their usual place, and the sea-anchor, should we need it, is behind the companionway steps; as are all the spare warps." He indicated again. "The flares are under the chart table in the yellow, plastic, waterproof container; and you all know how to use the radio and where the 'emergency' hand-set is – and you all know where your life jackets are . . .

"I also think that it would be wise to update the chart regularly during the watch, and religiously at the end of every watch; that's because we won't know where we are if the 'electrics' suddenly go. Lightning, water, or whatever could wipe out this box of 'white-man's' magic." Ramsey affectionately patted his new computer (the pleasures of material possessions) before proudly adding, "Though it's guaranteed to still operate underwater – up to . . . well, down to three feet actually."

The sarcasm in Potter's voice you could cut, "Very handy, I'll remember that when I'm driving around on my underwater torpedo."

Nick's grinning-serious voice broke the strained, humorous, clamp-jawed, tongue-biting hush. "Helmut and I are supposed to be on watch, I've come down to get dressed, that's all – we're perishing up there. I'll change then, and then I'll send Helmut down; he'll just about be finished by then." Nick bobbed his head at the deck above. "He's lashing the roller reefing to the stanchions – and everything else in sight – it'll take us a day to undo all the rope-work he's put round everything." Nick quickly glanced at each of them before continuing on. "Gary said he'll be all right for the moment . . ." He hesitated. "Um, I'd better get a move on – he'll be getting cold too."

"Good," Ramsey said encouragingly. "There'll be a meal ready shortly, we'll relieve and feed Helmut and you in turn. You'd better send Gary down as soon as Helmut's happy, he can eat and then get some rest – all right? Harnesses from now on, Nick," Ramsey instructed. "No excuses."

Nick's voice was constrained, and quiet, "No worries. We're getting organised, I'll take mine up with me now." Nick turned to go and then turned back. "By the way, before I forget, what course are we steering now? And Gary said, do you want the engine off now – he says he knows it's in neutral and that you are charging the batteries." Nick tipped his head to one side and raised his eyebrows. "He says that we seem to have been running it for a while?"

Brian's frustration began to show and he tutted – it'd been a long day. "Yes, he's quite right, I should have told him that – would you tell him to turn it off, please, Nick. The batteries are as topped up as far they are ever going to be, given our circumstances – we're just wasting fuel . . ." He half-pointed at Nick. "Um, Nick," and said slowly, "also tell him to put her tight on a starboard tack – whatever that is, that'll be our course – he'll understand. Also tell him to set the backstay hydraulics to half. Thanks, Nick – topside now."

Ramsey turned to Lincoln. "All right? That sort of bend won't put too much pressure on the rig, that and the pre-bend should be enough to eliminate any chance of the mast inverting – it won't be much good to us broken, will it?"

"Sounds good to me, Brian," Lincoln said lightly. "Bruny Island Light," Lincoln asked. "That's obviously the lighthouse we've been seeing: white? We could just make it out earlier, sat on a headland, high up," and admitted, "I haven't timed its sequence."

"Yes, Cape Bruny, that'll be it." Brian perked up a little bit. "One thing about all this that's comforting, so long as we can see and keep Maatsuyker Light in view we'll be right. We should be able to pick up its loom, if not the light itself, from about thirty miles out – it's as powerful as Bruny. Let's try not to lose it, it'll orient . . ." Ramsey stumbled over the word, "orient . . . ate us." He ignored their smiles. "Group-flash-two every thirty seconds." Ramsey gave a loud sigh. "That was a stupid statement, sorry. That light is the southernmost, and the only light west in this half-hemisphere of the world. As long as we can see it, then we'll be right." Ramsey raised his eyes to heaven. "Excepting Mewstone Rock, of course – that bloody thing's not lit – there's always something." Ramsey mused for a moment. "Actually, they did know what they were doing when they set up Bruny and Maatsuyker; you can pinpoint exactly where you are with them." Ramsey just had to add the proviso, 'That's providing that you can see them, of course – and only fog'll stop you doing that."

He turned and attacked Lincoln then, before Potter or Lincoln could add their two-penny's worth. "For Christ's sake, Pom," he snapped, "stick those fingers under the tap, you're dripping blood onto the carpet. Lionel's right, you know, you've got to start looking after yourself – move!"

*   *   *

"Who's got the watch, Brian?"

Ramsey looked up. "Lionel and Warren are up there. It's started, listen to it – 'Huey's' begun to move around." Huey was an Australian slang word for God, Lincoln had gleaned, or the supreme deity anyway. "Can't you sleep?"

Brian sat at the navigation table and the chart light threw a circle of illumination that highlighted and accented the deep lines of tiredness and fatigue on his face.

There were several spaced, vertical, hand-width, conveniently placed cut-outs in the wooden bulkhead just behind Ramsey, inside of the upright. Lincoln made a grab for the upper one and held on as *Worippa* lurched, the upright groaned very slightly as Lincoln's weight swung despite it being part of the mainframe to the entrance of the galley and saloon, and also an integral part of the bulkhead behind the chart table. That slight groan emphasised that *Worippa* was really beginning to plunge; and the wind moaning and whimpering through the shrouds was always disquietingly eerie.

"What was Lionel doing earlier," Lincoln asked, "he was making enough bloody noise to wake the dead?"

Brian's face turned a touch grimmer. "He was re-running the jacklines." Ramsey hurried on, obviously thinking that Lincoln was going to interrupt, "Don't say a word – better late than never. There'll be no excuses for being washed off the deck now anyway – lifelines to be clipped on from the inside of the top of the hatchway, irrespective."

Lincoln closed his eyes and nodded his agreement. Another mistake: they should have run them prior to leaving Hobart! They'd stowed them in Hobart because if the uninitiated stood on one it tended to roll his, or her, foot under their bodyweight and unbalance them. With so many guests that they had had on board they had been a hazard – and again, there was just no point in pursuing the obvious – they were a complete set of irresponsible tits.

"What's it doing up there now?" Lincoln asked.

"Six, a force six, about twenty-five knots: gusts of thirty and it's backed maybe a couple of points." Ramsey indicated a place on the chart with the point of his pencil. "We're here, forty-three, fifty-two minutes south; a hundred and forty-six and thirty-six minutes east." He turned back away from the chart and looked up at Lincoln directly. "I'd anticipated – I'd have thought that we'd have been further on, wouldn't you – what do you think?"

"Any rain?" Lincoln asked.

"No," Ramsey replied, "some incredible lightning displays to the south of us though."

"Our heads'l's all right at the moment, isn't it," Lincoln ventured. "Didn't you say it was good for – up to around thirty-five knots?"

Ramsey nodded his confirmation. "Yes, that's right."

"I think I'd be tempted to put a tack in soon, Brian, as you said earlier, there's no point in losing touch with Maatsuyker, and if it backs any more, then we'll be able to sail directly to the South West Cape!" For the first time in a good few many hours, it seemed, Brian Ramsey looked slightly happier. "There are probably two or three knots of stream running against us, maybe – the set of the Southern Ocean Current – plus maybe five degrees or more in leeway. I guess that'll be why we haven't made as much headway – if we tack and the wind continues to back as it should then she'll have her nose into it. At the moment she's sideways on and there'll be a lot of drift with the current pushing her down – everything'll be catching her exposed length." Lincoln sighed. "She'll still make leeway, just the same though, if you see what I mean."

Ramsey was thoughtful. "We can't do much about that, can we – I'll do that course-change on the change of watch. More crew – we'll get her tight on the wind again and settle her down, and then take another look."

"And you'll have an added bonus, Brian, with a bit of luck you'll be sailing away from the centre of the 'low' – it all helps."

"Mmm, makes sense – sounds like good advice." Ramsey began to pull himself along the chart table bench. "I think I'd better take this opportunity while you're about – I'll get changed."

He answered Lincoln's look. "I'm on watch with Gary." Ramsey grunted as he stood. "One thing, Sharon's sleeping like a baby – and that's a bit of a relief. If she can sleep then she'll be fine . . . She's not a bad kid, you know."

"Hmm," Lincoln muttered noncommittally.

Ramsey ignored Lincoln's obvious dubiousness. "She tried to help when Gary got her up, you know, but she was too crook to be of any real help." He looked at Lincoln directly. "It's a good sign; it shows, despite her seasickness, that she's not fully out of it." He went on before Lincoln could reply, "He got her dressed and back before she actually 'threw up'. Oh, and by the way, he also fitted her with boots, so she's fully kitted out."

Up until that point Lincoln had been quite prepared to let it ride, but Ramsey's next sentence really set him off. "She's a lucky girl, Chris, Judy's boots fitted her . . . What's the matter –

why that look?"

Lincoln snapped, "He should have got her organised ashore – that's the very least he could have done – it's a bit late now that we're out here, isn't it! Boots are the one thing we couldn't have got over; it would have been catastrophic for her without wellies. The whole thing's been a bloody fiasco from the start, and the more you think about it the worse it gets. I've a good mind to take his bloody boots," Lincoln added pettishly, "and throw them over the side and then we'll see how he likes sitting around with freezing wet feet for two or three days!"

"Whoa, hold up." Ramsey held out his hand, palm upwards. "Come on," he objected, "don't be so hard on him." Ramsey smiled faintly. "He's not thinking straight, that's all," he didn't allow Lincoln to interrupt him, "he's infatuated with her . . . and to be fair – she's keen on him, you know." Ramsey raised his eyebrows and at the same time gave Lincoln a sideways, knowingly humorous, conspiring glance. "And I saw the reason why today – when he was dressing her. I don't think that girl ever wears a bra – God, she's got the most wonderful pair of tits – I could have grabbed and bitten each one of them myself."

Lincoln snorted and coughed at the same time, and had to grin. "Naughty, naughty," he tutted, "what would Judy say!"

Tactful was Ramsey, and Lincoln was grateful to him because it struck him as soon as he'd uttered the words, that Ramsey hadn't exploited the chink and hadn't come back with an obvious rejoinder concerning his, Lincoln's, own domestic backyard and associated shambles!

"Ah well," was his only comment, "good luck to him. Come on," he gave Lincoln a light push, "you'll be better off in bed, it'll be a help even if you only doze – go on, we can manage – it'll be your watch soon enough."

"Um, I'll just pump out the bilge and get changed ready, and then I will."

"You really are expecting the worst, aren't you – what about . . . how are the fingers?"

"Looks worse, you know how fingers bleed – the remaining piece of nail came away," Lincoln absently lifted and looked at and rubbed the offending remainder of his index finger nail with his opposing thumb. "They'll be better now – nothing left to catch."

"Good." Ramsey nodded and then shivered.

"What's the matter?"

"Nothing," Ramsey flapped his hand, "someone walking over my grave, that's all!"

Chapter 11

Slowly, very very slowly, and taking an age, Lincoln was subconsciously aware as *Worippa* began at last to right herself. Tumbled and tipped from the base to the would-be side of the bunk and then partially back and up again was not an experience he would be recommending, nor, from having been through such an extremity once, have it repeated. Another wave from the feel, he again subconsciously concluded, must have rolled right over her and knocked her down again, and knocked her down below the horizontal, and that after she'd only partially lifted.

The excessive rise then sudden drop of *Worippa* and the thud of returning to and, presumably, re-hitting the bunk, despite the drastic drop, in truth, only half awoke him – and though actually asleep he had been aware of deteriorating conditions. *Worippa* descending and partially falling off waves had left Lincoln partially airborne too many times to count already and such a motion of a yacht making its way in very heavy weather wasn't that unusual in itself – that last had been though!

Lincoln snapped suddenly awake after he'd drowsily felt with a hand – he was not in his bunk at all, but was lying flat on his back and snug in his blankets, and actually well up on the side of the hull!

His waiting became a nightmare: Sharon's screaming, the confused shouting, equipment falling and the wind whistling . . . and the periodic shrieking of the wind after a slight lull was particularly unnerving. That periodic shrieking was accompanied by a vibrating and a drumming on the hull, and behind those noises, and felt as much as heard, were loud and disquieting screechings and groanings – of metal and wood working under too much stress.

The sound of cascading and incoming rushing water was starkly and ominously distinct to Lincoln's ears, despite the cacophonic agony from *Worippa* already under grave duress. That noise of invading water was encouraging an already primeval survival instinct to turn to blind panic, and he could almost clinically observe his own brain classically splitting and separating into two warring parties: the thinking and primal. If *Worippa* didn't attempt to right herself very very soon, then there'd be little doubt as to which one of the two would dominate and run amuck! And even now that 'run amuck' side would not stop its insistent, semi-hysterical, overwhelming clammering and whispering and was inexorably pushing the calm counselling half to the back. Lincoln could hear and was listening to himself and yet he couldn't stop – was that really him who was praying, begging, swearing, cursing, threatening and whimpering! Unbelievable!

He would be back to childhood soon and *deja vu* flashed, and a memory: not an actual incident and not what he was actually doing, but that he was searching for a tiny 'vital' that he'd clumsily dropped while assembling something at the kitchen table. On hands and knees and not being able to find it for looking – palm flat on the floor and sliding back and forth – and feeling for and scrutinising and then actually laying flat on the smooth linoed floor and squinting at eye-level along the surface – and oh, so desperate. And then finally trying to do a deal and wishing 'Him' to help: *'Where is it, please God help me find it, just this once – if you let me find it then I'll never disbelieve that you exist, or doubt again – and I'll always be good. If you don't then I'll never . . .'* And, of course, any intentions he had had of honouring that commitment were immediately forgotten should that illusive object eventually be stumbled upon – and 'Him' dismissed without hardly a second's thought; and again dismissed contemptuously and an heretical disbeliever if the object was, after the bouts of pleading and tantrum, in fact, finally never found!

Pathetic – and he was about to try and do the same deal!

Sharon's screams turned to screams of pain – Lincoln had trodden on her. Despite the lee cloth she'd been spilled out of her bunk and onto the cabin sole – and her outline was, when Lincoln really looked, vaguely visible in the weak reflection thrown by the diffused galley light. Lincoln reached down and grabbed her top and shook her. "Shut-up, shut-up you silly little tart," he snarled, half-shouting to be heard, and as he did so and to his shame realised that he was venting his own fear on her. With almost a physical effort Lincoln pushed down what was bordering on erupting terror, realising that if he didn't, she, and the people around him would hear the panic in his voice and react accordingly. "Climb into the bunk above you," he leant closer and ordered, hoping that the forced calmer inflection sounded genuine, "and ignore the water, don't get any wetter."

He would be eating, he admitted, humble pie for some time: Brian's initial assessment of her had been uncannily accurate – he'd seen something he had missed. As Lincoln reached to help her up she actually tried to punch him, not a punch from a distraught girl either, but a sober, calculated, solid blow – that missed, but only just!

She yelled back into Lincoln's face, "Don't you call me a tart!"

Lincoln just looked – what did they have here, just who was she – was she either so stupid that she didn't realise the seriousness of their situation – that he didn't believe.

Lincoln grabbed a scruff of her top and pulled her viciously. "I'll come back for you, if necessary," he ground out in her ear, "you can't help at the moment, you're in the way." He started to push her. "Go on, into the bunk – shut-up and wait." Lincoln paused, and with his hand still pressuring her, added nastily, "Oh, and by the way, don't lie up there hiding – watch what's happening – get off your arse and climb down and help Bill when and if he needs it. Go on," Lincoln let her go and gave her a final dismissive push and hoped to God that he was right, "we're not sinking yet, you can keep an eye on things from there."

Her indecision and stubborn leaning resistance lasted only a few seconds – abruptly she turned and clambered.

Worippa didn't seem to be fighting – Lincoln just steadied himself and stood for a moment – she wasn't struggling? For some reason her heart didn't seem to be in it – it was almost as if her soul had flown!

Lincoln shouted across the cabin, hoping to be heard above the din, and thankfully Helmut acknowledged, his bulky outline was easily distinguishable amongst the other fleeting and scrambling figures. Using anything available to cling and hold on to, Lincoln struggled across. It was difficult to make out exact detail because of the shadow, but from what he could see, he, Helmut, looked remarkably cool and disgustingly calm, and considering their circumstances, embarrassingly collected.

Helmut's aura of control had its effect. "Get dressed, Helmut," Lincoln bawled, trying to make himself heard above the din, "and then would you make sure that Nick gets dressed,

143

if he isn't already, and Bill as well. Don't go topside without your gear on, you'll not last ten minutes." Lincoln held up his safetyline to emphasise the point, and despite the fact that Helmut couldn't possibly see it, and yelled, "And your harnesses."

He, Helmut, so dispassionate . . . and Sharon, in her way, hadn't been much better; and their world falling apart around them and death by drowning imminent . . . What with *Worippa* lifting and falling and her irregular twisting, staggering lurches so vehement – and so infuriatingly inconsistent. There was no respite from it and it left them with so little dignity, and then, as if to emphasise the point, Lincoln was sent sprawling by a particularly violent dip and yaw. Just holding on was exhausting – and he was very close to panicking again. Yes, him, bloody Helmut, Lincoln could see him in his mind's eye standing there: riding, stolid; and indicating with and acknowledging with a wave of his hand that he had understood – and quite without fuss . . . And bloody Sharon as well, just to add insult to injury, and her temper and apparent lack of fear! Lincoln paused for a split second mentally to consider. He put Sharon to one side because she might not have fully understood just how desperate their situation was, yet that wasn't really true – anyone with half a brain would realise their plight and her ignorance of the sea would, or should, theoretically add to her already overpowering assumed hysteria and overwhelming terror! And Helmut, thought Lincoln, why was Helmut coping so much better than him? He sighed, this emergency was proving that he didn't quite measure up to the mental image he had had of himself, and it hurt to know that he wasn't quite as good as he thought he was!

Lincoln let those thoughts hang, something about *Worippa*, something . . . There was now a certain inevitableness in her motion despite constant sudden changes: a slight muting; a dampening of minor lurches and the short vicious pitchings. A slight change had occurred, though minusculely subtle, and it didn't in any way significantly detract from the overall, comparatively long, extreme rolls and, to understate it, the excessive angles reached . . . To directly and almost malevolently contradict his, Lincoln's observation, *Worippa's* next dip down was by far the most extreme and frighteningly acute.

From where had that tiny little well-spring of optimism that Lincoln faintly felt sprung? Helmut – from him, of course.

Trying to struggle from the double-tiered bunks fitted to the hull on either side of the mast to the entrance of the galley and saloon was enough: *Worippa's* inclination was too steep, and from there Lincoln was forced to crawl. Most of the journey he made with one knee on the engine cover's side and the other on the cabin's sole – with the vee of their meeting points vertically beneath him!

Despite the chaos and the meagre light, a movement caught Lincoln's eye which stopped him dead – below him and athwartships a minor tidal wave's peak was keeping time with *Worippa's* long, deep undulations. The mini-roller was surprisingly broad and travelling, with minor changes of direction, fore and aft along, and its deepest point was in the angle where the floor sections butted against the hull lockers. Lincoln watched with a kind of blinking, mesmerised fascination as it travelled from one end of the yacht to the other. That wave was only partially interrupted when it hit, splashed, and surged around an odd obstruction – just how deep was it over there, Lincoln wondered, not having the wherewithal to check the high-water mark staining the locker doors, to flood and flow like that, and virtually without hindrance!

Lincoln eventually pulled himself upright once more by using the frame and the cut-out handholds built into the same strengthened entrance frame aft of saloon and galley, and from there he floundered from the chart table to the bottom of the companionway steps. The crawl from Lincoln's bunk and getting upright again had just about winded him and he was forced to rest . . . and he used the opportunity to once again take account. He leant and jammed his back into the corner and against the partition behind and beside the short, steep, exiting companionway ladder and the side of the ladder itself, and closed his eyes in disbelief. The stupid bastards, he hadn't the breath left to even swear – the washboards weren't in place! As Lincoln pulled himself around to climb a fresh flooding, cascading torrent of incoming water poured over the lip of the hatchway like a river – the stupid, stupid bastards hadn't locked themselves out!

Lincoln's mental cursing was abruptly curtailed as he was knocked down, and he was aware next of lying flat on his back and of looking up and just making out, in the weak illumination from the chart light, where the partition top met the edge of the deckhead! It took him some seconds to orientate and as he was doing so he became quickly aware of water seeping: of freezing water finding entrances; of finding ways into and up his cuffs; of creeping further up already wetted trouser legs. An uncontrollable involuntary stiff-armed, fist-clenching, teeth-biting shiver racked through Lincoln's body as the cold fingers explored, and a particular one, a trickle, reached and passed under his collar and started to creep down between his shoulder blades. That trickle brought Lincoln bolt-upright in a dizzying instant – he hadn't made it out of the hatch, someone had . . . Somebody had shoved and had punched him out of the way in their hurry to get in – and with a strength and determination that had been both frightening, and frighteningly fast in its merciless execution – and overwhelming!

And then the anger came – and so angry, so very angry. It'd been many years since Lincoln had allowed and had not been able to control and had let such a killing, all-consuming anger boil over. Being hit first and then trampled didn't suit – didn't suit at all – and that someone was going to pay, really pay!

Helmut had blocked and trapped Lincoln before he was fully aware, and with a hand on either side he gently chested and herded Lincoln back until both his hands, with Lincoln caged in-between his arms, were holding on or resting against the partition behind the companion steps and the steps themselves. He lent his bodyweight against Lincoln as Lincoln began to push him out of the way and, as he did so, he shouted into Lincoln's ear. "Listen, that vas unadulterated fear, that is vat it vas." He pushed back against Lincoln as Lincoln went to move again. "Ve cannot help Varren now – now ve must save the ship."

Help him! Help him, he'd fucking-well murder him, ranted an enraged Lincoln, he'd wish, the scrawny, wimpy little bastard, when he got hold of him that he'd never been born. Through the red mist of temper a thought flittered through Lincoln's brain: Lincoln was really taken aback that it had been Warren – and he certainly hadn't realised that it had been him and nor should he have guessed it. The strength and determination which he had used to despatch Lincoln somehow, in Lincoln's mind's eye, didn't quite match the character . . . but then in his panic had . . . *Worippa* suddenly lurched heavily and leaned further at the same time and it was only due to Helmut's weight and him holding on that Lincoln hadn't gone sprawling. Lincoln sagged and the fire went out of him: how to explain to Helmut, or, come to that, even explain Helmut! How did you tell or talk to someone whose soul is completely white, and not a stain on it. His, on his, to his shame, you'd have a job finding any white left at all – truly, his past sins, to his chagrin, were all encompassing! With him, Helmut, there was, and Lincoln had no doubts, only the question of help: revenge, punishment, violence, physical chastisement didn't seem to be in his vocabulary . . .

Any more thoughts along those lines were drowned, literally, as water poured in over them, and it was just as well that Helmut was strong, for again, it was only his strength that held them. The force or the sheer volume of that water that had flooded in and over, or rather, through the hatchway had been frighteningly powerful and should otherwise have washed them away and back down into the boat. *Worippa's* acute angle was such that they were now lying virtually on their sides, whereas, normally, they should have been just about upright!

The force and the quantity of that incoming water, for microseconds in Lincoln's mind's eye, had had echoes of one of those flickering black-and-white films where submariners, or matelots, were desperately trying to escape by scrambling and fighting their way up the conning tower, or engine room ladders, and that panic that was portrayed in those types of films was, in his case, very close to the surface!

"Helmut," Lincoln yelled, his mouth close to Helmut's ear, "she can't take much more of this, that's the forth knockdown that I know of – she's not righting herself as she should." Lincoln thought as he talked, and that helped to quell his rising despair. "It must . . . I can only think of . . . unless the mast's gone? No, we would have heard, and felt it – we'd be hearing it now hitting the side." Lincoln pondered for a moment and then shrugged. "We'll have to go and look – I wonder if it's something stupid like a sheet . . . like a jammed foresail sheet, Helmut, something like that?" Damn, Lincoln cursed himself in his mind, in his numbed state it was all he could think of, or come up with. "Helmut," it was a request and Lincoln had the awful feeling, or premonition, that he would probably be sending him out to his death and that he would never see him again, "would you go and check, and if it is jammed . . . just cut it at the . . . if it is the sheet, cut the damned thing as near to the tack as you can." He hesitated; there was no other way. "Can you do that?"

Lincoln could almost feel Helmut nod his head as he absorbed what Lincoln had said and the implications – there was no change or a sign of emotion in his voice, just stoic unquestioning acceptance. "Ja, this I vill do – it is trapped somevhere, you think, ja?"

Good, he understood, concluded Lincoln. "Yes," Lincoln yelled, and the anxious stringency in his voice that he couldn't quite hide, as against his, which Lincoln again found embarrassing. "If we can bring her up," and Lincoln hoped to God that what he was saying was true, "she'll sail in this with the 'try' – we'll just leave the headsail flogging." Once again Lincoln could see, or sense, Helmut's questioning look in the near-darkness. "Ignore the trysail," he instructed, "I'll see to it," Lincoln rode over any objections that he knew Helmut was going to make – about him going on deck and two taking risks instead of one et cetera, "and anyway, I don't believe for a moment that the 'try' could hold her down like this on its own – that sail is too small." Lincoln was striving desperately to instil a firm, confident inflection in his voice to finish. "We'll get the Number Three off her," he said with a positiveness that he certainly didn't feel, "and the storm jib up when we can."

How Lincoln knew that *Worippa* was wearing the Number Three headsail and not the storm jib – again, as often happened, he didn't know how he knew, but he did.

Helmut seemed to have understood everything that Lincoln had said though how they were communicating above the resounding noise and din and the darkness was another thing, only due to their proximity probably. Lincoln smiled to himself – what would they look like in other circumstances – they would look like two lovers locked in an intimate and impassioned embrace!

"Would you tell Nick to fit and lock in the washboards after we go topside, and tell him to keep the hatch closed," and then he stated the obvious, "there's too much water below already."

Again, Lincoln could feel or sense Helmut's nodded

understanding.

Despite the muffled screeching howl of the wind, the clatter of falling articles, the shifting and the groaning and squealing and creaking of fixtures and fittings, and of stores and other gear moving and things sliding; and the water that had been sloshing around; and the frighteningly extreme and the horizontal angle that *Worippa* was laying at, and the pounding on her hull; and her dramatically steep, dropping, twisting, acute heaving and beam-end dipping and long bone-jarring motions . . . Nothing, but anything, had prepared Lincoln for the world outside. Even though he'd experienced some very bad white-water squalls in the North Sea, the Irish Sea, and the Dutch coast and elsewhere, this was in a different league – this, this was premier!

The flying spume and presumably rain, hurt, really hurt, and air and water were indistinguishable. Even trying to breathe when facing the wind was near to impossible; and its lashing fury when trying to glimpse around the corner of his own stung and pin-cushioned forehead and cheek inflicted instant blindness. The roar was deafening: a sea flying horizontally and paralleling the noise of a continuous alpine avalanche sweeping all before it: immeasurably more powerful, thousands of times more, and generating power unimaginable. This was nature unchained and releasing her ultimate: a band of uncontrollable, wild, unrelenting, merciless, malignant, wilful, rampaging, tramping, smashing titans – and all intent on stamping their destructive will upon them!

The muffled relative silence after struggling out of the hatchway and down onto the side coaming of the cockpit was uncanny and disorienting and bewildering. The shock of that first encounter was slowly subsiding; and that Lincoln's eyes, albeit for practical purposes useless, were beginning to clear and that a very meagre night vision was slowly re-establishing helped.

It was a strange phenomenon and theoretically impossible, yet, despite the appalling conditions, Lincoln knew that there was somebody on the helm. There was, and only just discernible from time to time, a faint, pale, suspended, floating red blob above the stern of *Worippa*: a ghostly orb: an orb that could have been a fleeing, fleeting, obscured moon, or planet, and barely glimpsed in the scudding murk, but was, Lincoln appreciated, in reality, a luminous face and made so by the diminutive reflected glow thrown by the compass light.

Lincoln felt for it: one of the waterproof torches was still jammed in its usual place, so at least he wasn't going to have to feel his way. He held on with one hand and flashed it quickly on, then off. Well, Lionel would not be going anywhere, and as far as Lincoln could just make out, he was practically hanging by his safetyline – and not unmoving . . . Or rather, he was moving, but in a different way: he was rolling back and forth in time to *Worippa's* excessive crests and dips. He was lucky, was Lionel, in a sick kind of way, for it was only his rotund shape that was saving him from further injury – he was, for all the world, like a ball on a string penduluming back and forth against a wall! So, he was obviously, Lincoln surmised, either very badly hurt, unconscious, or both!

It was Gary on the wheel . . . and he'd not and wasn't reacting to the beam of light that should have been, or was, blinding him! Lincoln sighed, he'd have to wait, and so would Lionel – neither looked capable of helping for whatever reasons and *Worippa's* survival had to take precedence. Lincoln gingerly eased himself around to face *Worippa's* bows – and was confronted by a solid wall of darkness that stood beyond the barely discernible glow of the instrument lights immediately forward of the hatch. His torch beam cut a swathe and Lincoln followed the outline of the rig – and it seemed, from a first cursory look, to be intact . . . At least, the majority was – the top quarter was not quite visible and despite him trying to cup his eyes and hold the torch steady and hang on, it remained obscured and was completely blotted out by waves and driving spume most of the time. It was, Lincoln found, just about impossible to keep independent of *Worippa's* dipping, twisting motion whilst trying to isolate and examine with the torch. At this distance and in these conditions a hand-torch, this hand-torch anyway, simply wasn't up to the job – the beam just wasn't strong enough.

Lincoln concentrated and somehow managed a closed-mind to the tempest and turned and swung the beam till it rested on the heavy, starboard sheet-winch – it was bare! Lincoln swung the beam again, to the sheet lead, deck block. The end of the sheet rested there and he was relieved to note that its knotted end had fulfilled its function and had done the job that it had been tied in there to do – to stop the sheet running right through the pulley and irretrievably away into the sea.

It was impossible to trace or highlight further from where he stood, or spot where the sheet was trapped . . . Lincoln was not prepared to think about 'if'!

Another glimpse of Lionel was a cruel reminder – Lincoln had initially and stupidly forgotten, despite his insistent reminders to the others, to secure his own safetyline! He fumbled, found and clipped it to a U-bolt beside the hatch. If Lionel, he chastised himself, had not remembered to clip on his then, aside from whatever injuries he may have sustained, he'd not be with them now, but out there – and the very thought, to be washed overboard and to drown alone out there . . .

It was just as well that Lincoln had secured his harness, for, as if a reminder from God and to underline the point, the next sudden down-lurch dislodged one foot and left him half-hanging – and he desperately clutched for a handhold as *Worippa* dropped into a well between two huge, long, impossibly high, rogue waves.

Irrelevant thoughts in the comparative stillness: this was why 'topsail-schooners' had topsails, and this moment in time was a frightening, unwanted and unwelcome practical demonstration. In troughs as deep as these only the topsails on topsail-schooners protruded above wave summits and they drove a boat when she was in the valleys – the lower sails being sheltered, as now, would have been flogging and impotent! Those vessels had been built for these conditions and one could only but admire the courage, or the madness, of the men who had sailed them! Lincoln shook his head; as to why these sorts of facts, perversely, had a way of surfacing in his brain at the oddest of times he didn't know . . .

There was no pressure at all on the trysail sheets – well, the trysail was innocent then and Lincoln prayed that he'd find the guilty party elsewhere!

Why wasn't she righting herself? Why wasn't *Worippa* coming up – she should be trying harder . . .? Could it be the tremendous windage, Lincoln asked himself, which was hitting on the underside of the now sideways-on, exposed hull: all of fifty feet, and by the feel, over half her breadth – say five feet? Was there enough wind pressure to keep her on her beam-ends on the top of a wave, he wondered, maybe – but surely not enough in the valleys! Certainly she should be making more effort in the troughs, or when she commenced ascent on the lee of the slopes, there was a little protection there ... It was almost as if she'd lost her centre of gravity ...? Lincoln buried that thought quickly, and besides, they'd already have been upside down had she lost her keel! She seemed to be on the very edge of very nearly turning turtle though, or, at least, her angle felt so acute at times that it felt like she was about to go. *Worippa* especially seemed, it seemed to him, to be teetering on that knife-edge as she topped the odd, particularly steep peak, before completely sliding down the other side – almost as if the wind were actually getting under the keel and as if the keel itself was acting like a sail? Lincoln finally pushed that thought aside as well because there was no point in dwelling on that disquieting possibility either!

Not to let one's imagination run wild, Lincoln knew, that was the trick: tiredness, panic, cold, fear, all those factors would contribute and try to distract away from a hard, cool, factual appraisal. Sheeted sails filled with tons of water wouldn't usually be enough in normal conditions to cause this phenomenon – but the trouble was, these were not normal conditions. Perhaps ... was it possible, and he was aware that it was just conjecture, that *Worippa* had found a point of equilibrium: a fluke *status quo*? Was she like a pole-vaulter at the point of equal effort, as it were, and the weight of the mast and water-filled sails digging in and that equalling the forward force of a wind-lightened hull and keel? He pursued that thought, was the awesome velocity of this wind like a pole-vaulter's forward effort, and it was that, that force, that was overcoming the counterweight of the cast-iron and lead fin keel! Lionel had indicated that the mast was over-specified – and he hadn't thought to ask if they'd compensated – a foam-filled mast would at least have given some buoyancy. What if they hadn't had it foam-filled and it had filled with water, God knows what, and he couldn't even begin to guess, a mast of *Worippa's* exceptional size and height would weigh if it had! *Worippa*, by Brian's and Potter's albeit reluctant, own admissions, was much too tender for whatever reasons, and again, speculation was probably not going to help them at the moment ... It'd have to be down to Helmut then, one thing at a time for, and despite all his hypothesising, Lincoln still couldn't think of another logical cause for *Worippa's* distraught dilemma!

Lincoln reached across and transferred the Gibb hook to the jackline and began to feel his way aft, he closed and deliberately didn't turn to nor look down at Lionel, intentionally shutting him and his awful predicament out from his mind, and simply crept on past. It was a slow business because Lincoln only dared to move or edge slowly and crawl along the top of the cockpit coaming when *Worippa* was between peaks. Actually, there was no logical reason why he shouldn't have moved continuously – only fear and that and the thought of her overbalancing, imagined or no, and also the threat and possibility of being trapped under *Worippa's* inverted hull! That threat caused Lincoln involuntary immobility at the top of each wave, and that combined with the increased howling of the wind, stinging rain, and the resounding vicious smack of the sea hitting the partially bared underside of the hull, froze him every time.

The features of that floating face, the bottom half at least, were becoming distinguishable in the light from the compass, and what Lincoln saw there he didn't like ... That haunted, fixed expression, as Lincoln quickly found out, to his dismay, after clambering and half-sliding down.

Despite all Lincoln's efforts his state indicated what he'd suspected, that Gary was frozen and wouldn't, or couldn't, respond. He was standing partially on the side of the starboard coaming, his shoulder leaning against the cockpit sole, and rigid: he couldn't talk, he was too far gone for that: tiredness, cold, fear, apprehension, shock, exhaustion and responsibility had all combined and exacted – and Gary's empty face and apparent paralysis reflected that, and a too higher price paid. It took persuasion rather than force finally to relax his grip, brute strength Lincoln had tried to no avail – Lincoln simply hadn't enough power, his hands weren't strong enough to break Gary's hold on the wheel – nobody in the world could have! Nobody was going to force him out from behind that wheel either and in the end Lincoln didn't even try: instead he stood there facing him – facing the stern – with his back to *Worippa's* bows. Some glimmer of comprehension, some flame in his brain, Lincoln saw, was still burning and together, and slowly at first, they turned the wheel to lee; how long they waited, what Lincoln talked to him about he didn't know or remember – the universe rotated many times.

If anything the storm's ferocity was increasing and even behind, in the vacuum produced by the sloping hull, it was furious – up to force ten, maybe eleven, Lincoln estimated. Succession after succession of mountainous, white-crested combers passing under – their tops usually tumbling and any loose water was instantly scavenged away by the savage wind.

Lincoln kicked annoyingly at whatever had caught and hooked onto the 'tightening' strap at the bottom of his oilie trousers – an irresponsible, thoughtless act, he forgetting the fact that the sealing ankle-fasteners of foul weather gear these days were held by 'velcro', and that they came undone before an individual could damage or rip them. Lincoln looked down and felt eventually for the cause of the snag, an act that he should have done in the first place – to be flipped over the side on a night like this, and it had happened before, by a loose, wind-blown, curling rope-end would be Murphy's Law! Lincoln grimaced and silently cursed in exasperation – it was one thing after another . . . No, better and wiser, he cautioned, to take the time and secure whatever it was.

It wasn't sane – disbelief stopped time – it simply wasn't sane! Lincoln stood immobile as she clawed her way up, using Lincoln for purchase, and Lincoln didn't even try and make any sense out of what she was screaming – any relevance was carried away by the storm's pandemonium anyway. She'd defied him, and presumably, Helmut too; against all common-sense Sharon had ventured out here . . . 'Cuckoo' – her sanity must have flown – now Lincoln had her and her bloody boyfriend to deal with!

His temper flared and he dragged and roughly forced her down to the coaming and sole of the cockpit and put his mouth against her ear; she'd clipped herself on, he noticed, well, at least she'd had the presence of mind to do that.

"Did you replace the washboards?" he yelled.

She held up a thumb – cheeky cow!

"I thought I told you to help Bill?"

She held up her thumb again and Lincoln caught the flash of her teeth – she really was bloody cheeky, this one. She yelled an explanation once, twice, and even then Lincoln's comprehension was instinctive: partly lip-reading and partly an educated guess. Lincoln crouched there with her next to him and he was thoughtful for a moment – she'd done a lot, she'd gone a long way to placating him – how she and Bill had got Potter below, Lincoln couldn't guess, it should have been a feat beyond them; Lincoln looked forward, he'd gone though, and that was a fact!

Lincoln stood better to see, someone was going forward; what had initially attracted his attention and what was catching his eye now and again was the flash, or reflection of . . . or from an erratic torch beam tracing a senseless, weaving pattern.

Lincoln glanced back and around, and again, time stood still for a moment – them three, underlit by red compass bloom and their faces streaming water – reflective and gaunt – Satanists in a tumbling, howling, nightmare world of unreality!

The defiant little moo shook her head every time Lincoln indicated for her to go back – and it was she, this time, who dragged Lincoln down to the bottom of the cockpit. They struggled once again to make themselves heard – the gist, as Lincoln understood it, was that she was not going to die like a rat in a cage . . . Well, he agreed, one could sympathise with that sentiment. Then the illogical 'icing' – but she would go back if she could take Gary with her! They squatted there looking at each other and comprehension only dawned after she'd pantomimed and spelt it out yet again. She wasn't insane, as he'd assessed her a bit earlier – but just totally and utterly mad – insane was too polite a word!

And there they sat in a force ten, maybe eleven, and it gusting beyond anything Lincoln had ever experienced, and him at stalemate with one raving mad, female berserker – and one helmsman who was completely shot and a boat that was about to founder from under them – bloody hell!

It took some moments – illogical, but . . . and Lincoln paused to consider for another moment and finally raised mental eyebrows and shrugged philosophically . . . Well, maybe, and he thought about that . . . She wanted Gary down below, in the rat hole, and with him it would apparently be an illusory place of safety – safety! Her two wishes on the surface were totally contradictory, but that didn't really matter because Gary below was better than Gary topsides. Yes, Gary dried out, fed and with a warm drink inside him made much better sense. And furthermore, somehow Lincoln knew she'd get him there too, given the chance, she'd already moved Potter's dead weight

– a conscious Gary wouldn't exactly be a cinch but . . .

A party, a bloody party, and now bloody Corsham had come to join the celebrations. Lincoln gave up and squatted down yet again – they said you could get used to anything! Lincoln was instantly ashamed, Bill informed him that Lionel was below, conscious, but not quite lucid, and his, Bill's subsequent request was beyond criticism: he pointed to Gary for emphasis with his forefinger and the meaning of a thumb over his shoulder was unmistakable – and his pantomiming eating and drinking left no doubt as to his intentions.

In the end the problem of Gary solved itself; all four of them took the force – the full brunt of the blunted aftermath of a wave over the top. That wave left them coughing, gasping and battered, and hanging on for dear life after its destructive passage. It is a powerfully strong and wonderful thing, Lincoln observed from somewhere, the human spirit and its indomitable will to survive: Gary, as if that cold little dip had revived him was suddenly completely coherent, or at least Lincoln assumed him to be: and, more to the point, willing, despite his chattering teeth and shivering body and obvious anxiety.

The poor sod was into the second or third stage of hypothermia, assessed Lincoln, and his ability to move woefully and pathetically limited. Somehow, and Lincoln watched in admiration, the three of them fought, helped and clawed their way along the coaming of the cockpit, and Bill, then behind, managing somehow to bundle the lovers forward from there. The whole enacted little episode would have been funny anywhere else, or heart-endearingly touching – the two of them, the two lovers helping each other while Bill shepherded, and Sharon's concern obvious – love will overcome.

Lincoln thought about that: comradeship, despite that all-consuming tenacity for life and animal base-instincts for survival, had triumphed. These people had been and were true, none of them had tried to neither climb over nor take advantage of another – Lincoln was impressed and felt a blinking, belittling humility!

Bill, after helping the two below replaced the washboards and closed the hatch, Lincoln lost sight of him then, the light issuing from below had just about killed his night vision. Lincoln heard or rather sensed his presence as he clambered back down into the cockpit, and was, nevertheless, taken aback when his face finally appeared in front of him, lit by the binnacle. He lingered there and they stood facing each other, the wheel between – Lincoln understood his question.

He grabbed at Lincoln with a cruel strength when Lincoln didn't answer, and pulled him half-over, round and across the wheel and he forced Lincoln, and Lincoln hated him for it: to face, admit and confront.

He asked again, yelling savagely in Lincoln's ear, and Lincoln couldn't fight him. "Where's Brian?"

Lincoln kept, or fought to keep his mind blank after he'd let go – for long after he'd gone. There had been no sign, no trace, and no evidence that Brian Ramsey had ever been – had ever existed!

Chapter 12

The flickering of a very dim torch beam on the foredeck, sometimes seen, sometimes not, was distracting, yet somebody was making his or her way along and back from the bows. Yes, Lincoln could just catch a glimpse, now and again, of a silhouetted, bobbing head occasionally against a white-topped crest above the dark, blurred, curved outline of *Worippa's* hull. If he used periphery vision to try and shield the rain then Lincoln could also just distinguish and catch the movement of that person's shadowy, fleeting body in the luminiferous backwash created, presumably, by the white of the waves and spume, and reflected by and from the all-encloaking, opaque scud.

Visual recognition wasn't necessary anyway, because there was only, Lincoln knew, one person on board *Worippa* who was nimble enough and could move that fast in these conditions. Moments later Nicolo Frascati's shiny wet head and shoulders were illuminated and the high points reflecting in a rain-softened glow escaping and radiating out from below decks. His, Nick's, ducking, overhanging upper body quickly smothering most light liberated by a slid back, half opened hatch, and Lincoln could discern only a faint candescence and the odd distinct gleam which broke the unintentional blackout.

Almost immediately and after collecting, or informing, darkness reigned again, but not before, like a flash bulb going off and freezing the instant, an image was stamped indelibly in Lincoln's mind. Immediately visible in the short afterglow and in the moment after he'd stepped clear and before the hatch re-closed – a snapshot of the nearest huge, tumbling, licking, white-breaking top of a long, steep, overwhelming and menacing roller had been taken . . . *Worippa* had lifted and that wave had passed under before Lincoln's brain could process – and words couldn't describe the awe . . .

Nick's retreating progress and the retracing of his original climb went unseen and only the sudden reappearance of a second form in the mostly obscured, illuminated spot of the erratic beam of the torch forward confirmed his safe arrival back on the foredeck. Lincoln shook his head and cursed: if they carried on wasting time as they were doing, then none of them would be surviving this. Lincoln seethed, and Helmut, what on earth was he up to – how long did it take to cut through eight millimetres of braid! What in the bloody hell were the two of them doing?

A slit of illumination from the companionway showed again and the area of reclaimed darkness increased and then was blinding as the first washboard was slid out and removed; the others must have also been removed for the outline of the shape eventually emerging could only be that of Bill Corsham. Lincoln watched, concerned about the amount of water that would be entering – and his, Bill Corsham's safety – but, nevertheless, beneath his frustration Lincoln was curious . . . That curiosity turned to amazement and then to dumfounded shock and anger as Bill Corsham turned and helped and assisted another to struggle out – and that someone else he'd know and recognise anywhere too – he'd let bloody Sharon out again!

They couldn't or wouldn't hear Lincoln and Lincoln watched helplessly as, with his back to him, Bill finally replaced each washboard with what seemed to Lincoln like exaggerated, unnecessary care. Lincoln's temper slowly turned to perplexity – and by the time his night vision had partially returned they were halfway along to the foredeck – they must have been moving very cautiously because of the time lapse involved. The two of them were even now picking their way forward in a wild darkness – forward on a sluiced and steeply sloping, invisible deck. Lincoln watched intently, squinting behind a shielding, cupped hand – as far as he could make out they were moving, one behind the other, carefully, and on their knees – they also were obviously crawling to and making their way towards the bobbing, torch-lit area of activity.

A glimmer of understanding and a sliver of their intentions had already formed – and a hope that he wouldn't allow to expand until proof was presented. It was a harsh and unforgivable and selfish thought and Lincoln pushed it away and looked out into the lee with blank eyes. Yet that thought still lurked below the surface – their sentiments and concern were admirable, only their priorities were wrong – they'd sink them with their misguided efforts. If they didn't cut that sheet soon then they'd end up pulling, presumably, Brian Ramsey back onto an already foundering and sinking ship . . . No, and Lincoln braced himself for it – better to drown!

Lincoln turned to look forward once again and another thought crossed his mind – perhaps he had underestimated Helmut's or Nick's capabilities, which he was prone to do with people, and one of them had already cut, or had discovered that the sheet *was* free! Or perhaps it had nothing to do with Brian Ramsey and that there was such a tangle, or whatever, up there that it was going to take the four of them to sort it out! That being so, or whatever which way, whatever the problems they had, or were encountering, then their present actions and priorities were entirely correct . . . No, their and also Sharon's and Bill's actions and priorities had been, he admitted, perfectly correct from the word go, period. And that glimmer of hope still glowed in that what they were doing was about Brian Ramsey, because, without a shadow of doubt, it would be infinitely better, if they finally had to take to the life rafts, to have Brian Ramsey with them.

Next, as if to underline Lincoln's thoughts about underestimating people, the deck lights came on – someone below certainly was thinking.

Heartfelt and thankful admiration welled up in Lincoln: the company that manufactured their deck lights should surely deserve some sort of recognition: that they worked in these conditions was a testimonial. And that especially applicable to the one attached under the starboard spreader, which came on and stayed on when immersed, and was, to Lincoln, nothing short of a miracle.   They, the deck lights, shrank their world further again and there was now only an inky, black, impenetrable wall outside the glare of their blazing, expanding cones.

This scene, as Lincoln's eyes adjusted to the glare, triggered another fleeting mental snapshot: it was not unlike, or at least it had echo's of and was reminiscent of looking up from behind a lamppost on a winter's night, and watching rain and sleet rush past in that lamppost's light. Such a spectator could watch the wind-driven, backlit spindrift and rain sweep past in much the same way, only, of course, there the faint parallel ended. Here the picture viewed was much larger and the onslaught, unlike that seen from behind that mental lamppost, was not constant, but rather the spume and precipitation came in agonised, speeding, twisted ropes and snaking, fast-drifting streamers – in clouds and sheets and torrents, and endless curtains of horizontally staggered, scudding, blustered water. Those streamers and curtains of rain and spume were seemingly slow to approach at first, as well, but then they accelerated and whipped past and away until finally hurtling into infinity and into the darkness of the night.

Riding the roller-coaster was not so bad, it was when on an odd, irregularly, extraordinarily high, rogue peak, that was the moment in time when, for him, time stood still: when looking over the side at that point of hesitation and on the edge of the void and imagination running, and just before and waiting to drop down into a bottomless black abyss. It was, Lincoln realised, the deck lights that sharply and harshly accented and caused that contrast – at least without them, surprisingly, the world was a softer combination of darker greys and blacks. The well of a trough then, in the dark, was not quite an acrophobic's ultimate nightmare, not quite a featureless, bottomless, perpendicular black hole of terror as it was now.

Patches: reflective, silver, oblong strips stitched to the group's individual jackets and trousers bounced impossible minute heliographic flashes as each moved. The deck, even through a veil of gusting spume and rain, was a brilliantly lit, steeply inclined, plunging, see-sawing, double-circular joined stage, and the players on the far edge and on the periphery of shadow were bulging, distorted red-clad figures moving in and against a backcloth of impossible effects and scenery.

Awareness jolted Lincoln back with the next dousing wave, and yet went unheeded – them, the group, were pressing against each other as they crouched in a huddled semicircle – they were pulling and straining for all they were worth. Hauled up the side, grabbed, lifted and physically dragged over awkward lifelines like a landed, stunned, helpless, harpooned whale – and suddenly there were five in that group, whereas, formerly, there'd been four!

Nothing else happened for an age and for an eternity all five simply clung and lay.

Helmut, Lincoln couldn't help but notice, had recovered first and was quickly followed by Bill Corsham. Ramsey alive though not looking too good, and Lincoln laughed with pleasure – and Helmut and Bill lugging his, Ramsey's, waterlogged body, heavy and awkward, and his feeble efforts to help just about ineffective. He was alive! Poor Ramsey, understandably, had nothing left to give, he must have been hanging and regularly dipped, immersed and battered for some considerable time. Brian'd be thanking his 'maker' later for that harness and safetyline – and then there arose that sour note again in Lincoln's mind: that was providing they survived the rest of this, of course!

Nick, after starting, held back and stopped as *Worippa* momentarily tipped towards upright while ascending on the back of an excessively steep roller – and clinging by whatever he dropped down on his knees and was hanging and looked to be examining something on the deck down on the lee. The kid's agility had always impressed Lincoln – Lincoln peered and saw that he had quickly caught and was gesturing to Sharon with a hand and was talking into her ear; finally both of them, the girl and he began to crawl and make their way back. Nick was crawling and following simply to make sure of her safety; and Lincoln admired him for that because Lincoln knew he could have made his way aft like a monkey swinging through the trees! Lincoln watched them, especially Sharon, because she was a novice.

They'd surprised Lincoln, Sharon and Nick – they'd stopped before they'd reached the companionway . . .

He, Nick, eventually sat her behind the big, three-speed sheet winch – and finally and carefully placed both her feet, heels together, on its wide, diametrical base. Lincoln peered through half-closed eyes – Sharon was virtually standing on the winch's barrel and her bottom on the deck, and knees slightly bent at a comfortable bracing distance. His, Nick's instructions, were obvious even from where Lincoln stood.

Then Lincoln knew what they were up too – Lincoln had known when he'd sat Sharon down – and there was, God forbid, Lincoln could hazard, a sort of twisted illogical logic to Nick's thinking!

Swearing, and a stream of it substituting impotency, frustration and an underlying, deepening concern. Lincoln hadn't the means to lash the helm and though he knew from the lack of bite and feel that the thing was all but useless – nevertheless, to let it go and they'd probably end with a smashed rudder. Lincoln, literally, had screamed himself hoarse and to no avail – it was useless – the wind, as before, had whirled away any sound. Lincoln knew that he, Nick, had found a twist in the sheet – in the sheet trolley – and the twist, he guessed, was probably jammed between the heavy, free-running sheave, or pulley, and the base and the supporting side-frames . . .? It didn't matter, Lincoln knew that Nick had missed the point though, and couldn't see the wood for the trees: he should have cut it when he had found it: and by the time he'd messed, and if another giant wave hit them while he was messing, then they'd be under and gone.

Indecision: risk the helm and cut the sheet himself or wait for him? Dear Lord . . . Lincoln mentally rubbed his forehead . . . Trouble was, if *Worippa* did lift then steerage and way would be crucial – and they'd perhaps have to bear away – and, anyway, it simply wasn't in Lincoln to risk the rudder!

Nick, Lincoln surmised, must have pulled the sheet end that he himself had glimpsed earlier from the deck-mounted, horizontally fixed turning block, which was positioned down nearer the toe rail and aft from the sheet winch. In the circumstances seven or eight turns round the winch drum did not seem excessive – Lincoln watched. Sharon's stance took on a pose of grim determination; she held that sheet as if her life might depend on it. Nick had primed her well – and the ability to 'tail' and keep tension on, probably, in her mind did mean all their lives.

Disbelief again froze the moment and they, Lincoln and Sharon, held eye-contact only for a second in the scattered light . . . and Lincoln had to close his mouth – the cheeky madam's water-drenched, momentarily wrinkled face and stuck out tongue had only just been visible under a soaked and plastered, skull-clinging curtain of hair. Her attention had gone directly back to the task in hand before Lincoln had had time to react – she hadn't looked across again. Despite Lincoln's frustration and temper caused by her not glancing up again and communicating, he had to smile – you could but only admire and give it to her. There she stood, or in her case, sat alone, and yet, in these conditions, in the wet and the cold and in a plunging sea and hurricane wind she still had the verve, the courage and the audacity to make rude gestures – foolhardy or no, they'd broken the mould when they'd made her!

Nick took a second to position himself comfortably; actually, he was just about standing – with each foot spaced and conveniently placed, assumable, on the bolted-down, parallel running sheet track.   His burst of energy took Lincoln by surprise even though he'd been expecting it – and Nick, using one hand only, span the big, long, two-handed winch handle so fast that all Lincoln could see was a flickering, spinning, silver, propeller-bladed blur. As tension came on his circular motion slowed – and his turning speed momentarily increased again for a few rotations after he'd shifted himself and employed both hands. Nick ground on after that, and Lincoln felt for him, slowing and straining harder with each turn until he finally ran out of strength and was forced stop.

Despite everything, Lincoln had mentally been straining in sympathy with him – Lincoln hadn't been consciously aware that he had been – and only releasing held breath and relaxing locked fingers on the wheel in unison with Nick's pause informed him that he had.

Sharon nodded her head to his mouthed enquiry, or instruction, and Lincoln was sure that she, as he, matched his, Nick's, deep inhalations and tensed themselves just the same. And that girl, what about her, Lincoln hadn't taken much notice of her because all his attention had been focused on Nick, but she had hauled in, hand-over-hand, the excess of sheet produced by Nick's efforts impeccably. Yes, she'd performed like a veteran and hadn't faltered or fumbled, or missed a beat, and Lincoln had nothing but admiration for her.

Nick rotated the handle in the opposite to previous, and thus engaging a higher, slower ratio. As Lincoln knew only too well, he'd have to wind more for less line taken in – a fair exchange for increased pulling power – nothing is free! He, Nick, was forced to give 'away' that grinding, circular action in the end, as the load became too much and his strength finally began to give out. He wasn't one for giving up, Nick – and pity began to replace Lincoln's mental urgings when he was down to managing only short, mindless, robotic, deep-winded, long-spaced, heaving, full-bodied, feeble, sporadic jerks.

He was laid motionless across the winch for what seemed an age . . . At last – and Lincoln answered his hopeless, helpless, exhausted look with an excessively exaggerated negative – nobody surely would, could, misunderstand the meaning of his frantically beckoning hand. Nick slowly raised himself and hesitantly pointed to the winch (oh, the recuperative powers of youth, flashed as an aside, through

Lincoln's mind). Lincoln frantically beckoned for him to come – and desperately hoped that he'd sense the urgency in the action. He bent, Lincoln assumed, to tell Sharon to sit and wait.

Nick was young and to balance those enviable recuperative powers, he also had that impetuosity of youth – and Lincoln knew Nick, and knew that for him there was no middle road – and either he got it brilliantly right or he got it horrendously wrong! They'd won and lost races because of his uncontrollable impetuosity – his thoughts and actions often couldn't be diverted once his head was down – and only with a 'four-by-two' lump of wood, more often than not, could you do that. Nick, and Lincoln understood, hadn't yet really learned nor did he have the patience, experience or maturity to consistently think that little bit ahead and to think problems out, although, to be fair, he was getting there and getting there fast. No, and Lincoln to a degree was philosophical about it, he hadn't quite conquered that impulsiveness of youth, especially not in an emergency – he'd usually achieve the right result in the end because his heart was in the right place, though the price was often too high in cost and pain. As now, though he actually didn't know it, but he'd completely missed the point!

His reluctance to come back to the companionway and across the cockpit to the helm was palpable. Lincoln encouraged and beckoned him on, and once committed he had come quickly – and had timed his moves across the cockpit with enviable ease and at any other time he'd have been a delight to watch. As soon as he was in range Lincoln grabbed and pulled and placed his hand on the wheel, which in turn forced him to hold onto the wheel while regaining his balance. Lincoln let go at that moment in time and climbed before he could object, and left him no choice – he had to stay and mind the baby.

"Keep the wheel in that position," Lincoln mouthed while pointing to the wheel at the same time. Lincoln drew a curve with his finger and indicated to the usual helmsman's place. "Climb behind."

Nick probably hadn't heard a word, but he'd understood the gestures; nevertheless, Lincoln had to pantomime and go through the whole thing again and insist that he clamber around. Actually, Lincoln couldn't blame him and perfectly understood his reluctance – to be tied behind a seemingly useless wheel, and inaction, and in these conditions, to him, after his and Sharon's prodigious efforts would be the equivalent of giving up – and it was obvious from his stance and body language that all he really wanted to do was to race around – and that was, Lincoln confessed and conceded, his doing!

Still, climb round he had to, and quickly – it would not be wise to allow someone so inexperienced on the helm to look behind – and it was essential and psychologically important for him only to face forward. If by some mischance he did catch sight of a rogue wave coming in from the stern, then Lincoln knew that he'd likely run, even though, odds on, *Worippa's* stern'd lift and the wave'd pass directly and harmlessly beneath. It took iron nerve, or rather experience, and gradual exposure to get used to and quell and overcome terror when gazing way up at an inevitably life-threatening, oncoming, mountainous, tumbling cliff face – and, understandably, some people never did – and Lincoln, for one, wouldn't blame and would be somewhat surprised if Nick didn't, in such circumstances, yield to panic.

Irrelevant-relevant, unsought and uninvited knowledge surfaced in Lincoln's cerebrum: the horrors of a following sea were not unknown and were well documented, and the old 'windjammers' went to the trouble and solved the problem by having a specially built, forward-looking shelter. It was not, literally, physically possible to see behind or look over your shoulder when on the helm aboard one of them!

Lincoln struggled up and out of the cockpit, and shuffled along the top of the coaming and then along the deck – searching next and forward, step by hesitant step, and feeling for the same sheet track that Nick had used. Lincoln crabbed slowly along feeling his way on that track in the same way that a mountain climber would use a narrow rock ledge . . . Or, more like, in Lincoln's view, a scared, witless, would-be suicider on a New York skyscraper window ledge who had changed his mind!

Lincoln had a job believing it, Sharon was still holding like grim death and still had the headsail sheet under tension – this girl! Lincoln gently took it from her and expertly flicked the turns off the winch using the same action as she would have used as a child in the playground. It was an automatic thing for him to do; and the same wrist and arm movement she would have used at one end of a skipping rope ensured that a cleanly released line would, all things being equal, run through the various leads quickly and without hindrance.

She had the last word, Sharon, metaphorically speaking: she reached out and caught and then deliberately handed over the free end of his safetyline – the end that Lincoln had unclipped from the steering U-bolt and had then ignored. Words were not necessary – her look was more than enough!

There was a difference almost immediately – and subtle, but there. Further waiting, anticipation, and feeling and sensing what was happening to and how *Worippa* was lying in the water were quickly curtailed as a different instinct overtook Lincoln. It came out of the night without warning and its impact coincided with Lincoln's scrambling and reaching the mast. He just may, with the deck lights off, have spotted that approaching monster, but as it was all that Lincoln did observe in that moment of grace, and when a sixth-sense told him that it was there, was the dull, minute, reflective flickerings and glintings off of a rain-misted, vision-filling, vertical wall of black, bottle-green glass.

The cold wind and returned hearing informed his body to breathe – that plus lack of oxygen. It took another minute to actually become aware and a bit longer for fragmented thoughts to assemble – Lincoln had been under and totally immersed – and the afterimage of that wave still dominated, and even with hindsight Lincoln wouldn't have tried to hazard a guess at that wave's height! Another thought quickly chased that one; that they'd never survive if many more brothers or sisters chose to visit – and even younger ones at this moment of time would badly wear them.

In fact, and truth be known, Lincoln had personally come through it surprising well – he was lying and hanging prone and his hands were still instinctively gripping the circular steel hoop that encircled the bottom of the mast – though they, his white-knuckled hands, told their own story. That hoop, thankfully, was built to take a lot of stress – all free-hanging pulleys and turning blocks were shackled to it – and every line on the mast eventually led and 'turned' through one or another of them. Lincoln thought about that and why – that wave would have had to have hit the mast before him, and it explained a lot, it explained why he was still there!

Lincoln just hung there for a few moments longer, just resting . . . and slowly it dawned, despite the wave, *Worippa* had risen another couple of degrees more again than that prior to the wave – and the change in her inclination was that much more perceptible, more substantial. In the wind maybe, through the deck perhaps – and a different motion again when lifting to the next wave – *Worippa* was defiantly lifting in spite of the punishment she'd taken, albeit agonisingly slowly.

Inspection of the forward sheet trolley confirmed, there was no twist in the sheet aft the carriage and the foresail was at last free – Nick, and Sharon, had successfully winched out a twist in the foresail sheet.

Worippa came up a touch further during Lincoln's climb back to the mast – and another confirmation was taking place there – water was draining, cascading and pouring out of the many vertically-spaced, staggered, built-in, from base to head height, pulley and roller cages. The sparkling gushers were quite distinguishable in floodlight – an Italian Renaissance fountain with multiple spouts jetting out water as from those stone-sculptured, ornamental, carved faucets.

Nick looked to still be functioning behind the wheel. Sharon to all intents and purposes was not so lucky – as far as Lincoln could tell, her back was against a leeward stanchion – but for her head slowly turning towards Lincoln she was inert. She was up to her waist in water and her safetyline, and going by the way she was being jerked on the declines, was fully extended and taught – and she'd not be going anywhere for the moment.

Up *Worippa* struggled, millimetre by millimetre, inch by inch – exultation, adrenaline pumping, Lincoln struggled upright and finally with the mast at his back, stood before the storm, arm raised and only her to hear. "Come on, *Worippa*, come on. Up, my love, up you come." And to the storm and without malice and quietly. "Fuck you. Fuck you. Fuck you, you fucking bastard." And then louder, "We'll beat you." Lincoln shook and half saluted with his fist again. "We'll beat you, you fucker – we'll beat you yet."

Quickly to silence – it was stupid to tempt fate!

The next lurch underlined that thought and overbalanced Lincoln: a nudge from God, a little reminder: don't push your luck!

Helmut was wiping a very bloody nose at the bottom of the companionway steps, wiping it away with the back of his hand – and next he was inspecting, gently feeling and tenderly squeezing and lightly pinching that proboscis. Even from where he was, Lincoln could see that Helmut's eyes were very slightly glazed – and there was tension showing in the lines round his mouth.

Lincoln bawled down, "She's lifting – a trapped sheet. You with it, Helmut?" His nod at least told Lincoln that he had understood the question. "Is everybody down there in one piece?" Helmut nodded again. "Good, get whoever's still mobile to start, will you, take turns pumping – both pumps." Lincoln ploughed on without waiting for another acknowledgement, "Those who can't will have to anyway – we'll survive this if we pull together. Move it, Helmut," Lincoln brusquely and harshly ordered, "you're like a big girl – shift your arse."

There was hate in his look, and it glowed in his eyes – he took a step forward, placed one foot on the first step before stopping. His relatively quiet voice contrasted Lincoln's hoarse shouting. "You are a bastard, Chris. I know vot it is the game you are playing." He twisted his neck from side to side and rotated his shoulders. "You do not vorry, I vill sort it out, you do not have to play mind games silly vith me."

His incorrect speech, mispronunciations and defensive stance – Lincoln's heart went out to him. "I'll need you topside when you've got 'em happily pumping, all right? Oh, and would you turn off the deck lights, please. Don't let them give up, Helmut," Lincoln advised, "hassle 'em, make 'em hate you. Cuff an odd ear if you have to – stir them up – no need to be shy."

Helmut's half-smile and half-grimace, and his shaking head told a story – good, he was back with them.

Helmut held onto the companionway steps and Lincoln grabbed onto the side of the hatchway for support as *Worippa* lurched, tipped and slid down another huge wave. Part of Lincoln's brain had been monitoring as he knelt there: there hadn't been a deluge down the hatch during their conversation, maybe, just maybe . . .

Lincoln crossed to the lee and using any handhold available for purchase, he half-crawled and half dragged himself along the cockpit's side. For some reason that Lincoln couldn't fathom, a winch handle was still locked in the top of the spinnaker winch; Lincoln collected it and passed on. He found the tail end of the 'running backstay' knot in the braided line's end, jammed against the heavy, deck-mounted, shackled swivel block. The idea was to tension the 'runner' and thus help take the strain on the upper third of the mast, Lincoln didn't like the idea of that part of the mast being unsupported, especially if the foresail was still trying to shed any excess water. Though logic told Lincoln that the crisis in that area was all but over now, it nevertheless still couldn't hurt, and furthermore, it'd stop or damp any flexing should they be lucky enough to eventually get under way. A little insurance couldn't hurt – and it'd be a bit stupid to break the top off now, especially after what they'd already been through!   Lincoln grabbed the runner's tail end and wound the runner around the runner winch and pulled in the slack and then cranked on till there was just a touch of tension on, and then cranked on a touch more. He'd have to match that same tension on the sister runner on the other side of the boat – and that for safety's sake because at this stage he didn't know what tack they'd be on! Lincoln considered and then turned and then eased out a couple of lengths of trysail sheet, and then re-cleated the end of the remainder – if he did exactly the same to the other twin trysail sheet on the matching winch on the other side of the boat then . . . Better to get *Worippa* upright and let the trysail flog a little and see where they stood, because in a wind such as this *Worippa* might well sail under bare poles!

Lincoln rested a moment before carefully making his way to those self-same, twin winches across and on the other side of the cockpit.

Nick had been watching Lincoln from behind the wheel – Lincoln could feel his eyes – he'd just have to cope.

The top of the spinnaker winch felt cool to his forehead, job done, and after a moment's rest Lincoln turned from that kneeling position – and as he did so *Worippa* reared on another exceptionally large and steep crest. As Lincoln overbalanced and teetered, the airborne, wind-whipped wave-curl of that crest slapped into him and helped him on his way, washing and rolling him off of the coaming and off of the cockpit seat and down into the well of the cockpit proper. Lincoln lay sprawled on the cockpit sole for some moments, catching his breath, before clawing his way up and into a sitting position. Lincoln sat there, still bewildered and recovering. It was some moments before it dawned and he realised with muted surprise – *Worippa* had come up enough to allow him that much at least – he could now sit in the cockpit conventionally, albeit, hopefully, not short-lived, with legs braced and knees locked, and feet pressed hard on and against the edge of the opposite cockpit seat.

It was the first chance he had had for some little while to look around, and the first thing Lincoln was aware of again was the howl of the wind and the spume and whipping rain . . . And next Sharon, she'd moved and she now had her back against the lifelines – and her arms outstretched – and each hand clamped onto the top lifeline . . . as if crucified. Lincoln couldn't see her face in the stark shadowy light, but she looked dazed and was not taking notice of an odd wave flooding and washing around her backside!

The trysail was shivering and flogging above, but restricted by its now jerking, partially slackened sheets. *Worippa's* headsail though was not restricted, and it was not going to last – it'd flog itself into ribbons . . . Lincoln observed with indifference – let it.

For no particular reason and after watching the flogging headsail, Lincoln glanced aft – Nick was automatically and instinctively adjusting the helm and guiding and trying to allow *Worippa* to find her natural position for lying a-hull – he seemed to be coping. Lincoln inspected the buckled and bent wheel under Nick's hands, it must have taken one hell of a thumping to have distorted it that badly, and Nick, Nick wouldn't be feeling too well if his rebounding body had caused that damage. The deck lights, as requested, flickered out before he could get a closer look – and to be truthful, there wasn't much Lincoln could have done for him at the moment anyway. No, it was better to pretend and not to notice, and ignore for the moment – and that was because they were already getting dangerously short of people to drive the ship. There were not many more fit and capable bodies left to come after Nick – and his demise didn't bare thinking about.

More detail could be made out as vision adjusted once again – it was lighter. Lincoln wasn't so sure that he welcomed it, the daylight; you couldn't worry about nor be afraid of something that the eye didn't or couldn't see!

Nick's sight was that bit keener, and the panic in his faint, urgent call over the wind demanded attention, and his pointing hand brought shock and gut-wrenching fear. If he listened carefully, and once aware and under the wind and at an octave lower, Lincoln could hear a booming: it was the thunder of surf announcing and heralding in a shy, tardy, reluctant new dawn!

Chapter 13

The misery caused by the stinging barrage of rain and drifting spume and trying to see through the murk with a face wet, streaming and dripping, it wore a person down in the end. It was akin to two people throwing buckets of water at someone in slow motion and taking turns, one after the other alternately, without pause and without let up. The irritation became too much at times and he hurting himself with an impatient hand, or fist, and childishly losing his temper when knuckling and trying to brush away the running water – and futile!

Another punch regained him Lincoln's attention and Nicolo indicated the wheel and then pointed to himself, and then pointed forward. He yelled in Lincoln's ear, "Helmut and I, with Bill, would do it faster." Lincoln leaned back and away from him, Nick indicated the wheel again and signed Lincoln to him with a back and side movement of his head. "I don't know that I'm going to be able to steer her in this."

Lincoln climbed around; his, Nick's, statement had an element of truth in it and Nick was not one to admit incapability lightly. He was right too, to broach her now would be fatal, and they would be quicker providing Nick was still fit – and he seemed to be.

He and Nick conducted their shouted conversation crouched and squatting in the shelter of the cockpit, and Nick on one side of the wheel and Lincoln the other. The cockpit coaming and their backs provided scant cover and it was not very dignified, nor comfortable, but it was effective. Words were unnecessary for the first question and reply, and Lincoln's raised eyebrows and caress of the buckled wheel and Nick rubbing and inflating his chest followed by a raised thumb was answer enough – good, apparently he hadn't hurt himself.

Lincoln had been firmly grasping the wheel with one hand and he gave it an exploratory turn, there was hardly any bite on the rudder – *Worippa* would either eventually broach, or, with luck, she would finally find her own point of natural equilibrium to the sea and wind . . . The trouble was, he didn't really believe in luck!

Lincoln turned back to Nick again and shouted a request. "Would you wind in the trysail weather sheet, and then the trysail lee sheet on, straight away, Nick; now before you do anything else, okay." Lincoln blew and directed his breathe upwards towards his nose with a protruding lower lip and wiped away the dripping rain from his mouth and nose and spat out the residue. "Follow my hand signals, Nick – all right."

Lincoln grinned at Nick. "You never know, it just might, might, with a bit of luck, give us enough to hold our own if we reset it." Nick nodded his reply and gave a sickly half-grin in acknowledgement. "We'll get the storm jib on her then, after. We'll not really get going properly till that's up, but the 'try' should be enough to get us under way." Nick nodded again, despite the puzzlement written there on his face. Lincoln pointed at the violently cracking, flogging mad thing of a loosely restrained Number Three for emphasis. "The foresail's the 'driver', Nick, the trysail alone won't be enough, we need that storm jib – we won't be able to get the power on – we won't be able to sail out of here without it."

Lincoln could follow his line of thinking and pre-empted after Nick had pointed a finger at the engine throttle and ignition. "The engine'll be doubtful, it's probably flooded, though you never know; the prop'll be more effective, anyway, if we can get her upright and stable. We'll get them to start the engine anyway – belt-and-braces – the engine may well finally end up to be our last resort . . ." Lincoln added and speaking to himself as much as to Nick, "Yes, of course, start the engine." It was difficult to admit, but, in truth and in his panic, he'd quite forgotten about the engine! Lincoln restrained Nick before he could stand. "Get one of them to call Radio Melbourne as well, Nick, not a 'Mayday', just inform them of our situation and have them standing by." Lincoln grabbed him again, and again shouted into his ear with a cupped hand. "Wait; ask also, whoever's down there and still mobile, for a fix on our position – we'll need a course to sail."

Lincoln had tried to sound confident, but Nick wasn't daft and Lincoln doubted that he'd been taken in. It hadn't, obviously, been necessary to tell him 'quickly'; he'd turned and was on his way before he could anyway.

NO ENGINE! End of message.

Worippa was undecided for what seemed to be forever: hovering, trembling and stalled. She came alive slowly and reluctantly, gradually gaining momentum with each half-inch of the trysail wound in, until at last the rudder began to respond sufficiently and Lincoln could finally bear away. He'd had to ease the 'try' out considerably after they'd gotten some power on because *Worippa* had been heeling too much – they had achieved some sort of balance after having only cranked on barely, in Lincoln's estimation, a turn or so of tension on the try weather sheet winch overall! Lincoln glanced quickly up and then forward again, the sail was barely filling and they were spilling most of the wind and it was flogging more than it was pulling. *Worippa* was on a knife-edge, and in-between driving, too much heel, and stalling – but for that odd turn on that weather try sheet and the damping effect of the lee sheet, then *Worippa's* ridged canvass trysail would be thundering and crackling and streaming like an unresisting, comparatively paper-thin, bunting flag! Yes, Lincoln concluded, and after signalling Nick to put more tension on the lee trysail sheet, the handkerchief of trysail was going to be more than enough!

Nick turned again towards Lincoln, and his face across the cockpit was just visible in the half-light, and written on it was pure unadulterated panic. It was their heading straight for the half visible, smudged, looming, white neck-laced cliffs that had put the fear of God up him. There was nothing Lincoln could do, *Worippa* was too light and too tender on the wind and they had to have speed or these seas would knock her round too much and slow her down and eventually leave her wallowing again. Bearing away initially would give them the extra speed and subsequent power that they would need to punch through these tumbling rollers and keep going, that and the option of picking exactly when and at what angle to bring her round and onto a reach.

It was different, and Lincoln did not know whether to be exulted or afraid – of having some control, even if limited. Riding across and up the huge waves and crashing over the top, and then the descent, which was a sliding, breath-holding, heart-stopping, surfing plunge – which surpassed any fairground ride anywhere.

Not all of it was due to her angle of attack or her riding higher; the wind was not ripping the top off of every crest now and the waves were tumbling less often than during the night. There was, and if he paid careful attention, the odd respite in the stinging rain and spindrift as well. *Worippa*, Lincoln observed, was definitely not burying herself quite so deeply either and the deck was not taking as long to clear after each flooding; and happily, fewer and fewer wave curls or broken crests were coming over the top and into the cockpit. Had the storm centre been imperceptibly edging to the east – Lincoln fervently hoped so – and pray it was not just a lull!

Now or never, Nick carefully eased the lee trysail sheet and cranked in the weather try sheet as per Lincoln's request. They were past hand signals and were now in harmony and all Lincoln needed to do was glance at him and almost imperceptibly nod his head, and Nick would react accordingly. They were, Nick, *Worippa* and Lincoln, silently communicating and as one. Lincoln had gradually and gently nosed her bows round into and as close onto the wind as he dared, and he had kept the groove wide, thus to allow plenty of room for error. They were not a piece of swirled, wave-flung flotsam any more – Lincoln glanced at the log, three, three and a half knots, not much, but just enough maybe to hold her off those ominously hungry, glistening, foamed, serrated, schisted, stone teeth.

Lincoln's thumbs-up and a raised arm with a downward pointing finger, that and waving him away was enough to galvanise Nick again into action. He quickly crossed to and crashed open the hatch and removed and dropped each washboard unceremoniously down inside. He had to wait for what seemed an age before he was passed and received the storm jib. Nothing happened after, nothing happened; whatever he'd told them hadn't had an effect – unbelievable!

It had though: it was that 'time slowing down' aberration, distortion thing, and his brain running too fast, and . . . and anxiousness. Helmut came first and he signalled to Lincoln with a raised thumb before climbing out, he didn't even try to emulate Nick, but sensibly following him forward to the foredeck on hands and knees. 'Thoughtful' Corsham came next, he didn't go forward at all directly, but stepped across and wedged himself down on the cockpit seat in front of the wheel – he ignored Lincoln's questioning look and after steadying and bracing himself he produced and passed a pocketed, sealed, plastic beaker. Lincoln knew he could be a stubborn old bugger and all Lincoln's requests and pleadings he ignored, and to placate him finally and in a fit of pique, swallowed and drank the lot in one gulp. That had been a mistake: the tea was piping hot and scalded Lincoln's mouth and burnt on its way down!

There was, despite the still atrocious conditions and their lurching, desolate, wind-swept world, a quiet humour there; he took the beaker back and carefully replaced the top and, ignoring the indicated cliffs and white water now easily visible, Bill Corsham calmly pocketing the beaker and then produced and passed to Lincoln, from a seemingly bottomless pocket, a huge, bulging, thick-crusted sandwich.

Moving much slower than the previous two and stopping only to partly open and drop the plastic cup down the hatch, Bill Corsham made his way forward. Lincoln half-smiled as he paused now and again to carefully lift his attached safetyline clear of various obstructions before eventually kneeling and settling himself behind the mast and in front of the foresail halyard winch.

Gary, when he appeared, unfortunately caught the brunt of Lincoln's temper, caused by lack of sleep and apprehension – that and anxiety, and fear. Lincoln had run out of patience and although he knew he was being unfair, he just couldn't help it. Lincoln waved him away and forward; and although Gary wouldn't have heard any of the shouted abuse over the wind, he'd not have misunderstood the content. "Enough!" Lincoln finally stated without realising he'd spoken out loud – and still unaware, completed his sentence, "the ship first and then we'll see to Sharon, and anything else afterwards."

*   *   *

Come on, come on, come on, come on. Despite and beneath his desperate urgings Lincoln knew that *Worippa* was not making over the ground; it wasn't obvious, she seemed to be making way, but, in fact, she was being pushed sideways and slowly and inexorably being edged towards the shore. He watched as the Number Three slid down and was quelled at last, and it was such a relief to get rid of that viciously snatching sail – it had been like a frenzied, bucking and kicking, wild-eyed bronco that was prancing and jack-knifing away and trying to pull free from a cruelly restraining halter. To be rid of the underlying vibration that it had caused to run through the ship and rigging, and that they had had to put up with for, seemingly, hours on end, was a blessed relief too. Nick and Helmut sat on it – the re-clipping and shackling of the halyard to the storm jib seemed to be taking forever.

Gary sweated it up . . . "Come on, come on, come on."

Lincoln's muttered litany fell on death ears . . . as did his resigned, whispered imprecation, "You bloody fool!" Helmut's frantic signals he didn't see, or ignored!

The headsail halyard exited from the mast's interior at eye level, and it then led down to and was turned by and via one of the usual swivel block's attached to the welded ring at the mast's base – the same welded ring that Lincoln had held onto during the night – and the sheet being led from there to finally terminate at the winch in front of and between Bill's knees.

Gary, with one foot on the mast was blindly heaving horizontally on that exposed length of sheet that exited the mast at head height. He had his head down and was rhythmically using his falling-away bodyweight when pulling – and there was not, as far as Lincoln could see, another thought in his idiot brain! "God preserve us!" As before, only the wind and Lincoln heard Lincoln's involuntary utterance. And when they did eventually catch his attention, then the opposite, and in his hurry to make amends he allowed the sail to drop completely out of the foil! Lincoln looked down at the deck and mentally counted to ten – Christ! Helmut's raised clenched fist and Nick's mouthings were ineffective, and in the end it was Bill who had to, literately, crawl and stop him physically.

The storm jib finally went up again, and this time hoisted in controlled stages. Helmut quickly tied each 'earring'; they were spaced down the storm jib's leading edge and were attached to the foil with a traditional reef knot. They were the same lengths of braid that Brian Ramsey, years ago (was it only yesterday), had found time and had threaded through each spaced, circular metal cringle pressed into and up the storm jib's reinforced luff. Each length of braid, or earring, had an integral knot tied into it on and against either side of the metal cringle, which thus trapped the earring permanently. As Lincoln had pointed out to Ramsey, they were left in place for obvious reasons, and to state the obvious yet again: one couldn't afford to fumble about when a yacht, as now, was in serious trouble, and neither could one afford to have a storm jib part or peel away from the foil for the same reasons! They would, the earrings (Lincoln remembered concluding lamely) incidentally, usefully double-up as telltales when the storm jib was in use, and when conditions and wind speed didn't warrant the precautions of tying them – as in local club racing on a flat sea with a robust inshore wind, for instance.

Nick, coming out from behind the forestay, left them to it and crabbed his way along the deck with the bundled Number Three. Sharon surprised Lincoln and impressed him again, she had obviously sufficiently recovered and had seen the necessity and had gone forward to help without being told – needs must, but many a crew member that Lincoln knew of, and who would consider themselves more than competent, would have sat licking their wounds in one form or another and wouldn't have had the wherewithal to react in these conditions as she had – and she a novice! The trouble was, after the bashing she'd obviously taken, Lincoln wasn't at all sure that he wouldn't have been one of those 'competents' sitting down there licking his wounds and ignobly watching the proceedings had it been him in her place!

Mind you, mused Lincoln, it was just as well that she did have the wherewithal, because the Number Three proved to be too awkward for one person to trap, drag and contain, and the wind-plucked, would-be escape artist eventually had to be pushed, punched, kneed and fisted below.

Nick, before he'd come aft, had remembered to re-tie the sheets, and as Lincoln had said, either he got it brilliantly right or he got it brilliantly wrong. Sharon had got it brilliantly right too, she was quick to learn and was already waiting for him – she'd sat herself behind the big sheet winch and was poised and ready.

There was not a man born who'd have the strength to winch in that sail, Lincoln waited . . . Nick had though and he'd got the foot of the storm jib in tight before any of them had fully realised that there was a problem. Once again he'd hyped himself up and had been so concentrated while grinding in the sheet that he'd not paid attention nor had he heard Lincoln's shouted supplications. Lincoln finally had had to bear away slightly and was struggling to keep *Worippa* something like upright and under control, yet, beneath his temper and concentration, Lincoln could but only feel sorry for him. Unlike Gary's earlier effort, such an astonishingly explosive burst of fierce, frantic, portentous, Herculean energy needed that kind of focus, and Lincoln could only imagine Nick's disappointment and heart-breaking despair when resistance became too much and he was finally forced to look and check . . . Only then did he become aware and realise that he'd forgotten to reposition the sheet trolley from the Number Three sheet position to the storm jib position!   The sheet 'car' should have been slid forward to a place clearly marked on the track – to a position where an imagined line from the head, or top of the sail, to the bottom trailing corner, or clew, ended.   Nick collapsed over the winch when he realised and sympathy Lincoln had to feel – he was a real 'battler'!

Lincoln squeezed his eyes shut: none of them could point the finger – they hadn't – he hadn't thought to move the bloody thing either!

Nevertheless, even with the storm jib half set and with a disproportionately slack leach, *Worippa* had gained a knot . . . two maybe. They'd have to fix it, the trailing excess of canvass had formed an exaggerated, uncontrolled, outward bulging curve and, unlike the Number Three that had been only loosely restrained by its slack sheet, the wind was jerking this sail's restrained slackness back and forth and the frightful, erratic, trapped, plucking and tugging power was transferring to and causing the mast to judder and shake.

Lincoln looked to heaven and whispered, "Lord please reward Helmut in the 'after-life'." The big German had calmly pulled the portside sheet through and out from all the leads.   He was just aft of the bow and on the weather and the peaks of cresting rollers were irregularly trying to wash him away – and seen in a lull, in the blown rain and spume, he grinned and Lincoln simply laughed. On a lee shore and edging, even if minutely, closer to and under the cliffs, the mad bugger grinned at Nick and at the same time raised an accompanying middle finger, and the wealth of meaning in the mimed, blown kiss was beyond belief and added so much insult to Nick's already injured pride. Lincoln grinned and shook his head: for once Nick was obviously speechless and his open-hanging mouth closed with a snap, and as in Helmut's blown kiss, there was a wealth of meaning in Nick's pointing and gently wagging you're-for-it-now, warning finger.

Helmut's antics, and whether designed to or no, and knowing Helmut, he probably had deliberately done so to cool the whole situation. Lincoln grinned to himself again, they were acting, and yet you could hear Nick swearing in his mind, he'd hate it, Lincoln knew, he just hated for Helmut to get the upper hand – to have Helmut permanently on his back foot he preferred. If you knew them, as he knew them, and then you knew that for them to be playing their game in these conditions was not irresponsible; it was a measure of their inner strength and unassuming awesome courage.

Promptings from Lincoln were unnecessary now and Lincoln watched as Nick slid the rear trolley down until it was against its wrongly positioned twin, and Helmut threaded through what had been the port sheet. Once done, they returned back along the weather deck, one behind the other. Helmut stopped at the big sheet winch while Nick continuing with the substitute sheet.

Lincoln glanced at Sharon – poor Sharon's eyes were as big as saucers – she'd only have seen an imbecile helmsman apparently and insanely laughing in the face of death!

Nick swung into the cockpit and handed Bill the substitute jib sheet, and keeping on the trysail's tension, he cleared the spinnaker winch and cleated that sheet. Bill, in the meantime, had wound around the new, re-ran jib sheet that he'd been handed, and had hauled in its excess and had refitted the winch handle and stood ready to tail. Nick swung on the spinnaker winch with a vengeance. He'd gone forward again before the rest of them had had time to think – he was towing and controlling his safetyline with one hand and that umbilical miraculously cleared every obstruction – he passed Helmut in a crouched run. Helmut had the original starboard sheet slackened ready; Nick slid that trolley forward easily till it was over its correct 'felt-tipped', deck-marked position. Bill paid out and gently released the substitute sheet after Helmut had wound on and had taken up the slack with the now correctly positioned, starboard sheet.

Lincoln observed the needle on the electronic log as it began to edge round: five, five and a half, six, six and a half!

Helmut paused, strength spent, Nick rejoined him, together they wound, and both collapsed exhausted on either side of the big sheet winch after Lincoln's thumbs-up had told them to stop. The big sheet winch was designed to be operated by two people and its special winch handle was double the length for that very purpose – which only went to further underline Nick's prodigious prior feat of strength and determination.

Helmut's heroism quietly spoke for itself and didn't need

commenting upon – Sharon's did though, because, Lincoln didn't know whether she'd been consciously aware or not, she'd read it right just the same. Most of *Worippa's* winches were self-tailing, but in an emergency situation such as these, there simply wasn't enough time to fiddle around with the self-tailing jaws. All through that final episode Sharon had tailed for them, and once again, through the whole episode she hadn't missed a beat!

Lionel's face appeared in the hatchway and Lincoln nodded in answer to his raised questioning eyebrows. He raised a foolscap pad and on it and in thick, black felt tip was written, 'COURSE TWO-FORTY DEGREES – TWO HUNDRED AND FORTY DEGREES MAGNETIC', and beneath that 'HF RADIO NOT WORKING'. Lincoln shook his head: when on earth would it end, it was one continuing disaster after another; he pursed his lips and then shrugged – better not to make a lot of it. Nevertheless, the HF was by far their most serious loss: it was the second of their two guaranteed links with the outside world gone – and they would really be in the 'mire' now should they want to communicate – should things go really badly for them!

Seven, seven and a half knots.

Lincoln signalled Sharon with a gently extending, palm-up, half-closed hand and arm for her to ease out her sheet – she allowed it to slip out on the winch and stopped doing so on his command. That done, Lincoln beckoned them all to come back to the safety of the cockpit, and Helmut followed Sharon after relieving her of and carefully paying out and keeping the storm jib sheet taunt as he came. Helmut again, Lincoln just looked at him: you could trust him – you didn't leave a sheet untended at any time, let alone and especially not in these conditions.

Helmut had cleared the, now redundant, port sheet from the sheet spinnaker winch and reloaded its replacement; he next unwound the runner from the runner winch and, still under tension, cleated that off. Finally, he uncleated the trysail sheet and, under tension, rewound that sheet onto the runner winch, and Lincoln could only look on with admiration, Helmut had set them up so that both the jib and trysail sheets had their own winches and they could now trim both those sails from the cockpit with ease. He was right too, Lincoln confirmed, the runner would be comparatively happy living there, cleated off, under these circumstances.

Nick hadn't joined them, he'd gone forward once more: re-running the port sheet again and repositioning the port sheet 'car', as appropriate. He was a good kid, acknowledged Lincoln, you never knew, it'd be fatal if *Worippa* broached and survived the broach only to subsequently find themselves on the opposite tack, or if they had to tack for some other reason, and only realised then that they hadn't a port sheet!

The compass needle was wildly swinging, but the centre of swing was above two-forty degrees and it was the best average Lincoln could manage on that point of sailing – *Worippa* was on a full-blooded reach and had the 'bone' between her teeth. Lincoln could feel and sense that she was close to the edge and she needed his total and constant attention and concentration – and slowing her down, he knew, would be their next problem!

Eight knots – hull speed!

*   *   *

They had a full complement topside, bar three, Lincoln glanced around, Helmut, Bill and Gary sat in the cockpit to weather and Sharon they'd squashed in on the end and under the protection of the cabin bulkhead. Only Nick was sitting to lee, watching and tending the storm jib, he'd taken a couple of extra turns round the spinnaker winch as well – for a little extra insurance!

Lionel appeared in the hatch again and a bemused Lincoln almost unconsciously witnessed him hand Gary a long, metal, rubber-handled tube from below. Lionel pointed to the sole of the cockpit and Gary, without demur, inserted its end into the flush, rubber-faced bilge pump – and his back-and-forth strokes were paced for endurance rather than speed – penance perhaps?

Worippa's balancing over and through the crests and waves still called for total attention and concentration, and Lincoln had observed who was and what was going on in the cockpit before him with the merest flick of the eyes and another part of the brain. *Worippa* heeled savagely on the next roller and he had to desperately spin the wheel to counter its brutal power. Just one more of those, Lincoln promised himself, and they'd have to get the trysail off her; they'd clocked in excess of twelve knots surfing down the thing and that was with him sawing at the helm! The roar from their created, swirling, seething, bubbling wake was such that it drowned the howl of the wind, and the two wings of ploughed-up water on either side caused by

Worippa's churning counter and her pell-mell dash down the slope threw up two spectacular roosters' tails that rose up well above their heads.

It was exhilarating stuff, but Lincoln knew that the risk was too high and that this sort of thing was all right if they were racing, had help near at hand, and one or two more competent helmsmen fresh in reserve and waiting on the sidelines. No, the odds were too much, this was no good for them, they were all too tired or exhausted, and he was well aware that they'd broach and, or break something vital sooner or later – it was inevitable.

Lincoln indicated for the trysail to be eased out again and waited to see the effect, and then asked again – just a minuscule of difference. Should they take the trysail down – they could just try feathering it . . . Unfortunately, he had to balance taking it down against an exhausted and somewhat inexperienced crew, namely Sharon, and the risk to their lives while handing that 'try'. No, he decided, they'd have to persevere; to get sea room and get away from this lee shore as quickly as possible was their first and only priority at the moment . . . And, as an afterthought, all the odds had to be weighed and all counted; and there, as he'd noticed earlier, definitely had been a painfully hesitant and even if somewhat meagre moderation in the weather, though Lincoln had to admit that the time-factor of improvement (if it continued) would be too long to help them immediately . . . Still, every little bit helped!

All relevant dials that a helmsman needed to consult could be clearly viewed on *Worippa*: they were built into a horizontal consul at the back of, and bridged the sliding hatch of the companionway. Neither the 'close-hauled' nor 'wind speed' instruments were working, Lincoln peered quickly up. It was difficult because he couldn't risk or divert his attention away from the job at hand, but on first glance, and as difficult as it was, he couldn't see the wind direction sensor or the spinning anemometer cups on the tubular extension that was fitted to the leading edge of the masthead crane.

Bill tugged on Nick's jacket answering Lincoln's mimed request. Nick handed over his sheet, he'd no trouble understanding the meaning of Lincoln blowing out his cheeks and looking up at the mast's peak. Lincoln using an upright, sideways, wagging finger and pointing to the stationary needles of the instruments on the instrument panel was also self-explanatory. Nick had to go forward again because they needed to know what had happened and if there was any further or more serious damage up there. He was forced to make his way to the bows for an uninterrupted view in the end, despite several intermediate stops for inspections – and even if the sea had moderated just a little it still took their collected breath away to watch him there, squatting in and with his back in and against the pulpit and with the sea regularly breaking over him, and the wind and the sea combining to pluck or wash him off that foredeck should he make one false move. Seeing him there was like . . . Lincoln searched for the words . . . It was exactly like being in one of those awful swingboats at the local fair in earlier years, the one's where as a youth (his youth anyway) one stood in the swing's end and your friend stood opposite, at the other and both pulled in rhythmic alternate harmony on the equivalent of a bell-ringing rope to increase the swing. That used to be where the girl's screamed and the boys showed-off, and it was, in those days, one of the focal points at the fair. Nick's presence forward in the pulpit emphasised *Worippa's* extreme seesawing motion and it gave a person a measure and reminded one, it reminded Lincoln anyway, as if he needed reminding, of just how steep and raw these seas were!

After what seemed to be an extremely prolonged inspection, Nick, with deceptive ease, quickly made his way back aft, and instead of returning to his original place in the cockpit, descended and turned and swung himself around when initially clambering down into the cockpit, and finally trapped himself in the companionway facing them. A downward stirring, turning, rotating finger and then wagging it horizontally referred to the anemometer and wind vane, his shaking head meant either they were broken, or, more probably, Lincoln guessed, not even there at all! He got his next meaning across in the end by flashing the torch on, then off: the masthead light had also disappeared.

Nick went forward without complaint in response to another crucial question and one that they also had to have an answer to, and one that Lincoln had unforgivably forgotten to ask him originally. Him talking into an imaginary telephone, followed by a stiff, upright held arm and a pointing finger, Nick had instantly understood and he was scampering forward again after Lincoln's nod: was the aerial still there? Lincoln glanced up to where Nick was also now looking, the wind vane of the Windex, which he already knew about, was bent over at sixty degrees, and, as far as he could see, there was not a sign of the thin, white, four-foot, VHF whip antenna!

Consequences? Lincoln questioned, what were the consequences? It meant that they'd have to rely on the emergency aerial, and that they had one was thanks to Brian Ramsey's forethought – it was one better than the handset. The backup VHF aerial was permanently attached to the pushpit, and the only drawback with it was that its low position severely limited its range: that was fine in his, Lincoln's comparatively crowded home waters of Europe, but no good for out here in these wastes.

The initials VHF stand for 'Very High Frequency', and unfortunately, VHF is only effective over line-of-sight, that is, its range is limited to how far the naked eye can see, and thus, of course, the higher the aerial, the further its range! Conversely, the big, now useless, 'High Frequency' radio set below did have the capability of sending a radio wave for hundreds of miles, and unlike VHF, its signal had had the capability of bouncing itself off of the ionosphere and thus, indirectly, could travel around the curve of the earth!

Lincoln had not needed to wave acknowledgement, he'd followed Nick's progress to the foredeck – and then suddenly there was acute agitation and naked panic in his attitude and body language, an agitation in Nick that Lincoln had never witnessed before. Nick was, and with a repeated jabbing finger, frantically pointing to off of, and just shy of their port stern quarter, and directing their attention out to sea; Lincoln turned and stared – nothing. Nick began to run, in that same half-crouched scamper, but in frantic haste.

There nothing to see; Lincoln half-noted that the others were also peering round and some of them were struggling to stand, turn, or kneel: there was only the now usual, if daunting, windswept desolation: onward, as far as the eye could see, marching, frothed, spume-blown, white-topped rollers. And yet . . . Lincoln searched for it . . . something wasn't right, something . . .? Then it hit – no horizon – there was no horizon! Or rather, the horizon had changed . . . It was . . . higher, and . . . and closer – and apart from those between that puzzling horizon and them, and as per any horizon, there were no distinct valleys at a distance, just the close-packed peaks – it had to be an illusion, surely?

Nick's return went unnoticed and it was moments even then before Lincoln became aware of him behind – he was hanging onto *Worippa's* backstay, and even in the panic of the moment Lincoln could not but notice and admire how easily he swayed there, not fighting *Worippa*.

A solid wall of water was coming towards them and probably, he estimated, in this visibility, only now a quarter of a mile out. It towered above its nearer minions, cousins and neighbours, and was coming out of a dull, grey, wet, depressing, wind-swept, rain-spattered, ugly morning. Yes, once Lincoln had seen, it was easily distinguishable – and getting more distinguishable by the second!

Forced together by a cross-sea? Made one by a hurricane gust? It was a freak, a rogue, an aberration: a giant comber made up of two or three amalgamated Southern Ocean specials. Relentless, and a convex wall growing taller as retarded time callously ticked on, Lincoln could see quite distinctly, even from where he stood, its top tumbling down its front – there was too much cascading water for even these winds to whip completely away.

It was mesmerising – and hypnotic. Time crawled – almost standing still. The world moved in slow motion.   Lincoln knew, or sensed, or felt Nick unclip and re-clip his Gibb hook and swing back into the cockpit – good, he'd be as safe, or in as much danger as the rest of them; Lincoln had to grin – in the 'same boat' didn't seem appropriate, given the circumstances.

Lincoln observed that wave dispassionately and floated above the oncoming and overwhelming paralysing awe and dread of this world. Bear away a touch, his brain instructed, ride up it at an angle: not too much, just enough for the bow to slice through: too much and the frothing, breaking top'd roll them over like a piece of timber being toppled and thrown about in the surf on an exposed beach.

The rest, Lincoln instinctively knew, were still not fully aware, they had not quite picked it yet – they were overbalancing and hindered and their views partially restricted and obscured by each other. That, and the fact that they hadn't had time or the desperate need to adjust and protect their eyes from the violent gusts that made the eyes water, and from the irregular whipped flurry's that stung them so excruciatingly. Yes, Lincoln dispassionately stared, this visitor was not yet fully appreciated, which was probably just as well – that their attention was split. Lincoln could see that they were puzzled by the contrast, it was still confusing them, and yet, nevertheless, they knew that something ominous was out there. Nick's face during his seemingly unwarranted, frantic scrambled return and questing stance at the backstay must have really contrasted and emphasised Lincoln's involuntary grin when he'd thought about 'in the same boat', which was something quite, quite alien to humour.

Lincoln's request, subsequently, and coupled with their natural curiosity must of taken a fair amount of self-discipline to accept, and yet, despite that involuntary grin of his, the urgency, fear and apprehension lying beneath were obviously catching. Nick's yelling, miming, and he physically pretending to half-pull an odd head down finally convinced, and Lincoln was glad that it was because, in the short time allowed, they would all be as safe as they could be with heads down, body's folded low, and their harnesses clipped.

They just had time, and quickly and half-climbing and swinging round and hanging onto the wheel with one hand, Lincoln caught onto the upper sleeve of Nick's jacket.

"Ease out the jib on the rise, Nick." Lincoln shouted, and while pointing to and beckoning Helmut, Helmut half-stood and lent towards Nick and Lincoln to hear. "Nick'll ease out the jib on the rise, Helmut, would you let go the trysail at the same time – you can release the lee sheet now." Helmut nodded accent. Lincoln pointed to himself and addressed them both, and though he tried desperately to disguise his feelings while he did so, Lincoln couldn't quite and was too scared to but momentarily take his eyes off that incoming monster. "Crank the jib and the trysail back on after. Watch for my instructions." He nodded to Nick, and then to Helmut as Helmut poised to shift across to lee. Lincoln hadn't let go of Nick's sleeve and gave it another tug. "Warn them below, Nick, quickly, then get back here and settle yourself as fast as you can."

That's, of course, with regard to his instructions to Nick and Helmut, if there was an after!

People were amazing and although perhaps it wasn't such an odd reaction, Nick actually looked relieved – something to do, Lincoln concluded.   It would be on them imminently – and Lincoln picked the angle – they were in God's hands.

Their looks of awed fear at once informed, they, while Lincoln had been talking to Nick and Helmut, had seen, and a lifetime passed and the jib slatted in the microseconds that passed while they were staring up from the bottom of their ravine. They crouched, ducked down and waited for the inevitable.

There was one exception, and Sharon turned as they began to lift, their eyes, hers and Lincoln's, locked for a moment – just a look – and her face calm and strangely serene in the shadow of that impossibly high, steeply-sloping, towering, tidal mountain of water.

Chapter 14

The rudder was effective and there was still plenty of way on as *Worippa* rose, and she lifted gently at first and deceptively slowly when gradually ascending, and then she suddenly accelerated towards the peak. The wind caught and heeled her, which in turn levered her around by the stern. And thereupon those in the cockpit were drenched and crushed and next buried under the tumbling crown, and Lincoln could feel the mounting pressure and relentless power exerting itself on and pushing through the steering quadrant – and the surge trying to force *Worippa's* bows sideways and down and away.

Glimpsed and laid out from high above on the peak, and in a frozen moment in time and as far as the eye could see were humped, white-capped rollers – row after row and line after line. *Worippa* had hesitated, undecided, and then she was through. Through to nothing – to vacuum, to emptiness!

She pendulumed back upright again as she plummeted straight down for thirty . . . forty . . . fifty feet? It seemed more, and to Lincoln it seemed never-ending; an uncontrolled drop on a descending, unbraked, ten-ton, express elevator! The sea was like bedrock, with no elasticity and no apparent give: *Worippa* crashed down and hit the trough's bottom as though onto solid concrete. She actually landed on her port side and the impact of that bottoming reverberating through *Worippa* in an abrupt knee-buckling, neck-snapping, jarring dead-stop.

The shock wave transferred itself from the keel directly to the mast and Lincoln could almost see the harmonic travelling from its base and continuing up in an imagined 'S', through each set of spreaders, to terminate at the crane. The top of the mast whipped and vibrated and snapped back and forth like a wild thing, and that despite the tensioned runner. The pronounced flexing, banging and rattling of halyards and rigging was extraordinarily loud and prolonged. The initial, main shock of hitting was followed by a lesser and continuing vibration; and both the former and the latter travelling the hull, and both were distinct through the deck.

Water flowed away through the large, three-inch cockpit drains – thigh-deep to empty in minutes . . . No feelings, no thoughts, no reactions. Left to her own devices *Worippa* struggled, righted, and shook herself – and although still in shock, Lincoln noted somewhere that after she had eased herself around somewhat she shrugged off and shouldered away the next wave. *Worippa* found her own equilibrium after turning further and her stern quarter lifted as each long-fetched hill of water easily passed beneath!

Awareness came slowly – the night and the succession of events and emergencies had taken their toll. They would have to check the keel for damage first – Lincoln stared, looking through the deck in his mind's eye – all of those forces, all of that stored kinetic energy would have focused and would have been concentrated and spent there, at that point below, where the mast was stepped.

The rig of a sailing boat could be likened in set-up to that of an arrow in a bow. The standing rigging holding up the mast, and their tension and the combined tension of all stays causing considerable vertical pressure – the equivalent pressure of that as on an arrow's notched end from a very powerful, fully sprung bow. The concussion of their impact, Lincoln knew, would have created and momentarily exerted a tremendous downward force on top of that permanent pressure, and the resulting accumulation would have just about rammed the mast through the bottom of the boat!

Nick, as usual, Lincoln noted, was the first to react to their situation and had enough presence of mind, while ignoring the distraction and intimidation of the noise from the cracking, flogging and unfettered jib, and to a lesser extent, the trysail too, to scan around for signs of obvious damage.

It only registered then, that Nick and Helmut must have released their respective sheets as they crested that monstrous wave . . . Lincoln had no memory or recollection of them performing that feat of brinkmanship, but it was, indisputably and without doubt, one of the reasons why they were still here!

Lincoln eyes automatically following and looked to where Nick was looking – an involuntarily staring in the same direction because of Nick's facial expression and stance – something fascinated! There was a difference, but it took Lincoln a moment to sort out – a moment to clear away disorientation, confusion and afterimages. Yes, the mast . . . Lincoln shaded his eyes . . . the top . . . the top section of the mast had been sprung. The mast had acquired a bias above the second set of spreaders, and not radical, but distinct enough – distinct enough to cause concern! The distortion tipped away to port, Lincoln moved to one side of the wheel in order to get a better view – he looked down and closed his eyes before looking up at it again. God, they were dogged with an unfair share of bad luck – it didn't look much, but, and experience had taught him the hard way, that that bias was now automatically suspect and to add any undue or unfair stress and eventually that'd be where it would inevitably and finally buckle. They'd exceeded the thing's in-built flexibility, in-built tolerance, and, as Lincoln knew, and as experience had taught him, they were never the same after – the punishment had been too harsh.

It was a relief to see Lionel in the hatchway, unhurt and apparently calm. Lincoln felt for him, it'd not have been much fun below. Down there it would have felt as if in a drum, the noise magnified two or threefold in that confined, enclosed world. It would have been far worse than up here – the not knowing, the wondering, and imagination running riot. A world where equilibrium had ceased to exist: a world that seesawed violently back and forth, from side to side, with no rhyme or apparent reason – and then that drop and final resounding crash!

They looked at each other, Lincoln nor Lionel, neither of them commenting by gesture or otherwise, apart from his only eventual request that is, his pointing and Lincoln's nodding assent – and Gary went without objecting below to help.

There had been no sign of Brian Ramsey; Warren would be a different story . . . Lincoln immediately dismissed any further considerations along those lines; and anyway, it didn't matter, they'd be someone bobbing up and telling them soon enough – should they be taking water!

With another part of his mind Lincoln had followed Helmut as he had made his way forward to the mast; Helmut was kneeling before it and examining the collar and seal around its base. He was right too, acknowledged Lincoln, damage could have been inflicted there, that was where the 'stick' pierced and passed through the deck: the edge of the padded aperture where the mast passed through hadn't been designed for what had occurred. Helmut was not happy: his face told Lincoln that much after he'd stood and turned – all was not as it should be. He came back along the weather and stopped and explained while clinging to the top rail of the pushpit – and the wind was still blowing and the gusts heeling *Worippa* alarmingly on the crests, and blowing every other of Helmut's words away.

Lincoln's mind ranged elsewhere while he listened, interpreted and pieced together what Helmut was saying. It was strange, thought Lincoln, everything was relative. Although *Worippa* was wallowing around and lurching and tipping like a stuck pig on the crests, and those on board still had to hold on for dear life, and the storm jib was jerking and banging around like a wild beast on the end of its retaining tethers. And that jib, despite it having been sheeted in enough to stop it being positively lethal and yet putting minimum strain on the mast, was making enough noise and was distracting enough to disturb the dead. The trysail by comparison was just filling, despite Helmut apparently easing out the sheets just prior to cresting that huge rogue wave – there was enough tension still on to just power *Worippa*. Just as well, Lincoln concluded, it was why *Worippa* was riding these swells as she was.

It was, he further reflected, strange, and that indeed everything was relative, because although conditions weren't as bad as during the night, and excepting that one crushing mammoth wave, of course, and apart from everybody, including him, looking apprehensively around and scanning the horizon when they remembered . . . They had . . . Well, they had all somehow gotten used to it!

He'd heard enough to understand the gist of what Helmut was saying: there were stress cracks in the deck! Lincoln thought about that, and that the actual area that Helmut was talking about wasn't, in fact, an integral part – it wasn't a vital load-bearing part of *Worippa's* structure . . . It'd be all right and they could get away with it just so long as the deck had given and not the mast, or the keel, of course! . . . They could live with it, if the damage was limited to that – and it'd probably look worse than it actually was!

He, Helmut, went directly below to check after their short analysis, and no fuss, and understanding immediately that he'd partially missed the point and by the expression on his face he knew it: that the damage to the deck was superficial. Helmut would check the mast step around the keelson thoroughly; Lincoln had faith in him, his engineering credentials he respected.

They finally and collectively sighed – those in-the-know topside had understood the gist of Helmut's and Lincoln's answering gesticulations – and they all breathed easier after Helmut's nod and thumbs-up from the hatchway, and Lincoln could feel those breathing easier below as well. Their confidence in Helmut in such matters was absolute.

*   *   *

Helmut pointed to the trysail and then to the weather winch, and Lincoln replied with a negative and pointed to the trysail's lee winch, and held out an index finger and opposing thumb with a minimum gap between. His same finger pointing to the weather winch and the same sign, and then a hand held vertically, and Helmut understood: tension the trysail as is. Lincoln gazed while he deliberated: by rights and as before, they should be taking it down – trouble was, the little power it was providing was the only thing that was enabling *Worippa* a scanty semblance of sea-kindliness . . . It'd have to stay up till they got going, he decided; sheet in the storm and then see how they stood? One thing, whatever configuration they finally decided on, it must be the one that exerted absolute minimal stress on *Worippa's* mast – time to move!

Nick beckoned Sharon across to lee and making room, sat her in front again, she facing forward next to the cabin bulkhead. She nodded and took the handed jib sheet and kept it tensioned while and after Helmut had followed Nick forward – she was to tail from the cockpit this time.

Bill moved up and turned and fitted the winch handle, and pulled on it tentatively to get the feel of it before looking up; he too was waiting for confirmation and was ready.

For the second time that day, though not as close into the cliffs, they bore away off the wind, only this time *Worippa* had only the storm jib to set. Nick again, with Helmut, sheeted in and Sharon tailed as *Worippa* came about. They nearly mistimed it and nearly broached her on the first wave before gaining control – their attention was on . . . they'd all of them been . . . all of them had been anxiously monitoring the mast. Relaxing just a little once and they were sure, and after utilising the winch again and the runner had been carefully re-tensioned and re-cleated, did they breathe easier.

Only after they had settled her down did Nick and Helmut

returned to the cockpit, Helmut sat himself next to Bill and Nick relieved Sharon and sat to lee again – minding. Lincoln eased the wheel; they had been lucky, very lucky in a perverse kind of way, the bend in the top of the mast was to port and the prevailing wind from the south, the combination of which fortunately would tend to straighten out the bias rather than accent it.

It was over, and the strangest thing was that somehow they all knew, and Lincoln knew that they all knew: it was almost as if they were now living and were in coordination with nature, and that they had just paid the final instalment to whatever god ruled the elements and was omnipotent and all-powerful here! Oh, no doubt they would have further problems, perhaps serious ones, and Lincoln expected that as part-and-parcel, but not on the scale as previous.

Confidence took time to re-establish itself and though seemingly contradictory, there was therapy in *Worippa's* discomforting and uncomfortable and ungainly rhythm, which they all again somehow quickly adjusted to.

One of their main and disconcerting and disruptive problems for Lincoln was trying to stop her pounding, which occurred as or directly after they'd just topped the crests. Not on every wave fortunately either, for which he was thankful, but frequently enough and always on a steepish one, which *Worippa* seemed to encounter with a regularity that was almost mathematical! No matter how or what techniques he tried or trialled initially, *Worippa's* bows would hang clear of the water on the crest for a moment – held proud by her aft weight until gravity took over after the point of balance had been passed – and then her bow would smash down onto the back of that same wave. That impact sent a shuddering vibration through *Worippa,* which resonated through to her very core – and the subsequent rattling of her mast and rig, also on a particularly heavy impact, literally, rattled Lincoln's teeth – and at the same time also sent, imaginary or no, a cold shiver of foreboding and acute anxiousness up the mast and up his spine!

Excepting *Worippa's* suspect mast, no boat anyway, unless very substantially reinforced, which *Worippa* wasn't, she was comparatively lightly displaced, could suffer this kind of punishment for a moment longer than was absolutely necessary – and that aside from their personnel discomfort, which had also to be a major consideration because of their combined exhaustion. One might have – Lincoln might have put up with it and risk it for a while during a critical period on a race, but in their situation and condition – no! The main example of what pounding could do to a boat was during Australia's world-famous rival race, the Sydney-to-Hobart: year in, year out, and with boring regularity, boats in that event had to retire because of damage to their bows caused by pounding!

Worippa had been or was surfing down the back of every wave, but on those particular ones, to Lincoln's consternation, the 'speedo' was recording ten, twelve, fifteen knots – and that despite all his and their efforts and conservatism. Conversely, *Worippa's* slowing and almost stopping in the troughs was bewildering and in complete contrast: sails emptied in those deep, steep hollows, and then there was an overwhelming and convincing illusion of going backwards just before lifting on the next roller. And after that the jib filled again, not sedately, but with an explosive crack if not controlled, and then the power came on – until the whole clockwork cycle started again.

Using the rollers rather than fighting them, that was the trick, and Lincoln eventually learnt to recognise which wave – steer her off the wind and climb at an angle and then correct and slide diametrically down the hill at the opposite angle. The technique wasn't that difficult, once learnt, and there was a bonus, if one could call it that – one cancelled out the other, more or less, so *Worippa* would not stray too far away from her overall course either!

Further, *Worippa* often reached and passed through the magical vibration point, a point on the acceleration curve where she would shudder and shake for a short moment. It was exhilarating, if tiring and exacting work, and would have been fascinating at any other time, but *Worippa's* crew were too weary and wary now to enjoy – they had sustained too much. Anyway, it'd be short-lived, hopefully, and Lincoln knew that it was not sensible and that it was pointless to prolong the risk, especially to *Worippa's* now vulnerable mast, and also the boat and other gear, and to take unnecessary risks after what they'd been through and survived. He would have to think about slowing her soon – but only when they were further out and well clear of that ominous rock-strewn shore!

Lincoln looked down: Sharon didn't look too bad, it had been some introduction to sailing – and they'd broken the mould after, he keenly and willingly acquiesced – she was something else! Gary had better start 'wooing' with a vengeance, or he would not hold onto her. Sharon had charisma, and whether consciously or not she attracted. Lincoln wasn't aware that he had been staring at her until *Worippa's* resident madcap spitfire smiled and hunched her shoulders, pulled a face, and grinned through clenched teeth and gave a little wave at the same time. Lincoln smiled back and grinned as another thought crossed: one thing was certain, no one on this boat would be climbing over her in order to get to him – Gary that is!

'Him', coincidentally, climbed out of the companionway, he clipping his safetyline and interestingly, then another, somebody else's, to the bulkhead U-bolt! Something was going on, Gary had turned his back and was pulling – and not, Lincoln noted, gentle persuasion either. The expression on Warren's white-green face Lincoln fleetingly saw before he tumbled: there was panic, fear and resentment written there.

He'd not have volunteered to come topside then – two sets of hands had pushed him out, and neither considerate. Lincoln watched as he succumbed to the inevitable: he stood, undecidedly half-turned and finally squeezed himself in between Sharon and the cabin bulkhead. Once there he laid his head on one arm, faced the corner and closed out the world with the other. Gary shifted Sharon up one further, and after he'd sat, once again picked up the rolling bilge pump handle from the cockpit sole and without a word grimly resumed his previously interrupted chore.

Brian Ramsey appeared next and not looking at all well, immersion, struggle and cold, they'd all taken their toll. Lincoln glanced away, he'd aged ten years, they all looked a bit shabby, Lincoln guessed, but Ramsey had fared the worst and looked as if he had; there were deep black smudges under his eyes and his face was lined – almost emancipated with fatigue.

Lincoln nodded back as he climbed up the steps, stopped and wedged himself there, at waist height. His surveillance was slow and studied, and Lincoln saw afresh what he saw, through his eyes: a dripping, glistening world: and sporadic blusters of fine rain and rollers as far as the eye could see – and their crests white. There were, now virtually mute, combers

197

booming and breaking on the northern horizon, against the darker base of the rugged cliffs, which contrasted the slightly lighter hills and crags above. Many of those peaks were hidden and shrouded in cloud, and distance had softened the picture and there was a fascinating beauty, which was enhanced by the violence of the mauling, rampaging, white and foamed, exploding waves beneath.

Home-sickness struck Lincoln with painful suddenness, the scene somehow strongly reminded him of home – as above a ploughed field on a clear, freezing, autumn afternoon – a mist like frozen breath, just the same, floated above the sea, hazing detail and hanging like a partially opaque, white gossamer curtain.

Ramsey turned in the hatchway, taking his time; he slowly inspected his pride-and-joy. Lincoln discretely watched as he carefully inspected the rig, and although his expression gave nothing away his eyes returned and stayed focused on their newly acquired irregularity after his general perusal.

Nick clipped Ramsey's handed hook to the lee jackline, his journey across the cockpit was painful and a lot of effort was spent climbing around Lincoln. He gently took the wheel and Lincoln stood-by until he felt comfortable – till he'd learnt *Worippa's* rhythm and the technique of dealing with those reprobate rollers.

He leant close. "Are you all right, Chris?"

"Yes," Lincoln answered. "I've been trying to avoid taking down the 'try' – I think that we might well be able to carry it, providing the weather moderates further."

Ramsey grunted noncommittally and half-pointed. "How bad is the mast?"

Lincoln considered. "It'll be all right if we're careful." He looked to the top of the mast and nodded at the same time. "There's nothing left on the top, the light and the VHF aerial have gone." Lincoln pointed to the instruments. "And so have the wind-direction and anemometer."

Lincoln felt Ramsey nod before he answered, "Right. Okay . . . Oh, while I remember, would you make sure," he requested soberly, "that the emergency aerial has been plugged in and the set is on, and on standby – and on sixteen." He indicated the hatch. "Before you climb – I'll take over now, that is."

Hoping to reassure him and cheer him up a little, Lincoln shouted two words over a sudden gust and flurry, "Storm's over."

He glanced around at Ramsey to see his reaction, and Lincoln was just in time to see a little smile play across his lips, and his eyes held his. "I know," he answered, "the glass is rising."

*   *   *

An invisible toxic cloud and the smell was so offensive that it made him pause at the bottom of the companionway steps, and he was unable to go forward because of it. Lincoln had to put a hand over his nose and mouth to stop himself from actually gagging.

With eyes streaming, Lincoln quickly looked forward into the gloom, the boards of the cabin sole were no longer awash – the poor beggars, they'd have not stopped pumping – it took a while to pump out hundreds of gallons of water by hand.

Curiosity overcame disgust and Lincoln quickly slid in behind the chart table and reached out a hand, the needle responded to a gentle tap: one thousand, zero-twelve millibars and rising. That took a bit of absorbing – just how low had the mercury gone during the night! Everything seemed to be working, 'Sat Nav', 'GPS', and no reason why they shouldn't be, he thought, because their aerials were, of course, mounted on separate stainless steel posts and each an integral part of the pushpit.

Forty-three degrees and forty-two minutes south, one hundred and forty-six degrees and thirty-eight minutes east. They'd survived and were practically out of the danger zone – that was good news. Lincoln allowed his mind to roam back – barely twenty-four hours at sea! The ticking brass, mechanical chronometer confirmed the electronics, zero-eight-thirty hours – it didn't seem possible, a lifetime had been crammed in since the previous night – twelve hours of adrenaline-pumped, concentrated living.

He went forward, swinging from grabrail to handhold, Potter was forward, still pumping – he looked round and watched Lincoln approach.

Lincoln forgot to ask Lionel about the frightful smell – he looked completely exhausted and concern about him took precedence. "Are you all right, Lionel – have you recovered?"

It was a stupid question, he admitted, because he obviously hadn't.

Lionel sort of sidestepped his enquiry. "I just didn't duck in time, that's all, matie." Lionel tiredly leant his weight against the edge of the bulkhead. "I'm getting too old for this game, Chris," Lionel's voice was flat and without inflection or expression, which Lincoln found disturbing, "I don't think I'll be sailing again after this trip." He glanced at Lincoln, and before looking away again added quietly. "My nerve's gone."

"Gently, Lionel," God, Lionel really was in a bad way and it really concerned him to see him like this, "it takes time. Food, rest, some sleep, you don't recover from . . ."

Lionel interrupted, "No . . . it's deeper than that, matie." He looked at Lincoln again and again quickly looked away. "I'll work it out, don't worry."

There was nothing more that Lincoln could say; he was obviously in no mood to be cajoled or babied, so best ignored. Maybe, given time, it'd go away, Lincoln hoped so, a morose and depressed Lionel he hadn't seen before and didn't like.

Lincoln indicated back to the navigation area – to the radio. "Completely stuffed, is it, the HF?"

"Not transmitting, nor receiving. I've double-checked the earth junctures and they're okay – actually, the set seems to be fine as far as I can tell, that is." Lionel pointed. "I suspect the aerial connections; one of them has probably got water in it." The tone of Lionel's voice took a nasty turn. "The fucking thing's supposed to be waterproof." Lionel contemptuously flicked the imaginary set with his finger. "Fucking useless."

Lincoln commented mildly, "I don't think they quite envisaged the punishment that we've put it through, Lionel, it's been half under water most of the time."

"Don't you excuse 'em, Pom," replied Lionel tartly, "the one time you'd really need the thing to fire a shot in anger would be in exactly these conditions, not on a summer's day, for Christ's sake." Lionel's voice really was venomous, still, his temper was better than that jaded resignation that Lincoln had first encountered – anything was better than that. "Fuck 'em, I've got no patience, if they can't make it properly then get out of the market and make room for someone who can."

Lionel had a point, but then again, most cautious skippers would waterproof and silicone all critical points personally –

had Brian?

"We'll take a look when the weather moderates," Lincoln told Lionel placatingly, "we can't do much in this. By the way, Brian said to take a look . . . Where does the emergency VHF aerial lead terminate, Lionel?" Lincoln had decided that it was pointless telling Lionel about the mast at the present time, he'd find out quickly enough and there nothing he could do about it anyway, and it would be a pity and an unnecessary burden for his recovering spirit. Lincoln answered his look of enquiry and added casually, "The mast aerial disappeared sometime during the night."

Lionel wasn't really curious . . .

"It's taped to the mast lead, matie, behind the set, you just have to change the cables over – come on, I'll show you."

Then the enormity of what Lincoln was asking hit him: for crying out loud: why hadn't Ramsey and Potter already sorted it out and tried? He stood frozen, just holding and swaying to *Worippa's* rhythm, and held his head mentally: why?

Lincoln breathed out slowly . . . it was so difficult to understand people at times – and beyond his ken. Things seemed so clear-cut, absolutely clear – the answer and action written there, as in a book . . . He sighed. It had always been a problem for him, how their minds worked. 'Don't do unto others' – reverse the roles. Lincoln had lived by that code for many years and it was, he'd found, after following many ideals to a dead end, the only one that worked – it was one of those overused, but nevertheless, true cliché's of true wisdom. The memory of the man from whom he'd gleaned that so-simple, yet so profound principle for living, never mind all the doctrines and dogma, was at that time, in the early years, teaching an industrial psychology course. He had come across to Lincoln as a learned, yet unassuming lecturer, and it wasn't until much later and after many heated debates that some kindly soul had informed him that he was, in fact, a nationally-renowned and quite brilliant professor! He was to become to Lincoln, and sadly was until his death, a close personal friend.

Anyway, as an aside, in Lincoln's professional life it had always, with very few exceptions, been the answer to settling an industrial dispute – or any dispute, for that matter. In a nutshell, in Lincoln's nutshell anyway, all one had to ask oneself was: 'if I were part of their work force, would I like that, is it right, is it

201

fair'? People would argue with ardour if right, they'd argue black was white if forced, but not with the same total conviction if wrong. The trick: to concede if wrong, albeit with dragging feet and a bit of face-saving nonsense thrown in!

That philosophy had failed Lincoln this time; Lionel's logic was beyond him (and for whatever reasons, Ramsey hadn't realised either). "But why haven't you got it on, Lionel?" Lincoln asked. Lionel didn't answer; he just looked at him. "If the other one's down, wouldn't you put this one on standby? Brian does know, doesn't he, that the HF is out?"

"I told him." *Worippa* took the opportunity to tell them that she was alive and kicking and they both held on as she lurched heavily and partially fell off a wave. After a shrug, Lionel matter-of-factly resumed, "It's only got a range of three to five miles, you know."

That illogical logic again, at least Lincoln could follow that. "That's us, Lionel, that's our range, not somebody else's." Lincoln pointed, as if to the outside world, "There might be a ship out there, another yacht just over the horizon, we don't know, do we? We should have scheduled in hours ago, Christ," he was thinking on the run, "it gets worse, Lionel, we should have scheduled in last night." And then it hit. "We're both a pair of bloody idiots, Lionel, there's Maatsuyker sitting out there, Maatsuyker's a thousand feet high," Lincoln fell over his words, and what he asked, even to his ears, sounded for all the world like an accusation "Is that 'light' still manned?" he harshly demanded.

As he voiced the words he realised that he was being unfair, and to place the burden and to blame him, or even imply, meant or no, was to insinuate that it was all his fault – Lionel had spent most of the night rolling around in a bunk concussed. And, come to that, Ramsey hadn't fared much better – too late anyway. Lincoln took a deep shuddering breath. "Sorry, Lionel," he apologised, "the old brain's only just started to work."

Lionel had not, for which Lincoln was thankful, taken umbrage at his words. He waved a dismissive hand. "Yours is quicker than mine, matie," he replied, "quicker than anybody's," and he voiced Lincoln's thoughts. "We're all getting tired, that's all. Um, Maatsuyker . . . I honestly don't know, they must be due to go over to automatic, if they haven't then they must be one of the last. Mind you, I've just got a feeling . . ." Lionel paused for a fraction of a beat. "And furthermore, if they haven't yet then they'll have the 'bee's knees' in radio gear." Lionel jabbed the air with a pointed finger to express his point. "If it is, manned, I mean."

Lincoln turned as Lionel finished his sentence and was quickly making his way back to the chart table, Lionel following closely on his heels. The cable to the emergency VHF antenna was exactly where Lionel had said it would be. Lincoln unplugged the lead for the mast aerial, and cut the adhesive tape and plugged in the emergency, and turned on the set. Nothing!

"Christ, the bloody thing won't come on. Help me, Lionel?" Lincoln pleaded; he was desperately trying to reign in an overwhelming explosion of rage caused by frustration. "What the hell do I do now?"

"You calm down, matie," soothed Lionel, "you've been too long without sleep. Come on." He eased Lincoln out of the way. "Get out of the road and let me take a look." He lent and peered behind the set. "The spare fuses are in holders, there're built-in, they're behind and on the back of the set – we'll try them first." Lionel opened the chart table lid as he forestalled Lincoln's next comment. "Here," he said and handed Lincoln a chocolate bar. "Shut up and eat this while I sort it out."

Lionel had put his finger on it, Lincoln admitted, they were all beginning to get too tired – and their judgement, or at least his, was starting to go – and unimportant things were beginning to get out of proportion and important things forgotten . . . His nudge brought Lincoln back.

"Come on, Chris, wake up – don't go to sleep on me now. Actually," he said with an accompanying grin, "you can in a minute; we're in business, it was a fuse."

Lionel held him down with a reassuring hand as Lincoln tried to jump up – Lincoln looked at the little red glowing LED on the front of the VHF set. "Are we on the speaker?" he asked.

Lionel nodded confirmation. "We sure are."

"No traffic then?" Lincoln had a job keeping the disappointment out of his voice.

"Not a bloody tweet, matie, and before you ask, there's nothing wrong with the set."

"'All Ships' then, Lionel," Lincoln said excitedly, perking up again, and impatiently instructed, "put out an 'All Ships'.

And . . . and, if you get an answer, then . . ." He pointed at him with both his hands and wagged them to emphasis the point. "Then you can ask them to relay our position to Melbourne and . . ."

Lionel interrupted Lincoln in full flow. "You do it." He'd gone red. He answered Lincoln's astonished look. "What the bloody-hell do I say?"

Exasperation flared again. "Get on with it, Lionel." Lincoln ordered, half-shouting.

The point was mute because they had lost the initiative anyway, because a booming voice had interrupted.

Potter broke their stunned after-silence, "Oh fuck." He whispered and spoke through the fingers and thumb of a hand, which he had inadvertently placed over his open mouth, "We're in it now; they'd have sent it out from Hobart." Lincoln could see the grimace Lionel had pulled his lips into behind his hand. "In this!"

The call repeated, "Yacht *Worippa*, *Worippa*, *Worippa*. This is Air Search and Rescue. Echo, X-ray, Sierra – over."

"Answer it, Lionel." Lincoln ordered. "Go on."

"I can't," Lionel hastily replied, "you answer it."

"Lionel, come on. Get a grip." Lincoln peered at him. "I'm not even awake."

Potter had to wait even then, as did Lincoln, until after the third call. A stuttering Potter he had not experienced before – this was new! "Search and Rescue. Search and Rescue. Search and Rescue. This is the yacht *Worippa*." He nearly forgot. "Over."

"*Worippa*, this is Search and Rescue. Echo, X-ray, Sierra, your signal broken. I say again, your signal is breaking up." He added distinctly, and Lincoln could almost taste the patient boredom in his voice. "Check the 'high output' on your set, *Worippa*. I say again, switch to 'high output' – over."

Potter looked at Lincoln, Lincoln looked at Potter; he flicked the switch from 'stand by' to as directed. Lincoln shrugged in answer to his shaking head – too late, they had both forgotten! Lincoln berated himself – elementary and unforgivable! You switch, on a VHF set, to 'Low Output' for 'guard duty' and receiving, which, as he well knew, was fine for local calls – it conserved and saved power. 'High Output' one used for maximum range and emergencies, and, of course, it conversely used much more power.

Lionel spoke into the microphone again, "Search and Rescue, Search and Rescue, this is *Worippa* – over."

They tactfully made no references to their, his and Lionel's incompetence: they'd have, Lincoln surmised, seen, and, no doubt, heard worse. "*Worippa,* this is Search and Rescue – Echo, X-ray, Sierra. Your position and status, please? Over."

Potter read off their position from the GPS and then explained and then clarified. "Search and Rescue, welcome. Um, we have no HF. Umm, I say again, our HF radio out of action. All we have is VHF, with an emergency aerial only." Lionel coughed. "Um, we sustained a bit of minor damage." Potter just couldn't help himself – he smirked at Lincoln. "Mind you, we're still rocking and rolling. Um, over."

The silence lasted for what seemed to Lincoln to be at least a minute – they were, no doubt, absorbing Potter's radio blasphemy . . . and their reply when it did come was terse. "Search and Rescue. Echo, X-ray, Sierra, to *Worippa*, Romeo, stand by – over."

He was absolutely hopeless, was Potter; and Lincoln had to look away as he raised his eyebrows above the microphone and pulled a 'please yourself', 'so sorry I spoke' face.

The tension had gone from his voice when he came back on air again, "Search to *Worippa*, we have you visual." He'd get a 'bollocking' from his skipper, but then, as Lincoln only too well knew, Potter tended to corrupt anybody who came into contact with him. "Enjoying yourselves down there are you – tripping the 'light fantastic'. Bit bumpy, is it? Over."

Letting the cat out of the bag, that's what you did when you let Potter loose on the airways – he was, Lincoln with resign conceded, an old hand now.

"Search – *Worippa*. Up and down like a whore's drawers, mate, it's like being a pair of knickers in a washing machine. Oh, by the way, while I think of it, you haven't got the next forecast for the next twenty-four hours, have you? Over"

Lincoln studiously studied the bullhead in front of him.

There was a slight frown in the voice from above. "*Worippa*, this is Search and Rescue. Moderating over the next twenty-four hours, you'll be glad to hear. Southerly four to five, I say again, southerly four to five. Over."

Potter was immune, "Search. Thanks, matie, received –

over."

"*Worippa* – Search and Rescue," said the voice from above formally, "please broadcast 'All Stations' on original 'sched' time from now on for possible relay." Potter held the microphone away from his mouth and whispered to Lincoln, "What the fuck's 'sched' mean?"

Lincoln whispered back, "Schedule."

Potter nodded sagely and then snapped his fingers and wagged his index finger. "Of course," and added hastily, "I'd forgotten – that's right."

Search and Rescue were still advising them, "We will instruct vessels in relevant areas of your "sched" time – over."

Potter acknowledged.

All party's were unanimous and had agreed apparently, Lincoln cynically concluded, it was only 'wimps' who turned back!

"*Worippa* – Search and Rescue, do you require further assistance? Over."

Potter answered and there was genuine sincerity in his voice that was palpable and that one just couldn't take offence to. "Search – *Worippa*, further assistance not required; I'll buy you a beer when I see you, matie – over."

Their angel from the skies must have also heard that sincerity because Lincoln could hear the warmth in his voice. "Search and Rescue to *Worippa*, we'll hold you to that, good luck – out."

Potter and Lincoln scurried and then hotfooted it for the hatchway.

Chapter 15

Silver-white and high-winged . . .? Potter and Lincoln had just been in time to catch a glimpse of the 'Search' aeroplane. In his mind Lincoln had almost contemptuously and dismissively labelled it 'Search', and not 'Search-and-Rescue', because their would-be rescuer had been a light monoplane, which had been a surprise and a disappointment because he had expected to see a helicopter, and naturally it made him put a bit of a question mark against the suffix, 'Rescue'! Actually, 'Spotter' plane would have been a more accurate description . . . Lincoln revised that assumption as he thought about it, he supposed that they were still capable of dropping encapsulated life rafts et cetera, and pondering further reluctantly admitted that it would be a bit pointless . . . Lincoln meant, to be sending a helicopter wandering around willy-nilly in the Southern Ocean without a specific destination, and especially in search of a lone yacht, which for any number of reasons other than rescue had failed to radio in (as in their case) would, of course, have been a criminal waste of precious resources . . . Lincoln considered that small fact further: and what if while it was doing that Murphy's Law had been invoked and a genuine distress call did occur, and that helicopter's winch and rescue capability were paramount and lives at risk! No, it was just . . . Well, he had convinced himself in his own mind that a helicopter it would be, and he had been a bit shocked and disappointed to subsequently realise that it wasn't!

Lincoln abruptly abandoned further thought on the subject: to be babbling in company was one thing, to be babbling mentally to himself . . . Well, a person could easily disappear up their own certifiable backside before they knew where they were!

The noise from the twin engines of the Search and Rescue plane increased as the pilot applied more power and continued to climb. He quickly and finally disappeared into the low-hanging mist that hid the top of and shrouded the skyline, and which partially obscured a rugged, steep, desolate, remote and indented mainland.

The noise of those fading engines was accompanied by a very faint, rogue glint of much diffused sunlight, and it lit and by comparison basked the awesome beauty of the scene before and around them – and that momentary and unexpected suffused illumination expanded the distance and dramatically exposed the horizons of their circular world. What assaulted and hit Lincoln between the eyes first were the lone monoliths standing before.

How could a person begin to describe such a landscape? Those cousins of Lot, those Medusan observers: isolated, remote, indifferent and standing alone on the edge and knee-deep in the Southern Ocean. Lincoln could only speculate: they must have been sculpted over millions of years: wind-scoured, frost-cracked and formed and carved by the elements. Nature and erosion had been hard at work, wearing and washing away surrounding softer soil and rock, flake by flake, grain by grain, millennium after millennium, till bare. The core of those huge, ragged, chimneyed, grass-topped, petrified pillars had been made of sterner stuff than Lot though, they were bedrock sentinels and hardened stone escarpments that had stepped out from the mainland and had been left to guard Tasmania's south-western approaches. Some were a thousand feet high and the ocean was breaking against all their legs – even out here, out to sea, once Lincoln realised what it was, the continuous, underlying, varying, louder and fading, pitched grumble of booming violence was quite audible. Viewed from afar through a mist of water-laden air as they were, it looked as if they were being alternately dressed in streaming white cloaks that was rebounding spray up-thrown by hundreds of feet. The curling, over-flung, flying, scudding, wind-whipped spume and smoke enhanced and mystified their already majestic, statuesque, awesome, gull-circled beauty.

Potter, a little earlier, Lincoln remembered, had quietly commented something about they being flees on a dog, and in his own way his statement though perhaps not eloquent – or perhaps it had been – had been deeply profound. Nature did humble and did try the nerves: to see the Maatsuyker Group from the sea: Maatsuyker itself, De Witt, Flat Top, Round Top, Flat Witch Islands and the rest. Few had seen them and this might well be a once in a lifetime privilege, for her, Sharon's, and perhaps his as well for that matter. Only the 'once in a lifetime' because of a compelling feeling and an overwhelming conviction deep in the psyche that one shouldn't be here – of, for Lincoln anyway, an instinctive shying away and a peculiar sense of trespass – this was not a place where man should tread, or, if one had to bandy with words, sail – this, Lincoln instinctively knew, was chancing your arm. One visit and survival instincts: fear, intimidation, not dread, but close, would be tolerated: one visit they were allowed, God looked after simpletons, half-wits and the insane, and only the foolhardy would dare to go back.

To go back . . . and yet, love-hate, love-fear, attraction-fascination, dare-death wish? Having seen it once he'd go back, and even if he couldn't physically, he knew he'd visit here, in his mind's eye, regularly, for the rest of his life!

In Lincoln's mind, and he'd seen his share of places, it was one of the most desolate, isolated, Godforsaken home's in the world – all there was, was that one solitary, silhouetted, thin white tooth – and built at what cost? The 'light' stood at three hundred and fifty feet and was situated at a third of the way up on the south-western slope of Maatsuyker Island – Maatsuyker Lighthouse.

It was the most southernmost abode in the Australian dominion and so remote that only the wind, albatrosses, sea birds, seals and the odd whale were there for company. Lincoln gazed intensely and was fascinated: white building, no . . . buildings, were slowly revealing themselves and coming into view, most were still partially hidden by the lighthouse itself – they'd all be fully visible shortly. They were the keeper's residences and outbuildings – powerhouse and engine rooms – it obviously had to be, or had been, a self-sufficient little community. Lincoln knew a bit because Gary had filled him in on some of its history, he had told him, for instance, that there had even been a school teacher in residence there at one time – and the twenty or so children on Maatsuyker hadn't gone untutored, or had had their education neglected! God, to imagine it here in winter – and it probably would have been a minor 'blow' to them, what they had experienced!

Gary broke into Lincoln's quiet musings when he excitedly pointed to their cruising companion; it was their first and was quartering the wind and effortlessly skimming above the cresting, spitting sea. The Albatross, as Gary had informed, would not be found above the equator – it didn't frequent northern waters – and the only place that an observer could see them, a human observer anyway, was down here in this half of the world, in the southern hemisphere. They gazed in awed fascination, despite its long establishment with ships and the sea, and its *Ancient Mariner* fame, and its romanticised and much-quoted and often revered reputation, nothing prepares or arms against the reality of its grace and magnificence and . . . the sheer poetry of beauty and movement. This, this was truly one of God's creation's, so beautiful and so envied by Jonathan Livingston in his premature years – it is surely one of the most graceful living thing's on God's earth.

They grinned, there wasn't an actual specific reason, and it was just, well . . . Lincoln hadn't the words . . . It was . . . It was their surrounds . . . and that bird out there, sitting on the wind, and the wind in the sails and the angle of heel and the hiss of *Worippa* making her way through the water, and the backdrop and, and . . . and everything. It was the beauty and wonder of it all, and the joy – the joy of just being alive and out here before and under God's sky. For just that one magical moment in time it overcame everything – fatigue and tiredness – it simply belittled whatever other worries had been or were nagging at them – at him!

*   *   *

"God, that is terrible, Lionel. Poo – the toilet's flooded, has it? For God's sake, don't tell me it's broken?"

Lionel shook his head. "No, it's bloody Warren, you won't believe this, but he's shit himself." Lionel answered Lincoln's disbelieving look. "Honestly, I kid you not." Lionel raised his eyebrows and nodded downwards. "You'll be treading in it now – it's every bloody where."

There was nothing to see; only sopping carpet. "Jesus, Lionel." Lincoln muttered, fighting rising bile. "Where's the disinfectant – how the hell can you stand it down here?"

"Priorities, matie; I hate to say this, but do you know, I can't even smell it anymore." Lincoln simply closed his eyes after he'd made that statement. "The bottle's trapped in the sink, in the galley, don't use it all," Lionel cautioned as Lincoln began to move aft, "what's in that bottle is all we've got left."

Lincoln sluiced with a mix of salt water and disinfectant and scrubbed the whole place with a deck broom, from the heads in the bow to the companionway steps – 'priorities'!

Cooling sweat caused by exercise was causing the cold to start and to really seep in – the job was done and it was time to change into dry clothes – it was always a problem in adverse conditions, or even in cool conditions, was the cold, and Lincoln was by no means immune. It was an ever-accompanying problem with sailing and was due mainly to long periods of inactivity, and that wasn't helped when it was interspersed with short bursts and moments of intense exertion and bustle and the accompanying body moisture that intense activity caused. Not so much on a trip like this though, not while cruising – on a trip like this a body could usually disappear for a quick 'warm' down below. And a skipper, if he was worth his weight, would attach canvass dodgers to the pushpit and stanchions on either side of the cockpit to keep off the wind – their worth, in Lincoln's view, was way beyond their actual material value and (he smiled at the unintended pun) they helped enormously.

Personal lockers were forward, forward of galley and saloon, in the bunkroom, as it were, abaft the mast. Lincoln had made his way forward for a change into clean clothes after he had been topside to empty the bucket over the side, and to wash it and the deck brush out in fresh saltwater. The personal lockers were housed in a double-shelved, two-doored locker facing the bow and built against the bulkhead that separated that area and the saloon.

Lincoln stopped and, while hanging onto the overhead grabrail as a commuter would while travelling on the underground, drowsily contemplated the lower bunk – and the longing to climb into that bunk and simply go to sleep and let the world go-hang was overwhelming. The inclination was a dangerous one and was to be fought and avoided at all costs, no matter how exhausted. He'd been down that path before and had given in, in the past, thinking that he'd manage and be better off if fresher and with a clearer head – it sounded, even as he thought about it, very logical, and even more logical when, as he was now, very close to exhaustion, but it was, in fact, to use a cliché, a formula for disaster.

On a lone ocean-going yacht one kept going, to plan to lie a-hull, or whatever, was one thing, but to stop before that soloist's chores were completed was quite another, and to do so would inevitably lead to only one conclusion – catastrophe. So, with a one last wishful and regretful glance, Lincoln reluctantly moved on.

One had to be while trying to change in this seaway a master of acrobatics, and with his thermals and trousers round his ankles Lincoln hopped around on one leg and staggered across from bunk to mast, and then back again, from mast to bunk. *Worippa's* constantly changing inclinations, especially the odd extreme one, overbalanced him and no matter how secure, or how well he tried to trap himself, or how far or at what angle he leaned, it was still impossible not to avoid being regularly tumbled. The only answer in the end was for him to lie down in that 'inviting' lower bunk and change while lying down. The last and final straw was when he was even tipped out of there – and that with the aid of a malevolent lee cloth of who's securing knot to the eye attached to the hull above magically untied itself – and that, of course, was precisely when he was in the most awkward, painful and contorted position of final undress!

Potter helped him out of the dilemma he had gotten himself into in the end; he re-threaded and re-lashed the miscreant lee cloth and helped Lincoln climb back in afterwards. It had been just as well that Lionel had ridden to the rescue because Lincoln had been heading towards and was on the edge of either tears or temper – and Lincoln wouldn't have put money on that it wouldn't have been the latter! That little incident had evidently amused Lionel and had obviously lightened his day a little – and he couldn't quite keep a straight face and he was trying just a little too hard not to show it . . . Well, Lincoln was glad someone had found it so bloody funny.

Fortunately, it proved only necessary to change the bottom half in the end – the soggy seaboots they'd all have to live with, and Lincoln wasn't alone there, they had all been squelching around with frozen feet for hours. Potter emptied them thoroughly though, and Lincoln forgave him all his sins for that seemingly minor, thoughtful act of charity. He went forward while Lincoln waited and it crossed Lincoln's mind while he was laying there that he hadn't been thinking, he should have thought to empty them and should have wadded them with kitchen paper to soak up the worst, and more to the point, he should have done that barefoot – before he'd put on dry socks! A repeat performance there wasn't going to be – over-trousers went on again, wet. Lionel, his concern appreciated and touching, tried to persuade and to push him back into the bunk to sleep, and there was nothing he would have liked better, but he had to desist in the end and hand Lincoln his boots, there were still jobs to be done – one that was, Lincoln thought, essential, anyway.

The galley had been built into the port aft corner of the saloon and it consisted of a working surface with a double sink and attached draining boards, and there were lockers and cupboards against the immediate aft bulkhead.   On the same port side, forward of the sink and draining board (and between them and the freezer), and beneath the 'fiddled' work surface were more cupboards and lockers, and in a recess built into them, that obviously broke the continuation of the work surface, was fitted the gimballed cooker.

The only place they'd stay put was in the sinks, Lincoln counted: three tins of soup, two beef, one oxtail, one tin of potatoes (large), a tin of carrots, one of mushrooms, one . . . no, two of baked beans – peas would go and so would flaked onion, dried.

Lincoln swore out loud: "God damn, God damn the blasted thing!" He'd always had trouble with *Worippa's* 'methylated spirit' cooker, even in harbour: they just didn't get on. The thing hadn't liked him from the word go and had always been spiteful – their last joust it had won and his eyebrows had been its spoils! The enemy had to be pressurised as a 'tilly' lamp, and was fitted with a fitted hand-pump for that purpose; cracking the appropriate burner control knob allowed a small amount of the same inflammable liquid into a cup in-built around the burner ring. This, as he had, was physically lit and only when hot enough would the 'spirit' from the reserve vaporise and form a gas, and only then would the 'ring' be fully efficient and burn properly.

A flair-up from the ignited spirit licked the thin, curved, aluminium sheet that was screwed to the hull and to the deckhead behind and above the cooker – extended flames had left a sooty, blackened trail from the deckhead above, to the horizontal limit of the gimbals.   The protective aluminium followed the arc of the cooker and was a safety feature placed there, behind and above the cooker, to stop imbeciles like him burning the boat to the waterline.

Dancing around in front of it ineffectively didn't help; Potter came to the rescue yet again and Lincoln wasn't in the mood to be beholden. "Bugger off, Lionel," Lincoln dismissively waved him away. "It's not that funny, it's not a comedy act just for you – bastard thing. Now, piss off"

They finally brought the thing to heel and once tamed it seemed to accept its predicament and settled down to emit a pleasant hiss, which became a purr, and the warmth from the 'beast' cooker was so welcome – and comforting.

He, Potter, leant and watched while Lincoln punched and opened.

"One hell of a wave last night, Lionel," Lincoln idly commented while he peeled back the lid of another tin. "That wave must have come very close to rolling her over completely – I found myself lying above the bunk, actually on the side of the hull."

Lionel wouldn't . . . he wouldn't quite look at Lincoln directly, which was not surprising, subsequently, considering the circumstances.

"It wasn't a broach." They made eye contact, and Lionel sighed wearily before looking away. "That storm was directly overhead and the lightning was flashing all round us – it was lighting up the sky like day." Lincoln quietly stopped what he was doing and gently leant against the sink. Lionel continued on, "It scared me bloody witless – the thunderclaps were deafening." Lionel was gazing into the neverland. "And what you could see in the flashes, Christ, a sea running the likes of which I've never seen before . . . not nice." Lincoln waited – something was to do. "Two, three, four bolts hit the water around us, I actually heard them sizzle into the sea, my bloody hair stood on end, literally – you could smell the ozone even in that wind." Lionel's eyes re-focused and there was defiance in his stance. "I don't blame him," he belligerently said to Lincoln, "you've read about it the same as the rest of us, you'd have thought about it and don't say you haven't, Pom. Echo sounder transducer blown out the bottom of the hull – all that crap."

Puzzled for a second, and then taken aback, and then incredulous. "Just what exactly are you saying, Lionel", Lincoln quietly asked, "are you telling me . . . I hope you're not telling me what I think you're telling me – did he let go," and then the penny completely dropped, "he didn't let go of the helm, did he?"

Lionel's not answering was answer enough.

Lincoln was incredulous. "The circuit's broken all round, Lionel, there's ceramic strain insulators built into the backstay, for Christ's sake, and the rest. Even the lifelines through the stanchions are broken."

To say Lionel looked momentarily miffed was an understatement. "You didn't know then . . .? No, of course you wouldn't have." He bit his lip. "I don't know why I've let the cat out of the bag, I must want my bloody head seeing to – you won't tell him that I said so, will you?" Lionel's anxiousness was so uncharacteristic that all Lincoln could do was shake his head and mouth a 'no'. He smiled, Lionel, after a moment, after he'd realised that Lincoln had meant what he said – they were in confidence and he instinctively knew that Lincoln wouldn't mention or pursue it further. "Bloody father confessor, aren't you – I can see the funny side now," Lionel looked strangely relieved, and faintly bemused as he plainly saw the scene from the night before once again in his mind's eye, "he just let go and cuddled and clutched himself every time a bolt hit – it was like, well, it was like the wheel was burning him – like the rim was red hot – too hot to hold." Lionel must have read something in Lincoln's face that Lincoln wasn't aware of showing. "Come on, Chris," he admonished, "you're out of order this time, you really are," he waved his hand in emphasis, "everybody's not as brave nor as experienced as you." He glared. "You're an uncompromising, intimidating bastard, do you know that. A kind word now and again instead of that look wouldn't go amiss, you know."

"Yes, all right, Lionel." Lincoln expelled a deep breath and then looked at him directly, "there's no need to labour it – point taken. It just . . ." He hesitated. "It just nearly cost us all our lives, that's all – especially Brian's." Lincoln nodded to him and added dryly, "And yours."

"Change of subject," retorted Lionel forcefully, and by way of answer. "What about Warren then, what are we going to do about Warren?"

Lincoln blinked and then shrugged, he was right; there was nothing to be gained by hashing over last night. If he knew Gary, for him, remembering would be punishment enough, he'd chastise himself far more and harder than Lincoln would, or anybody else could!

"We, Lionel?" Lincoln raised his eyebrows questioningly

and sublimely added, "Nothing. I'm going to eat this and then I'm going to bed – I've done all the cleaning I'm going to do."

"No, come on, Chris, seriously?"

"I am serious, Lionel, it's over. All these people," and Lincoln waved an arm to encompass everyone; "all they . . . Well we . . . all we need now is hot food and rest, in that order. It'll be a pleasure trip from now on – a holiday of a lifetime. A tropical cruise."

Lionel scoffed, "Those ancestors of yours told you that, did they?"

His grin froze.

"They did, Lionel – feel it, it's starting to flatten off – the wind's abating all the time. It'll back to east of south for a while, and it should then veer to west-of-south – take it from me, 'matie'," and Lincoln had emphasised the 'matie', "just a mere gale now, with an unusually big sea running, is all."

A gust of violence shook the boat, heeling her further, rattling the halyards, loose objects and cutlery, and calling him a liar.

Lionel concentrated on the stew. "They'll not want this, they'll be past it, and they're too tired: stomach-ache, nauseous and too seasick to eat."

Lincoln elbowed Potter. "They'll have to force it then, won't they, and anyway, once they taste my . . . This succulent, delicious cuisine, believe me, they'll scoff it down." Lionel had a point though, Lincoln had to admit. "All right, getting them to try might be the problem, still, plenty of bread'll be the answer, you watch." He elbowed Lionel again. "It'll bring 'em back for a time, regardless, Warren especially. Anyway," Lincoln observed, as the thought struck, "it's ridiculous, Lionel, everybody being awake at the same time – we'd pay for it later, in the night, you watch."

       *   *   *

Hustled, forced into a corner and confronted by Helmut.

"Ve cannot allow him to suffer, Chris, even a dog you take pity on and bring in out of the rain. Varren, I vill help him, clean him up."

"Good on you, Helmut." Lincoln patted Helmut on the arm and grinned at Potter. "Helmut's going to clean up Warren, Lionel, what do you think?"

Lionel laughed outright. "Helmut, old friend, come this

way."

Potter sat, and Lincoln sat next to him; both of them settled themselves on the padded engine cover, their backs against the table and their feet braced against the kick-boards of the cooker and freezer bases.

There was no doubt about it, their beaming faces worried Helmut, he stood swaying, holding onto the deckhead grabrail and his face in contrast to theirs was both puzzled and wary.

"Vot? Vot? I do not like. You are both no good – vot is it that you both are cooking?"

Potter pointed to the large saucepan on the stove. "We're cooking water, Helmut." Potter redirected and jabbed with his pointed finger. "Bucket, soap, and cloth's in the sink, and paper towels – it's all yours, cobber."

Helmut accused them, "You had planned to vash him, all ready?" He looked, sounded – was annoyed, "You have led me down the garden, that is not right."

They solemnly and innocently gazed at him.

"I apologise, you vould not do that." He massaged his eyes. "I am just a little tired."

Lincoln contemplated: the more you knew him . . .

"Have some coffee, Helmut." Potter filled three cups from their back-up kettle. "The thing is, Helmut . . ." Potter held up a thumb. "One: Sharon's never seen Maatsuyker, she's tired, she's wet, but she'll remember. I . . . we'd not forgive myself . . . ourselves – unforgivable for her to sail past and not see, do you see?" Potter hurried on before Helmut could interrupt, "Two", he lifted his index finger to match his raised thumb, "I don't quite know how to tackle it . . . him, I mean, his nerves – Warren's nerves are stretched to breaking point already, right?"

Helmut examined them, his eyes inspecting and switching: travelling from Potter to Lincoln, Lincoln to Potter – one to the other and back. "How long to clear Maatsuyker Island, Chris," he asked finally, "how long?"

"About an hour, Helmut, maybe two, give or take."

Helmut nodded, satisfied, presumably, with both his answer and the fact that they were sincere. "Ja, okay, Varren can vait vun hour." Helmut's next comment caused acute discomfort; Lincoln had not given Warren a second thought. "Varren should see Maatsuyker too, despite his predicament and discomfort, ja

– I vill clean him up then." Helmut was emphatic, "Sharon must go below though – ve must leave him . . ." Helmut hesitated, looking for the words. "Ve must preserve vot little dignity he has. Ve must clean him up then – I vill clean him up, he is not comfortable, he vill get sore, ja. And the cold, I vill have to be quick."

"Use the old favourites on him, Helmut," suggested Lionel, "make him take . . . it might be worth shoving two or three seasick pills down him. Sedate the mucky bugger a bit, make him sleepy, clean him up and then put him to bed – he's no good anyway as he is, four or five hours and he'll be a different man – he'll feel better anyway, yes."

Potter's depression had certainly begun to lift – an echo of his old sarcastic, former self – beyond niceties and personal considerations had begun to surface. "And not only that, Helmut," Potter, always the natural anecdotalist, paused momentarily before delivering the punch line. "He smells of shit."

They exploded, roared, and at what Lincoln couldn't exactly say, Potter's attempt at humour just wasn't that funny. The three of them below stood and sat, or curled, and laughed uncontrollably – aching, fit to burst, and with tears streaming!

Potter caught hold of Helmut's sleeve as he turned to return topside, after they'd got over their hysterics. "Where are you going, Helmut," Potter rode over any objections Helmut was about to voice before he could utter them, "you're not going anywhere yet, matie, change first, you're wet – you know better. Rule Number One: stay dry. I'll sort out Warren's stuff – his dry clothes'll be ready."

It was impossible for Lincoln not to repress a smile – Rule Number Ones were flying everywhere! Helmut understood the wink, he could be as astute as the next man – no arguments, he went forward to change.

Lionel shouted after Helmut's disappearing back, "And after you've done that, send Nick down – the dicks up there'll sit around wet and then wonder why they're cold."

Potter was back, and Lincoln sighed deeply with relief, he'd seen the 'elephant' and had survived.

He, Potter, turned and gazed at Lincoln for a moment, and was suddenly serious. "And what's the matter with you, what are you thinking about?"

"Watches, Lionel," Lincoln replied slowly, "we're all desperately short of sleep. We've eaten, and you're right about getting everybody dry – we also need sleep..." He was puzzled. "Why, Lionel, why aren't they lining up – you'd think they'd be fighting over the bunks, wouldn't you?"

Lionel tried to explain, "They're all still living on their nerves, matie, we all are. They probably aren't even really aware, but it would have scared 'em last night." Lionel smiled a lopsided smile. "They'd like to die with their boots on – and I know exactly how they feel."

"They should be coming round by now surely?"

"Give 'em time, matie," Potter said it with feeling, "give 'em time."

"Hmm. Yes, well, I guess we'll have to start somewhere and it makes sense to sort Sharon out next – as Helmut said, get her out of the way and then we can pay attention to Warren. Actually, thinking about it, she's been up a long time, you know, she'll be dead on her feet anyway." Lincoln commented further, "She did well, didn't she, Lionel, people surprise you."

"A bloody hero . . . Um, a bloody heroine, matie, that's what she is."

*   *   *

"Bed, Sharon, come on, it's time to call it a day." The look of relief on her face told its own story. Lincoln nodded to her. "Not seasick any more then – are you going to keep your dinner down?"

A violent lurch overbalanced and Lionel caught and gently eased her down behind the chart table. "One hand for the ship and one hand for you, easy now." Potter grinned, as far as he was concerned she'd worked her ticket – she was crew!

"No." She considered. "Do you know, I haven't even thought about it," she perked up her head, she was obviously pleased, "not a twinge."

"There you go," Potter beamed, Potter being nice was a sickly sight at any time, but listening to his being ingratiatingly nice to a female was particularly cloying. "I knew it, told you, didn't I, Pom, a born sailor." Potter turned back to Sharon. "Come on, Sharon, off you go, strip off, dry off and into a bunk – it's just plain stupid to sit around in wet gear. Come on, Brian'd kill us if he knew you were still up, best to give it away. Nice hot drink, then bed and Uncle Chris'll tuck you in." He turned. "Port or starboard side?"

"Starboard'd be better." Lincoln turned to her. "Down the bottom, on the starboard side. Um, on the right, Sharon."

*   *   *

"What's the matter?" Lincoln flicked on the bunk light – pathetic, everybody was doing it. She'd got one step further than he had though – at least the lee cloth had stayed tied! The question was rhetorical anyway; she was just lying there in a half-undressed state – one boot off and one leg bare. "What're you snivelling about?" Lincoln asked resignedly, and using that tone was a mistake because she hadn't the strength, or the will, or was too upset to answer. It was kindness and understanding she needed now – there was no retaliation, she just shook her head. "Where are your dry clothes?" he asked gently.

She pointed out the obvious, she was half lying on her track pants and knickers, and the rest of her clothes were jammed down the side. Lincoln swallowed and inadvertently voiced his thoughts. "It's a bit risky this, Sharon, I'd better call Gary?"

Strength surfaced, and a flair of temper, it made Lincoln look at her twice – the delicate little flower!

"Don't fuck about, seen a fanny before, haven't you? Just get the bloody things off." "First time," she grumbled and accused, "that anyone's . . . anybody's ever complained, or hesitated."

Lincoln looked up to the deckhead: the sacrifices one had to make!

Lionel stood between the freezer and the engine cover, blocking the way. He voiced what was exactly on Lincoln's mind, "I hope you weren't taking advantage of the crew, Pom?

"Aw, shut up, Lionel," Lincoln retorted brusquely, too brusquely, "it's a bloody circus already, without you starting." And over his shoulder, like an apparition, appeared the one person he really didn't want to see at this moment in time. "What do you want, Gary?" He asked, both aggressively and defensively . . . and guiltily, if that was possible!

The question was definitely too sharp, even to Lincoln's ears and it was little wonder because of the consequences, the potential misunderstanding, the stupidity and embarrassment and fright – and above all, his conscience!

Gary's reply was quietly reasonable, "To see Sharon and then catch a few 'zeds', anything wrong with that?"

The look from Potter, Lincoln ignored. "Not yet, Gary, and

anyway, it's not your turn – there's still jobs to be done. We'll restart some sort of watch system then – soon, I mean – and Sharon's asleep anyway and not any wonder, she's been up all night." He took Lincoln's needlessly spiteful meaning and there was no call to embroider further. "She doesn't need you at the moment, but we do," and he added before Gary could interrupt, "we'll be turning the corner, we're late now – and we'll have to change back to the Number Three.

"Do you want to change into dry before, or after, you'll have to be quick though, you've only the time it'll take us to get organised . . . Hot drink?" God, what a pig he could be – Lincoln had tried to soften his tone during that last sentence, but he hadn't quite succeeded and that fact showed on Gary's reddening face.

Potter, now sitting behind the chart table, interrupted their would-be confrontation. "Better tell Brian to turn now, Chris, we're going to overshoot by a mile if we don't, we've gone too far already, by the looks – here." Lionel held out a scratch pad. "I've written it down – show it to him – our new course."

"I'll do it." Gary stepped across and snatched the proffered calculation, and he did so with his eyes not leaving Lincoln's. "She'll not take a Number Three," he stated flatly, "we're having to let go the 'try' now and again, in the gusts, as it is."

Salvaging wounded pride, or no, he was okay, was Gary, admitted Lincoln, a better man than him!

Lincoln switched his mind with difficulty and tried to envision *Worippa* currently, and the consequences and requirements of her new course in his mind's eye. He spoke slowly, considering, "We'll be running with the wind on our starboard quarter, Gary – we're going to need all the sail we dare to carry – *Worippa'll* pendulum and wallow like a pig otherwise – she'll be underpowered . . ." Lincoln looked directly at him, all other thoughts, bar *Worippa's* status, had been magically and thankfully dismissed from his mind, "Won't she – we'll also have to get the trysail off of her at some stage and get the main up?"

Gary placed his cup in the sink, turned, and with one foot on the step and without further bitten-back comment, simply stated, "I'll tell Brian."

Potter had the last word, and justified, "Who's contradicting themselves now, eh!"

Warren the last – he'd taken a few sips of his hot tea, but that was all, and nor would he respond to Lincoln's questions. He must have answered Helmut though, Lincoln knew, somehow Helmut had gotten through – which wasn't surprising, one didn't not answer Helmut. Helmut was a personality that one didn't ignore – even Warren! Lincoln considered: actually, the 'why' wasn't easy to answer, but it had something to do with the fact that genuine caring, concern, or whatever, came through. It got more complex as he, Lincoln, thought about it – or perhaps it wasn't, perhaps it was very simple. He'd force a person, physically, if necessary, would Helmut, and one instinctively knew it – and that same instinct definitely warned that same person not, or in this case, Warren, to mess with him in that way!

Helmut's nod confirmed – he'd gotten the pills down, but a held-out, full, food bowl and a negative indicated that Warren hadn't eaten and had stubbornly refused to do so!

Worry, and any thoughts of insisting were given-away after Lincoln had glanced down. The heels of Warren's boots – the heels were coated, caked, and a watery, rust-brown stain of excreta was seeping and spreading and creeping across the deck from his half tucked-under feet!

Chapter 16

They barely had any way on and were virtually hove-to, and stomachs were churning: *Worippa* was twisting and gyrating horribly under trysail alone. Nick and Helmut had taken a little time to clear the storm jib, they had to cut away the 'earrings' in the end – the knots had turned to solid lumps of locked braid. A 'bare-headed' change on the foredeck – they had learned, the Number Three was not to be allowed topside until the other was stowed and out of the way – a forgotten practice on a racing yacht.

It had been a bit of a job below, but they had checked and had minutely gone over that sail – as best they could anyway. To Lincoln's relief and surprise there was no obvious damage to the Number Three, despite the abuse it had been subjected to during the storm. As Ramsey had said, he'd buy his sailmaker a beer the next time he saw him!

*   *   *

"The wind's right up our backside," complained Bill. "We're on the wrong tack; we should gybe her now and then back again, later, if he wants – we'd be more comfortable off the wind, and faster anyway." Bill, Lincoln could see, was beginning to get the wind-up, "We should never have changed in the first place, Chris, he only did it because we altered course, not because we had to – or needed to."

Actually, and Lincoln had been in accord with Ramsey, Ramsey had been right in deciding to change headsails, if anything he'd been reticent in doing that chore. *Worippa* had been somewhat sluggish for some little while and he would have suggested that he did so should he not have already made that decision. Still, tact, Lincoln felt, was a better approach under the circumstances. "Give Brian a chance to think, Bill, he'll get there, he's tired, like the rest of us. He'll gybe and bear away again as soon as, don't worry, and then he'll sort out which tack once we're at hull speed; there won't be much in it anyway." Lincoln shrugged. "And whichever way, it'll be quite pleasant – he'll get the best out of her – he doesn't want to lose complete touch with the mainland, maybe."

Bill wasn't going to be placated so easily. "Never give up, do you, Pom. No, I've got a feeling about this – he's going in because we've overshot." Bill took a deep breath. "Like I told you, he's already late turning – it'll be dangerous, to be going in, we'd be compounding a mistake – now's the time to gybe her back." He pointed. "Especially while we've only the 'try' to deal with." Bill abruptly turned to face Lincoln and he asked, and the edge of his temper was really beginning to show, "What's the matter with you – that's the 'Cape' in there, strewn with rocks – don't you care?"

They rested; both beside the mast and each hanging onto a shroud; and after a moment of pregnant silence, Lincoln asked, "You think he needs a hint, do you?"

"I just think it's safer out, that's all," was Bill's surly reply. "Why risk it?"

Lincoln caught Helmut's eye and signalled for him and Nick to wait – they were about ready to feed up the new headsail.

Nick left Helmut to it and joined them at the mast, "Party, is it?" he asked, and Lincoln's immediate, fleeting thought of 'cheeky little sod' was gone before it had even crystallised.

"No, Nick, do me a favour, would you," he requested. "Wind in the headsail once we've tensioned – starboard winch, Bill'll tail. Gary and I'll take care of the hoist, okay?"

He was indignant, was Nick, and with good reason, "I know what bloody winch to use!" Nick sensed something was going off – he looked from Lincoln to Bill slowly and questioningly. "He'll have to gybe her back again, then?" He turned to look back at Brian. Bill grinned, pushed a puzzled Nick. "Come on." He turned to Lincoln as he began to move off. "You're a crafty bastard, Chris."

Potter, minding the trysail, standing in the cockpit, raised his eyebrows – he'd not missed the point nor misunderstood the direction of Lincoln's nod and look. Brian Ramsey grinning behind him hadn't either, and he was, fortunately, not one to take unnecessary offence. 'Gybe-ho' was just audible above the wind.

*   *   *

"Chris?"

"Brian?" Lincoln yelled back, mimicking his voice.

He ignored Lincoln's ill-mannered pettiness, and rightly so. Lincoln couldn't believe that he had answered in such a rude, humourless, infantile manner. He himself detested being answered in that way, and it annoyed him intensely when somebody, instead of answering properly, parroted their name back to them in the same belittling, pantomiming tone. Fortunately, Ramsey was mature enough and ignored his, Lincoln's, offensive and ignorant rejoinder. "I can't believe it," he bellowed, "the difference, it's a pleasure just to be able to talk, isn't it?"

Talk? Lincoln smiled to himself, they'd need new ears!

He was right though, Lincoln allowed, and it was always a shock: the contrast between beating and running.

They had been too tired or busy to notice, it had been dead on the nose the night before and the wind since had slowly and imperceptibly backed through the hours of darkness – it had been a little aft of the beam off Maatsuyker – and now, now they just about had a following wind! In truth, despite Bill's reservations, or insistence rather, they could have gybed should they have needed to, which they didn't, at anytime once under way, hence Brian's tact and lack of concern. Nervousness, shock, fear, all showed up in different ways in different people, and Bill, Lincoln appreciated, had still not come to terms with it yet: that it was over. Bill was still dealing with his own particular brand of demons!

'Into' the wind, boat speed and actual wind speed combined against a sail boat: as the breeze in a cyclist's face when peddling into the wind on his bicycle. Conversely, 'with' the wind, the wind took away the boat speed from actual wind speed: it blew a sail boat along. The most obvious example: should boat speed and wind velocity coincidentally and exactly match, then the illusion was that of standing still – as that same cyclist being blown along by the wind!

Ramsey shouted again, "Have you noticed how the sea is flattening off?"

"Almost as if it's turned, Brian," Lincoln observed, "not wind-over-tide anymore. I reckon it'll flatten off even more as the wind dies and the 'stream' gets a grip – that's assuming there is one, of course."

The waves, or rather, rollers, were still huge, but were now domed rather than broken. The same principle applied: wind and sea not fighting and both going, blowing and flowing in the same direction. Lincoln had been below when the rain had stopped and that fact had only just . . . really registered.

"Anybody's guess," commented Brian, he was referring to

the tidal stream. After a moment he asked, "Do you believe that's it, Chris, do you really believe it's over?"

"I'd put money on it, Brian," Lincoln replied, "I reckon the wind'll veer as the 'low' moves east, and then it'll shift a touch north with a bit of luck. The 'high' in the 'Bight' will probably become predominate, which'll bring balmy breezes from the southwest. You'll have to gybe her before then, of course, and gybe back eventually again – when we close the coast."

Ramsey nodded and leant closer. "That's what Bill was whinging on about, was it – had a cold sweat on, did he . . . It was about us jibing her, or rather, not jibing her, wasn't it?"

It wasn't really a question and it was his only comment on the subject – and not daft, Brian, Lincoln acknowledged, he'd read between the lines and he certainly knew Bill Corsham far better than he did – he was a good skipper.

And then he was yelling again and repeating his previous question, "We've survived it then?"

Lincoln smiled. "Yes."

He waited a minute and then held out his hand. "Thanks."

And so they shook hands and to hide and cover his embarrassment, Lincoln pointed. "You can ease the backstay," he said shortly, and after swallowing. "I'll get Nick to release the babystay too."

Ramsey's only reaction was to grin, and neither of them moved – and it was he, Ramsey again, who broke the silence eventually, "Would you organise immediate watches, Chris, we all appreciated the meal, but now you've got to go to bed – it wouldn't do for us both to be below at the same time." Ramsey paused for a moment. "I'm pretty 'stuffed'."

Lincoln indicated with a downward nod. "I'll sort out Warren first, yes."

Ramsey looked; he shook his head. Potter was standing, unaware, in the mess: brown footprints tracked around the bottom of the cockpit!

Lionel turned; Lincoln tapping on his shoulder distracted his attention from forward, his eyes following Lincoln's arched, downward, finger movement. "Stay where you are, Lionel, and I'll be back in a minute and then I'll give you a hand, you'll tread it everywhere otherwise."

Nick sat on the coach roof between the sheet winches; Lincoln climbed round. "You're off watch, Nick, time for bed, okay?" He pointed. "Don't tread in it – drop down the hatch from here."

Nick rolled onto his side, pulled himself forward and peered over and then sat again. "Is that?"

"Yes," Lincoln replied, nodding.

His eyes closed for a moment and his lips pursed, then, "Helmut? You and Helmut . . .? No. I'm in better condition than either of you . . . I can help?"

"Nick . . . you're off watch – below, now . . . Go on."

Nick was genuinely angry. "No, you're not my father. I'm a man," there was desperation in his face, "not a child."

Lincoln hadn't an argument with that. "I'm fully aware of that, Nick." Their eyes held. "I'd sail anywhere with you, at anytime." Lincoln sighed and gave in. "I'll pass you a bucket from below; would you sluice down the cockpit, and then help Lionel with his boots? Use the deck broom if you have to – it's not the nicest of jobs. Oh, you wouldn't release the babystay first, would you?" Lincoln stopped him. "Be tactful, Nick, ignore Warren – right?"

Nick looked away and he raised a finger to the corner of one eye, and then turned back, and not bothering to hide his emotion, quietly agreed. "I'll do that."

*   *   *

Lionel had put on the lid; the burners under saucepan and kettle were on simmer. Not good housekeeping, leaving them unattended – and not like him.

Nick quietly descended the companionway steps. "I've done that – here's the bucket. It's clean; I've scrubbed and disinfected it."

He looked tired. "Thanks, Nick, bed now." Lincoln pushed on, not letting him interrupt, "Come on, don't look like that, think about it, if we don't start watches now we're all going to fall-over – it's going to be a bloody long night for all of us."

Even then, he didn't give up. "You're not going, are you, and nor is Helmut; if anyone, it's you who hasn't slept?"

He looked away, now was not the time for harsh words. "I will," Lincoln assured him, "after we've cleaned up Warren. Sh . . . ush. Listen . . . Don't you see, Nick, you're too close to his age, it'll be the last straw for him were you, or Sharon, to be around, yes?"

Nick thought about that – Lincoln didn't doubt.

"Does it matter which bunk?" he asked.

"No."

"You'll call me if . . .?"

"Yes," Lincoln said, "I won't hesitate."

"Good night then."

"Good night, Nick."

*　　　　　　　*　　　　　　*

A bucket of warm water, plus washing-up liquid, Lincoln passed to Helmut; and Warren, the poor little 'sod', just stood there, goose-pimpled and teeth chattering. It was impossible for Lincoln not to but notice that his genitals were in-drawn, and his scrotum was drum-tight under a stumped, blue-tipped penis. Warren, like a very, very young child getting undressed for a bath, was bare up to the waist and wearing only a rippling, fluttering vest!

Helmut nodded. "I'm going to need another, Chris."

"I can see," Lincoln said, "I'll put on a reserve after that, as well, okay."

Gary climbed across and round and down. Lincoln stopped him. "No, bed now, Gary, you can't help here – are your boots clean?"

"Yes," he answered shortly.

Hot water from the kettle Lincoln put into another saucepan, Gary stood by the chart table watching. "Don't say it, Gary."

"Say what?" he asked with pretended nonchalance – fooling nobody.

"Don't cast the first stone, judge not, all that."

"Yeah, but, Christ . . ."

"Go to bed, Gary, it's going to be a long night." Lincoln took a deep breath, why he had to explain . . . "In yesteryear he'd probably have been the only survivor: the only one who'd have had sense enough to run away and hide from the sabre-tooth – get it?"

Gary was silent for a moment and then he sighed. "Can I help there?"

Lincoln nodded, acknowledging his generosity of spirit. "Bed." He indicated with a thumb and added gently, "Off you go now."

"Any bunk," he asked.

"Yes, it doesn't matter."

The bucket Lincoln refilled and offered from the top the steps. "Want more washing-up liquid in it, Helmut?" he enquired.

"No, Chris, I can manage vithout now," he took the proffered bucket, "I vill never be able to vash the remainder of the soap residue off othervise." Helmut dried his hands on the towel and with that felt for, produced, and then opened his clasp knife, and without hesitation cut away Warren's vest. God, Lincoln confirmed in his mind yet again, he was competent, this man, and a couple of levels up above the rest of them, both morally and in kindliness – the vest's hem was soiled – and taking it off over his head would of spread the 'cack' further.

Helmut washed him as a baby, both hands soaped and massaging in and around every crevice: working up a mud-hued lather – deft but firm. There wasn't a ha'p'orth of him, Warren; thin, hairless, narrow rounded shoulders – huddled and shivering.

He still completely bewildered Lincoln . . . What he was doing on an ocean racer God only knew . . . Bloody Brian had some explaining to do, his, Warren's, was not a body that would stand the cold, little wonder he was at rock bottom. What had he, Warren, been thinking of: wandering around without thermal underwear nor lined second layer was verging on criminal . . . No, it was verging on the side of suicide and, and . . . incomprehensible!

The kitchen towel would have to do, Helmut took it with the next refill – it would carry a goodly amount of water and was, in the circumstances, the quickest way Lincoln could think of to wash off the remainder of the soap.

Lionel climbed down and indicated. "His underwear's on the top of the chart table, matie."

"Your boots clean, Potter?" Lincoln demanded roughly. "I've washed this floor, you know; they're no bloody good either." He pushed his offerings aside. "He needs thermals." He ranted on, "What the hell was he doing, Lionel, wandering around in ordinary underwear, that is absolute bloody lunacy. Bloody Ramsey should have checked . . ." And that set Lincoln thinking: no, that wasn't fair . . . Well, yes it was, but he was equally guilty and to blame too, of course, because he hadn't bothered to check either! And yet, who would have expected someone to come so woefully and inadequately dressed on a trip like this! And what about the race down – had he sailed all that way, in those conditions! And another thought quickly rode on the back of that one: he must have been dressed like that through the storm! Christ, it didn't bare thinking about.

Lincoln voiced those thoughts, "It's our faults, you know, Lionel, we should have checked." He then asked quietly, thinking it through at the same time, "If he was dressed like that on the race down, Lionel . . . It's not as if he didn't know what he was in for, was it, coming back – do you see what I mean?"

He always had an answer, Lionel, "He probably wore two pair of everything, Pom. Listen, some people you just can't seem to help. At the end of the day every man has a responsibility to himself: to help himself. He's a 'wowser' anyway."

"No man is an island, and all that, Lionel." Lincoln abruptly pointed and curtly requested, "Would you fill and put the kettle on again, please." He felt aggressive and strangely defensive – both at the same time. "I'll have to bloody well lend him some of mine then, otherwise it'll keep me awake knowing." The trouble was, Lincoln admitted, there more an element of truth in what Lionel had said. "I've got a couple of spare sets . . . we'll need blankets, as well." Lionel read the signs and said hastily, "I'll take care of it, matie; you take care of the kettle." He went forward, not waiting for a reply.

Lincoln climbed to help – Helmut held one of his arms from above and Lincoln held Warren's other, and feeling for the steps, backed down – they managed!

"Come on, Warren, I've got you, it's over now – stand there." One blanket Lincoln wrapped round his waist, the other over his shoulders. He hissed threateningly, "Don't fight me, Warren, otherwise I'll punch your bloody lights out." Lincoln ordered, "Sit there, behind the chart table, on the edge – go on." Lincoln physically pushed him down, while asking in his mind for God to forgive him his harshness.

He couldn't drink it – his teeth were rattling so violently on the rim of the mug and his hand shaking – he spilling most down onto the blankets.

"Take your time," Lincoln said gently, still feeling a residue of shame, and took the mug from him. "you're safe now, the storm's over – gone away – finished." He turned to Potter, "Do you think that's very wise, Lionel?"

230

Never one to be reticent, Lionel, "Fuck 'em," he said, "different this, all he has to do is sleep – a drop of rum in his tea won't hurt him."

"Christ." Lincoln was watching him pour. "That's enough; he hasn't eaten since God knows when."

Lionel ignored Lincoln outburst; he indicated the chart table. "Had a rummage round in the old 'slop-chest' – those should do him."

Lionel placed one of his knees on the seat and braced his other, and in that position he fed Warren: one hand holding the cup and the other supporting Warren's neck and head.

Slop-chest? What bloody slop-chest? Lincoln didn't dare ask.

Lionel turned back to Lincoln eventually. "Right, matie, that's got that down him."

"We'll do the top first, Lionel – get the blanket off him and then move out of the way." He looked to Warren. "Right, raise your arms, Warren, come on, the quicker we get you dressed the quicker we can get you to bed – you'll soon get warm tucked up in there."

"Chris?" Lionel pointed. "His feet." And with that he continued on conversationally, "It really amazes me . . ." Lionel inspected more closely – he ignored Warren, and Warren's feelings! "How could it have gotten down there, do you think – how the hell did it get in from outside on his boots, as well – do you know what I mean?"

"Lionel!"

"Sorry."

"Get the bucket", Lincoln ordered, his patience really was wearing thin. Sorry Lionel wasn't, and it was only when Lincoln looked at him directly did he realise that Lionel had been winding him up, "and fill it from the kettle," Lincoln yelled after him, "whatever's bloody-well left – and bring the washing-up liquid that Helmut used – and a sailbag for him to stand on after, please?" He apologised to Warren, "Just wait, Warren, won't be a minute, I've just got to wash your toes and then we'll be finished."

Lionel hadn't finished though, he had silently returned, handed Lincoln his requested items and after a few minutes he observed from behind Lincoln, "Like what's 'is name washing what's 'is name's feet – Last Supper, an' all that."

"For Christ's sake, Lionel, help or go."

"That's him – I knew it began with a 'C'."

From Warren, Lincoln noted, an upward pucker in the creases, where they terminated around the edges of his blue, shivering lips, that was all – something at least, there was hope for him yet.

Warren was quite placid, like an automaton obeying instructions. Lincoln threaded one leg of his underpants, long johns, track pants onto one lifted leg and then threaded them onto the other – they got there eventually. "Stand up and we'll pull 'em right up, Warren." Lincoln commanded, after placing and positioning the sailbag.

"How is he, is he varmer?" The companionway steps groaned under Helmut's weight. "Ah, you have found my skiing top, I see, that is good, it is very varm." Potter, wisely, kept himself busy at the sink and didn't look round.

"Would you help me wheel him down to a bunk, Helmut," Lincoln asked. "Um, try to keep his feet out of it, I've still got to dry them – the carpet's . . . Well, you know . . . We'll put him in the pilot birth forwards," he directed, "it'll be quieter there and he won't be disturbed."

Helmut gently edged him, Lincoln, out of the way . . . Lionel and Lincoln watched him – it was one hell of a feat in a seaway – Helmut, with a hand under each armpit and at a fast walk, with Warren in front, dangling, carried him through. Lionel and Lincoln, after one quick, all-telling, silent look at each other, followed.

"Socks." Lionel passed them to Lincoln. "That's him." Lincoln pushed Warren's feet under the piled blankets – he was already asleep. He commented, more to himself than to present company. "Well, we'll not see him for a while."

Helmut hadn't finished with Lincoln yet though. "You and I are to go to bed also," he said with finality. Then in a softer tone, he had caught his, Lincoln's, look. "I am sorry, Chris, the skipper has ordered and I must obey him, he is the captain, you know."

"What, together, Helmut?" Lincoln asked.

"Vot . . .? Ah, a joke, ja." Not a glimmer of a smile, he continued on, "I must insist, if necessary, Brian said. The old guard, the old school can manage, ve have three hours. Brian, Bill and Lionel – the three 'muskets'."

"Musketeers, Helmut," Lincoln absently corrected him, "a musket's an old-fashioned rifle. What about Warren's gear," he asked. "What've you done with it?"

Helmut repeated the word. "Musketeer; ve threw them," and their disposal of, he emphasised with a flicking hand movement.

"Not overboard." Lincoln asked, shocked, "not his boots and over-trousers as well, Helmut, surely – bloody hell."

"No, ve have them," Helmut somewhat smugly replied, "they are in the cockpit still – vhy?"

"To clean 'em off," Lincoln said briskly, and then thought about it and echoed those thoughts." "We'll have to wash off the boots and then swill 'em out with disinfectant – we can't do much else. We'll tow the trousers," he said brightly, "we'll pass a warp through each leg."

"Not you," said Helmut sternly, pushing Lincoln back. "One of them vill do it." There just a glimmer of a smirk on his face now. "Lionel vill do it, before he goes to bed, von't you, Lionel?"

Lionel, surprisingly, smiled at Helmut, and his placid, sublimely serene, cherubic face belied his mildly spoken words. "Go and fuck yourself, Helmut."

*   *   *

"Chris? Come on, wake up. Time to get up."

"Gently, Bill," Lincoln mumbled, "don't shake me, I feel very fragile – what's the time?"

"Sorry," Bill apologised, "five-thirty – seventeen-thirty hours in seamanlike terms." Bill was quickly brusque again, "Come on, either take this tea or move over."

"Got any aspirin?" Lincoln asked.

"Got a headache, slept too heavy, did you? Only Paracetamol."

"I don't know," Lincoln answered slowly, "I feel like a piece of board – I daren't move too quickly, something might fall off."

"Are you that bad," he asked, suddenly concerned. "Get over onto your side, get an elbow under," he advised, "you'll spill the lot otherwise." That was what Lincoln liked about Bill, no unnecessary 'ooing' and 'ahing'; the rough concern in his voice was nice ... comforting. "Christ, bloody-hell, can't you even do that; just a minute, there's some straws somewhere, do you . . ." There was real concern in Bill's voice now, "Would it be easier to drink through a straw?"

Lincoln's groan was involuntary. "Bill, you're a 'one-off'," he told him. "What would we do without you. No . . . right, I'll manage, thanks – Paracetamols then?"

They were interrupted, "Vot, Mister Mate, you are too vorn out – are you staying in bed vith tea and breakfast served like a king?"

"Morning . . . Um, evening, Helmut – sleep well?"

"Ja, vot is it, you are crook?" Helmut bent over the bunk.

". . . Christ, Helmut," Lincoln protested, "turn your head, your breath smells like a camel's arse."

"Ve have had no time to clean our teeth," he apologised, "sorry. It is bad?" He moved back.

Lincoln said it as casually as possible, "Going to need a hand here, Helmut, to get out of the bunk, I've stiffened up a bit."

His legs braced, upturned soles against the base of the bunk tier, and back against the mast – wedged. Lincoln seemed to remember that semblance of patient, stubborn repose – when Lionel and himself had volunteered him to wash Warren – only theirs had been pretended, and he wasn't one hundred percent sure that Helmut was pretending – poetic justice maybe! In that position Helmut contemplated. He enquired slowly, "How bad is it that you are damaged, not the 'toughie', but vot hurt truly? I vill not move you – the truth, ja?"

"I'll do it myself, then." Lincoln retorted.

Bill, using his no-nonsense voice, innocently entered the arena, "What's up, Helmut, they're waiting for you up top, you know."

Helmut snapped at him, "Don't tell me vot I have to do, Bill, I know my duty, all you have to do is mind your own business." He turned back to Lincoln. "No, you von't get up, I vant to know – no bullshit, here ve stay – the truth?"

Bill didn't pause for breath – and no recriminations. "Tell me, Helmut?

Helmut apologetic and in a conciliatory tone, did, "He is a bullshitter, Bill, I know him . . . ve know him, he vould not ask!"

"What do you mean, 'he wouldn't ask'?" queried Bill.

"He vants me to help him out of the bunk?"

He, Lincoln, apparently was the ship's cat and didn't come into the conversation!

Bill handed the packet across and was silent.

"Vot are they?" enquired Helmut suspiciously.

"Pain-killers," answered Bill.

Dear God, Lincoln lay back and sighed, it now a case of having to wait it out, they'd have to explain it all to Potter too.

The man in question pushed – bulldozed his way through without ceremony, as usual. "Come on you lot, super-crew's waiting to be relieved; out and at 'em, Pom." Not slow, Lionel, it only took him a moment. "What's up, matie?"

"Stiff, that's all, Lionel," resigning himself to the inevitable, "all I need is a hand up." A thought occurred – it could, and Lincoln grasped at that straw, also be used as a diversionary tactic, though feeble. "Brian hasn't been on the helm all this time, has he, Lionel, he was all ready dead on his feet when we came below?"

Potter was contemptuously dismissive, "Do we look like a set of morons, matie. And don't get too smart, Pom," he held up a warning finger, "and no smart cracks either, all right." Lionel lowered himself to his knees, hands on the bunk's side. "How serious?"

"You listen to me, Lionel . . ."

Lionel objected strenuously, "Not so hard, matie, that fucking-well hurts."

Lincoln let go of his arm. "Sorry, but I know my body, Lionel, I don't abuse it, I'll be all right once I'm moving." He came as close to begging as he could, the others wouldn't be able to see his face clearly in the half-light. "Please, Lionel?"

Lionel lent back, arms stiff, moving easily to *Worippa's* motion; he looked away and sighed. "How?"

"Get me round onto my stomach," Lincoln explained, relieved. "Lift me out of the bunk and onto the floor – I'll take it from there."

"You're fucking mad, Pom, do you know that." Potter shook his head, and then to Helmut, he ordered, "Get his legs, Helmut."

Helmut eased Potter out of the way, leant against the top bunk, back against bulkhead and got comfortable again. He folded his arms.

Lionel fronted, and Lincoln could almost see the cockerel's

comb rising on the top of his head, "Listen, Helmut, I'll only say it once; you square-headed, wooden-topped, thick-headed, German refugee." He put his face close to Helmut's. "Get out of the way."

The noise of *Worippa's* passage through the hull was distinct and gurgled in the silence.

Quietly, "I object to refugee, Lionel, I am a citizen – I have sworn my allegiance to your English Queen, and God."

Corsham first, in the background, and there they stood, God help him – three little schoolboys tittering.

Lincoln looked up in the silence and all three were looking down, and realised that he must have been away for a short moment.

"What?" he asked.

Lionel broke it, "Look, Helmut," and he nodded down at Lincoln, "we can't guard the little prick all the time, can we?"

It was his turn. "Not so much of the little," Lincoln said.

Lionel continued to ignore him. "He'll manage by himself eventually, won't he – really fuck himself up in the process, right, besides . . ." Potter looked from Helmut, then down to Lincoln again. "I believe him."

Helmut moved and stood before the bunk, he was a man not to waste words once the decision had been made – and by way of acceptance he said, "It vill be easier to lift you out of the bunk, then ve turn you over on the deck?"

Lincoln nodded agreement.

"I vill lift your top, Lionel vill lift your middle and," he indicated to Bill, "Bill your feet." He really was concerned. "You vill remember, Chris, if you have a spinal injury, bend your back, break the spinal nerves – you never valk again, ja?"

Potter, as usual, had the last word, "You're a cheerful fucker, Helmut, life and soul of the party, you are. If I, or Chris, thought he had a spinal injury we wouldn't be even trying to get him up, now would we. Here, put this sailbag down," he ordered, "the carpet's sopping, it belongs to the storm jib." Potter casually gave Bill a sarcastic backhander in passing, as only Potter could, "some lazy fucker hasn't bothered to repack it yet."

Then the usual performance, even if a variation: up onto his hands and knees first, and next shuffling around until in front of the mast, and thereon pulling himself upright, only this time he was helped by three willing pairs of hands. He turned finally and leaned his back hard against the mast for the final straightening.

"You all right, Pom?" a really concerned and worried Lionel enquired. "We're fucking mad, we should be calling in a helicopter to lift you out, I'd never forgive myself . . ."

"Lionel," Lincoln interrupted gently, Helmut and Bill were both silent during their exchange, but were watching closely, he could feel their eyes. "I told you, I know my body and I wouldn't put it at risk for you, or anybody else, be rest assured. I'm all right," He made another stab at lightening the atmosphere, albeit again feebly, "and besides, this is the only one I've got!"

Lionel just looked at him for a moment, finger to his lips, and then abruptly asked, "Ready for boots and oilies, or do it later?"

"Now, Lionel, let's get it over with, now."

"We'll have to change your socks as well, Pom," sighed Lionel, "seeings you've fucked up a perfectly good pair – they're soaking."

They got Lincoln into them, over-trousers, socks and boots: all done with his back against the mast and each arm supported – Bill was the baby-dresser.

That's it, matie," said Lionel finally. "How do you feel?"

Lincoln nodded to him, to Bill, then Helmut. "Fine, thanks – thanks a lot." Back still against the mast, he stepping sideways cautiously and thereupon waited for the pain to subside – and then circled once.

Some instinct made him look up, round and back again: three more pairs of eyes: Nick, top port and Sharon and Gary, both starboard. They'd not have noticed him, hopefully, flushing in the tenebrous shadow.

Lionel couldn't be avoided, he stood in his way, he gently asked, "How's it feel – everything working, matie?"

"Fine, Lionel," Lincoln replied.

Lionel exploded, "Liar then." He brushed Lincoln's lips. "You're a fucking idiot, and we're even bigger ones for helping you. Not lipstick, is it," he held out his hand, "this!"

Chapter 17

Gary, after they had ducked below for a quick warm-up, voiced his thoughts, "That view, Chris" He shook his head. "It reminds me," he said quietly, "of what I'd imagine South America would look like, from the Pacific Ocean side. You know, sailing up the coast from Cape Horn, and then the Andes before you, rising sheer out of the sea and their peaks shrouded in cloud."

Lincoln knew exactly what he meant, and like him he had also stood in awe and was not a little subdued and intimidated by the vast panorama that, even with their offing, had towered before them. "Some of those behind must be getting on for two, three, four thousand feet, Gary, more. I have to admit, I've never seen anything quite like it – its glacier country." Lincoln paused, just thinking. "It's too hostile for me, Gary – it's just a mountainous, rugged, barren, moonscaped wilderland. It's too . . . it's too forbidding. The loneliness and the isolation of the place, I don't know, like I said before, it makes me nervous."

Lincoln continued on slowly, remembering, "Do you know, your parallel might not be too far off the mark, I once read an account of Drake's voyage up the piece of coast you're talking about: it's called Patagonia. That's the country below Chile – it described," ignoring *Worippa's* hull, he pointed shorewards, "exactly that." He sighed. "A different breed of man, Gary, imagine him, Drake, or better still, imagine Abel Tasman: circumnavigating the worst seas and oceans of the world in a leaky, wooden boat – and his first landfall is here – it doesn't bear thinking about."

Gary's viewpoint was slightly different from his, Lincoln's, and there was a lot of bravadic enthusiasm underlying Gary's tone. "It's not barren, there's plenty in there, Chris, it's one of the most ancient, undisturbed pieces of land – piece's of real estate in the world. Most of it's never been explored, even now. Some of the forests in the interior and on the hinterland are the oldest in the world, and the trees are the oldest trees known to man. The bulk of it, the majority's undisturbed right to the edge of the sea, even the beaches – especially down here." There was now a certain relish in Gary's tone as he expounded, and there was also, Lincoln noticed, for all Gary's bravado, a certain amount of . . . Not fear exactly, well partly fear – partly fear mixed in with apprehension – and something else laced in with that too . . . something akin to a rabbit mesmerised by a snake.

"Prospectors used to disappear without a trace: experienced men. You'd disappear just the same today, despite the helicopters; a search'd never find you. Tasmania's getting a world reputation for its ecology and bush walking; you wouldn't dare go in without a guide, you'd get yourself lost within the hour."

They were both silent then – and standing and unconsciously and gently swaying in time with *Worippa* – and contemplating that thought. It was Lincoln who broke the silence; he leant around Gary and indicated on the chart. "I see I've missed Port Davey, what's Port Davey like, Gary, you ever been in?"

Gary, after he'd turned to look at what Lincoln had pointed to, pursed his lips. "We both missed Window Pane Bay too. I particularly wanted to see that, for one reason or another I've missed it every time, the 'pilot' describes it as remarkable. You know how dry those tomes are, if they say it's worth seeing then it'll be something else!" He explained, "The rock there has been split over aeons, which has exposed the mica within: the massifs apparently look like windowpanes when caught in a certain light from the sea." Gary tutted, presumably over the lost opportunity. "No, I haven't been into Port Davey, we tried once but there was too big a sea running, and I wasn't too sorry at the time." Lincoln had to remind himself that he could be quite canny, could Gary. "You have to be a special kind of person to wander around in there, like you, I feel very uncomfortable and yet fascinated at the same time." He quickly went on, "Lionel's been in, years ago: there's a huge waterway in there, deep water and protected, it extends for miles; it'd take you weeks to explore it. It's never been settled either, apart from the aborigines, that is, and there's still evidence of their occupation here and there, by the way. They used to roam up and down this coast; you mentioned Tasman, Tasman was supposed to have seen their campfires on his way south – but for some reason he never landed." No, Lincoln thought, he was probably put off by the forbidding air of the place – just like him! "They, the aborigines I mean, they no longer exist, of course – genocide. We killed the whole lot of them off in double-quick time. A black stain on our nation's soul, and no pun intended – ethnic cleansed in eighty-five years." There was that certain satisfied relish again in Gary's voice that Lincoln again couldn't help but notice. "A bit of timbering in the early days, and whaling here for a while till they ran out of whales. A bit of mining, tin mostly, long since closed, and that's it."

Gary brooded and seemed suddenly pensive; happily and much to Lincoln's relief, he perked up again after a moment. "Rumour has it that there's supposed to be one family living in there still – we don't know for sure. But what I do know is that it's an ornithologist's paradise: parrots, rosellas, cockatoos, robins, wrens, honeyeaters; a lot of them and other stuff are peculiar only to this part of the world . . . to this country. Duck, geese, swan, teal – all the water birds." Gary swept his arm around. "Every seabird imaginable, of course – huge colonies of everything."

They were silent, picturing and seeing the world that Gary had conjured up.

It was Gary who broke the silence this time. "Brian's said he'll probably give the race a miss next year, sail down with the fleet, peel off and take a look at Macquarie Harbour and Port Davey instead. He will too, Chris, that's if we survive this and it hasn't put him off permanently!" He asked pointedly, "Would you be interested?"

Lincoln didn't hesitate: "I certainly would, Gary, it'd be quite different once you were in there, and from what you've said, there'll be plenty of natural anchorages and protected water. We've an in-built prejudice at the moment; it's difficult for us to picture anywhere safe in this part of the world." That thought jogged Lincoln's memory concerning another subject, and he asked, "Talking about safety, Gary, Low Rocky Point, according to the chart, there's a light on it, do you know it?"

Gary nodded and picked up the dividers. "We alter course when it's off our beam, it'll be about at the end of our watch, three-forty degrees true." He indicated. "Smack bang on the forty-third parallel; our present course should give us an offing of five miles. To answer your question, there's not much to see – it's just an unmanned light on a square, metal framework tower . . . No, that's Port Davey . . . " He was silent for a moment, and then explained, "I tend to get them mixed up, it's one of the new one's; Low Rocky Point, it's a stubby, white

240

fibreglass, space-age affair with solar panels down one side. Hmm, that's right; they replaced the metal one some years back. Port Davey's probably been converted by now, as well." It always, for some reason, surprised Lincoln, concerning the depth and extent of Gary's local knowledge, and just how brim-full of relevant and irrelevant bits and pieces he was. "Not in time to help the *Brier Holme* though, she went down with a bang just after the turn of the century, literally." He smiled. "She hit a reef inshore near here and exploded – her holds were full of dynamite."

And after importing that intriguing piece of trivia, Gary turned to the chart again and traced with a finger. "The next light on is Cape Sorell." He looked up. "Remember that one, the lighthouse that we thought was another yacht – remember? It looked just like a white sail for a while? We'll never get in there in this though; we'll never get across the bar."

Lincoln nodded. "I remember, the entrance to Macquarie Harbour is around the back, you could see the first leading mark."

"That's right," said Gary. "I'll radio in our 'sched' to there, I imagine that the Harbour Master, Tidal Officer, Port Officer, or whoever'll be waiting for our call – it's an obvious choice. They should be in range after Hibbs."

Lincoln had to end their conversation abruptly. "God, I'll have to go topside again, Gary, this motion's bloody awful – she's not happy, is she, and I'm starting to feel queasy." A thought occurred. "Oh, while we're on the subject, is there anybody on Maatsuyker still – a light keeper – you never actually said?"

Surprise, surprise, thought Lincoln, as Gary nodded. "Yes, there is, though it must be one of the last, that and Bruny. It's a rearguard action, Chris, Maatsuyker's really a weather station now – it's only pressure from the aero clubs, divers and local fishing communities, they are insisting that it should remain manned. You've seen how quickly it can turn along this coast, someone or other phones them at least once a day – for sea-state and all that – so it is used. Actually, the light side is already fully automatic, but even so, there are still two families on there. They service the power plant, do all the maintenance and meteorology, although that side's just about fully automatic now too, the meteorology, I mean – old habits, I suppose."

Lincoln swallowed bile and let Gary ramble, the sort of information that he had at his fingertips you couldn't find in books – his seasickness would have to wait. "There used to be four families on there at one time, on rotating shifts; everything was supplied from the mainland by boat. They were often isolated for weeks at a time and they ran out of essentials more than once, by all accounts – they're supplied exclusively by helicopter now." Gary took a breath before adding almost irrelevantly, "The light was built in the late eighteen hundreds, it's built of brick and has cavity walls; all those, the bricks and everything else were also brought in by boat." Gary gesticulated. "Imagine the problems, hauling those bricks and the rest up there – up that incline – the mind boggles."

*   *   *

Echoes of cold were beginning to seep in around the edges; Lincoln stood there, at the top of the companionway steps, half-in, half-out, looking around. Helmut signed 'hello' with a hand; and Lincoln couldn't help but notice: he was sawing the helm. The wheel was moving too far and too often – he was compensating much too much. Nick grinned; he was not holding onto the sheet now, but simply sitting next to the winch and ready to adjust should it be necessary.

Worippa's motion was exaggerated: she was rolling far too much: she was heeling over on her beam when lifting to the long steep swell, and her toe rail was only just clear of the water at the end of that heel. She hesitated at that point, before coming upright, and she hesitated again on the peak, before continuing her arc. She, once again, was halting at the same, opposite inclination towards and at the bottom, before coming upright again. Lincoln felt for her, *Worippa* really wasn't at all happy: the sails where tending to slat in the lop – five and a half knots and way under-powered. They might as well get it over with, while the light still held: to finally hand the trysail and set the mainsail. For whatever reasons, and up until now, and Lincoln suspected he knew those reasons, there had been a unanimous, unconscious consensus not to take down the trysail – it was time to now.

They were silent, Nick finally asked, "You'll be wanting the mainsail back up then?"

"Yes."

After a moment he admitted, "We knew."

"I know you did," Lincoln replied. "The point is, I guess, that that was then and this is now – the storm's gone." He sighed, "We have to push ourselves, Nick, and I should know better than anyone, it's all psychological – we're all still living it. The silly thing is, we're making life unbearable for ourselves, the motion's awful and, more to the point, *Worippa's* suffering." Lincoln looked up as a fresh thought forced its way into consciousness. "More to the point and I've only just realised – so is poor *Worippa's* mast!"

Gary and Nick climbed out of the cockpit trailing safetylines, Helmut beckoned and half-climbed around while holding the wheel with only one hand. Lincoln didn't argue because there was no question of his helping, his ribs and leg would never take the strain – and he and Helmut both knew it.

None of the three musketeers appeared, which said something to Lincoln about their exhaustion: almost head to wind, *Worippa's* sickening motion must have been just about tipping them out of their bunks! Lincoln took a firmer grip on the wheel: 'one hand for the ship' was relevant now, otherwise broken limbs and lost teeth were going to be the order of the day.

Handing the trysail and bundling it below hadn't been a problem. Untying the reefing ties had been fine until Nick came to the last one, and only then did Lincoln realise and admit that they should, with hindsight, have perhaps left everything on: tackles, downhaul and mainsail sheet – and all bar-tight. Nick's present chore was unintentionally comical and looked to Lincoln for the entire world as if he was gamely trying to ride a bronco while trying to undo that final tie at the clew end – on the boom end. Nick was being flung and jerked around like a rag doll, or more appropriately, and Lincoln's mind conjured up an unbidden picture of a colourfully dressed monkey on the end of a stick: airborne a lot of the time and legs flying! Lincoln quashed an upwelling urge to laugh. To divert his mind he focused on Helmut as he also watched helplessly: he, Helmut, had anticipated and had just started to haul up the main prior to also realising that there was a problem – and despite Gary's heroic efforts at containment – the wind had done the rest! At least Helmut had had the sense, Lincoln acknowledged, to secure the halyard before coming round to help. The trouble was that at the same time, while he and Gary were trying to contain the rest of the loosened, wind-tormented, half-slabbed canvas, they were also having trouble with keeping their footing. To hide his face and hiccupping convulsions of perfidious humour, Lincoln bridged his brows with the edge of his hand as if to shield his eyes from the sun, and tipped his head down to look at the wheel, only to glance up again, after barely containing his imprudent treacherous mirth, to see that the boom was still surging back and forth horizontally, according both to and in time with *Worippa's* general angle of heel. This in itself wouldn't have been too bad but for the erratic, incidental and unpredictable lurches interspersed and in-between the general pattern! Their, Helmut's and Gary's, forced stumbling back and forth run could be also likened, in his mind, to the handlers of an uncooperative horse taking its novices from the pony-club with it, as it objected and danced sideways and back! The mouthed curses were not hard to interpret: something beginning with 'f', he believed! Nick would kill him – they'd all kill him! Dealing with that sail was like dealing with a wild animal, no sooner had they trapped one piece of *Worippa's* untamed mains'l then the wind caught, jolted, and released another. It was, and Lincoln's imagination again supplied an involuntary erroneous metaphor: like a corpse that wouldn't lie down: push down the head and the feet came up, push down the feet and the head came up . . . and what, with Nick's antics too – to Lincoln, in his present mood, it was hysterical!

The bugle sounded eventually and spoiled the fun, the cavalry had appeared once again – Sharon climbed out of the companionway, and she made the difference, she helped Gary try and hold and try and contain the unencumbered beast. Helmut, meanwhile, had stepped aft, he dropped to his knees once there and winched in the slack in the mainsail sheet – the slack that had allowed the boom an amount of freedom of movement, and that, as Lincoln well knew, had been the cause of all their problems. That done, Helmut quickly stood, stepped, leant around and actually cut away the offending reefing tie. Glowering faces and accusations flew every whichway – that before they turned as one and then vented their full spleen on him!

Helmut hesitated before returning to the mainsail halyard and completing the hoist, and called, "How many reefs do you vant out?"

Lincoln held up one finger.

After releasing the cringle at the tack on the mainsail and reefing line, re-hoisting went, despite energetic bids for freedom and some more indelicate language, comparatively smoothly. After familiarising themselves with all and setting the mainsail to their satisfaction, and settling down the boat generally – finally they turned again, as one, and, again, more harsh words were spoken!

*   *   *

Sharon had, after a small delay while commiserating with Nick and Helmut and talking with Gary, followed Lincoln below. Lincoln stood at the sink, and, in truth, he was not really doing anything, just taking five minutes. Despite the open main hatch and the armoured glass hatches inset into the deckheads, semi-darkness always prevailed below – like the opening of and inside a prehistoric cave – all half-light and shadow.

Sharon leant against the edge of the saloon entrance bulkhead, letting her eyes adjust, presumably, and contemplating Lincoln – Lincoln could feel her stare.

She ventured finally, quietly and conversationally, "You can be a real, tactless bastard, can't you?"

"Did the trick, didn't it." Lincoln glanced at her. "Feel her: she's comfortable, or as comfortable as she's going to be anyway."

"They would have killed you, you know." Sharon shook her head. "When you gave that little wave. Helmut . . . God, Helmut was furious."

"He'll be more furious when he realises that I was at it," Lincoln said.

Sharon was piqued. "At what?"

"Never mind," he replied.

"He sent you below, didn't he?" Sharon looked smug about it.

Lincoln put on his all-wise, superior face. "I like my head where it is, thank you, on my shoulders."

Sharon raised an eyebrow and asked with relentless, blatant, pretended innocence, "Pity he fell over, wasn't it?"

"You going to help, Sharon," Lincoln asked, "or are you going to stand there sucking blood – kill chickens for entertainment, do you?" Lincoln hurried on, quickly changing the subject – when it came to repartee, she was at least two levels above him. "What're you doing up and about, anyway?"

"I don't know," Sharon gave him a knowing look. "You're bloody rude, do you know that." She then let him off the hook, for which he was thankful – she stepped across and leant close. "What exactly are you doing?"

"The hardest lesson to learn when out here, in these conditions, is to eat," Lincoln said, "and eat well – I feel like a broken record. The only substitute for lack of sleep, serious lack, I mean, is food with guts in it – Mum's special stew." He pointed. "Meat's cut-up and in, would you chop up the carrots and onions, do you mind? It should be ready for the change of watch with a bit of luck."

"Two saucepans?" asked Sharon.

Lincoln affirmed "Yes, equally into each – there'll be eight, maybe nine of us . . ." He explained, "What we'll do is add to it – top it up – and then keep it going. Two stock cubes crumbled into each, right, bring to the boil then simmer – throw everything in." He pointed. "That's the potatoes, already peeled, chip 'em over the pan and drop them straight in too. Don't bother peeling the carrots, just dice them."

"Yes, 'sir'." She actually saluted.

Lincoln ignored her sarcasm and pointed again. "There's wine in that top locker, in the rack, a good cupful in each saucepan – and don't be shy, pour it in"

"Chris?"

Something in her tone made Lincoln look.

"There's blood on your chin." She was silent for a moment, then, "Just how bad are you, you never say a word?"

Lincoln looked away. "Split lip, that's all."

She grabbed his arm, rose onto tiptoes and kissed his cheek. "Lionel says you're a schizophrenic: a cross between a pussycat and a tiger."

"Oh, does he." Lincoln looked at her. "And talking about pussy's, Sharon, stop waggling your arse, you're wasting your time – Gary'll catch you, sooner or later."

That pretended blatant innocence again. "I don't know what you mean."

"Don't you?"

Lincoln sighed: everybody had to have the last word; she turned on the steps. "I hope it hurts – you'd let 'The Doctor' look at it though, wouldn't you."

The minute pause at the top of the companionway before exiting took the sting out of her words: her bent over and taut bottom defiantly and perkily wagged from side to side – just once – but heavily accented!

A cruel, pleasant reminder though: all through the storm her face had appeared in Lincoln's mind's eye, the doctor's presence felt, they were inseparably linked.   Her grandfather, James Montrose, had hinted as much: all their women had always been medical, he'd said, and Elizabeth the brightest – there'd been a respect in his voice when he'd talked of her ... awe even, almost fear. Medieval England, especially Scotland, almost without exception, had a local village soothsayer, wise-woman, midwife, medic, curer of all ills. Knowledge had been passed from mother to daughter, over generations. Their power had eventually been broken by a jealous church – and many had been burnt as witches. Her lips, Elizabeth's lips, creased into a smile, which was followed by a gentle nod.

Hygrometer, thermometer, barometer and ticking clock slowly came into focus. Sitting behind the chart table and with no memory of moving away from the cooker – tiredness and lack of food. Hallucinating, he'd done it before, he recalled ... off of Southern Ireland: off of Waterford in St George's Channel: Mother and he had chatted for an hour. Anybody who knew his mother would verify that she was a bloody witch, a dragon, anyway.   Lincoln half-smiled to himself: he would be second only to his father in the race – to light the faggots under her – she could irritate! It'd been his first and only solo voyage – single-handed sailing and vivid imagination, he'd found to his cost, were not good seagoing companions. That combination being too dangerous an affliction, the trouble was, of course, that a person, especially a lone sailor, could hallucinate himself straight off the back of the boat because acquired imaginary company often wasn't, nor needn't be, necessarily friendly!

Peas, baked beans, sweet corn, dried garlic, and a touch of curry powder – Lincoln put it all in – and finally, dried potato powder. Dried potato powder thickened it beautifully; it was going to be a fine cawl. Lincoln's brain started again: cawl, a name direct from fireside cookery: pot-au-feu, potee, hotchpot. An iron pot hanging from a tripod ... Macbeth – 'witch's brew'!

Running lights – where that thought surfaced from Lincoln didn't know – they should be on. There'd be a bigger drain on the batteries now: three bulbs instead of one: port, starboard and stern light. They would miss that masthead light, he knew, apart from only burning a single bulb, unlike the running lights, it could always be seen above the waves! Lincoln switched off the now defunct instrument lights – compensate and conserve – every little bit would help.

Low Rocky Point was off their beam and its light was quite distinct in the early dusk.

"What's up?" asked Nick, he was still easily recognisable in the fading light at the rear of the cockpit.

"I was just going to check the running lights, Nick," Lincoln explained.

"I'll go," he volunteered.

Lincoln grabbed him as he began to climb past. "Not without a harness, you won't – it's getting dark."

Nick held out his formerly obscured safetyline, which Lincoln hadn't seen, for inspection.

"Sorry." Lincoln apologised. In for a penny, he thought, no point in putting it off, "Could you stand an extra hour on watch, Nick, do you think?" His face told of his disappointment. Lincoln covered quickly, "I know, I know, but . . . But . . . If we delay an hour it'll establish four-hour watches, three hours just isn't practical – it just isn't long enough." He explained his thinking, "Don't forget, we delayed their getting to bed, or should I say, I delayed them because they had to get me up – my fault, I know." He hurried on, "Dinner won't be ready for three-quarters anyway, it'd be wiser to wait, if you can?"

Nick nodded consent and then went forward, neither Helmut nor Gary objected.

"Ven do we alter course, Gary?" asked Helmut from behind the wheel.

"Now," answered Gary. "Go to three twenty-five magnetic, Helmut."

Lincoln interrupted, "Hold on, Gary, hold on. We're going to have to gybe her."

"No," he answered without hesitation, "the wind's been veering all the time, it'll just about cancel out, it's very nearly due south."

Helmut heard the confidence in his voice too, and Gary was not often wrong where theory and figures were concerned, in that area they all took a backseat. Helmut eased them off the wind. *Worippa* objected straight away, definitely not happy and up to her old tricks, yawing and sloughing like an old drunk.

Nick climbed back down into the cockpit. "Thanks very much, couldn't you have waited two minutes?"

Helmut shook and hung his head, a picture of dejection . . . but it was not quite convincing somehow – each quick furtive peep from under inclined brows gave him away. Lincoln shook his head: an actor he would never be.

Not slow, Nick, he read the signs more quickly than any of them and he really let fly, "You should be bloody sorry too, you big 'wuss', you nearly had me over the side." As an aside he said to Lincoln, "The lights are working." He then slid along the seat and kicked out at Helmut. "I feel better now." He turned and Lincoln could just discern his wink before he kicked out again.

Helmut was behind the protection of the wheel, Lincoln saw, and only had to step sideways to be well out of range. Nevertheless, Helmut looked up, with spaniel's eyes. Nick gave him another vigorous feigned kick for his pains. For Lincoln it was priceless to watch: Helmut's bottom lip pulled back, upper front teeth sucking onto it; he leant out and kicked back tentatively.

"Right, you fucker," Nick yelled, loving it, and with that span around on his bottom and onto his back – his legs bicycled in the air as he pulled himself further and closer along. He froze for a moment in mid-motion. "You've asked for it," he leaned up on an elbow and pointed a finger, "and now this is . . . it!"

Helmut could only hold out and flap a protective arm; to see someone laugh like that was a joy. The likes of Nick he had never met and it was obvious to Lincoln that he simply had no idea of how to cope.

Lincoln waited until they'd more or less settled down again and then gave them the good news. "We'll have to shake out the third reef."

All of them moaned, they knew they had to do it – they were, Lincoln knew, just moaning for moaning's sake.

Nick pushed his head close to Lincoln's. "Laugh this time, Pom," he threatened, "just laugh when we're taking this reef out, that's all, and you'll be dead meat, right?" He pulled a finger across his throat. "Chop Suey."

"Nick . . ." Lincoln hung his head, as had Helmut, not daring to look up. "Nick . . ."

He yelled, "Fuck me, you've started already."

"I haven't," Lincoln denied.

"You fucking-well have."

"No, honestly," Lincoln gasped out, "not the same, is it, anyway, all you have to do is pull it up."

Nick grinned and then shouted over Lincoln's shoulder and inadvertently into Lincoln's ear. "Come on then, 'Elmet, 'urry up; and try not to fall over this time, right."

Lincoln climbed round behind.

Helmut held onto the wheel for a moment, he asked, "Are you feeling sick, Chris – I suddenly am not very vell at all, I am now sweating."

"We'll eat after we've done this, ready or not, Helmut. Would you call Sharon up from below, make sure she locks the saucepans on, would you – she can tail, it'll be quicker." Lincoln took a closer look at him; he did look a little green round the edges. "Take a ticket out of Lionel's book," he advised sympathetically, and handed him a crumpled chocolate bar. "Force it down, Helmut, even if you gag on it. It's sugar, instant energy, carry a few provisions on you, like Lionel – don't get beyond it, don't let yourself get to that stage." Lincoln patted him on the arm. "Give it a couple of minutes to digest and try not to throw it back up – you'll be right then. All right?"

Helmut ignored Gary and Nick's yells and beckoning gestures; they were now just outlines vaguely visible at the mast – it was almost completely dark. His comment came unexpectedly out of the blue and Lincoln was unprepared. "Ve marry, Margaret and I, ve talked as friends . . . Ve are lovers, and friends. Can you understand vot I mean, Chris?"

The words that he had spoken were merely words; the wealth of meaning in his earnestness went, Lincoln instinctively sensed, world's deeper, almost to a telepathic level. "I know exactly what you mean, Helmut, was she with you during the storm?"

His silence spoke volumes to Lincoln, finally, "Since Hobart." He asked softly, "The doctor, she and you are in love, you love your vife also, ja, you have serious problems." Helmut constantly surprised him; his physique and strength beguiled a keen, astute and sensitive brain. He summed up, "Still, better to have loved – ja?"

No answer was required – nor expected!

*   *   *

"Is it done, Sharon?" Lincoln enquired.

"Damn, the bottoms of the pots have caught – just about, it'll be a bit on the raw side, but good enough."

"Let's dish up then," he said. "By the time we've all eaten the watch'll be over – it worked out just right, didn't it?"

Gary climbed down. "Can I help?"

"Yes, you're just in time, if you'd just give Sharon a hand, Gary, and then you can sit and eat, and while you're doing that, I'd better go and relieve Helmut before he collapses from hunger at the wheel. The kettle's on, by the way, would you wake up the other watch ten minutes before – you'll be a hero if you wake them with a cup of tea – is that okay?"

"You're sure you don't want me to take the wheel?"

"No, I can only stay down here for a short time, this motion gets to me, I'll be sick if I stay down here much longer."

Sharon gazed up at the deckhead and Lincoln couldn't help but notice and recognise that, now familiar, silly, annoying, supercilious expression on her face; she turned, sweetly, "A bit bilious are we?"

"Gary!"

"I know."

*   *   *

Not fair – Nick and Helmut ate topside – easier to look the other way. Lincoln just unconsciously swayed in time to *Worippa's* motion. Both had started half-heartedly and neither sure that they wanted it. They'd already stuffed the remains of a half-consumed loaf and were well on their way to consuming a second – the pigs.

He gazed forward, looking for the horizon: forward, in front of the mast: above, below, one side and then the other. One, two, three, four and more, seen through a gap in the scudding clouds: stars unblinking, diamond hard: minute pinpricks of light.

. . . Later, at home, Lincoln remembered, after returning from that solo trip, his mother had commented about the self-steering: specifically and pointedly about one particular sheared-off bolt! What his mother knew about his world, sailing, a person could write on a stamp, let alone what self-steering was . . . and as far as a sheered-off bolt – not possible!

Chapter 18

The oil lamp, hung from the central deck beam, swung round in a slow lazy circle and its light was soft, gentle and comforting. An acquisition Lincoln had not known about, and he'd thought it out, Lincoln acknowledged, had Brian – that lamp, apart from its comfort, saved the batteries and took off the chill. Its only disadvantage, as far as Lincoln could see, or smell, rather, was that it gave off a very vague, faint odour of kerosene. The lamp looked an antique, he looked at it closely: the cylindrical brass burner and fuel reserve base was separated from the matching brass chimney above by a ball – a circular orb of caged glass. There was a steeply coned, inverted, brass, scalloped dish, which was, in fact, a heat shield and was braised horizontally to the top of the chimney. The shield was shaped like an umbrella and it protecting the deckhead from the lantern's rising heat.

Lincoln lay there, at peace with the world, and not thinking, just dozing. He was warm too; safe and snug – and it seemed days . . . No apprehension, he realised, that was it – he felt no apprehension at all. His grey matter had recorded somewhere: that the light swung in a lazy circle rather than violently jerking around like a mad thing!

Suddenly he was into shadow as a form passed, going forward silently, and seconds later Brian's illuminated upper body and face he glimpsed briefly in the flicked on-then-off yellow of a bunk light. And then into shadow again and he a silhouette once more – he caught hold, as he stood there, of the deckhead grabrail as *Worippa* lurched, and after he'd steadied himself he reaching up with his other hand and minutely adjusting the oil lamp's wick. He spent another couple of minutes undoing a mushroom ventilator – his action caused no rush of water – presumably then, he'd have tasted the faint fumes too.

Ramsey turned and checked the two bunks opposite and then stepped across and checked the one above – he thereupon kneeled and their eyes locked. Lincoln quietly enquired, "How's Warren?"

Brian gently bobbed his head. "He's dead to the world." And with that he pursed his lips. "Anyway, what are you doing awake, Chris, you're not due to be on watch for half an hour yet." He leaned closer. "You're not in pain, are you – that's not what's keeping you awake, is it?"

"No, actually I'm lying here luxuriating, Brian." He nodded to the lamp. "Nice."

Brian grinned. "To be honest, it's no credit to me; it was a Christmas present from Judy. I put it on board as an after-thought – to keep the peace." His raised eyebrows said everything. "I was going to use it in Hobart, a romantic evening with Judy, and all that." He looked away and Lincoln imagined his blush rather than saw it. "She sensed my slight disappointment," he admitted. "To be honest, I was only half keen: another piece of useless, impractical junk lying around – cluttering up the house – that'd never get used. Insensitive bastard, aren't I – now who's sorry!"

There no answer to Ramsey's question and none expected, instead Lincoln asked, "How much fuel have you got for it?"

"Enough to last about a year." There appeared a whimsical smile on his face. "It's little wonder that we got stuck on the Derwent, wasn't it, all the scrap we carry . . . Sorry, I carry."

No, that wasn't altogether true, and he wasn't being altogether fair and he was doing himself an injustice – and knowing him as Lincoln did now, he'd have sat and weighed the odds, generally – it was just that Ramsey, despite all his talk, simply wasn't a fanatic, or remotely like . . . Plenty of skippers trimmed too close to the bone, and Lincoln had sailed with a few, a dribble of fuel in the tanks, a minimum of food and water, spare anchors, chain, warps et cetera, all left behind. Everything sacrificed – no excess carried at all – and only suffice to cover regulations and some not even honouring those! He was right though, Brian, in a way, because as far as safety equipment was concerned, happily, they were into overkill: light bulbs, batteries, nuts, bolts, lengths of threading, odds of stainless steel and aluminium. A comprehensive tool kit: pop-riveter, twelve-volt drill, hand-drill, saw, files, soldering iron, fuses, wire and the rest; clevis and split pins, spare halyards, rigging wire with U-bolts to suit, shackles, pulleys, blocks, snatch blocks and whatnot. There was even a wet suit and facemask stowed under one of the bunks! He'd have a sextant tucked away somewhere too – the accompanying tables on the bookshelf were the give-away. Those tomes of tables were snuggled up against the 'Sailor's Easy Recipe Cookbook', another volume that he had missed when trying, unsuccessfully, to lighten the boat and to relieve *Worippa* of all the unnecessary (as if any of them would be able to remember how to shoot a sun-sight anyway!). They didn't actually carry a sewing machine – he'd have to ask about that! ... And yet, mused Lincoln, for all that they hadn't, in fact, and despite getting stuck on the Derwent, come in too far down in the race placings, finally!

Lincoln nodded once again to the light. "It must have flattened off quite considerably, that'd have got smashed to pieces earlier?" There was disbelief on Ramsey's face ... mingled with bemused wonder ... and obviously tiredness ... and relief perhaps. "It's cold out there, you know – you need everything on. You won't believe this, Chris, but it's a beautiful night. There's still a long swell running, but nothing like."

Lincoln remembered then and enquired. "The engine!" he asked. "Have you tried the engine?" The worry lines round Ramsey's eyes deepened and Lincoln gave an inner sigh, the question could have waited.

Brian shook his head. "There's a dead short somewhere – nothing. It won't fire at all." He took a deep, wavering breath. "I'll look at it tomorrow; I can't face that, not without more sleep. I've got a feeling that we're going to have to take it to bits and dry out half the electrics. You saw it; it was under water half the time." He looked away and again shook his head. "I never thought I'd see the day – came close, didn't we?"

"Yes," Lincoln replied, "we did, and lived to tell the tale." There was no point in them dwelling on it, so he changed the subject. "It'd be worth removing the engine cover, you know, Brian, there'll be a lot of trapped moisture under there – it'll help dry it out. You never know with diesels, they'll surprise you; they're not like car engines, are they. Have you got a handle for it – it'd be worth a try, if you have?"

Brian was adamant. "Not this time, Chris, it's a bloody joke, the thing's seventy-two horses. The handle's there for maintenance and repair only – takes all your strength just to turn it over." He shook his head. "No. There's still plenty in the batteries, though – let's just hope that there'll be enough juice in them to get her started – it's a bit of a worry."

Lincoln nodded. "You're right, better to wait for daylight – we'll be fresh and at least then we'll be able to see what we're at."

"Yes." Brian was quiet for a moment. "The ironical thing is, I had it in mind to buy a solar panel." He sighed. "Bloody hindsight, if I had then we won't have been totally without power should the worst happen." He didn't leave Lincoln time to interrupt – a sounding board Lincoln was happy to be. "And another thing, we'll take a look at the aerial in the morning too, there can't be much wrong with it – there's only the backstay connecting joint, water could have got through the deck gland but I doubt it – I sealed and checked all that myself.

"Anyway, close your mind to it, we'll sort it all out tomorrow." He tacked on an afterthought, "That's if we see tomorrow, of course." There was a flicker of something on Brian's face – caught in the light from the lamp – something suspiciously like suppressed humour! He explained, "Lionel's been playing around with your eternal stew pot, he reckons we can purchase the antidote at a price – you're not included." Lincoln waited, apologising to him in his mind for doubting – he had waterproofed the radio connections then – and from his demeanour and stance there was obviously more to come. "We shook out the second reef, not easy with just the two of us. Lionel wanted to shake out both," Brian raised an eyebrow. "That was the first he'd heard about our little hiccup – in the mast, that is. He wasn't pleased, not pleased at all, I can tell you: that we all knew about it and he didn't." Brian said solemnly, "He blamed you, of course."

"Oh, of course," Lincoln muttered.

"Really peeved . . . got real shitty, reckons he'd have been nicer to the 'fly-boys' had he known: mast bent, on the edge of snapping; communications kaput; engine fucked . . . Not a happy boy, Lionel . . . his words." After a slight pause Ramsey asked innocently, "Are you going back to sleep . . . No. Be back in a minute then." He nodded, and the bugger walked away.

Lincoln tried to turn, aware of the watching eyes of his comrades-in-arms who were also due to go on watch with him shortly. Lionel stood in the entrance, easily swaying – and no hands! Then he was yelling: there was no consideration for any recumbent form that might have wanted to doze for their last half-hour. "You never told me, did you, Pommy. Bloody mast about to fall over, bent like a bloody banana." The volume increased, "Oh, you can bloody grin, matie."

There something in Lionel's face, as Lincoln tried to sit, he didn't or couldn't keep it up; he picked up a pillow instead and stepped across. "Lay back – tea's ready – can you lift your nut enough for me to tuck this under?" Gently, carefully, Lionel eased Lincoln and eased up his head.

He asked, "How stiff?"

"Thanks, Lionel – stiff, stiff. I'm going to need some help again."

Brian returned, tea in one hand. "He ready for . . . Are you ready to drink this?"

Lionel interrupted, "He won't be needing that, the only thing he'll be needing is a doctor – I've just beaten the shit out of him."

Across from and out of the shadow a female voice, embarrassing and tactless, both Lionel and Brian looked anywhere but ahead and down. "Don't mention the word 'doctor', you'll embarrass him, I don't!"

*   *   *

Lionel laid more slices of bread on the mesh-topped frame of the camping toaster and Brian added to his pile after buttering. Zero one-twenty hours: twenty past one in the morning and breakfast for a king!

No longer a crew this, Lincoln glanced around at them, a chemical psychic bonding had taken place, they had . . . including him, been through the fire and out the other side. They were family to each other now and more intimate than most kin ever would be – he knew, in the future, company and help would only be a phone call away. Two faces were missing, Bill, he was looking after the shop above, and Warren. Warren? Warren, Lincoln somehow knew, was also indelibly entwined with all their futures, that tie was, despite everything, perhaps the strongest, and his weaknesses causing concern to all his new cousins.

"Chris?" Brian touched Lincoln's shoulder. "You listening? More cereal? There's still some hot milk left?"

"No. No thanks, Brian, couple of slices'll be fine; I'll wait till tomorrow and then we'll really eat." He ventured, "Makes a real difference, doesn't it, four hours sleep without the worry nagging at you – and Bill up there on his own – a bit of a contrast!"

Lionel broke a concentrated hush of people preoccupied

with eating, "I've managed to salvage the stew," he ignored the grinning reception, "don't eat it all, I'll be having some for breakfast, it'll be nicely flavorous by then."

Sharon leaned away from Gary and broke the stubborn silence. "I'll regret it, I know. Nobody else is going to so I'll put you out of your misery, seeing how I helped to make the original . . . How?" Then sweetly, "Old socks, I bet?"

Potter elaborately examined the nails of one hand. "Funny you should ask me that." Another pause. "Lamb chops, more potatoes, fresh runner beans and a few peas."

Silence again ensued, the old bugger, Lincoln admitted, had got it right and no denying it.

"Change of watch folks," Brian gently reminded them. "Daren't burn the lights any longer, we're going to need all available power tomorrow – to try and start the engine."

*   *   *

The night sky ablaze with stars – wheeling their unbroken timeless way across the sky. Ramsey had been right, it was cold, and it had long since swept away the last vestiges of sleep. That was him though – that was any vestiges of sleep that he, Lincoln, still might have felt.

They stood side by side, with Bill waiting for Lincoln after Lincoln had taken the helm, to adjust and get used to the feel of *Worippa's* motion again.

It was just an innocent enquiry, "Are you all right, Bill?"

His reply wasn't what Lincoln had expected, "No, Chris." He was looking forward, into another world – a different world. "I've suddenly become very, very tired – I was all right ten minutes ago – it's just sort of caught up with me . . ."

"Bed, Bill," Lincoln touched his arm, hit by compassion. "It's caught you up, you've been through an awful lot – you're done your stint anyway. Go on," he urged," grab something to eat and go back to bed. You're dead on your feet."

"I've gone beyond that stage, Chris." Despite the comparatively light wind, Lincoln heard him swallow. There was slight bewilderment in his voice after that brief pause; he was almost musing to himself. "I'm aware of what's going on . . . I'm outside of myself watching. A strange experience, you know: I can't focus on the compass anymore, my eyelids are quivering so badly – I can't control them – and I can't stop them fluttering . . . A sort of nervous reaction, I suppose."

"You're in the danger zone, Bill," Lincoln said, "bed for you – it's called battle fatigue." He gently pushed him and then grinned into the darkness. "Helmut and Nick're washing-up – you wouldn't just make sure they haven't murdered each other, would you?"

Bill still hesitated, that was until Sharon very quietly wished him 'good night'.

Gary stirred after Bill had crossed the cockpit and had made his way below, Sharon leaned against him.

Lincoln anticipated one of them breaking the silence and spoke first. "Tell us about Macquarie Harbour, Gary, you're up on all this." He gestured into the night, "It's obviously been settled: the town of Strahan's marked on the chart."

Gary was silent for a moment, accepting and acknowledging that Bill Corsham's inner weariness wasn't a subject for discussion, before brusquely asking, "Are you really interested?"

"It's our low spot, Gary, this time in the morning. We're at our lowest ebb – the worst time – our spirits are beginning to flag." Lincoln cajoled, "It'd be nice if you'd take us on a journey." He gestured again. "In there. I, for one, haven't come all this way not to be interested – tell him Sharon."

An apparent elbow from Sharon and an accompanying grunt started the flow.

"Four men in a whale boat led by a man called James Kelly; he's been credited with being the first." Gary sat up straighter. "A local lad, first-generation Australian, and no 'dill'. He went to sea as a boy and he eventually became a Master Mariner in his own right. He named the place after the governor of the time – he was apparently a political animal, as well – James Kelly, I mean.

"The only place you'll find Huon Pine is in there, by the way, and the most sort-after wood for ship building in the world – strong and impervious to everything, and light . . . Or was." There was that bitterness again, "As per usual, the stupid, shallow, unforseeing idiots have stripped the place bare, with no thought of tomorrow. There's not one tree left, not one tree – can you believe that!"

They were silent – what on earth could one say!

Gary took a long breath, collecting and putting his thoughts in order before continuing. "Cape Sorell was supposed to be

Tasman's first sighting. There's a huge inland waterway in there, as well, and deep. The entrance is protected by a bar, between ten and sixteen feet over it, that's all – depending on local conditions. The place is littered with wrecks, Port Macquarie's tricky – it has its own peculiarities – you need local knowledge. There isn't much of a tide, comparatively, in this part of the world – two or three feet, depending on wind direction. Macquarie's fed by the mountains and water can run out of there at eight or nine knots after the rains: the outward flow's so powerful that it can even hold back the tide. It doesn't run straight out either, it sets sideways across Hells Gates." Gary sat back. "That good enough for you?"

Gary had been waiting for the chance to ask, that much obvious.

"What are you doing here in Australia, Chris?" There a puzzled curiosity in his voice. "You seem to have 'upped stumps' and just come – completely blind. Have you – and why here?"

"I wanted to see the southern sky, Gary – I've always been fascinated – I wanted to see Centaurus. Proxima Centauri is the closest star to the earth – well, Alpha is anyway. Alpha and Beta are, as, no doubt, you know, ' the pointers', they and the Southern Cross point to the Southern Celestial Pole – and the Magellanic Clouds and all that; I wanted to see for myself, that and plain old curiosity."

Gary was doubtful, "Is that really true . . .? Yes, it smacks of you . . . No – it's too pat.

Lincoln, almost in despair, closed his eyes – he hadn't the nerve nor was he game enough in the present circumstances . . . It was one thing to admit that his main reason for visiting Australia had been to attend a christening and the wedding of a very close friend and associate, but it was quite another to admit he had been in love with and still loved the bride to distraction!

Too complicated, Lincoln thought, and my business, besides, even though platonic – theoretically – he wouldn't put it past Sharon to hear something in his voice, and once heard she'd . . . Time for him to change the subject and time to steer them away. "You read about weather systems in the southern hemisphere, Gary, at home, in England, and about depressions rotating clockwise instead of anticlockwise, and the highs vice-versa – the Coriolas Force and all that. Water disappearing and rotating down plug holes the wrong way et cetera. The sun high in the 'northern' sky at noon especially takes some getting used to, you have to think, suddenly things aren't automatic: all very well in theory, but a bit more disconcerting, the experience." They waited, expectant, knowing there was more to come. Lincoln obliged, "The most well known constellation in the northern hemisphere is Orion – you know it?"

Gary nodded, movement seen, caught in the faint reflection of the remaining instrument lights – he'd know from his navigation. He, Gary, shushed Sharon with an, 'I'll show you later'.

"We know it as Orion the Hunter – in mythology he's a hunter . . . obviously. The three bright stars in the middle are supposed to be his belt, and another couple of stars and a nebula his sword hanging from his belt, the two stars above and below his arms and legs. He dominates northern sky's in winter months – automatically and almost subconsciously in the UK you'd look for him, he's part of the landscape . . . nightscape rather. Following him around is Sirius the 'Dog Star', needless to say, Sirius is supposed to be his hunting dog. It's bright blue in colour and one of the brightest stars in the northern sky. That star has been worshipped since ancient times, associated with the Pharaohs and before, they used it as a calendar: their astronomers used it to anticipate when the Nile would flood and hence when to plant their crops." Lincoln grinned into the darkness. "Something like that.

"One thing that nobody ever mentioned and I've never read about it either – not a hint. The bloody thing's upside down here: the hunter's doing a handstand, and his poor old dog's on its back and floating – paws in the air!" Lincoln sighed. "I must have got very ridged in my dotage: the old brain synapses seem to be habitually connecting, or misconnecting, and the old signals are still automatically flowing across, if you see what I mean." He paused for a moment, bemused still by his own feelings of outrage . . . and the foreignness that the sight of that inverted constellation still caused. "I still haven't got over the shock; it's as if something you utterly relied on and had total faith in, isn't there – and has let you down." He was talking half to himself now. "A violation of something deeply embedded in the fabric of yourself – and hard to come to terms with . . . Actually, to tell the truth, I'm surprised at the depth of my own feelings."

Nick climbed into the cockpit – it was obviously going to be a party. Plates though were a delicacy he'd not heard of, nor frugality. He slapped them into their hands before wriggling his way in between Gary and Sharon; they gave up trying to push him away. Doorstep sandwiches, and the wedges of bread only there to support a half-inch of cheese. The internal contents of tomato squirted under the pressure of their teeth!

"Brunch." He looked either side – there a flash of white teeth. "Can't you leave it alone, you two; you're like a pair of bloody rabbits."

"Could you not sleep, Nicolo?" Lincoln quickly interjected. "Nor Helmut?"

"Nar, you're a long time dead – who needs it."

Just as well Bill Corsham wasn't present to hear that little bauble, Lincoln thought, it made him, let alone Bill, feel ancient!

The silhouette of Helmet's head and chest appeared in the companionway – he placed steaming mugs on the cockpit seat. Gary gave up trying to yet again oust Nick – he was distracted by being passed and passing the hot drinks.

The silence lasting as long as the food.

Helmut had been assessing while they were eating. "Ve are going to have to shake the last reef out, Chris, this is not good – if ve do it now, then ve can settle down for the rest of the vatch, ja?"

They should have done it a while ago, Lincoln knew, though, in truth, they should be changing the headsail . . . Better to wait for daylight to change that . . . For now, shaking out the reef would be easier – and safer, they'd be inboard – though they'd never get home at this rate! Cape Sorell Light was still clearly visibly off our beam: five and a half, six knots: he was right, Helmut, it was not good enough.

Lincoln enquired, "Do you want her head to wind, Helmut?" He asked the others, "Have we all finished brunch?"

Nick was grinning in the darkness; Helmut was mentally scratching his head. He, Helmut, tentatively asked, "Brunch . . .? You mean . . ." He gave up, for which Lincoln was truly thankful – it was going to get too complicated, explaining that. "No Chris," he said, instead, "maybe bring her up a bit – to keep the sail clear of the lower stays . . . the shrouds. Ve do not vant to trap a batten!"

Neither Gary nor Nick commented, they simply made their way forward; Helmut gave Sharon her instructions and she stood to the side and leaning against the companionway bulkhead ready, and waiting to ease out on the mainsail sheet winch. Nick undid the sail ties, freeing the trapped excess of sail; a hand signal and a call from Helmut and Sharon let go the mainsail sheet. Nick quickly went forward freeing boom vang and reefing line.

Humped shapes in the starlight, and Lincoln mentally visualising, discerning and following their every movement.

Gary eased the halyard – the reinforced metal reefing cringle in the leading edge of the mainsail would have dropped free, or would have been easily pushed from the inverted hook welded to the boom gooseneck by Helmut. Nick made sure the sail's boltrope slid smoothly up the mast's track. Helmut raising the unfettered, rattling sail with a minimum of fuss, hand-over-hand on the halyard, total bodyweight unnecessary. He'd surprised Gary, Gary had been left behind and not able to tail fast enough: the winch sang and there was panic in Gary's movements as he pulled off arm-length after arm-length of braided line. Nick waited, ready to re-tension the vang. Helmut, anticipating, waited for Gary to organise himself and then dropped to his knee and cranked on and carefully tensioning as appropriate. Sharon had a good retentive memory as well, Lincoln now knew, the mainsail was correctly sheeted and *Worippa* was back on course before the three were seated again – full circle.

Each of them an island, solitary – and private thoughts for company. *Worippa* cut through the night, now comfortable and the wind just forward of her quarter – and broad-reaching into infinity.

Lincoln picked it up again. "Hell's Gates, Gary," he asked. "Sounds like something out of Norse or Greek mythology – a mariner's boneyard?"

"What do you mean," Nick queried quickly. There a spontaneous curiosity underlying his tone. "Hell's Gates? What are they?"

It almost palatable: the swashbuckling pirates and buried treasure that he was imagining in his mind's eye, and Lincoln had to grin – that enthusiasm of youth again! "That's the name of the entrance to Macquarie Harbour, Nick, back there." The flashing of Sorell Light was still very visible over the stern quarter. "The lighthouse is next to the entrance."

It was Gary who disillusioned him, "It isn't a maritime reference, it was named by the convicts." There was, once again, resentment in Gary's voice, only it was directed at Lincoln this time. "Your lot again, Pom. The worst convict settlement of them all: untold horrors and atrocities were committed in there. Hell's Gates contained the naughtiest boys – the worst recalcitrants. The place only lasted for eleven years: it was too isolated and harsh even for the warders. I can tell you, not too many were shipped out finally: after that ordeal, either they died of the brutality metered out, or were lost in the bush after running for it . . . As good as executed if they came back, or got caught. No, they couldn't win and they knew it, so most simply gave up and died." Gary took a shuddering breath. "Bloody way to start a new world – tainted before it ever got onto its legs."

Only the sound of wind and sea filling the vacuum.

. He eventually continued on, but in a calmer tone, "The miners moved in then, gold, tin, copper and silver-lead were found in the region. Strahan, the town you mentioned, Chris; ore was shipped out from there – the place existed for no other reason. It was all . . . the whole shebang was linked by a network of rail that connected, directly or indirectly, to all the significant mines on the West Coast – it stretched up as far as Burnie." Gary breathed deeply: from passion to pensiveness . . . to resignation, to sadness. "Those mines are all closed now: they never recovered from the Great War: the bulk of the miners were killed off. At Gallipoli, the Somme, Pozieres Ridge, Passchendaele . . . and all the other lunatic battle fields – bloody Krauts. The tracks have been ripped up and the sleepers burnt for firewood – slagheaps still litter the countryside. Strahan's a holiday resort now and Macquarie's a huge nature reserve – the only good thing that came out of the whole sorry bloody mess."

Well, Lincoln concluded, he'd really well and truly soured the atmosphere – a little too emphatic – just a tad too overwrought. Tired, testy; fatigue, depression – out of proportion . . . Maybe?

Lincoln sighed. "Fiery stuff, Gary – I hadn't realised, I hadn't a clue that you felt so strongly . . ."

His mentioning the Great War had touched a nerve and had started Lincoln thinking: the very fact that he had quoted Pozieres Ridge, and his tone of voice indicated that he knew more than a bit about the subject. The horror of that war had haunted Lincoln for most of his life and it sounded as if it had done the same to Gary – and they hadn't even been alive then!

It was the way they had died: the mud and the filth: the carnage and the rats. A million dead in just one day – in one engagement! The brain, Lincoln's brain, couldn't accept nor comprehend it! The mind shied away from such abhorrence – one skipped over the surface of that war and clung to the staggering numbers and dared not to allow one's imagination to glimpse at the pictures that wanted to form.

Yet . . . and yet, Lincoln pondered, it was all too simple; no nation was blameless for that madness, including Gary's. Why? Why did it affect them so: a communal guilt? Had they all a collective scarred psyche? Maybe it was because their generation had been too close to it – their grandparents – that age-group had told them about it personally, albeit snippets. And Lincoln and co. had seen some of the results – the maimed and the gassed . . . and 'World War' was the right title too; and it was quite beyond comprehension, in the sense that little isolated communities even out here, and in every one-street town across Australia – halfway around the globe – had not been immune . . . Yet none of them, he knew, had the remotest prior connection, in any way, with that conflict!

Strangely, though the results also evident, the Second World War hadn't had the same effect – probably, Lincoln surmised, because that war and the reasons for it could be fairly easily understood – on the surface anyway . . . It was all too deep.

There no point in him trying to explain the whys and wherefores of English settlement policy to Gary either – he wouldn't, in his present mood anyway, want to know.

The gradual change in Gary's voice brought awareness and dispelled Lincoln's musings – there was that underlying poignancy in his diction again, of acrimony and acerbity! "It's all still going on – they've learnt to keep a low profile, is all. Open cut mining, apart from the ordinary – that's rape in my book. Dam-building for power we don't need, indiscriminate logging – that Huon pine that I was telling you about – they just never seem to learn.

"Tasmania's the last citadel – it is a land that time really has forgotten. It's the jewel in the crown: untamed and comparatively unspoiled. To be cosseted – God's creation – and beautiful. It is a fortress, you know, not much of it is below a thousand feet, most of the central interior's a plateau of two thousand feet or over; but whether or not it's going to be strong enough to withstand the final assault is another thing!"

Sharon pushed Nick out of the way indiscriminately, ignoring his protests. She pulled Gary's head down into her lap, kissed his ear and then turned to Lincoln. "Isn't he a passionate, romantic, clever, little walking encyclopaedia." Gary struggled; she wouldn't let him up. "No, no, no, mother's little baby."

She was doing something to his ear with her tongue, and his muffled objections ceased to be quite so loud – time to look the other way.

And, as Lincoln did so, he realised . . . Helmut! Helmut was sat there! He had been as quiet as a mouse throughout the whole conversation – and little wonder. God, they had all forgotten that Helmut was there, and that he was of German descent – bloody hell!

Helmut stirred, rose, crossed, stepped down the companionway steps and turned – his comment before disappearing below left them silent. "Both my great grandfathers died at Ypres." He stood there. "My grandfather died on the Eastern Front – he is buried somevere between Germany and Leningrad. My mother and I, and my family, ve do not know where. All my family history place of birth vas Dresden, my father vas young boy ven bombing vas doing – he vas alvays not so vell, there vas no food there after that var – I do not remember him so much . . ."

Cold indifference. The temperatures of the stars clearly denoted by their colours. The night sky spangled with a background of pearls on black velvet: diamonds, emeralds, sapphires and rubies sprinkled and sparkling amongst them. The misty haze of the Milky Way tracked in gold dust across the firmament; God's creation he'd said – insignificant little ants, more like!

Chapter 19

A cool, invigorating, refreshing draft was blowing gently through, and the forward open hatch was full of watery, dappled sunlight. Cheerful tinklings and murmurings were being conducted through and could be clearly heard from the other side of the hull – and those harsh noises and strains of *Worippa* were now just a bygone memory.

Bacon ... Lincoln could smell the tantalising aroma of frying bacon and fried bread that was now and again wafting back through on a reverse upper eddy and mixing with that fresh air above ... Well, that was one thing; they certainly weren't going to starve to death!

Rolling over for Lincoln was not easy, but easier – his old body had begun the process of repair. Slightly bent at the waist and with his upper hip resting against the padded hull proved comfortable – head supported on a hand and elbow and an unrestricted view forward was enough. Swirled dust motes caught in the streaming sunshine that had been admitted by the square of the forward hatch were reminiscent of light through a church window – of flickering patterns playing on ancient flagstones ... of childhood.

"What are you thinking about?" Sharon asked quietly. "You're miles away. Are you going to cry?"

There was no real aggression nor overtones in Sharon's voice; she wasn't looking for a fight, it just her way of telling him that she too was awake. The final sentence she had tacked on just in case – she was just testing the water.

Lincoln inwardly sighed: privacy was not an abundant commodity on a sailing boat, though surprisingly, solitary moments of contemplation and peace were not rare. Most yachts with regular crew had an untalked of, unwritten, unthought of respect for temperament, and extremes of mood were part and parcel of the package. Lack of sleep, worry, stress and tension guaranteed a visit from the 'black dog' from time to time, and his form ranging from deep depression, lassitude, to flashes of unreasonable, welling anger. The unwanted guest could only be pandered to, hoping for a short stay – and aggressive retaliation to the recipient of this dark malady was out of the question. Such taciturn moods of contained, suppressed emotion, and Lincoln wasn't different from anybody else, were not uncommon: to sense and respect them, and better to ignore: to interrupt and jolly rather than leave them be was to risk, or invite, an unmerited attack of verbal abuse . . . Or worse! Aware that one had things out of proportion, one was – to be reasonable, a person suffering from such a malady couldn't be.

Potter, Lincoln felt, had accessed her well, whether uncanny insight or flattery another thing, Sharon was a natural: she knew when to stay quiet until encouraged, sensed what type of approach to use and was unoffended and happy with her own company, it was, as far as he was concerned, a rare gift. She'd, thankfully, laid one of his original main objections to rest: that novices and long trips were an unknown quantity and taboo!

Lincoln twisted his head around and up on his palm and brought her into view, she was opposite, but on the top bunk and on her side and looking down, and cocooned in blankets, even around her head – an unlikely Madonna!

The half-smile came unbidden and he cursed inwardly, but without rancour. Unintentional affection had crept and bloomed – and the bond was there – and another had gotten, somehow, in through a chink and under the armour.

She'd seen the green light. "Ah, by the way. Um . . ." A shy and bashful Sharon Lincoln had not seen before. "How do I wash?" she quietly and discreetly blurted out finally and glanced inadvertently down at her body. "I stink like a polecat."

His, Lincoln's, bland, indifferent, supercilious countenance and raised haughty eyebrows followed by a mouthed 'Oh' and a tutted sigh of lofty disdain, needless to say, had the desired effect, and his barely concealed smug, interested-disinterest, exasperated and niggled her – as it was meant to do.

"I don't have to spell it out, do I – a girl has to wash, least ways, this one does." She cut off his look of sudden comprehension and said impatiently, "No, I don't mean that, I mean wash, pure and simple – a girl has to. You . . . you pig."

Her head was now also resting on her hand and her eyes pleading – she was serious.

Lincoln laid back. "It'll disrupt the whole boat," he said. "It'll be a pantomime." Unfair, but a little more salt, "There's only one way and it's as the same as before – warm water, bucket, sponge and soap."

There was a three-inch grated drain moulded into the sole

forward and in front of the toilet, which ran straight into the bilges. An ankle-high coaming stopped water from escaping aft: he had not thought about it before, the sink they had always used as a harness and safetyline receptacle! Hand hygiene had always been, and was maintained with a diluted, disinfectant-filled, small, hand-operated, garden spray. Their only other concession to cleanliness: tooth brush, paste and beaker taken into the cockpit. The area, he realised, had been designed with strip-washing in mind: the curtain that they used for privacy forward in the heads, just inside, ran athwartships above the retaining coaming. As far as Lincoln knew, the tap worked, so at least she wouldn't have to wash in her own dirty water.

There was both panic and disappointment in her voice, "Not in the cockpit, surely. God, not in front of everybody . . ." She pondered out loud, "If Gary steered and everybody else went below – could we do that, d'you think?" She'd not thought it out – Lincoln waited – it took a minute. "No, course not."

He spoke while still contemplating the underside of the bunk above. "You can strip-wash in front of the toilet." He casually explained, "Use the sink, you can splash away in there to your heart's content – the water'll drain away – there's a drain built in the floor. That's why we store our foul weather gear in there, it can drip away without contaminating the rest of the ship – it keeps the boat dry. Oh, and when you've finished, don't forget to scrub and sluice away any soap residue – use seawater for that – use a bucket." Lincoln added dryly, "It'd be a bit naughty if someone was to slip over while walking through after, wouldn't it."

How long had he been listening, Lincoln wondered, it didn't matter, Gary broke the happy silence: his voice tentative, low-loud, intimate, half-begging – and full of contained wanting and yearning – full of something . . . "It's easy to climb out of the forward hatch from there: it'd be just above you, this side of the curtain, there's foot and hand holds built into the sides of the sail lockers."

Now what was going on – what on earth was this about? And not only his – Sharon's puzzlement and enquiry Lincoln could sense, she hung over the side, trying to make eye contact with Gary. Gary wouldn't look up. She asked, shaking her head slightly, "What's that got to do with anything?"

"You could climb out of the hatch," explained Gary, "and

walk around the bow, and then climb down again."

Sharon shook her head again. "I could do that anytime?"

Only their silence for an answer, Lincoln began to see a glimmer of light – genuine superstition, or sexual excitement? There no question, by his voice and the look on his face, obviously the later! This was another, unknown and vaguely disturbing side of Gary that he hadn't expected, or suspected, and yet, for some reason, Lincoln found the whole thing faintly humorous. The things that happened at sea – he, Gary, ignored Lincoln's look.

She was not slow, Sharon. "Something funny here, mister." She reached down, nearly out of her bunk – Gary squawked and his head following the hand that twisted his ear. "Tell me?" she insisted.

He hadn't a high pain threshold had, Gary, he yelped. "It's lucky," his voice went up half an octave, presumably extra twist, "since ancient times: all-seeing eyes painted on the prows of fishing boats; serpent's heads carved on the front of Viking ships looking out for danger – scaring enemies; naked figurehead's on the bow for luck."

Sweetly, quietly Sharon mimicked, "Naked figurehead's on the bow for luck?" She looked across. "Is that true, or is Gary Prestwick just another dirty little pervert?"

A lump of varnish from the base of the bunk above Lincoln removed with a thumbnail. He said it casually, "We accepted that he is a pervert a couple of years ago, none of us have felt quite safe in our bunk's since. Um . . . he does the skipper favours, that's the rumour."

"Pom, you bastard."

A tut of impatience from Sharon, they ignored Gary. "Not that," she said, "about the figureheads?"

Lincoln confirmed it, "As far as it goes, he's right. It used to be a traditional christening, a wench actually did walk around the bow of a ship, they were a bawdy lot hence figureheads of bare-chested women – bare from the waist were more popular." Lincoln took a breath. "She was supposed to placate storms and all that; they were usually the heavy-breasted Rembrandtian types." There no point in letting the pot go cold so just for good measure he added, "That rules you out."

Gary's mutter of 'spoilsport' was only just audible.

Lincoln caught the seemingly genuine petulance in Sharon's

voice, and belligerence – she'd immediately picked-up on that one comment and that one comment only – she was damned quick. "What do you mean by that, that I'm small, is that it, is that what you mean, is that what he means, Gary?" She didn't wait for an answer, "Huh," there disdain in her voice, "who was Rembrandt anyway, just a dirty old voyeur who got his rocks off by painting his big-titted wife. Stuff you . . ." As an afterthought she added, "And Rembrandt." She looked down and then outlined an adequate breast with her hand. "Big as the next girl, bloody sight bigger, aren't I, Gary?"

Gary, free from ear restraint, gently shook his head and his unspoken curse easily deciphered. Lincoln knew what he meant; they had touched on a sensitive nerve and had set her off. 'They', because if he was going down, then so was Gary – sounds of ice splintering from under, time to steer her away from the subject.

One thing Lincoln had noticed, as an aside, was that she knew that Rembrandt had often used his wife as a model . . . and for some reason, Lincoln found that interesting!

A vague hovering form in the shadow, betrayed by movement caught on the edge of periphery vision and somehow furtive, just beyond the entrance, and half sensed as much as seen. Lincoln said quietly, twisting his head around, "Come in, if you're coming in, Warren, don't skulk out there, man, somebody else might think you were listening in . . . To other people's private conversations."

He would have the last word if it killed him; Lincoln turned back to Sharon. "It's too late anyway, we've had our storm . . . though you might try standing naked in front of the engine, and then the aerial – Brian'd appreciate a bit of luck."

Such words young girls, Lincoln felt, shouldn't even be aware of, let alone use!

*   *   *

The entrails of the exposed metal beast were strewn around the saloon and Ramsey was wiping his oily black hands on an already soiled wad of kitchen paper; and strain, perplexity and worry were reflected on the countenance of his tired face.

Bill Corsham replaced the kettle and lifted the steaming bucket. "Enough, Brian," he chided. "Come on; wash your hands – breakfast and bed." Bill turned to Lincoln. "There's tea in the pot, Chris, would you be mother. Lionel first, he's had the helm for most of the watch." He pointed. "The cups are in the sink ready: sugared and milked."

The tea was delivered despite *Worippa's* disruptive efforts. Lionel nodded his thanks and waited, patient and silent, while Lincoln looked around, absorbing and processing.

"Where are we, Lionel?"

"Just off Pieman Head." He pointed and directed. "There's the entrance to the Pieman River – follow the beach down – between the two rocky points."

"Doesn't get any less rugged, does it; nor friendlier, is it, even in the sunshine?"

Lincoln just stood: the cliffs and crags were uninviting, drab, sullen, sinister, threatening and indifferent, and the sun not strong enough to burn away the perpetual mist that clung stubbornly to the shrouded peaks. The beach a washed, yellow, forever-strip with a dark green and khaki canopy behind. The foreground of the tableau was an undulating, odd, white-flecked blue – and all quite distinct from the background pastels of the rising eminencies.

Lionel thought differently, he tapped for attention and then shook his head. "You're gone." He pursed his lips into a half smile, half grimace. "The place has already worked its magic on you, I can tell from your face – it's touched an inner chord, hasn't it, admit it." He raised an encompassing arm and not waiting for an answer. "A wild, untamed country with a beauty all of its own. You were warned – I told you before, didn't I. Now it'll really get under your skin – this'll haunt you for the rest of your life." He indicated again. "Look at the sun on . . ." and continued indicating, ". . . and behind the clouds." Lincoln knew, despite himself, precisely what he meant. "Look at the chart, some of those summits are well in excess of two thousand feet – nearer three. A beach of virgin sand – never been trod on." He nodded in the appropriate direction. "It runs northward for miles – it's a speculator's dream. Look at the colours of the sea – not a speck of pollution in it."

He turned slowly around, looking the other way, out to sea – he changed the direction of his conversation too. "Difficult to believe, matie, bloody winds been dying all the time – we're going to have to change the headsail again soon."

*   *   *

Squatting and standing, wherever – and a working breakfast –

and listening to Ramsey's monotone. Like the rest of them, he was not an expert on diesel engines – and he'd covered everything in sight, and out of sight, with a moisture-absorbing, aerosol spray. Into places where no man had ever gone before – and all to no avail.

Helmut coughed discretely, Ramsey focused and mental gears meshed – and from frown to welcome in seconds. Lincoln hid a smile: a long lost brother wouldn't have been disappointed, the penny had dropped – Helmut the engineer!

Helmut commented on cue, "If you have a dead-short with your motor vehicle, vot is it you do?"

Nick was in before anybody else had a chance to answer, "If you can't fix it," he blurted, "as a last resort, try fucking it."

Lincoln inwardly moaned and mentally held his head in his hands: Nick's quick, flippant, unthinking answer caused other groans and frowns, and studied resignation for the, yet again, ever-surfacing impetuosity of youth . . . Lincoln looked up and inadvertently directly at yin and yang standing next to each other opposite: Gary the 'x' factor, frowning – Sharon, the only description apt, smirking!

Helmut broke the collective silence without a sound; in his book, and Lincoln didn't doubt, Nick's comment had been unforgivable in female company. Helmut took a step towards Nick; and not a garner of a smile on his face.

Nick responded quickly – panic, survival-driven and nowhere to run – his answer stopped Helmut, "Something wrong with the starting motor, the spray can't get in there." Nick took a crestfallen breath.

Helmut surveyed the sea of grins. Nick nodded to the warning finger: he gestured like a choir boy with both hands held up in front of his chest, palms together, that and a mouthed 'sorry' was just enough for a last-minute reprieve. Lincoln expelled air, not realising that he had been holding his breath: the little bugger really did sail too close at times.

They decided between them, there were no objections from Brian: Helmut would take the starting motor to pieces and dry it out, as necessary; Gary and Nick would change them back to roller reefing; Sharon volunteered to cook lunch, she'd be heating hot water on the stove for her promised wash anyway; and last, but not least, he, Lincoln, would be the helmsman.

*   *   *

Worippa quietly under way, but there was no distinct wake streaming from her stern – just a telltale swirl of pale green bubbles around her rudder.   Just three and a half knots on the clock, which wasn't bad considering – they were cresting the long, lazy, subsiding swell under mains'l alone.   Lincoln felt her through his feet, hands and being: she had been built for this, *Worippa*, the extra on the mast was paying dividends – the quartering wind was pushing her along effortlessly.   This was as near to heaven as any mortal would get in this part of the world, not quite a soldier's wind, but comfortable enough.

In a serene, torpid malaise, Lincoln watched as they handed the Number Three sail without trouble, however, undoing the hitches that secured the roller reefing was obviously proving to be problematic, and was starting to try their patience. Helmut, who had originally lashed the roller reefing to the forward stanchions, was no longer popular with Gary and Nick!

Their problems just didn't seem to matter; what was time. Lincoln had not felt like this since leaving Hobart, and in truth, long before that – contentment.   Face and body like a flower, drawn to the sun, and absorbing every ounce of warmth. He pulled the reinforced velcro overlap free and undid the heavy zip. Knee between the spokes and his foul weather top first, fleece-lined jacket next; braces unhitched, over-trousers down to the knees, followed by towel neck-scarf and second layer. He had trouble with the elasticated foul weather bottoms, as usual – leaning, then sitting on the coaming, with one hand on the wheel, while hooking a finger under to ease them, one at a time, over the heel of each boot . . . His temper solved that, and they were eventually flung onto the cockpit sole, but were inside-out and with his boots still caught in them. They lay there with the other discarded miscellaneous items of clothing – it didn't matter.

The smell, rising directly, wasn't nice, and Lincoln wrinkled his nose: there was an odd tang, a faint cloud, a puff of body, armpit, crutch and foot odour caught, now and again, wafting up despite the light breeze.

Lincoln, racked on the wheel, facing astern instead of forward – looking astern and out to sea, and his back, instead of his chest, as it were, leaning against the circle of spoked stainless steel – and hands hanging behind grasping and exerting only enough pressure to counter *Worippa's* weather helm. They would, he mused, be searching the desk of the chart table for dark glasses soon: accumulated bits and pieces always ended up there for some reason, but only until Ramsey threw a 'wobbly' and ditched the lot.

A sky full of shine and everything glittering bright. Not the subdued colours of yesterday and before, they, to Lincoln, full strength – garish even. Cobalt blue at the zenith and fading gradually – meeting a pale cobalt green sea at the horizon. Gaining vitality then: those waves nearest, their intense emerald tops spun, shot with white thread; down through the blue-green spectrum, darkening till azure-tempered, with viridian-mauve in the hollows.

There wasn't, accepting *Worippa's* wake and beautiful in itself, a break in the trackless, pathless wastes, only solitude and peace.

A voice of higher pitch than the rest, yet softer, with a built in 'nag' interrupted, "How the hell can you steer like that?"

Nothing lasts forever! Lincoln answered lazily, without turning or moving, "I tried standing on my head, but I kept losing me balance and falling over."

Sharon didn't react too well . . . what had he done?

"Nothing worse than a smart-arse, there's always one. It doesn't matter where you are or where you go."

Silence more ominous than chatter, Lincoln glanced over his shoulder.

There hissing venom in her voice, "And there's . . . yours." Tumbling and turning overhead and travelling in an arc from behind: white bread blinking – catching the sunlight. "And . . ." Soft impact between the shoulder blades. "There's the other half."

It just wasn't worth getting out of bed on some mornings; she'd gone forward by the time he had struggled round. The 'other half' lay where it had fallen, there was nothing wrong with it as far as he could see, the cockpit sole had been scoured clean by the sea.

Lincoln bit into it: spam and pickle, bread not quite fresh, the edge gone off it, but crunchy and delicious. How long had they been watching, he wondered: Nick and Gary stood on the foredeck, too close to be observed by the shrew, both grinning over each shoulder of Sharon's still taught back. And there below, in the foreground, was Helmut, framed in the companionway and shaking his head – he climbed, said one sentence and then went back down below again. Lincoln spat it out over his shoulder and viciously rubbed his lips, the rest of the sandwich he instantly jettisoned.

Lincoln cursed, with Helmut you couldn't tell: deadpan face, different background, different upbringing. He'd mixed with Nick long enough to learn though – the dirty little sod – he'd have pissed outside the cockpit, and not 'in', surely?

*   *   *

"Try for a little more tension on the halyards, Nick, try to take that slight sag out of it – don't worry about the mast, it'd have gone by now if it was going to. Both together, Nick, tension the same on both – the backstay's completely off. Let him do it, Gary," Lincoln advised, "it's a one-man job – let him feel both of them on." Lincoln pointed, "Umm, please would you slack the main sheet right off when he's ready and then stand-by the fore sheet." Gary held up a thumb and Lincoln thanked him.

They waited; this was the last and one of the most important parts of setting up the roller reefing: eliminating the sag from the foresail luff. The fore halyard winches were by the mast, Lincoln watched as Nick sweated them on, straining for the last ounce of tension. He finally stood and signalled; Gary ground in the foresheet till Nick called a halt – he had a clear view of the foresail by the mast.

Lincoln felt *Worippa* as she picked up her skirts . . . Only to knee-high though, five and half knots maximum, and that with the main set and all available heads'l unwound.

*   *   *

Both Nick and Gary began to strip off too – the condensation inside foul weather gear was always a problem despite various manufacturer claims. They'd be smelly too, Lincoln knew, exertion causing both oilies and bodies to sweat.

Gary eventually enquired, "What do you think?"

"We're definitely losing it, Gary, and it'll get worse towards midday – I can't see us getting an onshore breeze, can you?"

Gary didn't answer, eyes only for, even with heavy wing beats, the graceful 'Concord' of a sea-bird labouring its way south. The odd puff of cloud, to Lincoln, had looked to be pure white – sun-caught plumage proved them to be grey!

The three of them tracked it, Nick voiced his question, "Big mother, ain't it – what is it?"

276

It was Lincoln who answered him, "It's a Gannet."

Gary knew more, "It has a six foot wingspan and is a fisherman by trade. They can dive from a height of over a hundred feet." They watched the bird in question while Gary continued his semi-lecture. "It looks exactly like a German Stukka dive-bomber when, at maximum height, it folds up its wings to dive. They impact the surface so hard, their foreheads and chests are specially reinforced with extra bone, gristle and cartilage. Nature has also provided them with air bags: this bloke pumps up protective air into sacs at the last minute." Gary was silent for a moment, then, "There's a tremendous splash, you know, you don't appreciate it unless you're close – incredible sight. In my opinion, the best, the most graceful diver, there is."

Nick and Lincoln looked at each other from behind his, Gary's back; Nick's raised eyebrows said everything.

Gary picked-up and continued on with their previous conversation – it was almost as if there hadn't been an interruption! "No, not much of a sea-breeze down this coast, we won't be able to get another forecast till we fix the aerial. Still, I can't believe there'll be other shipping around here anyway, though I'll keep trying. I'll take a look at that, the aerial, in a minute, when I catch my breath. We're on our own now; Macquarie'll be out of range."

'Catch his breath'! Lincoln repeated silently.

Nick interrupted Gary and casually nodded at the distant shore line, "Did you know," he said and lifted a careless finger, "there's some sort of structure on that point?"

They turned, Gary and Lincoln – he had a pair of eyes on him, did Nick, acknowledged Lincoln – if he looked carefully, he could just pick out an almost indistinguishable, stark, squat, upright oblong: a tiny, white, lonely tooth amongst a jumble of comparatively low-lying, predominately ochre rocks.

"Is that Sandy Cape Light, Gary?" Lincoln asked, knowing that it must be.

"Yes," and he added, matter-of-factly, "it's made of concrete, it's unmanned and only visited periodically by maintenance crews." Another silence, anything man-made on this coast a novelty, but not necessarily a comfort, it accented their isolation somehow. "What's your gut feeling, Chris, or bottom, or bum feeling, as the case may be?"

"No different, Gary." Lincoln grinned. "Everything feels fine. I don't foresee any more problems with the weather, apart from no wind . . . it might even veer a touch more later."

Gary was obviously thinking out loud. "Umm . . . the barometer's rock steady – it's not moved."

"What about tides, Gary?" Lincoln asked. "Worth going right out to sea, d'you think – might we pick up and catch the 'ocean' rather than chance bucking a local inshore tide?"

Gary shook his head, and in his own way chastised Lincoln. "Your guess is as good as mine, Chris, there's very little data available, it's not like the English Channel, you know. They say they can't justify the research expenditure, and they probably have a point, I suppose – just. There is hardly any shipping down here."

Gary changed direction suddenly, "Those pundits talk in the yacht club about a north flowing current as if it were running at five or six knots." He turned to Nick, as if Nick knew all about it. "The offshoot of the Southern Ocean Current – it's all bullshit. Ocean currents run at around a knot an hour at most – the official figure up this part of the coast is about six knots per twenty-four hours, that's all. Point two-five of a knot per hour, at most. Bass Strait is the only exception: Tasmania and the Islands cause a bottle neck: up to three knots an hour depending on wind and where." Then almost to himself, "It'd be interesting to check out the GPS and see what that says, that should tell us something." Lincoln, with a tolerant half-smile, looked shorewards again, after he had discretely observed Gary returning from wherever he'd been and him refocusing his eyes back on them. "Actually, the wind's the key factor; the wind's more relevant than anything else: the set and stream'll run where the wind dictates. We wouldn't still be here if that weren't true, we'd have never survived that storm had the wind not turned the current round and created a following sea. Imagine the waves had that current shown the least resistance, it would have lifted them to undreamed of heights – that storm wave that we experienced would have been a minor issue!"

A little walking encyclopaedia, he was!

      *   *   *

They thinking their own thoughts; Lincoln turned to Nick finally and in the silence said slowly, "Listen you." He lifted a threatening finger. "You urinate . . . I catch you urinating in this cockpit," Lincoln leant close, really close, "I'll feed you to the fishes a piece at a time – right!"

"What do you mean," Nick replied indignantly, "I've never pissed in this cockpit in my life." He shook his head. "I use the lemonade bottle like everybody else."

His response had been totally instantaneous: shock, puzzlement, disgust: hurt, righteousness were written there for Lincoln to see . . . Bloody Helmut!

Chapter 20

It took some minutes in the comparative darkness of the shadow below for Lincoln's eyes to adjust, though, in truth, sight was unnecessary to walk to the chart table anyway. There was no glow from any of the navigational aids nor instrumentation; all unnecessaries had been turned off in an effort to conserve power. Lincoln slid in and sat at the chart table and examined the log; the barometer matched Gary's last log entry, which was not unexpected. There was very little reaction to a gentle tap – a hair upwards a fraction, if anything. There was just a low hum with an occasional muted burp from the VHF; still, he would have been very surprised if there had have been any traffic. The VHF wasn't going to provide them with a link to the outside world, which would be wishful thinking – a chance in a thousand.

There was no suntan cream to be had, that there used to be a tube in the chart table desk, Lincoln could have sworn . . . He remembered then and recalled the actual incident: Ramsey, Ramsey had thrown it overboard in a fit of temper, objecting to the mess, especially to stuck and wax-stained chart edges – and they had hidden, or made themselves scarce when he'd spat that particular dummy!

And suntan cream because one of the golden rules in Australia is never to underestimate the Australian sun. One of the first painful lessons he had learnt here, down-under, was that, for a white Caucasian, it took only ten to fifteen minutes to acquire severe, grade-three burns. Acclimatisation didn't come into it simply because a body couldn't get acclimatised, even if one were born here! Treating the sun as a giant three-bar electric fire, or the equivalent, he had found, saved a lot of pain and grief – better still, treat it as an inefficient, yet effective death ray – it took time, but eventually kill you it would.

These guys aboard *Worippa* were older and, as far as Lincoln was concerned, had nothing to prove – body-beautiful and overly worrying about a girl-enticing image was, more-or-less, a thing of the past – they wore a hat and neckerchief, if appropriate, as a matter of course. Thankfully, they'd looked after and educated him – for which Lincoln was grateful. Potter and Ramsey both swore that its vicious strength was a recent acquirement and both insisted that problems with the ozone layer were much more serious than publicised, and, as Lincoln knew, they were both conservative people and certainly not prone to 'green' hysteria. Shepherds, graziers and farmers, according to them, now had to cover their four-legged helpers with 'factor-fifteen' suntan cream: dogs with blood-raw, pink-scabbed, painful, peeling, burnt noses they had not seen as children!

Lincoln walked on through, Helmut looked up, his grin was infectious; the 'sandwich' incident was going to be put down in the annals and he would get a lot of mileage out of it yet! They both understood that Nick had never urinated in the cockpit; it wasn't Nick and for all his bluster, for Nick, as Lincoln well knew, was finicky in that way. Helmut's effort at humour and his reaction had created a land-bridge between them somehow: a catalyst for a lifelong friendship and from now on he'd always be there for him. Helmut would never be short of a talking point, no awkward, pregnant silences for him from now on – the aforesaid could be raised at any time and if necessary embellished and embroidered upon. Nick was a lot of things, but not slow, he'd quickly understand the significance of Lincoln's answering grin to his indignation (once he heard the full story), nor, Lincoln guessed, would his future relationship with Helmet cause him petty jealousies – Nick was already mature enough to be above that sort of childish nonsense.

Relationships so complex, they'd never be understood or unravelled by an outsider – nor by themselves eventually.

Whatever Sharon had simmering smelt delicious; there were no saucepans on the top of the oven so it had to be a casserole.

"You haven't seen the suntan cream, have you, Helmut?" Lincoln asked.

Helmut sat behind the saloon table: casing, armature, carbon brushes, and other bits and pieces were laid out on protective kitchen paper . . . However, Lincoln asked himself, did they survive before the introduction of kitchen paper: it had a million wasteful uses and was a godsend on a yacht.

Helmut put down his screwdriver, stood, turned and climbed onto his knees: he searched in the recessed shelves above the saloon settee. He sat again after handing across a large plastic tube.

"Thanks," Lincoln said. "Sharon forward, is she?" he enquired, and then nodded to the starting motor. "Found anything?"

"Yes, she is vashing – I am to check the oven." He frowned. "A little condensation, maybe."

"Let's hope it puts her in a better mood after then, as you saw, or heard, she just about bit my head off earlier."

Helmut shook his head and then peered carefully in either direction, his exaggerated, clandestine behaviour closely resembling something from a second-rate 'B' class movie. He'd clam up, Lincoln knew, if he so much as sensed a smile, and, by the look on his face, it was serious. Lincoln sat and pivoted his legs under and slid along the shorter length of settee: the side that was attached to the same bulkhead as the chart table: the side of the saloon alcove nearest to the companionway steps. Helmut moved too, along the base line and closer to the corner and to him, which was because in this corner of the saloon, with their heads together at right angles, though not ideal, it was in the circumstances a natural choice for a semi-private conversation.

"Something vent on down here," said Helmut, he pointed. "Up forward, before or vhile she was showering – something just before, I think . . . It vas something to do vith Varren, it vas he who had upset her – something said or something done."

"What?" Lincoln asked. "Had a bit of a 'blue', did they?"

Helmut shook his head. "I vas not paying that much attention – I heard it only in the background." He indicated to the starting motor parts along from them. "I vas looking at the motor and vasn't taking too much notice of them . . . not consciously taking notice, you understand?"

Lincoln nodded.

They both sat back.

There something odd here, Lincoln sensed, Helmut was obviously uneasy. "Where's he now then? Warren, I mean."

This time it was Helmut's turn to look puzzled. "Up vith you."

Helmut and Potter were alike in one respect; they could both be amazingly fast when they wanted to be. Helmut's instincts operated on something of the same level – and told a story – he'd slid along, round and out of the forward opposite settee while Lincoln had automatically slid back and along to the edge and observed. Warren walked through from forward as Helmut stood, Warren was now in shirt and jeans and apparently oblivious to their combined stares. They watched silently until his legs had disappeared from sight and were both staring, finally, at the empty companionway steps.

Helmut said slowly, reluctantly, "Maybe better if ve fold up the pilot berth?"

Instinct and their minds as one – the pilot berth was directly in front of the heads curtain, apart from the pilot berth there was no other reason for a person, that Lincoln could think of, to legitimately loiter in that particular section of the boat!

"We'll need a place for the Number Three, Helmut, where the pilot berth is would be ideal – it's too useful a sail to stow out of sight anyway, we should have it handy – the trysail can live there too." Lincoln followed that trend of thought. "I'll re-thread new braid into the storm jib, to replace those 'earrings' we cut – best we keep the two of them together, yes?"

They both turned in unison, Sharon stood there: vulnerable, healthy and cuddly: clean and scrubbed: wet hair combed back. She had that indefinable, ageless, comely freshness that children and women have after a bath that had been preceded by a busy day – monitoring the children in the children's playground or similar.

Not quite happy, Sharon – better to ignore that for now.

Lincoln enquired of Helmut instead, after nodding across, "Will you be stitching the patient's appendages back on before the end of the watch, Helmut?"

The uncovered engine was an anomaly, upsetting and an affront to the eye; it was spoiling the comfort of the saloon.

It took a moment for the puzzled frown to clear. "Oh. Ja, I just have to screw it back together. I fit his 'pace-maker' in a minute," he next added, trying to contain himself, "then ve hold the pads to his chest – a little shock treatment, ja. Ha. Ha, ha . . ."

God, what on earth had he . . . they, done – they were going to regret it, unlocking that part of his brain – Margaret was going to get a real shock! Lincoln shifted the blame, more Nick's fault than his – this, Helmut was, without doubt, a different person.

Head down, shoulders heaving silently, Helmet tickled pink . . . and infectious; Sharon and Lincoln had to laugh too – and thereupon, Helmut spoilt it. "Is not this, hardly vorn and is not vet."

Lincoln, perversely, felt like complaining, "We're doing well, Helmut, Gary says the same, there's nothing wrong with the aerial connection on the backstay!"

Curiosity got the better of her, Sharon's sharp brain again – her femininity made a person forget. "Why the backstay, the aerial's on that post, surely? Isn't that the aerial – behind the steering wheel?"

It was Helmut who answered her, "That one is the VHF emergency aerial, Sharon. Ve actually utilise the backstay for the main radio, it is our aerial for the broken set – it's much higher, you see." He turned. "Ve maybe should have had an emergency vip aerial for our MF radio on the stern rather than the VHF, that vould of covered all emergencies Chris, ja?"

He meant 'whip' aerial, of course.

"You're right, Helmut," Lincoln replied, "and knowing Brian, I'm sure that that'll be his next priority. The trouble is, how far do you go, an emergency VHF makes a lot of sense and is ideal for local waters – the only way to go." He pointed out albeit somewhat defensively, "What I mean is, you can end up towing a spare yacht in the end, can't you, if you see what I mean?"

The screw that was holding and securing the aluminium framed, armoured, smoked glass skylight above the table took a bit of moving: pure oxygen-saturated air poured in, completing the flow. A hand gently rubbed up and down, gently caressing his, Lincoln's, up-stretched arm; a nod was enough for her – the hatchet buried.

Nick tumbled down the companionway steps; he was slightly breathless. "There's only twenty-five minutes to the end of the watch, put the billy on, shall I, they'll be wanting hot tea?" He pointed to the oven, turned to Sharon and at the same time turned into that earnest, obnoxious, whining, nuisance child that, at one time or another, they had all met. "Eat ours now, can we? Go on, can we? I'm starving."

Sharon didn't seem to know quite how to react, she was strangely defensive, Nick was accenting each question with a slight irritating push – pretending to be trying to get between her and the oven. It was the pinch finally that did it – she reacted to that all right!

Through gritted teeth, just coherent, and in time with the effort – the flying, cack-handed punch luckily missing by miles.

"You little Italian git." She moved in. "Your balls are going into that casserole."

He, Lincoln, had guessed right, it was casserole.

She grabbed, her aim painfully true the second time and resulted in Nick laughing and crying – and begging. His back finally against the sink and standing there with both his hands covering and clutching hers – hers had a firm hold on his crutch!

Sharon said sweetly, "Say you're sorry."

Nick gasped, "I'm sorry."

"Really sorry?"

Nick parroted quickly, "Really sorry."

"Sharon's lovely?"

"Sharon's the most beautiful girl in the world and I'll never pinch her big fat ars . . ." he yowled, tears and laughter mixed, until finally and squealing hysterically like a big girl, he answered correctly. "Pinch her wonderful bottom again."

She let him go. "You little sod, I suppose you'll be wanting bread too?"

Nick wiped his eyes with a piece of that torn off, indispensable, kitchen paper and then pulled out the elasticated waistband of his track pants and looked – his hand disappeared down inside and he tentatively and judiciously felt about. He only made the one comment – and it expressed everything. "Christ!"

He finally sidled across to the saloon table after his self-examination, they watched, fascinated. Poor Helmut was going to catch it, as usual, surmised Lincoln, he, Helmut, knew too and was moving uncertainly – squirming.

Nick addressed Helmut, lording from his superior height, "What are you looking at, you great big pudding, taking your time, aren't you. We do want to be home before next Christmas, you know."

Helmut kept his head down, dejected, a picture of sorrow. He ignored Nick and directed his question to Sharon, "Ve have aspirins, Sharon – I feel a headache coming on."

He'd never win.

Nick turned abruptly and flounced across to the steps, and stopped there, with one foot on the third step for effect. His eyes turned to Sharon – one sentence before departure. "He's German, you know, you'd better make that four aspirins. He has four – one for each corner of his square bloody head."

Best to look the other way – and keep busy.

*   *   *

Ramsey now sat where Helmut had sat at the end of their previous watch – to starboard – on the settee in the centre of the saloon. Helmut had been and was quizzing him and Ramsey had gone full circle. He had answered Helmet's questions calmly, initially, and with patience – he'd lost his temper slowly and had got to the stage where he had been almost shouting the answers to the merciless, third-degree probings – and he was fading fast again now.

Helmut asked in a bleak voice, "So, you have rechecked that I had cleaned the connections to the starting motor?"

Brian ground out between clenched teeth, "Give me a break, Helmut, I had to just in case, I wasn't questioning your competence, you weren't around to ask at the time, were you?"

Helmut looked at him for a few seconds, and then nodded slowly. "You vaselined the connections again, as found?"

Not quite positive, Lincoln sympathetically noted, was Brian's voice, "There was already sufficient on them."

Helmut ignored his answer. "You have dried and cleaned all the connections on the starting relay – including the low current energising switch?"

No mug Brian, he could see which way the wind was going to blow and he gave up and resigned himself to his fate. "Fuck, Helmut, how do I know? I could tell you if I knew where or what the low 'whatever-it-was' switch was."

Lionel cut Nick's stage whisper off midway. "The SS had nothing on Helmut . . ."

Sharon also shushed him.

"It is in the cockpit, it has a key in it, ja?"

Brian looked relieved, then triumphant, he nodded. "Checked and done – the ignition switch, right?"

The next question Ramsey greeted with a glum silence. "You have turned on the power and felt all the cleaned and vaselined connections – from the battery onwards – nothing vas burning hot to touch? Especially you have checked the solenoid, including the (Helmet emphasised the next word with disdain) 'ignition switch'?" Helmut well and truly had his arrogant head on now, he was merciless, "Have you screwed and resealed the 'ignition switch' without doing that?"

There were basic nationalistic differences here: a different upbringing, a different culture – different traits. Helmut's race generally, and Lincoln was very familiar with that mentality, were not given to flights of fancy: they weren't encouraged, from an early age, to follow intuition or hunches. Also, one thing they wouldn't tolerate, which he again knew from hard won experience, was open criticism, especially from one whom Helmut considered a rank amateur.

Tact the lubricant, life's lubricant, and a word that unfortunately wasn't in the Australian dictionary. Most Australians wouldn't have been privy to the industrial experiences Lincoln had had in Europe. It is a dangerous game, to lump or label nation's into categories, he knew that, but still . . . They were light years apart, these two cultures, Aussies through need and necessity, and isolation, used string and brown paper given that nothing else, very often, was available. Germans, on the other hand, were used to and expected the very best.

Helmut would automatically and methodically work down through the list and be totally disciplined – Aussies, to be blunt, would start any bloody where!

It was Nick who pre-empted Lincoln, it was he who realised in his own way that they hadn't asked the obvious, and it wouldn't occur to Helmut that he himself should take the initiative.

Nick pushed his way through, and there, with his hands on hips again, he stood looking up, almost eye-to-eye and nose-to-nose (and, incidentally, he had saved Lincoln asking his question – and Nick's involved advanced psychology!).

"Why don't you admit it, Helmut," he belligerently asserted, "you don't know what the fuck's wrong with it, do you?"

Neither moved and the strangest thing, and in no sense homosexual – Helmut reached up and gently and affectionately caressed Nick's cheek. Nick's hand came up slowly, placing it over Helmut's, and holding it there for a second.

Nick whispered, "Fix it for them, Helmut . . ." Nick gently shook his head, "Please?"

Helmut turned to Ramsey.

Ramsey nodded to the unspoken question, a big man too. "I'd be obliged."

Helmut gave good advice and his sincerity glowed through

– he could surprise you, he had surprised Lincoln once already that day!

"There is no point in getting over-anxious over the engine, Brian, it does not help, you are making yourself ill, ja, and you do not sleep. So. Then you are more anxious about the engine . . ." Helmut reasoned, "Does it matter, ve are on holiday, you are on holiday. My friend, the Mister Mate, he has said no more storm – the mast vill hold. Ve should be back on two-hour vatches, the three muskets have done – they have vorked hard enough." Helmut's eyes rested on each of them in turn. "Maybe a little vine, red – Sauvignon from the Barossa, ja," Helmut added a blatant plug, "it is made by Germans." The fleeting grin faded and he concluded, "Better to play vith the engine if ve have the extra energy, ja: a hobby, something to pass the time?"

Sharon took her arm from around Nick's shoulder. "Where?" she asked.

Brian looked at her. "In the cupboard above the freezer."

"Yes, of course," answered Sharon.

To Helmut, Brian said, "You'll have to slum it on this trip, Helmet, South Australian wine is all we've got!"

Helmut simply nodded good-naturedly and shrugged.

Bill Corsham roused himself, declaring concurrence, "I'll do crackers – we've some nice cheese."

And Lionel, "I'll drink to that, matie."

Brian couldn't contain himself any longer, "Tell me?" he asked.

Helmut knew exactly what he meant, it almost as if he'd been waiting for the question – and in Lincoln's estimation, he probably had! Helmut held up a thumb, jerking that appendage outward to forty-five degrees, emphasising the first point. "Vun: ve turn over the engine by hand, it maybe that the engine has seized and there is nothing vrong with the electrical system." He held up his index finger. "Two: ve go through all connections again, it is vun of those, I think." Then his middle finger. "Three: ve check that we have a ground."

Brian held his peace, "Earth."

"Ja, earth." Helmut finally held his ring finger up with the finger and thumb of his other hand. "Four: ve check the solenoid – you have a spare?"

Bill intervened, "Only an old one that was becoming

unreliable – we kept it for some reason."

Helmut covered his disapproval well, "So . . . it has occurred to me, ve should check the pockets of the first battery, a pocket not vorking vould cause a dead failure – ve change them round."

Brian absent-mindedly corrected him again, "A pocket we call a 'cell', and a failure is a 'short'. What else?"

Helmut didn't take offence. "So, then ve see. You have no meter, maybe ve make up a test light, ve maybe use a globe." Helmut advised again, "You should use alkaline batteries – nickel-cadmium for starting, ja. This vould pay you: longer time, more stronger and you vould not have to look at so much." He pointed. "Automobile batteries are good for lights only . . . And alvays you must carry a second solenoid." He brooded, without acknowledging, or perhaps he simply hadn't heard Ramsey's 'right'. "We must not try until ve are sure, even if ve mend, ve vill need all power, an engine vill sometimes turn for forty-five seconds before starting. The quicker it turns the more chance ve have." He rotated his hand to emphasise the point. "Must go fast . . ." Another thought occurred to him. "Your engine, Brian, it has a thermostart?"

Brian shook his head, there was hesitancy in his voice and he quietly side-stepped the question. "Never had problems, not in this climate."

Helmut had missed it and from the ambiguity of Brian's answer it was obvious that he didn't know what a thermostart was, still, that didn't really matter because Helmut would look for it himself later and find out. Helmut pre-empted Lincoln's train of thought with his next disdainful and dismissive comment.

"It is an English engine, not German."

So. So much for theory, Helmut had obviously assumed that, naturally, an incompetently-made English engine wouldn't have one! He'd turned up his nose and had casually condemned a whole nation to the refuse heap, to boot – Lincoln's nation! Lincoln had to bite his tongue and had to be tactful in the circumstances, and take his off-hand effrontery and impudence on the chin like a man. There was, he ironically concluded, poetic justice in there somewhere!

"You have some 'ether'?" Helmut asked next.

Bill Corsham answered him, "There's some in the stern

locker, out of harm's way – it's an aerosol." Helmet nodded his approval. "The trouble is," Bill continued on, "it might have bled away; we haven't used it for years."

Ramsey voiced his reservations, "I hope you know what you're doing with that stuff, Helmut." He turned. "I didn't know we still had that shit on board, Bill, fucking stuff." He quickly put his hand to his mouth, and thereupon apologised, "Sorry, Sharon."

Sharon shook her head.

Ramsey clarified his doubts, "We nearly blew the engine out the bottom of the boat the last time we used it. The engine very nearly knocked itself to bits initially, after finally starting, that is."

Brian stood, the obvious strain had, thankfully, disappeared from around his mouth and his eyes were bright: relief, and something to do with the fact that he was now on his second glass of wine, no doubt. "We'll leave you to it then." He looked at Lincoln. "Would you make ours the last four-hour watch, Chris, two obviously won't be enough – I don't know about the others, but I'm just about dead on my feet . . . I guess I've overdone it – do you mind?" Lincoln shook his head and mouthed a 'no', and with that he half-asked and half-instructed, "You can split up your watch, if you want to – revert back to original times, or as near as practical anyway – you can tell us what times later." He looked at his watch. "From twenty-one thirty – fair." Lincoln nodded assent. Ramsey turned back to Helmut again. "The start-up procedure, Helmut, Chris knows it – and Gary as well as anyone." He put down his glass abruptly and held up a hand, palm outwards and nodded to everyone. "'Night all."

It must have taken a lot, which Lincoln could only guess at, for Ramsey to say that, especially to walk away, drop it and let it go – it was often a very hard thing to do when in earnest and tired. Burning curiosity and the wondering would kill him – he'd desperately want to be there should they try to turn her over!

*　　　　　　*　　　　　　*

"I've had a look at the watch roster," Lincoln said, "and it'll put us back where we were if we leave them till ten." He held up a piece of paper. "What I suggest is, if you go now, Warren, and you, Sharon: if you and Gary go too then we'll be just about right."

Sharon said grumpily, "We don't need any favours, you know, not from you or anyone else – you don't have to carry us." She looked around belligerently, challenge written there.

There was a high-pitched coo from Nick. "Well, aren't we the tough one – I'll tell you what, if you're so keen you can take my watch, and I take two lumps with my tea – around nine'ish would be nice." Nick sweetly pursed his lips and mimed a kiss to her before he said it. "And you could wake me with a kiss."

"Piss off," blunt if nothing else, "I'd rather bare my arse in Bourke Street than kiss you." She pleaded to Lincoln, "Does he have to stay on board?"

Lincoln's mind boggled, Bourke Street was one of the main streets in Melbourne's city centre. Lincoln had to turn away and take a few deep breaths; if they caught a glimpse of his face then there'd only be more trouble!

Lincoln made a quick aside to Helmut while he was at it, and Helmut closed his mouth as requested – it not becoming. Lincoln faced them again eventually, with an expressionless countenance . . . just; it was not easy to ignore Nick's grinning face. "It doesn't work like that, Sharon; we can't afford concessions nor favours. You may well be fine, but Gary isn't, don't forget, he's been on the helm all this time." He carried on before she could interrupt, "Warren's original watch was two till four, with Lionel – yours was four till six, right?"

Sharon stayed silent, just a moody reluctant nod from her. "You've finished then," Lincoln rode rough-shod over her, "your watch is already finished, so you can go to bed now. Bill and I are on watch next, then Helmut and Nick – therefore, we three, us three would have been up anyway." He finished his train of thought, "If Lionel and Warren come back on at ten and you and Gary at midnight – then bingo – we're back where we started. Brian was probably too tired to realise, but now that Warren is up and running, he can pull his weight, and Brian as skipper is a free agent as far as watches are concerned – he can sleep on, if you see what I mean."

Sharon's comment dripped sarcasm, "Really smart, aren't we." She'd turned before Lincoln could answer. Sharon had got to have brothers, he surmised, she had practised somewhere; she hadn't learnt that killer technique in a day. She feigned, coming in low and fast with a left, Nick was faster, arms jerking, hands instinctively covering his testicles – unfortunately, he'd not monitored Sharon's right hand. It was a bad mistake; it left his head exposed. They winced: forefinger and thumb only, and no quarter given, taking her time: two or three hairs from his head, which were casually removed with an expert twist of her wrist!

*   *   *

The exhaust gate valve Lincoln tried to unscrew: there only one water intake fitted to *Worippa*, everything was fed from there, and Lincoln certainly didn't disapprove: Ramsey didn't believe in having unnecessary holes in the hull. The valve was already open; he was, out of habit, just checking. He knelt and felt for and depressed the lever of the fuel lift pump several times for luck. He made to turn the master key to the electrical system to 'on', but didn't do so.

"Turn the master key to 'on', and that's all there is to it, Helmut," Lincoln said, "I can't think of anything else."

Helmut nodded. "Good, ve turn over the engine by hand now, that will prime the injectors and break the oil seals in the bearings – then ve try."

"Aren't you going to give it a quick blip just to see first?" Lincoln queried.

Not a subject to be pursued, a contemptuous, withering glance from Helmut was enough to silence the most critical of critics, let alone him!

Helmut asked instead, "You have started the engine many times, Chris, you know the throttle setting and exactly how, Nick must stand on the steps and be the middle man." He turned, oil-smudged face deadly serious, and instructed, "You must not stop the engine turning, only if Nick signals, ja – only if Nick signals." With some slight condescension in his voice, he added, "If you believe in heaven above, or are superstitious, now is the time, Chris?"

"God, the Lord help us, no – no Helmut," Lincoln replied ruefully, "I don't believe in that sort of nonsense myself. There's no substitute for logic and scientifically thinking it out," and added, "it'll work . . ." He was silent for a couple of seconds. "Touch wood."

There was only a little telltale, extra crinkling in the crows-feet around Helmut's eyes – that was all!

Chapter 21

There was no need for over-trousers yet, Lincoln decided, despite a slight nip in the air, a jacket would suffice for now. More and more layers, he knew, would be required as evening progressed, it was going to be a clear night, and fresh – and a fair amount of insulation when inactive would be needed to combat and keep the ever-present cold out.

Nick was curiously reluctant to go off watch – he was hovering – there was obviously something on his mind. They studied each other; and indecision was written there on his face and in his stance and plain to see. Nick looked behind and down and then stepped over the hatchway coaming and climbed down the companionway steps backwards until he was at chest-high – and there he stopped. He chewed his lip before coming to a decision – and with that climbed back up again and out into the cockpit.

He stepped across. "Are you all right for a quick word?"

Lincoln nodded. "Sure, just tell Helmet you'll be following him down in a minute – you're minding the wheel while I put on my over-trousers." He added, "Bill's just called into the heads, you know what he's like, he'll be a while."

Nick hesitated.

"Go on," Lincoln said quietly, "whatever you've got to say won't go any further than me, not if you don't want it to, that is."

Nick turned and crossed back to the hatch and dropped onto his knees, his head and shoulders disappeared inside, he having a word with Helmut, Lincoln presumed. Nick eventually and with obvious reluctance came back to the helm. "Um, I'm not trying to 'dob' anybody in, Chris, or anything like that, or talk out of turn, only . . ."

Lincoln interrupted him, "This isn't school, Nick, and I'm not teacher and you're a bit too big to be a pupil." Lincoln cocked an eye at him. "We're just a couple of friends quietly chatting, okay – it's no big deal."

Slowly then, he was thinking it out before speaking – and working out how best to phrase it. "Um, I went forward earlier; to tidy up and check the halyards and see that everything was all right with the roller reefing."

Silence.

Lincoln prompted, "And?"

"The forward hatch was open," quickly now and words tumbling, "and I couldn't help but notice, Sharon was washing in the dunny, she'd left a vee at the top – between the curtains."

This was a bit of a surprise for Lincoln, he had always pegged Nick as having a clean mind: wild, passionate and fun, but not yet ready to be serious. Nick was the sort who was liable to fall deeply in love – and out again just as quickly! A confession of this kind was out of character and he had never, as far as Lincoln knew, had problems with the opposite sex and always seemed to have, much to everybody's chagrin, a different beauty in tow every time. No, this was something different, it was not in him: he had that indefinable interest-indifference to girls, and it made him irresistible to them: even Sharon couldn't help herself, she never left him alone.

Lincoln didn't really know what to say, nor to where all this was leading (or did he), so Lincoln sidestepped. "You're a naughty boy, Nick, you shouldn't peep – you'll get yourself arrested, sooner or later."

He in no mood for it, Nick snapped back, "Be serious," and then more calmly, "I can't . . . I don't know quite how to handle this one, as you said, he's a bit too close to my own age for comfort."

"Warren?" Lincoln asked.

Nick nodded. "He was forward, kneeling on and practically hanging out of the pilot berth, watching. I didn't think much of it when I went forward." Lincoln heard disgust, puzzlement, bewilderment, frustration, temper – all mixed in. "A bloody Peeping Tom, as well as – he was right, was Jamie, about giving him the creeps – he gives me the creeps as well." He shook his head. "There's something sick there – he's bloody weird, isn't he – I wouldn't trust him to lay straight in bed." Nick shook his head again. "He was still there when I went to return to the cockpit – he's thick with it, too. He disappeared like a rat up a drainpipe when he realised that I was watching him – and that's what made me connect. I obviously haven't said anything to him . . . or Sharon . . ."

Lincoln contemplated their surroundings: the sea was slowly turning to slate: and sombre, like viscous oil. An odd star glimmered away in the east and south, it was now dusky overhead and the westward curve of the sky was haphazardly dabbed with delicate, coral pink-edged, almost transparent filaments of fleeced cloud – and the sun now was very low down and almost obscured by red-gold streamers and haze.

"It takes all . . ." Lincoln started to say.

Nick interrupted, "Bullshit. Two friends talking, you said, equal."

Lincoln countered an awkward wallow with a turn of the wheel, the wind had died with evening – it was fluky and *Worippa* was not a happy lady. Her attire was like worn out, second-hand clothes hanging on an old lady too: the sails drooping: a curving flutter of canvas running up from foot to head in time with fore-and-aft, side-to-side roll: and loose gear tugging and jangling, and creaks and squeaks and gurgles and plops heard from under the hull. The mainsail was undecided: swing then back, swing then back and hesitant: and wondering whether to go across and explore the port side or not. The foresail should be poled out and now was the time, if ever there was one, for a preventer on the main . . . Lincoln, to his shame, just couldn't be bothered.

"What am I supposed to say, Nick, I can't figure him out either – what do we do, keep an eye on him, warn Sharon, perhaps? Um, I don't know, I . . . We'll have to think about it – maybe warn him off if it happens again." Lincoln shook his head as Nick went to speak. "One thing I do know though, Nick, I've seen it before and it's not nice: we mustn't start a hate campaign under any circumstances, right. The thing is, they can so easily get out of hand and the consequences can be serious – it's not the path to follow."

A reminder for Lincoln – that Nick wasn't slow.

"Not enough reaction." He was intent and daring Lincoln to look away. "You already knew, didn't you?"

"No." Lincoln bit his lip before qualifying that negative. "Well . . . suspected." He explained, "He came through from forward when Helmut and I were talking – a sixth sense, an instinct, I don't know – he'd been out of sight too long."

Lincoln re-looked at this affable young man and was reminded yet again and anew: he really was growing up, was Nick, and his next observations and conclusions simply confirmed that.

"Do you know what springs to mind, it's a bit twisted but comforting somehow, my mother used to read to my brother and myself every night – we're second generation Australian-

Italian." He said second generation Australian-Italian as if that explained everything! "She's the most wonderful person, you'll meet her; she passionately believes in education – and loves books. Those bedtime stories are still vivid, and she was totally democratic – an English book read in English followed by an Italian book read in Italian." Nick paused for breath. "One book really got us going – fired us up. It was so real to me, I used to hide under the covers while listening – it was *Treasure Island*." He asked, "Have you ever read that book – Jim hiding in the barrel of apples?"

"I remember, Nick, I also remember that book as being slightly macabre somehow: a bit evil for young children: creaks on the stairs in the night – and all that."

Lincoln didn't quite get his drift, but what he was saying was leading somewhere and he was curious.

"Yeah, that's right." Lincoln heard and ignored the embarrassment in Nick's quick laugh. "I used to sleep with a little pocket knife under my pillow – in the morning I'd find myself laying on the golf club that I kept in the bed with me – I never admitted it to my mother, naturally, because she'd have stopped reading it to us, but that book raised the bogey men." He sighed. "Completely lost you, haven't I, I associate the two: it's part of the story to me now: all mixed up and yet I remember it like it was yesterday.

"One of my mother's chores, as a girl, was to sort through trays of stored apples – on the farm in the old country. Once peeled, she said, they were delicious – the skins were wrinkled and tough, like soft leather." Dreaming was Nick, Lincoln discerned, and seeing. He came back to reality. "Sorry. One bad apple, she said, as with the apples in the barrel, one bad apple would send those around it the same way – strange how some childhood memories stay with you." He was brusque then, "We can't throw him away, can we. We can't get rid of our bad apple – couldn't be that easy, could it?"

Well . . . Lincoln gazed forward . . . follow that!

He said gently, "You have to learn to live with them, Nick, there's always one – always; they're not an endangered species. It seems to be a natural law; I've never actually been on a yacht where there hasn't been at least one." He indicated around them with a raised hand. "We're very confined and our closed little world accents – and you're right, it's impossible to do as you'd do normally, to simply walk away." Lincoln shook his head, thinking. "Believe it or not, and looking back, I've even had them when there's been a crew of only four! One's good intentions wrecked my first boat – he let the sheet go too late – he'd been daydreaming and panicked. We screwed up to wind and collided with a cardinal buoy that we were using for a turning mark; it split the side of the boat open like a sardine can."

Lincoln started the usual admonishing, moralising clichés after a moment's silence – as one seems to automatically do when talking to the young. "Be wary of labelling people too quickly, Nick, they can surprise you, people, they often come through," that was until he saw the look on Nick's face and then he quickly changed tack, "and more importantly, don't let him sour your trip. It's difficult, Nick, I know, but try to acquire a protective shell of indifference – polite but distant – there's no need to be rude." Lincoln grinned at him. "Even better, adopt Helmut's attitude, if it's in you – be charitable."

*   *   *

Again, on and on and on, harshly rotating, over and over. One doubtful sign of life – a cough, that was all.

Did he believe in 'heaven above', Helmet had asked – Lincoln was praying now, all right.

That Helmut had fixed the 'dead short' and that the engine *was* turning over was incidental, that fact had not really registered and they, at this moment, were too intent to even notice let alone give credit where credit was due. Lincoln found the urge to twist the key back and stop, as when starting a car, and then try again, almost irresistible.

They had blown it, the batteries were giving out and she had started to slow down – the imperceptible easing Lincoln felt as much as heard. Another cough interrupted the monotonous high, then low grinding – a cough and hiccup – and grinding again. The engine was straining desperately, and Lincoln was straining with it, and turning slower still: a cough, hiccup and cough, and cough again, but still not firing. An agonising crawl, an animal's death throes – to a painful, muted stuttering. And a double-cough finally, before the last rites . . . but the last rites didn't occur because the engine was tentatively catching and missing and thumping, as was his heart . . . and then banging.

His gritted teeth and breath releasing occurred not with the expected death rattle, but in time with the limping, struggling, uneven, straining revolutions. Lincoln felt his head and body nodding and urging, and moving in time to the fluttering heartbeats – eventually they flattening out and his fierce wishing forcing the beautiful, wonderful monster to a lumpy grumbling – and then to what sounded to him like an exalted, contented, too-fast rumble. The billowing clouds of choking black smoke were slow to clear in the erratic, tugging zephyrs; Lincoln could hear it anyway, before confirming it visually, water was exiting with the spent gases and healthy engine cooling spurts of water were being flung out from the low down, stern exhaust.

Helmut and Nick's grinning faces materialised through the thinning, swirling smoke, one behind the other – with a rare display of feeling, he, Helmut, took a step forward and his out-held hand Lincoln shook delightedly. Although aware that Lincoln had already done so, Helmut, nevertheless, lent over the pushpit checking, and confirmed for himself, as any good engineer would – Lincoln forgave him and Helmut accepted the heartfelt praise with a pleased nod.

Lincoln, with a grin, nodded to Ramsey as he appeared and climbed out of the hatchway, his modesty was covered by underpants only, and with a bottle and plastic glasses in either hand. Sharon came next, her modesty . . . Lincoln rephrased that, her modesties, were covered by knickers and a silk top – and erotic enough, he hazarded, to cause Warren an epileptic fit! Bill, Gary, and Lincoln noted, and talking of the devil, Warren – and finally, and bringing up the rear with extra beakers, came Lionel.

These, for Lincoln, were now haunted, treasured memories: there they sat or stood, off-watchers swathed in blankets, and the muted thud of the diesel accompanying the *Dire Straits* cassette tape, *Brothers in Arms*. There was only a pale yellow-red stain above the corrugated skyline to the west, and Bluff Hill Light was winking a friendly hello from a coastline now in deep shadow. Chattering like magpies over the music, and tired, but safe – they were at peace with the world, and whiskey-lined stomachs were loosening tongues. They were laughing and reminiscing, and the waves, built by imagination, were getting higher and bigger by the mouthful!

Nick staggered across and cursing a leg that wouldn't lift

high enough, climbed around behind the wheel. Hesitant at first, until Lincoln got the idea, they, Lincoln and Nick, were eventually swaying in exaggerated unison to an internal beat and natural rhythm of the boat and *Money for Nothing*, shoulder to shoulder and both of them grinning at the world.

Nick, when the first half of the tape ran out, turned to Lincoln; Lincoln could literally see his glassy eyes trying to focus. "I saw you, Pom, I saw you." He hiccupped before stepping away from the wheel and holding out an admonishing finger. "You are absolutely fucking mad."

Gently, filling the sudden and embarrassing hush, Lincoln said, "I know you did, Nick . . ." and with that he persuasively and hurriedly urged, "Time for bed now, Nick, what say? It's another day tomorrow."

"In a minute." There was now a look of secretive cunning on his face. "Not yet. Nobody knows but me, you know." Nick's eyes had lost their hard-won focus. "It's something I'll remember till the day I die." He stepped completely back around the wheel till facing Lincoln, at two steps distance – just out of Lincoln's reach! He held up that erratic wavering finger again, despite the embarrassment, Lincoln could see the funny side, at any other time he would have laughed. "I saw you," the finger jabbed, "I saw you." His head nodded up and down slowly. "Some storm, wasn't it. The wind, fuck, have you ever been in a wind like it?"

Lincoln tried to humour him and at the same time placate – and shut him up. "I haven't, Nick, I've never seen such a wind." Lincoln grinned. "It was so windy; it even blew my penknife open!" And all he got for his troubles was a silly bobbing smirk. Lincoln pleaded, "Come on, Nick, bed."

"No, Pom, you'll not laugh this one off, I can say anything I like and you can't do anything about it." He had, Lincoln saw, that intense concentration that only the drunken are capable of. "In the light from the spreaders on the side of the hull, and with the wind and the sea rolling right over us." Nick's hand touched his mouth and he, in that stage-carrying whisper, whispered, "I was so scared, Chris, so scared – I was sure we were going to die." He was oblivious to his surroundings now. "And you just stood there, I could see you through the rain, as clear as day in the lightning flashing all around." He shook his head. "You were screaming, and shaking your fist, defying it." There was half-accusation and half-awe in his voice, "You were threatening God himself."

Only nature's voices trespassed the silence – starring eyes and embarrassment – Nick not noticing and ignorant of their sublime, undivided attention. "You carried me through," there wonder in his voice, "I surprised myself, I got beyond the fear stage: I was resigned to it: dying. I felt quite calm. I regretted that I'd not be able to say 'good bye' to my Mother, I remember thinking that, that was all – still, she'd have understood, I know she would have."

There puzzlement in his face and he asked. "Where does someone get that kind of courage? What goes on inside your head . . .? We'd all be dead if it wasn't for you." His face suddenly twisted. "I fucking hate you, Pom, you'll always be there in the background and I'll never be able to live up to that image." He stood, unashamed, defiant, eyes blinking away tears. "When will I . . . will I ever be a man?"

Potter pushed through, gently helping him round and through the whispering encouragement – through the parting of caressing, touching and patting guard of honour.

Lionel's voice was just loud enough at the hatch, and heard by everyone. "You've been a man for some time, mister, that storm only confirmed it, matie, only . . . Only you're the only one who hasn't realised it yet, and that's as it should be." Lionel looked round slowly. "You're got nothing to prove that's not all ready proven, Nick, you're as bigger man as any of them – just a little unworldly, is all," Lionel grinned. "And they're not daft enough to drink a gallon of malt whiskey on an empty stomach either, and get weeping drunk, are they?"

Their voices came echoing back as they descended the companionway steps.

"I don't feel very well, Lionel."

"You'll be right, matie, once you're in bed."

"Do you know what, Lionel?"

There never-ending patience in Lionel's response, "What, matie?"

"D'you know – I'm never going to drink again."

Lionel's voice was faint but distinct, "Ah. Well. Well there's a thing – and welcome to the fraternity of men, matie."

        *   *   *

"No, no, come on, wake up. No, no turning over. Here we are, a nice cup of tea for our little hero."

Her voice came from a long, long, way away. Lincoln pulled the covers over again, she pulled them back – he pulled them viciously, not playing. Telling her to go away was successful, but short-lived for some reason, maybe he should have phrased it in another way! All Lincoln vaguely heard and ignored was a muttered 'right' and with that silence. Deliberately, he held on to that semiconscious state and was soon back to the twilight zone, until finally fading again to a deeper sleep.

The shock signals took moments for his brain to register: a freezing cold hand was slipping from middle back till cupping his bottom. The response automatic and the fingers of Lincoln's out-flung, jerking arm hit the deckhead above with a painful thump. The cold hand ignored his reaction and expertly followed the curve of his thigh – Lincoln quickly rolled over. She'd removed her hand before he had had time to grab it.

Her face was in half-darkness, and the lantern, which was the source of the soft light, swung partially and gently into view from out behind her: flickering moving shadows and dark corners: a picture of the *Potato Eaters* for a second, unbidden, came into Lincoln's mind's eye.

Sharon was unperturbed, "Awake are we, big boy. You've got a quarter of an hour before you're due on watch." She flicked on the bunk light, the light blinding Lincoln – a minuscule colouring of sympathy entered her voice. "God, you look like shit."

Ah well! Lincoln muttered in his mind, deep breaths brought him round slowly, his head was woozy – it was like coming out from a drugged coma.

Sharon asked abruptly, "Can you sit up a bit – the tea'll help."

Onto one side and failing to get an elbow under, and slumping down after the effort. He mumbled, "In the words of one of the world's great philosopher's . . ."

Sharon moved out of sight before reappearing a moment later with a patch-worked cushion. "Lift again," she said, "and I'll tuck this under." She paused, "What great philosopher? Come on, lift."

"Nicolo Alessandro Domenico Frascati."

Sharon's response was not quite the kind of response

Lincoln had expected, but then . . . "Never heard of him – always 'he' isn't it? You, buster, and your lot have had it too good for too long, it's about time us girls got a few 'thinkers' racked up – men are going to have to move over, whether you like it or not." There was no apparent pause for breath, "What did he say?"

"Who?" Lincoln asked.

She looked down suspiciously, "What are you grinning at?"

"I can't concentrate," he complained, "There's a bloody parrot in my ear, squawking away . . ."

She reached across.

"That hurt."

"Good, it was meant to."

"I'm never going to drink again."

"What?" Sharon asked – he could see her temper slipping.

"That's what the immortal philosopher said." Lincoln pointed. "Lying over there, in the bottom bunk."

Sharon turned and stepped across; she bent down and lifted the blanket gently before turning back. She was incredulous, "That's never Nick's name?"

"Yup," Lincoln replied, "and true too, we should all know better: we fend off seasickness till we're over it and then undo all the good work by having a drink. I'd better get up before it's too late – I'm feeling very queasy myself." Lincoln looked at her. "Do you mind?"

"What?" she asked innocently.

As if she didn't know, about his underpants, or rather, the absence of them!

"I'm not getting up while you're standing there – push off."

This one, Lincoln resignedly admitted, always seemed to have an answer.

"You didn't feel particularly big to me – what are you worried about?"

God, Lincoln swallowed, if Gary was listening in, or anybody else for that matter – he'd, they'd, draw all the wrong conclusions. The tone of her voice suddenly changed, there was real concern in it, "There's blood on your hand, it's smeared on the cup."

Lincoln looked down, she was right; hitting and catching the bunk above, he concluded, had reopened a nicely healing fingertip.

Sharon took and wedged the cup and gently lifted the offending hand: she held the wounded digit up and inspected it in the direct candescence of the bunk light. She nodded. "I'll get you a band-aid." And then she ruined the whole Florence Nightingale scene, "You're not going to puke up a 'technicolor yawn' straight away, are you?"

"What?" Lincoln recovered quickly, and to be truthful, the concern and pampering had lulled him – it'd been nice. "They're like pearls," he muttered, "the poetic little utterances that drip richly from your red-wine lips."

"I thought you'd like it," there was just no answer to Sharon's supercilious smirk, "that's one of your Nic . . . Um, that's one of your Nicolo's descriptions for being sick."

Lincoln half-heartedly objected, "That's bloody disgusting."

Sharon picked up his hand again and held it in both of hers; she lifted it high and before he could object, licked at the blood. Lincoln watched, fascinated, as she sucked the fingertip for a few moments – before biting softly.

Lincoln added quietly, "And so are you." Lincoln looked from his finger to her eyes, and tried unsuccessfully to make light of it. "Seriously, you don't know where that's been."

Sharon paused, and her answer so sarcastic, "Well, I can hardly hold onto you in any other way – the way you struggle."

She would shock the senses back into anyone, "Here," Lincoln said, suddenly aware, "the engine's not labouring – it's not under load – what's going on?" He snatched his hand away. "Come on, help me out – help me to climb out."

Some words got said, and he would go to the grave regretting them, but, God forgive, in the wrong tone, say them Lincoln did. "Gary'll kill you, you bloody little tease, and me – and I'm old enough to be your father." He quickly over-rode and bulldozed through any reaction when he realised what he had said and how he had said it – he pretended that he hadn't uttered the words and ordered, "Ease my feet round, damn you, and then pull – and don't," he blustered, "don't, pull away the blanket."

Sharon didn't argue, there was no pretended hurt innocence though, and Lincoln wondered if that indicated real hurt, he didn't know . . . but suspected. For some perverse reason, Lincoln did notice her terminology and her words betrayed her keen ear – she'd only been on the boat a few days and already she was using sailoring terms. "The wind's been filling-in for over an hour" she stated matter-of-factly, "and we're making about four knots. Gary says there's two of tide under us so we're only using the engine to recharge the batteries." She gave him a disdainful push. "Move. I haven't got time to waste hanging around here gasbagging with you; Bill'll be wanting his tea too."

Not quite quick enough, opposite, above Nick in the top bunk, but not before Lincoln had seen, did Warren's eyes shut!

*   *   *

Forward to the bow and in the dark of the night and swallowing great mouthfuls to rinse out his lungs once there, and then waiting for the oxygen-impregnated blood to clear away the cobwebs.

Lincoln positioned himself in front of the forestay, and with a foot on either side placed against the end of the toe rails and fully stretched, and with his bottom actually just touching the forestay and with arms stiff and hands grasping the end-curves of the pulpit, he rode along with *Worippa* like a jockey. He was like a steeple-chaser urging his horse over the jumps and his taunt, hinged body rode with their manufactured stead, up and over easily: not fighting and catching the rhythm, and as one with *Worippa* and nature.

The radiance from the running lights was surprisingly faint and muted from his position, and their thrown arc, or horizontal sphere of influence, was negligible. Each light, one on each side, was screwed to a metal plate and each plate in turn welded to the rear of the pulpit. They were positioned, as per regulations, where they could be clearly seen: in the curve where the stainless steel tube of the top pulpit rail turned to vertical. They were, in Lincoln's secret mind, the glittering eyes of a mutant dragon: the one on the left a heated ember of red when looked at directly; and the other, the right, an intense, opaque green.

And then glimpsed at under the flared overhang – there was no give-a-way reflection and seemingly brighter in that black shadow. Lincoln leaned right out over the starboard side for a better view: a tumbling bow-wave of shining, glowing, unbelievable luminescence: the gurgling, golden-yellow, sequinned water at the cutting edge was heaped above the inky black surrounding water. Lincoln's mind and imagination drifted . . . No, sequinned was the wrong word, this was not a gaudy glitz, this was a scene of indescribable exquisite resplendence, and not, literally, of only surface beauty. The water somehow had an inner glow: a yellow to a deep bottle-green semicircle nosed before: thousands, billions – clouds of microscopic disturbed marine organisms suspended and floating in the soup of life. This deeply lit, frothed, nocturnal beard, he theoretically knew, was haphazardly and liberally sprinkled with isolated, black, minute blotches, which, if anything, accented and increased the contrasted therein. His eyes automatically followed the waterline; there was an immediate, thin, golden strip alongside and clinging to the hull too.

Lincoln felt the lifeline sliding between his fingers as he made his way aft, eyes bedazzled, until he was halted by and came to rest against the lower fore shroud – the line of shimmering radiance was unbroken until after the glowing after-brilliancy of their bubbling wake had stopped disturbing the water. Lincoln gazed, spellbound, and his brain recorded that fact somewhere, that it was very noticeable that their wake tapered quickly away to obscurity, and that that dark obscurity was all around and only the immediately disturbed water produced the phenomenon, and that it was only their passage that had created such an abrupt short-lived transplendency.

He stepped across and leant against the mast, this is what sailing was all about – the night crystal clear and the blazing stars crowding the sky in their thousands. A white crescent moon was hanging suspended above their stern and close enough to touch, and its light was noticeably fading the glory of those nearest stars and distant suns to insignificance. An oily black sea gleaming under that waxing quarter: molten silver reflected: flashing and flickering from near and distant leagues of dimpled undulations. Eerie, luminous, zodiacal white and contrasting shadow, and humps and hills ghosting past and marching away to smooth perpetuity.

Lincoln went aft eventually and back to reality. Instead of relieving Gary at the wheel as Gary obviously expected him to, Lincoln used his, Gary's shoulder, to steady himself, and as much as an acknowledgement of his presence as of necessity, and climbed around behind him and lent out to check and confirm that their stern light was on. *Worippa's* stern light was attached high up, comparatively, and screwed to the central post of the pushpit; the light's halo from the wheel or anywhere on the boat was almost impossible to distinguish. Lincoln marvelled, as he often did, at the efficiency of the light's design as he leant out and viewed the cylindrical oblong of blinding white ice directly: its horizontal arc of light was exactly calculated, as was the distance off from which the light could be seen (to enable shipping behind to ascertain their approximate course and position). The lens design of the thing, as before, was such that there was no escaping light to be seen onboard – to obviously preserve night vision – and hence the necessity for his periodic checks.

It was Lincoln who finally assaulted the silence. "Right, Gary, move over and I'll take her."

Gary shuffled to one side as Lincoln gripped the wheel, it took a moment to get the feel – she was balanced perfectly, and the sails sound asleep. It was like skimming through a dream in suspended time.

Gary's teeth were pink-white in the compass light and he grinning that peculiar grin that only camaraderie and shared knowledge and experiences can create. There were a thousand words in his countenance – and words that Lincoln knew were unnecessary and inadequate anyway. A night like this, apart from any other considerations, burnt itself into the memory and in isolation from earlier events and incidents and became one of those treasured gems that could be dredged up on a rainy day, but, more often than not, such a memory would be flashed up into the mind's eye at some unexpected time – either way, it was there to be marvelled at, mulled over and relived and savoured.

Gary eventually turned to the business at hand, the ship's business, and began to pass over the watch. "The wind's freshened nicely – and the wind shifts aren't big enough to worry about." He eased Lincoln's hand from the wheel to demonstrate. "She'll sail for about two or three minutes before she even thinks about coming out of the groove – beautiful." There was no need for him to reiterate but ingrained discipline, Lincoln knew, and habit made him automatically go through the ritual. "There's no course as such to shape," he held his hand vertically over the compass, "due north: we simply run up the one hundred and forty-four, thirty minute longitudinal meridian till we're off the 'Heads'. Three-fifty magnetic – easy." He took a breath, "Incidentally, the GPS 'off-course' alarm is off." Lincoln gave him a look – he explained, "I've been checking the aerial lead for faults and the thing's been driving me crazy – beeping all the time." He added, for Lincoln's ears only, "The helmswoman was a bit erratic."

Lincoln grinned. "Right, off you go then." Lincoln touched his sleeve as he stepped away. "By-the-way, did you find anything wrong with the aerial?"

Gary was silent for a moment, his shaking head seen in silhouette in the half-shadow. "I thought I'd found it – there's a joint in the cable just under the trailing edge of the locker above the double berth – you know, the skipper's berth – behind the navigator's seat. There was a lot of verdigris on it, I cleaned and vaselined it – it's not made a damn's worth of difference. You shouldn't really have a join in a cable if you can help it, apart from being vulnerable, it impairs the efficiency of the set. The plug going into the actual set was green-rotten too – I've cleaned that up – I had to take off the cover to get at the socket. There was some moisture in there so maybe it'll end up to be something to do with that." Gary, to Lincoln, didn't sound hopeful. "I've left the cover off in the hope it'll dry out, but I wouldn't hold your breath."

"Where are you getting your energy from, Gary," Lincoln asked, "you're an embarrassment – you're too bloody energetic and cheerful by half."

Gary laughed. "It's the end of the watch and the magic of the night, and . . . and I've just had a little tot." Lincoln tried to see his face – Gary held up an admonishing finger. "Now. I only had the one, and a small one at that – I've fallen for that one before and I'm not about to make the same mistake twice." Lincoln nodded his acceptance and concurrence. "You know," their navigator continued, "it feels odd, sharing the 'middle' watch. I mean, only two hours on the helm instead of four, it makes one hell of a difference – you'll be back in bed before you know it."

Lincoln enquired, "Did you find a 'U' in the aerial lead?"

"How do you mean?"

"A business friend of mine," Lincoln explained, "an electronics bod, he started out in life fixing television sets. On outside aerials, where the lead joins the actual aerial on the chimney, or wherever, you make sure there's a downward loop there in the cable. Water drips off the bottom of the loop instead of running directly down the aerial cable and straight into the junction box – he made a fortune, by the time he'd finished he had a couple of lads running around for him as well, repairing or replacing wintered aerials that had rotted out before their time." Lincoln added as an afterthought, "He was fair too, he explained the problem to them and didn't denigrate his predecessors – it snowballed – his customers always came back to him, and not necessarily for aerials only . . . And they naturally recommended him to their friends et cetera, et cetera."

There was no reaction from Gary – his attention was elsewhere. The panic and urgency in his whisper as his head, shoulders and torso turned quickly back transmitted itself and a cold chill ran through Lincoln – causing goose pimples to rise. The fine hairs on the back of his neck and those on his arms, stood up on end.

"There's something on our starboard quarter, Chris, and coming in – something big. And that's not the first time I've caught sight of it either, only it was further out before and I glimpsed it for only a second." Gary was bordering on babbling – until he uttered his stricken conclusion to Lincoln, that is, "I'm sure the bloody thing's been stalking us, I can feel it – Christ!"

Lincoln had turned quickly and was peering intently at the section of sea that Gary's silhouetted outstretched arm indicated.

"Where-away, Gary," he asked finally. "I can't see anything."

"It was there. It was over there." He pointed again. "Maybe a hundred feet off." Gary's voice was stringent and shaky, and yet, if Lincoln listened closely, it was laced with an underlying panicky, semi-hysterical excitement, "The thing disappeared," he hissed, "as soon as I called out."

Chapter 22

Bill had not fully recovered from the storm and Lincoln was concerned that he had yet again got himself over-tired, the galley strip-light accented the deepening lines etched into his face, his eyes were puffy and bloodshot, red-rimmed and sore. They must all have looked the same, more-or-less, and they just a little bit worse for wear. Unwashed and grubby, with four-day beards and uncombed hair – Lincoln was not unaware that in all probability his appearance would be as bad, if not worse – they would look like a gang of unsavoury, scruffy, greasy pirates to an outsider.

Bill placed the refilled kettle back on the hissing hob and confirmed and echoed Lincoln's thoughts in a round-a-bout way. "You don't look all that crash-hot, Chris. You've gone a nice pasty shade of green." Bill grinned and nodded. "Under the muck, that is." Despite his haggard looks he was reasonably buoyant and Lincoln's concern, he felt, was unnecessary – it was he, Bill, who was actually comforting him! "Try and hold onto it for a little longer, tea and toast'll settle you down and we'll have some soup later."

Lincoln admitted it, it would please Bill anyway, Bill liked to mother and it'd stop him brooding. "I think I'm paying for that little drop of poison, Bill. The old demon drink – bloody stupid – and I should know better.   Lack of regular sleep, irregular eating and a bit of tension and worry thrown in – it's a bloody formula for disaster." Lincoln shifted for balance as *Worippa* heeled.   "I'd just started to come good too, I was finding just a bit of excess energy, would you believe – I'd been waking up or dozing before watch-call."

Bill sympathised, "Don't worry, think about something else, you'll feel fine once we've got some tucker down you."   His demeanour then collapsed, "The very thought of food makes me feel squeamish too." Lips pulled back from clamped teeth; his head, throat and shoulders shuddering.   "We'll just have to force it down, we're both long enough in the tooth not to know, us old campaigners – eat and sleep and snatch our chances when opportunities arise." Bill closed his eyes for a moment and then glanced across – despite his own pallor there was a look of appraisal on his face. "Tell you what – I'll do a deal with you.   You get Gary and Sharon to bed ASAP – whatever he saw'll be long gone by now anyhow – it's pointless, them two hanging about." Bill gestured. "You can go first, after we've settled the boat down and eaten." He raised his eyebrows in askance and Lincoln looked in askance. "Let's take a ticket out of Sharon's book and take a bucket of hot water forward and strip-wash?"

Bill quickly continued on, not letting Lincoln interrupt, "You're skin's white with encrusted salt, it's glistening." He reached out and rubbed a rough thumb across his, Lincoln's, cheek. "It could almost be hoar frost the way the crystals catch the light." Bill dropped his hand and leant back. "You can't be comfortable, and anyway, it's unnecessary – your eyes look like piss holes in the snow. The next kettle'll be just about boiled by the time you're done and ready to shave – talc up, spray on a bit of deodorant, clean underwear and you'll feel like a new man. What say?"

Lincoln nodded his complicity; Bill had obviously not missed the gleam in Lincoln's eye, albeit a bit murky – he was talking to the converted!

"We may not have another chance, something's bound to crop up – it's steady enough up there and provided we stay clipped on . . . Whoever's up top, either you or me, can tap three times quickly on the deck with the bilge pump or winch handle, or whatever, should anything be amiss. And . . ." Bill left the word hanging in the air – before adding his clincher. "Our watch'll be over by the time we've finished messing about!"

Lincoln, with the backs of his legs braced against the engine cover and his head pounding in time to the engine's muffled, throbbing vibration, and his stomach protesting and churning and objecting to the very faint, lingering residue of diesel exhaust, gulped and tensed as a spasm hit. Only a gesture was necessary, after pouring a half-mug of milk during Lincoln's gasping lapse, Bill handed across two of mother's-little-helpers: pain-killers from the first aid locker.

Lincoln clutched the grabrail attached to the deckhead as *Worippa* yawed. "You go first, Bill," he half-pleaded, "these would have had a chance to work by then – fresh air should do the rest." The queasiness began again and Lincoln took another deep shuddering breath. "I'll have to get topside before I'm really sick – the atmosphere's too close down here for me."

Time spent exposed to a fresh, cool night breeze cleared out the cobwebs and, for Lincoln as usual, a spell at the wheel and thinking about other things eventually soothed the seasickness to a dull discomfort.

Still nothing . . . As them, Lincoln carefully scanned and quartered their dimpled lunashiney surrounds again – as much for therapy as anything else. That Gary had seen something Lincoln didn't doubt, probably a whale that had since, hopefully, sounded – and he didn't want to see it either, for a yacht to be sunk by a curious or love-hungry leviathan was rare, but not an unheard of occurrence in this part of the world. In normal circumstances he wouldn't give it another thought, but out here, as before, thoughts had a habit of getting out of proportion – and it didn't do to think nor dwell too deeply . . . about being stalked – Nick's bogeymen again!

Lincoln followed another and as it turned out, equally disturbing train of thought instead: something that European sailors could be thankful for . . . Not so much whales, but that shark didn't abound in those same European . . . his home waters. It didn't occur often in these particular waters either . . . Well . . . not too often, but there were just enough odd reports in the newspapers to keep a person on their toes: an odd shark attack here, a disappearance there; a diver snatched descending and neither seen nor heard of again. That shark preferred warmer seas he would take their word for, that the odd one or two frequented this far south also true – and that Lincoln didn't want to confirm personally – shark did though, it was said, follow refuse-dumping ships, so maybe . . .?

Lincoln and Sharon jumped to Gary's 'there', Lincoln's consternation instantly dissolved away contemplations. Gary was right too, Lincoln had glimpsed a vague, elongated, green-yellow lit blur well back and out and off on the starboard quarter, and just barely discernible. A very weak spot, or focus, of an underwater spotlight shining, describing and drawing arcs on the underskin of the sea. It disappeared almost as quickly as seen, leaving Lincoln with a strong feeling of self-doubt – did they see it? Was it the result of a reflected swirl caught in the moonlight? Even an odd patch of irradiant floating seaweed? Neither explained the moving circular track though!

Lincoln spotted it again as it suddenly reappeared, and on 'it' came as if it was aware of their awareness, and then suddenly it was accelerating and heading in and closing the angle – and on a collision course for the bow . . . And flashing and streaking past them at a phenomenal speed. The after-image etched forever in Lincoln's brain, of breathless beauty beyond imagination or description, and engraved in his memory. The outline of bottlenose – long aero, water-dynamic, streamlined, finned body driven by a blurred horizontal fluke – and all wrapped in a gleaming, glittering, sequinned, minute-spotted, comet-tailed body-stocking. Forward in microseconds and across *Worippa's* bow and then round in a large curving arc ahead. Their visitor veered off the circumference, on a tangent well out, before turning back to parallel their course – and finally settling in the same, but opposite, port, stern, flank position as when first seen. Their eyes had been glued, tracking and following till their protagonist met, till their concentration was distracted by another speeding, incoming missile.

Word had gone out, a foreigner in their patch – and they'd come and have a look-see. Lincoln was spellbound as they fanned and approached in a spreading segment from the stern. Coming in from way way out, one after and following another – singular and in pairs and in groups – and all closing. Distant silver, glistening, silhouetted, arched bodies leaping from a moonlit sea. Suddenly dozens: dolphins. Two, three, four riding in tandem abreast and on either side of the hull. Their antics and gambolling were finally superseded by serious escort duty: their protozoa-haloed bodies shimmering below, and coruscate quickly dulling to a ghostly radiance when they occasionally leapt clear; and throaty whistling exhalations of, clearly heard, expelled air from blowholes.

For no apparent reason that Lincoln could see or ascertain: perhaps because their curiosity had been sated, or because they had been called away, perhaps in pursuit of a more important quest? With bewildering suddenness they were gone; dispersing as quickly as they'd appeared, leaping away till as if they had never been. They were left standing in a void – such regret, something precious had been lost – Sharon, Gary and Lincoln tarrying till long after their final departure, earnestly watching and silent.

Lincoln had been unaware that Bill had joined them – his voice was a murmur and disquieting and heard by all. "Strange, isn't it: it always makes me wonder, that this is all going on out here. They simply don't need us, do they?"

He silent for a moment, his yearning, questioning sincerity requiring no answer. "I take the dog for a walk in the local park every night, you know – and I watch the birds, which are always busy and going about their business. Their world's also immune from ours, they're also on a totally different wavelength – they never have to question their existence or reason for being, do they?

"I'm on the wrong side of fifty," he said quietly, "I imagine and think about the world outside when I'm at work – I drop my guard sometimes and I keep getting this uneasy feeling of . . . I can't quite describe it but I can tell you, it's close to despair. We've . . . I've got it wrong," such anguish that Lincoln had never heard before, and his soul open and bare for all to see, "and I'm not quite happy. I'm unfulfilled somehow – I always seem to have been searching." Bill shook his head. "I've never quite found my niche in life, especially after leaving the navy – it all seems wasted."

There was no answer to his next question, at least, Lincoln hadn't one – or perhaps he was providing his own answers, if he did but know it.

"What is it all about? I've lived more in this last two weeks than I have for the rest of the year. That they're all at their benches in that factory-prison plodding along . . . That they missed seeing that storm and didn't . . ." He shook his head again. "They aren't aware that such things even coexist anymore, that's if they ever did!" He swept an arm round. "None of this is actuality for them, and you know what's starting to frighten me, that this is the real world out here, not there, and this life's not a practice run . . . and that we only get the one shot and I've bloody squandered it."

Raison d'etre – that old chestnut again. That question that had been worrying man since the beginning of time – and there were no simple answers, despite the mystics, the religions, and all the rest of the acquired baggage. Lincoln's heart went out to him, he knew how he felt, nevertheless, one had to push aside all the pomp and ritual, and trappings, and at the end of the day one had to live – and more to the point, perhaps feed a family! Not everyone had genius or was born with a superior natural talent – nor had the means to exploit it even if they had. Still fewer were lucky enough to be blessed with private means or a silver spoon . . . Too deep, way too deep; only that each person, each individual, had to come to terms and had to find a balance . . . Lincoln personally had come to quite like Lionel's direct philosophy anyway, as he'd said and to quote: 'you are responsible for you'; 'who gives a brass razoo anyway', and 'come on, get 'em down ya – it's your round'!

Lincoln kept quiet as another and unexpected side to Sharon was surfacing: sensitive, compassionate and understanding; this one fully professional, self-assured and bogglingly competent to the ninth degree. Suddenly, they were her students and she the academic; this was yet another Sharon that Lincoln had never seen before or even dreamt existed.

"Maybe, just maybe," she said in a practised lecturing tone that commanded their undivided attention, "society will bite its own tail. Practical, totally practical: our society is logically materially oriented." She had held her arms out at shoulder width and height, with the forefinger and thumb of each of her hand's closing like a crab's claws, and their tips snapping in unison for emphasis at the ends of the invisible 'logically-materially-oriented' headline between.

Who the hell was this? Lincoln asked himself. Who was this counselling persona, this . . . this scholastic rhetorician . . . this moonlit goddess?

She continued on, and obviously unaware of their astonished awe, and completely unabashed if she was. "'What's it worth'? Even I, a mathematician, at the other end of the scale – who has recently been through and am quite versed with the system. Apart from the children, who, of course, instinctively know. Parents, teachers and lecturers, some of many years standing – despite the successes, they're all aware, albeit sometimes a deeply buried disquiet, that something's not quite right. Those so-called enlightened guardians pushing the kids too hard, allowing or forcing them to burn the midnight oil – their golden youth spent chained behind a desk – and the other poor little souls written off as failures if they don't achieve the top five!"

There was obviously, Lincoln sensed, more to come and on a subject a little deeper than 'children growing up too-fast and no time to play'. This a guru to pupils and talking, dare he say, on a matter closer to their hearts – never mind the problems of youth, they were all, as far as Lincoln was concerned, chasing Bill's age too closely – and also, underneath it all and like him, in need of a little comforting.

It happened sometimes, and Lincoln had experienced it only too rarely – but, happily, it did happen occasionally, especially in good or interesting company – that fatigue fell away and mind and brain were stimulated for a time with bigger questions and issues. Lincoln couldn't but wonder though, despite her words, was she talking and approaching the problem from a top student's, or a keen top student's parent's point of view . . .? But what about the majority: those who didn't make it into the top five classes, let alone the top five places! He knew from personal experience that many of the traditional apprenticeships and associated skills and assumed job security had gone forever – and, as far as his limited knowledge went, not a thing on the horizon to fill the void; and what about those at the educational level below those again – the future unskilled!

The thought had flashed across while she was talking and Lincoln hadn't lost the thread, nor had his attention wondered, her tone and intentness didn't allow for that.

"The kids are fine. Quite happy, inventive, brilliant – till you take away the paintbrush. Just one area for example: how desperate we are for original, talented entertainers – those very people that make life bearable. Comedians, mimics, puppeteers, ventriloquists, storytellers, dancers, actors: all the ancient arts in their modern forms." Sharon momentarily paused for effect. "Yet to most people, especially parents, they think they're not quite 'fair dinkum' – not quite proper; in fact, we do our damnedest to knock it out of our adolescents: the very thing that should be coddled, nurtured and venerated. Most parents have a fit, really freak, if one of their children want to, or do go that way. That some people do rebel and go on to become artists, pop musicians, poets, writers, entertainers, to my mind is nothing short of a miracle. It says a lot for the tenacity and the resilience of the human spirit, doesn't it – that they do.

"There's a lot of work going on, you know, especially in the 'States' concerning the imaginative part of the brain. It's true, if you stop and think about it – when are you happy? When are you at your happiest? When does time stop?" She then answered her own question and delivered her *piers de resistance* before any one of them could answer. "Fulfilment can be found only in creativity," she stated, fixing each of them in turn with half-closed eyes – daring any dissent. "It's as simple as that.   Unemployment, crime, vandalism, problems with delinquents, suicide: it'll end up to be the only practical way, as close a solution as you're going to get, financial, or otherwise. If for no other reason than to shut them up, they'll be forced, sooner or later, to introduce – creativity!"

There were no comments in the thoughtful after-vacuum – talk about liberated woman! ... Had he been wrong to pre-empt her? Was she really socially aware? Did she truly appreciate the plight of the no-hopers and the never-hads; Lincoln doubted it – yet from small acorns ... Furthermore, where in truth would one look for an answer but from the academics – and when one considered the pre-eminence of graffiti in their cities, then perhaps, Lincoln concluded, her preoccupation with creativeness wasn't so far removed from the truth!

Bite its own tail it would, and then thinking another four or five moves ahead ... So complex and contradictory, and perhaps irrelevant – and she not old enough to really appreciate the worry, and a completely chauvinist thought maybe, Lincoln admitted, though most mothers were worse – and it was so personal ... No jobs for their sons – it was as simple as that!

*   *   *

Bill had looked one hundred percent better: clean, fresh and hair slicked back, that much seen in the subdued light, and cheeks baby-pink. He had supped on tomato soup before relieving Lincoln topside, and had left him the remainder. Lincoln had to force down his first half-cup – and from thereon he couldn't stop. He finished most of what was in the saucepan and then mixed a large packet of dry into it again, and next added milk, and then floated more crusts cut into inch-squares on the top – and only finally sated and full of good-will to all men after three mugs followed by crackers and cheese!

Bill had left everything for Lincoln, kettle simmering, and bucket and soap in the sink. Lincoln wasn't quite ready to commence the serious business of ablutions, and now tolerant of the rumble from *Worippa's* diesel, was quite happy to potter about for the moment and enjoy the rare solitude.

Forty degrees, twenty-five minutes south, one hundred and forty-four degrees, thirty-one minutes east. They had picked up the semicircular loom of Hunter Island Light just before the end of the watch, albeit well below the horizon. Lincoln had always found the looms and technological miracles of lighthouses fascinating, and this one had been no exception, and more or less of the standard mode: the light was similar to a weak, horizontal searchlight being rotated on its own axis. They had not been close enough to see the source, the lamp, directly, but they had watched the narrow sweeping fan of the beam, which was, due to the curvature of the earth, angled well above the horizontal; the beam overlaying a diffused background glow. The light periodically revolved twice before winking out, the cycle lasting ten seconds, and then, after a timed pause, repeating itself.

They had now departed Tasmanian proper; the descending coastline to Cape Grim had been hidden in the darkness. Other names on the chart threw images up onto the mental picture-screen in Lincoln's brain: most of it, including Cape Grim, Lincoln had seen on the race going down. He tracked with a finger; Ramsey had pulled him out of a deep sleep to see: and the rising humps of Three Hump Island were still vivid in his memory, which was where George Bass and Matthew Flinders had confirmed that Tasmania was indeed an island.

Lincoln's mind and his imagination once again roamed: ships had sailed under Tasmania and had braved rounding the self-same treacherous southernmost coast that they had so recently sailed, the world prior to that confirmation believing Tasmania to be part of the Australian mainland. Investment in exploration had paid Her Majesty's Government handsome dividends, cutting through Bass Strait to reach the Australia's east coast had saved weeks and hundreds of sea miles.

Not such a fanciful thought in reality: that the early explorers had thought Tasmania to be a part of the mainland. The lay of the land and general detail, from a distance, inferred an unbroken coastline. Snippets and facts were coming to the fore in Lincoln's brain: that if had they frequented that area and had they sent out a reconnaissance party some ten thousand years earlier, then their way through Bass Strait to the Tasman Sea would have been blocked by a land-bridge! The summits of Three Hump Island and other high country 'island' peaks would have looked down on wind-blown, grassy fertile plains. The would-be covering sea was then locked up in polar ice; hardly a millisecond of the astronomical clock and not even time for isolated human or animal life between times to evolve or alter significantly. It was perfectly understandable to Lincoln then, that they had initially missed that gap.

Hunter Island Lincoln barely remembered, though closer to Australia, it had only been a dark shadow interrupting a smudged horizon. They would have been well west of their present course: Albatross Island nor North or South Black Rocks could he recall seeing. Black Pyramid though stood in his mind like a still photograph with every detail recorded: an eminence rising vertically from the sea and climbing steeply to the overcast; a broad-based, perpendicular obelisk of rock circled and fringed in frothed broken white. The grassy polls imagined as much as seen, with grey-white guano droppings decorating shelves, stratums and ledges, and spilling down oblique, recumbent, chimneyed scarps and buttressed drops.

Black Pyramid: Lincoln recalled Gary's, and to a lesser extent, Brian's running commentaries – particularly Gary's, which was accompanied with his usual enthusiasm. Home and protected breeding sanctuary of the Albatross – that ocean vertebrate again. Called Mollymawks, Cape Horn Sheep and Gooney Birds by early mariners: they were hopelessly clumsy once on the ground and thus a useful source of fresh eggs and easy meat for any passing vessel. Albatrosses breed only once every two years and only on the remotest of islands. They had a suicidal stubbornness when protecting their one egg, or single chic, and steadfastly refusing to abandon their nesting sites hadn't helped – they had allowed themselves to be slaughtered by the thousand. Those 'not so ancient' matelots had salted them down into barrels, and thus preserved, pickled in brine, they had supplemented a ship's meagre stores on the homeward voyage.

Lincoln couldn't in his heart completely condemn them, it must have been needs-must, and either that or chance an extremely painful death on the way home from malnutrition and associated debilitating illnesses. But now those outstanding graceful fliers were no longer threatened, but rather studied: man's extreme, sporting, champion, distant gliders were designed around their extraordinarily long, thin, fragile, back-angled ended wings. Those starkly white senior microlights of nature were now left in peace – floating on still airfoils while skimming and soaring on the lifts – wheeling, banking and circling and cruising their rugged, grey, spume-dulled, wind-swept, lonely, basalt habitat.

The increasing volume from the whistling kettle brought Lincoln back to the present – personal hygiene first then. He went forward to his own locker and began to sort through the various wrapped clothes in the light of the overhead florescent; the noisy crackling of plastic bags was disturbingly loud even against the muted thumping of the engine. Underpants, thermal top, bottoms and clean socks came to the fore eventually, after seemingly emptying and examining every bag present! Lincoln stood there for an indecisive minute before mentally shrugging, and then began to strip. There was absolutely no reason for his curious reluctance and no point in his holding back, and now, in truth, was as good a time as any. Lincoln held on to the shelf of the locker and eventually figured it out – he was reluctant because, as far as *Worippa* was concerned, he would be out of action while washing. Well, that was no longer relevant – it was time to let go.

Damn the batteries, Lincoln thought, as he stepped into the heads. Spoil yourself, Lincoln, live dangerously, we'll have power enough – so he turned on both bulkhead lights!

He had had to wash his hair three times: it had taken two washes and two rinses and a quirt of their indispensable washing-up liquid before a lather would even form, and the water by then was hopelessly sudded. Lincoln was reminded and made a mental note: he would have to buy something for Judy, the angel: her light had served and comforted in their hours of need, and even here, in the heads, its ambiance was taking the edge off the chill and was making washing just bearable. As previous, Lincoln dumped the contaminated bucket down the loo; and with a towel around padded back to the galley for yet another refill. This final bucket would have to serve for a body-wash; he had used the second bucket trying to rinse his hair free of soap. He had given it up as hopeless when he realised that he had passed the point of no-return: when the bucket was so saturated with suds that he was regenerating a lather and re-soaping instead of washing the soap out! Lincoln grimaced, that would make three in all – so far! And another thought after that: he should have used the second sudded bucket that he had just dumped for the body-wash, then he could have used this new bucket for rinsing only! No, it had just been too soapy – period.

Still, Brian would never find out, hopefully, that he had

squandered a third bucket of fresh water, and, after all, it wasn't as if they were crossing the Pacific, was it? Lincoln tried more of the same self-justification: it had all been Bill's fault, and once he had started he had had to finish, and it wouldn't have happened had they used cold water. He shuddered; he would rather have slit his wrists than have washed his hair and strip-washed in freezing water. Lincoln tried another tack: he had had to use three buckets because ... Otherwise the soap residue would cause head, bottom and pubic hair to itch even worse than it had previously, and, furthermore, he had been rigorously scratching at those areas recently – and the soap residue would have made it worse! His 'bugger it' went unheard.

Lincoln checked the amp meter as he passed: good, there was only a minimal trickle charge registering, and they were wasting fuel now.

Bill shook his head in disbelief; Lincoln ignored him and continued filling their paintered bucket with seawater, and that he was as naked as a 'jaybird' was neither here nor there. Lincoln nearly lost it then, the bucket, when glancing aft at Bill and by being in too much of a hurry. It was unbelievable, the stopping power of a bucket: the trapped resistance therein would, if one were not prepared, wrench a person straight over the side. If that person were holding on to anything and let it fill too quickly, and he was daft enough to have the loop in the painter around his wrist, then it'd wrench their arm right out of its socket! The whole thing had been caused by him forgetting about *Worippa's* inexorable passage through the water – one got used to it as an everyday thing and forgot that *Worippa* had way on – the shock of being hauled up as with a braking parachute on a jet fighter quickly and violently righted that little lapse!

Lincoln couldn't justify using up three buckets of fresh water for washing, let alone another on sluicing down their newly acquired, for them anyway, strip-washing cubicle – hence him dashing topside for saltwater. Saltwater was better than fresh for dissolving and killing the dangerously slippery, soap-scummed film clinging to the sole anyway. Lincoln sat the bucket on the deck and signalled to Bill with a horizontal scissors action of his hands – and then pointed down. Bill understood immediately and was obviously pleased to throttle down and turn the key. There were quite a few more muffled thumps and clatters before the engine finally came to rest.

Lincoln hesitated before darting back below, savouring the silence. The silence hurt: and Lincoln knew that generally people had the habit of underestimating the 'noise-fatigue' caused by engines and similar, especially a diesel as big as *Worippa's*. One couldn't escape the continuing underlying thudding rumble – despite adequate insulation, and even though, as theirs, not under load, the vibration eventually wore one's nerves thin.

Questions about the meaning of life he would not have to worry about soon – getting too smart for his own good was Corsham. His question embarrassing, and Lincoln had had no ready answer to hand: why hadn't he got dressed and then cleaned and washed down the heads instead of freezing his arse off up here! He could be, concluded Lincoln blandly, a real indiscreet, blunt and tactless sod at times.

The contrast striking, *Worippa* so snug below, one didn't realise till a body came in from the outside – and being naked aside. The heat from Judy's lamp, human breath and bodies, the engine and the regular use of the oven and burners all accumulated and were contained in the hull. Lincoln took a fresh look around, sitting on the side-settee and only half-dressed. She wasn't the bitch any more, *Worippa*, she was home. Undisciplined, untamed, flighty, wanton – a bit loose maybe. Affection, love even – how did something made up of steel, fibreglass, metal and plastic take on such a personality and become a living entity?

Lincoln blinked and reality once more called: the floozy had a belly full of soapy water that would have to be pumped out – tea for Helmet and Nick first though.

They would have to do further work on Helmet, Lincoln grinned, his, Helmut's sense of humour when being woken was slipping badly again – there were other ways of expressing disinterest in the sale of a 'battleship'!

Helmut eventually came forward and interrupted Lincoln and Lincoln was only too glad to stop. He had got to the stage where he could only pump with one hand for a short period before having to change to the other.

"Too long that you pump," Helmut stated. "Ve must have a leak – a quite bad leak. I pump her dry last evening."

Yes, Lincoln said to himself – a three-bucket leak!

"No Helmet," Lincoln avoided his eyes and said aloud and

between pants. "Bill and I strip-washed. It's too bloody cold to do it out on deck." Lincoln nodded forward, "We used the heads; it's all right so long as you're careful and don't make too much mess." Lincoln found himself explaining with humiliating apology – the only thing he wasn't doing was hanging his head and toeing the dirt. "I sluiced it down with 'saltwater' after, you can't really do any damage, there's nothing in there to ruin."

Helmet was thoughtful. "Vould ve have enough fresh vater to rinse vith, do you think? No good to leave salt on the skin, vill feel dirtier – that is no good." He looked directly at Lincoln . . . Knowingly? Lincoln couldn't tell. "Vhy you aren't itching, I don't know."

Lincoln quickly turned his head and pulled a face – in half-despair and in half-humour – had Helmut seen his eyes or expression he would instantly have known.

Helmet continued his train of thought, "Too long to fill the bucket from the saltvater pump, Nick and I vill fill all the containers first and then bring them down." He then asked Lincoln that dreaded question that a 'side-stepper' of the truth couldn't side-step. "Does the *saltvater soap* vork? You and Bill are the first to use it – perhaps only a half-bucket of fresh water, ja . . ."

Poor Helmet, he had misinterpreted Lincoln's look as disapproval.

"I get the torch," he said and turned before Lincoln had regained his wits. He half-turned again after a couple of steps. "I vill check our fresh-vater levels first. Maybe ve vait till daylight to vash, and save a little power – which will be another hour, maybe an hour and a half perhaps."

Lincoln leaned against the sail bin upright, forehead against cold wood – get out of this one, Lincoln. There wasn't any doubt, his brain had finally given up the ghost – his ongoing senility was getting worse!

Bill interrupted Lincoln's guilty cogitative introspection, "What's going on, Chris? What the hell is Helmet up to? He's got the bottom of both bunks out." Bill was resentful as well as puzzled – as far as he was concerned, Helmut was invading his territory. "There's nothing in those under-lockers that he can possibly want. I can't think of anything – all you can see is his fat arse sticking up." Bill flicked Lincoln's shoulder for attention. "Answers up on the ceiling, is it?"

"That him and Nick were in the bottom bunks is an uncanny coincidence, Bill, the gods really are against us. He's checking the fresh-water sight-glasses."

Bill mouthed an 'oh' – there was no point, Lincoln dubiously felt, in mentioning pre-filled buckets to him!

"He's seeing if there's enough fresh water left for him and Nick to have a final rinse in fresh. Yes, Bill, they don't want to be like us and use 'saltwater' from the 'saltwater pump', it upsets their skin." Lincoln added nastily, "You do remember the 'saltwater pump', Bill, you can use that instead of – it saves you perishing up on the deck with a bucket."

Bill joined Lincoln – they inspected the deckhead together.

Lincoln carried on relentlessly after a moment, "Were we impressed with the 'saltwater soap', Bill?" he asked. "We were the first to use it, you know!"

Bill, after a tentative start, boiled up a case till he was aggressively unrepentant and he persuaded himself finally, and vehemently voiced his indignant justifications: "*Worippa* carries enough water for each of us to have umpteen strip-washes and then some, let alone one. We've hardly used any, anyway. One bucket to wash and shave in and another to wash away the soap with isn't asking too much. We didn't have time to drink any of it on our first two days, did we? Fuck him, if he's stupid enough to even think of washing and shaving in cold saltwater then he deserves all he gets." Bill added sarcastically, "He'll probably dive over the side for a rinse." He stabbed a finger at Lincoln. "You can forget Nick too, he'll go crook. He'll not have a bar of it: he'll not want to sluice down with cold let alone wash with salt."

One bucket to wash and shave and another to rinse? Lincoln had used three and hadn't had enough left over even then, let alone to contemplate shaving . . . He didn't voice his 'oops'!

It sounded like someone clearing his or her throat? In close proximity – very nearly intimate. They really should not have stood with their backs exposed and blind – it like a cough, it sounded like a cough to Lincoln, like a German cough!

Every man for himself then. Lincoln stepped forward, turned and faced Bill squarely, and fighting to keep a severe expression of outraged condemnation, voiced his deepest disapproval. "My God, Corsham, let me get this right, what are you saying. That you've been . . . You've never been using fresh water for washing, have you? That's a hanging offence that, man. You should be ashamed of yourself – you ought to be bloody shot!"

Chapter 23

Nice yet frustrating, and temper just beginning to slip – either do something about it or leave it alone. Sleep began to fade as Lincoln reluctantly swam up to semiconsciousness . . . And always fascinating this, this half-awake, half-dreaming state which he was drowsily experiencing – and thinking two distinct different thoughts at the same time . . . He was aware that the HF radio had been repaired, though asleep, and was now actually listening to the muffled radio traffic in the background. Too lazy and comfortable and warm to completely wake up . . . and half-nice and half-annoying to have one's penis wagged gently back and forth at its base, and that was because the pleasure felt was fighting the painful pressure of an over-full bladder stretched to bursting point.

Her hair tickling, and it could only be her, and when Lincoln half-opened his eyes her face was only a quarter of an inch from his and the faint, scented, musky smell of her unmistakable . . . and her quiet derogatory whispers were swimming around before finally forming a coherent sentence.

"Wakey, wakey, hands off snakey. Are you going to wake up, peewee?" Another wag. "Or are you going to laze the day away?"

Lincoln suddenly and without warning snatched at her hand, but she was quicker and she also immediately stepped back out of reach. This time she had gone too far, too far by half . . . But without doubt she was a quick learner because she had been sensible enough to warm her hand and he was fairly certain that it had not just been a coincidence: she must have previously caught his genuine flare of real temper – Lincoln seriously hated cold hands.

Those thoughts flashing through at the back of Lincoln's brain as he spoke. "Jesus Christ, can't you leave a bloke alone." He had meant it to come out as outraged indignation and not as it sounded: tired resignation. He looked at her directly and murmured, "Please don't do that again."

She'd caught the nuances in his voice and she considered him for a couple of moments before replying. "I've gone a bit too far, haven't I . . . once again?"

"Well, let me put it another way," Lincoln replied quietly, "if Helmut woke you up by grabbing your tits, you'd not be too impressed, would you?

"All right," she whispered huffily and tossed her hair back with a flick of her head. "You've made your point and there's no need to labour it, I won't do it again."

Lincoln simply nodded, and that was because she was covering well, but there was a well-disguised and yet distinct, for someone who knew her and had a discerning ear, underlying reserve of embarrassment and hurt in there that belied surface appearances!

Again thoughts fluttered, humorous thoughts – the furtive little 'madam', this was the first time anybody had ever got into his knickers without him knowing! Lincoln grinned to himself, this girl was one on her own and Gary was a lucky, lucky man, and she, despite surface appearances, was not of loose morals, just a fun-loving, somewhat brazen, exuberant, smart, healthy girl. She'd acted on an of-the-moment impulse, and a silly, childish, girlish thing to have done and yet part of that self-same shipboard life again. As he had noted many times before, people did things that in ordinary circumstances they wouldn't dream of – and after a few trips it paid to be wary of such impulses because one thing could lead to another, and very often did and had et cetera!

"No disrespect meant," Lincoln offered sincerely, yet firmly.

"And none taken," she replied coolly.

Struggling over onto a shoulder was much easier and it was much easier to move now than before Hobart. Well, at least she was big enough not to take offence and not go into a sulk, or so it seemed, and that certainly told a person something about her. The fear of a woman scorned had crossed Lincoln's mind!

Then, in an ordinary conversational voice, and as if the prior incident hadn't happened or had been dismissed, he asked, "What's the time?"

"Twenty-five to ten," she answered in the same, "and you've had five and a half hours of undisturbed sleep, how do you feel?"

Yes, Lincoln reflected, she wasn't as tough as she tried to make out and yet had, nevertheless, risen above it and her obvious effort to overcome her embarrassment and her still red face was . . . touching.

"I don't really know, I haven't moved all the parts yet. I'm still coming round, but better." He smiled at her – they had an agreement – from now on she wouldn't step over the line he'd drawn in the sand and neither would he. "And I'll feel even better'er after I've drunk the tea that you're going to make me – I'll wait and murder you after – after you've done that."

Again, Sharon's brain, Lincoln had noticed before: she thought in a peculiar way and not like any girl he had ever met or known. There had never been, that he could recall, in her case any offence taken after an order, half-instruction, or half-request given – provided that they were warranted. There had never been any sarcastic retorts about previous servants dying and the rest – she looked under the obvious – surface appearances fooled, the last thing she was, was shallow. Before this morning, that was, and it hadn't take her long to bounce back even then.

"Your tea's in the sink." Then she said nicely, as if an after-thought, and the false, sweet smile on her face contradicted her tone, "Why don't you pole-vault out of bed and go to the toilet while I fetch it. And then again, you could wait and balance your tea on that flag pole you've got under there and take it with you."

A parting jibe answered Lincoln's two-worded, mouthed reply.

"Oh very nice, and don't knock anything over with it on the way." And then capped that with a final rejoinder belatedly flung over her shoulder as she moved aft. "Sorry, can't stop – Helmut's waiting to play with my tits."

Lincoln laughed to himself – well, she'd not spent a youth of innocence. Lincoln thought about her: whatever she had been up to would have been colourful. That she had travelled, from her odd remarks and comments, that much was obvious – it had sounded like she'd backpacked all over the world. Lincoln didn't know why but he got the impression that she was comfortable with them, older though they were ... Safer perhaps; and that with Gary, her impulsive, misjudged, overzealous impropriety's aside, she'd come home – despite everything, Lincoln had to admit, the two did somehow make a whole!

No, he thought, it was not possible to take offence nor be overly serious, there was a pretty astute judge of character, despite the odd hiccup, under that blonde mop of hair and like the rest on board, and it surprised him to admit it, he had in his peculiar fashion come to love her. Not by any means beyond the physical either; he also, like the rest, was made of flesh and blood and was tempted – and he liked to look . . . and, he admitted it to himself, enjoyed flirting with her. Also, putting all that and associated aside, Lincoln would trust her with his life – and there was no higher an accolade that one could pay another human being than that!

Warren was opposite and in the lower starboard bunk, and was awake and not hiding the fact this time. He had had to have been privy to all that had gone on and was obviously not happy.

He looked away after a couple of seconds.

"Don't take it all too seriously, Warren, it all doesn't actually mean anything."

He deigned to answer him for once, surprise, surprise, but as far as Lincoln was concerned it would have been better if he hadn't!

"She doesn't like me, she chats to and talks to and flirts with and gives everybody else the come-on – she's just a whore."

An overwhelming urge to crack his useless scrawny, stupid, silly little neck blurred everything and Lincoln had the lee cloth undone and was twisting out of the bunk with hands involuntarily reaching forward before he was fully aware of what he was doing. Only his, Warren's, shrinking reaction stopped any further violence: his face white with fear – and terror plainly written there.

Lincoln sat back down on the bunk and took a deep breath before finally leaning across. "You'd best bottle those sorts of remarks, Warren, or you'll not live to set foot on land. I shouldn't have to remind you, should I, of people's worth?" He raised his eyebrows questioningly. "That storm sorted that out, didn't it?" Lincoln regretted those words as soon as he had said them, it a remark caused by his temper, and spite . . . and dislike – and just plain immaturity on his part. He sighed. "I don't know what goes on inside that head of yours, Warren, but here's a little piece of friendly advice for you and sincerely given: I'm concerned about your future happiness, and, any more remarks like that and you won't have to worry about your future at all! Do you understand?" Lincoln let the groundout, not so thinly veiled, implied threat hang in the air for a few moments and then tempered it with some well-meant advice. "Don't try so hard, Warren," he advised in a soft voice, "be yourself, do your own thing. Don't try to be someone you think you want to be, or ought to be – you can look over your shoulder like that all your life." And finally advised, "Believe me, there's a girl waiting out there for you, it's just a matter of confidence – and getting up and going out to look. She doesn't have to be the local beauty queen of the pageant, does she – be like the rest of us, don't be too ambitious."

Some fell on stony ground and his rolling over was his only reaction – face averted from the world, as usual.

Not far off the mark and no pun intended and much too worldly-wise for her own good, Sharon had had it to rights. Lincoln staggered with and after a painfully swollen penis to the heads, overbalancing and teetering to *Worippa's* playful rolling lurches and ups and downs, and hindered by a body that refused to work properly and handicapped with a befuddled head that was still, despite what had gone on before, woozy with sleep and tardy to clear. He couldn't nor did he want to come round. Eyelids drooping and gummed and tending to close on their own accord: to go to the toilet and go back to bed, that's all he really wanted to do – he needed another two hours at least to be right.

The damn thing refused to give any quarter, Lincoln virtually had to rest horizontally with one elbow resting on the crossbar forward of the toilet and the other hand pushing the stubborn member down to direct urine into the bowl. It was close to agony getting started and near to ecstasy once flowing . . . and then an impossibly long time before stopping.

'Like listening to a horse piss in a field'. That thought was an unwelcome intrusion: Rosemary, his wife's description of his morning ablutions.

They had married young, nineteen and twenty-one, and they had been together through thick and thin – through both good times and bad. He had never really been out of love with her, and now he had betrayed that sacred trust. She would find out about it too: she'd always had a knack of getting the truth out of him. Subterfuge, as far as she was concerned, was not Lincoln's forté. He had learnt early, when they were courting – trying to tell her anything other than the truth was a waste of time. Lincoln remembered back to the first and more or less the last time he had tried it – telling her lies . . .

It had been on a Sunday afternoon and they were having tea at her parents place – and they sitting down at the dining room table, formally, to plates of egg and cucumber sandwiches and dainty icing-topped, fairy cakes and similar on a tiered cake plate.

Lincoln recalled, to his everlasting embarrassment and shame, that he had said a long 'good night' to Rosie on the eve before the 'said' Sunday afternoon tea, and on the same doorstep just along the hall, at half-past eleven – her father's curfew time! He hadn't really been tired and after a few phone calls . . . Hammersmith Palais had thrown them, the 'likely lads', out at one-thirty, each the worse for wear, and acquired female partners not much better!

It had just popped out on that fatal afternoon, out of the blue – blurted out without thought or consequence – with no pressure nor any logical reason why: Freudian, or a guilty subconscious playing dirty tricks, or similar – one could take one's pick!

"Those girls last night," he had said enthusiastically, "Christ, they were as drunk as skunks, weren't they?"

Realisation came to him slowly – Rosie hadn't been there! An icy, disapproving silence filled the void . . . An insect pinned to a specimen board – and nowhere to turn and nowhere to hide, and no excuses to hand. Frigid conversation resumed, and his incredible gaff ignored – worse, much worse than further enquiry was him not being dragged from the tea-table for a full interrogation. Lincoln remembered that awful, humiliating sinking feeling even now: that the price was going to be high . . . very high. So very, very high!

On the same doorstep again and the frosty atmosphere of an agonisingly long afternoon and evening behind them. Presently, stealthily, after he being lulled, and attention and concentration distracted by a world of innocent asides, furtive caresses and intimate small talk. The question asked quietly, and wrapped in sugar and honey and without apparent rancour! Rosie, the very soul of reasonableness – and underlying barbs on the barbed wire not quite below the surface – and only the odd rusty tip grazing and catching his skin, and just the odd isolated bead or globule of blood showing here or there!

"You didn't go straight home last night, then?" she asked gently. "You met some girls, did you?"

His elder brother had owned, when they were children, a small explanatory booklet: he a 'wartime' baby. They still had had a lot of war paraphernalia around their home at that time. On his bed, for example, he, Lincoln, had had an eiderdown made from a khaki, camouflage-patterned, silk parachute. His father's old kit bag, at his insistence, had also lived in that bedroom, as had his father's army water-bottle – they had added ambience in his, a young boy's mind (their mother, always practical, had promptly delegated the kit bag to the role of super-hero's, dirty-linen basket!) ... That booklet had badly frightened and horrified him as a child – had chilled his blood. His brother had kept it in the top draw of his dressing table – that booklet contained pictures and diagrams, in brutal graphic detail, of how to efficiently kill ... murder a Nazi paratrooper, or invader, in cold blood.

All thoughts of caution Lincoln had pushed to one side – kissing and petting taking precedence – and her question was like that same stiletto portrayed in that wartime booklet. It was as that same cold, honed steel being quietly slipped under the rib cage and up into the heart – his heart!

Lincoln mused on the memories for a little and then sobered quickly. There was no doubt, he would betray himself again, sooner or later, and let something slip without thinking ... And Rosie would pretend not to notice at the time – said the spider to the fly. Lincoln's thoughts wandered: what about Elizabeth though, what had driven her to take blood samples and the rest? She was, is, a beautiful woman in anybody's book: she would only have to crook a little finger and half the male population of Tasmania would jump – and half of Australia too! And she was another one who was far from shallow and certainly not the sort who would chase after another woman's husband, or let a fixation for something she couldn't have override her common-sense ... And him no innocent party himself: electric had flowed and crackled; and exactly that same mutual attraction that he felt, and did feel for Rosie – bloody hell.

*   *   *

Ramsey asked, "What was the row about last night, Chris? You, Bill and Helmet, you lot woke the whole bloody boat ... What was going on?"

"Those two were being totally unreasonable," Lincoln replied and shook his head in mock despair. "It was just fortunate that I was there to keep order and keep the peace – at each other throats, they were." Bill climbed down from the cockpit – and time for him to change the subject. "A private thing and I'd prefer not to discuss it," and Lincoln added rudely, "and it's none of your business anyway." And what made him say the next bit, and mean it, Lincoln didn't know. "You're as bad as Rosie, you are – always nosing about."

Ramsey looked at Potter, Potter looked at Ramsey. Corsham looked from one to the other – to each of them. Ramsey mouthed an 'ah'.

Potter started it, and the other two were full-voiced too, after hesitant beginnings: "Love is a many splendid thing . . ."

All Lincoln could do was stand there and take it, and wait them out – they only knew the first few lyrics, for which he thanked God! Little did they know – Rosie would make mince-meat of him!

"Finished?" Lincoln asked and shook his head. "Shipmates and bastards."

An infuriating and considerate Corsham: "You going topside," he asked Lincoln mournfully, "Gary's not unduly worried, but we should relieve him. You go on up, all right, and I'll get us some late breakfast."

Lincoln gave him a long look, there was a suspicion – just a hint of a suppressed smirk round his lips . . . The bugger was getting his pound of flesh. There was no malice in him though, it was only his tongue-in-cheek way of telling him that he had been forgiven for last night's attempted betrayal – Lincoln would give him his bloody spaniel eyes. Unsummoned and instantly recalled, and reminded of, was last night's debacle that had backfired anyway, because there simply was no defence against Helmet and he had had to stand there in the end and take a severe reprimand and lecture about an uncompromising and unreasonable attitude; the squandering of resources; irresponsibility and undisciplined selfish behaviour . . . Setting an example, and . . . well . . . all deserved, Lincoln supposed! He wouldn't have minded but it had been Bill who had finally undone them: he had acted the aggrieved party! To keep a straight face with him nodding wisely at and slightly behind Helmet's shoulder had been what Lincoln had found impossible – and the more he had tried to keep himself from laughing, the worse it had got. He had nearly had a hernia while trying to contain the rising mirth and he had spluttered into helpless hysterics in the end and . . . needless to say, it had given the game away.

"We've got a few more minutes yet, Bill." Lincoln said brusquely, and turned back to Ramsey. "You managed to get the radio working again, then?"

"Gary fixed it up this morning," explained Ramsey, "it was the internal socket to the aerial, water'd got in. I've talked to Melbourne, by the way, I think they were starting to get worried again and that, I think, was because they couldn't understand why we hadn't raised King Island." Ramsey grinned. "They put me directly through to Judy after all the rigmarole, on 'radphone'. She says she'll contact all the girls and loved ones and let them know we're all safe, and she'll give them our ETA – okay?" After Lincoln's affirmative, he added, "If you want to talk directly to your loved one." He looked at Lincoln quizzically. "Be my guest?"

Lincoln looked at him suspiciously. "Um, good, I might want to later, if that's all right with you. Anything else?"

Ramsey gave him a knowing look that Lincoln didn't much care for, before turning to indicate Potter. "Meet the international celebrity. According to Judy, pictures of *Worippa* have been flashing across the world. They had a television camera crew onboard that spotter plane, they filmed us battling it out 'underneath' – and with Lionel's fruity conversation accompanying the footage – can you imagine it! Anyway, it apparently caught the public's imagination – and the television people, they played the story right up to the hilt and according to them, apparently, we were lost without trace after that . . . Judy's shock when she realised it was me on the phone." Ramsey's face was wistful. "It's nice to be loved."

Lincoln asked, "Has there been anybody else in trouble?"

"The fleets scattered all over and a fair number have had to be towed in: broken masts, failed rigging, shredded sails, structural damage. A few with ill and battered crews: concussion, broken limbs, cracked heads, but no fatalities, thank God – we were the last to be accounted for."

"Lucky." Lincoln murmured.

Ramsey mouthed a sombre 'yes'.

"What's the forecast?" Lincoln asked.

Lionel answered, "A cold front's coming in. The wind'll veer before then, and then back to south-southwest after it's gone through. Scattered showers; force five to six – twenty-five knots."

To himself as much as to them – and thinking about something entirely different. "Better to start now if I'm going to start at all," Lincoln murmured, "everybody'll be awake by then."

Bill checked the time and then looked questioningly at Lincoln – Ramsey and Potter also looked in askance. Lincoln slowly lowered an eyelid, an eyelid that Bill couldn't see but Ramsey and Potter could.

"Don't bother looking at your watch, Bill," Lincoln grumbled petulantly. "I might not even go topside today – it depends on how I feel."

Lincoln turned back to Ramsey and Potter, and they raised their eyebrows, and they and Lincoln exchanged knowing looks – Ramsey and Potter would play the game.

Lincoln snapped his right arm to horizontal and thumped his left hand in the elbow crook and raised his forearm to vertical in an age-old expression – he added a raspberry as an encore. "To the watch." He stood there for some moments with a disgruntled pout on his lips. He turned abruptly and finally, and after a suitable pause, barked at a bewildered Bill, "How many chickens have we got?"

Bill stood there for a moment, looking puzzled – enlightenment slowly dawned. "I'll find however many 'chooks' Sahib wants."

"Two then," Lincoln ordered imperiously.

"Yes, oh Master," answered Bill brightly, and then added, "that's good because that's all we've got."

"And make sure they're big," Lincoln waved him away with an imperious hand.

Potter intervened, probing cautiously and innocence hollow, "Curry would it be?" he asked.

Lincoln pretended to look round, as if he had heard some sort of faint annoying noise – Potter, Lincoln ignored.

Ramsey tried next. "Something Indian, perhaps?" he asked and raised his eyebrows to underline the question.

Lincoln examined his nails with an elaborate nonchalance. "A pig-up." He looked at them and gritted and bared his teeth in a grinning mask. "I'm starving," he yelled enthusiastically, "I could eat a bloody horse."

Ramsey looked at Potter with a grin on his face, Potter looked at Ramsey with a grin on his face – Ramsey after their unspoken conversation said, "You stand down then, Bill, if that suits you – Lionel and I'll take yours and the Pom's watch."

Lincoln interrupted, "Not so fast, not so fast: there are rules: clean hands, faces scrubbed and hair combed – and teeth brushed. You're not sitting down there like a gang of coarse, hairy-arsed hooligans." Lincoln adopted a haughty pose and said, "Its ten o'clock now, so sherry and liver pâtè'd hors d'oeuvres will be served on the promenade deck at thirteen-hundred hours."

Potter barged in, "I'll stick to the old 'amber nectar', if that's all right with you?"

Lincoln looked down his nose at him. "No, Mister Potter, that's not all right with me – you uncouth sod. Pig-up, I said, not piss-up. In Australian parlance – no neck-oil. I can't afford to have any two-pot screamers, we have to stay sober – a boat's no place." He glanced at Potter's crestfallen face and said directly, "Look, we'll have two large glasses of cold white, believe me you'll like it, it'll enhance the meal." Lincoln put his head close to Potter's and said confidentially, "It's from my own private stock." He straightened up and addressed everybody generally, "It'll put most of us on our backs, the state we're in." Lincoln looked at Potter again. "Including you."

Ramsey agreed. "That sounds fair, Lionel."

Never one to give up, Potter, "A glass of port to finish with then?"

Lincoln sighed, "With the cheese board and coffee after." He wagged a finger. "But just the one."

Ramsey, Corsham and Lincoln cracked up into hysterics. Potter looked serious, sounded serious, was serious. "What about farting?" he enquired.

         *   *   *

"It'll be handy if those two chickens are of a reasonable size, Bill." Lincoln pondered the deckhead. "Hmm . . . We'll be better off if we duplicate in two saucepans. It'll be better, under the circumstances, to make too much than too little – fair? The tighter each chicken fits into each saucepan, the better."

Bill shook his head. "We didn't have a choice in the matter, we had to take what Brian and Judy could get in Hobart, there wasn't time to really shop around. They're about average, from what I can remember."

"They'll do, Bill, they'll have to, won't they. We'll make-do-and-mend – wash 'em off in fresh water, ay?"

Bill smirked. "I'll just go and check with Helmet first, just to see if . . ."

"All right, all right," Lincoln interrupted him, "let's not pursue that one."

They packed potatoes, carrots and onions around each bird and covered them with cold water after adding garlic, bay leaves and salt and pepper to taste.

"No Bill," Lincoln instructed, "don't bring to the boil, straight onto simmer – it'll keep them tender that way – there's plenty of time." He stood back. "They can look after themselves now – the timing's important – we shan't need them to be ready for a good couple of hours."

The original curry sauce recipe, Lincoln recalled, required four whole bulbs or heads of garlic, not single cloves. The chore was too arduous and they had had enough by the time they had peeled the cloves of three bulbs. They accepted that it would detract a little from the final quality – it was simply too much work, given the conditions, for the end result.

Bill sensed Lincoln's disappointment in the compromise and saved the day: he poured two-thirds of a container of dried garlic flakes into their ingredients. He also solved the shortage of fresh ginger in the same way, substituting a second golf ball of unsalvageable mildewed with three teaspoons of powder. He and Bill took turns to mash the lot down, a large steel drift from the tool kit substituting for a blender. They added five diced onions that they had already peeled, and a cup of water, plus oil. They took turns, frying their concoction in the bottom of a third saucepan with tears streaming – the stink would contaminate the whole boat for days.

"Right, Bill," Lincoln said, "the onions're nicely soft, time to add the rest."

They counted them out carefully: six pieces of cinnamon stick, ten cardamoms, four bay leaves, eight cloves – and another half-cup of water. Lincoln fitted the lid.

"That's it then," Lincoln gestured. "The onions should break down and provide extra liquid, and we can always add stock from the chickens if there's not enough.   Give it just the occasional tentative stir and also spoon off the scum now and again from the surface of the birds at the same time, if you feel so inclined.   We can sit on our backsides now and take the air; it'll be another hour and a quarter . . . an hour and a half before we need look at any of it." Lincoln grinned at him. "Strip the carcasses; throw in some runners and a few peas to keep the dreaded scurvy at bay – and Bob's-your-uncle. Mix up the lot: half an hour, three-quarters for the Basmatti rice before serving up: finish."

Bill wouldn't be put off nor be fooled, Lincoln admitted, and he asked the inevitable question, "There's only half the sauce in there, when are you going to make the other half?"

"Ah Bill." Lincoln shook his head.   "I don't know whether I can actually show you that. I promised the old Maharajah that I'd never break nor betray his sacred trust.   It was while we were shooting tigers from the backs of elephants, it was – in Madras National Park.   It was too late to save him from one of those man-eating, striped dervish's that we'd been tracking: an unexpected, ferocious, savage, suicidal attack – and he badly clawed and half-eaten. He passed on the secret recipe," Lincoln added solemnly, "with his last dying breaths."

Bill looked at him in disbelief, his mouth open. "Bloody oath. That must be the biggest load of rat-shit I've ever heard, where do you get them from?"

With his eyes large pools of innocence and pained hurt, Lincoln enquired, "Don't you believe me, Bill?"

Bill apparently didn't. "You're the biggest bullshitting no-hoper I've ever come across."   He considered. "Tell you what?"

"What?" Lincoln asked.

"You show me that recipe and I'll steer on tonight's watch?"

"Done," Lincoln said.

"Bastard!" he replied.

Chapter 24

There was a vague aromatic fragrance on the wind: a faint scent of land and not offensive and not industrial; the olfactory membranes were delicate and extremely sensitive after the clean air of the sea. Lincoln breathed deeply and smelt the salty tang of exposed seaweed, rack and tidal; of earth and growing things. That rich, mixed, aromatic bouquet and from whence it came sent the gist of another of Gary's semi-lecture's echoing round ... No, not gist, Lincoln could recall his words with surprising clarity.

Smack-bang in the way of any locals going across or, more importantly, ocean traffic making its way through Bass Strait, he had said, either incoming to Melbourne and the east coast of Australia, or outgoing to Adelaide, Western Australia, or European-bound. King Island, whose subtle perfumery now tinged the air, sits there patiently waiting for the unwary, careless, unlucky or negligent; and indifferent to the calamities of careless navigators, innocent seamen and passengers alike. Lincoln had been and was aware of, in Gary's words, the unforgiving, surrounding, offshore rocks and razor-edged ledges and reefs, and aware too that they still did and still do occasionally take their toll, but not that it was, and currently still is, Australia's most notorious and infamous graveyard for ships!

Sea captains weary after a voyage of twelve thousand miles through the worst seas and oceans of the world, and lulled before landfall into a false sense of security by hundreds of previous nautical miles on an open ocean. Though by no means all, the majority of founderings occurring on the island's incoming west coast; and again, as per records, the vast majority occurring before the commissioning of beacons to the western approaches. The said beacons, as Gary had explained, being Cape Otway on the Australian mainland and Cape Wickham Light on the northern-west tip of King Island, these two marking the natural sea route between Australia and the rugged islands that haphazardly dot and extend out from the northern coast of Tasmania – and King Island, of course, being the main outermost island.

Lincoln pondered and envied Gary's evident ability yet again: to retain and recall facts and trivia, apparently at will . . . There had been tens of previous shipwrecks and numerous lives lost before the wrecking of the *Neva* in 1835. Her foundering had underlined the urgent requirement for navigational aids: bureaucracy had withheld finance despite that tragedy and despite acknowledgement for the need. Of *Neva's* human cargo of women convicts and their children, a small number of passengers and crew, only fifteen, Gary had said, out of the two hundred and forty odd had survived!

Mounting losses of vessels and an ever increasing death toll cumulated some ten years later in a public outcry that finally loosened the official purse strings – and shelved lighthouse plans were dusted off once again – and this immediate action, according to him, had been prompted by Australia's worst sea disaster. On the southwest of the island the *Cataraqui* had struck in the darkness of early morning. Outward bound from Liverpool and an emigrant ship carrying over four hundred souls, and the majority again women and children – only nine innocents, this time, survived the surf to the beach!

They had erected Cape Otway light three years after that – and still the whole sorry tale, Gary's sorry tale, had continued. One gatepost is better than no gatepost, Gary had admitted – and yet still only half a job – and skipper's got confused, whether through tiredness or bad conditions, poor visibility, whatever, and sailed the wrong side of the light! A pair of gateposts, one on either side of the entrance to the safe water through Bass Strait, was required for complete orientation, and Lincoln had confirmed that for himself after a look at the chart later. Some fifty more ships were wrecked and more untold drownings and deaths occurred before the eventual construction of Cape Wickham light – and not built, even then, till sixteen years after that fateful night!

Yet, and Lincoln didn't doubt that officialdom couldn't win regardless of its good intentions, ships had still piled up on King Island's unforgiving shores despite the two lighthouses; some skippers mistaking Cape Wickham Light for Cape Otway's apparently, and bearing away accordingly! Lincoln had sat up when Gary had stated that a final tally of sixty or so ships and hundreds of accompanying souls had perished before the advent of modern-day Radio-Beacon navigation! The trouble was that Lincoln, like anyone with experience of the sea, could see only too well, even now, those ships, hauntingly, foundering in the surf . . .

Like all good storytellers, Gary's recount had finished with a final hook: shrouded in mystery and distorted by the mists of time. That magical something that roused the curiosity and made a person remember and wonder . . . Those first intrepid European explorers had found a wreck on King Island: a wreck that couldn't exist and that shouldn't have been there! Imagine, he had said finally, the equivalent of the first Apollo astronauts finding a wrecked alien spaceship when exploring in the lander-roving vehicle. How long had that wreck lain there? From whence had it come? To whom had it belonged? What of the people who'd sailed her? Nobody knew . . . and nobody, to this day, knows a blessed thing about it!

*   *   *

A good twenty-six miles or so off their port beam there would be that selfsame light: Wickham. It just below a misty, pale, blue-white horizon – they would not sight it.

How long, Lincoln queried, would that 'race' last now that they had shut the 'mine' – the writing on the wall surely? That 'race' was a yacht race that went out from Melbourne each year to Grassy – Grassy being a small mining and fishing community three-quarters down on King Island's southeast coast.

Lincoln had stark memories of Grassy and he knew that many personal relationships and friendships had been formed there, over the years, between individuals and yacht crews and the residents of Grassy – and that already many residents had moved and most of the remainder would soon be forced to decamp and relocate away similarly!

He also knew too that the community's main source of income there had been a 'scheelite' ore mine – a tungsten ore used as an additive, amongst other things, during steel manufacture. There was now not enough scheelite left, they had told him, and what remained was too difficult and expensive to get at and that the financial losses had been simply too heavy to warrant further investment. Gone, just like that, finished, and mining scheelite now simply just another part of the Island's colourful history.

Lincoln's thoughts drifted . . . on the King Island race the tides dictated – and the time required for the yachts to assemble on the start line – and the fact that they all had to be back by Sunday night to be ready and fit for work on Monday morning – and that time was dictated by the slowest yacht. Yachts from berths and clubs all around Port Phillip Bay and further, and Lincoln could clearly see that fleet, in his mind's eye, amassing off Queenscliff on the Friday night ready for the start. Those 'crazies' started their contest at zero-one-thirty hours – in pitch darkness. A yacht race involving that many competitors was nerve-racking in daylight let alone at night; a fleet of thirty or forty comparatively heavy, blue-water yachts jostling for position on a start line with limited room was not easy at any time! Confusion and screaming reigning and yachts ghosting in, appearing from nowhere out of the darkness; close-encounters and hair-raising involvements leaving an already fatigued and tired brain from a week's work a quivering jelly. Lincoln mentally shook his head – it was one of the very few regular races in the world with a night start that he knew of.

The King Island Race had been one of his first introductions to the Bass Strait, and some aspects of the closing stages of that race Lincoln could remember in picture detail – and clearer than yesterday. His first glimpse of the island, or a man-made addition to it, had been from low down on a deck in disturbed water and then only seen between the crests – and the distant, solitary, white tower of Wickham stark and rising, without apparent foundation, directly from the sea. Only when really closing did one realise that it was built a third of the way along on a seemingly low, rocky, extended, stretched finger of lashed, wind-swept ledging – a ledging that prompted, for him, recollections of WW2 film clips, in scratched black-and-white, of a U-boat's foredeck being repeatedly washed and swamped by a sudded, storm-tormented, torn Atlantic swell.

Distance belied the strength of that apparently delicate elegant tower; and Gary's penchant for natural and local history came to mind yet again: Wickam Light had been built, as seemingly per usual now, by convicts, from locally quarried granite and was reminiscent of fortification construction. The base had first been hewn out, and excavations going down tens of feet, before the huge ten to eleven feet wide foundation blocks had been laid, and subsequent base-tiers being of the same dimensions. The light, as he could confirm, was, or rather, is enormously high because of its low location, and immensely powerful for the same reason: the tower is some one hundred and fifty-seven and a half – one hundred and fifty-eight feet tall. The light itself is two hundred and eighty feet above sea level – and Australia's tallest, apparently!

They had arrived much too far out with wind-over-tide throwing up a confused and ugly sea – there had been a wild beauty about that blustering afternoon. The heavy contrast between the grey, blue-green, jumbled yet marching waves and their severed tops – and the sheer distance enhanced by an indistinct land in the background. The reflection from broken and scattered white-water had been blinding in the early afternoon sun – and all seen through a multitude of tiny, cobwebbed rainbows that formed in the smoke of blown away spray that was the immediate aftermath of the broken waves that regularly exploded over their bow.

They had put a tack in off Lavinia Point in order to reach calmer water inshore, they had planned to follow the coast and go inside Sea Elephant Rocks and Councillor Island and thus avoid the tide. Wind, sea and leeway had proved too much and had forced them finally to go out to sea and around Councillor Island – the miles of sandy beach with an uninterrupted scrub and bushed grass backdrop of King remaining tantalisingly distant. They had crashed and rattled their way through and over a steep chop, working their way carefully to windward so as not to be blown away and lose contact with the island as well. They had tacked inshore again as soon as they had dared, and in contrast to Wickam Light and yet similar, and again a picture sprang into Lincoln's mind: of the white, pencil-thin light in the centre and on the highest point on Councillor Island and catching the sunlight, and it like a thick mast above the bridge of a half-submerged vessel in heavy weather. The thrown up white-water around adding to the illusion – that the low-lying island was also under way.

Huge, circular fuel tanks that were indicated on the chart were quite distinct behind and finally marked the end of that seemingly, never-ending, sandy foreshore of the main island; and from then on an unfriendly, steep, undulating, rocky, rugged coast till . . . Even a reasonably keen observer wouldn't have picked it easily unless he knew: and there, low down and practically obscured in the misty, water-laden air and distant tumbling swell between and against and blending with the earth colours behind, was a breakwater. The comparatively, and at that time, unknown crew and the skipper obviously had known what they were about and there was excited consternation and a pointing of fingers and then a ragged cheer – apparently they were through an imaginary finishing line that extended out, at right angles to the coast, from the outlying tip of that low, man-made, surf underscored and explosively covered, crooked finger of protective concrete.   Lincoln remembered the two or three small fishing and motor boats that had laboured their way out to them; and after a number of sarcastic and ribald shouted welcomes and replies, they had escorted and guided *Worippa* in. The contrast had been astonishing; and finally they were nestling below Grassy, glad to anchor in a surprisingly large, calm, protected expanse of crystal-clear, flat water.

*   *   *

That garden-party hadn't been the sort that Lincoln was used to and for some reason, be it tiredness, depression, anticlimax or whatever, he hadn't been able to settle. He had felt isolated and uncomfortable . . . and vaguely threatened. Those were his personal feelings and probably not prevalent, although to his ears a lot of the laughter and conversation had seemed overly loud and not a little forced – no, it had been his imagination and mood, surely? He had glanced around at the view, and then had looked around more slowly – their venue had been set out on a grassed area next to the quay – and they had been, he recollected, huddled in the shadow of rolling surrounding hills. The quay itself and its environs, including their grassed area, had been immediately overlooked by the town, which was spread out along and on a shallow, arcing crest above, or near the crest, and there was nothing between them and the town atop, just a steeply rising, grassed and bushed incline. The road that wound up to the town had been hidden and obscured by the overly long grass and profuse, wild foliage – and the town was further away than it looked – and to walk up would be a fair hike. The reason for Lincoln's discomfort at that time had lain before and around him: isolated, desolate, unfriendly and lonely. The yachts, he recalled, had seemed to be crowding in and their whiteness, chrome and plastic glitter and newness accented – and playthings in those surrounds against the working fishing boats anchored further out. The yachts had been moored bows-on to the wooden jetty and comings and goings, callings and shoutings, even from that little distance had also sounded echoingly harsh and intrusive. There's was a temporal pocket of chatter and laughter infringing on an indifferent hostile landscape, and none of it, for him, had dispelled the alienability of their presence.

Like a lot of people brought up in industrial England, Lincoln had always had a starry, deep-seated yearning to live in the country and lead a simpler life – something died within him on that afternoon, and all the thoughts, musings and dreamings and the romance of going back to the grass roots, self-sufficiency and the country-life had fled and in their place only a hollow feeling of loss. Those pleasant dreamings of playing the country squire killed by reality – that he was a city-boy, on that day, Australia had forced him to accept.

Another thought followed and the truth of long-ago advice once given, now realised – and spelled out with a capital 'T'. Lincoln smiled to himself: 'go where all the lasses are, boy,' that old mentor had advised, 'all the comforts and amenities of home'll be there: clean sheets, hot water – civilisation. Girls'll not rough it, they're not that daft, you'll not find them far away from where they can plug in a hair dryer!'

The local womenfolk had barbecued beefsteak, lamb chops, sausages, mushrooms, tomatoes, sliced potatoes, plus baked beans, and all for a nominal sum – and bread, side-salad and accoutrements they helped themselves to. There would not have been an individual displeased nor who begrudged that their efforts were rewarded – and profits made from the tucker and the sale of beer apparently more than covering all their expenses, and that included the fact that they kept on adding to out-held plates so long as they were out-held!

One particular woman, who was a 'no-nonsense' type and whom Lincoln had liked, had humorously and contritely admitted to him that they had seriously underestimated quantity – and had been shocked at the consumption. It had been interesting to watch too: they, the women, had coped with the first onslaught of ravenous yachties cheerfully; were quite happy about the second, there were a few who raised their eyebrows when a fair section came back for a third helping, but were definitely taken aback and not a little bewildered when the younger ones began to dribble back for a forth! It hadn't been a question of money either, each individual insisted and paid happily each time – no, the women had forgotten just how much growing boys and young men could consume, especially lads who wouldn't or couldn't be bothered to cook on such a short trip and had been living off of Mars bars, crisps and the like since Friday dinnertime!

As one of the awed, breathless servers had explained later: George, one of the lady's husbands, had spent the whole day driving the local rattletrap back and forth, and it fully occupied transporting beer and supplies from the nearest stores. They, the fleet, had apparently drunken dry and eaten out the first and the second store – they had emptied the third by mid-afternoon and there had been a major depletion to the stocks in the fourth, which was one of the larger supermarkets, by the time they had finished!

Lincoln remembered himself standing there watching and grinning, and better hosts there were nowhere on earth: rough, rude, bawdy humour had quickly surfaced after the breakdown of initial reserve; and the ladies giving better than they got most of the time.   For them, and underneath it all, that event had been a serious business, he had belatedly realised, and news and company from the outside and a bit of pocket money to be made on the side far exceeding the obvious and apparent surface values.

For Lincoln, people-watching had nearly always proved to be good fun; and the women's men-folk had started with all the right intentions – that is, with an overwhelming urge to earn strong. Famed King Island beef and cheese changed hands; and sackfuls of live crayfish were carried onto yachts and hung over the side in cool water till ready to sail.   One innovative fisherman, Lincoln was reminded, had begun a separate party on the beach and he selling buttered fresh fish wrapped in foil and cooked in a driftwood fire lit under a forty-five gallon drum, and not coping with demand and unable to net out steaming red 'crays' from the boiling water above, nor had he been able to wrap fish quickly enough from embers below!

Contrariwise, the husbands had fought valiantly initially, before they had been finally dragged down to their guests' drunken level – and eventually succumbing to temptation and pressure, despite the good talking-tos, the waggings of skillets and the shirty warnings. Raucous, local male laughter and shouted comments could be heard more and more often above the general hubbub as the afternoon wore on – and some husbands intent on drinking away their own potential and their wives hard-earned profits – till, ironically, stronger contents from bottles had been brought onshore, and whether intended or not, had put a stop to that.

A walk up the hill to and through Grassy had killed, on Lincoln's part, any personal inclination to party; the town was silent and deserted and only the wind blowing over and between the buildings had been a sighing companion. Rows of annex-type 'company' houses lined the street, and all empty, and some, presumably the last occupants to leave, hadn't bothered with boarding up – and they, with their starring windows, accented the bleakness of it all somehow. The signs were there already: of nature reclaiming: hedges, flower borders, abandoned lawns; and grass verges overgrown and beginning to run wild. And Lincoln had trudged on. The death of a community depressing beyond belief and the air of desolation had been especially strong around the local stores: a shuttered post office; and paper, leaves and litter trapped and heaped in doorways of the grocer's and butcher's; and the dark brown leaves in stark contrast against the patchy, streaked, whitened-out, opaque plate-glass of shop doors.

Made up from squares of pastel card: and a haphazard, epitaphic line had been pasted across a huge picture-window of one of the classrooms. On each card there was a background of smaller overlapping oblongs and squares – and articles and black-and-white and coloured pictures cut from newspapers and magazines, and each one telling or depicting something of local everyday life and events. Imposed above them again and using the lion's share of the card were huge letters, each of a different colour. Lincoln remembered standing there before and just looking . . . before walking away; he remembered that he had turned on impulse to look again at the whole, and again at the message left by the children of that local school. So simple yet so powerful – and his emotions flooding out. 'GOOD-BYE GRASSY', the letters had spelt.

*   *   *

"Chris?"

Lincoln looked round.

"That's the third time I've called you, Bill's below, he says he's ready."

The smell of curry just about knocked him over as he descended the companionway steps. Lincoln had to grin to himself; Bill's face glowed, as much from anticipation, Lincoln could see, as from heat from the stove. Parts, as usual, had to be played and acted out, and his exaggerated checking for spies and listening-ears were calculated to exasperate him to as close to the teetering edge of his losing his temper as he dared. Lincoln sidled on past and stopped with Bill just behind him, but in peripheral vision and where Lincoln could keep an eye on him and calculate his mood to the ninth degree – and run for it if necessary! In a parody Lincoln just peered: eyes roving back and forth and up and down. He stalked forward finally, prompted by the beginnings of Bill's first muttered oath. Lincoln stopped at each locker door and paused for a second for effect before quickly pulling each open – and nobody should have been more surprised than Lincoln had there have been a body in one of them. He carefully examined each bunk on the way back, and round Bill again for a look in the skipper's berth behind the chart table, and in the double on the other, port side. Bill watched, reconciled to the performance and knowing that Lincoln would take even longer should there be any sign of impatience on his part . . .

Enough was enough, and yet when Lincoln at last stood at rest next to Bill he still could not help but push his luck a little further: he leant back behind Bill for a final furtive, exaggerated glance on either side. He only then produced a small spiralled notepad from inside his shirt with a flourish – just as Bill was about to blow! Lincoln congratulated himself; the timing had been perfect. Lincoln held the notebook directly in front of him while Bill calmed down, and pretended to study the instructions therein intensely again while watching for Bill's reaction out of the corner of his eye. Bill's hand came up involuntarily: he was wanting to move the notebook closer to himself and, as Lincoln had anticipated, he was unable to read the scribbled writing in the bad light. Wicked, so wicked. Like a snake mesmerised, Bill's head moved: turning and bending to follow the gently descending, ascending, sideways-moving and retreating open page. Cruel, not nice; and Lincoln admitted that he really shouldn't do this sort of thing to him.

Always attack first, that was Lincoln's motto. "What are you up to, Bill?" he asked crossly. "Even if I allowed you to, which I'm not, without your glasses you can't even see the bloody book let alone read the writing."

Bill turned, looked up and just stared – he had spoken not a word.

"All right, all right," Lincoln said petulantly, feeling guilty all of a sudden – and retreating away from the 'Poor Bill' countenance and giving in. "I'll read out what we need and you can make your own notes later if you want, or I'll write them out for you." Lincoln looked at him in askance. "Satisfied?"

Bill nodded, and from what Lincoln could see, also accepted his unoffered apology – bloody cheek!

"You spoon off all the excess oil and rubbish first: splinters of cinnamon, cloves, cardamom seeds, bay leaves. Bite into any one of those." Lincoln pulled a face. "And you'll know it."

They patiently sifted through, taking turns to fish out the bits and pieces.

"Right," Lincoln said, "once it's like this, like a lumpy apple sauce – you carry on. We'll put all the next ingredients into a separate jug, pour in chicken stock and mix after, okay. As I say, that way we'll keep it separate and you can see exactly how it's done."

Bill's intensity was really a surprise, he really was keen, but then Lincoln had gone down the same road when he thought about it: originally bullied into trying, and nothing more satisfying on earth once converted. One never really suffered stomach troubles after an authentic curry – chronic, satisfying flatulence, yes, but a real stomach-ache, no. And not surprising really, the stuff had first been developed and evolved to cope with questionable stringy meat in a hot climate. Like the forbidden fruit, once over the shock of tasting something so thoroughly alien, a person was never quite the same after. Lincoln had never bothered to find out and isolate which, but he was convinced – one of the spices, one of those spices had to be mildly addictive.

"Ready?"

Bill nodded.

"Right, one tablespoon. No." Lincoln held his hand in the way of the spoon. "A tablespoon, not teaspoon." He waited while Bill exchanged the teaspoon for a tablespoon. "Right, one tablespoon of each of turmeric, cumin, chilli powder, tomato sauce."

Bill frowned and then asked. "Tomato sauce. You sure?"

Lincoln stepped back away from the working surface and once more looked theatrically on either side and around. "It should be puree," he whispered, "but sauce'll do." He held a finger to his lips. "Not a word."

Bill's temper finally began to fray, "Christ, you can be bloody hard 'yaka'." He sighed. "Can we just get on with it?"

"You can't be too careful," Lincoln said half-heartedly, "you never know who's listening in." He was right, Bill, the humour had worn thin. "Right," he said brusquely. "Two tablespoons of coriander, and then all the rest are teaspoon measures." Bill spooned the rest in: garam masala, curry powder, paprika – hot. "That's it then, Bill, there we have it: fill with stock, mix it up and pour it in. Bingo."

Bill wasted no time in clearing an area of scum on the surface of the first of the chicken saucepans; he cupped off half a jug full of juice and then did the same with the second. He rubbed his hands with satisfaction after pouring the pungent spice concoction into their sauce saucepan.

"One thing you should know, Bill." Lincoln put his hand on his shoulder to placate him. "There's no need to look so worried, the recipe's fair dinkum. Leave the sauce for twenty-four hours, minimum, if you make it at home, and freeze the excess. I can't explain it but some sort of chemical transfer takes place if you let it stand – without doubt, it's much better for it."

Bill nodded, he obviously knew about standing food already. "What about the basmati rice?" he enquired.

"What about it?" Lincoln asked.

"Don't give me that, I noticed you dropping stuff in by sleight of hand. Come on, what was it?"

"You don't want much for your tuppence-halfpenny, do you, just all my hard won culinary secrets acquired over the . . ."

Sharon came down the steps, and grinned a false grin: a typical reaction to their silent hostile stares. "Sorry boys," she said in a sweetly provocative singsong voice, her nose in the air. "Not interrupting anything, am I?"

It wasn't actually a question and she sailed on through without waiting for an answer.

"All right," Lincoln said to Bill, "talking of bad pennies – in for a pound. You put in a drop of oil, a touch of chili powder and garam masala, a chopped onion and a clove of garlic – and stir. Fill to about an inch above the rice with ordinary cubed, chicken stock, and then bring to the boil and cover . . . Happy?"

Bill nodded. "The basmati makes it, it's sort of nutty – I've never tasted anything like it before." He then added, "Least you're useful for something, Pom."

"Bloody charming," Lincoln said. "You sweet-talk me into giving away all my secrets – and abused me after."

Bill grinned.

"What we need now, Bill, is . . ." Lincoln said, considering. "Have we got any pickled onions on board?"

Bill put a finger through an inch circular hole in and halfway up and near the edge and undid the inside catch of a locker above them. He handed across a glass jar. "They're not in the recipe, surely?"

"No. I need two sheep's eyes, that's all." Lincoln looked at him. "They're a delicacy in the Arab world; you've seen the old films: in the Bedouin tent?" He made a 'picking-up' gesture. "The old hand dipped into the communal cooking pot – and then a dirty great, dripping eyeball looking at the audience between finger and thumb, and the audience squealing as the evil Arab scoffs the thing down – all that." Lincoln grinned. "I'll have one on my plate and you can point it out and comment. The other eyeball." He nodded forward. "Can go on Crazy Mytle's – she needs a bit of revving up!"

Bill shook his head. "That's not very nice." There an air of false innocent wonderment in his voice and expression. He added after a moment, "And it's childish."

Lincoln grinned. "I know."

Bill held up a finger before dropping to his knees, he opened and started to rummage through one of the locker's below. "Raisins," he said. "We've got a whole box-full of packets somewhere." He explained while he was looking. "If we carefully cut out a hole to size and fit a raisin in flush . . ." He held up a box triumphantly. "It'll look just like a pupil at first glance."

"You wicked bugger, Corsham," Lincoln admonished. "You're worse than me!"

*   *   *

Rapidly cooling food underlined the silence and they, and Lincoln, even though Lincoln knew, were intent like pigs

350

interrupted and frozen at the trough, which was the only way to describe them . . . Concentration on the interrupted and now closely studied meal was absolute and caused by Lincoln's little joke, or rather, theirs, Bill's and his, which would shortly eventuate and finally fire them all up!

Sharon had watched in horror, alerted by an aside from Bill; and, as he explained later, he had also added a little zest of his own to their little plot – and for some reason only known to himself he had told her that Lincoln had a jar of baby lamb's eyeballs stored away for treats and special occasions et cetera! The optic Lincoln rolled and rotated in his fingers, nodded without a change of facial expression, and then crunched one half before casually swallowing the other. Sharon hadn't really reacted, she had carried on, head down, cautiously pushing around and sifting through the food on her own plate – and hence oblivious to the sly glances exchanged. Her reaction when it came exceeded all their expectations . . . and more. She stood suddenly, and with her hand over her mouth forced her way out and round and up the companionway steps. The half-hidden orb, when they looked, was in the middle of her plate, and a quite convincing visual organ – uncovered, sitting there – staring up! Gary had been furious (they had somehow forgotten to tell him about the plot!). While Gary had loudly remonstrated with Lincoln, Helmut, the only one topside, had sympathetically commiserated with her, believing Sharon to be deadly serious. He had put her in the picture before sending her back down. They all stared mutely as she descended the companionway steps, grim of face as she forced her way back around to her seat, with no consideration for other people's feelings, or legs and feet! Gary, still standing and ready to sympathise and comfort she ignored, pushing him back down into his seat as she passed. They waited as she sat – women, Lincoln thought, you can never tell how they are going to react – flirty and friendly one minute, moody and quick to take offence the next . . .

She caught Lincoln completely on the hop: picking and standing up and throwing in one quick fluid movement, at full strength, and so unexpected; and that other eye, that other onion had hurt, ricocheting off the top of his head and then rattling away like a bullet into the fore cabin and beyond.

The shocked silence had lasted for only a moment, and

while Lincoln rubbed the bruised wet spot and teased out the odd grain of rice from his hair; they were so incredibly and impressively quick, and once started, like verbal diarrhoea, they couldn't stop. Lincoln thought it was Nick who had started it, who else, and so it went on: 'One eye for the ship and one eye for the pot'; 'Eye, eye, captain'; 'Eye see no ships, only hardships'; 'Keep your eye on that for a minute, please'; 'Well – I just can't see it' . . . and so on.   Lionel's background accompaniment, showing his age and bad harmony, of 'Jeepers, creepers where did you get those peepers' added to the cacophony. Ramsey finally cracked the mask, she couldn't hold out – and not a word from him, he just sat there looking, a hand over one eye, innocently peering around with the other.

Sharon winked at Lincoln from across the table, and a wealth of meaning there was in that wink – she had obviously not been fooled for a minute from the start. Lincoln laughed to himself and looked on; they would all be snapped up by the next travelling troop passing through – a credit to any drama school – and their acting so real that they were nearly believing in their own charades. How they all enjoyed it: the shouted, mock arguments, the ad-lib jokes and the rest . . . Some sort of tension-release mechanism was obviously operating – and that, Lincoln mused, could only be to the good.

Nick finally sat down again and they were only half-aware of him buttering two crusts of bread, and slowly a hush spread and the chatter slowed down to a whisper and finally to silence. Onto the bottom slice he finished knifing from his plate the remaining curry and juices. On went dollops of brown sauce poured from the bottle kept in the table's centre recess, and elaborately smoothed flat then with the same knife – he added the top slice next. Potter's half-disgusted, half-awed comment on the first bite echoed all their sentiments.

"Fuck me dead," he whispered, "that's it . . . Well . . . I've just about seen everything now!"

Chapter 25

Ramsey was on his bicycle again – Ramsey pressed another button. "It's going to revolutionise Australian yacht racing this, there'll be no point in even leaving your mooring unless you've got one of these thing's on board. There's no Decca out here, as you know, only transit satellite navigators – Sat Nav and whatnot. This GPS'll upset those boys, Decca, I mean, all that investment in those coastal stations around Europe and elsewhere." Getting quite excited, was Ramsey. "Bush-walkers've even got 'em hanging from their belts, they're making 'em that small now; they know exactly where they are when they go out into the bush." Ramsey half-laughed. "Im-bloody-possible to get lost. For what they are, they're bloody cheap – and, what's more, the prices are coming down all the time. You can grin, Chris, it might be old hat to you, but to us, it's the next best thing since sliced bread . . . You get lost out here and the odds are . . . Well, you know what I mean." He didn't give Lincoln a chance to answer him directly before he asked the next question. "This'll just about put us on par with Europe, do you reckon?"

He looked across expectantly. His anxious, slightly belligerent attitude didn't sit well with Lincoln; there was a faint trace of envy in there, or something similar. He was right, of course, Lincoln conceded, strictly speaking this new technology did put Australia and other remote areas of the world on par with Europe navigationally. But . . . Well . . . Recent navigational aids were only part of the picture: European waters have been sailed upon for hundreds, probably thousands of years and therefore an unbroken string of knowledge had been collected accordingly; the usual thing of a father passing his knowledge on to his son, for example, and the subsequent dynasties. One could go on and on: bearings, depth of water, tide and currents, wind direction, prevailing wind, time of year, colour of the water, behaviour and type of bird – migrational habits . . . Sailors from Lincoln's part of the world could and can pinpoint pretty much where they were, or are, or the vicinity anyway, by simply dropping a waxed lead over the side: the detritus from the seabed stuck to the wax is, whether broken shell, sand, gravel et cetera, pretty much uniquely particular to only one specific area or place.

No, there simply wasn't, or isn't, a subsidy for that sort of familiarity and accumulated knowledge – so he wasn't on par and it would probably be many years before he, or rather, Australia was . . . Brian wasn't unintelligent, Lincoln acknowledged, and his aggressive-defensive stance and his being slightly on his back heel said to Lincoln that he already knew that but hated the thought. It sounded very much like he was looking back over his shoulder to the old country – with its associated culture and that accumulated knowledge – and in a way who could blame him, that knowledge was something to envy . . . But, then again, what a person loses on the round-a-bouts he gains on the swings, and the people of this new world had so much more going for them if they did but know it – their population, or the lack of, rather, for example – in a nut shell, push too many rats (or people) into a box or confined space and they would eventually begin to bite each other!

Another thing to consider was modern survey ships, satellite observation, space technology – in the near future, with a whiz-bang infrared camera or something similar, they could and almost certainly would (if they hadn't already) capture, compute, plot and colour print to a chart, and all that hard-earned knowledge amassed over the centuries, it would all be collected in one afternoon's orbital sweep!

Ramsey interrupted Lincoln's thoughts, "Well, does it?"

"Hmm," Lincoln said absently. "Decca'll give you almost exactly the same data – that's the junior model for yachts – it's been around for about . . . Well, it must be all of . . ." Lincoln shook his head. "Five years – at least ten or fifteen years for the big ships . . ." And Lincoln even had to qualify that, "Probably longer, I don't really know." He peered across at the GPS. "As I say, that thing's giving the same information as Decca – it's just a different technology, that's all." Lincoln looked at it again. "It's a little more advanced than the Decca Navigator I used two or three years ago, it has a few more functions, but then, you'd expect that." Lincoln looked at Ramsey directly and he still didn't like the disgruntled yet smug look on Ramsey's face so he pointed out, "Ground stations are a bloody sight cheaper to build and maintain than satellites, Brian, let alone the expense of launching and repairing – that's your luck."

Ramsey had the decency to look slightly embarrassed and maybe just a little dismayed, and then he bounced back –

constructively this time, though not without a touch of sarcasm, "It's going to have a much bigger impact over here, and as you're so fond of reminding us, there's very little data concerning tidal information on our charts. This'll change all that, we'll be able to do our own now." Ramsey sighed. "There's not much more on them than when they were first published, is there? Which was . . ." Ramsey turned the chart over and examined the top left-hand corner. "Look at this: *'Surveyed by Commodore J. L. Stokes and the officers of the HMS Beagle 1839-43'* . . ." The incredulousness and disgust in his voice was something to behold. "The HMS-bloody-Beagle, for Christ's sake." He read again from the chart, and this time from the bottom right-hand corner, "The latest reprint according to this was in *'1982'*!" Brian pushed the chart away from him with contempt and then looked at Lincoln directly. "And the latest addition won't be that much better, will it?"

Ramsey's disgruntled attitude was, in fact, Lincoln's fault, Ramsey had been happy in his ignorance until Lincoln had shown him a few charts of European waters. He had been very, very upset after he had seen his Dutch Tidal Atlas and the detail therein – there wasn't anything remotely like it published in Australia. Original information, as he had said, from the original admiralty surveys seemed to be the only information available, and he was right on his other point, there did seem to be very little extra, modern, additional input, if any at all!

Lincoln could only confirm – and give the knife a little tweak. "It'll have been made from the original hand-engraved plate, Brian, photographed and then revamped . . . and I didn't say there was very little information on there either, I said there was none at all!"

Ramsey gave Lincoln a knowing look; he knew very well that Lincoln was stirring him up. He pointed a finger at Lincoln. "Don't exaggerate." He turned and again gazed at the dimly lit face of the GPS. "Anyway, it's quite brilliant, how this thing constantly updates: speed and position over the seabed, plus how much we're deviating away from our desired course." Suddenly he looked pensive and a little glum. "How on earth are we going to cope with it all, the technology, I mean?" He confessed, "And there's me still trying to come to terms with the pocket calculator, and that's still a piece of white-man's magic as far as I'm concerned – I haven't really got over that yet. And don't look at me like that, think about it, they're now smaller than a playing card and about as thin – you press the buttons and it adds-up, subtracts, divides – every-bloody-thing . . . And half of the damn things don't even have batteries anymore!" Ramsey pointed his finger at Lincoln. "I'm telling you, nine-tenths of the population, including me, don't have a clue how the damn things work!"

Lincoln could sympathise with him, and his words reminded him of the shock he had had when he had gone to replace the speedo cable on Rosie's car: He had eased back the dashboard after taking out the retaining screws (finding them had been a feat in itself) – nothing! Not a sign of a cable – just a printed circuit pasted on the back!

Ramsey touched Lincoln's shoulder for attention. "I was saying . . . You listening? The Americans own the satellites – did you know the system was developed and built for their military." Ramsey's voice was taking on a slightly petulant quality, "They degraded the system for civilian use, it was only accurate to twenty-five metres, or something, instead of being exact."

Lincoln just looked at him – to be quibbling over twenty-five metres!

"Still," Ramsey hurried on, "that's so small, it would've been neither here nor there as far as we're concerned . . . I suppose." He brightened slightly. "The signal's not been scrambled since the Middle East crisis; you know – our friend Saddam. Nigh on pinpoint accuracy – it's important, I guess, that you don't park your Sherman tank in the wrong place. No doubt they'll re-scramble it again as soon as they think of it." Ramsey contemplated on a point just above Lincoln's left shoulder and frowned. "That war was a fair while back though – maybe they're not going to bother."

Ramsey's eyes blinked him back into the present world. "The point is, I now know if there's any tide under us, that's after she's settled down on the course dictated by the GPS, and I can ask how far we've been pushed off our rhumb line – at any time. It'll even tell us which way to our destination and by how many degrees to compensate . . . and, and the time it'll take to get there. It'll tell you your elapsed time, as well: that and the difference between the mileage on *Worippa's* log and that of the GPS'll be the tide – you can plot it exactly. I know you can already get that information from the GPS exclusively, but it's interesting." There was awe on Ramsey's face, literally. "Take now, the wind's on our quarter so there'll be negligible leeway – so . . ." Ramsey pressed two buttons. "We're being pushed out very slightly." He glanced across at Lincoln quickly. "What're you grinning at?" he asked suspiciously.

"Nothing." Lincoln sighed. "I'm just smiling at your enthusiasm." Lincoln quickly pointed out before Ramsey could interrupt, "What you've said is right, but it's an over-simplification, and overly complex at the same time: as you say, leeway . . . And what about your compass, it's unusual, isn't it, for there to be no deviation at all?"

Brian was just a touch defensive.

"Like I told you when you first stepped on board, the deviation's negligible. If you were doing a great circle voyage then I'd have them swung professionally, but as it is, it's not enough to worry about – we only ever do short hops. Why are you looking so sceptical?" he asked. He pointed to the GPS. "I checked ours against this after we'd installed it, in the 'Bay': we motored for half a mile in every direction." Brian gestured with his hand. "It only confirmed what I already knew, our deviation's negligible – it's not worth complicating everything up with a deviation card, it'd be a pain in the arse."

That was the trouble, and Lincoln refrained from answering, everybody thought it was a pain in the arse and side-stepped the chore – and it was only when they bounced off some rocks on a dark wet night that folk regretted not putting themselves out . . . That's assuming, of course, that they lived to realise and had the gumption to work out the cause of their accident! On the other hand, Ramsey was right in another way, when one thought about it, that was one of the good things about GPSs and similar navigational tools: if there was a large deviation present in a compass then the discrepancy between the two: it and the GPS, or whatever, would quickly become obvious!

Lincoln let it go, he was no mug, was Ramsey, and anyway, Gary would not let something so elementary pass by. "Sorry, Brian, it's just a pet hobby-horse of mine, it's such a simple job and yet so many people neglect to do it – and the consequences can be so disastrous. I also take your point about understanding the electronic side of it all – we're just another pair of old dinosaurs. I guess there's no point in worrying: use it like you do your pocket calculator and press the buttons and enjoy life: it frees us up to enjoy the scenery rather than trying to work out in a seaway a complicated position while being over-tired and feeling sick."

Lincoln didn't bother to state the obvious, that they three were old-school and automatically noted their actual position on the chart, and double-checked, even if roughly, with dividers and parallel rules – that their position as quoted by the GPS made sense!

They watched the yellow-green digital figures change and update, and it was Lincoln who finally broke their mesmerised silence, "It's not quite what the chart says, is it – the chart indicates that the set runs either north-north-east, or south-south-west, depending. At least I think it does, there's not a tidal diamond to sight," Lincoln said, as much to annoy Ramsey as anything else, "and these engraved little arrows are," he pointed to two or three on the chart, "so faint they might as well be invisible – they look a bit tentative to me . . ."

Ramsey shook his head. "No," he denied, "the set'll be biased that way if that's what it says, even if not by much, it depends on conditions – it's not all black-and-white, you know. You'll find the most relevant information under the title." Brian didn't, Lincoln noted, need to look at what it said under the title on the chart, he obviously knew the words by heart. "It says there's a light east-setting current throughout the year; two to two-and-a-half knots near the mainland reported occasionally." Ramsey looked at him directly. "I've been sailing here for twenty years and I can tell you, never yet have I gone out into the Bass Strait without being or ending up east of where we've wanted to go."

Lincoln looked down again at the chart, for a stretch of water that was notoriously treacherous, the lack of information was actually scandalous – if Lincoln were approaching Bass Strait for the first time, the absence of information given would have badly frightened him. Apart from that, local information was always worth its weight in gold, especially from reliable people like Brian and Gary. Also, Brian and Gary's enthusiasm for Bass Strait intrigued him . . . so Lincoln probed further. "Gary says that water funnels through Bass and is much faster than the average ocean current, from what you've read out from the chart, that's obviously so, and you seem to be confirming it too?"

Ramsey shook his head again. "It's not so much that, or rather, that as well – this is a highly complex piece of water, you know, and there are all kinds of forces at work. What gives me the shits is there's been masses of work and research done; did you know, Bass Strait was attached to the mainland one time. I mean, it was dry land – it wasn't always under water."

"Gary told me."

"Ancient plant life under the earth equals oil, and all that?"

"Mmm." Lincoln encouraged.

"That's what it's all about really," there was an edge of disgust in Ramsey's voice, "the rest of it's just a spin off. It's about oil – it's as simple as that. Oil and mineral resources. The bloody Government, private enterprise and the oil companies have spent millions on research: seismic charts, core samples, tidal information, currents, waves, wind, and all for future rigs . . . and mining." Brian quietened somewhat, and then judiciously explained, "I've got no real axe to grind there, it's all got to be paid for somehow – and it's paid off for them handsomely. Australia'll be self-sufficient till well into the twenty-first century as far as oil is concerned, and that's putting export revenue to one side.

"None of it gets back to Joe Public, that's what pisses me off – and we pay for most of it. We don't seem to be capable of organising all the information into a comprehensive format." Brian lifted the corner of the chart and then pushed it away dismissively. "Imagine how detailed that chart would be with all that information on, it doesn't bare thinking about." He added bitterly, "They're fucking useless."

He was getting genuinely annoyed – it was time to defuse the moment, before he started spitting blood. Lincoln looked at him for a heartbeat and in an exaggerated reasonable voice, asked, "It wasn't our curry that upset you, was it, Brian? Do you want some stomach powder for that bout of the gripes you've got?"

And although indignant, a slight crease appeared around Brian's mouth. "It's all right for you, Pom; you haven't lived here long enough for it to get to you. I reckon they'd be able to simulate a pretty accurate computer model of the Bass Strait should they pool their knowledge, as it is we have to make an educated guess from snippets heard from here and there."

He went on, "I'll never forget it, it must have been two, three . . . it might even be four years ago now: I sat idly watching the 'idiot' box: one of those nature programs was on. Do you know, it was all about what we've just been talking about: upwellings of cold Antarctic water on the upper west of Tasmania and its influence on Bass Strait. 'Upwellings'! Have you ever heard anything about upwellings, Chris? The one this woman was talking about – the one on the west tip of Tasmania, the one that nobody's ever heard of till she just happened to mention it – it effects the East Australian Current on the east side . . . I still can't believe it, even now. She said how the research they were doing and the subsequent information would help control pollution: pollution spills, fish, fish yields, navigation, fuel economy for shipping: it was all good stuff, no doubt about it." Ramsey then asked the crucial question – the frustration and exasperation in his voice one could cut. "Well, where the hell is it, the results of all that research? From that day to this, as far I know, never has anything been subsequently published . . ." He said slowly, "Unless it was in-house, or in some obscure limited edition – if it has, then that would be bloody typical!

"The lady's there explaining, as cool as you like – her talking about and confirming an upwelling was shock enough, I can tell you." Ramsey looked at Lincoln directly; he pursed his lips in indignation. "She then casually drops this other bombshell – it was right in the middle of her bloody narrative."

Lincoln almost chuckled out loud, Ramsey was building up quite a head of steam and he was getting more and more annoyed as he recounted his tale of woe.

"Actually, it wasn't a bombshell – it was a fucking great nuclear explosion." He took a breath. "It's apparently called the Bass Strait 'cascade': water from the old land bridge at the eastern end apparently pours down into the less dense Tasman Sea. If you sit down and work it out, as I've done, that's from say, Gabo Island to well outside the Furneaux Group." Ramsey held out his hand in front of him – horizontally, with its palm down. He dipped it as he spoke to emphasise his point. "The water drops down nigh on half a mile off of a two hundred mile long ledge." He shook his head in wonderment. "It's scoured away the seabed as clean as a whistle – it's actually eroding the seabed away!"

They were both silent then; Lincoln didn't quite fully understand all the implications of what Ramsey was telling him, but for Ramsey in his passion it was very relevant, if not profound.

He said quietly, "I've got my own theories: it clarifies so much. It goes a long way to explaining why there are so many anomalies. I swear to you that at times and depending where, the tide runs like a rip. Across the top of Tasmania for instance – why should it?" Ramsey answered his own question, "It should if there were an upwelling at one end and a fucking great waterfall at the other, shouldn't it? Wouldn't it?"

Lincoln's mind boggled – and he wasn't finished yet!

"I read somewhere, it might have been Alan Bombard; you know, the guy who deliberately set out in a rubber inflatable and nothing else. To see if he could survive living off the sea and then pass the information on – in his opinion, too many seamen were dying after abandoning ship. Do you know of him?"

Lincoln nodded gently; Lincoln had read his, Alan Bombard's story.

Brian continued on, "Him, or Rachel Carson anyway, it doesn't really matter, the point is, where there's an upwelling there's food. They're dotted all around the globe and well documented apparently. Wherever they occur there's prolific life: the upstream brings stuff to the surface . . . The undersea current that feeds the upwelling – that'll flow from somewhere way, way west of Tasmania, God knows from where. That undersea current stirs up the seabed, which in turn releases all kinds of goodies from the disturbed sediment: trace elements, bacteria, nutrients . . . food. Hence plankton, and where there's plankton, there's fish – a sort of chain reaction, do you see?" Brian pushed his way out from behind the chart table. "I'll get us some coffee, the kettle's on simmer."

Lincoln followed him into the saloon; he was intrigued; Ramsey looked up from the sink. "I don't know if you've clicked on, but for comparatively shallow water there's not that many fish: not like your Dogger Bank, for example. For some reason, which I don't really understand, we aren't traditionally a fish-eating 'state' – that's Victoria, I mean . . . Meat, yes, shellfish and stuff like prawns, yes, fish, no – we haven't even got a fishing fleet to speak of.   You've been around the coast, there's usually only two, three, four fishing boats in any one port, isn't there?"

He was right too: Lincoln had noticed a scarcity, though it hadn't really registered.

Brian gave him a knowing look; and conformation of his statement must have registered on Lincoln's face. "Umpteen fishing companies," he informed him, "have come and gone – most of them went down the 'gurgler'.

"Flake's our most popular fish – bloody flake. They wouldn't touch flake with a barge pole up north: it's the scavenger of the seas. Did you know, flake's actually shark – we hide that fact by calling it flake."

Lincoln said quietly, after thinking about it. "There's nothing really wrong or unusual about that, Brian, one of the most popular fish in the UK is called 'cod' – it's also a bottom feeder, it eats any crap going, that hasn't detracted from its popularity though!"

Brian sighed. "It's not that, it's that we shouldn't be guessing: we shouldn't be putting forward pet theories: the point is, is that the information's already there!

"Apart from Australia, Tasmania's also quietly done a lot of work, on all aspects of Bass, especially on fish – after all, it's one of their main industries.   Why aren't these waters richer in plankton?   What quantities do you fish before you fish out an area?   Where should you fish and at what depth? Fish quotas, in other words: plankton analysis and distribution: food chains, all that."   Brian took a breath.   "All those sorts of things – and lots of other stuff too probably – stuff I can't or wouldn't even think of . . ."   Ramsey smacked his fist into his palm.   "None of the information gets back.   You talk to Gary, the Bass Strait Islands support, or used to support, an untold quantity of wild life. Matthew Flinders, one of the first to see and explore this part of the world, watched a fly-past of petrels.   According to him it was never ending: he calculated that there were hundreds of thousands just in that one flight.   He actually quoted millions, you can't dismiss him, he was a highly trained surveyor: a map-maker, a hydrographer of the first order: he wouldn't be given to speculation."   Ramsey pointed across to the chart table.   "A lot of his work'll still be on that very chart, won't it?"

Lincoln nodded conformation, and now was not the time to

break into Brian's flow, not often would he open up like this.

"You can take his observations and work them out for yourself if you want." Brian looked directly at Lincoln again. "He states how wide, how deep and how compact that fly-past was, and for how long he watched.

"The islands also supported a seal population of god knows how many; and the islands have been a regular calling point for whale since time immemorial. They must have all lived off something, especially the seals, they all can't have lived off fresh air, could they, and one thing they all had in common . . ." Brian paused for effect with one questioning eyebrow raised and a half-grin on his lips. "They all frequented that upwelling, didn't they!" Brian's mood then changed. "Now they tell us there's no fish, I don't believe it: not unless we've broken a vital link in the food chain or something similar, like . . . The whalers came first – the whales have gone. Next came the sealers – two species of those they killed off completely, and only a few of the third are left. The fishermen are shooting them still, would you believe: they reckon they pinch their fish!" Brain shook his head. "Whole islands of roosting and breeding birds wiped out: used for food, or even worse, turned into oil, or plain fish bait to turn over a buck, because the birds were too trusting or stupid to fly away." His mood changed again then, as he speculated, "Or is it simply that despite everything there's fish only around the 'islands', because the islands break up the current . . . And it's shallower, of course, and there's little life elsewhere, comparatively, because, as I said, the bottom's swept clean of any food by a combination of that 'cascade' and what local fishing there still is!"

Lincoln followed Ramsey back to the chart table. "You and Gary," Lincoln said, "you both really care, don't you – you're both in pretty deep?"

"It's our backyard." Brian answered simply. "You look after your own backyard, don't you – you try to keep it clean and tidy." The sincerity of his matter-of-fact next few words moved Lincoln deeply. "I love it out here."

Lincoln reluctantly stated and it was only an outside possibility, that was all: that he sometimes suspected that the superpowers, including the United Kingdom, deliberately didn't make such similar information easily available either. He asked, "It's not the Australian Navy, is it, Brian, suppressing information?"

Brian opened his mouth then shut it again.

"Don't take offence," Lincoln said, "but the 'Defence' and 'Fisheries' in Europe wouldn't give the sort of information you're talking about away lightly, nor cheaply either." He added as an afterthought, "Not to mention the oil companies!"

Ramsey clicked off the navigational computer and said slowly, "I hadn't even considered that – it hadn't even entered my head. If anybody else had suggested that, other than you, I'd have dismissed it out of hand." He was silent for some moments. "Do you know, I've got a master-chart at home, I religiously transfer all the tidal information from the log to it after every trip, and any other information that I think might be relevant as well. I'll have a bloody good idea about what's going on in the neck of the woods I'm interested in, in two or three year's time." Ramsey grinned and then answered Lincoln's previous question, "No ... I can't believe that: a set of intellectual fucking morons disappearing up their own arses is more likely."

He had a point.

"Chris?"

Lincoln looked up from watching him walk brass dividers across the chart.

"Say eleven'ish hours at six or seven knots – the home run from now." Brian mentally calculated as he spoke, "That means we'll be entering the 'Heads' at around eleven or twelve tonight, right. So, if you get your head down now you'll get five hours before your next watch – that dinner you cooked entailed a lot of work – back into bed at eight again, that's another three. You'll be up then, and Lionel and I will be anyway."

Brian wasn't really asking a question, as far as he was concerned he was stating a fact ... And he was right too, Lincoln would be on deck when they entered the Heads: and if not from a safety point of view then simply because they would be entering their home waters: in other words it marked the end of their voyage, all bar the shouting, that is.

Lincoln tuned back in; there wasn't any real resentment in Brian's voice despite his look of reproach. "You'll not trust me to take us through, and nor will Gary." Brian held up a hand. "No offence taken, I'd do the same was I sailing with somebody else.

"The temptation is to stay up, because of the daylight – I'm just making the point, you'll be more of a help tonight were you fresh. Lionel and I have timed it just right – we've got the second half of the 'first' watch anyway."

His reasoning was all very well, but . . . "You're in a worse state than I am, Brian, you've had less sleep than any of us. Your little swim, and hanging around in the Bass Strait wouldn't have helped either – you haven't really got over or recovered from that yet, have you – be honest?"

Ramsey shook his head, and dropping the act for once. "It came in so quickly, didn't it, that storm. So incredibly vicious: literally out of the blue like a giant line squall. If we hadn't been warned . . . God, I've never been so cold. I went forward to sort out the sheet, and it happened when I actually, accidentally, stood on the sheet: it must have been the sheet: it rolled as I stood on it. I remember jerking back to regain my balance – and the wind did the rest . . . The strength of it, it just tumbled me straight over the side – just like that." Ramsey murmured, "I never thought I'd give up and lay down on my back with my legs in the air – I wasn't scared, I didn't have the time . . . I was actually preparing to give it away, do you know that, I was at that stage when they pulled me out. It seems like light years ago now, I can hardly remember it: a spark of annoyance, a few curses, and Judy, of course: yes, Judy. Plus a few things I'd like to have done – and that was all. Even now . . . I feel so placid about it – it's really strange."

Ramsey contemplated for a few moments and then abruptly stood, thus effectively closing and changing the subject. "We're under control, Lionel'll cover me with Warren if I want to follow you and get some shut-eye. I'm going to get Nick to go up the mast first though, while it's calm, I'll get him to secure the remains of the aerial and the cable end." Brian glanced forward and up, to where the top of the mast, though obviously not visible, would theoretically be. "I can hear the damn thing tapping now and again, can you? It's rapidly getting on my nerves. I'll send him up with some insulation tape and tie-wraps, he can seal the various wires and tidy up – that'll be the last of our chores, as far as I know."

Lincoln found it kind of interesting: Brian, as skipper, was not supposed to be attached to a watch – his duties as skipper dictated that he should be available and monitoring the boat and associated at all times. There was no debate there – a conscientious skipper worried and had less sleep than anyone on board. Nobody in their right mind resented nor was enviable of his so-called, independent, watchless existence. No, what was interesting to Lincoln was that he had continued to partner himself with Lionel on Lionel's watch. It was also interesting that Brian, though desperate for rest, hadn't mentally disassociated himself from Lionel's watch prior to that: when Warren had been declared fit enough and had reassumed his watch with Lionel!

*   *   *

A shadow passed by – Lincoln rolled over slightly just to see who it was. Sharon must have heard him stir, she stopped and glanced back and she smiled before turning and carrying on. With his head resting comfortably in the crook of his elbow and half-asleep, Lincoln idly watched. Sharon laid an empty sailbag carefully on the deck; she removed one boot while supporting herself between the bulkhead and bunks opposite – before stepping onto the dry sailbag. She somehow managed to remove the other while preventing the sailbag from sliding out from under on the wet carpet – a feat in itself. What a difference, she had got her sealegs now, a few days ago she would have been staggering and hopping around, unable to keep her balance and making a pig's ear of it!

Once again, this girl, despite her limited experience, could already teach them, the so-called old hands, a thing or two about changing below.

She took her jacket off and then her track pants, and then base thermal bottoms! Lincoln went to look away but her next antics forestalled that: she clutched onto the deckhead grabrail furthest away from her, and hanging onto that, slid her feet, sailbag and all, across to her locker. And there she stood, the little innocent, wearing top layers, knickers and socks: and nothing to see, her jumper hanging down and over, and all very decent. Lincoln rolled onto his back and concentrated on the bunk bottom above him and the ribbed deckhead above that – and trying to blot out the image of the curve of flesh that had been exposed when her top had ridden up, and the splash of her stark, glowing, almost incandescent, light-blue, minuscule silk knickers that barely concealed that flesh!

Sharon's soft, knowing, innocent voice invaded the

darkness, "Not disturbing you, am I?"

"Yes," he said.

"I won't be two minutes – just going to change my underwear and socks, that's all – won't be a minute." She asked reasonably, "You wouldn't want me to go around in smelly drawers, now would you – it might damage my reputation."

There was no answer to that, or if there was, Lincoln wasn't brave or game enough to voice it. "Why can't you turn them inside out each day like the rest of us," he asked. "Do that twice each side, alternately, and they'll last a minimum of four days – what's so special about you!"

Lincoln squeezed his eyes tightly trying to shut out the picture that her next disgusting comment evoked.

"There's a couple of them I wouldn't put it past – getting a bit ripe – some of them are getting a bit cheesy down there, wouldn't you say?"

"God." Lincoln rolled over, facing away as she began removing her top layers.

Sharon's scream followed by an audible thump brought Lincoln round and over quickly. Warren accelerated through the entrance from forward and past a half-naked Sharon – and his overbalancing and trying to run at the same time before finally sprawling to his knees would have been funny at any other time, but not today. Lincoln just half sat there, observing the scene from somewhere and not really with it and robbed of initiative by the speed of events. Echoes of a statement someone had made recently surfaced unbidden: *There's going to be trouble between him and Gary before long, if Gary catches him hanging around!*.

Well, Gary apparently had, and in the meantime he had followed Warren and had calmly grabbed him by the hair before running his head into the louvred locker doors – they had splintered under impact. Better if he had lost his temper: there was a death knell in the slow, merciless, methodically spaced arm movements: Lincoln doubted whether Warren was even conscious by the time he had reached him.

Lincoln twisting with everything he had, Gary's fending hand and arm gave ever-so slowly – Lincoln's best thermal top started to rip: the seam was parting under his clamped grip! Gary held him at arm's length for far longer than Lincoln had believed him capable of . . .

Sharon's screaming, pulling and begging went unheeded by either of them; she pleaded hysterically, "Let him go, Gary, you're killing him."

Gary turned his head and his face more frightening for its calmness. "Yes." He nodded. Warren's head again thumped sickeningly. "I am."

He couldn't quite not hide nor faintly acknowledge Lincoln's aside: it showed in his face – a response anyway, Lincoln determined, that was something. "You're damaging the cupboard, Gary, Brian'll be furious. Hit his head somewhere else, something more solid – use the mast."

Sharon crawled in between that (Warren's) head and the locker remains, she held Warren protectively, her face and voice again pleading, "Leave him, Gary . . . please? You've hurt him enough – poor, pathetic little man."

She had his, Gary's, attention; the strength went out of him. Everybody crowded round; Lincoln, for one, wasn't that surprised by his, Gary's, damning explanation.

"He was hiding: skulking around inside the heads, behind the curtain – take a look." Gary's shoulders slumped and he said disgustedly. "You'll find his flies are open!"

Lincoln stood there and calmly thought about it: well . . . when all was said and done, and to be truthful, Sharon hadn't been nor was she entirely blameless: what with her seemingly casual immodesty, her blatant sensual wiles and her provocative little exhibitions . . . and her apparent looseness . . . Yes, a person could really fall for that act and misread all the signals, that's if they were as thick as a plank or didn't know better – or both! And Lincoln knew that he was just as guilty as she was – in participating in and playing their silly games!

He sighed, and ruefully examined the tear in his new thermals – it really wasn't, on some days, worth the getting out of bed for!

Chapter 26

Lincoln was drifting on the edge of consciousness and yet as usual was aware and was waiting for confirmation and hoping, should it prove to be a false alarm, to be able to dive back down again into that luxuriant darkness. He mentally and subconsciously groaned, seething at the thought of being awake prematurely . . . Nevertheless, something had happened, something different – some discord: ordinary everyday sounds would never have brought him out of such a deep slumber. Again: a muffled thump and followed by two or three lesser, similar . . . not so much thump, more a resonance, a tremor: a vibration felt rather than . . . as much as heard.   There was the scraping of feet on the deck directly above, and always in the same vicinity and not moving away – one pair only.   Lincoln did not actually remember literally hearing it; he knew though that a winch had been used recently and excessively . . . or erratically – in use anyway!

He listened to the calling and yelling from above, and the muted cheering in the background – it was fun they were having up there and certainly not panic – the use of the winch nor the obvious enjoyment occurring on deck would not have woken him . . . And then, felt as much as heard, and not quite masked by the noise above: a twanging and strange drumming . . . of something working . . . a particular noise of something under undue stress!

Lincoln gave up and swore and threw back the snug blankets – no sleep for the wicked – and clambering down from the top bunk, and toes curling to the repulsive touch of the still slightly slimy, damp carpet. He shivered in the cool air flowing in from the half-opened forehatch and waited, dressed only in tee-shirt and underpants, for the next onset of bangs and quivers – contact with the cold caused huge goose pimples to form.

The origin, the source of the foreign 'something' that woke him, Lincoln discovered straight away and more by accident rather than by search and elimination.   It was quite distinct through the hand that rested lightly on the mast, casually placed there as support against *Worippa's* subdued rolling motion – and that noise and especially the vibration was something that he'd not heard nor sensed before!   He lent an ear against the mast directly and it amplified the popping and clicking, and the screeching tingings to a hair-raising degree – the mast was acting like a soundboard and the noise travelling down from throughout the mast's length. Lincoln was hearing the flexing of distorted metal under much too much torque – much more than that, there was an element of real pain there – and torment! It was something like ice trying to expand in a confined space, or like an animal writhing and twisting under torture – something in brutal agony.

Lincoln blinked and shook his head, he had actually been mentally drifting whilst leaning against the mast – he had thought that he had got over that deep inner weariness that invaded the soul and caused the type of stray flights just experienced, obviously he hadn't . . .

It was uncharacteristically quiet there below: deserted and vacant: an air, an atmosphere of abandonment prevailed. It was unusual, very odd, for every bunk to be empty – there was nobody, when he glanced through, in the saloon nor behind the navigation table either! A momentary increase of volume in the blurred and indistinct immediate merriment and chatter coming down from the cockpit drew his attention and drew an involuntary smile on his face – he was intrigued, they really were enjoying themselves up there. Lincoln stopped and cocked an ear whilst slowly making his way aft, and the noise coming directly from the cockpit couldn't mask the intermittent yahoos followed by shrill screams of objection and an almost inaudible reverberation of background speech coming from further forward; and they, and especially the screams, almost squeals, carried – they were louder . . . No, the pitch was different . . . and the excitement and the laughter and the fun from there, forward, and the distance, of course, was quite distinguishable from the now closer voices coming directly from the cockpit.

Helmut's far away questioning rumble from forward was distinctly audible from halfway up the companionway steps. There was no surprise there, Lincoln had also guessed, or rather, recognised, that it had been Nick's distant, muffled, hysterical screaming and begging replies under duress that he had heard from his bunk.

Another almost inaudible faint groan came from the mast, followed by more metallic clickings, it galvanised Lincoln into action – that noise was definitely no dream – he shot up the companionway steps.

Warren moved his feet as Lincoln exited; he was seated in his now usual place: furthest forward in the cockpit and against the companionway bulkhead. Lincoln noticed in passing that there was no drastic visible physical damage to his face, and only a dark bruise showing just below the hairline on his forehead. Lincoln had also caught a smile on that face before the mask dropped, he had obviously been watching and enjoying whatever had been and was going on forward – he was proving to be resilient, if nothing else!

Lionel was behind the wheel and Bill was above and behind him, Ramsey was in front of them both and partially obscuring Lionel. Ramsey stood with one leg under, with the majority of his weight on a knee that rested on the port cockpit seat; he was leaning out and like the other two his attention was focused forward. Bill acknowledged him with a nod; he was half-seated on the pushpit, to lee, with one hand around the extended stainless steel, port pushpit Sat Nav pod stanchion post and grasping it for balance and support.

It was never really warm at sea, especially this sea; and the wind off the water was biting and making a liar out of the benign afternoon sun. Occasional white froth broke on the broad dappled expanse and was blinding – hurting his unadjusted eyes. Even worse was the agony caused by the reflective glare from the white sails above, and impossibly painful when looked at directly. Actually, these were fairy tale conditions: blue-water sailing under a blue sky on blue water; there were only a few mares' tails high in the west, they, as far as Lincoln could see, were the only sign of the cold front forecasted.

Gary was sunning himself between the main sheet winches, legs out in front and feet crossed, one ankle over the other and his upper half propped on stiff arms and spread hands behind. He would be just out of the wind there, Lincoln knew – and the slant of the deck affording just enough protection – that and being low down, of course. Sharon sat nearby, next to and just behind the aft lower port shroud, in the lee, with her knees close in to her chest. She had her back to him, one hand she had on the shroud and was holding onto the top lifeline with her other, the left.

Shocked to the core, was Lincoln, that Ramsey had

allowed, considering *Worippa's* stressed mast, let alone condoned, but . . . All eyes were focused on what hung out from *Worippa's* beam, attached to a halyard from the mast's peak – like a weight hanging from a crane's extended jib. Nick sat in the boatswain's chair as on a garden swing – on a short, polished, threaded wooden oblong of thick ply. Lincoln laughed, despite the mast, Nick was hanging there, in the lee, circling and turning, with his toes just above the tops of the licking crests. He pulling strongly on each vertical braid now and again, his feet thrust straight out and they dropping in time to his tugging hands, and pulling and pushing as a child would and gaining momentum with each heave. He moved in a slow, lazy, overall ellipse as well, rotating on the end of the line like an erratic, slow spinning planet orbiting an invisible sun.

Helmut sat aft of the mast, controlling the winch-wound halyard, and Nick indirectly, with both hands: children playing, letting off steam after a hard few days.

The wind had veered a touch, pushing *Worippa* over to a not too uncomfortable slant, and on a white-sail beam reach and ploughing through a lazy loping, sparkling sea at seven knots.

Helmut yelled again and heard easily on the wind, "There vas not enough feeling in your voice, I do not think you really meant vot you said."

Nick bottomed and bounced a second after, in answer to an inch of slack let out by Helmut. Water touched Nick's toes at the bottom of the arc; he screamed and lifted his feet to horizontal. He pleaded, "I said I love you – what more do you want?"

"Vas not loud enough, you must say it vith more feeling. Oh look, your feet are getting vet. Vot a shame."

Nick's voice dropped to a conversational yell, which spelled retaliation. He asked, "What will Margaret say?"

Helmut couldn't help, he knew, as did Lincoln and everybody else, that it was coming, yet, despite himself, he just had to ask. Nick had thought of another weak spot to probe – anything to do with Margaret . . .

"Vot do you mean?"

Communal breaths were held.

"Does she know?" Nick grinned at them as he swung slightly round and into their direction; he pulled on the appropriate rope and faced Helmut again. "Does she know about that spot on top, you know, where you're losing your hair?"

Turning within his fore-and-aft biased circle Nick fought desperately to keep himself facing Helmut. Despite his bravado one could see, while he waited to see how far the barb had sunk and what the reaction, that he wasn't really quite game enough to completely turn his back.

Helmut stood after cleating the halyard; a hand unconsciously brushing over a practically unnoticeable, thinning, taboo circle at the back of his pate. He walked across and stood beside and above Sharon, one steadying outstretched hand on the same aft lower shroud as she held. He leant forward and slightly down, his eyes never leaving Nick's.

Nick spoke around uncontrollable forced eruptions of nervous laughter, and they, including Lincoln, were unsuccessfully trying not to react – his bubbling, apprehensive high spirits were catching.

Nick quickly glanced at them, including Lincoln, before turning back and up to Helmut. His unmeant 'sorry' they were meant to hear, and him heaving jauntily with both his hands and lifting his feet till his arched tensed body was practically horizontal unmistakably told of a different story: one of playing to an audience and of blatant defiance. The explosive energy he had used had increased his swing over the waves, and their attention was on him and his grinning face as he circled and turned, rather than on Helmut. Lincoln thought that they must have all mentally shaken their heads at the same time, and a glance at Helmut's calm face and stance clearly hinted to him that comeuppance surely was to come – and of the folly of letting bravado overcome caution when dealing with someone like him.

Still silence from Helmut, he was just calmly looking down at Nick.

Nick couldn't help himself. "Bald . . . going . . ." He brushed the back of his head with a showy flourish of hand movements and finally emphasised the point with two or three exaggerated slow pats. His raised eyebrows and a perkily raised, questioning head finishing the statement.

Helmut looked their way, so Lincoln looked round too. Survivors all of them: Potter, head turned and looking out to sea; Corsham, hand over mouth and nose was examining the deck; Ramsey was inspecting the top of the mast; a frozen smile from Warren; Gary lay on his back, his 'beany' hat over his face; the up and down movements of Sharon's back and shoulders told their own story.

Lincoln turned again in time to see Helmut nod, and one finger on his outstretched hand wagged. "So," he said. That was all.

He abruptly spun on his heel; he ignored Nick's half-hearted, too-late, belated pleadings and stepped back across the deck.   He undid the same appropriate halyard from its cleat from behind the mast and carefully led the tensioned tail to a place where he could clearly see and monitor: aft of the mast again, but closer to the lee.   There he sat himself and got comfortable.

They waited. There was no action for what seemed an age, during which Nick tried everything he could think of, from threats and promises and promised rewards; to sorrowful pleadings and profound apologies – and he, like them, could guess at exactly what was coming. Helmut just sat, immune, watching Nick squirm – a fixed 'cat to victim', 'you are all mine now' smile on his lips – and savouring the moment.

The big German finally stirred; he gave Nick an uncharacteristic, delicate little finger wave – Nick screeched as he dropped.

Lincoln took the opportunity to duck below. Brian's dark glasses were trapped on the top – and in their usual place at the rear of the chart table – one curled wire arm hooked down into a handy knot-hole kept them there. Nick's short abrupt drop had been hint enough.

Once back on deck, and so as not to detract from their enjoyment, Lincoln casually made his way forward along the weather – everybody's attention and concentration was still riveted on the game being played out between Nick and Helmut anyway, so nobody really took much notice. Lincoln leant against the side of the mast and peered round, and grinned: the thrill of being out over the long swell could be better appreciated from where he stood.   Speed accented by close proximity and the hiss and gurgle of *Worippa's* way through the water would be echoing back to Nick: soundboarding off the hull. An apparently smooth sea a swirling, twisting, heaving, live confusion of welter close up; its own inherent noise adding to that of *Worippa's* – the roar would be deafening from where Nick hung.

The mast neither felt nor looked any different from previous; the bias to port above the second set of spreaders was quite distinct when he viewed up the sail track from behind. A slightly bigger flex to port than was normal though, it seemed to him, was occurring each time: just after *Worippa* had shouldered her way over each scend.

The mast, as Lincoln assessed, could be thought of as in three sections: a third to the lower spreaders, another third to the upper spreaders, and the last to the peak. The top third always took the lion's share of the punishment: the sideways flexing and bowing near or just above the top spreaders on *Worippa* when on the wind, particularly on *Worippa*, was sometimes extremely pronounced – hence the addition of the runners! Lincoln followed their leads with his eyes just to confirm . . . As previous, running backstays were . . . was their official name: they were wires that led, one on either side, from just above the top set of spreaders to, via an appropriately placed deck block, a point at or near the stern. Only one was used at a time, on the weather side, and was tensioned when in use by its appropriate winch. *Worippa* being a masthead rig and with her extra mast height and all – the runners were used purely for support and were not, as on many modern, 'bendy' three-quarter rig's, used for altering the sail shape – not to any significant degree anyway. The runners Ramsey had fitted did, as Lincoln could affirm, effectively dampen the mast flex up there too, especially in heavy weather or when ploughing and plunging her way through and over a steep sea.

Helmut must have dropped Nick another inch – the top third in question gave a bit and then sprang back.

Lincoln released the bitter end of the runner from its cleat at the stern and took a turn around the winch and hauled in the inordinate amount of slack; the bite of the runner when not in use dropped down virtually parallel to the mast and then ran back parallel to the deck; the centre of the bite was loosely secured by a pendant of elasticated 'bungy' cord that was attached close to the mast's base; the runners were thus kept out of the way when not in use. Lincoln gently tensioned-on while watching the mast – movement above was less and then was dramatically dampened. It was always prudent to allow some flex in a mast and he was satisfied when Nick's next jerk of descent proved to be little different from the normal flexes that occurred after the topping and tipping down off each standard wave. Lincoln was as happy as he was going to be: one could only surmise that Brian had considered that there was no risk involved in allowing Nick and Helmut's antics . . . Or, perhaps more probably, that their playtime had started before he had been aware – and by the time he had been aware, he had taken the attitude that if it was going to happen, odds were, it already would have!

Lincoln nodded back in answer to Ramsey's mouthed 'happy' – a touch of extra support from the runner had done the trick.

Lincoln looked across and laughed yet again, Nick now stood on the boatswain's chair; and the domed crest of each wave was, on average, just kissing its underside – with just the odd one splashing over. Nick, trying to anticipate which wave was going to wet his feet, periodically pulled himself up and hung by his arms; and the freed chair when he did rotated on its own volition. Getting his toes back between the rope bridle and onto the plyboard again was proving to be a major problem, Lincoln saw, and trying to look down and foot the chair round to the right position was awkward, especially while hanging by one's arms when trying to do so! A wicked man, Helmut: he was pulling Nick to him now and again via a length of braided line attached to the end of his safetyline, and just when his feet were going to make contact – it wasn't nice.

Brian took his sunglasses back without comment and a knowing look his only acknowledgement.

Sharon, Lincoln had noticed, had moved away and her and Gary had ceased their animated conversation and were now both simply staring at Ramsey. They all watched as she clambered into the cockpit. Sickening ingratiating obeisance: a wheedling little girl's voice asking for sweeties . . . Fluttering lashes – bold, demur – and simpering eyes full of future promise – the whole bit!

"Brian?" Her hand gently snaked out and she trailed the back of her fingernail sensually down the back of Ramsey's hand.

Potter from the background voiced his thoughts, "Let me puke."

Like a serpent's tongue licking and flicking out. "Shut up, Lionel!" Lincoln blinked as the smarmy composure instantly returned to her face. "Can I have a go on the chair, Brian? Gary'll say 'yes' if you say 'yes'. Please, Brian?"

Ramsey looked at her, his face straight and obviously flattered by her undivided transparent attention despite himself – or so they all thought!

He looked away, then back. "I don't know, it's got its risks even if you wear a safety harness like Nick, and a life jacket . . ."

Sharon butted in before he could finish, "I'd wear them, of course, Brian, Gary'd insist anyway."

Ramsey ignored her, "Even then, if you slip off there's no guaranteeing we'll get you back on board in time."

Sharon started to speak and then stopped; the reply she had received wasn't quite what she'd expected. If she was curious, they . . . Well, Lincoln, he was even more so.

Sharon asked the expected, "What do you mean?"

Her question was greeted with silence. Sharon looked from face to face, seeing no help in any of them. They were, including Lincoln, as much in the dark as she was.

Ramsey again, "You can get picked off before you know what's happening, we haven't even a rifle on board."

A quick glance at Potter gave the game away: head down on his chest and forcing a double chin and looking from under his brow; and his flicking eyes met Lincoln's before momentarily disappearing upwards.

Sharon's eyes wide, questioning; she asked the inevitable, "What . . . What do you mean, get picked off – shark, do you mean?" Lincoln had to give it to her, she was not backward in coming forward – her temper flared. "Just because I'm a girl. You've let Nick, why can't you let me?" It had taken a moment to penetrate. "I don't believe you."

Brian shook his head, clenched his teeth and bit down. "No . . . you're right . . . There's no sharks in these waters." There were groans from all quarters; he got it half out before exploding. "They've all been eaten," he spluttered. "Eaten by the crocodiles!"

Sharon turned on her heel and crossed her arms and waited – knees and shins against the port cockpit seat for support and gazing at the sea, her face grim. They just couldn't stop laughing; it wasn't at her as she obviously believed, except for Potter exacting a little revenge maybe, it was at Ramsey – his mirth was contagious.   Him, and Bill surprisingly, were the worst. As soon as they had quietened they'd start again, and off they would all go too. Brian particularly took an age to wind down. Lincoln grinned; he was like an old engine with its neglected timing too far advanced: one that after the ignition had been turned off would keep going in hesitant stuttering bursts. Like that engine the gaps between Brian's outbursts grew longer and less loud and of shorter and shorter duration – till there was just an odd, final putt and hiccup. It would have stopped there but for Gary's coming aft and trying to commiserate with Sharon, that set them all off again: she shook off Gary's arm like a child having a classic tantrum: elbows out from her hips and clenched fists against either side of her waist, and a shrugging and twisting torso.

Not used to being laughed at, Sharon, nor not used to not having her own way either from the look of it, Lincoln concluded.

Nick and Helmut clambered around the sides, their game finished, intrigued by what had diverted everybody's attention and to find out what was going on.

Ramsey tapped Sharon on the arm finally. "Sorry, Sharon." He sighed. "You have to understand, we're not laughing at you, it's just . . . It's just a way of letting off steam, that's all. A way of getting rid of the tension: a safety valve. A sort of mass hysteria – childish, I know."

Sharon didn't turn nor look at him and Lincoln was disappointed with her; and so was Gary, Lincoln suspected, that she'd not risen above it.

They had misjudged her, and all eyes looked to where her outstretched arm and finger pointed. "Not eaten him, have they," she said. "He seems to be staying in one piece?"

Well forward off the beam and floating comfortably on his back, with the top half of his stomach out of the water and the bottom half and tail under – and the big, black, inquisitive, soulful eyes as curious about them as they about him.   A smooth grey, elongated, egg-shaped head and mouth gently opening and closing under a pointed whiskered snout. Flippers extended out before folding and resting above on his tummy: like an old raconteur, Lincoln thought, preparing to start his after-dinner speech: arms out in welcome before clasping lapels . . . He only needed spectacles!

They watched him silently and there was no fear there as *Worippa* approached, just a weather-eye kept on them as they closed.

Gary half-laughed as he identified him, "That's an Australian Fur Seal. Nice isn't he." The timbre of his voice changed then, "They're about the only species left in Bass Strait – and they've been hunted virtually to the edge of extinction. There're pockets of them coming back in places now – since men have left them alone." Gary didn't take his eyes off their aquatic companion and he said in a puzzled speculative tone. "He's miles away from where he should be, I wonder why . . . They're not supposed to frequent the open sea; usually you only find them close in – around rocky prominences or islands and the like. I'd say he was completely lost, he'll starve to death out here." Gary added regretfully, and yet his voice had a sort of fervour in it, "He'll not be long for this life."

Potter was outraged, "Prestwick . . . I've never heard such a load of old shit in all my life. Where do you get it all from? I'm sure you make up half the twaddle you feed to us." Lionel wiped dribble away from his mouth. "Blind Freddy can see he's not starving – look at him. Does he look distressed to you! He's floating around trying to digest a gut-full of fish; he's not got a care in the world. The thing's swanning around like a dog with two cocks – look at him."

Gary stuttered, "No, I've read . . ."

Lionel interrupted him, "That's just it, isn't it; a couple of armchair naturalists, silly old farts, see a few seal on their 'perve' along the beach and that's that. They write a few words in one of your soppy magazines and you fall for it and believe 'em. It sucks." Potter held up an arm. "No, you listen. You go and stick a transmitter up its arse and show me some proof – and then maybe, just maybe . . . and then perhaps I'll believe you. All right?"

Gary lost his temper, "Fuck off."

Lincoln looked down: no match for a heavy-weight like Potter, was Gary.

Lionel turned to Bill. "Here, take the wheel, matie." He turned back to Gary, "If I had that rifle that Brian referred to, I'd fucking-well shoot you with it, believe me." Lionel climbed round and gave Gary a shove. "You silly dick."

Sharon flared, doing her own shoving. "Don't you call him a silly prick."

Lionel shoved back. "And you can shut up, you old bag. And I didn't . . ."

Gary was not normally physical, his retaliatory push was slightly effeminate and his retort unworldly. Ramsey's snigger didn't help. From where he had found the strength to 'do' Warren and fend him off for as long as he had, Lincoln would never know.

"Don't call her an old bag – book a hearse – be Springvale Crematorium, will it?" He turned and shoved Ramsey hard. "You, as well."

Everybody started to laugh, including Gary himself, his threat had sounded ridiculous even to his own ears – and in doing so conceded that his statement might have been just a little over-enthusiastic.

Nick loved anything like this and always game and happy to stir up the pot: the unspoken calling off: the cessation of hostilities had gone completely over his head. "Aren't going to take that are you, Brian? Give him another serve, Gary." Lincoln stumbled forward. "In you go, Pom."

A regretful error of judgement on his part, Lincoln pressed his fingers to his lips, it was just the opening Sharon needed – someone to vent her temper on. Her push was strong enough to upset Nick's balance; and her turning her back before seeing the result and her remark was all the more insulting for her indifference, her apparent immediate and subsequent disinterest, and her casual, off-hand dismissal.

"Silly little fuckwit."

She cleaned up further, her punch caught Lionel in the middle of his chest – his attention had been distracted by Nick's ignoble, sprawling demise. It was just fortunate that the steering pedestal was as strong as it was.

"Don't call me an old bag," Sharon rasped, she turned and in the same breath said to Brian, all sweetness and cream, "Can I have a go on the swing now, Brian, pl-ee-ea-se? Now that Nick's busy with other things. Pl-ee-ea-se, Brian?"

Chapter 27

Bill's admonishments were relentless, he'd followed Lincoln down; and he took the plastic mug gently away a few minutes later. "Go on, I'll make it, go and put your thermal stuff on. You've gone and allowed yourself to enter the first stages of hypothermia, of all people you should know better than anyone; you might as well not wear anything as wear a tee-shirt."

Lincoln didn't answer Bill directly for two reasons, one: he was right and therefore there was nothing to be said, and yes, he should have known better; and two: his bloody teeth were chattering so much it was impossible to talk anyway. The cold had stalked and had finally leapt out and attacked like a hungry animal: nipping around the edges before getting into his bones.

Lincoln stood on the same sailbag that Sharon had stood on, and after removing the tee-shirt applied under-arm deodorant and then talcum powder below; he would have strip-washed properly again before changing into clean underwear, but it was the best he could do in the circumstances. Thermal top, underpants, long johns and thick woollen socks . . . Their, the combined thermals insular efficiency uncanny – and their life-giving warmth were gratefully and immediately felt.

Bill appeared and stood in the entrance. "Coffee or tea? In bed or in the galley?"

Lincoln compromised with the guilt that he always experienced when he felt that he was taking advantage of Bill's generosity of spirit – and dismissed tea in bed – and the fact that he wasn't averse to being unselfishly pampered when he was in the type of whiny mood that he was in. "I'll come on through, thanks, Bill. Thank God, I feel warmer already."

Bill nodded, before disappearing.

Lincoln sat on a bunk before pulling on solar fleece trouser bottoms and then boots. Apart from their incredible insular properties, and he never wanted to be as cold again, Lincoln also wore the solar bottoms if for no other reason than for the sake of appearances – the zip-sided legs hung outside of, when wearing boots. An exaggeration, but yellow wellies and long johns were not only unbecoming, call it vanity, but a person wearing such a combination looked so utterly bloody ridiculous, especially wandering around on deck, so Lincoln wouldn't . . . A person dressed in such a way one couldn't take seriously – the equivalent of a ballerina wearing wellington boots and about as elegant!

Lincoln also donned the matching solar fleece top, and although he knew it would be uncomfortable directly because he'd be too hot, as probably would be the trousers – nevertheless, he could always take either or both off once sweating!

Brian sat against the forward bulkhead of the saloon settee; and Bill handed Lincoln a cup after he had settled opposite.

Brian took a sip out of his; he nodded. "Are you warmer?" He nodded to Lincoln's cup. "Are you going off to bed again after you've finished that." It was an order rather than a question. He turned. "You as well, Bill."

Bill and Lincoln just looked at him – the muted chatter and laughter from above sounded louder in the silence.

"You have to let them let off steam," commented Ramsey. "They'll be paying for it tonight though." He then tacked on a little rider to the end of his sentence: to underline his point about them going to bed, and to cover his contradiction. "We're all more tired than we think."

Bill ignored Ramsey's not so subtle hint, "They won't, you know, they're young those kids – give 'em a couple of hours sleep and they'll bounce straight back." He sighed pensively. "I don't know about you but they sometimes make me feel really old." He pre-empted before Ramsey could pounce, "There's no point, Brian, it's sixteen-forty-five now and we've got the second dog watch."

Brian looked vague so Bill clarified his point, "Eighteen till twenty – that's six o'clock to eight."

Brian grinned, and as much to himself as to them, he had to think about the names of the various watches and the twenty-four hour clock, which conversely was literally everyday language to Bill, and the names of the watches aside, Bill thought, as Lincoln well knew, of the twenty-four hour clock first and then converted to civilian twelve-hour timekeeping after.

Ramsey nodded. "Oh, right . . ." He then sighed. "Um. I take your point." He was silent only for a moment. "I've been thinking." His hand rasped over the bristle covering his chin. "We should be through the 'Heads' at around midnight, right, then it'll be eight or nine hours up the 'Bay'. We should be tied up and eating breakfast by nine tomorrow morning, all being well." He looked at them keenly. "And all snuggled up and in the lee of 'Bum Island' by tomorrow night!" His up-and-down eyebrows said more than any words, Bill and Lincoln grinned – and a reply wasn't expected nor necessary.

Bill asked, "How do we stand as far as the tide is concerned – timed it right, have we?"

Brian shook his head in reply. "No, that's the point, according to my calculations we're going to be too early – it'll still be on the ebb. I thought we may try and use the 'small boat' channel inside, providing that that cold front doesn't chop it up too much." Brian bared his teeth in a half-serious, mock grimace. "I always lose my 'bottle' when going through there, even in the flat calm. What do you think – we'll have to stand-off and wait otherwise?"

Brian and Bill were talking about entering Port Phillip Bay and their healthy nervous respect for 'The Rip' justified. Never, in all Lincoln's travels had he seen such a 'pinch the cheeks of your bottom together' entrance (and that was the only way to describe it!).

Port Phillip was one of the most beautiful, impressive, protected and safe inland shipping lanes, waterways, landlocked bay's that a person would ever see. Captain James Cook on his exploration voyage had sailed straight past the insignificant entrance, not even suspecting – and hardly surprising because a vessel, as Lincoln had seen for himself, would not see the gap unless that vessel was following the coastline in and out, literally, instead of cutting across.

They had sent round a launch from the just recently discovered Westernport – Port Phillip was first seen during preliminary scouting carried out by a William Bowen in 1802, and mate of the especially purpose-built, British coastal explorer – *The Lady Nelson.*

Most of this information Lincoln had gleaned from Gary, as usual – local Melbournian history being another one of his hobbies, and not unnaturally and to a lesser extent, Ramsey's too.

Lincoln had always found it fascinating and fun too: that of trying to get into a vanguard's mind and to imagine and to try to see through that original discover's eyes and feel as he would have felt: apprehension perhaps, anxiety, disquiet, fear of the unknown – and sober! They would have gone armed, he knew, because, as Gary had said, aboriginal hostilities would have had to have been considered. Conversely: curiosity, anticipation, excitement, adrenaline, intoxication, plenary concentration and arrant bravado might have come to the fore, and probably did, they being the sort of adventurous men that they must have been: to be first and history in the making!

It was not difficult for Lincoln to imagine either: the trepidation that they must have felt when entering from the open sea; and that comparatively insignificant, dangerous, treacherous gap of broken water; that entrance which pierced and flowed between sandy foreshores, low rocky outcrops, dunes and scrub. That crew, that band of brothers, would have felt their way in carefully, and a man in the chains (or the bow, in their case) casting a lead none stop and he calling off the distinguishing depth 'marks' and 'deeps' that were or would have been tied into the line in a sequence of fathom intervals – and the helmsman ready to tack instantly should the bottom, 'by the mark', or 'deep', shoal.

Unsuspected: to unexpectedly find and sail into such a vast, beautiful expanse of flat, panoramic, watery magnificence: and the distant low blue-purple hills peaking in the haze and an inland sea that must have to them seemed to have gone on forever. They would have felt what, Lincoln asked himself: wonderment, astonishment, entrancement, awe . . . struck dumb and dazzled surely! It was exhilarating and fascinating just to think about!

Port Phillip Bay has always been overshadowed by Sydney's spectacular harbour: Port Phillip Bay being relatively unheard of internationally, though known as one of the world's finest to mariners. A huge, virtually landlocked, irregular bay: thirty-six miles west to east at its widest. From the entrance to the mouth of the River Yarra, due north, the cause of the ancient, flooded, sunken plain that was now the seabed, thirty-two miles. Lincoln had sailed or driven around the majority of Port Phillip Bay, and its countless foreshores offered every variable to suit every palate: rocky for fishermen; exposed beaches that the wind surfers preferred; sandy bays and inlets for sand castles, picnics and dingy launching.   He had seen scattered man-made rock breakwaters built where appropriate and that of protected numerous havens, pontooned marinas, yacht clubs and the like. Yes, Lincoln had to admit, talking of 'man-made', modern Melbourne had got it right – most beauty spots and favoured recreational areas had public barbecue facilities. All a person needed for a great day was an all-popular 'Esky': a specially built, with handles and locking lid, evolved container: an insulated box filled with ice-packed steaks, sausages, chops and preferred cold beer or cooled wine . . . Those goodies and good company, as Lincoln could personally testify, guaranteed some very pleasant and agreeable leisure time.

A working port and then a playground, and as a yachtsman one tended to forget – Port Phillip Bay boasted deep water and deep-water channels. Lincoln had seen enough of and could attest to the various vessels arriving, crossing and departing the 'Bay' to be aware of their numbers – some turned for Geelong, but most heavy shipping crossing directly, entering the extended docklands at the mouth of the Yarra River and from there discharging directly into suburbia – the freight from there going either by rail, road or air to wherever – and, as Gary had said, it was one of Melbourne's main reasons for being.

Whether viewed from a heaving deck or contemplated and considered from one of the points, the wonderment of that unique, easily protected narrow entrance in from and to the sea never palled in its fascination: under two miles wide and within that only a meagre half a mile of deep water. Incredibly dangerous and not without justification called 'The Rip': confined water flowed in or out through that narrow gap at between five and eight knots! Lincoln shuddered when he thought of wind 'with' tide and thought of the build-up of associated water . . . He had sailed through once with a comparatively lazy wind blowing 'over' the tide, and it hadn't been a happy experience . . . The seabed around for acres was littered with wrecks, both old and new . . . No, 'The Rip' was a place where a cautious skipper didn't take chances, nor liberties . . . One really needed local knowledge, no cargo vessel, ever, came through without a pilot . . . There were no guarantees even then, and as Gary had once pointed out, more than one pilot boat had tragically been lost while attempting the entrance in heavy weather! The point: those pilot boats had been the world's most seaworthy and supposedly unsinkable vessels – it was a grim inference!

Lincoln had gone through that entrance for the first time,

Port Phillip Heads, with Brian and *Worippa* on a bright, sunny, spring morning. They had been participating in a race from Portsea, which was at the bottom of the 'Bay', to a small harbour and host yacht club on that other fabulous piece of water around the corner, and just as beautiful as Port Phillip, if not more so in many ways, and comparatively unspoilt – called Westernport Bay. Imagine thirty or forty yachts going hell-for-leather and all striving to get into clear air and thus to exit through those selfsame Heads first. That they were all mad, there wasn't in Lincoln's mind a doubt: three of them, he remembered, had run aground, and many more had touched bottom whilst trying to take shortcuts and nip inside various cardinal buoys. The moral as far as Lincoln was concerned was that in Port Phillip Bay, and especially in the vicinity of the Heads, unless one knew absolutely it paid to follow the leading marks and buoys because, sooner or later and probably sooner, a vessel would inevitably pay the consequences!

They had arrived at the actual 'Heads' and had gone through earlier than anticipated – the tide had still been on the turn. It had been one hell of a ride and something that Lincoln would not quickly forget: they had gone from flat water to a frothy, racing millstream in minutes. Short, heavy, vicious, steep, utterly confused, clashing seas and sucking whirl pools; and dotted haphazardly in this maelstrom there had been strange, large, circular, oval, flat, mirror-like platelets of water between. There had been no time to be frightened, being too desperately occupied with hanging on – the fright had only occurred after, and after that and on reflection: *'if it was like that on a comparatively calm day, what would it be like on a. . .?'* A short, gut-wrenching, shocking, exhilarating run of the gauntlet and then it was over and one was through to, if one was lucky, the long calm swells of Bass!

*   *   *

Lionel clattered down the companionway steps and the sound of his weight recognisable: he waited for a few minutes at the bottom, giving his eyes a chance to adjust, Lincoln presumed, and then he came on through.

Brian asked him, "How are they doing up there, Lionel?"

Lionel was unusually polite considering the debacle that had gone on in the cockpit. "Just about to launch the little . . . the lovely little lady. Actually, she'll get a good ride; it's just beginning to pipe up a bit." He changed the subject then. "Lunch, dinner, food, fuel, matie." "What do you want? What do you fancy?" and added magnanimously, "I'll be mother."

Brian was obviously pleased, it helped the *bon ami* all round and oiled the wheels when people volunteered their services and took their turn. "Good one, Lionel, nice of you to offer – I'll give you a hand." Brian hesitated for a moment, and Brian being Brian, he offered, "If you'd like to get yourself organised, I'll find something to throw in the pot."

Lionel had other ideas and carried on conversationally, "A 'sheila' I used to know." He looked at them innocently – there was a wealth of meaning in his opening words. "Amongst the other things that she used to do . . . She used to cook a chicken paprika casserole." He looked at Lincoln directly. "Have you ever cooked a paprika casserole, Pom?" He continued on before Lincoln could answer him. "I really fancy it." He sighed. "I must be pregnant – I've got a chronic urge. She used to do it in cream – or something. Yoghurt! No, not yoghurt . . . It was cream – sour cream. That was it, I remember now – it was sour cream. Do you fancy having a go, Pom? I'll do the work if you instruct – and Bill, if he wants." Lionel followed his train of reasoning and though he was going to involve them all there was neither malice nor intent in it, he was simply an innocent (in that way anyway). "I'll tell you what; if all four of us muck in we'll have it fixed-up and in the oven in a trice. We have got paprika, Brian?" he asked.

There was a resigned, benign, elusive grin on Brian's face. "Of course. You'll have to use milk though, it should do, it's full cream – unless you'd rather condensed?"

"No, at a pinch, full cream'll do . . ." However, Potter had been watching Ramsey closely. "We have got chicken?" he asked.

He just didn't look innocent, did Ramsey. "Oh yes. Ye of little faith."

Potter was a lot of things, but he wasn't slow and he smelt a rat: and his questioning look was enough.

"Thirty-six chicken legs," stated Brian. "In the freezer, semi-frozen: I keep the temperature only just, so you can drop 'em straight in the pot."

Potter looked at Ramsey in disbelief. "Thirty-six? Thirty-six chicken legs? What the fuck were you doing . . . buying all those?" He gave Brian no time to answer. "You're bloody bonkers."

Not a bit fazed, Ramsey, they, Lincoln hazarded, weren't going to stand much more of this, Ramsey had started again. "I borrowed them off of Stumpy and his mates down at the farm." He gasped it out before folding sideways onto the settee. "From where the hell do you think I got them from?"

They collapsed: squeezed eyes, sighs and cringing and grinning faces: Ramsey caused them to laugh, as usual, at him as much as with him.

After he had caught his breath he advised, "Look, don't bother with the casserole dish, Lionel, it's not a good idea on a boat, it all slopping around out of sight – it can make one hell of a mess in the oven."

Lionel looked disappointed and replied sulkily. "Sharon did. Can't we do it then?"

Ramsey explained, "It makes no difference, you know, Lionel, between a casserole and cooking on the top. You'll find it'll be easier on the top, that's all, that's providing that the lid fits properly. Actually, thinking about it, I . . . well, Judy anyway, she usually seals the lid with aluminium foil, that way . . . Well, then everything'll cook in its own steam – and, of course, it being on the top then it means you can alter things. Umm, to taste perhaps, stir it, and we can throw anything in that we think of . . . and, and furthermore, we can place all those chicken legs in such a way that they'll be evenly distributed – you can't do that with our casserole dish, its oval, and it's not deep enough, not for all of them, anyway."

Yes, a lot of thought had quietly gone into the buying of those chicken legs, Lincoln allowed, joking apart, he was a deep one and a modest one, was Brian: chicken legs needed little preparation and took a comparatively short time to cook, and, as he had said, they could be packed in efficiently: like as the spokes of a wagon wheel, head-to-tail as it were, from the centre et cetera.

So Lincoln added his weight to Brian's argument and stated the obvious and ignored the fact that he wasn't personally convinced by Brian's argument: that there wasn't a difference between cooking in the oven and cooking on the top. "You can clamp the pot on the top, Lionel, a casserole dish'll slide around all over the place – it'll be a bit iffy, it'd be better on the top."

A lot happier, Lionel, and . . . and he had found some energy: and that he had got enough enthusiasm to cook was a good sign – he had surprised Lincoln.

They stopped to listen, nervous, excited, elated shrieks of delight pieced the hull from outside, they grinned at each other – and then there was a different, minute, high-pitched squeal which wiped the smiles from their faces: of a rope running out freely and unrestricted through its blocks. A thump from above was followed by a twanging, bouncing vibration. *Worippa* shuddered after a muffled groan, and then there were wires snaking and being pulled and rattling through a long, hollow, echoing, metal tube: from inside the mast . . . and then being pulled along the deck. Muffled shouting, screams and babbling confusion followed.

Just two words from Brian – a horrified statement. "The mast!"

Worippa dipped and heeled and they held on as she slewed and tried to turn on a sixpence; there was a competent helmsman on the wheel up there, for which Lincoln would be forever grateful; whoever it was, wasn't fighting her, he was letting her find her own equilibrium.

Ramsey raced straight up; Lincoln followed Potter, Potter lifted the heavy wire cutters from their place on the bulkhead at the bottom of the companionway steps. Lincoln quickly found what he wanted: two sets of pliers from the tool kit, and from behind the hinged companionway steps, some heavy elastic shock-cord that they used when experimenting and playing around with the self-steering.

Calmly girding for a fight: Potter turned and looked at Lincoln and took a deep breath before climbing: a quiet orderly foot-soldier mentally sighing and philosophically preparing to enter a war-ravaged battle zone.

There was nobody else to come up from below after them so Lincoln had time to stand on the top of the companionway steps and assess. Immediately to view was Warren, still seated; there was a look of total bewilderment and imbecility still on his face. Better he should stay seated and keep out of the way, Lincoln thought fleetingly. Helmut was on the wheel, Lincoln should have guessed, and his face contrasting Warren's: and he fuming helplessly: and the frustration of inaction written there. His immediate responsibility, as Helmut himself well knew, was to safeguard *Worippa* and if possible steer her in such a way as to stop her from hurting herself further. Satisfied that he could do nothing in that direction and that *Worippa* was in good hands, Lincoln slowly turned on his heel and allowed his eyes to travel up a backstay that was now snaking and sagging uselessly.

The mast had folded where he would have expected it too, just above the second set of spreaders. Lincoln closed his eyes and breathed deeply, swore, and looked again. The top third of the mast hung down well below the horizontal, and not actually broken off but folded; the mainsail, now not tended, was wrapped hard against, or rather pasted against both sets of port spreaders and the remaining two thirds of the cap shroud. Lincoln could see the outline of the intermediate through the canvas, and most of the rear lower shroud too, and against which obviously the boom was hard against. That the sail was plastered against the standing rigging, or what was left of it, was their luck and at least it dampened any violent flogging and shaking, which was just as well, so long as it all held!

Nick, Bill and Brian were clustered round and struggling to lift Sharon back on board, the combined weight of her and her water-logged clothing, presumably, and their awkward positions was making it difficult for them . . . Something else was wrong . . . Lincoln looked again, Gary lay on his side parallel to the lifelines, his upper body resting against the base of the cap shroud and his thighs against the lower aft – and he wasn't moving! A thought registered briefly: that the cap shroud should still be taunt, and that despite the weight of Gary's body lying against it, and it's lacking attachment up top – it wasn't sagging! It told Lincoln that it could only be the locking arrangement in the eyes at the ends of the two spreaders, the upper and the lower, that was still keeping the thing taunt! That fact was, surprising, a happy surprise though – every little helped!

Presumably, Lincoln calculated, the main sheet or one of the pulleys had broken; the boom must have caught Gary and thumped him good and hard. He, Gary, then, was their number-one priority; Lincoln had just started climb round when Gary's legs moved and Lincoln saw his lips part, as if he was sucking in or blowing out air. Good, Lincoln nodded, Gary could wait for the interim – on his side there he would come to no harm – and better that he be left where he lay and be allowed to come round in his own time.

The foresail was still marginally pulling – the belly of the bottom third anyway. That they had not lost the mast completely was a miracle, whether by accident or Helmut's design, with the forestay gone there was nothing holding the mast up from forward! Lincoln followed that train of thought: the only thing holding the mast up now was the pressure of the wind on and in the remnants of the sails, and should they deviate off their course in any way then they would surely lose the lot. That thought must have registered on Lincoln's face as he wheeled round and quickly stepped past Lionel and across to inform Helmut.

Helmut pre-empted him, "I keep her down wind, ja," he said calmly. "Otherwise . . ." He indicated the mast collapsing by holding his hand up vertically and then folding his fingers.

Lincoln nodded, relieved, his summation of their situation was just a bit too graphical for Lincoln's taste, however, as far as Lincoln was concerned, he knew.

Lincoln turned once more, eased Lionel to one side and stepped forward again and placed his hands on either side of the companionway and lent on his arms – and just looked. The tangled mess slowly sorted itself out, and then it really dawned. Forestay and backstay and cap shrouds, for all intents and purposes, were down and only the fore lower shrouds were holding the mast forward, and the rear lower shrouds and the starboard runner behind – 'lowers' because they were designed to support the 'lower' mast only! So what was stopping the whole thing from collapsing forward, he wondered . . . only the starboard runner! Lincoln pushed Lionel out of the way yet again and quickly lent across and looped the tail of the port runner round its winch and reeled in the slack, the shock-cord that held the runner out of the way, parallel to the mast, simply broke – he felt the runner on gently. He checked the tension on the starboard one then – just to make sure that they were even and would hold. He glanced around at Helmut, Helmut just nodded.

Lincoln turned to Lionel who was, going by the expression on his face, obviously having a job coping with the situation and coming to terms with it. "Lionel?" he enquired quietly. There was no response. Lincoln said his name again, but louder. "Lionel!" Lincoln touched his arm and requested,

"Would you put the inner forestay on, please – the babystay. Make sure it's really on, Lionel," Lincoln said quizzically, "because there ain't not nothing else holding up the mast forward till you put on that babystay." Lincoln grinned at him albeit, he was sure, a little sickly: and he trying desperately to quell his own rising sense of panic and hysteria, and the overwhelming frenzied urge to dash forward and do everything for himself: just like the proverbial chicken without a head. Lionel, Lincoln felt sure, saw through his attempt at collected calm and glimpsed at the tremulous turmoil that he was actually in . . . Something in his voice as well, no doubt: the mast literally was teetering on the edge of collapse. "Apart from fresh air, that is." There was comprehension in Lionel's eyes suddenly, for which Lincoln was thankful, and horror but not panic. "Don't cut anything, Lionel, hear? And don't allow anyone else to either, please. Leave those cutters here – put them behind the wheel, by Helmut's feet, where they'll be handy but out of harm's way." Lionel didn't move. "PDQ, Lionel," Lincoln murmured gently, "please – as I say, we'll lose the lot otherwise."

As Lincoln had noticed before, for such a heavy man Lionel could be surprising light and fast on his feet – he quickly stepped aft and around Helmut and placed the cutters before Lincoln had turned completely around and forward to face the next problem at hand.

The two lifelines, one above the other, that threaded their way through the spaced stanchions along *Worippa's* sides, that stopped them falling over the side, ran from fore to aft: that is to say, they were attached to the pulpit at the bow and the pushpit at the stern. Unlike at the bow, where they were, more or less, permanently secured, the stern lifelines were tied or bound to lugs with thin nylon cord. They were lashed there instead of permanently attached to the pushpit for two reasons, one: they broke the electrical circuit produced should they be struck by lightning, and two: they could be cut and the lifelines pulled out (to facilitate helping a person back on board) – Lincoln cut them. Helmut eased the wheel to the lee a touch, not questioning the instruction, and he ignored Lincoln as Lincoln climbed around behind him to weather. Helmut stepped a little aside at Lincoln's request, and then instead of asking him to go forward which Helmut had obviously anticipated, he instead, much to Helmut's disbelief, began, at knee height, opposite the wheel's rim, to tie and knot shock-cord to the steering pedestal.

Finally, once satisfied, Lincoln did request the wheel from him, which Helmut gave up without demur. "Get them to move Sharon along to here, Helmut," Lincoln requested, "they'll never lift her over, it'll have to be here – the threaded plastic insulation and eyes attached to the ends of lifelines'll never allow them to be pulled through the holes in the stanchions, will they? They'll need your strength, and there's no point in cutting them." Lincoln answered Helmut's sharp and accusing look. "Sharon, by the looks," Lincoln said dryly, "is not in immediate danger of drowning, is she, not like Brian was, not when she's making that amount of noise?"

Helmut looked distinctly relieved and went forward – it just wasn't in him to stand by and watch while others were doing.

With a knee jammed between the spokes and looking, reassessing, and at the same time preparing the other ends of the shock-cord – *Worippa* was already settling to a uncertain rhythm and if they had learnt nothing else they had learnt that *Worippa* would look after them and herself if basically left to her own natural devices. Get the foresail off her as soon as they could because they knew, or, at least, Lincoln knew, that she would ride nicely with very little canvass on – and there would be minimum pressure on the main that way, with the helm lashed, once she was happy, and shock-corded in place.

Lincoln moved across to weather because they needed room – room to find purchase and prepare.

He stopped Nick after he had crossed and had begun to climb around. "Um, leave them to it, Nick; they don't actually need you now." Lincoln said sympathetically, "They'll be tripping over each other as it is – help is needed elsewhere." Nick ignored Lincoln and made to go around anyway – he had that look on his face. Lincoln touched his arm. "I wouldn't put her life in danger, Nick, you know that – I love her as much as you do, you know, in my own way. They can manage, Nick, it's *Worippa* who needs our help now . . . and me."

Lincoln waited. They stood there under the sky and each moving unconsciously to *Worippa's* ragged motion, just looking at each other with all the emergencies and bustle going on around them; they, for that one moment, were once removed.

Something passed between them, not a battle of wills, but . . . but some sort of understanding . . . something . . .

"Double-check . . ." Lincoln delicately pinched together the material on the arm of Nick's jacket and shook gently. "Ask Lionel: make sure he has put the babystay on? If you look, there's nothing else holding the mast up forward!" It showed in his eyes, Lincoln saw, the significance of his statement. "Then let the fore sheet go. Cut the damn thing if necessary, but don't mess with it." Lincoln pointed. "See how the wind in the jib's pulling on the bend up there – collar Lionel, tell him to leave Gary, we'll sort him out after." Lincoln answered the sudden look of concern that had appeared on Nick's face, "He'll come to no harm if left on his side where he is . . . Tell Lionel just to place a cushion under his head and just to make sure his arms and legs aren't restricted . . ." Lincoln was starting to lose his temper – exasperated at his own lack of vocabulary. "You know what I mean, tell him to make sure none of his limbs are twisted."

Their attention was on Lionel and he must have been reading their minds, he had already folded up his jacket and was gently placing it under Gary's head.

"Right, we've done all we can for Gary under the circumstances – once we've got the mast sorted out and Sharon back on board, then we'll see to him. Okay, what I want you to do, you can't do it on your own, Nick, it'll take the two of you – and I don't care how. Right, let's move . . . Wait . . ." Lincoln cautioned and grabbed his arm and in doing so, contradicted himself. "I haven't told you what I want yet." He pointed. "Release the two fore halyards holding up the roller reefing and then ease the whole lot down onto the deck. Once we've got that lot down and laid alongside, then maybe we'll be able to make some sense of the mess – and sail her under jury rig, even yet." Lincoln held onto him. "We need that weight off, Nick, understand; even with just the roller reefing foresail only flogging the windage and tugging up there will be considerable, and sooner or later even that'll bring the mast down completely – it's on the edge." Lincoln pulled Nick to him slightly to emphasise the point. "So I don't have to tell you to go gently, do I; the halyards are wire so they'll probably pull round the bend. Make sure there are no twists in their tails," he added, "we'll all look a bit stupid if . . ." There was no need to explain further –

Nick understood. "Should you not be able to move them then attach a line somehow and winch down – use one of the sheets."

Lincoln supposed that he probably should not have uttered the next sentence, it was tactless, yet he was nervous and the exercise that Nick and Lionel were about to perform could mean the difference between their surviving, or, more to the point, Sharon's surviving, or a watery grave. An exaggeration perhaps, Lincoln admitted, but things at sea had a habit of escalating – like many aeroplane accidents, in the final analysis the cause often wasn't just the one single factor, but rather a chain of them!

"I'm relying on you, Nick – judge it as best you can. Try not to bend the mast anymore; we're going to have trouble releasing the main as it is. And listen to Lionel, don't just dismiss him – use him as a sounding board if you're in any sort of doubt – there's a lot of experience there." Lincoln pushed him gently away finally. "Go on then – good luck."

"Chris." There was panic in Ramsey's voice. "We can't lift her." He panted, "The cold's got to her already – she's gone – she can't help herself."

Damn, Lincoln couldn't redirect Nick, he had already reached Lionel and they were both on their knees with their backs to them, tending to Gary – they were deep in conversation.

"Warren?" Lincoln snapped. "Come here."

He just looked.

"Warren," Lincoln snarled. "If you don't come over here then I'll bloody well put you over the side." Trouble was, he meant it, and he would have done it; Warren knew too – they had no time for silly games of peek-a-boo.

"Climb around," Lincoln ordered.

Like a rag-sodding-doll: he moved at his usual automatonic pace – Christ. Bite your tongue, Lincoln, Lincoln ordered, and keep a leash on your temper – patience; this is neither the time nor the place to teach a competent sailor to helm, let alone . . . Despite their crisis and the growing seriousness of Sharon's situation, and the general disorganisation all around, the thought still managed to flitter across Lincoln's brain, and he found himself shaking his head: *what on earth were they going to do with this fellow?* That momentary deliberation skittered away as he quickly leant forward and grabbed him, pulled him around until he was in front, and once there Lincoln placed his nerveless hands on the wheel; he was putty till realisation dawned and only then did he try to pull them away – a reaction at least. Thank God for small mercies, thought Lincoln!

"It's just like a car steering wheel, Warren, turn the wheel and she'll go in that direction – understand?" Lincoln gently relinquished his own grip. "Can you feel her?" Lincoln ignored his slightly vacant look. "Just hold her as she is, she's only just sailing so there's no real pressure on."

Actually, that statement wasn't true, *Worippa* had much too much way on, but to call attention to that fact now wouldn't help. The whole point of the exercise was to have *Worippa*, and as quickly as humanly possible, stationary in the water – and with the rig still intact, if possible, but that would be secondary. Not the most fantastic master plan in the world, but it was the best off-the-cuff plan Lincoln could come up with under these circumstances. He had already concluded that part of the problem of trying to lift Sharon was *Worippa's* speed and the subsequent drag on her.

Lincoln leant around Warren and touched the glass of the compass dome with his finger. "Watch the compass, pretend the compass needle's attached to the steering and the rose underneath is fixed instead of turning – you'll find it easier that way and less confusing. If the pointer moves to either side of seventy degrees then turn the wheel accordingly." To Lincoln's surprise, Warren did exactly as instructed after *Worippa* had yawed slightly. "Good," Lincoln said encouragingly; and then qualified that, just in case. "If you get confused and you really aren't sure then right hand down, but gently." Lincoln demonstrated. "Don't, don't," he emphasised, "do not bring her head-to-wind, not yet anyway, and whatever you do, don't panic – I'll be here right next to you, just yell out. No drastic movements – okay. Keep an eye cocked on Nick and Lionel if you can, Warren." Lincoln pointed forward. "If they can get the roller reefing off her they'll signal to you, and if and when they do and I'm not in earshot or you don't hear anything to the contrary, then left hand a touch up. At the end of the day, Warren, we want to just edge her towards head-to-wind – just wallowing in the water. You know enough about sailing by now – ease her into the wind till the main just idly flogs – just like a flapping flag on a flag pole – and hold her there." Lincoln then doubtfully admonished, "But gently does it, that way everybody'll be aware of what you're doing and there'll be a minimum of stress on the rig.

"Once she's dead in the water, Warren, turn the wheel even further to the left, till she feels comfortable and is just sitting . . ." Lincoln lent down, stretched and let go of the shock-cord attached to the steering pedestal. "Tie the wheel finally, in that position when you feel that you have done the best that you can, with this shock-cord – tie it around a spoke as well as the rim, all right?" Warren nodded; Lincoln kept looking at him, waiting to see if there was any doubt – strangely, he showed no signs panic or apprehension. Lincoln shrugged mentally, when all said and done, unstable at times and somewhat odd he might be, but unintelligent . . . probably not. Lincoln added a few more words of advice and encouragement, "Like I said, feel for it – that sense of balance – she'll tell you when she's happy." He patted him on the shoulder. "Well done."

Lincoln quietly stood and watched him for a moment and for the first time in their acquaintance they were as one, and that indefinable silent companionship lay like a blanket over them. Lincoln glanced at him out of the corner of his eye – he would get to him, hopefully, should he really lose control. But then it didn't really matter, better to lose the mast than to risk the loss of Sharon. Besides . . . some instinct, some sixth sense told Lincoln that this time Warren would not let him down!

Chapter 28

The usual standard fitting was manufactured out of and caste in a light alloy. *Worippa's* triangular stanchion baseplates were unusual in that they were made of stainless steel and were a lot stronger than the standard, but were also similar to the weaker caste alloy ones in that they were secured to the deck through a hole drilled in each apex, though with heavier counter-sunk bolts than the standard. To each of *Worippa's* triangular baseplates a strong three inch length of heavy tubing was centrally welded – this the female for the actual stanchion. At sometime in the past, and knowing Ramsey as Lincoln now did, he would not have put up with them for long: not only had he replaced the usual stanchion assembly, he had also abandoned the cheap method of securing the lifeline stanchions to their baseplate sockets; and he had, in addition, employed stainless steel, 'allen-headed', through-bolts instead of split pins. Folded split pin ends even though usually taped over with electricians' heavy insulation tape were spiteful: and always managing, despite the tape, to scratch, tear or gash somehow: Lincoln had caught and had slit open two or three perfectly good pairs of seaboots on the odd one over the years.

Lincoln deliberately didn't even look, having decided early on to ignore Sharon's predicament, just one step at a time till the decks were clear and then and only then was he willing or did it make sense to face further problems. There was one thing, one almost insignificant thing that Lincoln had picked up on: and that was that Sharon had been wearing Nick's harness under her life jacket. His, Nick's, was the type of harness used by foredeck crew worldwide and designed especially with hoisting and the safety of a falling human cargo in mind – designed for climbers. A central 'quick-release' locking mechanism at the front with an integral lifeline 'eye' joined the four, wide-woven, nylon, cross straps: one over each shoulder met the two other straps that threaded up from the groin – at least, and that although adjusted to Nick's body size, that harness would not accidentally slip over her head and off, that was something!

The allen screw from the stanchion baseplate socket next to the pushpit Lincoln attacked first, he forced it undone with pliers and removed it before removing the next – around Ramsey and the next after that. Helmut understood immediately and following Lincoln, pulling the stanchions from their sockets; the third, unfortunately, he couldn't budge. Ramsey was a little upset after telling, or rather dictatorially instructing Helmut, to kick it out of the deck. A mind of his own had Helmut, he just sat and braced himself against the cockpit coaming, placed his foot high up on the stanchion before putting his full weight behind his foot, he stopped and scrambled up when it was sufficiently bent – he had then merely to turn his newly acquired, angled lever back and forth until free!

Lincoln would have words with Ramsey later, it was all right for Lincoln to comment, but Ramsey's references to and concerning his mother's morality were not appreciated – and he was sure that Helmut felt the same way!

Helmut gently laid the stanchions, complete with lifelines, out of the way, on the deck forward, and then the onus was suddenly on Lincoln again: a magician who without more ado was expected to pull a rabbit, a great big white 'thumper', out of the hat! Unfortunately, a master plan Lincoln didn't have – only brute strength and ignorance!

Sharon had given up the fight – poor little waif. Lincoln looked down at her: blue-purple, slack, still lips contrasted her pallid white face – bedraggled hair plastered to her scull – and already beyond shivering. She was floating – Ramsey had her pulled against the side of the hull via her harness safetyline. Her too-heavy hands and arms were as much below the surface as in front: ineffective and blind and yet still feebly, and looking at her state Lincoln assessed, probably subconsciously trying to fend herself off the hull. It was only her life jacket, he noted, that was effectively cushioning her – its bulk was protecting her face as each licking wave slipped beneath.

Thoughts flashed despite his compassion and flustered, debilitating, panicky, aching concern: the emergency steps from below would not help; they would have to lift her straight up and over – no other way. 'Awful' was the word that came into Lincoln's mind, it couldn't have been more awkward: the distance from deck to waterline was just that tiny bit too much and a fully outstretched arm unable to reach her in the valleys, and yet the waves were frustratingly lifting her to just beyond their tantalising finger-tip touch on the peaks . . . Bastard!

They would not be able to stop *Worippa's* accented rolling

without sails either, when heaving-to . . . Lincoln just stood weighing up the possibilities . . . and the windage on her hull, her rig, and especially the remnants of that main would be more of a hindrance than a help too – *Worippa* would tend to get 'way-on' every now and again and when she did, then she'd drag Sharon through the water instead of over before stalling again . . . They had no choice, Lincoln finally concluded, they'd just have to pick their moment if they could, that was all!

Even now, despite the tautness of her tether, surging crests were slapping, buffeting and bumping her against the underside of the curving tumblehome, and the waves were thereon rebounding and the foaming out-wash was next lifting her away – and each hollow trough was popping and sucking and the undertow was pulling her down, under and against again!

Lincoln sensed as much as heard a single, distinct, isolated, soft, metallic thump above the confused array of smacking hills, retreating eddies and indifferent swirls – then blood was pouring down and the water red-tinged within minutes. The metallic clink had been the sound of the stainless steel eye and perhaps part of the gibb hook attached to Sharon's harness hitting the hull, and that last bump must have been so hard as to have momentarily crushed the flotation foam in her life jacket – the harness eye was normally tucked well down between the deep, square, meeting edges of a life jacket! The collision had probably, he guessed, at least broken her nose; how much more extensive the damage and in how many places he could hardly guess? Lincoln was appalled, and he could now see, after the next sea had washed over her, that her forehead had been opened too and that blood from that particular wound had began again to stream into her eyes – they were cleansed, as was the rest of her face again, shortly after by the next wash.

It hadn't been Ramsey's fault, Lincoln knew, that bump, he had been fighting to protect her and the cause had been a combination of a lifting wave meeting, or rather colliding, with a particularly bad, staggering, heeling lurch from *Worippa* – with Sharon betwixt and between. He simply couldn't have done anymore, and in Lincoln's estimation he was taking too many risks as it was – Bill Corsham had his hand in the back of Ramsey's waistband and was holding onto him for dear life. Ramsey was like a fisherman playing a fish, reeling in the big one, but leaning out much further than he should: a human fish below human fishing rod and fisted tip, and waiting for either landing net or gaff: and not successful in holding Sharon off and away from the hull because the 'arm' of his make-do fishing pole was too short.

Lincoln called to him, "Brian?"

Ramsey twisted his head; there was fright, anguish and panic written there on his face. "For fuck's sake do something, Chris, look what I've done, look at her face!"

"Engine oil, quickly then," Lincoln snapped. "Where is it?"

Ramsey blinked and Lincoln could see the gears turning and him trying to cope with and find an answer to an apparently irrelevant question – the penny finally dropped.

"Under the saloon settee, in the locker under the . . . under the one aft, in front of the chart table."

Bill knew better than any of them where.

"Take over from Bill, Helmut, please," Lincoln directed, before turning back to Brian. "You're not going to win there, Brian, try her back in against the hull again."

Brian ground out, "It's worse if I pull her back in, why do you think I'm in a position like this – for the good of my fucking health!"

Blind panic and no point in arguing – concentrate on time, Lincoln . . .

Helmut and Bill changed positions: "Oil in a gallon container, Bill, please?" Lincoln repeated his request, "A one-gallon container – where?"

Repeated because Lincoln would not have put it past Brian to have a five gallon one tucked away somewhere!

Bill dryly nodded his confirmation. "A gallon can – right."

Lincoln added more instructions as Bill climbed around and began to descend the companionway steps. "Up here with it – as fast as you can, please?" Lincoln grabbed his arm. "Once you're back up and when we're ready, Bill, punch three holes in it – three holes only, right?" Bill again nodded his understanding. "Do that with the can hanging over the side – any on the deck and it'll be like a skating rink." Lincoln paused for breath, and then pointed. "Secure it forward, Bill; drop it in as near to her as practical . . . Go, Bill."

Lincoln started to scramble forward then, to the loaded but dormant, sheet winch – they would need that sheet to help haul Sharon back on board. Nick and Lionel, he saw, had somehow managed to douse the jib, so Lincoln couldn't tell whether Nick had actually freed the sheet from the clew of the jib or not, Lincoln just prayed that he had – he would have to go forward and cut it himself otherwise. Nick hadn't cut it and Lincoln mentally and with relief called him a hero: he had untied it; the foresail sheet pulled free through its leads without resistance.

Lincoln scampered quickly back to Ramsey only to realise once there that the 'gibb' hook on the inboard end of Sharon's safetyline already had a line attached, Helmut had used it, he remembered, to control Nick when in the bo'sun's chair, an ordinary safetyline would obviously never have been long enough to reach! Lincoln cursed: it was what Ramsey had had a hold of all the time!

Lincoln took a deep breath; he was yet again successfully impersonating his decapitated, feathered, farmyard friend, and beginning to run around without a thought *in* his head! He closed his eyes and admonished: Christ – think, Lincoln, think. There's a girl's life at stake here – and you're running around like a half-demented, brainless idiot!

Bill appeared as Lincoln opened his eyes – somebody's God had been smiling down – and Lincoln took the gallon can from him and squatted and quickly tied the end of the now spare sheet to its handle – while Bill found and opened his knife.

Another penny dropped as they stood. "Not here, Bill, don't throw it over here, on this side here, it needs to be on the other side." Lincoln pointed. "To windward – and forward."

Bill led, and directly across the cockpit they went, and then he suddenly stopped and it took a moment for him, Lincoln, to catch-up with Bill's intent: he quickly then realised that Bill was going to puncture the oil can there. Bill waited patiently while Lincoln pulled in, as Lincoln should have done before crossing the cockpit, and properly coiled the excess sheet! Bill waved Lincoln out of the way as he knelt, and with knife in hand and oil can extended overboard, ready to spike the side or bottom of the can. Lincoln uncoiled and trailed the sheet outside of the stanchions as he went forward. A nod from him and Bill shook his head and let the out-held weeping oil can go: a splash, a bob, and then it was gone. "The bloody thing was full, you bloody fool!" Lincoln muttered and chastised himself yet again – knowing that he still wasn't, as Bill already knew, thinking coherently! Hand-over-hand Lincoln hauled the gallon can to him until it was directly below and its silver top just showing above the surface in the hollows. Lincoln moved forward again until he judged it right and its position a little ahead of the mast, before finally kneeling and securing the sheet to the toe rail.

That Lionel and Nick had stopped and that they were watching registered somewhere – Lincoln ignored them, as he had a prone Gary.

Incredible, and even in the time it took to get back and re-cross the cockpit – a magic wand had been waved – the sea had already flattened right off in the lee-shadow of *Worippa's* hull.

Two halves of the same unbroken continuous line hung from Ramsey's hands, one end of which was attached to Sharon's harness, and as before, it was the other half that concerned Lincoln – that is, the free end of the same line! Brian must have accidentally allowed or accidentally footed over the free end and excess during his struggles – Lincoln needed that excess. Another thought flittered across: if he dropped that line then they would really be in trouble – they would have a devil of a job on to fish the thing out again . . . It was braid, he confirmed, the damn thing would sink out of sight if freed!

Lincoln shuffled as close as he dared to Ramsey; Ramsey glanced around at the sound of Lincoln's voice.

"Hold her steady, Brian."

Lincoln then made a grab for the unattached half of the line hanging below Ramsey's hands – and missed. Lincoln turned on contact, Bill had grabbed his other hand while he was unbalanced and still teetering on the edge, and Lincoln's initial reaction, despite his stupid predicament, was to try and pull free.

Ramsey screeched, "What the fuck are you doing?"

They could but ignore Ramsey's anguished, gritted shout. Bill placed his feet then braced, Lincoln clenched his wrist in return – he pulled Lincoln in. Bill then picked up and offered Lincoln *Worippa's* boathook from where he had handily placed it – Lincoln had no time to be embarrassed, he just took the boathook without a word and easily hooked and retrieved the slack unattached half of the line in question from below Ramsey's hands.

An explanation was not needed and Lincoln just pointed to and Bill led it across to the spinnaker winch and put four wraps round the barrel before starting to tension; Lincoln took a hold of and held onto the line while Bill went forward for a winch handle.

"Chris?"

Lincoln turned to the touch, Helmut stood there, and Ramsey was behind him, sideways on, watching the water below – and Ramsey giving them a quick and desperate and imploring glance now and again. Helmut's look was also accusing: and pity, anguish, desperateness, censorious reproach and smouldering anger were all there for Lincoln to see. His calm statement belied the messages apparent in his eyes.

"Sharon is just floating now, ve have a little time."

The three of them all attention and waiting: and Ramsey held . . . was holding the now slightly slack line attached to Sharon's safety harness; Bill stood ready at the winch, handle in one hand and sheet tail in the other; Helmut just stood.

"Right – decision time . . ." Lincoln took a deep breath and then stepped forward and took the line from Ramsey's unresisting hands.

"Helmut and I'll lift her." Lincoln looked Brian in the eye and daring any dissent. "Brian, you and Bill haul and winch in the slack – we'll do it in two or three stages rather than one big hit." Lincoln glanced at Bill so as to include him. "Our first lift is going to be our best and the most critical – she's completely waterlogged – she'll weigh a ton." Lincoln glanced round and down at Sharon. "There'll not be too many second chances – we'll lose our strength quickly." He was talking to himself as much as to them finally. "We'll have to hurt her a bit if we fail – we'll simply have to winch her up – brute force and ignorance." Lincoln shrugged that thought away and took a deep breath. "Come on, let's get on with it."

Helmut stood for a moment after Lincoln had gestured to him, looking down and before dropping to one knee as well.

"We lift her up as far as possible with the rope, or strap, on the first hoist," Lincoln half-instructed and half-suggested, "from crouched to standing, then we let her hang. Okay?"

Helmut gave an affirmative nod.

Lincoln pointed and traced with a finger. "Inside the 'U', made by the top of her life jacket and the start of the life jacket's shoulder straps, do you see?"

Helmut looked down, studied, and then back to Lincoln. Again a nod, but no comment and no change of expression, and no panic: and there just patient intelligence – just waiting for his, Lincoln's, master plan to unfold!

Lincoln pressed on, "On our knees this time; we each reach in and with the backs of our hands together we grab a harness strap apiece, and then lift; if we can pull her straight up and over, fine – if not, then we let her hang again. If one of us fails to secure a proper handhold or isn't comfortable then we both let go, right; time's on our side so we can have a little breather between each heave if we want . . . We can't waste our strength, besides, one of us'll never hold her on their own – she'll slip back into the water again before we can get tension on if we don't watch it – another bloody potential, maybe fatal disaster in the making." He was babbling to Helmut and Lincoln knew that he wasn't entirely coherent, but nevertheless Helmut did seem to be getting the drift: he simply nodded his understanding at each pause: at where and when Lincoln had stopped to draw breath. "Um, we'll lift her on the crest, Helmut, yes – any help, no matter how small, has got to be a bonus!"

Helmut stood and moved around to the left, a measure of his worth, and found his balance and then crouched down, his right foot and knee forward and his left leg back, and both well apart. He placed his right hand below Lincoln's left, and his left hand in-between and below Lincoln's right. He was going to use his right hand, Lincoln saw, and right leg to lift! Lincoln glanced at him, observing him: he was, it seemed to Lincoln, bloody confident! He a thinker too, he had thought it out: and he knew, if anyone, it would be him, Lincoln, it would be his right knee and ribs that would let them down. Lincoln's immediate impulse was to resent that assumption, but on consideration he had to admit that Helmut's thinking was sound – Lincoln wasn't as fit as he had ever been at this moment in time, and in ordinary circumstances he wasn't anywhere near as strong as Helmut anyway – and it wouldn't do to even contemplate bungling the job, let alone argue, Helmut had the rights of it and that was that!

Helmut's instructions cut through Lincoln thoughts: "Ve vill hyperventilate, ja?"

And there they crouched; and Lincoln managing to balance, his eyes closed and deeply inhaling and exhaling.

Helmut carried on with the initiative – he turned inboard. "Ve vill lift on the count of three, you must take in the slack

405

quickly, votever you loose ve vill have to lift again!"

Brian and Bill nodded.

Just absolutely unreal, Helmut, thought Lincoln as an aside – Margaret just wasn't going to believe . . .

"Ve vill pretend that we are pulling a horrible man off, he is raping your sister who is Sharon, ja, you understand. He is having intercourse vith her against her vill – Lionel maybe?"

Lincoln cringed at the thought and didn't dare to glance around at Bill and Ramsey, and swallowed the bubbling laughter that was trying to erupt through his clenched teeth – the hyperventilation was completely wasted . . . Lincoln ineffectually tried to curl his top lip from a smirk into a horrible grimace, and before theatrically snarling: "He's really got me annoyed now – and angry! I'm mad, Helmut, really getting mad." Lincoln finally hissed nastily, "Potter you say!"

Snickering was the only word to describe them, Helmut and Lincoln – a wicked, wicked pair of bastards . . . and Sharon inert, floating in front of them in the oily, lazy, swell, and her distressed, bruised, unaware, bedraggled face pink with diluted blood. God forgive them, Lincoln entreated – they had completely forgotten, or had ignored her!

Then, like a switch being flicked, they were ready. They looked at each other and took a deep breath, and gently pulled Sharon to *Worippa's* side; Helmut hyperventilated as he spoke loudly, so that Brian and Bill could hear.

"Relax now. Vun . . ."

Lincoln braced.

"Two . . .

"Three-ee . . ."

Every muscle, every sinew and every joint creaking and cracking – and slowly they struggled upright. Good fortune, providence, luck: and Lincoln's left leg doing the work and taking most of the strain; and his right arm across, gripping hand upward and forearm lodged and resting naturally in the soft spot above his knee. And a thought incidentally flittered, that Helmut had been entirely correct, and that his right leg would never have taken it, and he knew in his heart of hearts that it would have failed, and one of the fractures, or whatever, would simply have buckled and given in!

They stood together, momentarily frozen finally, braced, and with shoulders hunched and bodies half bent over: and

Lincoln's knee joint, leg and forearm shaking uncontrollably: and face glowing and eyes shut.

Brian and Bill had got it just right – they were a good team – and Helmut and Lincoln did not have to fight them as well.

"Ve lift to waist height on the count of three again – deep breaths, Chris."

Jesus Christ, Helmut, Lincoln thought, reserves nearly gone, get on with it!

"Ve step back as vell, ve drag her over the side – after three again, ja."

Lincoln nodded faintly.

"Right. Vun. Two. Three. He-ee-eave."

They managed to get her to waist height and after that Lincoln just couldn't do it, it wasn't in him – he simply had nothing left to give! The line then suddenly went slack – and Lincoln nearly knocked out his own teeth! Surprise, bewilderment, disorientation, and eyes quickly open to look down, that and the sudden release of blood pressure from a bursting skull sent Lincoln staggering – Helmut's hand steadied and eased him back and out of the way. Lionel had her under one arm, Lincoln saw, and Nick the other, and Helmut nodded phlegmatically before bending – and before reaching out and gripping Sharon's waistband.

"Ve lift and pull on three," he counted down, not waiting for affirmation. His overhand and their underarm finally secured her – she was safe at last.

They stood and sat, catching their wind: Lincoln was, at least.

Bill bustled round. "We'll get her below – blankets, hot drinks?"

Lincoln didn't answer immediately, but crossed and sat in the cockpit opposite – head bowed, arms on knees and still taking deep breaths. Between gasps and too exhausted to employ diplomacy, he instructed, "Best stanch any cuts first, Bill." He looked up. "And better to strip her here – she's saturated with oil, it'll get everywhere. We'll be able to lift her then, without all her wet clothes, it'll be hell of a job to carry her below otherwise – she's much too heavy and with that oil we'll never get a grip."

Ramsey spoke then, and there was a bitterness in his voice that Lincoln had never heard before. "Don't you get bored,

Pom, with never being wrong – he's right, is Nick, I could fucking-well hate you as well . . . Trying to live up to the likes of you is beginning to be a real pain in the arse."

Nothing to fill the silence, just the silence; Lincoln stood and climbed around, and stepped slowly to the stern – and there the seascape and nature better company. Nick's comment had been from the heart: youthful enthusiasm, inexperience, misplaced admiration. There had been no malice in his envy, just a misguided urge to emulate. Brian's different – and from the black part of his heart – and it was the end of a friendship. Lincoln scanned the sea and sky and almost subconsciously summed up: that him and Ramsey would act out and play out their parts, and pay lip service – a stand-off. He was sadly aware though that they would part company at the end of this voyage, just the same!

The wind had died with evening, but enough cool breeze still sighed to chill drying sweat – and enough to send *Worippa* tripping. Time didn't stand still and the earth turned regardless – and their little drama played out in a radiant, indifferent, summer evening. The sun was well over halfway down towards sleep in the west, and its orb obscured, glowing behind banking clouds building on that horizon. It always surprised Lincoln that the sun at these latitudes and at this time and when comparatively high up before twilight had, when he turned his back, dropped suddenly and quickly and almost vertically! Just now it was like looking at . . . into a streaming tunnel, and the forward-leaning, yellow, rimless sunbeams above the clouds spreading as spokes from a hub. The contrasts were muted, smudged – and oils to pastels – but not yet to the wash of watercolours. Sky-blues, sea-blues, sea-greens, and mauves weaker . . . and now tinged with misty yellow, and even the sea and the foam tending towards lemon. Impersonal, beautiful, cruel world . . . the words surfaced from somewhere: *'something rotten in the state of Denmark'* . . . *'what a piece of work is a man'.*

The gentle tug on his sleeve repeated itself; Lincoln squeezed the moisture from his eyes and handed and cuffed it away from his nose and mouth as well before turning.

Warren stood there, tentative and hesitant, with a shy stuttering smile on his face. He waited for Lincoln's full attention before turning and touching the wheel – a wheel that had been quietly helmed and then lashed – they had forgotten about him, Lincoln had forgotten about him, because he had done a complete and very competent job!

Lincoln nodded conformation and approval, and then stepped down and stood next to him. He the hero, Lincoln acknowledged, and to him the place of honour. Sharon was aboard because *Worippa* had lain quietly: Warren had, in their time of need and without fuss, taken care of it!

An affirming sideways twist of Lincoln's head and wink, and then two or three confirming up and down silent 'well-done' nods – and how wrong, conceded Lincoln, how very, very wrong could one be!

"You did it, didn't you," Lincoln congratulated.

Warren really grinned. "Did I do it right?"

"My word," Lincoln said in all sincerity. "Nobody could have done better: a bloody hero." He put his arm around Warren's shoulders and bent his head down and placed his mouth close to Warren's ear, Warren lent closer in response – two conspirators. "Don't tell the rest of them," Lincoln whispered quietly, "they'll all want the same." Lincoln looked around with conspiratorial exaggeration. "Just between us – a secret . . . You'll find an extra few bucks in your wage packet on Thursday – a little gift from me to you – a sign of recognition and appreciation." Lincoln hugged him with his arm.

Warren laughed, and genuine too, a laugh that Lincoln had never heard before – Warren really and truly and actually laughing!

Potter interrupted, "Chris?"

Something in his voice, the set of his stance, and the tension around his mouth . . .

Warren clammed up immediately.

Lionel got no further; Helmut was backing carefully, crowding Lionel – Lionel was being gently pushed till trapped against pedestal and wheel. They had stripped Sharon, Lincoln saw, to base underwear, and her oil and blood-stained clothes they had dumped or thrown in the helmsman's area; Warren had had enough sense to foot them out of the way, he noticed, forward and under the wheel and around the pedestal. Helmut was holding Sharon under the arms and Brian her feet and Bill was in his usual caring role – and holding an already red, blood-soaked towel to her face – an administrating angel.

Helmut paused, twisted round and said to Lincoln, "You vill come down and check her?"

Sharon though muzzy was already moaning – making noises anyway.

Lincoln said quietly. "I'm not a doctor, Helmut . . . Let Bill have her – he's right, blankets and hot drinks. The usual thing: sit her with her head forward and down and wait . . . Keep her in that position until her nose stops bleeding. Um, use the time to clean her up – you'll have to 'butterfly' if there are any really deep gashes . . . She didn't collide against any really sharp edges, as far as I could tell – the hull's smooth, so apart from that one really bad thump it'll probably be mostly grazes; either way, I'm not qualified to stitch anything – just so long as she's coherent."

Bill asked next, Helmut waited patiently, ignoring both Brian . . . and Sharon. "Pinch her nostrils gently together," he asked, "do you think that would help to stop it?"

Lincoln actually laughed, circumstances notwithstanding. "It'll be a brave man who tries pinching her nose, Bill." Lincoln pointed and nodded. "It looks to be swelling nicely now and 'oh' so painful – it's already putting 'Rudolf' to shame. If you do – squeeze her nose, I mean – then give us a shout, I wouldn't mind to watch!"

She and Gary were going to look like a pair of invalided bookends – they'd make quite a couple . . . Gary. Gary? Something stopped Lincoln . . . stopped him from asking . . . speaking his name out loud.

Bill grinned despite everything: despite the awkwardness, the weight and worry and the responsibility of Sharon. "Sorry. You'll come down and double-check – just to be sure then?"

Why he needed him? Lincoln asked, he, Bill himself, was more than capable, in fact, better than . . . He sighed mentally and then nodded. "As soon as we're secure and safe."

Lionel turned when allowed and after Helmut had stepped forward with his arm-dangling load. "You've done first aid, haven't you?" Lionel demanded.

Lincoln climbed around – another subject . . . Something . . . something bad!

"Only industrial, Lionel, I'm afraid," Lincoln replied reluctantly. "Wrap it in a handkerchief or shirt: stop the bleeding and straight to hospital – nothing very deep."

Lionel tried to continue: Lincoln's wasn't or hadn't been the response he had expected: nor to be ignored and pushed aside.

The harshness in his voice would have frozen hell over. "Wait a minute . . .?"

He went to grab Lincoln's arm, temper flaring – Lincoln got to his first and squeezed. Lincoln talked over his shoulder, "Got it down, I see, Nick, the roller reefing, I mean – much trouble?"

Lincoln momentarily increased the pressure on Lionel's arm before relaxing his grip, and he didn't let go though, just in case, though he knew that Lionel had understood.

Nick shook his head, as far as Nick was concerned there was a bigger, more important priority – and everything else, including roller reefing, was irrelevant.

"Sharon," he asked, "how's Sharon, is she going to be okay?"

Lincoln smiled. "She's young, tough and strong like you, Nick, with the strength and resilience of youth." He advised cheerfully, "You'd better watch out, she'll come looking in a couple of hours: you know it'll end up being your fault: she'll say you led her into it – she's bound to blame you." Lincoln nonchalantly studied the sky, and then gave him a nod and a wink. "I don't much fancy your chances, you haven't done that well against her previously, have you?"

Nick's smiled ruefully and then his face clouded. "You don't really think it was my fault, do you?" he asked.

"Course it wasn't. Don't be silly. One of those things – forget it." Lincoln changed the subject. "Did you have much trouble with the roller reefing?"

Nick didn't answer directly; he said instead, "You've got blood on your face, and on the back of your hand, quite a lot – are you all right?"

"Ay, Sharon's, Nick, her nosebleed, she also had small cuts and grazes on her forehead." Lincoln added in blind faith, "There's a lot of blood vessels in those areas . . . they always look worse than they really are."

Oh, the resilience and innocence, and Lincoln thanked whatever god was out there, that Nick dismissed that concern from his mind and without thought returned to Lincoln's original question. "I'm afraid we might have bent the mast just a tiny bit more." He held up his hand before Lincoln could comment. "Only a tad – really. We had to winch the halyards out in the end, there was no other way . . . still." He gave Lionel a playful shove. "We didn't do too badly, did we?" Nick raised his eyebrows and indicated Lionel with a thumb. "He did quite well after I'd shown him what to do, that is."

Lionel held on – held his peace – so Lincoln filled the pregnant pause.

"Mm. I need time to think it out, Nick – what to do. I have to admit, I still feel a bit winded from that lift – I'll need a few more minutes." Lincoln hesitated while quickly examining *Worippa's* condition. "Would you do me a favour, would you nip below and get the handy-billy, and then find the boathook?" He pointed. "Attach the handy-billy to the toe rail or wherever and ease the boom off of that rear lower shroud – about an inch, Nick, do you see . . . Twenty-five millimetres to you – all right?

"She'll ride easier with a touch of main on too." Lincoln waggled a hand for emphasis. "Only just pulling – she'll be a lot happier with the load off at that one point."

Nick nodded his understanding. "Right."

As usual, Lincoln had to grab him before he prematurely raced off. "Hold on, hold on – wait." Nick waited; he was shivering like a highly-strung stallion. "We're going to have to motor after we sort the main out – something around the propeller'll finish us. There're two warps still in the water that I know of: the bo'sun's chair for one, you'll need the boathook to reach that; and the gallon can that Bill and I dropped over the side. Would you reprieve and secure them, and check for any other stray lines? Um, the oil can: the best thing, I think, is to consign that to the deep – any of that oil on the deck and we'll never get rid of it – it'll be like a skating rink otherwise."

Nick stood – now a frightened doe ready to run . . . he knew!

Lincoln added gently, "Do those things for me, Nick – I'll take care of the rest."

He went to ask – Lincoln wouldn't let him.

"The handy-billy is under the companionway steps and the boathook's around somewhere – would you go down now." Lincoln indicated. "Get the handy-billy first?"

A hesitant, knowing, not wanting to know, scared, agonising, indescribable look before he moved off.

A moment for Nick to step out of earshot, and them, Potter

and him, to step forward beyond Warren's too.

"Gary's dead, Chris."

Chapter 29

Bill stood blocking the entrance through to forward, and he wasn't going to let Lincoln pass and he wouldn't let Lincoln push through either, and the only alternative would be to physically knock him down.

"I can't understand you," he reproved, "it can't be that important whatever you're doing up top, it can't be more important than this girl's well-being – for Christ's sake, Chris."

Brian and Helmut stood at the back of Bill.

"Quickly then," Lincoln said impatiently. "What's her problem?"

Bill didn't bother to hide his disgust, he shook his head. "Sorry to fucking-well trouble you, I'll try not to waste too much of your precious time." A tension-filled moment passed before he broke the silence again. "She won't respond," he burst out. "She won't or can't talk. I can't even get a drink down her; though she's stopped shivering . . . It's almost as if she's gone beyond that stage." He pleaded, "She's in a bad way, Chris, and I don't know what else to do!"

Lincoln didn't know why he hadn't thought of it before, but Gary had always carried a small torch hanging by a cord around his neck when night sailing – it wasn't actually a pencil torch, he remembered, but it did have a beam that would be narrow enough. It was a good idea in many ways to carry a small torch and he knew that some crew's did the same with their knives' though it was not his cup of tea: he always somehow managed to get the thing twisted, tangled, or caught up – and it would swing when in a hurry, and the thing had managed to hit him in the face more than once! Gary, though navigator, would often come forward to help should they have problems, and his torch, Lincoln had to admit, had proved exceptionally useful at times: on overnight races when trying to see; when having trouble starting the bolt rope of a new headsail up the foil groove on a sail change, for example. It had also proved to be useful when removing or replacing an odd split pin, tracing a twist or jam in a reefing line in the dark, or similar – that kind of thing – there were no end of odd uses . . . No . . . No, that wasn't really true, all during Lincoln's sailing career he had never found a real need for such a torch of that sort – a powerful, spotlight type, yes, a pencil torch, no. Well, perhaps just the odd instance, but certainly not worth the bother of carrying it around. It had been Gary's peculiarity, that was all, he had turned it on as required and just let it hang – it left his hands free.

Gary had been a fiddler . . . had been! He had driven them all mad, and it would be nothing for him, Lincoln recalled, to open the doors to their personal lockers half a dozen times on his watch and root haphazardly around and amongst his belongings. They squeaked, the doors, and for some reason they never afterwards remembered to oil them; the chore always got superseded by the next incident or forgotten by the next morning. They had turned on Gary when he had broken his own record, and had managed somehow to find a reason to come down five times on one four-hour watch. His visits had and without fail always followed the same weary pattern: clump down the companionway steps; light on; squeaking doors opened; noise of plastic bags loudly crackling as he rummaged around; squeaking doors closed; light off; and lumber back up the companionway steps. Lincoln could envision and hear him, and nine times out of ten he had not made the steps halfway before coming back down and then another patience-trying repeat pattern: and on went the light and doors opened yet again, and then questing noisily and longer for a final forgotten item – doors closed, light off and back up the steps. Not only his, Lincoln's, but other breaths, sighs, grumbles and grinding teeth had filled the immediate vacuum of his departure. Individual objections they had found, no matter how strongly worded, didn't pay, they were always fielded with an apology and a stubborn effort to start up a conversation – he would often take on everybody rather than simply go. Most of them, including Lincoln, employed two short words, and their only defence: it was the only sure way to shut him up . . . though, even then one still might have to listen to and endure an injured, half-reasonable, half-sarcastic, prolonged reply! His excursions into their sleeping time also were almost always accompanied by an irritating, under-breath whistle and an irritating feeling that he knew and was being deliberately provocative, and yet for some reason couldn't help himself!

During that first night at sea when they had all been unable to sleep despite the desperate need . . . That was right, he had acquired his torch, and Lincoln smiled, after they had trapped, or rather, jumped him on his umpteenth visit. Potter had taken his boots and socks off while they had sat on him – Potter had extracted promises – the soles of Gary's feet had proved to be unbearably sensitive to a feather touch. He had promised, after they had extracted their pound of flesh, to tread lightly, never to turn on the light, not to whistle, to oil the offending doors and not to enter at all unless absolutely necessary, viz., a life-and-death situation.   Lionel had dropped the act finally, Lincoln remembered, and had seriously accused Gary of being thoughtless, selfish and unfair – and the message had struck home.   Despite Gary's obvious, genuine contriteness, Lionel hadn't finished, not till he'd finally extracted 'the promise': Gary would have to suck a certain part of Potter's anatomy should he break his word! Yes, and Lincoln distractedly wiped a hand across his eyes, Gary had acquired his little torch by the next trip!

Bill was close to losing his temper.   "Are you going to look at her, or what? Bloody-oath!"

Lincoln finally asked, "Just what exactly is wrong with her? I told you, I'm not a doctor – can't you handle it for once?"

Bill's embarrassment jolted Lincoln fully back to reality, Bill was simply reacting like the gentleman he was.   He admitted reluctantly, "I had to invade her privacy on the toilet, she was sat on the loo gradually freezing to death . . ." The blush on Bill's face was spreading as he spoke, "I had to wrap her in more blankets sitting there. She was straining and straining to have a wee, but couldn't."

The obvious compassion in Bill's voice awoke an acute sense of guilt in Lincoln, but Bill didn't understand . . .

"She was sitting in there with her teeth rattling and crying, all at the same time." He shook his head. "I didn't really know what to do to help her; it's not an experience I'd like to repeat. I finally persuaded her, or rather forced her to give it away, she simply couldn't go – to the toilet, I mean. She's quietened down a bit since . . . after we'd got her back into bed." He was close to shouting in the end. "So don't bloody-well stand there and casually tell me you can't bloody-well help!"

Brian and Helmut moved aside after Lincoln had nodded, as Lincoln stepped through.

Sharon first, if it was to hand, that is – they would have to make-do with one of the big torch's otherwise. A piece of card with a pinhole through it, or something, or he would end up permanently blinding her otherwise.

It was amongst Gary's underwear and tucked into a pair of socks; Lincoln could feel its hard outline through the protective plastic bag. A dark-blue, man-made polar he shook out after pocketing the torch – a one piece. The socks that Gary had wrapped the torch in were thermal too.

Sharon lay in the bottom bunk on her side and swathed in blankets – three stark sticking plasters patched her sunburned forehead, but it was the one across the bridge of her nose that caught Lincoln's eye, and that was because a glistening, fine line of blood was still dribbling from beneath it. She already looked a mess and there would be more swelling and bruising to come out yet – and a picture she wasn't going to be. Her eyes were open, and they flickered, which caught Lincoln by surprise – for some reason he had assumed that she would be unconscious!

He went down on one knee and put his face close to hers – he pushed a strand of hair gently away from her forehead – her breathing was loud and ragged.

"How do you feel?" Lincoln murmured gently.

She didn't or wouldn't answer.

"Do you hurt," Lincoln asked, "do you hurt in any particular place – do you feel any pain?"

She was aware, of that he was sure – recognition had been there when their eyes had met, fleeting though it may have been.

"Do you want . . . Do you need any painkillers?"

A slight negative shake of her head was all – and acknowledgement at least.

Lincoln put a hand inside the blankets, her tummy was cool to the touch, but it wasn't the iced chill of someone suffering from severe, life-threatening exposure.

Sharon's pulse beat strongly under his fore and middle fingers; her irises responded to the beam of the torch – and dilation clear to see (a comparison Lincoln desperately hoped he'd need yet knew he wouldn't – worldly-wise was Potter, and it was highly unlikely that he'd not have been mistaken).

Lincoln lent close to her ear again and their heads not quite touching – and intimate. "Listen, Sharon, I'm going to have to leave you down here with Bill for a little while, it's not that I don't love you, it's just that we must tidy-up the mast. The top of the mast buckled, you remember, that's how you ended up in the water. We have to move quickly before a forecast . . . before a forecasted cold front comes in. We'll motor then; we're only about six and a half, seven hours to the Heads once we get going, you'll be home and in your own bed by tomorrow." Lincoln kissed the side of her forehead, and felt even guiltier about manipulating her thoughts . . . Still, better for her to concern herself with someone else's woes rather than dwell on her own. "Don't mess Bill about, Sharon, if you can help it, it's not fair, he's not equal to it, he's not a young man anymore – he's on the edge of a breakdown now and he doesn't know the half."

Sharon swallowed bile and whispered, "I'm going to pretend none of it happened – I can't face it yet – please don't tell me."

Lincoln nodded, and ignored what was uppermost in both their minds . . . though how she knew . . .? "Okay . . . Listen, as I said, there's things we've got to do: the safety of the boat and everybody on board – please cope – please hold onto it for a little while longer. Look after Bill for me?"

Another thought occurred. "Listen, Sharon, we're probably going to have to call out a helicopter, would you like to go home on it . . . it may be for the best?"

Sharon immediately became agitated and there was a surprising amount of strength in her grip. "No. No. I want to stay with you. Please . . ." She took a shuddering breathe. "They'll give me a check-up, then I'll be sedated and be put under observation, and then they'll send me back to that empty unit." Such anguish in her voice, "It'll be just the same as before Christmas – I'll be on my own again. No. Please?"

"Whatever you want is okay with me," Lincoln said quietly. He pushed her gently back down and ran a finger gently down her cheek. "I think you've got it wrong, my dear, remember, whatever, like it or no, our lives are now entwined." He sighed, as if exasperated by the thought. "We're stuck with each other – we'll be with each other so much it'll be a pain in the arse – we'll get on each other's tits."

Sharon hissed with venom. "Don't you patronise me."

Lincoln snorted.

Her mood changed again and the fight went out of her, and she lifted her hand and her fingers gently caressed, and their touch cold. Her concern was obvious, though her voice oddly matter-of-fact, "You've blood on your lips and chin again, you've upset whatever's wrong inside of you again, haven't you – rescuing me?"

There was no point in hiding it. Lincoln sighed. "I'll be all right so long as I'm careful from now on, like I said, we'll be home soon." He changed the subject, "Sharon," he said quietly, "I want you to do a couple of things for me?"

Sharon looked in askance.

Lincoln held up Gary's thermals. "Get changed into this 'teddy bear' suit." He held up a placating hand. "Please, Sharon, it's the only way you're really going to get warm. Also, I want you to eat and drink whatever Bill serves." Lincoln ignored her little headshake. "Try. Look, think only nice thoughts, seriously, it works, believe me. Close your mind, think of nothing other than vicious sunlight: sunburn, the desert, The Centre, Alice – sweat, heat . . . Please, Sharon, for me. If you do then it'll be something less for me to worry about." And then Lincoln was deliberately cruel, "We really don't want to have to worry about you on top of everything else – we've got enough on our plates as it is."

Lincoln knelt there, silent.

After a moment she gasped, "God, I need to pee." She held her stomach and folded as a spasm hit. "It's killing me!"

"You want to go to the toilet, you mean," Lincoln said harshly, "you won't be able to till you relax. Like I said – think of other things."

Lincoln stood and turned to include Helmut and Brian, and ignored Sharon – it wouldn't matter if she overheard and it might even do the trick. "She's in shock, Bill," he said matter-of-factly. "As far as I can tell, that is. All her body fluids have been withdrawn and absorbed into her vital organs – it's a survival thing – it's the body's way of protecting itself. Um, anyway, we have to assume that because I've never actually seen it before, but I've read about it and have had it described to me, and that's why I think she can't go to the toilet – her body's hanging onto everything that it may require, it's trying to cover every eventuality."

Lincoln stepped into the saloon without deliberately giving Sharon another glance – and out of her hearing. Lincoln glanced quickly at Helmut, Helmut's face was expressionless – if he suspected Lincoln of playing mind-games then he wasn't letting on. He would be right to stay neutral too, Lincoln acknowledged, it wasn't without its risks and dangers!

"Change her now, Bill, straight away, into that thermal suit – get those socks on her too, and then move her." Lincoln pointed. "Put her behind the table there, in that berth – where the action is. Don't let her sleep . . . you can let her take short naps if you can't stop her from falling asleep. The point is, if she goes too deep there's a small chance that we might not be able to wake her again – I know it sounds melodramatic, but it's better to be safe than sorry, head injuries are dodgy – she can sleep properly once we're sure there's no other complications. Normality's the next best thing for her after getting her warm. Talk to her as if she were her usual self, Bill, carry on and cook, the oven'll keep the cabin warm, bring Judy's oil lamp through – that'll help. You could even put some music on." Lincoln wavered his head from side to side. "Create an air of casual-everyday." He indicated again. "Get cushions under her, prop her up so that she's reclining rather than lying down: so that she can look around and see what's going on – involve her."

Bill nodded and then shook his head. "What was all that about – what you were saying to her, you lost me completely?"

Lincoln shook his head. "I'll explain later."

Ramsey interrupted and suggested, and oblivious to the bigger picture. "I'll put out a *Pan* call, shall I – tell them our situation, and get some professional medical advice?"

"There's other things going on, Brian." Lincoln indicated upwards with a thumb. "Better that you come up top before you do anything."

Lincoln left them to it then and went quickly back through to the locker room, and then on forward. He collected a blanket on his way and passed it up to Potter – there was no need for explanations, Potter had been listening in. Lincoln put his head through the lanyard of the torch and dropped it down inside his jacket for security – Lionel moved to one side as Lincoln cleared the fore hatch.

"Anything, Lionel? Did you recheck?"

Lionel replied calmly as they stepped across, "I can't find his pulse, no sign of life at all – he's cold already . . . even his groin. There's no colour, not even his lips – he looks dead, poor bugger, look at him."

"There's a thin chance he could have gone into a coma, Lionel, and his breath and pulse so shallow that you can't detect them?"

Lincoln knelt down beside Gary's head, and then moved round till in front. "Christ, Lionel, you didn't tell me he was losing . . ." Lincoln touched and then rubbed the watery discharge between his fingers. "You didn't mention that he'd lost fluid from his ears, did you!" Lincoln lent closer. "He's been losing from his nose as well."

Lionel said defensively, "Relevant, is it? There's not much there."

Lincoln looked at Lionel directly – it was a genuine enquiry.

"Hm." He explained distractedly, "As I told you, I've only attended the odd first aid course; the last one was about three years ago." Lincoln sat back on his haunches. "I do remember some of it – odd bits seem to pop out when needed. One of the symptoms of a severe blow to the head . . . of brain damage, or of a very serious head injury anyway, is a reddish, straw-coloured fluid discharging from the ears – that much I defiantly remember . . .

Help me?" Lincoln requested.

They turned Gary partially onto his back, and wrestled and lodged him into a position where he would not roll.

Just one lancing sword thrust of piecing acute agony when levering Gary over caused Lincoln to take a sharp in-breath, and to hesitate – Lionel didn't pick-up on it and did not notice.

He was right, Lionel, Lincoln confirmed, there was no discernible sign of a pulse, neither in the throat nor at the wrist. Lincoln pulled Gary's torch from over his head.

"Drape us both with the blanket, Lionel; I'll check his pupils, that'll tell us something. Just let me get comfortable first."

Lincoln shuffled round a bit further, kneeling with the torch poised, Lionel had got the picture and he carefully covered them. It took a moment to orientate: and gently, tentatively feeling for Gary's forehead – Lincoln switched on the torch. He opened Gary's eyelid fully and then shone the beam directly – no change. He opened his other lid in indirect light and then let it close after positioning and shining the torch again. There was no change in diameter of that pupil that he could see either, no reaction at all – absolutely nothing after opening and focusing on . . .

The blanket fell away; and Lincoln shook his head in answer to Lionel's unspoken question. "Nothing, Lionel."

Lionel nodded and then sighed. "I'd guessed as much."

Lincoln turned to a tread on the deck; and Nick was half-standing there, and watching and ready to bolt. There was no point in making him go away and no point in hiding the facts, Lincoln couldn't protect him further – he had to face it sometime. Lincoln ignored him and spoke to Lionel.

"I want you to lie down in exactly the same position, Lionel – exactly. I need a direct comparison – we can't check enough – we must be absolutely sure."

Lionel didn't argue, he simply stepped forward and laid himself down.

"On your left hip and left shoulder, Lionel, left hand extended above your head exactly the same as Gary's – that's right. Right hand across, thumb just touching the centre of your left armpit." Lincoln compared the two of them. "Your head resting on its crown, Lionel, tipped up and to the right – where it's naturally comfortable. Bend . . . lift your right leg, your right . . ." Lincoln pulled it into position, "and rest it against your left." He stood and re-checked again. "That's about it, hold it there."

Lionel's throat pulse, to the right of his Adam's apple, Lincoln located without trouble, was thumping like a horse – and it betrayed Lionel's outward appearance of calm.

Lincoln grabbed and cloaked his shoulders with the blanket and then pulled it over his head and over Lionel's. "Shut your eyes, Lionel, take deep breaths and relax."

Lincoln paused and waited for him to adjust and settle. He should really have let him lie there for some time, to calm down, unfortunately, in the circumstances, that simply wasn't going to happen.

Lincoln made conversation, "Don't open your eyes or fight me, Lionel, all I'll do is pull up your eyelid gently and shine the torch – it's important that you stay loose. If you can slow down your heart beat then do it."

They waited.

Lincoln finally clicked the torch on again and felt his throat, Lionel's heartbeat had slowed though not by much – and it was still very easy to find and very distinct. His pupils expanded instantly; Lincoln directed the beam away and then back – no question.

Lincoln straightened and let the blanket slide, and Lionel struggled over and onto his knees and then stood, and then he caught Lincoln's arm – he was harsh, upset, angry and blunt. "I'm not as daft as you'd have me think or believe, mate." He pointed to Gary and said brutally, "You carry on and you'll be joining him. I heard you and I saw you wince, and there's blood on your lips again – you're a fucking idiot."

Lincoln touched his chin with the edge of a forefinger, wiping, there wasn't much – their eyes held. "I'll check him once more, Lionel," Lincoln said quietly, "but I don't think there's any doubt."

Brian and Helmut now stood behind Nick; and there had been neither a word nor a comment from either of them. They were all swaying to *Worippa's* now muted motion – it was as if she too were holding her breath and awaiting confirmation.

Lincoln pressed his fingers harshly into Gary's throat after kneeling again, and then back and forth, of a pulse there was still no trace – not a thing. Lionel in point of fact had been right – Gary looked dead. Even in the short time they had attended his pallor had gone from very, very white, to, as now and lips included, a bloodless, lifeless grey.

Lincoln shifted around as before. "Drape the blanket over again when I'm in position, Lionel, and then when I tell you, find and grip Gary's ear – give the lobe a real vicious pinch when I say, and I mean really vicious!"

Gary's pupils remained fixed.

Instead of pinching Gary's ear, as instructed, Lionel silently and gently pushed Lincoln to one side and then eased Gary back over to his original position – on his side. Lincoln understood and stood and they draped and tucked the blanket around.

A hand suddenly spun Lincoln around.

Nick shouted into Lincoln's face, "What are you doing? Why, why are you covering him up? Why are you covering Gary up? What's wrong with him – let's get him below."

Eyes wild, lips quivering – naked aggression – demanding. Pleading, begging . . . tears welling.

Lincoln gently touched his arm. "He's gone, Nick."

He had not expected it; he caught Lincoln high on the

cheekbone and only a quick tip and then a reverse swing of *Worippa* had caused the blow to not quite connect. The next missed completely, which was just as well, it had been a haymaker.

He was screaming, "He's not dead, he'll get up in a minute, you watch."

He swung again and then a flurry delivered with determination: stinging Lincoln's upraised forearms and shoulders.

Helmut and Brian grabbed him.

Lincoln snapped out with a harshness that he hadn't intended, "Leave him. Let him go. Now!"

Nick raised his fists again. "He's not dead, you're lying. You're a liar."

It was half-hearted, the next flurry, and easy to smother. Lincoln dragged him to him, left arm round behind and right hand pulling down and caressing his neck. He struggling initially – went ridged – and then limp. Together, his head hidden and nestling in Lincoln's shoulder, resigned, they sank to the deck. His sorrow difficult and impossible to stand against, and endless whisperings to his God, pleading and begging on Gary's behalf.

They rocked back and forth till he had finally cried himself out.

Lincoln whispered to him, "I want you to start thinking about Sharon, Nick, she doesn't really know . . . I can't really explain, but inside she knows but hasn't accepted yet – don't ask me how. She's hurt and in pain physically and it's going to take a lot of time and understanding for her to recover. She's down there still trying to get warm." Lincoln tried for the right words and despised himself for the hypocrite that he was. "You're like her, but to a lesser degree, Nick, you're suffering from shock, and grief. It's good, and right, and natural to weep only . . . Only we need you now, Nick, Sharon needs you now, and it'll help her if you can bear it. Come on, she's going to need us to lean on – especially you. Her need is greater than yours. Put it away, Nick; put it behind you till we get home, if you can." Lincoln added quietly, "Gary wouldn't have known anything about it, you know, he wasn't expecting it, it came right out of the blue – instantaneous – a millisecond. He wouldn't have felt anything; it would have been over before his brain had time to record."

Gently easing between them, whispering sweet nothings, and the depth of communication and feeling beyond their ken: slowly to silence. Sharon led him and he blindly following as a child, weeping silently as no child would: to the snug womb of Bill Corsham's world: to the comfort, to that secret place reserved in a woman's heart for infants and babes in arms.

*   *   *

"Did you check his throat for any obstructions?"

Lincoln heard him and understood, but it didn't really register, Brian touched his arm.

"Did you clear Gary's mouth and throat?"

Lincoln looked at Potter – he shook his head.

"No." Lincoln answered.

"Give me the torch, I'll do it." Brian sighed. "I'll have to confirm anyway, me being skipper."

Lincoln looked at him . . . Really looked at him. Ramsey wasn't looking much better than Nick: his face grey and a nerve under his right eye was pulsating, stopping, before pulsating again. He was also continually licking his lips, yet, Lincoln noticed, missing the white flecks at the corners each time.

"Leave him in the position's he's in after, Brian, on his side with his head not completely smothered – allow the air to flow." Lincoln added without any hope. "It's not unheard of for a corpse to wake up two hours later, or whatever."

Potter could at times be unbelievably insensitive. "They used to put a final stitch through the nose, you know, when burying them at sea."

He had said it without thought, but not callously. His 'sorry' followed Helmut's back as Helmut stepped to and hung his head over the side – painful pauses between forced gagging and heaving retches followed.

Potter and Lincoln climbed down into the cockpit, Warren was still behind the wheel and his eyes large in his bloodless face – he was shivering.

"Below Warren," Lincoln ordered, "*Worippa's* riding beautifully – well done. Get dressed properly if you want to stay topside – go on, off you go." Lincoln added a cautionary, impromptu word of warning as he put a hand on the wheel, and it was cruel and probably unnecessary. "Don't barge in on Sharon, Warren, if she's changing – you'll catch your death if

425

you do."

Regretted as soon said and Lincoln shook his head in answer to Potter's look.

Ramsey waited for Warren to get clear before stepping down; and they sat in silence for a few seconds.

"You'd better move, Brian," Lionel advised, "and check Gary if you feel that you have to – and then radio in." Lionel touched Brian's knee. "We need to speak to a doctor – we need professional advice and confirmation – we've waited too long as it is."

Ramsey didn't look up when he answered, "I'm quite aware of that, Lionel – there's only one small problem." There was a two second pause before he lifted his head and looked directly. "We lost our aerial when we lost the backstay!"

Chapter 30

Aluminium mast burnished and reflecting a weaker yet deeper vermilion. A rallying point, a broken standard: a lance of ancient tempered steel broken on some *Champ de Mars* – on the playground of the God of War – on some forgotten undulating field of combat. And the banner, the huge battle flag different: and the mainsail totally transformed from blazing white to a dyed pink. A flag of a simpler monochrome design, and *Worippa's* inverted sail numbers bisected to three-quarter and half-size and indecipherable below the angular fold. The black camber lines and residue block letters of a previous sponsor could still be seen ghosting through and helping to form an effective, primitive pattern.

Silver winches scattered around the deck looking like pounds of mirrored, raw flesh. Other narrow, shiny, smooth, metal lengths and fittings reflecting the colour of the sky: crimson muscle, tendon, cartilage, lumps of gristle – and the highlights bone. Froth of a lung wound: a watery, tinted plasma: a russet, sepia-tinted 'globin'. Gore of friend, companion – and enemy and foe alike stained the decks and washing all around.

And not possible for Lincoln to remove or take off – his were rose-tinted glasses of a different kind.

Lincoln turned as Ramsey pulled up his collar; the smouldering sunset behind Ramsey belied a cold wind that was beginning to pipe. A heralding, probing forerunner: the wind was creating the effect of falling dominoes where it touched the smooth, languid sea: blush red acres of corn rippling and bowing to the strong regular forays of the erratic, embryo, evening wind. The improbably and somehow cool, great red ball dominating in the west would be quenched by a bloody-tinged, molten, liquid sea in not less than half an hour.

Worippa's accented curtsies were no longer consciously noticed and sealegs automatically compensated, her motion and untiring convolutions were now so familiar.

"Are you all right, Helmut?"

Helmut shook his head and then nodded as he clambered down into the cockpit – and Lincoln's mind drifted whilst he settled.

Potter's description had also thrown up, for Lincoln, mental pictures that were shocking in their clarity. He could see that old and weather-beaten mariner sitting with his head bowed and oblivious to surrounds . . . and the profile of Gary's face. Gary's forehead, nose, lips and chin as in a sharply focused photograph: an enlarged, black-and-white glossy: and individual fine hairs, bristle and soft down standing proud of outline and they in silhouette and standing stark against an almost black background. Lincoln shivered as that mariner with a dimpled metal coin attached to his leather palm carefully pushed a curved sail needle through soft septum flesh between – that, Potter's, final confirmation before closing the heavy, shot-loaded, weighted, canvass bag . . .

"Chris?" Ramsey touched Lincoln's knee.

Lincoln looked up. "Sorry."

Ramsey was obviously forcing himself to keep going and to think. "It's going to be awkward, it'll take all four of us to manoeuvre and carry Gary below." Ramsey swallowed. "We probably should sort out . . . The priority should be the rig first . . . I just can't. It'll be dark soon and it's starting to fill-in – I just can't bear the thought of that blanket blowing away, or him taking a wave – him getting cold." Ramsey shuddered. "Let's get Gary below and comfortable and then sort out the rest, okay?"

There was no dissent – they all felt the same.

"How and where – where do we put him?" Potter finally asked. "What do we do with him, matie?"

They looked at Ramsey, Ramsey looked out to sea, refusing to answer, refusing eye contact – ignoring the question!

Lionel pivoted round. "Chris?"

Lincoln spoke quietly to Helmut in turn, "Are you okay with this, Helmut, it's going to be unpleasant. Can you cope – can you deal with it?"

Helmut nodded – not offended. "Ja."

Lincoln decided that it would be easier for them all and better to take the bull by the horns and get it over with. "The Number One sailbag'll just about fit him; we'll cut the end seam if it doesn't."

Helmut quietly settled any doubts, "It vill, it is nearly two metres."

Lincoln nodded. "It's waterproof as well, apart from the odd loose stitch – we can put him in that. We're also going to have to prepare him a little; sorry, but I can't think of a more delicate way of phrasing it – orifices weep, bodies leak – fluids leak from various . . ." Lincoln took a deep breath. "Gary's wearing his over-trousers: we can tighten the leg straps. A towel under his head . . . No, better to underlay him with towels – and another towel doubled under his head."

Lionel didn't make it; he threw-up over the side decking before he could reach the side. They moved to weather, except for Helmut, he went below before quickly reappearing again with the ship's bucket – he sluiced down as and after Lionel had re-seated himself.

"You're like a fucking machine, Pom," Potter stated harshly. "It's like you've got iced water running through your veins – you're a cold-blooded bastard, matie. You show no compassion, show no feelings at all, do you?" Lionel dropped his head and pinched his nose before looking back up again. "Sorry . . . Sorry. Sorry, Chris, my nerves are getting just a little frayed, that's all."

Helmut was silent and the bucket was, Lincoln absently observed, now between Helmut's feet and most of the bucket's manila painter Helmut had coiled inside; he was, as Lincoln couldn't help but notice, distractedly fiddling with the painter's plaited end and rolling the neat back-splice back and forth between his hands.

"Thanks, Lionel," Lincoln said dryly and after a momentary pause, "I needed that."

Ramsey spoke, he had not faced them through the whole episode, "What else, Chris? I understand that you're suffering as much as any of us – probably more – it's always worse for those who bottle it up." He turned, rubbed away the moisture and massaged his eyes and wiped his mouth and chin – his hand rasped over stubble.

"Take him down the forehatch," Lincoln said tentatively. "That way we'll save Sharon and Nick from seeing, I wouldn't want either of them exposed nor subjected to any more shock than they have been already – especially Sharon. Her's is delayed, and what with her getting dunked, it all hasn't really hit home yet: we'll think ourselves lucky . . . and I'm praying that it doesn't until after we berth."

Lincoln was thinking as he was talking. "Strap him to, strap

Gary into the pipe cot and then position him in such a way – so that he won't choke and can breathe should . . . should we have made a mistake. A lee cloth, perhaps, tied low down and wrapped over. It'd be better all round, I think, if we cover him – disguise him: we're going to have to use the heads, as will Nick and Sharon." Lincoln took a breath. "We'll simply pretend he isn't there – just treat him as if he's a sailbag . . . or he's asleep." He gestured. "You know what I mean."

Brian finally filled the void, "I can't raise a soul on the VHF; I tried directly after you and Lionel had failed to resuscitate Gary – as you'd expect, the MF's completely dead. I'll radio in on the half-hour and on the hour . . ." Ramsey stirred himself. "We'll raise someone sooner or later, providing . . ."

He was suddenly accusing and abruptly aggressive, and he indicated Lincoln with a wagging finger and said bitingly, "You don't have to be a blind man to see that you're in trouble." He demanded, "I need to know how bad you are exactly." And added, "What I don't require is another dead man on my hands – just because you're intent on playing the bloody hero."

Lincoln moved an involuntary hand to his lips, Brian's nod and his look replaced a thousand words – his eyes flickered away. He had been unnecessarily harsh though Lincoln understood that he needed – deserved a straight answer.

"A badly cracked or broken rib," Lincoln said matter-of-factly. "The two halves part very slightly every time I really strain; I think a sharp edge cuts or presses, which I think upsets and slightly disturbs the original wound. It goes back after relaxing, and then a quarter to a half-hour for the bleeding to completely stop. I may be taking a bit of a chance in the sense that I may be risking a collapsed lung, but, in truth, I don't think so." Lincoln sighed. "Nevertheless, I am breathing out the little bit of blood that you're seeing . . . obviously I can't really be sure but I suspect that it's coming from a minute puncture: the bone realigns, the pressure eases, the pinhole re-seals – my luck." He added slowly, and truthfully, "I think I could be in trouble if I don't take it easy from now on, I've noticed that there's a little more blood after each strain – and my breathing's a little bit more difficult for longer."

Nobody interrupted Lincoln.

"I can do a trick at the wheel, I'll be good for that, as I said, I'm not in immediate danger." Their silent looks were beginning

430

to intimidate, which in turn inclined Lincoln towards babble. "I certainly don't need a helicopter, or anything like that – they wouldn't make me sit in a wheelchair even if I were at home. I also know for certain that they wouldn't treat it – they'd not even strap it. Oh, they'd fuss . . . but I'm ninety-nine percent certain that at the end of the day all they'd recommend is time and rest."

Ramsey shook his head; and Lincoln was taken aback by the disgust and disdain on Ramsey's face. "Lionel's right, there's something missing, God left something out when he made you, something that I find frightening . . ." And then he became quietly furious and to Lincoln's mind, extremely and unacceptably offensive, "For better or for worse I'm the skipper of this boat and if you go against my specific orders then I'll site you at the Board of Enquiry: you'll not set foot on a rowing boat let alone another ocean-going yacht ever again. You should have taken better care – you've been irresponsible to neglect an injury like that – you're a menace to yourself and to those around you. I'm officially standing you down and logging it as such."

Lincoln looked at him wonderingly, and at the glittering intensity there in his eyes, and then he blurted it out before he could re-establish control. "Well, you can also put this in the log too while you are at it, Brian. You go and fuck yourself, and fuck your Board of Enquiry too. If you think I'm going to stand there and watch a young girl either drown or get smashed to a pulp, you can think on."

It was pointless . . . and Lincoln added quietly, "If you want bullets, Brian, if it suits, I'll give you bullets. You ask yourself, as I'm constantly asking myself, would Gary be alive now if I'd treated him on the spot instead of leaving him?"

The wind whined through the shrouds and the busy sea cuffed and mauled. Lincoln didn't really want to elaborate – the implication was clear. "We've all got our crosses, Brian."

Potter stood and moved between them and looked down. "You back off, Brian. You're completely and utterly wrong. You're not coherent and you're not making sense. You're flaying around, snapping like a wild dog – a bloody dingo. If you've got nothing better to think about than Courts of Enquiry then you're not the man I thought you were. Your time would be better spent thinking about how we're going to break the news to Judy . . . We're going to have more than enough time to hold an inquest later, matie, when we're not up to our arses in crocodiles. It's time to close ranks: we need each other more than ever: the fat lady hasn't sung yet and a lot can happen before we dock, and going by our track record, a lot more probably will."

Potter stood there, swaying easily and in command – he one less to worry about.

He turned, "What about Sharon? How's she going to stand up, Chris?"

"Lionel, I'm not . . ."

"Yeah, I know, you're not a doctor, matie – an opinion, that's all?" His face was sending messages – and begging Lincoln for co-operation. "All I'm trying to do is assess our immediate problems and situation: I'm thinking about whom, if anybody, does need lifting off – we don't need any more casualties, God, at least, that's the way I understand it – that's what Brian wants to know?"

Helmut nodded. "You are correct, Lionel, ve are men: ve solve nothing with fighting – Chris has said and ve must respect that – he has answered vith candidness a direct question." Helmut turned to Brian, "You vould have done the same, Brian, should your positions be reversed." Helmut indicated the overhead. "Ve need to move soon – darkness is closing. Ve put Gary below and sort out the rig – the vind, it is not stable – then ve motor home, ja?"

Ramsey stirred and then said to Lincoln, "What's your assessment of Sharon?" He sighed and then added a qualifier before Lincoln could answer. "A trick on the wheel then, nothing else." He muttered to himself rather than to them . . . initially, "'*Pride goeth before destruction'*," he looked directly, "'*and a haughty spirit before a fall . . .*'" He added, "They knocked that into us at Sunday school, and I mean really knocked – they're not just meaningless words anymore."

Lincoln was relieved and more than happy to meet Ramsey halfway. "She should be with Gary, by rights, that little foray that she took should have killed her." Lincoln shuddered at the harsh way his words had come out . . . A thought drifted: he was deep, Ramsey, and unexpectedly complex – had he been talking to him or about himself? The quotes he had quoted applied to them both, truth be known, and probably more to him. Lincoln shrugged the thought off – now was not the time.

"Her life jacket took some of the impact and the quick-release buckle most of the rest. Um . . . I'm sure I heard a ting of metal when her head hit – it wasn't her skull banging."

Helmut and Ramsey concurred.

"Ve heard also."

"She's suffering from cold and shock . . . but there seems to be no signs of concussion. The rest of her injuries are comparatively superficial, as far as I can tell, that is. She's tough and stubborn, far tougher than we give her credit – she's flatly refused to leave the boat – we're going to have to tie her up and throw her in the 'Andrew' to make her leave. Actually, in a sick kind of way I think she may be better off with us." Lincoln quickly qualified that before they could voice their obvious and hostile objections, "Hold on, umm . . . she cares for us, and when you think about it and more importantly, she knows we care for her." Lincoln rubbed an eyebrow while thinking, and, strangely, nobody took the opportunity to interrupt him. "She doesn't seem to have any family or close friends . . . and I, for one, haven't the heart. I think she'll be better off if we can keep her occupied rather than give her time to grieve – with Nick and the boat perhaps. He'll bounce, I'm sure, Nick'll bounce if we pressure and handle him right, and don't let him think – it'll be therapy if we can find important jobs for both of them. Nick we're going to need desperately: to climb the mast." Lincoln said thoughtfully, "They do seem to take solace from . . . comfort each other, don't they. If it just wasn't for Gary's presence . . .

"Anyway, it's all irrelevant at the end of the day, isn't it, till we can contact Melbourne, or perhaps another vessel – let's reassess then. I reckon it'll pan out in two or three hours either way – the decisions will probably make themselves."

Helmut interjected next, "It may be best, I think, to maybe think about airlifting them both off together – get them away from their place of nightmare – the mast ve manage one vay or the other, ja?"

Lincoln stayed quiet, Helmut's assessment had been far better than his had: thought out, rational and considerate: and more to the point, better for both Sharon and Nick.

"Lionel and I vill empty the sailbag." Helmut looked from Potter to Ramsey for confirmation.

Ramsey nodded.

Lincoln stood. "I'll go down before then, Brian, and put Bill completely in the picture. He'll only have half a story and he'll have to be one of your four. I'll also sort out some towels and prepare the pipe cot. I'll send Warren back up, if nothing else he can mind the wheel – he'll only have to shout – he'll manage."

Potter looked from Brian to Lincoln: gone again had Ramsey, they saw: he was oblivious, silent and just sitting there, looking out to sea.

Lionel offered, "Do you want me to tell Bill, Chris, would you rather I do it?"

It was just a gesture, Lincoln knew, though well meant.

"We've become close, Lionel, I'll tell him."

Lionel nodded. "Helmut and I'll use the forward hatch then."

*   *   *

Bill turned and Lincoln couldn't help but notice, there was an opened packet of powdered gravy-mix in Bill's hand.

He pre-empted Lincoln, "I heard all I need to know."

His mouth was working and it was time, Lincoln quickly perceived, to change the subject, "How are Sharon and Nick? It's the first chance I've had to come down, one way or another."

Bill scratched his head. "Sharon was whispering to him one minute, then they're both sound asleep the next." He held up his hand before Lincoln could speak. "I hadn't the heart to keep her awake despite what you said. Anyway," he defiantly added, "she's coping."

Lincoln didn't take him up on that as he had obviously braced himself for and was expecting a few harsh words. Actually, Lincoln accepted, and there was no point, what was done, was done, and Bill was upset enough already by the look of him – so Lincoln simply stepped on through. They were like two children: head and shoulders showing above Indian blankets: Nick on the outside and on his side facing the cabin, with Sharon trapped and snuggled up against his back.

Lincoln returned to the galley and nodded. "I see what you mean," and was silent for a moment. "We're going to need two or three big towels, Bill, to prepare the forward pipe cot for Gary." There wasn't any other way for Lincoln to put it nicely. "We're going to put him in the Number One sailbag, Bill: we're going to have to line it with towels, for absorbing; he can rest there in peace then till we get in." Lincoln hesitated. "If Brian can contact someone on the VHF, then things will change I expect – we'll just have to see . . . We'll have to play that one by ear, as to if and when, I suppose."

There was no need for Lincoln to elaborate; Bill turned and trapped his backside in the apex between sink and working surfaces and lent tiredly. "There's a bath towel amongst Gary's personal things, and one in my bag – I'll dig it out. You've got one, haven't you?" He took a shuddering breath. "I know it's not fair but I can't go forward, I can't help. I'm on the edge . . . on the edge of going to pieces. I've been keeping busy, cooking Lionel's Paprika Chicken – I've been hiding." He added miserably, "We still have to eat, don't we. I wish Jean were here – I wish we were home."

Lincoln stretched out a hand and curled it gently around Bill's neck. "Amen to that, Bill." He let his arm drop. "Just a few minutes, Bill, that's all, we'll lower him down through the forehatch." Lincoln glanced through and into the saloon. "Out of sight of those two." He added, as if as an afterthought, "My side's been playing up, Bill, I can't lift."

Bill took two or three deep breaths. "Reality knocking at the door then – words to real life – that means I can't evade . . ."

"Yes you can, Bill," Lincoln answered quickly. "It's the only way any of us can handle it – out of sight, out of mind. You'll have to pretend, like I'm going to do, that they're passing you down the Number One sail and that's all, and think of nothing else. I'll do the rest."

Gently they clasped hands – mutual comfort.

Bill then said brightly, "Right, you go and sort out your towel then, and grab anybody else's on your way – you're right, and it's more important than ever that we eat. I'll carry on after, I'll keep busy . . . there's a long night ahead of us. If I know anything about it they'll think they'll not want it, but as we both know a full stomach'll make all the difference – it's more important than ever."

Good, Lincoln looked away; Bill would cope too, somehow!

They found Gary's towel at the front and to the side of his locker, unwrapped like everybody else's: their dampness was an accepted part of shipboard life, anything wet and once wrapped, stayed wrapped – otherwise, even though clean, they smelt like rotting fish, or worse, after a couple of hours.

Bill half-climbed, passing on bundled linen to waiting hands.

They manhandled the storm sails, Bill dragged the heavier Number Three across – they threw it on top. The Number One sailbag they, Lincoln concluded, must have already taken.

Lincoln tried to anticipate: "It might be better if we leave the storm and the trysail handy, Bill, especially the 'try'; we may have to jury-rig it later."

Bill nodded his agreement while pulling down the pipe cot.

A thought occurred and Lincoln asked, puzzled, "Where's Warren, Bill, have you seen him lately?"

"He's in behind . . . He's at the bottom of the skipper's berth – behind the chart table." Bill shook his head. "He got changed, went halfway up the steps and then suddenly came back down again – for no reason that I could see. He'd crawled . . . when I checked he was right down in the stern, I could just see his feet. He wouldn't answer me when I called, I gave him up in the end . . ." Bill indicated with a gesture. "Him, at the moment, I just don't need."

"Christ, that's about all we need, for him to start playing up. I'll have to chase him out, we want him up top, there's nobody else to mind the shop – he's a bloody worry, isn't he?"

Bill refused to be left and stood by the cooker finally, monitoring in both directions.

The wound, chrome, metal, flexible stem of the chart light Lincoln re-directed – there wasn't a sign of Warren, just eventual darkness, although he thought he could hear him faintly moving – a frightened animal gone to ground!

Lincoln called softly, "Warren, it's Chris. Are you there? Warren, I need you, I need your help again." A stirring . . . imagined or real? "Don't let me down now, Warren, it's all hands to the pumps. Come on, I really do need you to help me, I was relying on you, there's nobody else to turn to. I need you to mind the wheel again, that's all – you did really well the last time – you don't have to do anything else." Lincoln waited for a moment. "Just give me a shout if there's anything untoward – what'd you say?"

There was no movement at all – just silence.

"You help me now, Warren, it'll be us who'll tuck Gary into bed – it'll not involve you. Then we'll sort the rig out after – we'll be home by tomorrow morning if you come and help. It

436

might be the next day otherwise . . ."

Like a rodent backing up a tunnel: a hole in a dirt bank. The white, patterned grip-soles of his wellies only visible to Lincoln at first, then the yellow of his oilie trousers and then his shiny seat and top; finally he sat and turned, swivelling on his bottom with one leg tucked under. His huge eyes blinked in the light: an emancipated bushbaby awoken from a deep nocturnal sleep.

Lincoln thought it better not to make too much of it and kept his voice matter-of-fact and quietly cheerful. "Well done." Lincoln reached out and gently pulled at his collar. "Have you got enough on under there to keep warm – it's cooling rapidly outside?"

Warren raised his eyes and Lincoln took that as an affirmative – and he did for once seem, as far as Lincoln could tell, to be well insulated.

"Good. A piece of advice, Warren." Lincoln held up a restraining hand and added quickly, "No, not like the other. Look, don't think, just grab yourself a chocolate bar from the locker above the sink and a piece of fruit – and go up there and watch the evening unfold. Here, come on," Lincoln encouraged, "I'll get them for you."

Bill turned before Lincoln as Lincoln stepped through, and handed the requested items across, those plus a small bag of raisins – Bill had been listening.

Lincoln held them out.

Warren, now standing by the bottom of the companionway steps, shook his head. "I can't – I feel sick."

Bill gruffly but not unkindly insisted, "Yes you can," and then gave in with a sigh. "All right, in your pocket then, you'll feel better up there in the fresh air. But do make the effort and try to get them down because it'll be sometime before we can eat." Bill assumed that what had happened to Gary, and what was affecting him, was affecting Warren too. "He's right, is Chris, pretend Gary's a bit crook and we're putting him to bed – that's the only way."

Warren looked from one to the other of them, went to speak, changed his mind, pocketed away the proffered bits and pieces instead and then turned and climbed.

Bill and Lincoln both jumped, the next shout was louder, "Bill?"

Lincoln followed Bill through to the forehatch; Potter stood there below the hatch with a third of the sailbag hanging over the edge and level with his shoulders.

"You vill mind?" Helmut gently eased his way past; he must have come down the companionway steps, surmised Lincoln, and must have virtually followed them through. Helmut switched on the deckhead strip-light, and Bill and Lionel were both forced sideways and backwards, blinking, as he pushed on through.

"You vill each vun of his leg's take, vith your two hands spaced," he indicated where – an ankle and knee, "like so. Pull and slide him through and down in vun movement. Do not hesitate – I vill manage the top of his body."

On Helmut's affirmative Ramsey lowered and as he did so Helmut walked his hands quickly along Gary's back, then, by his own instructions, caught him as he dropped. Ramsey removed his hand from the back of Gary's shrouded neck and let Gary's head slide gently free – he began to climb down himself then.

Potter reached up and gently shook one of Ramsey's swinging boots. "There's no need, Brian, we can manage from here on in – there's too many of us down here now. Better if someone stays up top anyway, and keeps an eye on things – on Warren, keep him company."

Ramsey clambered back out, his face reappeared and he looked around – a relieved affirmative nod and then he was gone.

Lincoln peeked at Gary's head through the gap, in the undone end-section of the bag. "Lift him over; roll him onto his side, Helmut, so that he's facing the hull . . . Please?"

Helmut parted the opening further, checking for himself, he then moved along until he was centrally placed, got his arms under Gary and then lifted and rolled him at the same time. He pulled on the zipper next and separated the bag nearly to the bottom – he rearranged Gary's legs before tipping him a bit more. One arm he next placed palm-down, next to an alabaster cheek: a cheek that was resting ironically and contrastingly on a cheerfully patterned, coloured, macabre towel beneath. Helmut placed Gary's other arm and hand down behind his back. He finally and once again searched for a pulse before at last stepping back – before motioning Lincoln forward.

Moist yet dry, oily . . . no waxy. Cold . . . and no pulse

under Lincoln's fingers – this wasn't Gary.

Helmut gently re-zipped the bag completely, and before Lincoln could comment unzipped again the small section that was directly in front of Gary's face. He reached down then and threaded the lee cloth cord through the eye above – and quickly tied it with casual dexterity, adroitness and proficiency.

A long shuddering breath sounded from behind, it was Lionel. "Would you put some blankets over him, matie?"

Helmut shook his head; he stepped around and behind Potter and began to gently herd and shepherd them all along.

"He is vith . . . He is in the arms of . . . He is being comforted by his Maker now, ve can do no more."

Chapter 31

Worippa's exaggerated wallowing with the remnants of her sails slating while hove-to had been exerting too much strain on her mast and associated standing rigging, and that would eventually and inevitably have bought down the whole lot, so they had had no choice other than to get way on and minimise the forces of wind and sea that were acting upon *Worippa*. They would also need, and especially so if that were to entail any work aloft, as stable a platform as possible for repairs.

The throttle setting wasn't quite so Lincoln gently butted it forward a touch more with the heel of his palm, and paused for effect before butting it again – three knots. *Worippa* was head-to-wind and holding her own nicely. The low rumble from the slow trotting, mechanical horses below him he could feel, but were hardly audible and the noise blown away on the wind. The engine was only just above turning-over – and only just a little faster than idle – and she wasn't quite happy. He could hear, feel and sense, there was just a little too much torque on for her to be really comfortable – she was barely cantering, rather a shuffling trot, and certainly well below cruising revolutions – Lincoln gave the throttle lever another tap.

Helmut turned and climbed around and down and perched himself on the edge of the stern coaming. There he balanced, and easily riding along with *Worippa's* nosing motion; the heavy torch rested in the fold formed by his lower body and thigh, and trapped there, in his lap, while he sat for a moment.

There were, that night, long, almost cyclically, periodic, slow moving, lazy, gently rising, shallow, rotund, travelling, sine curves abroad: a low, long, easy and kindly ocean swell. Things were beginning to favour them at last: there was a gently caressing westerly blowing over and flattening off – and smoothing the prominences and filling in concavities. And furthermore, Lincoln tentatively and cautiously observed, and not wishing to tempt fate once again, it was easing all the time – black tea to liquid bitumen.

Lincoln could glimpse an odd pinprick, an ice glitter, a gleam of an indifferent, tiny, distant sun in a dark patch overhead now and again – before being quickly obscured by tendrils of grey. And dominating in the western celestial tract of the night sky and not actually dominating the sky generally was the spreading luminescence from a slightly brighter areola, inside which was the white glow of a shy, riding moon hiding behind fleeing cloud. There had been no triumphant exposure so far that night and only a misty curve of lunar arc had seen fit to resolve itself now and again.

Potter stood himself before the winch to port of the companionway hatch, and when Lincoln gave him the okay he began to haul in the slack – there was a muted hollow thrum from bearings and internal ratchets and then a turning, spinning and quavering singing. He tightened the main sheet still further after gently taming, trapping and quelling the contained to-and-fro and up-and-down till there was only a quivering hesitation from the mainsail boom, and an uneasy shivering and tired flopping from the mainsail itself. Lincoln grimaced and held his breath and hoped nothing would give as Potter exerted gentle leverage on the inserted winch handle before tweaking on a touch more after that. It was obvious to Lincoln, and Lincoln couldn't blame him, that Lionel no longer trusted the tailing capability of that winch and added two more loops plus two half hitches for security.

There was a sudden and startling short moment of silence as the mainsail bellied and momentarily held, till they dipped on a wave and then there was another flurry of agitation. Lincoln watched intently as the luff fluttered and chattered in a succession of spasms – perturbations and puckers rippled and shifted and their highlights and deep shadows accented by the weak moonlight – and amongst those, caused by an occasional, more enthusiastic, periodical jerk and shake, was a single corrugation which travelled and shivered right across and diagonally down. Then to silence again as the main momentarily filled and bulged again, only this time in a direction from the other side, exactly opposite to previous – and a mirror-image cycle repeating.

They were not going to get an ounce of lift from that too deep-bellied and sagging sail, Lincoln knew, and the simile to a bird with a trailing broken wing occurred to him, but in their case not only had the wing lost its aerodynamic qualities, it had also been mutilated beyond repair . . . And there was at the moment nothing else for them to do but to let the poor thing flutter.

Helmut broke into Lincoln's depressing observations. "Vater

is pumping from the exhaust – that is in order." He stood and turned and then stepped down beside Lincoln and knelt. "Mind your eyes a moment, Chris." He shielded and then switched on the torch, and there were a few seconds of study before he switched the torch off again. "The ammeter it says is charging correctly – that is good." Helmut's teeth flashed white. "Ve all held our breaths, vas a long time again before starting, vasn't it. It needs to run, the engine, for a long time – to burn avay carbon deposit, ja."

Potter, who had been half-watching Helmut and half-watching the shivering main, commented, "Well, it's going to get its chance, matie – it's about to earn its keep." He pointed up and at the remnants of their mainsail. "It's going to take some time to sort out this little lot, let alone motor in." He turned to Lincoln. "I don't think we're going to need to rig the handy-billy, Pom, looking at it. I reckon the sheet slipped through the self-tail jaws, and once slipping, the wind did the rest: the pressure of the wind in the main caused the boom to come loose and that was it! Also, the braid's well used and worn pretty thin in that area – we should perhaps have pulled it out and re-threaded it through the other way, so that the worn end was at the other end, where it wouldn't of mattered." Potter took a deep breath before continuing, "Presumably, the downhaul on its own simply wouldn't have been able to hold it, and it might well have had some slack in it anyway . . ." Potter after a pause for breath laboured on, "The strain and momentum from the main must have been enormous, and once that boom was free there was nothing to stop it. Gary was just in the wrong place at the wrong time – it must have clipped him in passing – poor bugger."

Potter must have caught Lincoln's look of scepticism in the light of the binnacle or in the diffused moonlight – the self-tailing jaws were tapered and so-designed to accommodate for, within reason, any diameter of rope.

"All right," Potter conceded, "maybe it hadn't been tucked in firmly enough, no disrespect to anyone, it might have even been me, it may not have caught originally and then uncurled itself – and dropped out . . ." Neither Helmut nor Lincoln commented. "Ah look, it's anybody's guess, but I'll tell you this for free though, there ain't nothing wrong with that winch." Lionel straightened up. "And the mainsail track – we can forget that . . . that's solid – it hasn't moved an inch." He added an afterthought in a somewhat lighter voice, "There's something to be said for an old fashioned cleat, isn't there." Lionel breathed loudly before snorting through his nose – before stating decisively, "No, nothing's broken – I've also checked all the pulleys and fittings carefully, with a fine-tooth comb – I'd stake my life on it."

Lincoln raised his eyebrows: 'Stake his life on it!'

"We'd better attach it – the handy-billy anyway, Lionel," Lincoln said dryly, and then added hastily, "It's not that I don't doubt or disbelieve you, only . . . if it happened again, we'd really be for it, apart from the mast, that is. Anyway," Lincoln added tactfully, "we've a long way to go and I doubt . . . It's highly unlikely that we'll be using that mainsail again, don't you think . . . You know," Lincoln conjectured further, half-heartedly airing his previous theory, "the side-frame of one of the pulleys could have opened – and sprung back after. The same thing could have easily happened to one of the other fittings, or one of the eyes." Lincoln jammed a knee between the spokes of the wheel, and forgetting the darkness, demonstrated with his hands. "The rivets pulled, the side plate opened and the sheet forced its way out between, and by a fluke, or whatever, the thing clicked or sprang itself back into position after."

Now it was Lionel's turn to doubt, and it wasn't in his words but the implication was there in his tone, and Lincoln couldn't blame him – it was thin, thin to the point of ridiculous!

"Right, matie . . . I take your point."

"Where's Brian?" Lincoln asked curiously, ignoring Potter's scepticism and ignoring his own embarrassment, and suddenly aware of Brian's long-time absence.

"On the radio again, matie, nobody's home – as unusual. You'd think there'd be the odd fishing boat about, or an odd ship entering or leaving or steaming through, or another yacht, wouldn't you – there's not been a peep." Lionel straightened up abruptly and said without reflecting on his words. "Right, I'll do that right now, attach the handy-billy before the bloody thing kills somebody else. Where do we start then?" He gestured. "After, I mean?"

"Well." Lincoln hesitated, also looking up and around. "I guess we'd better double-check the babystay, just to be sure, and then check the runners again. I'm really nervous about messing about with them anymore, but we'd better make sure that they're still evenly tensioned – they'll have settled a bit – but gently, Lionel, if you are going to do it now . . . I don't have to remind you, do I, not to crank anymore on unless you have to: you'll be pulling against . . . There's only the babystay holding the thing up forward. You might even be able to ease the tension off a bit," Lincoln added, grasping at straws, "you never know!"

Lincoln could sense Lionel's impatience with him for stating the obvious and over-fussing, so Lincoln quickly hurried on, "You know, Lionel, I'd feel a damn sight happier if we could somehow rig a temporary forestay, the only trouble is . . . I must have a mental block or something . . ." Lincoln pondered for a moment. "Do you know, I can't actually think of a way of hoisting Nick up there. Oh, I know he'd free-climb it without a second's thought, but, under the circumstances, I don't think it'd be wise to let him." Lincoln hunched his shoulders. "Let's not even think about it – it'd be really tempting fate."

Lincoln glanced up at their fretting mainsail, the vibration caused by rippling and billowing was minimal now and had settled into a pattern, and Lincoln had minimised that again by juggling with the throttle and by keeping the headwind shy and to one side. Even so, he could now and again actually feel the rhythm of the mast's flexing caused by the sail's spasms and irregular undulations through the soles of his feet – it was different from the regular beat of the engine and very faint. Lincoln picked up their conversation as Lionel reached across with the winch handle.

"It's just as well there's plenty of stretch: plenty of elasticity in nylon, Lionel: in the nylon in the tails of the runners, I mean." Lincoln knew he was doing it again, talking too much, but he couldn't help himself – it was as if talking about it would make it so! "Just enough on to hold her, Lionel. They'll give . . . that nylon'll give . . . they'll absorb . . . They'll take any shocks before, rather than punishing and putting unfair strain on the babystay – it'll give us a fighting chance, at least."

Lionel barely gave Lincoln a glance as he stepped in front and across to the other runner winch, there was no comment from him nor from Helmut – and their silence somehow forced Lincoln, as usual, to babble on.

"Let's try to get the main off her then; I can't believe the lot hasn't gone over the side already." He looked up again; the slightly erratic draft deflected by the main was cool and distinct. "We'll have to winch it down if we can't pull it down – we'll have to see." Lincoln looked across to Helmut in the dragging silence and finally, hesitantly and tentatively suggested, "I suppose we'd better move then, had we?"

Strangely, and he'd noticed that same phenomenon with different people on different occasions, the noise of Helmut swallowing could be clearly heard over the wind, sea, engine and boat noises. "Ve clear the main first then see about jury rig, ja – one cannot climb vith it in the vay – there is novhere for hands behind." Helmut addressed Potter directly, "You finish the runners then, Lionel, I vill fetch and attach the handy-billy . . . You do not think it better, Chris, that ve use the two tackles that ve used to hold still the boom when ve use the trysail?"

Lincoln couldn't think of anything to say and his embarrassment was absolute, he had completely and utterly forgotten about them and of their existence . . . "To be honest, Helmut, I hadn't even considered . . . I had completely forgotten about them . . ." He had hesitated before speaking further, "They would be safer, but the thing is though, if we manage to get the main down and off her, then I was thinking that we may be able to use the 'try' as part of our jury-rig . . ." Lincoln admitted that at the present time he just couldn't think that far ahead and so he simply handed the question back to Helmet, knowing that he was being unfair. "Do whatever you think is best, Helmut, but whatever we do, we'd better do it . . . Like you, no doubt, I don't . . ." he jabbed a pointed finger at the mainsail, "trust that thing!"

Helmut hesitated for just a moment, and without drama and without fuss nor resentment, "The handy-billy vill be adequate, the end of the trysail ve can tie to the boom end, I think, and ve save our tackles if ve vant for tensioning for our new fore and backstays perhaps." And added, "I vill also turn on the deck lights vhile I am down below – you can think of no reason vhy I should not, Chris?"

"No, Helmut, I can't." Lincoln took a deep breath and grinned into the darkness; perhaps they had a point, although sincerely grateful, people like Helmut could quickly get on your nerves – Helmut had been at least four or five moves ahead of him! "Yes," he absently answered, still thinking, "we might as well get organised. Would you flick on the nav lights too, at the same time, please, Helmut, it'd be a shame if a bloody great cargo ship ran us down now – during the night – at this late stage, wouldn't it?"

Potter added his two-penny worth, a Potter that had been otherwise tactfully mute, Lincoln gratefully noted, "Always the cheerful fucker, aren't you, Pom!"

Up to that point Lincoln hadn't been panicking about getting started because, although it seemed like longer, very little time had actually passed; and also that a little time spent discussing might save hours of frustration, as per Helmut reminding them of the existence of the tackles and his other invaluable and crucial observations – nevertheless, they had just about, he judged, reached the point where it was going to be counterproductive – now was the time to move!

The glow, which called him a liar, from the companionway hatch was suddenly blocked out, and the dark, thin, backlit, yellow-glinting, edged outline of Warren resolved itself as he emerged and stepped into the cockpit.

"Bill said to give you these: over-trousers, hat, scarf and stuff." He tumbled the bundle onto the cockpit seat and began to clamber around. He mumbled tentatively – and there was also a pleading in there somewhere. "I'll steer if you want, while you get your stuff on – you can sit and do it?"

This was on his own initiative and without having to be asked! Had he gained that little bit of confidence? Lincoln shook his head – people! Lincoln used one hand to steady Warren as the deck lights suddenly came on, and gently guided and eased him in front of him and behind the wheel. Lincoln allowed time for their eyes to adjust – the compass numbers under their red illumination were still easily distinguishable despite the deck lights.

"Two-fifty degrees then, Warren." Lincoln pointed with a finger. "Use the same technique as before: pretend you're moving the needle; keep her just a hair off the wind – just enough to stop the mainsail from bellying the other way – feel for it, like you did before. If you can't maintain that or lose it, then drive her – just meet the wind squarely. Whatever you do, do not put any pressure on the main!" Lincoln stood behind

Warren for some minutes, till *Worippa* had erred and he'd corrected several times. Lincoln put a hand on his shoulder and squeezed before finally climbing around, and that squeeze passing on thanks, reassurance, encouragement, and without words, complementing him on his steering. And again, and Lincoln couldn't really say why, he trusted Warren implicitly and had entrusted *Worippa* to him knowing that he would competently do exactly what he had asked him to do!

Forward the stage was set – and Helmut and Potter the players again and the stage lit by the bright, expanding, coned brilliancy from the overhead spreaders – and each deck light projecting a wide, overlapping, spotlight pool onto the deck. Lincoln turned and glanced aft and away from the influence of the two circles of glare and waited a moment for his eyes to adjust – the bloom of the compass light though faint had not completely overwhelmed Warren's face: a vampire mask in red floated, ghostly, against the black back-cloth. Lincoln nodded to him; he could feel the faint breeze precisely on his face when facing forward, and he had been feeling it on the exposed sensitive flesh on the back of his neck when looking aft, and he knew that Warren had not been erring too far from his course. He was just a little too stiff, just a little bit too mechanical – and he had a tendency to steer around corners rather than guide *Worippa* through smooth, shallow curves, but it was not at all bad considering.

Warren was right, and if it wasn't for him he should have shortly been effing-and-blinding again with a vengeance, and his forethought and thoughtfulness, as Lincoln considered it, shook him – and another who's apparent shallowness had proved not so shallow! And, Lincoln allowed, it would be quicker and much easier to simply sit and rely on him than to do acrobatics behind the wheel while trying to dress. There was or would have been a distinct chance of losing it that way as well, and to risk the rig through something so silly didn't bare thinking about – worse things had happened at sea! Better odds were in trusting him, and moreover, though Lincoln knew in his heart the necessity wouldn't occur, he could simply reach out and grab the wheel from where he was at any time should the need arise.

As a rule, the legs of over-trousers were generally too tight around the heel: to quantify that, the elasticised leg-cuff, though fully stretched, tended to adhere, grip, stick and cling to the rear edge of the rubber heel of a person's seaboot – and with a stubbornness that defied belief.   Lincoln cursed, as he always did, and for the umpteenth time asked why they hadn't re-designed the inner netted, elasticated, drainage bottoms that were stitched into the end of the lining of foul-weather trousers – the answer, he answered, as he also always did – they should look towards velcro for the solution. Lincoln swore again as he struggled to force the stretched elastic over – it happened to him every-bloody-time, and, coincidentally, always in a seaway or at an awkward time, or in an emergency . . . It would, he stated yet again, be the 'final solution' for the designer and manufacturer otherwise, if he had to put up with much more of this!

Lincoln stood finally, and with the backs of his knees braced against the cockpit seat, wrapped the neck towel around and pulled on the woollen hat before shrugging into his top.   There had been a crackle of cellophane when he had picked up his jacket: from wrappers. Bill had filled his pockets with the same goodies that he had supplied to Warren: chocolate, raisins and fruit . . . People!

Helmut stepped down into the cockpit and Lincoln stood in his shadow and out of the glare of the deck lights.   "No vay vill the mainsail vinch down, Chris.   The sail is vell and truly trapped up there in the bend." Helmut shook his head and more thoughtful than desperate or despondent.   "All I do is stretch till ve rip the cringle from the Cunningham."

Helmut, Lincoln knew, was referring to a metal ring that was stitched a few feet up from the boom, and into the sail's leading edge – and just in from the boltrope. It enabled more tension to be exerted vertically on the mainsail at the mast – and thus obtain a better sail shape aerodynamically when close-hauled to windward. Although the tack was strongly reinforced around that area for obvious reasons – if Helmut said they would simply rip out the cringle trying, then rip out the cringle they would, and there was no point in pursuing that line of attack.

Another shadow suddenly materialised, pushing Helmut to one side. Harshly Ramsey, "Cut the fucking thing – I'm past the stage of worrying and I'm past caring – cut the damn thing away."

448

"I've been thinking about that, Brian," Lincoln said gently. "It's a bit too chancy without the security of a halyard for the harness."

He quietly thanked God when Helmut pre-empted and stated the full extent of their problem – as Brian had had enough of his, Lincoln's, seemingly negative advice, Lincoln had had just about enough of the edge of Brian's tongue. Brian turned as well, as Helmut pointed.

"It vould also be pointless, Brian – even if ve could get part-vay up there vun couldn't reach far enough across to cut the sail off horizontally. And even if ve could it vould still leave the top third or quarter flapping up there and ve vould not be able to control it – you understand. Also, ve dare not allow a person to swing, so." Helmut held his hands out with their palms facing and duplicated the swinging action that would be required. "The mast has not the support around it that is required, ja."

Simply to break the silence, Lincoln asked brightly, "No luck with the radio, Brian?"

"God fuck – not a fucking soul. I'm certain the set's operating . . . how can you tell?" The exasperation in his voice one could cut with a knife. "What about hacking out footsteps, Helmut, and a harness strap around, you know, like climbing for coconuts – or like the old loggers used to do when climbing up trees?"

They stood and just looked, considering – even Potter was silent for once. Each of them, Lincoln was sure, was thinking and imagining: being up there and swaying about while trying to cut holes in the stiff, heavy, reinforced, double or triple layered kevlar – furthermore, nor did what Brian had suggested solve the problem of getting rid of that top third! No, Lincoln concluded, it wasn't the answer, there was simply nowhere to go after climbing to the top spreaders, and Helmut was right, it would be impossible to reach across far enough and cut horizontally should they decide to saw the bolt rope through at the bend . . .

Not far behind, was Helmut, "Ve deliberately vork and break off the mast top, ja."

"No," Lincoln said slowly. "Well, yes, maybe . . . we may well be forced to if she yaws or wallows too much, but with this sea and boat speed . . . Just bare with me and follow my thinking with this and shoot holes in it if my reasoning isn't sound." Lincoln took a breath. "We take the boom off, that is to say, we take . . . Um, we pull the pin at the mast, undo the outhaul and slide it backwards so that the foot of the sail is hanging free." Lincoln turned and looked over his shoulder and then looked forward, despite the fact that he couldn't see a thing – seeing it, rather, in his mind's eye. "Then we pull the pins on the fore and backstay and detach them – we then wind them around and wrap the mainsail with them." Lincoln added quickly before one of them could intervene, "They're heavy, I know, and virtually inflexible, but they'll bend over a distance – if we cross them in opposite ways, maybe . . ." Lincoln looked up and decided it was time to push the problem over to them, that way they would tend to concentrate on debating and solving the problem rather than rejecting the idea because of from whom it came! Mind games again, Helmut would say . . . still . . . "It's a pity we can't easily reach the first set of spreaders," Lincoln was trying to avoid someone having to climb the mast, "but it would be a lot better if we could thread them through and cross them above there, and all the other halyards too, but as it is, the cap shrouds are going to get in the way . . ."

Ramsey hurriedly spoke out first, "It's not a problem to climb to the first set of spreaders, I could stand on the spinnaker pole fitting and then someone could winch me up on its slide. It'd be fairly straightforward to reach and climb from there. We could even throw or drop a line over and attach it to my harness – it'd be better than nothing." He was looking up and considering. "I could even cut the caps; they're not doing a lot anyway, are they . . . Are they?"

Well, he certainly was happier, and Lincoln was happier too, for Brian to be adding to the conversation and being involved.

"No," Potter burst out.

Here we go, Lincoln thought, and it serves you right, Lincoln, you conceited bastard, why don't you just play it straight for once – it really does serve you bloody-well right!

Potter was emphatic. "Nobody goes aloft in the dark – you're all fucking mad to be even thinking about it – if you lot carry on the way you are then we're going to end up with another hospital job. No, if you try to climb that mast, Brian, or anybody, or anyone else," Lionel indicated to himself with a thumb, "then that someone'll have to go around me."

450

They were all taken aback momentarily by his venom: his naked aggression, his so-obvious, concern: it was so out of character.

A smile appeared, Lincoln couldn't help himself, and then Ramsey – a grin to a stuttering; even Helmut was smirking.

Lionel lost his temper then and really began to shout, "It's not a fucking game, this, you idiots, it isn't fucking playtime, you know. I can't believe I'm listening to all this shit." He pointed. "The only reason the fucking thing's still vertical is because of string and brown paper, and you're all standing about seriously discussing climbing around up there.   I'll tell you, you all want your tiny heads looking at, you won't be satisfied until the whole fucking shebang comes crashing down and kills some other poor sap, like . . ." He paused at the edge, not voicing the name that they all knew he was about to utter. "I'm just fucking glad you lot aren't a set of brain surgeons and me your patient, is all – and I'm being nice, I can tell you." The flaming star in their midst was beginning to fade. "Think about it, there's no need for anybody to go up. That cold front doesn't seem to have materialised, or maybe it has and this is it – the wind'll probably back if it hasn't already. As Chris says, take the boom off, collapse and strap the main down as best we can . . ." He asked reasonably, "What's the problem: punch our speed up to six or seven, or eight knots – get her up to hull speed. It's no different from motoring – motor-sailing, is it, as far as I can see – just so long as it don't blow too hard. Whatever's loose'll just stream behind – who cares. It's virtually downwind either way . . ." He held out his hands expansively. "You know what I mean."

They were silent.

Helmut tried his luck, "It vould not be really vise to cut the cap shrouds, Brian, they still help support a very little, ja. The vire is trapped: grub screws, they hold the vire to the spreader ends and the bend in the vire straight above them, above, helps a little to trap, ja?"

Helmut's somewhat laboured and pedantic observations had irritated Ramsey; there was an edge to his voice, "Christ, another bloody upstart expert."   He was resigned then, and sarcastic – he gave up, "Why don't you just knock me down, why don't you, and have done with it!"

Lincoln didn't smile . . . it might have been funny at any

other time, his about-face – his capitulation. Nevertheless, he'd made his point, he was skipper and not without hard-earned skills and therefore, in Lincoln's book, he did deserve the respect that he was demanding.

Potter crushed from any of them any other thoughts of sympathy or consideration for Ramsey's feelings or position, and conveniently and incidentally blamed everybody else at the same time. "Tut, tut. Temper, temper, matie, they're trying to help, that's all."

Ramsey was silent; he was looking up again. "All right," he said quietly, "enough said. I have to admit," he nodded at the mast, "I don't much fancy climbing up there – I hate heights." His tone didn't invite comments and he finally observed, "The intermediates'll be in the way anyway."

They held their peace as he turned and hunched himself, presumably against the searching wind. "It's like a never-ending nightmare," he said, his voice just audible and as if talking to himself, "it's gone so wrong." He came back to their world then and said brightly, and with finality, "You're right, Lionel, one fatality's enough – let's motor straight off . . ."

Helmut held up a restraining hand and even in the faint moon and starlight Lincoln could see Lionel's eyes look up and implore heaven – it was lost on Helmut. "It is a much steadier floor, as is: the vork is much easier if ve do now. Ve ride on adrenaline – if ve try to wrap the sail vhile motoring speedily, it vill be much more difficult and ve vill soon become exhausted."

Ramsey said forcibly, "Don't push your luck, Helmut, Lionel meant just let the mainsail stream."

Helmut this time had the tact to remain silent.

Ramsey took the time to consider and he ignored the obvious, that the mast wouldn't for a moment stand the strain of a flogging sail at seven knots, or any meaningful speed, nevertheless, what he said was true. "All right, but it's going to take real nerve and willpower to pull those pins – the forestay and backstay pins, I mean. I know that the fore and backstays are useless, and their weight loosely swaying about even a handicap, even so, it goes against every instinct to actually disconnect them at sea." He sighed. "All right, Helmut, I take your point, let's get on with it unless . . ." Ramsey raised his eyebrows questioningly and said sarcastically and with foreboding, "Unless anybody else has any suggestions?"

Lionel sat behind the chart table, his face indirectly illuminated and half in shadow, and above the usual pool thrown by the shaded chart light. "You should have eaten earlier, matie, when it was ready."

Lincoln looked at Potter questioningly; the thud of the engine though well insulated still made normal conversation a little difficult – one needed to attune to it.

"I said you should have eaten that earlier – when it was ready."

Lincoln swallowed and held the spoon poised. "This has been the first chance, Lionel; it's been a race between getting this down and being sick – I feel like shit . . . Sorry."

"Don't be, you're allowed to swear, matie, fuck me, you're in Australia now and amongst friends – we're all shot – it's part of life."

Lincoln looked at him, his affection for this over-grown rogue, this rough-edged man had grown, Lincoln realised . . . he considered him a friend.

Potter looked at his watch. "Nearly midnight, why don't you finish that and get your head down. Helmut and Brian have got another hour yet – and we relieve 'em at one anyway. The timing's perfect if nothing else: we'll sight the Heads in four and a half hours if we carry on like this, and by then it'll be dawn – as I said, perfect."

Lincoln stepped across and placed his food bowl in the sink and then stepped back.

"Are you going to try that radio," Lincoln asked with exaggerated reasonableness, "or fiddle and break it?"

"I promised faithfully," Potter retorted, and there was a certain puffed-up, I'm-in-charge pomposity in his attitude. "I told Brian I would, I'm to call him straight down if there's any response. Actually," Potter confided, "it's a wonder he hasn't already been down to check." His inflated demeanour then suddenly collapsed altogether and his body seemed to sag. "You do it, you make the call – go on."

Lincoln half-smiled in exasperation and shook his head. "For God's sake, don't start all that again, Lionel." As an afterthought he added, "And don't forget to flick over from 'stand-by' to 'transmit' before you try this time, either!"

Potter's look as he extended a hand for the microphone

would have withered the stoutest of hearts, and then he hesitated. "You don't think . . .? Brian wouldn't have . . . he wouldn't have done exactly that and that's why we haven't had an answer?"

"No," Lincoln said, "he's not dumb, like us."

Potter didn't look convinced. "Well, there's only one way to prove it!"

Lincoln looked at Potter for a moment, and it made Potter hesitate again. "What?" he asked.

"Well," Lincoln said tentatively. "It's just an aside, but one thing that has been puzzling me, and that is that the MF aerial packed up when the mast buckled. I mean, the actual backstay didn't actually break, did it? I mean, there was no reason why it shouldn't have continued working, was there?"

"Ah, matie," Potter said with an elegance that had Lincoln desperately trying to keep a straight face, "the thing was flopping around like a loose pair of an old tart's drawers, wasn't it – I mean, the way it was sagging, lolloping and bouncing around up there." He leant his head to one side. "No, I'm not at all surprised that the thing gave up the ghost."

Lincoln nodded – he had a point.

Potter suddenly grinned. "God, did you see his face, Ramsey's, I mean, after Helmut had climbed up to thread through the back and forestays, he really went applexic, didn't he!"

Lincoln gently corrected him, "Apoplectic, you mean."

"That's right, matie," he said with satisfied aplomb, "he really cracked the shits."

Lionel, Lincoln was sure, as before, used the extreme Australian vernacular just so that he could watch his reaction – it was becoming a bit of a sport with him.

Lincoln shrugged. "It really wasn't a big deal, was it; Helmut could virtually reach the first set of spreaders on tiptoe, couldn't he." And Lincoln said pointedly, "And you didn't help, did you – and at the end of the day it had to be done, didn't it?"

Potter turned and looked at Lincoln directly. "I dunno, to tell you the truth, I agreed with Brian – no offence."

"And none taken," Lincoln replied slowly and sighed – there had been a wealth of meaning in Potter's words that he had intoned, but hadn't uttered. "You and Brian may both well have been right, sometimes it is better to simply sit down and wait."

454

Lincoln had to give it to Lionel, he was his own man – after a moment Lionel simply pointed to the radio and asked, "'*Pan*', do you reckon?"

Lincoln sighed again. "Not really, let's face it, whatever we do, either way we're going to be wrong – it's up to you."

"Really bloody helpful, aren't we!"

"You know what I mean," Lincoln said. "There's no life in immediate danger, is there? A ship's not sinking, is it? Bill's been waking Sharon, he woke her about an hour ago – she's coherent and talking sense and there are no serious, specific aches or pains." Lincoln shrugged. "She didn't want to eat, but I see no hidden connotations in that, do you? She's just . . . Well, she's just simply tired-out – in other words, she's stuffed. That little dip and the rest's knocked the wherewithal out of her and it's caught up with them both, and Bill as well – all three of them are dead to the world."

Potter finally lifted off the VHF microphone. "Yeah, well, I guess we just want someone to simply know our situation and be standing by, just in case, don't we – and there's no doubt about Gary, is there." Potter's was a statement, not a question. *'All Ships'* again then?

"No," Lincoln said patiently. "'*All Stations*', Lionel, not *All Ships'*."

"Right. Right. I'll get there, don't panic – you're a bloody smart-arse, do you know that!" Lincoln blinked as Potter changed tack yet again. "Brian thinks, and it'd be nice, wouldn't it, if they came out – the lifeboat people, I mean – even if they met us at the Heads." Lionel raised his eyebrows, and then started to fiddle with the VHF volume knob again. "We wouldn't have to navigate or think." Potter turned around, more to check for Lincoln's reaction; at least, Lincoln thought, he had some humour left – he was still bouncing. Potter held up his hand and made chopping motion at forty-five degrees. "In like 'Flynn'." He grinned that infectious grin of his. "Not an hour – straight into Queenscliff – and all details taken care of!" He sighed a deep sigh. "It would be nice, wouldn't it?"

Lionel's first call was a little hesitant, but adequate. His repeat, his second call was better and his third broadcast across the ether was without pause and authoritative. Unfortunately, the end result to all three was the same: just a muted hiss with the odd hiccup of static from the VHF speaker!

Lincoln tucked in to allow him to pass on through, and then called out to him as he put his foot on the first step of the companionway steps. "Hold on, Warren, there's no need, you might as well head off to bed now and catch yourself a couple of hours. We'll be entering the Heads by the time you're awake again, and we'll be needing everybody as fresh as possible – it's always a bit tricky."

Warren stopped, turned, and came and stood at the corner. Lincoln looked at him, really looked, and in him now was the seasoned beginnings of capability, and he was unconscious of the unnecessary need for support – and it was habit and just a gesture, that his fingertips were just touching and resting on the hinged top of the navigation desk.

"Have you eaten?" Lincoln asked.

"I've been talking to Gary," Warren replied matter-of-factly.

"Right . . ." Lincoln said slowly, and put a foot forward and stepped gently on Potter's foot.

"He says he understands – he's forgiven me. He knows I really didn't mean to – really didn't mean to undo it."

"Undo, Warren," Lincoln asked doubtfully. "Undo what?"

"My hand just went forward," he said, ignoring Lincoln, "on its own – I watched it. I just pulled the rope out, it came out easily. It went with such violence, didn't it? All from me just touching that one little rope. Hurt him, punish him – yes. He knows he shouldn't have hurt me. Yes, he shouldn't have hurt me: shown us up in front of her. Bad that . . . It should have been her." His voice had been increasing in intensity and now he was shouting. "She's the one," and then he was screaming and shrieking, "SHE'S THE ONE. OH YES, SHE'S THE ONE – SHE'S THE ONE – SHE'S THE ONE – SHE'S THE ONE . . ."

The voice from the VHF loudspeaker seemed to be in the cabin with them, it was so near, so close and so loud, and it froze them in their places.

"*All stations. All stations,*" the voice said, and so calm, so every day, and so competent. "*Worippa, Worippa, Worippa.* This is *Pol-Air One, Pol-Air One, Pol-Air One.* Have received *All stations*, your situation, please? Over."

Epilogue

The young nurse heard the door open, but she was at a critical point and was concentrating and carefully unwrapping a sterilised instrument and hadn't turned around. Her back was to him and his arms came around and held and she was trapped against the working surface by his gently pressing body. "Ah, my little angel," he teased in a whisper, "my little oasis in the wilderness, my beautiful flower of the desert. My, my little . . ."

"God, don't do that. God, you're a devil – you made me jump – where did you spring from, you so-and-so?"

"From down the corridor – in Casualty."

There was a rustle from her crisp, white, starched uniform as the doctor pressed his front against her back and kissed her neck and gently bit her ear, his hands began roaming lightly. She tried to wriggle sideways, but didn't dare to drop and contaminate the instrument that she was holding . . . He stopped and as she relaxed against him, his hand circumspectly began to pull down the zipper at the front of her handsome bosom.

She stiffened against him and her eyes rounded with incredulousness as his hand gently slipped down inside her bra and fondled her breast. "Get off," she hissed. "Get off my . . ." She half-heartedly struggled. "Get off my boobs – you randy sod . . ." She again half-heartedly pushed away from him, fully knowing that he was nothing like he pretended to be: she had seen him in all his moods and in all his tantrums and tempers and knew him to be an absolute gentleman: which was why her apparent and present insincere behaviour was as it was – she loved him with all her heart. "You could give an . . ." she pushed again, ". . . octopus lessons . . . God, stop it. You'll get us both . . . dismissed." She heaved again, and out of his encircling arms with a strength that he found mildly surprising and amusing, and she dropped, in so doing, the sterilised implement and its wrapper on the working surface of the bench. She chastised him roundly, "Now look what you have made me do – you bugger!"

The young doctor stepped around and grinned.

"You bloody Australians," she said breathlessly, after turning; she began to strip-off the thin, white, surgical gloves that she had been wearing.

He bent and looked before stepping away to lean casually

against one of the spotlessly clean, white cupboards that lined the small sterilising and storage room. "That'll be all right, the pointy end is still sealed – you'll be able to murder a patient with impunity with that!" He grinned again, and was smiling with his eyes.

"You cheeky sod, it'll be you who I'll . . ." Her heart fluttered – she just couldn't and never had been able to fight that grin – and those eyes . . . "Oh," she said, interrupting herself as she pulled down and tried to straighten her uniform, and having moved on without really realising it. "While I think of it, there was a message for you on the answering machine this morning, from your father, him and your mother will be landing at Heathrow at nine-thirty a.m. – our time."

"Right." The doctor raised his eyes to heaven and nodded.

"I'd better move my stuff out, they might take offence." And she added with a genuineness which he found becoming, "It would be so embarrassing – especially if they caught us?"

The young doctor laughed affectionately. "We're going to be married – there's . . . No, don't do that, it'll be all right – they're cool – they'll think we're bloody peculiar anyway, if we weren't sleeping together!" He saw the doubt on her face – and the embarrassment at the thought. "Anyway," he grinned and lied, "they know all about us, I told Mum all about you, and about us . . . about us bonking away like a couple of rabbits at every opportunity!" He added casually, "So there wouldn't be much point, would there?" He raised his eyebrows. "You'd look bloody silly trying to pretend you're just visiting, wouldn't you?"

The young nurse's hand had shot to her mouth. "You're . . . You're awful . . ."

"And," he interrupted, admonishing with a finger, "how many times do I have to tell you . . ." He stepped away from the cabinet and stood up straight with a pretended hurt dignity. "How many times do I have to tell you that I'm a Tasmanian, and not . . ." He paused for emphasis, "Not an Australian!"

The young nurse stuck out her tongue at him and pulled a face.

"There's a world of difference."

That same young nurse side-stepped quickly as he made to grab.

"Don't. Get your hands . . ." Her hand flapped him away.

"Off, off. James Christian, if you don't . . ."

"Doctor Lincoln, paging Doctor Lincoln – please call reception. Doctor Lincoln, paging Doctor James Lincoln," the tannoy repeated. *"Report to reception, please. Thank you."*

She grabbed him and promptly grasped that selfsame wandering hand, pulled him to her and placed it exactly on and where it had previously been tentatively exploring.

"Kiss me . . ." Her other hand went to his cheek and pulled. "Kiss me before you go!"

Glossary

A-hull: leaving a yacht, while below, to ride out a gale without sails and the helm lashed to lee.

Asleep: perfectly adjusted, noiseless sails.

Athwartships: sideways, across the boat.

Babystay: a single wire attached about midway up and supporting the mast from forward.

Backing wind: wind direction shifting, or moving, in an anticlockwise direction.

Backstay: a single wire attached to the top of and supporting the mast from the stern.

Beam: the breadth or the maximum dimension across a boat.

Beam-reach: sailing with the wind on the beam.

Bend/bend-on: to secure.

Bilge/bilges: the lowest, internal part of a vessel – where waste water collects.

Bilge pump: used for pumping out bilge water.

Block: a pulley.

Boltrope: a rope sown into the leading edge (luff) of a sail.

Boom: the spar to which the foot of the mainsail is attached.

Boom vang/kicking strap: a tackle used to pull the boom down.

Bulkhead: an athwartships internal wall.

Camber: fullness, or depth of a sail.

Cleat: a two-horned fitting to which a line (which will be under strain) is secured.

Clew: bottom trailing corner of a sail.

Close-hauled: sailing as close to or as tight on the wind as possible.

Close reach: sailing between as close to the wind as possible and a beam reach.

Coaming: a small wall, usually around the cockpit.

Cockpit: a recessed and protected standing or sitting space, most often near the stern, and where the helm is usually positioned.

Counter: the back or stern of a boat – directly above the waterline.

Crane: short fore-and-aft protecting bar or bracket attached to the top of the mast.

Cringle: a metal eye or grommet stamped or sown into a sail.

Cunningham: a line led from a hook on the gooseneck, through a cringle just above the tack of the mainsail, and back to an anchored tackle: used to tighten and loosen the luff for aerodynamic efficiency.

Deckhead: the ceiling.

Downhaul: a line used, usually via a tackle, to pull down the sliding gooseneck of the boom at the mast, also a line that stops the spinnaker pole from lifting.

Drifter: huge, light-weight Genoa used in light winds.

Earrings: a series of short lines tied through the evenly spaced cringles down the luff of a sail, used to attach a sail to the forestay, or similar.

Foot: the base of a sail.

Foil: an aerodynamically, double-grooved moulding permanently attached to the forestay: the boltrope of a replacement sail is fed and hoisted in one groove and the redundant sail lowered in the other.

Forestay: a single wire attached to the top of and supporting the mast from the bow.

Genoa: a large headsail.

Gooseneck: a metal fitting that attaches the boom to the vertical sliding track on the mast – the slide allows for vertical boom adjustment and the gooseneck for pivotal.

Gybe: to tack the stern through the eye of the wind.

Gybe-ho: warning call just prior to gybing.

Halyard: a line, via a sheave (pulley) attached to the mast, which raises (or lowers) a sail.

Handy-billy: a convenient tackle with hooks or rope-tails at the ends, or a combination of both etc.

Head/headboard: top (reinforced) corner of a sail.

Headsail: foresail.

Jib: smaller headsail.

Jury rig: an emergency or temporary replacement made when appropriate repair facilities are absent.

Kicking strap/boom vang: a device (usually a tackle) used to tension and stop the boom from lifting.

Lee: the side away or the furthest from the wind.

Leech: vertical trailing edge of a sail.

Lee-ho: warning call prior to tacking.

Leeway: sideways drift to lee, caused by wind pressure.

Log[1]: a book kept on board a vessel in which are recorded all relevant facts and activities that concern that vessel.

Log²: an instrument for measuring boat speed and distance sailed.

Luff: the leading vertical edge of a sail.

Outhaul: tensions or adjusts the clew and foot of the mainsail on the boom.

Port: left (red).

Preventer: a forward restraining line that restricts the movement of the boom (back-winding) when running before the wind.

Pulpit: a railed, metal security fence around the bow.

Pushpit: a railed, metal security fence around the stern.

Reach: sailing across the wind.

Ready-about: a warning call prior to tacking or gybing.

Reef: to shorten sail.

Rhumb line: a straight line or course between two compass points.

Running backstays (runners): attached to either side of the boat and usually led from near the toe rail at the stern to the vicinity of the top spreaders. Tensioned – to stop upper mast flex – on the weather side in bumpy conditions.

Running rigging: required, easily and handily adjusted rigging, i.e. halyards, sheets tackles etc.

Set¹: the direction that the tidal stream flows.

Set²: the drift caused by a current.

Sheet: a controlling line attached to the bottom trailing corner (clew) of a foresail, or indirectly via the boom, to the trailing corner of the mainsail.

Shock cord: elastic line.

Snatch block: a pulley that has one side hinged and rather than being threaded through, the side is opened and the line looped over the pulley.

Soldier's Wind: a perfect or ideal wind on the beam – a comfortable wind that calls for minimum or no adjustment of the sails.

Sole (cabin): floor.

Spreaders: a pair, or pairs, of equidistantly placed (from the deck), right-angled struts that are attached to the mast to reduce (via the cap shrouds) the sideways flexing and load on the mast.

Standing rigging: permanent rigging.

Starboard: right (green).

Storm jib: a very small, specially strengthen, headsail - hoisted in very extreme conditions.

Tackle: a rope and block combination employed to increase tension and pulling power.

Tack[1]: to turn the bow through the eye of the wind.

Tack[2]: bottom leading corner of a sail.

Telltale: a length of lightweight ribbon attached and placed to observe airflow over a sail.

Toe rail: a low rail built into the edge of a deck to aid footing, often slotted to accommodate for various blocks, leads and similar.

Topping lift: a line, via a sheave (pulley) attached to the masthead, which supports the boom when not in use.

Track: a metal rail set into each side of the forward deck, on which the sheet-lead, spring-loaded, locking pulley-trolleys slide (through one of which the headsail sheet runs) – two pulley-trolleys are often employed on either side, one being in use and the other being locked in position and ready for an anticipated sail change (re matching double-grooved foil).

Traveller: another name for a pulley-trolley, but usually refers to the mainsail track and trolley that runs and permits vertical, horizontal and athwarpship adjustments to the mainsail.

Trysail: a very small, specially strengthened, loose-footed substitute mainsail – it replaces the mainsail in very extreme conditions.

Tumblehome: the amount of inward curve from the widest point of the hull (maximum beam), to the narrower width at the toe rail.

Turning block: a pulley, often deck-mounted, which re-leads a sheet or halyard etc to a desired location.

Veering wind: turning or shifting clockwise.

Warp: a mooring, towing or anchoring line.

Windward: on the side towards, or nearest to the wind.

Weather side: the windward side.